No one captures the drama and excitement
of men at war as powerfully as . . .

MARK BERENT

*Veteran of three tours in Vietnam and
winner of the Silver Star and two
Distinguished Flying Crosses*

"BERENT WRITES WITH GREAT AUTHORITY AND
UTTER REALISM."
—**Dale Brown, bestselling author of**
Night of the Hawk

"AN EXCITING STORYTELLER . . . HE GIVES DEPTH
TO THE CHARACTERS AND ACTION."
—*Air Force Times*

"THE MAN KNOWS HIS SUBJECT, AND IT SHOWS . . .
HE'S GOOD."
—*Tulsa World*

"BERENT TELLS IT LIKE IT WAS!"
—**Chuck Yeager**

*Don't miss these electrifying novels
in Mark Berent's acclaimed Vietnam saga . . .*

STORM FLIGHT

"MILITARILY TRUE TO LIFE."
—*Kirkus Reviews*

"AFICIONADOS WILL RELISH THE WEALTH OF
MILITARY DETAIL . . . ALL READERS WILL BE RE-
WARDED BY THE ULTIMATE MISSION, WHEN
PLANES, MEN AND TACTICS ARE TESTED TO THE
SPINE-TINGLING LIMITS."
—*Publishers Weekly*

Continued . . .

ROLLING THUNDER

A *New York Times* Notable Book of the Year—the novel that launched Mark Berent's saga of American pride and courage . . .

"A TAUT, EXCITING TALE."
> —Tom Clancy, bestselling author
> of *Without Remorse*

"TERRIFIC—A NOVEL OF EXCEPTIONAL AUTHENTICITY."
> —W.E.B. Griffin, bestselling
> author of *The Corps* series

"POWERFUL . . . A LASTING TRIBUTE TO EVERY AMERICAN WHO SERVED HIS COUNTRY IN VIETNAM."
> —*Washington Times*

STEEL TIGER

A novel of Vietnam, 1967, when America's fighter pilots discover a new breed of enemy . . .

"MASTERFUL . . . GRIPPING . . . A REAL TOUR DE FORCE."
> —*The Washington Post*

"WHAT TOM CLANCY ONCE DID FOR COMBAT UNDER THE SEA, BERENT DOES FOR AIRMEN."
> —*Air Power History* magazine

"BERENT KEEPS THE READER IN THE COCKPIT!"
> —*Publishers Weekly*

PHANTOM LEADER

A novel of the 1968 Tet Offensive, as seen through the eyes of America's bravest pilots . . .

EAGLE STATION

A powerful novel set in a radar post in northern Laos—and Hanoi's prisoner-of-war camp . . .

STORM FLIGHT

MARK BERENT

JOVE BOOKS, NEW YORK

This is a work of fiction. All of the characters in this book are fictional and bear no resemblance to real-life personages either living or dead. (Sometimes I think the Vietnam War bore no resemblance to real life.) However in striving for authenticity, some of the organizations and public figures exist or existed at the time. Note that not all actual events occurred in the exact chronology presented.

This Jove Book contains the complete
text of the original hardcover edition.
It has been completely reset in a typeface
designed for easy reading and was printed
from new film.

STORM FLIGHT

A Jove Book / published by arrangement with
Berent–Woods, Inc.

PRINTING HISTORY
G. P. Putnam's Sons edition published October 1993
Jove edition / August 1994

ISBN: 0-515-11432-4

A JOVE BOOK®
Jove Books are published by The Berkley Publishing Group,
200 Madison Avenue, New York, New York 10016.
JOVE and the "J" design are trademarks
belonging to Jove Publications, Inc.

PRINTED IN THE UNITED STATES OF AMERICA

10   9   8   7   6   5   4   3   2   1

Acknowledgments

It is five years now since I started this five-book series. Five years of talking with and interviewing old and new friends, PJs and mechanics, B-52 crewmen, SF NCOs and officers, Thud drivers and intell types, tanker crewmen and test pilots, grunts, staffers, POWs, and many others. We talked and talked and there was an equal amount of tears and laughter. I thank you all so much. We'll have a glass together anytime you can make it.

And special gratitude to Chuck Baldwin, Jack and Kay Bomar, Bill Butterworth, Tom Clancy, Tom Carhart, Dan Cragg, Barbara De Angelis, Sandy Dodge, Casey and Gail Finnegan, Doris Jones, Joe Lopez, Jim Monaghan, Neil Nyren, Don Rander, Clyde Sincere, Kim Thomson, and Tom Wilson. You gave me the right words and encouragement when I needed it most. And special thanks and love to my sons and daughters and grandchildren who gave and still give me unrestricted love.

And special thanks also to the hundreds of you who wrote such marvelous and encouraging letters. I've answered most of them but this last year was very difficult and I still owe a few of you an answer. Bear with me, please.

This book is dedicated to the KIA, MIA, and POW aircrew from Air America, the U.S. Air Force, the U.S. Army, the U.S. Coast Guard, Continental Air Service, the U.S. Marine Corps, the U.S. Navy, the Royal Australian Air Force, the Royal New Zealand Air Force, and the men of the U.S. Army Special Forces.

And to Mary Bess.

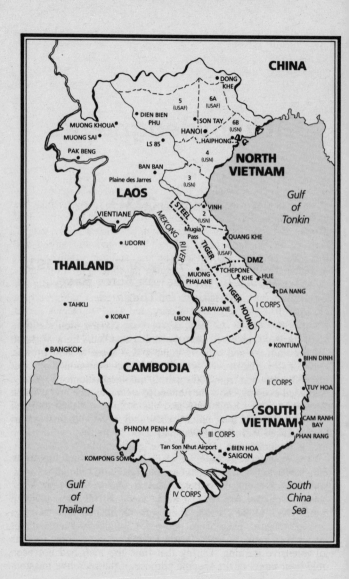

Prologue

On the day before the raid, the seventy chosen men test-fired their weapons, received satchel charges, and had a light workout. Five commissioned officers commanded three assault groups. Almost all were Special Forces senior noncommissioned officers, carefully selected from 300 superbly qualified volunteers. After a secluded evening chow they attended a final escape and evasion lecture, received E&E maps and blood chits, and then returned in a closed van to their billets, where they cleaned their weapons and checked their demolitions. By 2100 hours they were asleep in the secluded area of the air base in easternmost Thailand.

The next day was the *big* day. They rose early, ran a leisurely five miles, ate a light breakfast, received night-vision devices, and carefully rechecked their harnesses and webbed gear. They were given sleeping pills at noon chow and allowed to sleep until 1700, at which time they were awakened and taken to an auditorium. They wore two-piece jungle fatigues without insignia of rank, as they'd done for the previous three months of intensive training. During that time the men had not been told their target or the specific purpose of the secretive mission.

1

Early guesses had included raids on Mideast terrorist or Filipino communist guerrilla camps, but as the training continued, it became increasingly apparent that their objective would be inside North Vietnam. Their commander entered the auditorium.

Army Colonel Arthur D. "Bull" Simons had powerful shoulders and a thick neck, and his gray hair was cropped close to his skull. There was absolute silence as he strode to the front of the room and faced them, sweeping them with penetrating hawk's eyes.

His voice emerged in a rumbling, gravel tone. "We are going to rescue sixty-one American prisoners of war, perhaps more, from a camp in North Vietnam called Son Tay. This is something American prisoners have a right to expect from their fellow soldiers. The target is twenty-three miles west of Hanoi."

The raiders' average age was thirty-two. All but three had served combat tours in Vietnam—some had three tours. The faces remained impassive and the silence continued for several seconds. A smattering of low whistles broke the silence—then, as if upon command, the men rose to their feet and began to applaud. Hard hands beat together in a rising crescendo. Bull Simons' shoulders drew back. His eyes softened and glistened with pride.

When the applause had died and the men were again in their seats, Simons continued, the hawk's look carefully back in place.

"You are to let nothing—nothing—interfere with the operation. Our mission is to *rescue* prisoners—not *take* prisoners. And if we walk into a trap—if it turns out that they know we are coming—don't dream of walking out of North Vietnam unless you've got wings on your feet. We'll be a hundred miles from Laos; it's the wrong part of the world for a big retrograde movement. If there has been a security leak, we will know it as soon as the second or third helicopter sets down. That's when they'll cream us. If that happens, I want to keep this force together. We will back up to the Song Con River and, by Christ, let them come across that goddamn open ground. We'll make them pay for every foot across the son of a bitch." Hawk eyes flashed deadly signals.

Simons checked his watch. "We take off in three hours." He stepped down the aisle toward the door. Again the men stood and applauded. A man whispered to his companion, "I'd hate to have this thing come off and find out tomorrow I hadn't been there."

In the rear, by the wall near the door, stood Army Lieutenant Colonel Wolfgang Xavier "Wolf" Lochert. In his early forties, Wolf was broad-shouldered, stocky, and of medium height, and his dark hair was shaved so close to his skull that it looked a dusting of black powder. The sleeves on his fatigues were rolled sausage-tight on thick biceps, and his muscled forearms were matted with dark hair. Wolf Lochert was due for promotion to full colonel very soon. When he dwelled on it—which wasn't often—he thought of it as a chance to command more men in combat. That would be just fine with Wolf. He refused to accept the fact that the promotion to full bull might mean desk duty at some headquarters or other. He wasn't the type to endure that sort of thing, so he simply did not think of it.

Lochert noted the glint in the eyes of Bull Simons as the men applauded, and how his stout frame grew more erect as he strode through the door. Wolf fell in behind and followed Simons.

Outside, the sun was setting and the November air was cooling rapidly. "Lochert, go to the barracks," Simons rasped. "Be with them as they harness up. Have them put on their rank insignias. Don't let them miss anything."

Wolf Lochert saluted, climbed into a jeep, and drove toward the barracks, which was secluded in a remote part of the sprawling Udorn air base. Over 6,000 Americans were stationed at the base in northeastern Thailand. USAF fighters and rescue helicopters, Thai prop planes, and CIA-contracted transports took off and landed around the clock. Lochert parked, showed his entry badge to armed Air Force guards, and entered the large, empty, open-bay barracks. GI bunks were lined up in military precision, with blue USAF blankets drawn tight enough to bounce a quarter three feet into the air. The men's gear was stacked neatly under and at the foot of each bunk. They would soon arrive in the vans.

Wolf walked slowly down the aisle, absorbing the silence. The cloyingly sweet smell of Hoppe's cleaning fluid brought a torrent of memories. He'd been in the Army nearly twenty years, had seen combat with the infantry in Korea and as a Special Forces officer for three tours in Vietnam. The smell of cleaning fluid, Cosmoline, or gunpowder always evoked special and treasured recollections of hard training and dirt-level combat, of serving with professional soldiers who knew and loved their jobs.

Under Simons, Wolf and the others had been training these men unmercifully since August in a secret corner (known as Auxiliary Field Number 3 or simply Aux 3) of the huge Eglin Air Force Base in the Florida panhandle. They had exercised only at night, in an exact-scale replica of the Son Tay POW camp. The "buildings," made from 710 six-foot-long 2×4s and 1,500 yards of target cloth, had been dismantled before first light each morning to hide the operation (originally nicknamed Polar Circle) from the Soviet Cosmos 355 spy satellite. Postholes were covered with small, earthen lids. Trees were returned to their original planting sites on the base. The Son Tay replica was very precise, and the men had trained there until they were now familiar with every wall, ditch, rock, and tree in the compound.

USAF Special Operations crewmen flying helicopters and C-130 transports had trained with them. The HH-53s would carry Simons' raiders to the objective, then return them to Udorn with the rescued POWs. The C-130 Hercules would provide cover, deception, and command and control. They'd varied their call signs and made radio transmissions in such a fashion as to make the electronic intelligence operators in the ever-present Russian trawler in the Gulf think it was routine—business as usual.

The seeds of the raid had been planted six months earlier, in May 1970, when Air Force attachés in American embassies had obtained copies of East Bloc and Japanese television footage and radio tapes made of American POWs in Hanoi. These they had pouched to the Pentagon via the State Department. There, in a well-secured basement office, the video and voice tapes had been made available to a tiny group of USAF men, all holding very special compartmentalized clearances, so that they could study certain segments featuring a group of POWs singing a selection of seemingly innocent songs. "Aida" was the top-secret code name for *choir activities,* and the choir was conducted by a prisoner of war with the code name "Caruso."

They'd carefully decoded Caruso's choir renditions and found, along with other valuable information, that some fifty-five POWs had been relocated to a camp near the city of Son Tay, and that a number of the men were in extremely poor condition and dying. In fluted arpeggios, Caruso told them—sang to them—that the camp was relatively isolated and vulnerable for rescue operations. The USAF had drawn a tentative breath and quickly dispatched high-altitude SR-71 flights and low-altitude Buffalo Hunter drone flights to photograph the compound and its surrounding area.

Two days later, on May 9, 1970, intelligence specialists examining the photos for the USAF's 1127th Field Activities Group at Fort Belvoir, Virginia, confirmed activity and guard-tower construction near Son Tay. The site was located on the Song Con River, where it flowed into the Red River as it turned eastward toward Hanoi. The photos and choir music convinced military leaders in the Department of Defense to conduct a POW rescue as soon as possible.

They brought their plan to the Commander in Chief.

"How could anyone *not* approve this?" President Richard M. Nixon had responded, jowls aquiver. He'd paused thoughtfully. "But, if it doesn't work, I don't want this ending up putting even *more* of our people into those camps. And I can't stand for any more hippie riots on my doorstep. Remember when I approved going into Cambodia? Christ, they surrounded the White House. This time they'd probably knock down the gates." Nixon had shaken his head morosely. "But how could I say no? Go ahead with the plan. Bring some of 'em home. I just wish there was a way to get all of them."

Yet Nixon had delayed execution of the raid. Detractors said it was because he was playing political games in a congressional election year. The President's men said the original timing of the raid was bad because of the initial, critical talks with Communist China. It was early September before training began, and late November—after the elections—before Simons' raiders were in place at Udorn. The month's delay would prove to be momentous.

Neither Bull Simons nor Wolf Lochert nor any raider knew anything about Caruso and the choir. They did not have the need to know. Caruso and his choir was the best-kept secret since World War II's Ultra and the breaking of the Japanese code.

The men filed into the barracks, faces happy but thoughtful, talking quietly among themselves. A sergeant major took charge as they went through the drill of removing and packing away all personal items—wallets, pictures, photos, money—as well as anything that should be returned to their next of kin in the event they did not return. Next they were taken in the covered vans to Udorn's biggest hangar, where a big, four turbo-propellered

C-130 waited to take them to the forward helicopter launch site. Before boarding they performed a final equipment check.

There was a total of 111 weapons: two M16 automatic rifles (with 1,200 rounds of ammo), forty-eight CAR-15 assault rifles (18,437 rounds), fifty-one .45 caliber pistols (1,162 rounds), four M79 40mm grenade launchers (219 rounds), four M60 machine guns (4,300 rounds), and two twelve-gauge shotguns (100 shells). In special equipment bags they carried fifteen Claymore mines, eleven special demolition charges, and 213 hand grenades.

They checked the rescue equipment: axes, wire cutters, bolt cutters, coils of rope, oxyacetylene bottles and cutting torches, chain saws, crowbars, machetes, miner's lamps, handcuffs, a 14-foot ladder, two big aircraft crash axes, fire extinguishers, a set of hammer and nails, bullhorns, infrared flashlights, strobe lights, night-vision devices, baton lights, "beanbag" lights, and two cameras.

The platoon leaders went over each man's personal gear: goggles, AN/PRC-90 survival radio, pen gun flare, penlight, survival kit, strobe light, aviator's gloves, compass, earplugs, and a razor-sharp six-inch knife strapped to each raider's thigh. Each man pinned subdued rank insignia to his collar and used camouflage sticks to darken his face. The final preparations had taken an hour and forty-five minutes. The raiders were now ready. In one more hour they would be airborne; in three and a half hours they would assault the Son Tay camp and rescue the sixty-one American POWs imprisoned there.

1030 Hours Local, Friday 20 November 1970
National Military Command Center
Room 2C945, Pentagon
Washington, D.C.

USAF Lieutenant General Albert G. "Whitey" Whisenand sat at an elaborate communications console in the series of rooms known as the National Military Command Center (NMCC). He looked up at the huge backlit Plexiglas panels that displayed the raid route from Thailand across Laos to Son Tay. Primary fighter support would come from Takhli (anti-SAM and anti-

AAA) and Udorn (anti-MiG) air bases in Thailand. Route lines and scheduling times were depicted from those bases, and from Nakhon Phanom in northeastern Thailand (for the raiders), thence to air refueling routes across central Laos. From there, the lines shot directly eastward—into North Vietnam to the POW camp at Son Tay, just twenty-three miles west of Hanoi. Whitey Whisenand, silver-haired, almost portly, more closely resembled a venerable member of the Senate than a military man. He studied the tersely-worded messages which had been arriving over the High Command Communications Net.

The raiders were poised for takeoff, they said, awaiting only the final "Go" command to be relayed from the Commander in Chief through the NMCC. Time was short, and increasingly critical. Hurricane Patsy was moving relentlessly toward the Annamite land mass and would soon swoop into the Hanoi and Son Tay areas. All other conditions were optimum: the moon at half-light, the temperature predicted to be in the cool range, negative cloud cover. If the raid didn't get off within the next hour, the next such window might be months away.

An Air Force colonel dressed in impeccable Class-A blues hurried up to Whisenand and handed him a paper covered with a purple band and the emblazoned words TOP SECRET—yet another message. Whisenand scrawled his initials on the routing sheet, flipped open the cover, and read the decoded words. He grimaced when he read the last line, picked up a telephone from the console, punched a button, and within twenty seconds had secure voice contact with the vice commander of 7th Air Force, the headquarters at Tan Son Nhut Air Base, located in Saigon, South Vietnam.

A ludicrous situation had arisen. Bull Simons and Wolf Lochert, waiting at Udorn Royal Thai Air Force Base, could not obtain the current and forecast weather for Laos and North Vietnam because the USAF commander of the 1st Weather Group, Air Weather Service, had rigid security regulations that prohibited unauthorized access to its classified weather information. The Son Tay operation was so closely held that very few people knew about it, and Commander, 1st Weather Group, was not on that short list. It was a glitch in the plan—when the ops order had been devised, no one had foreseen the problem of obtaining critical weather information prior to launch. As a result, vital information, desperately needed by an unknown Army colonel, was being prudently withheld by an Air Force lieutenant colonel at an air base from which few combat flights had been launched over North Vietnam since the Johnson bombing halt ordered in March 1968.

"This is Kingpin command post with an ops immediate message," Whisenand told Vice Commander, 7th Air Force, in a brisk tone. "You are directed to inform Commander, First Weather Group, that he has no further career in the United States Air Force unless he gives immediate, full and *enthusiastic* cooperation to Wildroot in all matters. Acknowledge." Wildroot was Simons' call sign. Kingpin was the code word for the entire rescue operation.

"Christ, Whitey, I don't believe it. I'll take care of it personally," a chagrined three-star replied, and broke the connection. But Whisenand's problems weren't over yet.

Whitey looked up as an ashen-faced major general from the Defense Intelligence Agency approached.

"General Whisenand," he said, his mouth a broken line. "I have just received a new assessment." The words that followed were spoken in a quiet and bitter tone.

"You're sure?" Whitey said, when he was finished. *No POWs? Oh, God.*

"The new information is reliable, sir."

As much as he despised doing so, Whitey immediately picked up the phone, stabbed a button, and told the senior military aide to the Secretary of Defense he was on his way up with new and vital information. He then signaled his assistant to take over, picked up his Kingpin briefing book, and walked with brisk strides from the National Military Command Center.

A ringing sound echoed in his ears. He did not want it to end this way.

Up the south elevators to the third floor and down the bisecting halls to the E-Ring, then on, hating every quickened step, to Room 3E880. He entered the Secretary's office and quickly told him of the development.

"What do you recommend?" Secretary of Defense Melvin Laird asked.

"I recommend we go," Whisenand replied firmly, fully prepared to lay his career on the line for this operation.

"But if there is now a probability that no prisoners are being held there—why?"

Whitey kept his voice steady, trying hard not to allow the emotion he felt to interfere. "I've been studying the photos and reports since the plan was conceived. Granted, there have been recent indications of movement, but there is also hard intelligence showing something—*someone*—is still in place there. If we can bring out one prisoner . . . " Whitey paused and swallowed. Laird watched closely. "I recommend Kingpin launch as planned, Mister Secretary. We have a 95 to 97 percent confidence factor Simons and Lochert can get their men in and out without losses. They've practiced this operation over two hundred times. And—"

"I know all that, Whitey." Laird's voice was quiet, tentative.

Whitey held his voice very even. "If it turned out there *were* Americans in Son Tay and we *didn't* go, we would never forgive ourselves. If you'll recall, the Caruso messages stated that seventeen more POWs have died in the camps."

Laird held his face impassive. "You realize that I must tell the President of the latest intelligence development."

"Yes, sir."

"If this operation blows up, the President will be accused of invading North Vietnam."

"Mister Secretary, do you remember what Colonel Simons answered when that senior staff member on the Joint Chiefs said maybe we shouldn't go, that the public wouldn't stand for it? Simons said, 'These are American prisoners. This is something that Americans traditionally do for Americans. For Christ sake, what is it we're afraid of?' "

Laird did not comment.

Whitey's voice was low and hardly audible. "It's the right thing to do, sir. A signal to the North Vietnamese that we place value in our people. More importantly, a signal to our men there that we have not forgotten them."

Melvin Laird stared somberly out the window at the Washington Monument. Finally he turned back to face Whisenand. "I'll fix it with the boss."

0200 Hours Local, Saturday 21 November 1970
Son Tay Prisoner of War Camp
Democratic Republic of North Vietnam

It began with a suddenness which rudely shattered the early morning quiet. The Vietnamese People's Army headquarters, located in the Citadel in Hanoi, immediately passed from drowsy idleness into confusion and near-frenzy.

Forty miles to their east, multiple flights of USN A-7 Corsairs and F-4 Phantoms began appearing on radar screens, darting about on flight tracks which passed between Hanoi and Haiphong.

From the western sky, four-ship flights of sleek F-105 Thunderchiefs soared and fired AGM-45 Shrike antiradar missiles toward three different surface-to-air missile sites that came up on the air to track the growing numbers of blips suddenly appearing on their radar screens.

Special Operations C-130s flew at treetop level about the periphery of Hanoi, and the crews released special wares, which swung in great, black parachutes and added firefight noise to the confusion.

More Navy aircraft, then more fighters from the Thailand bases appeared. The sky was filled with Americans. The F-105 Wild Weasels launched more Shrike missiles as more radars came onto the air, vainly trying to discern which targets the Yankee air-pirate targets were going to attack.

In the midst of confusion a C-130 climbed and entered an orbit west of Hanoi, and dropped out a series of 200,000-candlepower flares, turning the darkness into brilliant daylight. Other C-130s released other flares and special wares at other locations, then quickly dipped back down to safer treetop altitudes.

"Shoot!" Air Force Captain Joe Kelly barked to the two side gunners as he slid his eighteen-ton HH-53 helicopter to a perfect hover at treetop level between two guard towers on the west wall of the Son Tay prison camp. Kelly's voice was calm and methodical. They had practiced the drill many times at the Eglin range. The gunners didn't hesitate. The screaming roar of their 7.62mm Gatling guns spewing 6,000 rounds a minute combined with the threshing of the huge rotor blades to drown out the screams of the guards as hundreds of bullets chewed the tower and the leg supports to splinters.

Simultaneously, a series of raucous gunfire sounds exploded from a half-dozen other locations east of them, made by firefight simulators—devices which amplified deafening automatic weapons noises—the special wares dropped from the Special Operations CF-130s.

Eastward, a giant pallet of napalm was ignited, giving off a huge rolling fireball that looked much like a nuclear burst.

Joe Kelly's helicopter was one of 105 United States Air Force and United States Navy planes launched from five land bases and three aircraft carriers that night to conduct or support the raid. It had taken astute coordination to choreograph the diversion raids around Hanoi and Haiphong without telling the Air Force and Navy commanders the reason for sending their pilots into the most heavily defended area in the world, many armed only with *flares*. Only the SAM-killer Wild Weasels from Takhli and those airplanes designated as rescue combat air patrol (rescap—in the event an American aircraft went down) carried offensive weapons.

As soon as the towers crashed to the ground, the gunner on the right side, Master Sergeant Manuel "Cat" Dominguez, advised Kelly on intercom, "We got 'em. The towers are down."

Following the plan—which allowed for precisely twenty-six minutes on the ground—Kelly moved his ship forty feet toward the entrance gate, holding his hover for six more seconds while Dominguez used his roaring gun to chew up a military barracks just outside the gate. Dominguez could not fire on the guard tower located at the gate, for beneath it was a torture hut that might contain POWs, and the tower could fall on it. After Dominguez put 600 7.62mm rounds into the barracks, stripping it like a flayed corpse, Kelly pulled pitch and moved the big helicopter just outside the camp and put it on the ground. He was to remain there until called in to pick up a group of the assault force and their rescued prisoners. Joe Kelly's job now was to monitor three radios and relay information between Simons, the on-site commander, and the off-site commander, General Leroy Manor, at his command post on Monkey Mountain near Da Nang Air Base in South Vietnam.

As Kelly, call sign Apple Two, pulled away to land, Apple One set down Bull Simons and Wolf Lochert's assault group in front of what he believed was the main gate to the Son Tay prison. Wolf yelled the order to disembark and the twenty-one men under Simons and Lochert swarmed off the chopper.

"Wrong compound," Simons yelled the minute he hit the ground. Wolf Lochert verified the mistake as he ran out the helicopter's ramp. He'd trained so many times at the stateside replica that he knew those trees should be *here,* these bushes *there, that* building and wall placed beyond.

A movement at the building caught Wolf's eye. He verified it was not a POW and cut the confused figure down with his CAR-15 assault rifle. As he fired, he realized where they were. The helicopter, Apple One, who'd just lifted off, had deposited them in what was known as the Secondary School, a place once used as a schoolhouse.

Just as Simons ordered his radio operator to get Apple One back to pick them up, a swarm of half-dressed figures began to pour out of the building. Even as the firefight developed—as Wolf and the others swung their guns on them—a feeling of familiarity tugged within Wolf Lochert's disciplined mind.

Wolf positioned himself and his men to most efficiently cut down the partially dressed men running out the door. There were fifty or sixty of them and their bodies piled up in neat rows under the flickering light as the Special Forces men shot them down. He studied them as they killed them. Several were bigger, much larger than they should be. The building began to burn from carefully placed grenades fired from M79 launchers.

Movement to Wolf's left drew his attention and he instinctively rolled to the right as several shots zinged over his head. In the same motion he leveled his assault rifle and fired two three-round bursts into two men he saw outlined against the flames. There was something odd about these too, Wolf noted, but turned back to complete the carnage to his front.

Only seventeen minutes remained!

He heard the helicopter returning. "Take over," he told his number two. "Cover me," he yelled at another. The firefight was dying out as the noise of the returning helicopter sounded over the trees. Dodging, Wolf ran to the closest bodies crumpled at the edge of the killing ground. Two were dressed in olive drab undershirts. They had Slavic features. Another body, bare-chested and barefoot, was clad in green trousers with a belt. Wolf knelt, yanked his Randall knife from its scabbard strapped upside down to his harness, sawed loose the belt buckle on the dead man's trousers, and stuffed it into the cargo pocket on his left leg. Next he searched and found a soldier with his shirt on, and deftly cut away the collar tab, which was royal blue in color. With practiced fingers he slid the knife up into the scabbard as he arose.

He quickly doubled back to the last two men he'd dropped with his CAR-15. Both were large, and wore dark civilian slacks and light-colored shirts, now rent and bloody. As he knelt beside them, he noted that they too were Caucasians, better-dressed and likely more important than the others he'd seen. A Kalashnikov rifle lay near one, a Makarov automatic pistol in the outstretched hand of the other. Wolf stuffed the pistol into his waistband, then rapidly rifled through their pockets, but found nothing. They were barefoot and one's belt wasn't fastened. They'd obviously dressed hastily before emerging from a nearby smaller, better-maintained building. Officers, Wolf decided.

"Load up. Get a move on," Wolf heard Simons' foghorn yell above the helicopter noise. Still crouched, Wolf looked back and saw in the flickering light the raiders boarding the helicopter. Simons pointed and beckoned.

Only thirteen minutes remained.

"Get on board," Wolf yelled to the man covering him, then again bent over the bodies. He lifted the closest man's hand and pulled a heavy signet ring from a finger, then rose and dashed back to the helicopter. He was the last to board.

"About fucking time, Lochert," Simons snarled, then turned to the pilot. "Put us where we belong." The pilot of Apple One lifted off and in one and a half minutes had them on the ground beside the south wall of Son Tay prison. In seconds they were in the compound, still brightly lit by flares from the orbiting C-130, looking like a football field under lights.

Ten minutes remained.

The firing had quieted as the two other assault groups secured the compound. The leader of one group, Captain Dick Meadows, repeatedly announced on his bullhorn: *"We are Americans. Keep your heads down. We are Americans. This is a rescue. We are here to get you out. Keep your heads down. Get on the floor. We'll be in your cells in a minute."*

Lochert raced with his men to their preassigned positions.

"About fucking time," a Green Beret said with a quick grin, and added, "Time to go in."

The men assigned to search for the POWs and carry them to the waiting helicopters ran to the low, one-story prison. The building was gray, with mildew and peeling whitewash. Men with axes smashed open the doors and others poured in, as they'd trained, some turning left, some turning right, some straight ahead to the exact position of the cell doors that CARUSO had spelled out in his choir chorus. One man was designated to take pictures.

"Keep your heads down, keep your heads down. We are Americans," Meadows' bullhorn boomed.

There were no answers. Instead, hollow curses and cries of dismay came from the men entering the cells.

"Negative, negative items. Negative," was repeated over and over in anguished voices. Lochert hurried down the concrete halls, glancing through each ajar cell door. There were no longer stocks or handcuffs lying about. Most telling, the bloodstains were long dried.

As hardened, tough and professional as Wolf Lochert was, he felt his heart slipping into his boots.

The Son Tay prison was empty of American prisoners of war.

There were three minutes remaining.

"Load up, move out," Simons' even, bullhorn-amplified voice roared over the din. Quickly and efficiently, the men did as they were told. Minutes later they were airborne and speeding back to the west.

Time was up.

"Negative items . . . repeat . . . negative items," Bull Simons advised General Leroy Manor over the HF radio net. "Negative items."

1530 Hours Local, Monday 23 November 1970
Press Room, Pentagon
Washington, D.C.

"Are you telling us the whole raid was a bust? An intelligence failure?" the reporter from *The New York Times* said to

Secretary of Defense Melvin Laird, who stood by the podium under the hot lights. Laird wore a dark suit, white shirt, blue tie.

With tired patience, Laird tried to speak. "What I'm telling you—"

"What you're telling us is a bunch of crap," a slender, blond man snapped. He was Shawn Bannister, California politician and sometime reporter for the *California Sun.* "We were told this press briefing was to start at eleven o'clock and it's already after three. You've kept us waiting for four hours to find out you invaded North Vietnam on the pretext of rescuing American criminals held in jail." Shawn Bannister wore a tan canvas photographer's vest, blue jeans, and combat boots. Several of his fellow newsmen gave low hisses at his use of the word "criminals."

"Bannister, shut the fuck up," a small man named Ramon Cragg sitting next to Bannister said in a quiet voice. "You're not big enough to spout off like that."

Laird simply ignored Bannister. The special mission, Laird said, had been deemed necessary, based upon information that some American men were dying in prisoner of war camps. Mission training had been meticulous, intensive, around the clock. "Regrettably, the rescue team discovered that this camp had been recently vacated. No prisoners were found."

"Was this the first time that American forces were used in North Vietnam?"

"No," Laird said. "We have regularly carried on search-and-rescue missions of downed crewmen in North Vietnam by helicopter and supporting aircraft."

The press people turned to Bull Simons, who stood in full uniform complete with ribbons and badges beside the podium. His impassive face was deeply lined with the efforts of the past months. He'd been en route from Thailand most of the last two days.

"How many men were on the mission?"

"I can't tell you that," Simons said.

"Did the mission have a code name?"

"I can't answer that question."

"Did you fly from an aircraft carrier?"

"I can't answer that."

"What kind of helicopter was it?"

"I can't answer that."

The questions went on relentlessly. How many men did they hope to free? Did they have an alternate target? Simons and Laird repeatedly said they could not answer or make comment. The press finally hit upon some questions that Bull Simons did answer.

"Did you fire your weapons?"

"Yes, we did fire our weapons."

"Did you kill anybody?"

"Yes, I would imagine so."

1630 Hours Local, Tuesday 24 November 1970
Oval Office, The White House
Washington, D.C.

"Those men," Richard M. Nixon said with fervor, "deserve the thanks and admiration of our nation. This mission will remain a beacon of courage and skill to military men everywhere." They were the same words he'd just spoken in the East Room to the assembled Son Tay raiders. Nixon, dressed in dark suit, white shirt, and red tie, now stood behind his desk, a hand resting on the surface. He was heavily jowled, yet appeared freshly shaven. Robert Haldeman, Nixon's tanned, stocky Chief of Staff, leaned arrogantly against the wall to one side. His hair was crew cut as short as if he were an active-duty military man.

The light through the window behind the President formed a frame, thought USAF Lieutenant General Whitey Whisenand. He wore his dress blues, and held a briefcase and an oversized manila envelope at his side. It was in this very room five months earlier that he'd first brought up the Son Tay raid concept. The vivid blue of the oval rug with its ring of gold stars and huge golden eagle depicting the President's seal of office picked up the light from the window and appeared too grand to step a mortal foot upon.

Whitey Whisenand had once been "fired" by the 36th President of the United States, Lyndon Baines Johnson. That is to say, two-star *Major* General Whisenand had worked for LBJ as a special member of the National Security Council, but had functioned as Johnson's adviser for matters relating to the use of air power in the Vietnam war. Johnson had placed him on the general officer retired list when Whisenand had accused his Commander in Chief of squandering American lives in his and his Secretary of Defense, Robert Strange McNamara's, half-baked attempt to run the Vietnam war.

Immediately following his inauguration on January 20, Richard Nixon had interviewed Whitey and offered to recall him as a three-star general, in essentially the same position. Whitey had been about to turn him down when Nixon had said he wanted him to be the chief mover in getting the American POWs out of Vietnam. Major General Albert G. Whisenand, USAF (Ret), had accepted and had soon been recalled to active duty as a lieutenant general.

Now Whitey stood before his Commander in Chief, representing what the press and many congressmen termed a definite intelligence failure. He did not feel good at all about that, yet because of what Lieutenant Colonel Wolf Lochert had discovered during the raid, along with other information from other sensitive sources, he had come to a conclusion which was so shocking, so sensitive and confidential, that he'd felt justified in jumping the entire military and civilian intelligence chain of command.

There had been a slight problem a half hour earlier when the media had requested a photo opportunity while the President was handing out medals to the raiders in the East Room. Whitey had quickly decided that Wolf Lochert's face should not be made known to the public as a Son Tay raider. Wolf's past was just too controversial. He had pulled the stocky man aside, out of view of the cameras' hungry eyes, and asked him to wait in a hallway until he'd spoken privately with the President about their matter of special concern.

"Mr. President," Whitey began, "I thank you for your kind words regarding the courage and integrity of our fighting men. And I am anguished that we weren't able to bring any of our boys home."

Nixon nodded but did not speak. His face remained composed.

"You hired me, sir, to bring our POWs home. Now, something has come to my attention that is so serious in nature that I felt compelled to bring it to your attention before that of any other person, military or civilian." He glanced at Haldeman, who returned his look with a steady gaze. "Even, sir, to the exclusion—for the moment—of your Chief of Staff."

Richard Nixon nodded at Haldeman, who exhaled audibly and left the room with a wooden face. He was unaccustomed to being ordered about by a mere lieutenant general.

Whitey Whisenand reached into his briefcase and drew out a 12×17-inch poster board, which he held up for his Commander in Chief to view.

"Ah, yes," Richard Nixon said. "Your famous blackboard."

LOSSES OVER NORTH VIETNAM AND LAOS			
	MIA/KIA	POW	Aircraft
USAF	441	232	905
USN	239	145	401
USMC	78	17	218
USA	173	63	512 (Helios)
TOTAL	931	457	2036

Whitey Whisenand had updated his "blackboard" daily and used it to impress upon his colleagues and his then–Commander in Chief, Lyndon Baines Johnson, that the count of missing and captured American aircrew fighting men was rising daily. And General Whisenand would not tolerate anyone saying, "It's a small war but it's all we've got." He was adamant in telling all who would listen that these air crewmen on his blackboard never thought of the Vietnam war as a small war.

Nixon rubbed his face. "Well, ah, you showed this to me, General, when we first met. Although I presume it is current, may I ask why the secrecy now that you didn't manifest before?"

"The board is to refresh your memory, sir," Whitey Whisenand said, aware that the sentence was overly patronizing, but wanting his current Commander in Chief to share his concern about these men who must not be forgotten.

"As to the classified part," he continued, "I have had reason to believe there were Russian troops stationed in North Vietnam in roles other than as advisers or air-defense technicians." He unfastened and opened the manila envelope and pulled out the Russian soldier's belt buckle and a photograph of the Makarov pistol liberated by Wolf Lochert. "These were found on Caucasians in a compound adjacent to the Son Tay prison. Both are Soviet military issue." He added the patch of cloth, the collar tab cut from the dead soldier. "That, sir, identifies the soldier as KGB. They're the only ones who wear the royal blue color."

When Nixon was finished examining the first articles, Whitey placed the signet ring on his desk. The blood-red stone was overlaid with the KGB sword and shield emblem.

"That is a KGB ring worn only by upper-level officers—colonels and above—and seldom when they're not among their own. The man who wore it either felt very secure in his surroundings or was very forgetful. He also carried that Makarov pistol, worn by officers in the KGB. Another Caucasian, wearing similar civilian clothing, was killed with him—another high-ranking officer, we believe. They were at Son Tay, with a company of their KGB soldiers, and there were no longer any American prisoners to be found there. I do not believe this to be coincidental. I believe there is a definite relationship."

Nixon examined the sword and shield emblem on the ring with interest. "Go on," he said.

Whitey spoke. "I do not feel we can ignore the implications, Mr. President. Since I also understand that your relationship with Secretary Brezhnev is sensitive and critical, I feel it would be prudent to conduct an extremely secretive investigation of the matter without bringing in or notifying any other members of our government."

The President stared without comment.

Whitey took a shallow breath. "If you agree, I'll need your approval to conduct a secret investigation with no questions asked by the intelligence community or any other agency. No questions, yet I might need their cooperation."

Nixon reexamined the ring, then the wide brass buckle with the Red Star in the center, finally the photograph. He looked up. "Who would you choose to run the investigation? Yourself?"

"At this level, yes sir. I would also like to use Lieutenant Colonel Lochert, the Army officer you decorated alongside Colonel Bull Simons. He was the one who recognized these for what they are when he was on the ground at Son Tay, and he made sure they were brought to my attention—and only my attention—when he arrived here for the ceremony."

"You? Why not his superior officers?" The President's eyes were narrowed. He had a liking for secrecy. The previous administration had been rent with leaks, and Nixon was determined not to let that happen during his own tenure.

"We worked together setting up the raid and he knew I had direct contact with you regarding POWs. I think it was shrewd of him. His discovery and my conclusions, if true, could have a massive impact on national security, as well as with our future relations with Russia."

"I see." The President gave him a look that told Whitey he liked what he was hearing.

"And to be truthful, Mr. President, Lieutenant Colonel Lochert isn't well regarded by certain members of the hierarchy in the Pentagon."

"Popularity is not always a good gauge of a man's worth," Nixon said.

"I agree, sir. Lochert is capable, a superb warrior, and a man of rare integrity. So," Whitey Whisenand continued, "I want to put him in charge of the operational aspect of the investigation."

Nixon pushed the captured items about on his desktop. "Is this *all* the evidence you have?"

Whitey nodded. "The only hard evidence. The KGB were Slavic and Mongolian in appearance. Two were obviously high-ranking officers. Several of the prisoners taken to Son Tay had sensitive backgrounds, possessing information the Soviets would surely like to have. Now they seem to have disappeared, as if from the face of the earth."

"Is that all?"

Wasn't it enough? He used his last bullet. Not a powerful one. "Colonel Lochert heard commands in Russian and curses in Uzbek."

Nixon took in the words, then sat at his desk and made notes on a yellow legal pad. He wrote swiftly before looking up. "You are cleared," he said, "to *discreetly* investigate the matter. This will provide proper authorization."

"And Colonel Lochert?"

"He's your man. I'll advise the Army Chief of Staff if you wish."

"Your letter of authority should be enough, sir. I'd rather not use a bludgeon when it's not warranted."

Nixon punched a button on his desk and a middle-aged woman entered through the side door. "Rose Mary, type this up for my signature, then give it to the General here. No other copies." He tore off the top sheet of the legal pad and handed it to her.

"Be discreet—and keep me informed," were the last words the President of the United States spoke to Whitey Whisenand as he departed the Oval Office.

After receiving the letter of authority, neatly typed on the White House stationery and bearing the President's bold signature, General Whisenand stepped into the hall and beckoned to Wolf Lochert, who had waited as he'd been asked to do.

"The President," Whisenand said as they started down the hall toward the entrance, in step as military people subconsciously do, "has decided to assign us an especially sensitive mission. We'll go to my office and discuss it in private."

Sixteen months passed before General Whitey Whisenand and Colonel Wolf Lochert finally made progress in shedding light on the Russian connection.

Chapter 1

"My God, they're all over the place," Rustic 17 transmitted in an excited voice. "Tanks, trucks, guns. You should see the troops. And they're all shooting. Unbelievable!"

Rustic 17 was a twin-engine OV-10 observation plane flying over the DMZ—the Demilitarized Zone where, according to the Geneva conference agreements, no military forces were supposed to be. The cloud ceiling was low, 500 feet, and the pilot flying Rustic 17 danced his craft nimbly about the sky at 250 mph, frantically dodging rugged hills and white, basketball-sized explosions from 37 and 23mm antiaircraft guns.

"One Nine, do you copy?" Rustic 17 radioed. He was young, just checked out in the area. He'd been told there wasn't much stirring, but to go up and sniff around just in case the bad guys were up to something. He was calling Rustic 19, a second OV-10 Bronco orbiting above the clouds in the brilliant sunlight. Both men were FACs—Forward Air Controllers—trained to locate and observe enemy troops and supplies, then to call in and coordinate air strikes.

"One Nine copies. Haul ass outta there, One Seven." The

22

pilot of Rustic 19 was Lieutenant Rick Scaling, at the age of twenty-four only one year older than Rustic 17, but with his ten months in Vietnam and 510 hours of combat time, he was wiser. His white flight helmet hid close-shorn brown hair. Another helmeted figure, an Air Force lieutenant colonel in his mid-thirties, was strapped into the backseat of the OV-10. Flying above the cloud layer, they could only imagine what was going on below. "Get out of there," Scaling repeated to the low-flying FAC.

"Negative, Rick," Rustic 17 said in a hardly controlled, excited voice. "I've gotta give you a count so you can tell Seventh. This is big! I mean there's hundreds of trucks, at least, oh, thirty or forty tanks, and so many troops they look like ants, and they're all hauling ass south. It's a no-shit invasion. I'm just north of the Boobs in the Ben Hai River. Let me give you the map cords."

"Negative, One Seven. I know where the Boobs are. Climb outta there . . . now!"

"Ah roger, One Nine. Stand by while I . . . *Oh, shit I'm hit . . . Engine blown off . . . Spinning, can't . . . move . . . can't . . . Move . . . Fire . . . I got . . .* " The carrier wave of Rustic 17's radio continued for two more seconds, then went dead.

"Rustic One Seven, Rustic One Seven, do you read?" Scaling repeated the call for a full minute, his voice measured and calm, with only a trace of sad irony. Finally he changed the litany. "Rustic One Seven, if you read me, come up on voice or beeper."

Although it did not sound encouraging, pilots had been known to bail out successfully under similar circumstances. Some spoke on their survival radios as they hung in their parachutes on the way down. The beeper was a special sound made by a pilot's small survival radio that he could switch on if he didn't want to talk because enemy troops were too close by. But there was no radio return from Rustic 17—not even the *whoop-whoop* of the emergency radio which was activated as a pilot's chute deployed.

"Doesn't sound good, Colonel," Scaling said on the intercom to the man in back.

"No, it doesn't," Lieutenant Colonel Court Bannister replied quietly. His immediate reaction was to say, "Better get a SAR going," but he knew better. To do so would be to order the obvious to a professional who knew his business. A SAR was a Search and Rescue effort, using helicopters and armed support planes to try to retrieve men who had bailed out of an airplane. Bannister also figured Scaling was resisting the urge to immediately plunge into the cloud and go down to search for One Seven. He heard Scaling switch his UHF radio to the frequency for Crown, a Navy radar vessel off the coast of Vietnam in the Gulf of Tonkin.

"Crown, Crown, Rustic One Niner on Uniform," Scaling transmitted.

Crown came up immediately with booming power. "Rustic One Nine, Crown, go."

"Crown, Rustic One Niner, go secure."

"Rustic One Nine, Crown, going secure."

Both men switched on their voice scramblers.

"Crown, Rustic One Seven is down—vicinity of the Boobs in the Ben Hai River in the DMZ—two souls on board." The Boobs were two curves in the east-west river which, from the air, looked like a pair of nicely rounded breasts. Scaling checked his map coordinates. "Cords are X-ray Delta 945681."

"One Nine, Crown copies X-ray Delta 945681. Any chutes?"

"Can't tell, I'm on top of a cloud layer and he was beneath. No beepers and no emergency locator beacons. Best put a SAR on standby. The weather's too bad to bring them out at this time."

"Rustic One Nine, Crown, placing SAR on standby now."

"Crown, also be advised that Rustic One Seven reported a heavy troop, truck, and tank concentration in the DMZ, moving south. I'm going down for a look-see."

"Rustic One Nine, Crown copies. Good luck. Crown listening out."

"Unless you've got any major objections, Colonel Bannister," Scaling said, "I'd like to take a look. I know a valley where we can let down and get below this stuff." An instrument letdown is normally made from a known navigation radio point using tested and approved turns, airspeeds, and a specified rate of descent to avoid granite-lined clouds. There was no such aid here.

Does this kid know what he's doing? Or am I going to bust my ass in the backseat with a lieutenant pilot who looks like a college freshman? Bannister wondered to himself. He stretched against his harness. At 6′ 2″, he filled the backseat, a fighter pilot with hundreds of missions over South and North Vietnam in the cockpits of F-100 and F-4 fighters. It would be different if Scaling were an old head he'd flown with under hairy conditions. With a proven buddy, you would go to hell and back if need be. But this squirt?

"Go ahead," Court Bannister said, keeping his voice neutral. He oriented himself on his map and took a bearing the best he could on the Da Nang TACAN, call sign DAG, nearly 100 miles distant. A typical fighter pilot, he trusted no one's navigation except his own. If something happened to Scaling, Bannister needed to know how to find his way. He felt and heard the sound of the two turboprop engines drop as Scaling pulled the throttles back a few percent, then lowered the nose of the aircraft. Within seconds they were in the white milk of sunlit clouds that rapidly turned gray then dark as the moisture content increased. The turbulence intensified, tossing the OV-10 Bronco about as they flew through updrafts from unseen mountains below.

The solid gray color grew lighter as they approached the bottom of the undercast, and light rain began to hammer on the canopy of the twin-tailed aircraft. Cloud wisps shot underneath and the ground appeared—a verdant world of greens and browns. A single glance at the altimeter verified that they were just 500 feet above the craggy hills.

Scaling threw the OV-10 into a sharp left bank and they looked down on an old French road crowded with khaki-clad troops, slogging southward through the red-hued mud. There were lines of vehicles. Here and there the road was choked by stalled or bogged trucks.

"Look at that," Scaling grunted as he maneuvered his craft south, jinking hard back and forth across the road. Machine gunners on the tanks and trucks frantically swiveled and opened fire. Red and green tracers chased after the airplane in lazy, graceful loops.

"God, I wish we had some fighters up here to put on these guys," Scaling lamented.

The Rustics were one of the many Forward Air Controller groups that patrolled the war zone for targets, then called in fighters to attack what they found. They lived and lusted for scenes just such as they were seeing below.

Court saw startled infantry troops unslinging their guns. The pilots were vulnerable flying at such a low altitude.

"Over there, ten o'clock," Scaling said, his tone altered. Court scanned and saw black smoke and an orange pyre. A crashed airplane. The fire was dwindling in the light rain.

Scaling nosed the OV-10 toward the wreckage, which littered a steep hillside. "Fly it, will you, Colonel? I'll use the binocs to try to see if they got out of the bird. We're out of range of their guns."

Court Bannister took the controls and set up a left orbit over the wreckage. The airplane had hit flat, scattering debris and fuel—no longer looking remotely like an OV-10. The Bronco's airframe is not made of metal and burns to a silvery ash, leaving only major components such as engines, the armor plates of the two ejection seats, and a few dented and charred avionics boxes and wire bundles. One engine had impacted two hundred yards from the crash site. Court noted the distance to the nearest enemy guns, firing ineffectually from half a mile to the east, then made a lower pass over the scarred hillside.

"Hell," Scaling said in a heavy voice, "I don't even need the glasses. The seats are still in it, Colonel. They didn't get out." As he made two more passes, Court could see the twisted and blackened remains of the pilot and observer crumpled amidst the armor plating. Their deaths had been mercifully quick.

Suddenly, 23mm automatic weapons rounds began exploding furiously about their airplane, and Court heard rapid drumbeats as pieces of shrapnel thumped through the fuselage. Without conscious thought he jammed the throttles forward and hauled on the stick. The plane shot into the clouds, out of view of the gunners.

"Kee-rist," Scaling breathed. "They must have towed a zipper over there." A zipper was a very accurate, very rapid-firing, Russian ZPU-23-2, optically fired, twin-barrel gun.

"I guess they heard us up above and expected we might come down for a look. You okay?" Court asked as he checked engine gauges and airplane instruments on the panel in front of him. All appeared normal, though they'd taken several hits.

"Yeah," Scaling said, taking back the controls.

They broke out on top of the clouds in the sunshine. Scaling performed a controllability check to make sure everything was operating and the plane could be safely flown. Finally, he lowered the gear and flaps and found he could slow to landing speed without any problems.

"Got your camera ready?" Court asked when Rick was finished.

"You mean we gotta go back?" Scaling sounded not at all eager.

"Only way they'll believe it's this massive is if we bring back photos. I'll fly the bird and make a single, south-to-north pass along the length of the column. You take pictures. Set up for low-light level using as fast a shutter speed as you can get," Bannister said, hoping to hell the enemy wasn't expecting them to drop down again. He took control and gingerly pushed back through the clouds, dodged a hill, then flew over the convoy, turboprops roaring loudly in the moisture-filled air. From the raised back "observer's" seat of the OV-10, Court had almost as much visibility as the man in front. He pulled the plane back and forth, periodically pausing briefly, wing-low over a concentration he thought might provide a good picture.

"Start snapping," he said, eyes roaming.

"I am. I don't want to have to do this again," Scaling said. He got a particularly good photo and exulted, "Yeah!"

Out of the corner of his eye, Court sensed motion from behind the airplane. He swung his head. A white smoke trail was arching skyward—streaking toward them.

"Hang on," he yelled, pulling the airplane toward the missile in a gut-wrenching, climbing turn. The dartlike missile whooshed underneath them.

"Kee-rist," Scaling breathed, "what was that?"

Court carefully looked about for more of them until they'd reentered the clouds. "That, young lieutenant, was a baby surface-to-air missile known as the Strela. A Russian-built heat-seeker that an infantryman can fire from his shoulder."

"If you hadn't seen it in time, it would have flown right up an engine exhaust," Scaling said in wonder.

"Yeah, that's probably what got One Seven. But clouds disperse the heat and up here they can't see us anyway. You got the pictures?"

"Indeed I do . . . even remembered to take the lens cover off." If the Lieutenant could joke at a time such as this, he was okay.

"Good. Without pictures, Seventh might think we're exaggerating and send another FAC to check it out."

"Man'd be crazy to fly down there," snorted Rick Scaling as he took over the controls.

1830 Hours Local, Friday 30 March 1972
7th Air Force Intelligence Section,
Tan Son Nhut Air Base
Republic of Vietnam

"These provide proof that no one can refute." Major General Leonard Norman said grimly to Court Bannister. They stood, hovering over a light table in the photo lab. "I've been predicting something like this, but my God. It's massive!" Norman was tall, slender, and straight as a stick, with a thatch of reddish-brown hair. He did not wear the wings of a pilot on his neatly pressed khaki uniform. He was a nonflier, a manager of information gleaned from intelligence sources. "Describe it all again, this time in more detail," he said doggedly.

The man before him, Lieutenant Colonel Courtland Esclaremonde de Montségur Bannister, wore a faded green K-2B flying suit. He stood two inches taller than the General and was broader of shoulder. His close-cropped hair was normally light brown, but was now bleached almost white by the relentless sun. He was in his mid-thirties and had been a lieutenant colonel for two years. He worked in the Standardization and Evaluation section of 7th Air Force, and his job was to ensure the flying units were following the rules, and to verify the flying proficiency and combat capability of pilots in the assigned units. He thought the job Mickey Mouse, and wanted to be in a combat squadron—preferably as commander.

Bannister described what they'd witnessed, giving, as accurately as he could, the numbers and types of troops and vehicles he'd spotted, in addition to what was shown in the photographs. A tech sergeant took careful notes. Bannister concluded with, "But the weather was bad, they were shooting, and I got to see my first Strela from up close."

"How does the SA-7 compare to the SAMs up north?" Norman asked. Court Bannister had flown combat missions over Hanoi in an F-4, and on several occasions had been forced to dodge the telephone pole–sized SA-2 SAM missiles fired at him.

"Well," Court mused, "the Strela's not much larger than a baseball bat, but my pucker factor was the same. It can kill you just as dead. Only difference is it'll leave you in bigger pieces." He made a wry smile. "Because of the damn thing, we couldn't stay down there long enough to follow the column back into North Vietnam and determine its length."

"We'll put out a warning to the pilots to expect large numbers of SA-7 Strelas. They're more of a hazard to the slow movers like the OV-10."

"Yes, sir. The jets can outrun and easily outmaneuver them."

General Norman wistfully regarded the wall map, where colored pins were being added to show the sightings. "It's a perfect time for the North Viet communists to invade South Vietnam."

Since 1969, both stated American goals of Richard M. Nixon—Vietnamization and withdrawal—had steadily progressed. Under the Nixon Doctrine, America would aid its South Vietnamese ally with material, technical advice, and, if necessary, air and naval forces. American military strength in South Vietnam was at 95,000—those troops assigned to purely defensive roles—down from more than half a million three years earlier. The majority of the men being sent home were from the Army and Marine Corps, but USAF strength in South Vietnam stood at a meager 20,000, a third of what it had been three years before. From Thailand, 27,000 more airmen were launching daily combat sorties, but only to Laos and Cambodia. The key areas, in North Vietnam, were not being struck.

"You've given me proof positive of what I've been warning might happen," General Leonard said. "I've got Black Bird and Buffalo Hunter photos showing a large-scale buildup in the North, but nothing showing the NVA have started into the DMZ." Black Bird was code for the SR-71 high-altitude, 3,000-mile-per-hour reconnaissance aircraft. Buffalo Hunters were unmanned recce drones that roamed over North Vietnam taking programmed pictures.

"Ever since the Viet Cong were destroyed as a fighting force in the Tet battle of '68 and the North Vietnamese Army got the hell kicked out of it," Norman said, "wily old Giap up there's wanted to put the hurt on us."

General Vo Nguyen Giap was Defense Minister for the DRV, the Democratic People's Republic of Vietnam. VC losses during the Tet offensive and NVA losses at the siege of Khe Sanh had been staggering. It had taken Giap four years of intensive training and recruiting—including fifteen-year-old children—to return his army to fighting shape.

"The communists are no longer even making an attempt to fool the world into thinking this is merely a civil war in the South," Norman said, tapping a revealing photograph. "These are hard-core North Vietnamese soldiers, with Russian tanks and guns, and this is an invasion just as real as Hitler's into France and the Chinese into Korea." There were photos showing T-34 and T-54 tanks, older PT-76 tanks, towed 130mm and AAA guns, and thousands of troops.

"Now," Norman said quietly, "we have to try to stop them, and we don't have much to do it with." He carefully gathered up the photos, placed them into a manila envelope, and started toward the door. "Sit tight here and have some coffee," he said over his shoulder. "I'm going over to show these to the old man."

The "old man" was COMMUSMACV, Army General Creighton W. Abrams, Commander, U.S. Military Assistance Command, Vietnam. Abrams, like his predecessor, General William Childs Westmoreland, ran the in-country war. The out-country air war—over Laos, Cambodia, and North Vietnam—was run by CINCPAC, Admiral John McCain, Commander in Chief, Pacific Command. It was not an efficient chain of command.

Court took coffee from a battered urn and scanned daily intelligence summaries (known as DISUMs) until General Norman returned an hour later, wearing a look of grim satisfaction.

"*Now* he believes me," Norman said. "We're putting our forces on alert and telling the South Vietnamese to prepare for the invasion. I've ordered an intensified recce effort so we'll know what we're dealing with. Things are going to get busy as hell here in the next few minutes." His eyes sparkled as he motioned. "Let's go to my office, Court." He led the way out of the room and down the linoleum-covered hall to a medium-sized office with plasterboard walls painted the standard, somewhat nauseous, military light green color.

Norman motioned to the couch and sat behind his desk. He studied Bannister thoughtfully.

"I don't like the fact that you're flying combat," he said.

"You've done your part. Two combat tours is enough for any man."

"I don't get to see much real action, sir," Bannister quickly replied. "I'm assigned to Stan Eval and I'm allowed to fly some, but combat missions like today's are out of the ordinary."

"You only fly *some?*" Norman raised an eyebrow.

"Well, in F-4s, for instance. We lay off the chickenshit as much as possible, but it's nice to know whether the guys are getting the proper training and are flying as safely as possible."

"And you're only cleared to fly in-country." It was a statement now, not a question. In-country meant within the borders of South Vietnam.

Court tried not to appear sheepish.

"And not on combat missions—just local area flights." Norman was not smiling.

"Yes, sir, but . . . "

"But *what,* Colonel?" Norman said before Court could answer.

Court wasn't at all sure where this was leading. He'd known General Norman since 1966, but only in a professional manner. Norman had always remained distant, as befitted a man fifteen years and four ranks his senior. This was the most open he'd been to his subordinate.

"I just do my job," Court said lamely.

Norman made a half smile. "Are you curious why I know so much about what you're doing?"

"Yes, sir."

"Your uncle, General Whisenand, dropped a line and asked how and what you were doing over here. He knows USAF policy doesn't allow three combat tours in the cockpit and he was surprised when you volunteered for the job you're in, since it meant you'd be assigned to a desk at Seventh Air Force headquarters, and he *knows* how you feel about desk jobs. So I checked up."

"I see, sir." When he'd heard about the two-combat-tour restriction, Court had phoned a friend in officer assignments for this headquarters staff job, which at least allowed him to remain close to the action. The pilots in his office at 7th Air Force Headquarters spent many days on the road, on TDY (Temporary Duty) to the flying units, ensuring the voluminous 7th AF Regulations were being adhered to. His boss, Colonel

Glenn Fricke, knew that Bannister was sniveling extra flights, even sneaking in an occasional combat sortie, and was not unhappy about it. He did the same himself. Fighter pilots do things like that.

As a lieutenant colonel, Bannister was not in the best job for his career's sake, and higher levels of officialdom kept track of their up-and-coming officers. He'd shortly be considered for full colonel, and running around the bases in Southeast Asia, cadging backseat combat sorties, would not be high on a promotion board's list of notable achievements. The board would look for managerial and staff time, for engineering and logistics experience. Combat time would be a cheap commodity.

"I've learned a lot about you," Norman said. "You've been flying in every damn airplane in the Southeast Asia inventory, not just the one you're checked out in, and not only in-country."

Court nodded cautiously. In addition to his instructor and flight examiner time in F-4 Phantoms at Da Nang, he also logged combat time in A-37s at Bien Hoa. In Thailand he flew in F-105s from Korat, B-57s and AC-130s from Ubon, and A-1Hs and AC-119s from Nakhon Phanom. He did not fly as pilot in command in those birds, for he'd not been properly checked out. He flew in the backseats of fighters. In large aircraft, like AC-130s and AC-119s, he was periodically given a few minutes at the controls, but never when they were approaching or over the target. Still, he was near the action, and it was important to him.

"You are a champion sniveler," General Norman said, not smiling. "You'll snivel flying time in anything. But no more, Bannister."

"Sir?"

"No more cheating the system. In the course of asking about you, I raised the eyebrows of a couple of generals who aren't at all happy about the way you're getting around the three-tour policy. I also owe it to your uncle to make damn sure you aren't destroying your career."

"There are things more important than my *career,*" Court snapped.

"Don't be insubordinate, Bannister. Just say yes sir, salute smartly, and don't try to cheat the system anymore."

Court glowered, trying to think of an appropriate yet evasive response.

"Or I'll personally see to it that you're grounded. Understand?"

A fighter pilot had to shoot down a minimum of five enemy airplanes in aerial combat to become an ace. On his second tour, Court Bannister had flown F-4 Phantoms from Ubon. In combat over North Vietnam, he'd scored four positive MiG kills, two probables, and so many possibles he'd become known as the *Ivory Ace*—99 and 44/100 percent pure. Now it had come full circle—he was not even allowed to fly combat from the rear cockpit. But being *grounded,* not allowed to fly *at all,* would be an even greater blow for a fighter jock who loved to fly.

"I understand, sir," he said begrudgingly.

"So be it," Norman continued. "I'll take you at your word and advise your Uncle Albert that everything's just fine with you over here. We back-channeled back and forth on several . . . ah . . . sensitive matters." General officers had the Blue Net on which they could send messages to each other in an unrecorded, "eyes only" mode.

Norman leaned back in his chair. "Remember when we met, Bannister?" He rocked forward and answered his question. "You were a captain flying F-100s at Bien Hoa, and came down here to develop a fast-FAC program. You ran around with that young lieutenant . . . Toby Parker."

Toby would be difficult to forget. Shortly thereafter he'd made headlines and earned his nation's second-highest decoration, the Air Force Cross.

"You were somewhat of a hot dog, but that's expected of a young fighter pilot. Trouble now is you're still trying to play the same game. No more combat, Bannister. None. Zip. Period. But don't worry. There'll be plenty for you to do around here."

When Court didn't answer, Major General Leonard Norman stood and changed to a softer tone. "You did a good job out there this morning, Court. Damn good. Thanks for the photos. Your pilot . . . what was his name?"

"Scaling, sir. First Lieutenant Rick Scaling."

"I'll see to it that he gets a DFC for his good work."

"There's also the young pilot of Rustic One Seven."

"The Lieutenant who was killed?"

"Yes, sir. He showed great courage by remaining in the area to report the extent of invasion."

"I'll take another look at the debriefing report and suggest a Silver Star be awarded posthumously." Purple hearts were automatically awarded to KIAs (Killed in Action).

"Thank you, General." Court delayed leaving, trying to think of a way to approach and argue the flying restriction which had just been imposed.

The General took his seat and picked up a pen. "You'd better shove on off. I've got to get the report on the wire about the invasion." He shook his head grimly. "Makes you wonder what Nixon will do. It will not be easy to stop the enemy, since they're massed in such great force size. This could make the President look mighty bad unless he takes some strong steps . . . and if he does, he'll be in hot water too. He'll be criticized either way."

Court was in a mixed mood as he walked from General Norman's office, angry and downbeat thinking of the prohibition against flying combat, but also wondering about the General's last words. What indeed would be President Nixon's response to the blatant invasion? With so few American ground troops remaining, there would be few alternatives. It was at times like this that you found what kind of mettle your leaders were made of.

"How're you doing, *Scheisskopf?*" came a growling voice.

Court looked up, and despite the long and eventful day, a smile grew. "Wolf!" he exclaimed.

Lieutenant Colonel Wolfgang Xavier Lochert, wearing his ever-present two-piece jungle fatigues with tightly-rolled sleeves, grinned back, then grasped and came close to destroying the minor bones of Court's hand in a powerful semblance of a handshake.

"Heard you were here in Saigon," Lochert said.

"I didn't realize you were in the combat theater, Wolf."

"Haven't been here much. Spend most of my time running back and forth between here and the Pentagon, and out in the field trying to help with the drawdown of forces."

"You're assigned here at Seventh Air Force?" Court frowned, baffled. Wolf was thoroughly Special Forces and it was difficult imagining him deskbound in a headquarters Intelligence shop, and particularly on the Air Force side.

"Sometimes," Wolf responded vaguely. "They gave me a cubbyhole to work in here. Got an office and another *scheiss*ing desk over at MAC-SOG." Military Assistance Command–Special Observations Group, also located in Saigon, served as headquarters for nonconventional forces in Vietnam, which included U.S. Army Special Forces, Marine Recon, Navy SEALs, Air Force Special Operations, and a number of CIA contract units, such as Air America.

"God, it's good seeing you." They'd been through much together during Court's previous two combat tours.

"Don't curse," Wolf growled, and Court recalled his penchant against swearing. "I heard you were here in the headquarters. I'll be looking for your help in the next few days. Something I'm working on." It was obvious that Wolf Lochert would remain evasive about the subject.

"Any way I can help, Wolf. You know that." He owed the man.

"I heard about your flight in the observation bird this morning. Lots of bad guys coming down from the North, I hear."

It was Court's turn to be careful about security. He glanced at Wolf's security badge, which showed that he was cleared for Top Secret SI/TK, which meant everything in the place, plus a few. "I've never seen anything like it," he responded in a low voice.

Wolf's hard eyes narrowed. With the drawdown of U.S. forces, the Army found itself in a tenuous position with a major invasion under way. Perhaps most vulnerable were the smaller SF camps which were rapidly being turned over to South Vietnam Special Forces in the Vietnamization process. Wolf Lochert looked back up at him. He was a few inches shorter than Court, but made up for the difference in sheer muscle and tough sinew.

"I'd better get on over to MAC-SOG and see what's cooking there. You going to be around in a couple days, say on Sunday?" The prosecution of the war extended their work to seven days a week, with twelve-hour days the norm. Both men liked it that way. Despite their physical and service differences, there were similarities. Both were warriors to the core.

Court didn't have another TDY scheduled for a week. "I'll be here."

"My cubbyhole's down the hall there. Says *MAC-SOG Liaison* on the door. Fourteen hundred hours?"

"I'll be there," said Court Bannister.

After they shook hands once more and he watched Wolf stalking down the hall, Court realized he was damned weary.

He'd been roused for the flight briefing at four o'clock that morning, endured the eventful flight, and rushed to 7th Air Force to brief General Norman and show him the photos. It was now approaching nine p.m. He decided to crash in his BOQ bed, with the alarm set for four a.m. With the invasion under way, the following day would be eventful. As the General had said, there'd be plenty for him to do, even if he couldn't get his real wish and be flying combat. He promised himself he would not think of Susan.

Chapter 2

Lieutenant General Albert G. "Whitey" Whisenand listened as Secretary of Defense Laird briefed his Commander in Chief about the North Vietnamese invasion of South Vietnam. Laird used white poster boards on a tripod in front of the President's desk and traced the invasion routes with a pointer. Henry Kissinger, Nixon's Chief Assistant for National Security Affairs, sat to one side. Bob Haldeman, arms folded, leaned against a wall. Rose Mary Woods sat in the rear, quietly taking notes.

"They came across the border in three places," Laird said in a matter-of-fact tone. "One was south of the DMZ, second was east across the border from Laos and Cambodia into the Kontum and Pleiku area, and third was from Cambodia toward the cities of Loc Ninh and An Loc, just sixty miles north of Saigon. In each case, tens of thousands of troops supported by tanks and big artillery pieces." He checked his notes. "The invasion force totals 125,000 men in fourteen divisions and twenty-six separate regiments."

"From the DMZ, Laos, and Cambodia," Nixon echoed with obvious anger. Since 1969, when he'd taken office, he had

37

been trying to dislodge the North Vietnamese from those very places, which had become communist sanctuaries because they were protected by law instituted by the Geneva Convention. He had found there was little he could do about it. Communist-bloc propaganda had been effective. American left-wing leaders had whipped noisy antiwar protesters into frenzies to gain attention from the media. They squealed that it was immoral to conduct secret wars against the peace-loving people of Laos and Cambodia. That these "peace-loving people" were the North Vietnamese Army didn't seem to matter.

"Yes, sir," Laird said. "And the ARVN is having a hard time."

"They're not holding?" Kissinger asked in a Teutonic rumble. He swung heavy eyes to his president. "You can hardly go to the Moscow summit with a defeat in South Vietnam brought about by Russian weapons."

The following month, on 22 May, Nixon was scheduled to attend a Moscow summit with Leonid Brezhnev to discuss relations between their countries. It was an important and much-sought-after meeting. Equally critical, just one month earlier Richard Nixon and his wife, Pat, had walked on the Great Wall of China during an historic state visit with Mao Tse-tung. No U.S. president had previously visited China, and it appeared to be the beginning of new and astonishingly cordial relations with the giant communist state.

"What's the status of our combat forces?" Nixon asked Laird, concern apparent on his face and in his voice.

"U.S. troop strength is at ninety-five thousand—in defensive positions only."

"And the air forces?"

"Fewer than eighty Air Force fighters remaining in South Vietnam. The Navy has two carriers off the coast that can launch as many as one hundred eighty aircraft. In Thailand there are more than one hundred USAF fighters. Those figures are about a third of what we had flying one year ago."

"And the South Vietnamese Air Force?"

"Approximately three thousand aircraft, but they are light-attack only."

"And how is the Vietnamization process going?"

"Generally well, but the ARVN reaction is spotty. Some units are holding, others not doing so good."

Nixon rubbed his jaw, looking gloomy. "Oh . . . I don't like this. I don't like this at all." He looked darkly at Kissinger. "Henry, what do you think?"

"I think, Mr. President," Kissinger began in his measured, deep voice, "that to simply leave things as they are would provide us with the supreme test of whether the Thieu government and the ARVN can handle the war. A reaction on our part would stir even more dissent from Congress and the press." He coughed lightly and paused. "And you do have an election campaign coming up this year." Richard Nixon had his party's assured nomination to run for a second term—against the Democrats' choice, which pundits predicted would be George McGovern, campaigning on a peace-at-any-price platform.

Nixon looked in Whitey's direction. "And your views, General?"

Neither the Chairman of the Joint Chiefs of Staff nor the Secretary of State wanted to escalate the war, for the very reasons Henry Kissinger had just offered. As a member of the military, Whisenand was, in theory, subordinate to the Chairman. But the President of the United States wanted Whitey's own views, unhampered by political or career motivations.

Whisenand's voice was resolute. "I firmly believe the use of American air power can be decisive in this campaign, and that without it, South Vietnam will surely fall. General Giap is doing as he did at Khe Sanh in 1968—launching an all-out offensive in hopes of achieving another Dien Bien Phu–style victory, this one is on an even larger scale. I've studied the same intelligence messages, and it is true that in many cases the ARVN are not holding. A number of the ARVN commanders are inadequate, and their command and communication lines are poor."

The others were regarding Whitey closely, Kissinger frowning, the others wearing more neutral expressions.

Whitey took a measured breath, nodding, as if he'd just convinced himself. "Massive air power is the only appropriate response if we wish to hold the enemy. Not just tactical air strikes in South Vietnam, but also a large-scale air offensive against North Vietnam, the source of the invasion and their supply line."

Nixon brooded. "Johnson did that for three years and . . . ah . . . where did it get him?"

"Yes, sir. The Rolling Thunder campaign. But that was applied as a purely political tool, conducted slowly and cautiously, and with so many restrictions imposed on our pilots there was no slight chance of success. We must take the kid gloves off, roll up our sleeves, and be resolute—act as if we are determined to win. We must seal that country so *nothing* can get in or out, and destroy the military supplies they have within." Whitey surprised himself at how vehement he'd become. He'd felt his pulse rising as he spoke, and he realized how much anger and frustration he had pent up inside him about this war.

There was a long moment of silence as the President considered.

Finally Nixon rubbed his jaw, and he made his determination as he muttered to himself. "Well, yes. Ah . . . what I think is . . . we must go beyond just helping out in South Vietnam . . . ah . . . I mean, extend the air strikes beyond the South alone." His expression and his voice became firm. "Yes, we should go North."

He made notes on a yellow legal pad, then looked up.

"The way I see it," he said, "I have three options: an immediate and final withdrawal, a negotiated peace, or military action to end the war. I reject the first option because it would be immoral to abandon our South Vietnamese allies to the communists, and further, it would encourage aggression throughout the world. Although I *prefer* the second option, it takes two to negotiate, and the North Vietnamese are unwilling partners." He nodded resolutely. "All right," he said to Laird, "here's what I want. I'd like you to start a . . . what do you call it?" He glanced at Whitey, then brightened. "An *interdiction* effort against North Vietnam. A big one, with a good probability of stopping them." He checked the notes. "Three objectives. First, stop the flow of supplies *into* North Vietnam; second, destroy the existing stockpiles *in* North Vietnam; and third, stop the supplies going *out* of North Vietnam to their invasion forces."

"No U.S. troop involvement?" Kissinger asked, his voice hopeful.

"Absolutely not. This will be an *air* campaign only, using Air Force, Navy, and Marine aircraft. No American ground forces are to be involved. The South Vietnamese will have to carry it on the ground. You get your test this way, Henry, and we'll see if they can hold."

"Sir," said Lieutenant General Whisenand, "for air power to be effective we'll have to increase our forces, since only modest forces are in place—deploy stateside Air Force and at-sea Naval forces to SEA."

"Do it," Nixon replied, now resolute.

Kissinger raised an eyebrow. "Large-scale movements will draw attention from the press."

"We must attempt to control that."

Kissinger, noting the conviction of the President, spoke again: "To be *truly* effective, perhaps we should use those big B-52 bombers in North Vietnam." Henry Kissinger had adroitly scrambled aboard his president's thought train.

"Ah . . . do that too."

"B-52s, Mr. President?" Whisenand asked, surprised. The Boeing B-52 was a huge bomber, and had never been used up north. The previous administration had been concerned about public reaction if one of its ten-million-dollar airplanes, with a crew of six, was lost.

"Yes, go ahead and use B-52s if you wish," the President said abstractly, obviously deep in thought about other matters concerning the air strikes, or perhaps the massive invasion under way.

"How do you want to handle the press release, Mr. President?" Kissinger asked, obviously impressed with the President's resolve.

Nixon blinked, emerging from a reverie, then looked at Whisenand. "What about it, Whitey? What will the reporters see?"

"We will be deploying from many bases, and the press is bound to pick up the activity. No way to hide it. If you wish, our military public relations people can keep it simple—just say in a low-key manner that we're dispatching combat aircraft to counter the communist invasion. There's no need to mention targeting or the fact that we'll be sending them up north."

"I concur." Nixon turned. "Rose Mary, have Ziegler draft a release with words something like: *Massive, unprovoked attack, violation of treaties, we must help our allies.* Things of that nature." He stopped thoughtfully. "Let's not use the word *communist.* That wouldn't sit well with Mr. Brezhnev."

General Whisenand was pleased with the outcome: that his

advice had been sought and—most important—he had been listened to. "Sir, do you wish to address the fact that the invasion could never have occurred without fresh Russian supplies, tanks, and long-range artillery?"

"I have the summit in Moscow in May," Nixon pondered judiciously.

"I suggest," Kissinger rumbled, "that we should have someone at the State Department point the finger at Moscow for complicity in the invasion. Coming from State, it won't carry the same impact as if from the White House, but still gets the point across about the role Russia continues to play in the war."

"Are the weapons different or newer than what North Vietnam has been using in the past?" Nixon asked Whisenand.

"Bigger and better artillery, new tanks, and upgraded surface-to-air missiles. This is the first time they've had SAMs in the South. They're obviously quite serious and don't give a damn about world opinion."

"Use the term 'sophisticated new Soviet weapons,' " Nixon said begrudgingly, "but leave out the word 'communist.' I want the weight of our displeasure to fall on North Vietnam, not Russia or Red China."

Whitey rose, and with Laird and Kissinger started toward the door.

"General Whisenand, would you remain for a few moments?" the President requested, then looked at Rose Mary and Bob Haldeman. "You needn't stay."

Whitey walked back to the President's desk as the room cleared.

"What are you hearing about our boys up north? Our POWs and the Russian KGB connection."

"Since the Son Tay raid, the North Vietnamese have brought more of our POWs together under one roof and are putting men into the same cells. Recently, for the first time they're being allowed to talk together. And thanks to the continued efforts of the POW wives and people like Ross Perot to mobilize world opinion, their treatment has improved. Less torture, more food packages."

"And the possibility that our POWs are being taken to Russia?"

"We still have no definitive information. I've tried to make a comparative study to determine whether more officers with specialized or sensitive backgrounds are missing than other crewmembers. But we have so many of *all* capacities missing that it's hard to come to a meaningful conclusion. Some may well have been captured but kept under wraps until transported out of North Vietnam, but I just don't have anything definitive. It's a tough project so far, sir."

The President mulled that over. "Well, stay on top of it. You know you have my support, but it would be nice if you could make a determination." He nodded vaguely, then said in dismissal, "Thank you for coming in today, General."

"Yes, sir," Whitey said and started for the door.

Nixon called after him. "By the way, whatever became of that Army colonel you wanted to help you with your . . . ah . . . task? The one I decorated."

"He's doing well, sir, so long as I periodically allow him to return to the war zone. In fact, right now Lieutenant Colonel Lochert is on an extended fact-finding mission in Saigon."

1400 Hours Local, Sunday 2 April 1972
7th Air Force Intelligence Section
Tan Son Nhut Air Base
Republic of Vietnam

Wolf waved Court into his office, which was indeed a cubbyhole. Since he felt such distaste for desk work, Lochert spent little time there and most of it in the field, ostensibly gathering information for General Whisenand's POW project, but also tending his flock of Special Forces warriors in this critical time of drawdown.

But he was very dedicated to the task he'd been assigned by the General almost eighteen months earlier. American fighting men being held in brutal captivity was an odious thought. If they were secretly being taken to another country—to face oblivion—the thought was even more unsettling.

"Mighty clean desk," Court Bannister quipped.

"I'm not much for paperwork," Wolf growled, surveying the place.

"How can I help?"

Wolf mused for only a short pause before plunging ahead with the sensitive subject. "I've been assigned a . . . um . . . task by General Whisenand."

"Uncle Albert?" Court asked in surprise. It was the second time the name had come up in the past few days.

"He mentioned that you two are close, and that he trusts you implicitly. He also said that if I must have a closer cross-talk with the Air Force guys here, you'd be a good source."

Court nodded slowly, wondering about the subject of the discussion.

Wolf noted his questioning look. "I can't tell you about the project, and I'd like it if you didn't try to figure out any more specifics than I give you." He paused. "And if nothing about this conversation goes out of this room."

Court agreed, intrigued.

Wolf proceeded carefully. "As you know, there is a large number of prisoners of war being held in Hanoi."

"Yeah." Court thought of his many friends there. Of good men like Flak Apple, to whom he had been especially close, shot down in flames and captured more than four years before.

"What I'd like to know from you . . . since you've got your nose to the ground about what's going on over there, is just who, among those being shot down, would make the choicest targets for interrogation by . . . um . . . perhaps the Russians."

"What the hell?" Court blurted. "Are the goddam Russians involved with our POWs?"

Wolf glared. "Quit cursing, *Scheisskopf*—and I already told you I can't tell you any more than I am."

"Dammit, Wolf . . . "

Lochert stared, closed-mouthed.

Court sighed, angered by the picture of Russians interrogating his friends but knowing Wolf would not tell him more. "Okay, you'd like to know which of our pilots have the most sensitive backgrounds, is that right?"

"Which types would the Russians most like to get their hands on? That's the question. No more than that."

Court took a moment to calm his outrage. Then he reflected on the men he'd known who had flown, and might be called upon in the future to fly, over North Vietnam and be in jeopardy of being shot down. And which of those could provide the most damning secrets.

"There are a lot of them," he began, thinking about pilots who had "sat on the bomb," meaning they'd been on alert to carry out a nuclear bombing mission in the event of a Soviet attack. Theirs was not in-depth knowledge which would be required to duplicate an intricate bomb design. He thought of others who had worked on new aircraft designs, and . . . Court turned toward Wolf, wearing a thoughtful frown. "I'm going to make a call over to the ops section. There's someone there I'd like you to meet. A couple of officers who're here from the fighter wing at Korat Air Base, Thailand, giving a briefing. I heard their pitch this morning."

"I can't disclose anything to them," Wolf cautioned. "Not even as much as I've told you."

Court was already at the desk telephone, dialing. "I just want you to listen and make up your mind. They'll give you an idea of the kind of people you might be looking for."

Fifteen minutes later, two majors entered the small office, wearing sage-green K-2B flight suits and carrying paper cups of coffee. Both were in their early thirties and wore pilot's wings imprinted in silver on black leather name tags. One was tall and pleasant-looking, and the leather name tag read FRIZZELL, W.A., MAJ, U.S.A.F. The other major was shorter, wore glasses and appeared somewhat dour. His name was SMYTHE, T.S.

Wolf had hauled in two more chairs from the next office, utterly filling the cubbyhole office. After a quizzical look about, both men took their seats. Court made introductions. "Gentlemen, this is Lieutenant Colonel Lochert, U.S. Army, and he's here to find out something about what we do. Wolf, I'd like you to meet Major Frizzell and Major Smythe, who are here briefing the staff on Wild Weasel operations."

As they shook hands, Court noted the frown on Wolf's face which had appeared at the mention of the term *Wild Weasel.*

Court nodded at the two men. "Go ahead and tell him what you do for a living. Colonel Lochert is cleared for anything you've got, and he has the need to know."

Frizzell, the more outgoing and articulate of the two men, spoke up. "We're a Wild Weasel crew, stationed at Korat Royal Thai Air Force Base, Thailand."

"What's a Wild . . . um . . . Weasel?" Wolf asked cautiously.

"Our job's to take out certain radar defenses to protect the other aircraft," replied Frizzell. "We fly a specially modified

version of the Thud, the F-105G, and carry bombs and missiles
to destroy surface-to-air missile sites that threaten the other aircraft. My bear is—"

"Bear?" Wolf asked, wondering if he'd heard correctly.

"Smitty flies in the backseat and operates the special receivers. We call the backseaters bears. Smitty locates the SAM sites
and I either bomb 'em or fire a homing missile at their tracking
radar."

Wolf liked the audacity of the concept.

"Wild Weasel's a relatively new concept," said Frizzell.
"Started back in '65 and '66 when the SAMs started chewing
up Air Force and Navy fighters flying near Hanoi."

"Does it work?"

Frizzell grinned. "Wild Weasels have taken out about a hundred SAM sites altogether. At first, when we were bombing
up there, they kept their SAMs around Hanoi and Haiphong,
and we killed them there. Then when the bombing was halted
up north, the sites were moved down to protect their supplies
coming over the Ho Chi Minh Trail. That's mainly where we
kill 'em now."

Throughout Frizzell's litany, the bear, the one called Smitty,
had held his tongue, looking on quietly.

Frizzell outlined the training they'd been given on Stateside
ranges, flying against simulators which electronically appeared
like Soviet radars, set up in southern Nevada. While the mission seemed innovative and technical, Wolf wondered if it was
enough for the Soviets to chance world disfavor by interrogating
such men. When asked, Frizzell outlined his background. He
was a fighter pilot with 2,200 hours of flying time, but there
was little which would make him a Soviet target. They had
many such men in their own air force.

"How about you?" he asked Smythe, thinking Court was
likely wrong. The Wild Weasel men and their mission were
interesting, but so far what he'd heard was not startling.

"I operate the homing and locating equipment," the bear
named Smythe said quietly.

"Very sophisticated equipment," Court Bannister added.

Smythe concurred. "It's state of the art. Likely the most
advanced in the world. The engineers in the States have installed
what used to take up an entire eavesdropping aircraft like a large
transport into a fighter, and that's no small trick."

Wolf was slowly nodding. "And you know a lot about how it works."

"Hell," Frizzell piped up, "Smitty could build it from memory. He's an electrical engineer and knows every transistor and resistor in his receivers."

Wolf felt his excitement growing—he was now getting somewhere. "What was your background . . . before you were sent to this Wild . . . um . . . Weasel thing."

"I worked in the war plans division at Wiesbaden, Germany," Smythe said.

"That's the headquarters for U.S. Air Forces in Europe," Court interjected. "The plans shop there has to know everything possible about enemy forces, including their best and latest equipment, and how to defeat them. That's what Smitty supplied for them."

Wolf smiled grimly.

Court nodded to Smythe. "Tell him a little about the Soviet Order of Battle over there."

For ten minutes Major Smythe outlined every piece of equipment, including the latest Soviet air weaponry which was stacked up against U.S. forces in Europe. When pressed he would go into minute detail, showing complete mastery of his subject as well as his technical intellect.

Although he understood little of what he was hearing, Wolf Lochert was impressed. "So you know a lot about their weapons and details of how they deploy them," Wolf said.

"No, sir," Smythe said quietly, his voice sure. "Not a *lot*. My job as an electronic warfare officer is to know *everything* about their weapons and how they use them."

Court looked at Wolf. "And how our forces will defeat their weapons."

"Give me an example," Wolf told Smythe, "of how our forces might get by their most sophisticated weapons in Europe."

"No, sir," was Smythe's immediate response. "I was debriefed four months ago, and no longer hold the proper clearances. I was told I could not discuss such things."

"But you know," said Court, "don't you?"

Smythe looked at the two lieutenant colonels and hesitated. He finally nodded.

"We're cleared for such information," Court tried.

"Sir, if you were the President of the United States, I would not tell you. I've been debriefed, and until my clearances are reactivated, I will talk to no one about our war plans. They are extremely sensitive."

Something rang in Wolf Lochert's memory. He'd been previously told that electronic warfare officers might be a likely target for the KGB. And there was something else. "You're wearing pilot's wings," he observed.

"Yes, sir."

"But you're not a pilot."

"No, sir," said Smythe. "I'm an EWO. Electronic Warfare Officers are navigators who attend additional, specialized training. We're not pilots."

Wolf stared at the wings, his shaggy eyebrows furrowed.

Smythe explained. "We'd lost a lot of Wild Weasels, but not many of the EWOs were showing up on the POW lists provided by the North Viets. A few years back, some of the EWOs began wearing pilot's wings and telling everyone they were pilots, and a larger percentage of *those* were listed as captured. So . . . some of us wear pilot's wings."

"Bingo!" Wolf thought exuberantly. He had found his Soviet targets.

A few minutes later, when the two majors had departed, Court looked grimly at Wolf Lochert. "What do you think?"

Wolf simply nodded. He was already formulating the message to be sent to General Whitey Whisenand. The Wild Weasels flying from Korat had discovered the most likely solution to the tragic puzzle. The wearing of pilot's wings by some of the electronic-warfare officers, so their specialties would not be known, and the fact that fewer of those were disappearing . . .

A thought occurred to him, and he immediately pinned Court Bannister. "Why do you allow people like Smythe to fly where they can be captured and compromised?"

"They've got one of the most important jobs in the Air Force, Wolf. Protecting our aircraft and pilots from SAMs is damned critical, and we want our best and smartest men doing it. When they're not flying combat, it's natural that the same smart guys work in the most sensitive jobs."

"Maybe, but exposing a guy like Smythe is going too far. You're putting some of our country's biggest secrets at risk."

Wolf was right. Court would advise General Norman about what he'd just heard. Major Smythe might be angered about it, but within a few weeks he would likely be sent back to the States, where his secrets would be safe. He hesitated then, for he knew how dismal Smythe would feel, not being allowed to do the job he was trained for and did best. Court decided to give the idea more thought before proceeding.

"Let's get together again tomorrow," Wolf said. "We're onto something."

After Court left his office, Wolf left the musty confines of the headquarters building and walked toward the M-151 jeep he'd been assigned, thinking hard as he absently unlocked the heavy chain securing the steering wheel to the brake pedal. The first time they'd considered electronic-warfare officers as prime targets for the Soviets had been when they'd decoded a Caruso message from an Eastern European propaganda film, as he'd led his choir and signaled with eye squints and melodic rhythms. They should have listened harder, he decided.

He prepared to drive to the comm center at MAC-SOG, there to prepare a pouch to be couriered directly to General Whitey Whisenand's Pentagon office.

0245 Hours Local, Monday 3 April 1972
Field Grade Officers' BOQ, Room 914A
Tan Son Nhut Air Base
Republic of Vietnam

Court Bannister had gone to bed late the previous night, after a full day at the Tactical Air Control Center, helping to schedule in-country fighters against the numerous targets offered by the invading North Vietnamese forces. He'd lain there for a long while, unable to sleep, thinking about Susan Boyle. He'd been doing that a lot lately.

He'd dropped to sleep fitfully, for Susan, the woman he'd truly loved, had been rudely taken from his life and he still could not cope with the fact.

He was roused by a loud pounding at the BOQ room door. An enlisted orderly told him he was to report to General Norman in Intelligence.

He did not see the General immediately after hurriedly pulling on his flight suit and boots and stumbling half-asleep to the headquarters intelligence section. Instead he found himself on a list of those authorized to receive a Top Secret briefing. He hastily poured a cup of stale and lukewarm coffee from a huge stainless-steel urn, and hurried into the large briefing room, where he was surrounded by intelligence officers and ops/plans officers from the Tactical Air Control Center, Out-Country. They were already bombing and strafing the invasion forces coming into South Vietnam, but the makeup of the group told Court that something new was afoot.

Although the speaker talked in a boring monotone, the audience was rapt, their attention undivided. A chill of déjà vu ran through Court.

They would be returning to the focus of the war, to bomb their primary enemy—North Vietnam. An OPlan was being devised, to be called *Freedom Train,* in powerful response to the invasion of South Vietnam by the North Vietnamese Army. Strike forces in Thailand were to be alerted and prepared to bomb the targets in North Vietnam which had been withheld for the past four years. They would at first concentrate on those targets from the DMZ to the 20th parallel, and from the coast to the Laotian border, but they were also to select targets in the Hanoi and Haiphong areas for possible escalation.

The U.S. Navy would participate, and they and the Air Force wings in Thailand were to be augmented by massive unit movements from Stateside bases.

"At last," exulted a fighter pilot from the control center, and a stir of excitement ran through the assembled officers.

The group was then told that their particular task would be to dust off the old Rolling Thunder OPlan—which evoked a groan—then they were to strike out the restrictions which had made Rolling Thunder ineffectual—which brought smiles. They were to immediately submit target lists, with recommended ordnance loads and specific aircraft. The team leader of the assembled twenty-five officers and twelve intelligence specialist noncoms was to be Lieutenant Colonel Courtland Bannister. The briefer asked that Colonel Bannister please meet with General Norman, who was waiting in his office, to receive additional directions. The others were to await his return and instructions.

Court hurried down the hall to Norman's office, alternately wanting to smile and frown. Happy that they were at long last going to be turned loose to win. But it would be difficult to help design a plan involving massive air combat, and then not be able to participate. He wondered if he could convince General Norman that he should . . .

The two-star was outside his office door, sipping at a paper cup of coffee and conferring with a full colonel. He nodded vaguely at Bannister and motioned his head toward his office, not interrupting his discussion.

Court went inside and was immediately joined by Norman.

"God, but that's awful coffee," the Major General muttered with a grimace. He sat down, stared at Court, and slowly grinned. "I guess my question about what the President will do has been answered. We're going to hit the bastards and hit them hard."

"Yes, sir. And sir, I was wondering if I might be able to fly in the—"

Norman raised his hands. "All arranged, Bannister. During the important strikes you'll be in an EC-121 command and control aircraft, flying off the coast over the South China Sea. You'll be my eyes and ears out there, and I'll want you to help with the after-action reports."

Court started to argue that he could see even better from a fighter cockpit, but was quickly cut off. "But first I want you to help with the Freedom Train operations plan. Take what we've got from the Pentagon and make damn sure it's properly integrated with Linebacker."

"Linebacker?" He'd not heard of it.

"There's an old Top Secret plan called Linebacker made up by the people here at Seventh Air Force with major inputs from Strategic Air Command. The thing dates from 1965. Shows how they planned to use the B-52s if they ever sent 'em up north in large-scale operations."

Court's response was immediate. "Sir, I'm not qualified to make inputs about strategic bombing." Like most fighter pilots, Court was not enamored of either bombers or anyone who would want to fly in them. Theirs was an entirely different world.

The General had long known of the antagonism between fighter and bomber people, and his tone was firm. "The B-52 crews stationed at Anderson and U Tapao are accustomed to flying here in South Vietnam in Operation Arc Light, and haven't faced the godawful threats up north. You have. From what I've seen of the Linebacker plan, they'll need your inputs."

Court still could hardly believe what he was hearing. "You

want B-52s included in the targeting in North Vietnam?"

"They'll be an integral part of the Freedom Train OPlan. For the first time, they'll be going north beyond the DMZ. Help 'em."

"In the briefing we were told to devise targets below the 20th parallel, *then* up in the Hanoi area. You don't want the B-52s targeted up in that area *too,* do you?"

General Norman nodded. "They're to be used in all phases of the operation. That's one big reason they'll need your expertise, Colonel. You've been there. They haven't."

Court withheld a disgusted sigh. "When will the Freedom Train missions begin?"

Norman could no longer contain his smile. He looked like a kid about to bite into a candy bar. "Just as soon as we can devise a proper plan, pick out some meaningful targets, and get the word to the combat units. The initial *suggested* target list is coming in right now from PACOM. You just put a good massage on it all and make sure it makes sense."

As Court left the General's office, heading back for the briefing theater and his waiting group, he saw Wolf Lochert emerge from his cubbyhole. Court nodded grimly, not surprised that the Special Forces officer would be here at this hour. The Army liked to begin their day early and do most of their work before daylight; by midafternoon they turned into pumpkins—at least, Court thought, the khaki-wearing staffers did. Wolf—always in fatigues—probably went back to MAC-SOG.

"I've just been assigned a hell of a task, Wolf. I won't be able to give you any help on your project for a few days."

Wolf Lochert grimaced at the curse word, then shook his close-shorn head. "Same here. I'll be working out of MAC-SOG. Things are falling apart at some of the ARVN posts and I'm making a few trips out to get a first-hand look. Give you a call when things simmer down some."

The POW matter was shifted to back burner. The two friends stared at one another for a short moment, then hurried away to tend to their immediate and very different responsibilities.

Before Court reentered the briefing theater, he was hailed by the two majors from Korat, Frizzell and Smythe. The Wild Weasel crew came down the hallway with sleepy expressions.

"What's up, Colonel?" asked Frizzell, the frontseater. "We

were rousted from our room at the BOQ and told to come here and report to you for a briefing."

Court nodded a curt greeting. "You guys have to get back to Thailand right away?"

Frizzell looked at Smythe the bear, who cocked his head and shrugged. "Yeah. According to what's going on here, we both have things to do back in the Weasel Squadron."

Court needed their expertise in his planning group. "I could use you here for a few days. I believe you'll find it interesting." He quickly outlined the Operation they were about to help fashion.

Smitty nodded, his eyes somber. "I think we can help."

"Damn right," exulted Frizzell happily. "If they're going to let us go up north again, let's make damn sure we do it right this time."

Court continued looking at Smythe. "Got any ideas how we can get a string of B-52s in and out of North Vietnam without them losing their asses?"

Smythe mused thoughtfully. "If SAC's willing to listen," he finally said, "we'll be able to come up with some tactics that work. If they don't listen, and SAC usually doesn't, they'll just kill folks up there with falling aluminum."

Chapter 3

A tremendous double boom sounded in the clear air five miles above the California desert floor. Streaks of blue flame shot from huge exhaust pipes as the twin afterburners of the big airplane ignited. The mighty addition of thrust rocketed the jet along a curve that the pilot, Captain Toby Parker, was using to set up an attack on two winged specks flying low and five miles to his left. Parker had determined he needed the extra speed to make his attack. With eyes fixed on his target, he instinctively made corrections as he positioned for attack.

Parker, call sign Salem One, sat in the front seat of the F-4 Phantom, blasting through the eastern portion of the air-to-air training range used by the instructors of George Air Force Base to teach air-combat maneuvering to pilots who were new to the airplane.

Parker had firm intentions on this, his first air-to-air training mission, to wax a couple F-4 pilots' asses in a wild dogfight. They used camera film instead of bullets, and Parker was pumped up about jumping on the two faceless foes and later thumbtacking

54

camera shots of them—squarely in the firing reticle—onto the squadron wall.

Fighters! It was what Parker had lusted for since he'd entered pilot training five years earlier. This was the same assignment he'd been given and then lost because of an attitude problem as a student pilot. As a student, Parker had lit a cigarette, then performed a flawless barrel roll during an instrument-approach descent. It was a definite no-no, and his instructor had wanted him washed out of the program, but the training wing commander had diagnosed that Parker had seen too much combat in Vietnam as a nonpilot before entering flight training. Besides, the commander knew Parker was under special observation from the Pentagon.

The Colonel was right, for Toby Parker was a genuine, well-known hero who wore his sensitivities openly and drank far too much, vainly attempting to wash away bad memories. In Vietnam, as a lieutenant, Parker had earned and been awarded an Air Force Cross, Vietnamese Cross of Gallantry, and Purple Heart. He'd saved a Special Forces unit after taking the controls of a tiny O-1 propeller-driven spotter plane when the pilot was shot. Because of that deed, which proved he was both courageous and a natural pilot, the Director of USAF Operations at the Pentagon had opened a slot in pilot training school, then had monitored his progress.

When his instructor pilot (IP) had determined to wash him out for "unprecedented lack of judgment," the training wing commander urged him to back off. The IP, putting his own wings on the line, said he'd agree only if Parker's coveted assignment to fighters were given to someone more worthy. Furthermore, the IP said he never wanted to fly with Parker again. The deal was struck.

Shortly afterward, Toby Parker had quit dwelling in the past, which had been at the core of his problem, and stopped drinking. He'd graduated, then been sent to Vietnam as a Forward Air Control pilot, where he'd performed flawlessly. Upon his return to the United States, he thought he'd earned the assignment to F-4s, but the USAF, in its wisdom, had decided he should instead teach young men to fly. He'd completed a four-year tour as an IP at Randolph Air Force Base and today, the brightly sunlit 3rd day of April 1972, Toby Parker was finally doing what he'd 'been born to do—fly at the controls of a powerful and deadly fighter aircraft.

When the airspeed indicator on Parker's instrument panel showed he was knifing the thin air at 500 knots per hour, he brought the two throttles under his gloved hand inboard to cut off the afterburners' extra thrust. He estimated he had 100 knots overtake speed on the "enemy" planes, and that should be more than enough.

In the rear cockpit of Parker's fighter was his instructor pilot, Captain Frank Owens, with an F-4 combat tour behind him during which he'd shot down one of the first MiG-21s to take to the air over Hanoi. Parker was confident and sure, as good pilots are, but knew he had a lot to learn if he wanted to fly and fight the Phantom with skill. Owens, he hoped, was the man to teach him. Parker did not yet fully understand the concepts of multiaircraft maneuvering at the airspeed of a .45 caliber bullet.

"Think I should pull it in tighter to stay in position?" Toby asked over the hot-mike intercom. He started to ease farther back on the stick and tighten his turn.

"If you think so, have at it," Owens replied cheerfully.

Toby grunted as he tucked the stick back into his lap.

Although the big Phantom came around swiftly to parallel the flight path of the other two F-4s, five thousand feet lower and now at his one o'clock position, Parker realized he'd pulled too hard and bled off too much precious airspeed. He decided to regain speed when he dove at them.

Toby was at 18,000 feet, preparing to roll in and attack the two Phantoms, call signs Camel One and Camel Two, who were returning from the Cuddyback ground gunnery range. The three airplanes were tuned to a common radio frequency. Fighters returning from the range knew they would be vulnerable to being bounced (attacked) any time after pulling out of their final practice dive-bomb, until twenty miles from the traffic pattern at George Air Force Base.

George AFB was home of the 479th Tactical Fighter Wing, which had been designated as the training unit for pilots and weapons systems officers who'd been selected to be upgraded into the McDonnell Douglas F-4 Phantom. The frontseaters were officially designated as aircraft commanders (ACs), but since that smacked of bomber lingo, and since they were usually the only ones aboard who were pilot-rated, many preferred to be called pilot. The backseaters were navigators, officially designated as Weapons Systems Officers (WSOs), but the pilots called them Woosoes, Wizzos, Whizzoes, GIBs (for *Guy-In-Back*), and pitters. In response, the backseaters called them FUFs, for *Fellows-Up-Front*. At any given time at George, five F-4 Phantoms were in the landing pattern, six were practicing air-to-air refueling from KC-135 tankers, fourteen were attacking ground targets on the Cuddyback multiple gunnery ranges, two flights of four each were in the air-to-air gunnery pattern shooting 20mm cannons at a thirty-foot metal dart towed by an F-86H, and ten Phantoms were swirling in various mock-combat dogfights, called air combat maneuvering (ACM). All told, the gunnery ranges covered 16,000 square miles of California desert and mountain territory, and included Death Valley, Panamint Valley, and goodly portions of the High Sierras.

"They're at six thousand feet slant range, sir—four thousand feet low, and we have one hundred knots overtake," Frank Owens called from the backseat, with the same deferential tone he'd used since they'd been introduced. As Toby's instructor pilot, he also had to act as the Weapons System Operator, and operate the intercept radar, radio, and navigation gear. In addition, a Phantom backseater provided an extra pair of eyes and noted the relative position of adversaries.

Toby again engaged the afterburners of the two J-79 engines, giving the Phantom 14,000 more pounds of thrust. He nudged forward on the stick to attain zero gravity, which allowed the fighter to accelerate even faster as he headed down the slide.

"Four thousand feet slant range, twenty-four hundred low, one-fifty overtake and increasing, sir," Owens said in a staccato voice.

As Toby slashed down, Camel lead looked up, saw him, and called on the UHF radio for a rapid turn: "Camel, break left!" Both pilots immediately racked their birds into a portside turn, directly toward Toby, hoping to force him into overshooting and sliding past. If that happened, the Camels could reverse their turn into Toby's vulnerable six o'clock position.

"Two thousand slant, five hundred lower, two hundred overtake, sir."

"Hell, I'm overshooting," Toby muttered angrily. His fighter was approaching the tightly turning Camels too fast to remain on the same plane and turn with them, and he was forced to choose one of several options. He could chop back the throttles and use speed brakes to decelerate and stay inside Camel flight's turn—but he'd lose his airspeed advantage. Or . . . he could continue in and pull tighter—but he'd likely enter a high-speed stall and possibly go out of control and into a flat spin. Or . . . he could go ahead and overshoot the turn, staying on the same plane, then try to turn back before the Camels had reversed direction. He didn't think much of any of these solutions.

"What do you think, Frank?" Toby asked, pulling five Gs and grunting out the words in the split second he had available.

"You're . . . doing . . . great . . . Toby," Captain Frank Owens forced out against the G force.

Toby let his fighter overshoot with a great swoosh. Then he traded airspeed for altitude, zooming three thousand feet over Camel's head, and rolled out inverted, looking down on them through the top of the canopy. He brought his throttles inboard, shutting off the gas-guzzling afterburners. The zoom maneuver had cost him the two hundred knots of overtake speed he'd gained in the dive. This solution occurred naturally.

"At least I've got altitude advantage, and they're still out in front," Toby muttered hopefully as they floated upside down. If Camel Lead was behind Toby, he could raise his nose and get a shot off into Toby's airplane. Being out in front, Camel Lead could not do that.

"Yes, sir," Owens said evenly. "Good job."

"I'm going to pull down and drop right in on his tail," Toby said with a grin.

"Yes, sir, shit hot, git 'im," Owens said, his enthusiasm obvious.

Toby started the nose of his airplane down, as if he were completing the back half of a loop, carefully keeping the Phantom's nose heading in the same direction as his opponents. As his gunsight slid behind Camel Two, he rolled upright. Frank Owens called out his speed and attack information. The gunsight on the Phantom was a lighted dot, called the pipper, projected on the windscreen directly in front of the pilot's eyes, and it was surrounded by a circle which presented overtake and range information sent from the radar and fire control systems.

Toby picked his target, Camel Two, who was flying behind

and off to one side of his leader. He pushed his plane's nose lower to stay behind Camel flight, and rapidly gained speed. He was still well behind Camel Two, still diving to get underneath, preparing to pull up for a camera shot from that concealed position.

"Three thousand slant range, eight hundred lower, no overtake," Owens chanted.

"Okay," Toby said. "Is this the way to do a one-on-two stern attack?"

"I'm not about to tell *you* how to do it, Toby."

"You're the IP, Owens," Toby said in frustration. "Do some IP-ing. I never flew this bird before last month."

"Toby, you've got a lot more combat time than I do. Do what you think is best."

That was not what IPs were paid to say.

Toby maintained his dive, wondering. "Okay, pretty quick I'll pull up and we'll have him . . . about . . . *now.*"

He drew the stick back sharply to raise his gunsight pipper to center on Camel Two—but he'd allowed himself to get too low and couldn't pull the nose up fast enough to get off the camera shot. As he tried, Camel flight abruptly pulled up and into a high-G barrel roll. Toby continued pulling on the stick in a vain attempt to follow, but it was too late. He watched helplessly as the two rolling F-4s moved from twelve o'clock level to twelve o'clock high, then to his right at three o'clock high, and finally as they dropped smoothly into his six o'clock position—directly behind him in the killing position.

"Gotcha, hotshot," Camel Lead said in a jaunty tone.

"Bang, bang," Camel Two called as he lined up parallel with his lead and took a picture with his gun camera. They were cocky from having operated as a coordinated team against a surprise attack—and, like all proper fighter jocks, they liked to win.

"Okay, Camel, let's break it off. I'm too low on fuel for any more play," Toby transmitted bitterly.

"What's your call sign?" Camel lead asked.

"Salem," Toby said with a sigh.

"You lost because you buried your nose at our six, Salem. Ta-ta." After imparting that bit of information, Camel Lead called for his wingman to change to the tower frequency and they were gone. Camel Lead had given Toby the information his IP, Frank Owens, should have related as it was happening, that he'd allowed the nose of his fighter to get much too low before pulling up when he was in an attack position behind the two Camel fighters.

Still incensed, Toby received landing instructions, fought his way into the pattern for runway 21, and landed. He and Owens went through the proper checklists, but spoke none of the small talk Phantom crews usually make after a landing.

Toby calmed himself as he taxied to the refueling pit and shut down the right engine. He and Owens rested their forearms on the canopy rails, hands outside in clear view, to let the ground crew know they weren't fooling with switches in the cockpit that might hurt them. They watched the pit chief on the right supervise the refueling with hoses from underground storage tanks. It was called hot refueling because an engine was running and the crew remained inside the airplane. Normal USAF refueling was provided by individual trucks trundling up and down the flight line, dispensing fuel to empty, parked aircraft. "Hot" refueling saved about thirty minutes for each airplane, giving the fighter's crew chief more time to prepare for his bird's next mission.

An observant Air Force colonel at Da Nang had picked up the hot refueling idea from the Marines, who started hot-pitting at Chu Lai in Vietnam. They had to. The Marine base was so bare, sort of just shoveled out of the sand, that there wasn't room for fuel trucks. After some initial resistance about "we've never done it that way before," the USAF adopted the idea. The USAF hated to admit it, but they'd also adopted three nifty things from the Navy: the F-4 Phantom itself, the idea of using an approach-end cable barrier to trap crippled airplanes, and the AIM-9 Sidewinder heat-seeking air-to-air missile, developed by engineers at China Lake Naval Air Station, not far north of George Air Force Base. About all the Navy would admit to adopting from the Air Force was how to ground attack.

Toby Parker taxied the big airplane back from the refueling pit to their parking spot on the flight line, both clamshell canopies open to allow cool air to blow in, Toby wondering just how he was going to handle the talk with his IP. It was obvious that Frank Owens was too intimidated to be an effective instructor. Something had to be changed.

An IP has knowledge his student does not, and his job is

to pass it on correctly, safely, and quickly. First lieutenants and captains are often called upon to train full colonels, and the rule is, "no quarter asked and none given." Outside of an occasional "sir" at the proper time, rank is inconsequential to an instructor pilot. The upgrading pilot, regardless of rank disparity, must learn what the IP has to teach him. He must pass the proper oral, written, and flight exams before being signed off as competent to fly that particular airplane on those particular missions.

The IP who is intimidated by the rank of his student, and consequently does not perform his job of transferring information from his head to that of the student, is not effective. Toby and Frank were of the same rank, yet Owens was obviously cowed by the fact that Toby Parker was so well-known. Parker had had no such problem with his air-to-ground IP, who hadn't given him an inch when it came to dropping bombs or strafing ground targets. Now it was time for Toby to chew Owens' ass, to impress him to be forceful and aggressive, for it was critical that he learn F-4 air-to-air combat maneuvering.

"We've got to talk," Toby said after Frank Owens finished debriefing him on their flight activities and Owens had completely omitted Toby's getting his ass trounced by Camel flight.

They were on their way to the locker room to clean up.

"Sure, Toby. What do you have?"

"I would like to know . . . ah . . . " Owens' friendly eagerness was so painfully apparent that Toby's resolve crumbled. "Just wanted to know where you're from, Frank," Toby muttered, cursing himself for lack of guts.

"Kettering, Ohio, sir," Owens answered. "Why do you ask?"

"Oh, no reason. Just curious," Toby lied. *Nuts,* he thought. *I can't chew on this guy, he's too nice. Besides, what would I say? You're a crappy IP?* "Look, Frank," Toby finally said, "quit calling me sir. We're the same rank." He glanced at his watch. "Well, got to go." Parker walked out of the locker room frowning, bottom lip stuck forward in thought.

1245 Hours Local, Monday 3 April 1972
4452 Combat Crew Training Squadron
George Air Force Base
Victorville, California

George Air Force Base was named after a luckless chap named Harold H. George who'd met his maker in a 1942 aircraft accident. All AFBs are named after luckless chaps. No pilots, of fighter or any other craft, want an Air Force base named after them before they reach the age of ninety-two, maybe ninety-five.

George was more than just a busy training base. It encompassed 5,300 acres, and the unit mission was the orderly but frenzied checking out of hundreds of aircrewmen in America's hottest combat aircraft, the F-4 Phantom. The students (called studs) were there not only to learn to fly the airplane, that is, getting it up and down without breaking anything, but also to learn how to use it as a weapon. The Phantom was the heaviest fighter around. It weighed more than a World War II B-17 bomber, and carried four times as much ordnance. Its two J-79 jet engines put out 350 percent more horsepower than the four piston engines of the B-17. It carried a crew of two men; the B-17 a crew of ten.

Toby walked down the busy hall of the squadron building, still wearing his flight suit, his short-cropped, blond curly hair matted with sweat. Parker had clear blue slightly oval eyes, a well-formed face, strong jaw, good shoulders tapering to a narrow waist. He stood just under six feet tall, ran many miles a week, lifted weights, practiced Tai Kwan Do, and considered himself in the best shape of his life.

He came to the open door under a small hanging sign that read OPERATIONS OFFICER, LT COL J. T. NEDDLE and looked in to see a cluttered desk in front of a stocky man dressed in a flight suit and chewing on a cigar stub. The man would scan a folder, write notes on a memo pad, put that folder down, and pick up the next.

Toby Parker knocked twice on the open door. "Yeah?" Neddle said without looking up.

Toby walked in. "Colonel Neddle, at your welcoming briefing, you said your door was always open, and I—"

"Yeah, but I didn't say you could just walk in." Neddle wrote two more lines, closed a folder, and looked up.

He read Toby's name tag. "What's up, Parker? You getting enough to eat? Did you write your folks this week? Counselors treating you properly here at the George Summer Day Camp?" Neddle grabbed a stained coffee mug next to his desk. It bore the Triple Nickel fighter squadron logo, with two red stars above Neddle's name. He'd nailed two MiG-19s one bright day while zipping around Hanoi at an altitude so low he was afraid to mention it in his after-action report. J.T.'s buddies called him "Lonesome George" because he looked so much like the World War II fighter pilot and comedian George Gobel.

"I need a new counselor," Toby said, straining some to get into the spirit of it.

"What's the matter? He chew your ass and make you cry?" Neddle rose and walked to the big squadron duty roster board on the wall. He traced out Parker's name and that of his IP, Frank Owens, who had three other student pilots.

"What's the matter with Owens?" he repeated. He chewed on the cigar stump, placed his hands on his hips, and looked up at Parker from his height of five-eight.

"He's a great guy. I just think I'd be better off with someone else teaching me."

"You want to switch IPs in the middle of the air combat maneuvering course?"

"Yes, sir. That's exactly what I mean."

Neddle looked at the soggy cigar butt, frowned, and put it back in his mouth. "He too tough for you?"

"He's not tough enough. If I'm going to learn how to shoot down MiGs, I need an aggressive instructor."

Neddle snorted and went back to his desk. "Look, Parker, I've got bigger problems to solve around here than that of some junior jock who doesn't like his IP. I can't be reassigning IPs and studs at the mere whim of one unhappy guy. The pipeline is really flowing now. There's a big push for pilots to be upgraded and go to SEA. We got more studs coming in here than we know what to do with. We've got ATC jocks, SAC bomber pilots, and PhDs from the Academy rolling in and we need super, shit-hot IPs for all of them. You don't need one as badly as they do, for Christ's sakes. I can tell just by looking at you that you've already had a combat tour."

"How's that?" Toby asked, perplexed.

"Three things," Neddle answered. "Your dog tags are taped together, you're not overawed by rank, and," he chomped on his cigar and winked, "your flying records say so. You think I don't study the records of the studs in my squadron?"

"My tour was in O-2s as a FAC. We did all air-to-mud work and I never saw a MiG."

"That's combat and you learned to make decisions under stress. Damn few guys coming through here now have that." Neddle's chair squeaked as he leaned back. "Okay, let's talk about your so-called problem," he said. "Most guys complain about their IP being too tough. Here you are bitching because yours isn't tough enough. Shit. You see all these folders?" He patted a stack on his desk. "These are for thirty new studs coming to this squadron in three weeks and I only have IPs for twenty-four. My guys are going to have to double and maybe triple the load they already have, and you want to change the lineup. Can't do it."

Toby blew a breath. He'd tried. "Sorry to take up your time, Colonel." He started to leave.

"Wait a minute." Neddle squinted at Toby. His chair squeaked as he leaned forward. "You're the guy who flew that O-1 from the backseat before you were a pilot and rescued that Special Forces team. Yeah, you got the Air Force Cross for that, didn't you?"

"Yes, sir."

"Well then, like I said, you're an old head at combat. Why in hell *can't* you make do with a perfectly good IP who has a MiG to his credit?" J.T. demanded.

"Owens is just teaching me how to survive in combat. Let him have the SAC guys and the math PhDs. They haven't been upside down since pilot training. They need to learn how to survive. I need to learn how to *kill*. He's not teaching that to me."

"Ahhhh, so you're one of the eager ones. Want to go out and kill a commie for Christ." Neddle regarded Toby with pursed lips. His chair squeaked as he rocked back again. "Want to become an Ace, do you?"

"Sure, but that's not my prime motivation. Since I first started flying airplanes I've wanted fighters, so now I have my assignment and I want to be able to fly them as well as

I can. And I happen to think there's more to combat than just making Ace."

"Not for most pilots there isn't. I'll ask you the same question at the end of your combat tour and we'll see what your answer is then."

"Dammit, Colonel, you're playing mind games. I know you're pressed for IPs. But what difference does it make to you which one I have? You got some shit-hot fighter IPs here like Madden and Wetterhahn, and I want one."

"These guys are already overloaded. They hardly have time to pee, much less go home to mama after a hard day. We're not hurting for airplanes. We're not hurting for maintenance. But we are sure as hell hurting for Eye-fucking-Pees. Sure, I can take you away from Frank Owens, but there isn't anybody available as ornery as you seem to want." His voice trailed off and he looked at Toby with pursed lips. "Wait a minute." Neddle pulled a manila folder from a rack and flipped through it. "Nope, sorry. That won't work either. Not available."

"What won't work?" Toby asked.

"Tanaka's on extended leave. I thought he was still on the duty roster, but he's not. He, ah, had a problem and has gone off to . . . sort of think it all out."

"I've heard of Tanaka. A buddy told me to try to get him as an IP, as a matter of fact, but I heard he'd shipped out. A problem, you say?"

"Serious problem. Spun a guy in on the gunnery range . . . an old buddy as I hear it." Neddle sighed. "What a guy." He shook his head. "Everybody in Phantom's heard of the Battling Buddha, Acrocka Tanaka. He's likely the world's greatest air-to-air IP . . . teaches what he preaches: lag displacement, high and low yo-yos, all the basic fighter maneuvers. And scissors, my God does he know scissors: flat ones, vertical ones, rolling ones. He's been Top Gun here in the IP shoot-offs so long we had to prevent him from competing to give the other guys a chance. He's been frothing at the mouth to get back to SEA."

Neddle continued. "He had a combat tour, got credit for an assist on a shoot-down, but a number of his students got a MiG or two and he couldn't stand not being back over there. We kept him on here an extra six months because we were pressed and he's so good. But after that crash, I don't know what he's going to do. He's been on leave."

"Where?" Toby asked.

"Not far. He has a cabin in the San Bernardino Mountains, up near ski country."

Toby felt excitement. He leaned on Neddle's desk. "Colonel, you say you're fat on airplanes and short on IPs. Suppose I talk Tanaka into coming back and taking me on. Would you put him back on IP orders and assign us a bird for two sorties a day for a couple weeks?"

"No problem there. Your problem's with Tanaka. He may not want to come back here—ever." Neddle examined the shreds of his cigar, tossed it into an empty waste can, where it landed with a soggy plop. "He's a tough guy to get to know. Hell of a background. He's Nisei, first-generation Japanese. When he was a kid, his family was interned after Pearl Harbor. His father was some kind of a hard case, so they wound up at Tule Lake here in California—not a nice place. The old man died of pneumonia there in '42. Tanaka was taking care of his mother until she died a few years back. Has one sister. Worked like hell in high school and got an appointment for the Air Force Academy, class of '62. He was a squadron commander and graduated number twelve in order of merit." Neddle pulled out a fresh cigar and bit the end off, but made no attempt to light it.

Toby leaned forward. "You just said he was a tough guy, and the most aggressive fighter IP you got, but he won't even fight to get himself out of his funk? That doesn't make sense."

"I told you he was a hard guy to get to know." Neddle wrote out Tanaka's address and handed it to Parker.

"How come you know so much about him?" Toby asked casually.

"None of your fucking business."

0930 Hours Local, Tuesday 4 April 1972
232 Kaiser Street, Crestline
San Bernardino Mountains,
California

Toby eased his white Corvette out of the last turn of County Road 138 into the town of Crestline. An AM station was featuring Doctor Timothy Leary, a noted Harvard mathematician, who was spouting his views on mind-expanding drugs. "LSD is Western yoga," Leary was explaining. "The aim of Eastern religion, like that of LSD, is to expand your consciousness and find ecstasy and revelation . . . " After listening to a few phrases, Toby no longer heard the words.

The program made him remember the time he'd been dependent on alcohol . . . being pitched into rugged combat as a young, immature lieutenant, followed by the loss of the first girl he had loved, had combined to create the downbeat mood, and drinking had been a natural next step. Drenched in self-pity, he'd wallowed in memories. His military career had suffered and his self-respect had fast deteriorated. After a bad drunk in Florida, he'd been braced by a Florida patrolman who'd shocked sense into him. From a pier that day he'd thrown, far out into the waters of the Gulf, the jade memento of his Vietnamese love, then run the white sand Gulf beaches near Hurlburt Field until he was retching from exhaustion. That was the beginning. Since then he hadn't drunk another drop. He'd studied and flown hard, working to overcome the bad reputation and rebuild his self-esteem. He'd been successful on both counts and become a long-distance runner while doing it. He made a small smile in mild appreciation for the way things had turned out, then lost it as he thought of Tiffy Berg, the stewardess who had loved him and whom he'd spurned when he drank until she had finally, judiciously, withdrawn from the scene. He had been unsuccessful in ever contacting her again.

From the one-bay Standard Oil station he got directions to Kaiser Street. There were few streets in the town of 180 souls, so it wasn't difficult to find. The streets were wide and lined with huge pine trees. The houses were older clapboards braced with steep-pitched roofs for heavy snow. Postseason snow lay glistening and melting in the brilliant sunlight. He drove slowly, thinking about his morning phone call to Captain Kenichi Tanaka.

"This is Toby Parker," he had said. "I'm an F-4 upgrade student at George and I'd like to come out and talk to you."

"Who? Talk about what?" Tanaka had replied in a remote voice.

"Toby Parker. I need your advice."

"Parker? Oh yeah. Advice on what, carving ducks?" Tanaka's chuckle had sounded far away, as though he had turned his head from the phone.

"Ducks? Well, no. Not exactly. I want your advice on how to kill MiGs."

"I'm through giving advice."

"J. T. Neddle said to call you," Toby had said. Tanaka hadn't replied. "And so did Court Bannister." After a long silence Tanaka had finally answered.

"Parker, I've heard about you. You've done great things, so they say, whoever the hell *they* are. What makes you think I can teach you anything?" Tanaka had sounded peevish.

"Let me put it another way. I want to talk to you about how to fight with the Phantom . . . and not just against other F-4s."

There was a pause. "Okay," Tanaka had said, "come on up." He'd given Toby terse instructions and hung up.

Toby found the cabin set back among pine trees. It was small, made of dark oak logs with a roof covered with dark green shingles. He parked next to a nearly new four-wheel-drive pickup.

"Back here," Tanaka said from behind the cabin when Toby knocked. Toby walked around to the small concrete patio off the back door. He wore gray slacks and a dark-blue cardigan, carried a small blue AWOL bag, and his eyes were hidden behind USAF-issue straight-frame aviator's sunglasses. He ran fingers over his hair.

Tanaka was sitting in a lawn chair, one of two, carving on an oblong piece of wood. He wore a red flannel shirt with the sleeves rolled up, dark corduroy trousers, and logger's boots. On newspaper at his feet were scattered curved chips of wood, looking like he'd upended a bag of potato chips. Resting on a wooden box beside his chair were several long-handled Buck wood-carving knives of various sizes. Next to them was a pair of USAF sunglasses identical to Toby's. A fishing tackle box open on the ground was full of small bottles of model airplane paint, the dull, not the glossy kind.

Tanaka did not rise. "Parker?"

"Toby Parker." Toby extended his hand.

The seated man shook it. "Ken Tanaka," he said. "Sit down."

Toby took the other lawn chair, placing the AWOL bag at his side. He looked at the tall pines and surrounding mountain views. The breeze was gentle and sweet with mountain air. "This is gorgeous. You a skier as well as a carver?"

"I ski. You?"

"Yes. We should go out sometime. Not many guys at George ski."

Toby studied Tanaka. He had a full, almost square face. His slightly oval eyes were black and clear, moderately slanted, and more lively than his small mouth and thin lips suggested. His black hair was shaped in a crew cut. His skin was a consistent brown, as if he had a well-established summer tan.

"Look, Parker," Tanaka said. "Let's cut the bullshit. Nice to meet you, but you're wasting your time." He picked up a piece of wood and resumed carving. Chips curled lazily off the wood as he slowly moved his knife, fingers guiding the blade.

Toby leaned back and crossed his legs. He breathed deep. "Great air." He breathed again, expanding his chest. Neither man spoke for several minutes. Toby debated the best way to get into Tanaka's circle of solitude. He decided, took a deep breath, and began.

"J. T. Neddle said the reason you're holed up here is because you spun somebody in."

After a while Tanaka said, "I'm up here because I like to carve ducks."

"You're not the first to spin someone in, you know."

Tanaka snorted.

Toby reached into the bag at his side and pulled out two jelly tumblers and a quart of Johnnie Walker Black. He pulled the cap off and carefully poured four fingers of scotch into each glass, then handed one to the silent Tanaka. "Cheers," he said, and raised the glass to his mouth. The liquid stung as he let it touch his lips.

With no expression, Tanaka quickly downed half his glass. "Cheers," he said, and raised his glass in a return toast. Toby again barely touched the scotch to his lips.

This time Tanaka took a smaller sip, then placed the duck to one side and stood up. "Drink up," he said, and raised the glass.

Toby wagged his head. "Can't handle the stuff. One drink is too much and a hundred aren't enough."

"Hunh," Tanaka huffed. He stared at Parker, then put the jelly tumbler of scotch on the side table, walked to the edge of the patio, and looked up at the mountains. Two hawks were soaring effortlessly in an updraft. After a moment, he started to talk.

"It was Colonel Tom Bakke. He'd been my Tac officer at

the Academy, and later my squadron commander. He taught me everything. How to be an officer, how to fly. When he went in, a part of me went in with him. It was my fault." He remained gazing over the mountains.

Toby put his full glass down. "How could it be? You weren't in the same airplane, and you weren't shooting at him. How about his backseater, did he get out?"

"Yes," Tanaka said, "he did."

"If the backseater had enough time, then so did your friend."

"No."

"What do you mean?" Toby asked.

Tanaka sighed. "We were in a six-G rat race. Colonel Bakke tried to reverse, tucked under, lost it, and spun in from 15,000. His backseater said he mumbled something, then never said another word or tried to make flight control inputs to recover. It was an inverted flat spin. The backseater was a young navigator. He kept hollering at Tom, then finally had to punch out."

"Sounds to me like he had all the time in the world to recover or eject. Sounds like he became incapacitated, like a heart attack or something," Toby said.

"Matter of fact, I think it *was* a heart attack. So does his GIB."

"Then what do you mean it was your fault, and he had no time? Doesn't add up."

"It does," Tanaka said. "See, we went on an F-4 cross-country together a few weeks before. He had some trouble in the plane. Vision and breathing problems. I could have, I *should* have, reported it to the Flight Surgeon and had him grounded."

"He'd have hated you," Toby said.

"Maybe," Tanaka said, "maybe not. But at least he'd be alive." He turned to Toby. "You see, I could have saved his life and I didn't." Tanaka's face was without expression.

Toby remained silent.

"I should have had him grounded."

"What does that have to do with your quitting flying?" Toby asked at last.

Tanaka shrugged. "I just don't want to do it anymore."

"That's a load of crap. You're a fighter pilot and fighter pilots fly fighters. They don't sit around and feel sorry for themselves."

Kenichi Tanaka scowled his eyes into black slits. "Not much on sympathy, are you, Parker?"

"Sympathy? That's between shit and syphilis in the dictionary. What do you suppose Tom Bakke would want for you? Certainly not to piss and moan about not doing something he wouldn't want you to do in the first place."

Tanaka returned to his chair and glowered at the forest. Toby looked at the peaks and thought how pure the sky looked. The sun was edging down behind the mountain, and the air was becoming chilly. Tanaka sighed and leaned back. Both men watched the sun slide behind the mountain and the snow turn from white to purple in the haze.

"How come you're not drinking?" Tanaka asked.

"Told you. I'm an alcoholic," Toby replied quietly.

Tanaka was silent for a long time.

"You say you want to learn how to fight the Phantom. What do you mean?" Tanaka's voice was deep and measured. His pronunciation crisp. He turned and regarded Toby with hooded eyes.

Toby leaned back and crossed his legs, breathed deep. "This is great air." He breathed again, expanding his chest. "What I mean is, I'm not getting enough from my air-to-air instructor. I only have thirty hours in the bird and—"

"How does it feel?"

"The airplane?"

"Yeah."

"Too damned big, but it has good overall characteristics. But . . . I haven't flown that many planes."

"How long you been in fighters?"

Toby sighed. "This is my first time. I was an O-2 FAC at Da Nang, then I put in four years at Randolph as an IP."

Tanaka studied Toby. "You say your current IP is teaching you how to survive? Since you're new to fighters, maybe that's all you're capable of learning."

Toby stiffened. "I want to learn how to *fight* with it."

"You may wear captain's tracks, but in fighters you're a second lieutenant," Tanaka said.

"A second lieutenant made Ace in Korea—shot down five MiGs with an F-86."

Tanaka didn't change expressions. "You're asking me to go to a lot of trouble for you."

"I'm on my way to combat. I want to fight the very best I can."

"You want to kill five MiGs and make Ace?"

"That's what Colonel Neddle asked. Making Ace would be fine. If I learn how to fight the Phantom, maybe I will."

Tanaka stared over the mountains for a few seconds, then sat back in his chair. "You still haven't told me why you want to learn how to fight the Phantom."

Toby stood and walked to the edge of the patio. He looked out at the peaks and thought how clean and white the snow appeared. "Nice."

"The view's therapeutic. Makes you appreciative. Lets you think. Answer my question."

"I was your usual dumb-shit college ROTC frat man who was having a good time in the Air Force, chasing girls and not really caring about much. Then several things happened." Toby paused. When Tanaka did not respond, he continued.

"I saw the war close up. Two people who meant a lot to me were killed."

The deaths of a Vietnamese girl named Tui and Air Force Captain Phil Travers affected Toby deeply. He'd fallen hard for Tui, then watched as she was cut down by machine-gun fire one dark night. "Phil the FAC" Travers had shown Toby the joy of flight in his tiny O-1 aircraft as he'd controlled air strikes in South Vietnam. Travers had taken a round in his stomach when Toby was in the backseat. Toby had taken the controls and rescued a Special Forces unit. Later Phil had died in the hospital.

"Too close," Toby repeated, staring at the mountains.

"That doesn't tell me why you want to be such a good fighter pilot."

"Anybody ever tell you you were relentless?"

"Yeah. And cruel. Now tell me why."

"It's obvious."

"Maybe. Tell me anyhow."

Toby spun around. "Tanaka, you asshole, it would be the only meaningful thing I've ever done in my life. The only thing I'm a natural at besides partying is flying airplanes. I want to develop that ability and go all the way with it."

Ken Tanaka stared at the young pilot. Something in his stubbornness reminded him of his early days as a cadet at the Air Force Academy. An upperclassman had tried to haze him out and he had successfully resisted. He had wanted to go all the way, too, as a cadet and in the Air Force.

"Okay, I'll buy that." Tanaka put his hand out. "Parker, I'll help you become the *second*-best fighter pilot in the world."

0545 Hours Local, Thursday 6 April 1972
Operations, 4452 Combat Crew
Training Squadron
George AFB, California

Parker looked on as Tanaka accepted the paper offered by Lieutenant Colonel J. T. Neddle—IP orders reestablishing Tanaka in his job.

"We've got enough airplanes for two or three sorties a day for the next ten days. And there's enough brand-new second lieutenant backseaters who want to log time in anything. They'll be delighted to fly with you guys when you go up against each other." He moved his cigar butt to the other side of his mouth. "One thing, Parker. You understand you won't be crewed up with a particular backseater here, like we normally do when we're sending a pilot to the combat zone. Since all your time will be spent training with Tanaka, you won't have time to get teamed up."

"Okay by me," Toby said. "I'm not all that hot to have somebody back there anyhow."

J.T. jerked around to face him. "You'd damn well *better* learn to like it. He may save your ass some day."

"Yes, sir," Toby said, convinced this was a subject best left unexplored in front of J. T. Neddle. Toby's previous combat experience had been spent alone in the cockpit, and he preferred it that way. An essential ingredient in a successful fighter pilot is his individualistic attitude, and that does not call for another person in the same aircraft. By all means rely on a wingman or another flight member—there's safety in numbers and you can develop more attack options—but another man in the same airplane?

"Have at it, you guys," Neddle said. "The schedule's set."

Toby, Tanaka, and their two GIBs went into one of the six small briefing rooms in the squadron operations building. Like others in the squadron, the GIBs had on black paratrooper-style boots with thick laces. Toby and Tanaka wore the canvas-sided jungle boots they'd been issued in Vietnam. The black paratrooper boots, while their tops shined nicely, had smooth soles and had proven to shot-down crewmen to be as gripping on the damp jungle floor as cowboy boots on ice. The ugly jungle boots had serrated leather soles as variegated as Alaska snow tires that gave them traction like a John Deere tractor.

In the room was a large, Plexiglas-covered table exhibiting local-area aeronautical charts and copies of checklists for weapons, avionics, emergency procedures, and radio frequencies. A wall displayed a large chart of the southwestern quarter of the United States, depicting Navy, Marine, and Air Force jet bases, air-to-air and air-to-ground gunnery ranges, and refueling tracks for the big KC-135 flying gas stations that replenished jet fuel to thirsty fighters five miles above the earth.

"Today it's a knife fight. No gadgets, no radar—just eyeballs. We'll start out one-versus-one," Tanaka said. "Later we'll do one-vee-two, two-vee-two, and so forth, but first I need to find out about you, and you need to find out about yourself and your airplane. For this flight I'm directing your backseater to give you minimum radar inputs. It'll be up to you to keep track of me. There won't be any surprises. I'll keep it one-on-one. Just you and me. You vee me, got that?"

Toby nodded, noticing how Tanaka was focused, obsidian eyes flashing, his body vibrant and alert . . . like a coiled rattler. "I'm ready."

Tanaka used a pointer to show Toby and the GIBs the aerial range where they would fight. They copied down the reference points that marked the corners of the giant box of airspace which measured 7,000 square miles, from the ground up to 50,000 feet.

Tanaka began his briefing. "Our call sign is Cigar. I'm Cigar One, you're Cigar Two. If you have to bail out, frontseater is Cigar Two Alpha, backseater is Cigar Two Bravo. Our station time is 0640, start engines at 0700, takeoff time is 0720. We're carrying two 450-gallon drop tanks, and we are simulating one 20mm cannon, four AIM-7 Sparrow radar missiles, and four AIM-9 Sidewinder heat-seeker missiles. You know that a Sparrow's a radar-guided missile, therefore your radar must acquire and illuminate the target. The Sparrow will home in on that radiation, so you must keep your nose pointed at the target until the missile strikes. With the Sparrow you can attack from any angle. Can't do that with the Sidewinder because it's a heat-seeker. You must be within a thirty-degree cone of the bad guy's tailpipe for your missile to properly pick up the heat from his engine. Once you get the growl tone in your headset, you can fire. The higher the growl, the better the lock-on. Unlike the Sparrow, once you fire a Sidewinder, you can break away. It will track the heat source all by itself." While he was talking, he pointed to pictures of the two missiles.

The Sparrow was twelve feet long, weighed 450 pounds, and carried a 66-pound warhead. Its top speed was just under Mach 4, range thirty miles. The long-range factor, however, was negated because before they could shoot, American pilots had to positively identify the target as an enemy aircraft. That reduced firing range to only four or five miles.

The Sidewinder was ten feet long, weighed 180 pounds, and had a 22-pound warhead. The range of the Sidewinder was less than three miles.

Tanaka continued. "Keep your backseater informed of what you're doing. He must know what weapon you select so he can give you proper radar information, like range to the target, and, in the case of the Sparrow, whether or not his radar is locked on. Your gunsight display on your windscreen will also show when he has a lock-on."

Tanaka went on with details. Cigar flight would take off in formation, fly in fighting wing formation to the air-to-air range, then separate to fly line abreast to begin the first skirmish. Rather than his hands, Tanaka used two eight-inch F-4 models attached to the end of pointers to demonstrate what he wanted. These were called fighter-sticks. The friendlies, the F-4s, were white, the MiGs red. Tanaka held a red and a white model side by side and parallel to the floor to show how he wanted the flight positioned.

"We'll begin at twenty-five thousand feet," he said, "with you off my left wing. Fly line abreast on me, about a thousand feet out. At that distance my airplane will look about one inch long. At my command, we'll make a thirty-degree bank away from each other until we each have forty-five degrees of heading change. Don't gain or lose altitude in the turn. We'll hold that heading for two minutes, until I transmit 'have at it,' and then the fight's on. At that instant you'll know I'm at your four or five o'clock position, level, about two miles away, heading ninety degrees to the right of your heading. When you hear me say 'have at it,' do whatever you think best to find, track, and kill me." Tanaka moved the miniature models to show what he wanted. "Later on, as you progress, you won't know where I'll be coming from, but this time you will." He hung the fighter-sticks next to the blackboard.

"If at any time," Tanaka continued, "either of us wants to stop the engagement, call out 'knock it off.' Minimum altitude is ten thousand feet. That is our floor. Go below that and you're dead. Remember, for today we have a special deal; don't use your fire control radar to find me. Today it's a knife fight using our eyeballs." He concluded his briefing with the details of communications and emergency procedures.

Each man then briefed his backseater on what he expected in the way of navigation, radio calls, and help in the dogfight.

"Don't talk to me unless you're sure what you have to say affects the flight," Toby told the young second lieutenant navigator who was to be his GIB.

"Yes, sir," the GIB responded in a neutral voice.

Fifty minutes later they had their airplanes in position and Tanaka called, "Have at it." The two planes were headed away from each other. Upon receipt of the call, Toby immediately made a hard right turn toward Tanaka's position. As he came around, he saw the speck that was Tanaka's F-4 and rolled out when it was on his nose. This was simulated guns only, no using the long-range, radar-guided Sparrow. As Toby bored in toward Tanaka, he estimated he needed several thousand more feet before he could open fire with his camera in a head-on pass. He didn't have much time, for their combined closing speed was 1,000 knots, 1,150 miles per hour. This looked suspiciously easy.

Then, while still out of range, Tanaka pulled up in a climbing turn to the right, presenting his belly to Toby. Toby pulled farther right and started to raise his nose, but Tanaka was still too far away for a shot. Ken seemed to be climbing away from the fight. Toby started a level turn so that when Tanaka rolled out, he'd be low and at Tanaka's six o'clock.

But Tanaka did more than roll out. When high at Toby's one

o'clock, he suddenly reversed his turn and dove toward Toby. He had traded a hundred knots of airspeed for 2,000 feet of altitude. Flying slower, he was able to make the sharp turn. Toby turned toward Tanaka in an attempt to spoil his tracking solution. The minute he did, Ken again reversed his turn, presenting his belly to Toby. Now Toby was worse off than before. He couldn't turn sharply enough to bring his gunsight to bear on Tanaka's Phantom for a quickie snap shot, even if he had been in range.

"I think he's turning away from the fight. Maybe he's lost me," Toby muttered into his mask as he looked at the fleeing airplane off his right wing. All he could do was continue his turn toward Tanaka. Suddenly Tanaka reversed again and Toby realized he was at the receiving end of what could be an angled shot at him. He did what he thought best; he slammed into afterburner and pulled up and to the left, hoping he had higher airspeed than Tanaka and could gain the height advantage. He found he didn't have anything. He pulled too tight, lost airspeed, gained very little altitude—and couldn't find Tanaka. He unplugged the burners and looked around. The sky was empty.

Tukka tukka tukka, he heard over his headset. He looked up at his mirror and saw the nose of Tanaka's Phantom in perfect gun kill position, 600 feet behind. Less than two minutes had passed since the fight had begun.

For the next thirty-five minutes, Tanaka gave Toby every advantage and whipped him six out of seven times. The seventh engagement was a draw because Toby dove away from the fight when he saw Tanaka closing and realized he couldn't gain an advantage.

A few minutes later Toby noted his fuel was at the predetermined *bingo* level, which meant it was time to return to base. As they joined up and Tanaka asked for a fuel check, Toby found to his disgust that he had twenty minutes less fuel than his instructor pilot.

Tanaka sat comfortably on the edge of the map table, arms folded, while Toby paced in front of the blackboard. Tanaka had sent the GIBs for coffee in the lounge. Tanaka kept an impassive face and waited for what he knew was to come.

"How do you do it? Dammit, we're both flying the same kind of airplane. Is yours specially modified?" Toby faced Kenichi Tanaka. "Hell, I know it isn't, but how'd you do it?"

"How did I do what?"

"Don't get cute," Toby said. "You know damn well what I mean."

"Say it," Tanaka said. "Put it in words."

Toby shook his head. "Okay. How did you *whip my ass?*"

"I didn't whip your ass, Parker, I whipped your *mind.* Got that? I whipped your mind, because all you were thinking of was putting your guns on me and never losing sight of me."

"Of course I didn't want to lose sight of you. Never take your eyes off the enemy, that's a cardinal rule, isn't it?"

"Another thing," Tanaka said, ignoring the question, "you give up too much energy when you maneuver." He'd been watching, waiting for Toby's face to change from anger to bewilderment. That was the crucial point a good instructor looked for—when the student's ego dwindled and he opened his mind to take in information. Tanaka judged the time was at hand when Toby flopped into a chair.

"I give up. Talk to me."

"Say please, round-eye."

Toby grinned. "Prease, you samurai plick."

Using the fighter-sticks and blackboard, Tanaka re-created the entire flight. As he touched on each encounter, he told Toby his airspeed and G-loading at particular points. As he did so, he diagrammed in excruciating detail each of Toby's errors. He never used the pronouns I and you, but instead "red" airplane and "white" airplane. Since the stick models were different colors, it wasn't hard to figure out who was who. Tanaka had assigned white to himself.

"I'm following what you're saying, Ken, but I have a lot of questions. Like how did you know my airspeed and G-load? How did you always gain position on me without using burners? And how did you keep me in sight, even when you turned away?" Toby lit his first cigarette of the day.

Kenichi Tanaka smiled. "You're asking the right questions. First off, I know my opponent's airspeed and G-loads due to spending so much time instructing and flying." He noted Toby's look of resignation. "But that comes quickly, you'll pick it up before you leave George air patch. I'll make sure of that. Second, I gained position without using burners by easing into the climbs and the turns. I don't yank in a lot of unnecessary G-loads that slow me down. Last, I had my backseater help me keep you in sight. I kept calculating your airspeed, turn rate, and G-load in my head so I'd know where you'd be when I rolled out. Even so, I never was turned away for more than ten seconds without easing off and eyeballing where I knew you'd be."

"How did you know I would or wouldn't continue the turns?" Toby asked.

"You became predictable in the first sixty seconds. The only time you weren't was at the end when you accelerated away. You hadn't done that before. So—you did one thing right."

"I thought the only thing I did right today was land the airplane without denting anything. But I'll take any praise I can get. What did I do right?"

"After the first turn of our seventh engagement, you accelerated down and away from the fight," Tanaka said.

"Positioning for a reattack," Toby added, nodding.

Ken sighed. "Then you were *not* doing the smart thing. You made the right move, but for the wrong reason."

Toby frowned. "You were close to getting on my ass, so I tried to get away while gaining enough airspeed to come back at you. What's wrong with that?"

"The smart thing would have been to keep on going and not even think about reattack."

"What in hell do you mean?" Toby demanded.

"You met a superior tactician who was going to kill you, so it was time to disengage—to get away and analyze what you were doing wrong. A good pilot is one who uses his judgment to avoid bad situations."

"I don't run from fights."

Tanaka laughed. "You sound like so many guys who come through here, and I'll tell you the same thing I tell them. There's no point in sticking your pecker down a gun barrel to pee on the bullet, just to prove you have balls. That's a one-time deal and they don't give medals to peckerless pilots." Tanaka stood. "Listen, if you don't have position and you can't gain it, if you don't have airspeed and you can't gain it, get the hell out of the arena."

"That's pussycat stuff."

"You try my patience, Parker. You know you can't fight without ammunition or gas in your tanks and so it is with tactical advantage. *Gain the advantage,* that's what I'm telling you. It's as vital as fuel or ammo. And if you can't gain it, haul ass and return to base so you can figure it out and fight on another day." Tanaka had his hands on his hips. "Like I tell anybody who will listen, ego can help you or it can kill you. It's like fire. It can cook your meals and smelt your steel or it can kill you most unpleasantly. A fighter pilot has to have the right mixture. Enough ego to get into the card game confident he can whip the shit out of anybody, but not so much ego he won't throw his cards in on a bad hand and—just as vital—learn what he did wrong."

Toby sprawled in the chair, arms hanging, receptive.

Tanaka took up the fighter-sticks again. "I am *here* and he is *there.* I don't have a direct reading of his airspeed indicator, but I know what he's done for the last thirty degrees of turn. I can look at his nose and see how fast he's going, his rate of turn. I can look at his nose to see where he's going and what he can do; and I know that right *now* he's going 250 knots and within ninety degrees turn with *that* G-load, he'll be at 180—and if he *continues* to do that, he'll have dumped all his energy. Now suppose he thinks about the bad spot he's in and acts—even then I know that the only other thing he can do is unload, ease out of his turn, and then he's going to be right *here.* I base my decision on the data I've taken in. I conceptualize the fight, and *act.* "

Tanaka was wound up. His eyes flashed, hands moving the stick-planes rapidly up and down, explanations emerging in staccato bursts.

"Bring your nose down across *here,* then up, a roll, a pirouette, now pull, down *here,* back across and now pull into the vertical, cross here, back over the top. Over the top, unload, roll, pull, bam, you're getting there. Now get down, fast." He moved the sticks, white plane after the red from a height advantage. "God doesn't care if you're upside down, right side up, or sideways. An unload is an unload is an unload. And you can't turn when you're pulling Gs. Unload, roll, pull. If you've got to pull five, six, seven Gs when you're fighting in the airplane, you're doing it *wrong.* "

"That's heresy," Toby said. He was absorbed with Tanaka's performance and trying to assimilate it all.

"Keep your mach up so you can maneuver. You learn to fight fast in this machine. Once you get slow, wrap it up—you're going down. *But,* go fast and you can use the vertical. Go straight up, fighting all the way. Energy to burn. I love the vertical. Why? Because so few adversaries know how to use the vertical."

Toby clapped, grinning. Tanaka looked momentarily embarrassed. "It will all come to you," he said. He hung the sticks up. "Now let's talk about that guy in your backseat."

"Lieutenant Whozit," Toby replied sarcastically.

"Lieutenant Whozit can either make you a hero or a bum. He can save your life or get you killed. He's as important to the proper use of this airplane as your control stick. More so. You get your stick shot away, he can use his to bring you home."

Toby shook his head. "I'm not comfortable flying with someone else in the airplane. It's going to take getting used to. I like to do my own planning, preflighting, airborne eyeballing, radio calls, even my own panicking, without help from anybody else. If the guy back there wants to tune the radio and radar, more power to him. But don't expect me to rely on his superior airmanship to get me out of tight spots." Toby laughed. "Come on, Ken, be realistic. These guys are navigators. They don't know how to fly, much less fight." Toby shook his head in disgust.

"They tried putting pilots in the pit," Tanaka said, "because there's a stick back there. They were unhappy as hell, and only wanted to upgrade to the front seat. These guys now are professional weapons-systems officers, and they like what they are doing just as much as you do. They give you an extra set of eyeballs, an extra pair of hands, and an extra brain. Use 'em. It's plain dumb to only use half a fighting tool. You wouldn't use only one barrel of a double-barrel shotgun, would you?"

"Point taken," Toby said begrudgingly.

"Or deliberately not use your wingman."

"I would not. Another point taken," Toby said. "You say so, I'll learn to use the guy. What about tactics? I talked a lot with Court Bannister when he was at Ubon. He got four MiGs. He said although we've been at war over there all this time, we still don't have our tactics updated."

"Not officially," Tanaka said, eyes glittering, "but me and a few others here go out on cross-country flights to various bases, talking to the guys who've been there. Particularly the Phantom and Thud drivers who went up north during Rolling Thunder. They all tell essentially the same story."

"What's that?"

"The Thud units attacking the heavily defended targets up north almost always had the same call sign, rolled in from the same direction and at the same time every day because they were fragged that way. They could only hit the two-bit targets picked by President Johnson and his civilian buddies, who didn't know diddley-squat about what they were doing. In those days the F-4s couldn't hit shit with AIM-7 Sparrow missiles because the son of bitches wouldn't work. The AIM-4 Falcon was twice as bad. The AIM-9 Sidewinder was fair. And even if they *did* work, the pilots had to get close enough to eyeball every target, since they couldn't tell if it was a Navy A-4 or an enemy MiG-21 in front of them. By the time they'd eyeballed the target, half the time they were too close to use a missile. And when you're that close, the yank and bank to stay with him usually has you out of the G-load parameters for a good Sidewinder shot. So the obvious solution for all this is to go for a gun kill. Only problem is, the F-4 *ain't got* no gun." Tanaka gritted his teeth angrily.

"The new F-4E models have a built-in gun," Toby said.

"Yeah, but most of the birds over in the combat theater are C and D models."

Toby mused. "They can carry a SUU-16 20mm gun pod."

"Sure," Tanaka said. "Damn thing weighs damn near a ton, takes up a hard point under the fuselage, and adds all kind of drag. Only thing is, it's better than not having a gun at all.

"Another thing," Tanaka said, wound up now, "Mikoyan and Guryevich designed their MiGs for air superiority work *only*. No air-to-ground for them like our trusty Phantom. We've got all these extra doodads for dropping bombs, and we dilute our air-to-air training learning how to drop them." Ken stopped and frowned. "Hell, I'm sounding like I don't like what I'm doing."

Toby grinned. "I had a ball up there this morning."

Tanaka stuck his head out the door and looked around for the GIBs, spotted them, and waved. "Let's get our gear on. We're going up again."

Chapter 4

When Major General Norman had temporarily commandeered Court Bannister from his job in operations to help set up Operation Freedom Train, he'd considered it would be for only a week, so they continued to work out of the intelligence briefing theater. That had been changed the day before the first combat sorties were launched into North Vietnam.

Court had been away, making a round-robin tour of the Thailand bases to brief the pilots on the intricacies of the initial attack plan, when General Vogt, the four-star Commander of 7th Air Force, had toured the Tactical Air Control Center on April 5 and asked about preparations for the imminent bombing operation. Before they started their briefing, the TACC plans officers had called Court's action group, requesting that someone come over to answer the General's thorniest questions. When Vogt asked who they were waiting for, he was told they worked closely with Court's people, who were the most knowledgeable group in the headquarters concerning the upcoming air operation. The General had immediately snorted and gained his feet,

83

saying he'd go there for his briefing.

The four-star General had visited the briefing theater/make-shift office with four lesser generals in tow, including General Norman. He'd glanced about at the men, who stood stiffly at attention, and demanded his briefing. It had been hastily contrived and supplied by Majors Frizzell and Smythe, the Wild Weasel crew from Korat on temporary loan to the head-quarters.

First Smythe had explained how they had coordinated with counterparts at the Pentagon, Pacific Command and Pacific Air Forces headquarters in Honolulu, Strategic Air Command head-quarters in Nebraska, Tactical Air Command in Virginia, and their sister office at the U.S. Navy's 7th Fleet. Next he meticu-lously spelled out each facet of the integrated plan. After each major point, Frizzell had stepped forward and with exuberantly waving hands, lines, and symbols on the blackboard, and vivid description, explained how the multiforce plan would be flown.

General Vogt was so impressed that he'd given a single terse order to Norman and his deputy commander for operations, making the interim group a permanent fixture for the duration of the operation. When Smythe and Frizzell made glowing remarks about Court's superb leadership, he'd assigned Lieu-tenant Colonel Bannister, in absentia, the job of running the group on a full-time basis. Before departing the room, Vogt had added a comment that the new organization should be moved closer to the Tactical Air Control Center so the effort wouldn't be spread out over half the sprawling headquarters. Smythe and Frizzell looked at one another, wondering when they'd get back to their units.

Within an hour the group had been assigned to a small struc-ture adjacent to the underground, bunkered TACC, a former warehouse where maps, forms, and office supplies had been stored. It was hastily caulked and sealed, air-conditioned, and dubbed as Annex F. It was made secure. The single entrance to the modest building was manned by two security policemen, a continuous dog patrol was established around it, and the highly classified documents and message traffic were brought from the makeshift office and placed in a secure bullpen inside while an army of South Vietnamese laborers from civil engineering piled layers of sandbags about the outside for protection against mortar or rocket attack.

When Court had returned to Tan Son Nhut and finally located his group in the warehouse, he'd been handed hastily typed orders reassigning him as "Chief, Special Activities Branch, Out-Country." His new chain of command was hazy, for although he worked directly for the one-star who ran the TACC, he reported to two-star General Norman.

Since Court had been away when he'd been reassigned, he'd had no voice in the matter. He might have been angry in other times, but he'd been working such impossibly long hours for the three days of preparations that he was numbed and weary beyond caring. He'd simply nodded at the news, taken a quick look around the small warehouse, asked Smitty where he was supposed to hang his hat, then sat at his desk and slept, head and torso sprawled forward. At midnight, still wearing the same raunchy flight suit and jungle boots, he'd gone across the field and boarded the EC-121, call sign Disco, and flown with them out over the South China Sea, waiting for the fighters to strike targets in the first major air operation conducted against North Vietnam since OPlan Rolling Thunder had been terminated in March 1968.

He'd continued the tough schedule throughout the initial strike period, from the 6th through the 9th—briefing and debriefing pilots, coordinating targets, flying on the command and control bird to monitor the air attacks, landing back at Tan Son Nhut and poring over bomb damage assessment photos, and writing after-action summaries for the brass. Sleep had come when he could find it, as it had for all of his group, which dwindled down to a hard core of six officers and four noncoms. Majors Frizzell and Smitty were temporary help, still on loan from the Korat Wing Commander, but they'd been essential to Court's efforts.

Bannister was at his desk, observing the forces status board across the small, open room.

Six Phantom squadrons, two B-52 wings, and four more EB-66s were shown, their status changed to blue, meaning they were airborne, en route from the States. When a yellow X was placed beside them, it would mean they'd landed. Green would mean that enough aircraft and aircrews were flyable that the unit could be declared operational and ready for tasking. Not shown were two carrier forces, steaming across the Pacific to join the two already in place off the coast of North Vietnam. They were all needed. By this, the fifth day of the Freedom Train air strikes, the Air Force and Navy had already flown a total of 2,800 sorties. One hundred of those had been made by B-52 crews, targeted on massed troop concentrations and supplies coming down through the mountain passes. All of the initial attacks had been in the southern areas of North Vietnam, south of the 20th parallel, considered low-threat areas.

Court was sipping coffee, reading a Top Secret message spread before him, entitled OPERATION FREEDOM PORCH BRAVO, with pursed lips, his mind considering the available options, when Major Frizzell approached his desk.

"Colonel Bannister, Smitty and I just got a call from our boss at Korat. He needs us back there ASAP."

Bannister passed a weary hand over his face. "Any way to talk him into letting you two spend a couple more days?"

"No, sir," said Frizzell. "I'm in charge of training for the squadron, and Smitty's the chief bear—the big kahuna for the electronic-warfare officers. Our guys have been flying their asses off, and they need us. The squadron commander wants us to return on the afternoon Scatback, which means we've gotta get packed and on over to base ops." Scatbacks were T-39 Saberliners used to take recce photos and intelligence information from the headquarters to the units in Thailand.

"Ask Smitty to come over. I've got something to show you guys before you go."

When he joined them, Smythe wore a smile. "Hate to leave you like this, Colonel, but we've gotta go earn our flight pay."

"Yeah, right," Court growled, wishing he was also going to a unit to fly combat. They'd become friends, the three of them, as they'd worked long hours on the operation together. Court's group could never have achieved the level of success they had without the Wild Weasel crew's inputs on how to deal with the enemy threat.

Court turned the Top Secret document around and pushed it across the desktop. "Take a look at that," he said, and waited.

The FREEDOM PORCH BRAVO message was from U.S. Pacific Command at Fort H. M. Smith, adjacent to Pearl Harbor. The Joint Chiefs had ordered a one-day, large-scale and coordinated B-52/fighter strike on targets near Hanoi and Haiphong.

PACOM had requested 7th Air Force, meaning Court's Special Projects branch, to provide timing and tactics inputs.

Both majors became thoughtful.

"What do you think, Smitty?" Court asked.

Smythe pointed across the room to the orderly sheaves of paper which made up the contingency plans they'd devised during the past week. "If they follow those, they'll get by with a single eighteen-ship B-52 mission."

Smitty had fought Strategic Air Command tooth and nail, trying to get them to change from their concept of having B-52s flying in a single long stream, one three-ship cell following immediately and directly behind the next, to the target, and then, after releasing their bombs, each making an identical, immediate turn toward the Gulf of Tonkin. He'd wanted them to use varying headings, feinting one way and another, and more importantly, varying altitudes, to baffle the enemy—and then to delay turning after bomb release until they were out of the coverage of the powerful SAM radars. An aircraft in a turn cannot jam effectively, he'd argued. Further, with its bomb bay doors opened in the posttarget turn (PTT) it made a huge radar return on enemy radarscopes. But the SAC generals said no, thanks, they'd fly to Hanoi just as they had to Berlin during World War II. There would be the stream of bomber cells, each cell handling its own self-defense. There'd be such an accumulative barrage of jamming and chaff issued by the B-52s that no radars could possibly track them, turn or no turn, and if the Phantoms couldn't keep the MiGs off them, their own tail gunners would.

Which was a bunch of bullshit, Smythe had told them, but no one at SAC would listen.

That was what he'd been left to work with, so Smitty a few days before had set his dour grimace into place and gone to work devising a plan which would provide massive tactical support for the bombers. Navy A-6s would pummel defenses near the ingress route and target area for an hour before the strike, pouncing on every surface-to-air missile site in the area. Multiple flights of F-4s, using ALE-38 dispensers, would fly line abreast and release chaff in wide, hundred-mile-long corridors just minutes before the B-52s arrived. Wild Weasel F-105Gs would fly escort and attack any SAM sites the A-6s might have missed. EB-66s would orbit north and south, over the water, jamming enemy acquisition radars. Multiple flights of F-4 MiG-CAP fighters would rove the area looking for interceptors. Other USAF and Navy fighters would suppress MiGs trying to take off from their bases.

"So if we stick to the plan, you don't foresee bomber losses?"

"Not on the first mission, even using the ridiculous tactics SAC refuses to change." Smitty shook his head and grew a wistful smile. "We'll take all the attrition in the fighter force."

"How much?"

"Not many. The enemy gunners will be rusty, since they haven't had activity up there for a long time. On that one mission, we're looking at ninety supporting tactical aircraft. I'm estimating one-point-five-percent attrition, which means we'll lose one or two airplanes."

"But no B-52 losses?"

"The Viets won't be expecting them, so they'll bring all their defenses up on the fighters. By the time the bombers get there, the Viets'll be hurting. Their MiGs will be back on the ground refueling and the SAM sites we don't destroy will be calling their depots for more missiles."

"What if we had a second bomber mission up there, say a few days after the first one?"

"Different ball game. The enemy will be gunning for the bombers, waiting for 'em, holding a percentage of their defenses in reserve. If the B-52s stay with their predictable tactics, I'd say a minimum of three-percent losses until they come down from their ivory towers at SAC Headquarters and make the right changes."

Three percent was high.

"Bomber people," Frizzell muttered contemptuously, shaking his head.

"There's nothing more we can do here, Colonel," Smitty said. "We gave you the best plan we could. When's it going to happen?"

"Within the week," Court responded, wishing to hell he could keep the duo at the headquarters, but knowing they were sorely needed at Korat. He remembered Wolf Lochert's reservations about allowing Smitty to fly combat, placing his secrets and formidable intellect in jeopardy. "You guys watch your asses," he cautioned.

"You got it all wrong, Colonel," said Frizzell with his wide grin. "It's the North Vietnam SAM operators who have to watch their asses when we're flying."

0110 Hours Local, Sunday 16 April 1972
Pilots' Lounge, 17th Wild Weasel Squadron
Korat Royal Thai Air Force Base
Kingdom of Thailand

Captain Woodrow G. "Bear" Woods, who unmodestly called himself the "world's greatest bear," wore a profusion of bright freckles, an incessant grin, and a dollop of carrot-colored hair that refused to remain in place. He was spare and of medium height, and from his looks and aw-shucks demeanor it was impossible to tell he possessed an intelligence quotient that had once caused the teaching staff at a small Oregon high school to purse their lips in awe. He sipped coffee from a paper cup and yawned, wondering why the hell wars couldn't be conducted during civilized hours.

Major Smitty Smythe came into the room, wearing his habitual frown and ratty flying suit. Bear Woods regarded his closest friend as he poured his coffee and started toward him.

"This is the big one I was telling you about," Smitty said quietly.

"It *better* be important, waking me up this early. I flew two times yesterday."

"Get anything?"

"On our second mission we rolled in on a new SAM site near Mu Gia Pass. Dunno if we hit the bastard. They were shooting like hell and I was flying with a new guy from the States."

The pilot Woods had initially been crewed with had broken his back when they'd ejected from a burning Thunderchief after making it out over the Gulf of Tonkin. He'd been med-evac'ed to a Stateside hospital, so Bear Woods now flew with whichever pilot was available, like one whose backseater was down with dysentery or wanted a day off. The new pilot he'd referred to, Captain Tucker, had a bear who constantly came up with excuses not to fly the dangerous Wild Weasel missions. Woods didn't think of him as a coward, but as a good guy who was allowing him, Bear, to get some missions in. He wished the man well, just hoped he didn't get a sudden case of big balls and want to start flying again.

"You'll be flying with Tucker," said Smitty. "Frizzell and I will be lead. You guys'll be number two. We'll be the hunters, carrying two Standard ARMs and two Shrikes each. Number three and four will be F-4Es, loaded with bombs and cluster bombs." Their mission was called hunter-killer. The F-105G Wild Weasels found the sites and the F-4Es helped kill them. Cluster bombs were shapes that, when opened, would spill out hundreds of softball-sized bomblets. Some exploded on contact, others when someone touched them.

Captain Tucker, the new pilot he'd flown with the previous day, was trainable, Bear Woods had decided. He just needed a few more missions under his belt. They'd carry no bombs on the mission, only antiradiation missiles that homed on radar beams emitted from SAM-tracking radar vans. AGM-78 Standard ARMs were huge, thousand-pound missiles, unwieldy but big enough to do heavy damage to a SAM site. Those were controlled by missile panels operated by the bears in the backseats. AGM-45 Shrikes were much smaller and less capable, often fired at radars just to keep the operators preoccupied while the Wild Weasels prepared to attack.

Smythe sipped his coffee, staring oddly at his pal, or, rather, through his pal. Bear Woods didn't like the look that had been stamped on his friend's face for the past few days, since arriving back at Korat from his extended trip to the headquarters at Saigon. "You okay?" he asked in a low voice.

"Yeah."

Smitty was the best electronic-warfare officer tactician at Korat. Woods felt he was just as smart and maybe had bigger balls, but Smitty had a way of outthinking the enemy that was downright canny. He was also moody.

A couple of evenings before, they'd been in a downtown bar, drinking rotgut Mekong whiskey and watching the Thai hookers work the guys. Smitty had told him about his stay at 7th Air Force headquarters, and how generally dicked-up most of the staff pukes around the place were. But if Woods got to Saigon, Smitty said he should look up a light colonel named Court Bannister, who had his shit all in one bag. Then, as the evening had worn on, when they normally began to get serious about rating the whores and maybe selecting a couple for therapeutic use, Smitty began to talk about the possibility of being shot down, which made Bear Woods feel downright itchy. They'd both come from sensitive jobs, and soon after they'd met, had conducted some long discussions about the ramifications of being shot down and interrogated.

That night Smitty had talked about the fact that too many electronic-warfare officers had been shot down and hadn't shown up on the POW lists. He'd mentioned that they were pressing the odds, because they hadn't lost a Weasel crew for a while, and maybe it was time. Then Smythe had confided, as he would do only with his close friend, that if he was captured and it looked as if he'd be interrogated and tortured beyond the threshold, he'd find a way to kill himself. His background knowledge was simply too sensitive to take a chance that he might give it away, phony pilot wings notwithstanding.

They hadn't picked ladies for the evening, but instead had returned to the base, and although Woods had tried to cheer him up, Smitty had retained his strange air of resignation, like he was dreading something that was inevitable.

"Our flight will be taking on the SAM sites between Hanoi and Haiphong," Smitty was saying. "We'll be Condor flight, and work the area to the south. Goose flight will be flying north of the target."

"Sounds good," Woods said. The bears often talked over the missions before they joined the others, discussing technical details which would bore and baffle the pilots.

"If it gets heavy, and there's more than four SAM radars on the air, you take the high frequencies and I'll take the lows. Don't make a radio call unless a site's about to launch at us and I don't have it, or you want to line up to fire a missile."

"Gotcha." Woods wrote on his flight data card.

"Ignore the gun radars. We'll just be after SAMs this morning."

Bear Woods made the note. Major Frizzell came in then, Captain Tucker looking nervous at his side, and motioned to the two men. "You guys ready to brief?"

"Does a bear shit in the woods?" Smitty asked, using their

standard joke. His voice was hollow.

"This bear *is* the Woods," grinned Bear Woods.

0227 Hours Local, Sunday 16 April 1972
Aircrew Briefing Theater
Korat Royal Thai Air Force Base
Kingdom of Thailand

Tuck Tucker's new-guy apprehension did not lessen during the mission briefing, Bear Woods observed. Throughout, he sat with his mouth a taut line, and when Woods joked with one of the F-4E frontseaters during a lull in the briefing, Tuck snapped at him.

The briefing was detailed. Under the cloak of early-morning darkness, Navy A-6s would attack and bomb all known SAM defenses throughout the area surrounding Haiphong, North Vietnam's largest port city, where vast amounts of war supplies were off-loaded from freighters. Navy F-4s would then launch and set up MiG patrols, and twenty Air Force F-4s would release a corridor of chaff. The two flights of Wild Weasel hunter-killer flights would then rove through the area as eighteen B-52s flew down the corridor and dropped their huge tonnages of bombs on the Haiphong petroleum storage area.

No armed American aircraft had flown where they were going for the past four years, and they expected the defenses to be formidable, if a bit out of practice.

Following the B-52 strike, two successive waves of fighters from Udorn, Ubon, Korat, Da Nang, and Navy carriers would attack targets near both Hanoi and Haiphong. Laser-guided bombs would be used almost exclusively. Other Wild Weasel flights would accompany the fighter strikes. Condor and Goose flights were to concentrate solely on protecting the B-52s.

Major Frizzell, the ranking Wild Weasel pilot for the mission, took the podium, grinning like a cat about to pounce on a nest of sparrows. "We're going up to sting the bastards," he exulted as he started his briefing. "If the Navy leaves any SAMs alive within thirty miles of the B-52 route, we're gonna let 'em know the Weasels are back in business up there."

Half an hour later, after they'd gone over the mission twice more, the Wild Weasel pilots and bears, and the Phantom pilots and wizzos, went to their individual squadron life-support areas in final preparation for the flight. They placed personal belongings into bins and pulled on G-suits and combat vests containing survival gear and .38 Special Combat Masterpiece revolvers. They tested their flight helmets and oxygen masks for leaks and placed them into nylon bags. Then the F-105 crews pulled on parachutes, and the Phantom people their harnesses, and went out to vans which would take them to the flight line and the waiting aircraft. Most were silent as the van drove through the darkness; all smoked with nervous inhales.

While Tucker began his walk-around inspection of the F-105G, Bear Woods flashed his penlight up on the nose of the airplane, illuminating the fierce snarl of the shark's mouth painted aft of the radome. He went from nose to tail then, inspecting the antennae of his receivers, ensuring they were tightly secured and not bent. Tuck and the crew chief were still out under the wings, examining the antiradiation missiles, when Woods crawled up the tall ladder and took his seat in the rear cockpit.

A twinge of apprehension tingled through him as he began to flip the switches of the AN/APR-35, his primary receiver, setting up for the mission. Woods angrily shook it off, thinking Smitty's gloomies and Tuck's nervousness were catching.

He made sure the receivers and missile control panel were set up properly. Tonight they would surely be firing their homing missiles at SAM radars, and as Frizzell had said in the briefing, Woods wanted to sting the bastards.

Twenty minutes later, Tuck Tucker fired up the engine and ran his controllability checks.

"You ready back there?" Tuck asked when he was done. His voice had firmed up only marginally between the briefing and engine start.

"Damn betcha," said Bear Woods, thinking Tuck would likely be all right as soon as he saw some hot action and realized they were the ones on the offensive. He wondered how his buddy Smitty was doing, and if he'd lost his blues. After they'd landed and debriefed, Woods decided to pull him aside and try to convince him they should go on a good rest and recuperation leave, maybe to Bangkok, and forget about work and flying combat for a short while.

The Korat tower cleared Condor flight to taxi.

0405 Hours Local, Sunday 16 April 1972
Airborne in an F-105G
18 Nautical Miles Southwest of Haiphong
Democratic Republic of Vietnam

"Got anything back there, Smitty?" Frizzell's voice was intense.

Smythe was staring at his primary receiver, at a small spike that protruded upward from the baseline. Not powerful enough to analyze, he decided. "Nothing much. There's four SAMs over to the west, but they're no threat."

"Five minutes until the heavies arrive. I just got a glimpse of the chaff-layer flights over at our three o'clock. Can't really see 'em in the dark."

"Yeah," grunted Smitty. "I'm picking up jamming from their ECM pods on my receiver. Lots of activity up here." He looked out, over at the dark shapes of the rest of the flight. Condor Two was at their four o'clock, the two F-4Es farther back, at their seven o'clock.

Smitty heard a rattling noise and pulled his gaze back into the cockpit. The sound had come from his warning receiver. He glanced at the APR-35. The tiny spike had grown. He flipped switches, correlating the signal. Smitty's voice rose an octave. "Joyride's over. We've got a SAM site in the corridor, at our five o'clock, tracking us."

Frizzell called the threat out to the rest of the flight as he started a hard right-hand turn, coming around to face the SAM site. Although the AGM-78 could be programmed to turn before homing on a SAM radar, its effective range would then be reduced. "I'm selecting the right-hand Standard ARM," he told Smitty over intercom.

"Roger," Smitty breathed. "Number-one missile selected."

"Got him on your missile panel?" Frizzell asked.

Smitty struggled to keep his hands on the receiver as they pulled G's in the turn. He finally had the new signal tuned and centered. "Yeah. Thirty more degrees and we'll be ready to shoot."

"Thirty more," Frizzell grunted in acknowledgment, continuing the turn.

"Damn! We've got another tracking SAM site at our eight o'clock!"

Frizzell calmly radioed for Condor Two, Tucker and Woods, to turn and take out the SAM site at their rear. He added for Condors Three and Four, the two F-4Es, to accompany them. Bear Woods was an old head, but Tucker was new to the game and seemed overly nervous.

"Condor Two's turning to port!" Tucker yelled over the radio, his voice falsetto high.

The SAM site in front fired. Smitty called it: "We've got a valid launch at one o'clock."

"Set us up," said Frizzell. He couldn't yet see the SAMs due to a cloud which lay in that direction.

They rolled out, the SAM radar signal directly on their nose. Smitty worked the missile panel until the number-one AGM-78 light glowed. "You're ready to shoot."

"Condor Lead is Shotgun!" Frizzell immediately pressed the trigger. There was a blinding flash as the big antiradiation missile dropped, ignited, and roared forward in a tremendous fury of fire and smoke. "Jesus!" he yelled because he'd forgotten to shut his eyes and was temporarily blinded. "I can't see!"

Smitty watched a glow streaking up toward them. "Break right! We've got a—"

At the same time Frizzell slapped the stick into his right knee, the sky about them turned bright red as they were enveloped in the fireball of the exploding SAM.

Halfway through their turn, Bear Woods decided that Tucker did not have time to complete it before the SAM would launch. He also estimated, from the power level of the radar signal, that the site was very close.

"You're in range and I've got the missile turn programmed. Roll out and shoot number one, Tuck."

"Are you sure we—"

"Dammit!" Bear Woods roared angrily. "Shoot the bastard!"

Tucker was breathing hard in the front seat. He did not level out or shoot.

The SAM site launched its first missile. "Now we've got a valid launch. Shoot, dammit."

The wings rocked level. The flash was bright as AGM-78 number one ignited and sprinted away with a roar. The missile became a fiery arc in the dark sky. "Condor Two is *Shotgun,*" Tuck called shrilly, meaning they'd launched one of the big missiles.

"Get ready to break," said Bear Woods, his attention glued to their two o'clock and the three surface-to-air missiles coming up toward them in the distance.

"What was that?" exclaimed Tucker.

"What was what?" Woods asked in an irritated tone, eyes glued to the airborne SAMs.

"There was a flash of light back behind us," Tucker said in his shrill voice.

"Yeah, well, you better watch the damned missiles so you can dodge them. They're at our two o'clock."

The rattling and squealing sounds, indications that the SAMs were guiding on them, suddenly stopped.

"We got the bastard!" Woods exulted.

"Where are the SAMs?" Tucker asked.

"Forget 'em. We took out the SAM site." Bear Woods confirmed that the three SAMs were no longer tracking them, then turned his attention to the sky at their rear.

"I just heard a garbled radio call," said Tucker. His voice sounded firmer than before.

Woods turned up his audio and listened, then he too heard a mishmash of squealing sounds, like someone's radio was screwing up.

"Condor Lead, this is Condor Two. You read me?" Tucker called in a hopeful voice.

The radio noise sounded again.

"Condor Two, this is Condor Three," called an F-4E pilot. "We saw a big flash back in lead's direction, just after he announced Shotgun."

"Yeah," said Tuck. "I heard it—"

He was interrupted by the mechanical wailing of one and then two emergency locator beacons, the ones activated when parachutes opened. They made eerie *whoop-whoop* sounds.

"Damn!" someone exclaimed over radio.

Bear Woods' heart dropped as he listened to the mournful sounds. Frizzell and Smitty had ejected. "Let's go over and try to find them," he suggested to Tucker, a catch in his voice.

"Yeah. I think—"

"Condor Three's got the heavy artillery in sight at our ten o'clock high," called the F-4E pilot over the raucous noise of the beepers. Heavy artillery meant B-52s.

Bear Woods monitored his receiver, examining the random spikes created by the bombers' jammers. He shook his head grimly, thinking they weren't nearly powerful enough to mask the huge aircraft. Thank God, he thought, they were flying in a profusion of chaff, and that the fighters had been beating up on the SAM sites in the . . . woops!

A SAM radar signal showed at their four o'clock, a potential threat to the B-52 force. Bear Woods called it to Tucker, who immediately reefed the Thud into a hard left turn. He seemed more in control of himself.

"I've selected the number-two AGM-78. Tune him in, Bear," said Tuck. His voice was calm. "Let's see if we can make it two for two."

"Roger. I'm centering him. Soon as I get a missile lockup light, I'll tell you."

As they continued the turn and their discussion, Bear Woods forced himself to forget that his best friend had just been shot down.

0412 Hours Local, Sunday 16 April 1972
Airborne in EC-121, Call Sign Disco
Over Gulf of Tonkin
South China Sea

Court Bannister sat at the small corner console in the large main cabin of the EC-121, ignoring the controllers working frantically at their stations about him, headset pressed to his ears, listening intently on the strike frequency as the Wild Weasel flight, call sign Condor, turned to engage their third SAM site. Condor Lead had just been shot down by a surface-to-air missile. Frizzell and Smythe. His heart thumped dully in his chest, and he wished to hell he could be there, flying over them in the dark morning hours and somehow helping out.

Goose, the second Wild Weasel flight, was near the B-52 target, the sprawling Haiphong petroleum-tank farm, and called

Shotgun, meaning they'd launched a missile at a SAM site. An F-4 pilot radioed that he had bogeys in sight, but his wingman identified them as other Phantoms.

One of the EC-121 controllers radioed in the blind that the "heavy artillery," meaning the B-52 bombardment, was about to begin. Goose Lead rallied his hunter-killer flight and hurried out of the target area.

Court glanced at the second hand of his watch. Ten seconds until the first B-52 time over target. He pulled at a latch and loosened the blackout curtain covering the window beside him. Since it was dark outside, it would not bother the controllers working at their scopes and radios, and a flight of F-4 Phantoms protected them from snooping MiG pilots. He oriented himself and stared in the direction of Haiphong, thirty miles distant, waiting.

A splotch of red marred the distant sky. Another SAM explosion? Court hoped to hell Smitty had been right with his estimate that there would be no B-52 losses. One had aborted the mission before entering hostile skies, leaving seventeen of the massive aircraft in the stream. Five cells of three, and one cell of two were now flying with opened bomb bay doors, preparing to . . . Lights began to flicker on the ground a few miles north of where he'd expected it. Then more and more, until it looked like a thousand fireflies winking away. A bright flash as something exploded on the ground.

Court became mesmerized by the continuous light spots emanating from the ground. Another flash, this one bigger, then yet another. Three secondary explosions so far, as the flickers continued, more than a hundred bombs belching from each B-52, concentrating their awesome destruction in the single area. Another bright flare. Two more. Court found himself holding his breath at the sight. The rain of bombs continued for eight long minutes. Six minutes after the last flicker on the ground, several fires continued to rage. The confirmation calls began to arrive over UHF radio. All seventeen bombers reported that they were undamaged and had released their bombs on target.

1430 Hours Local, Monday 17 April 1972
7th Air Force Intelligence Section
Tan Son Nhut Air Base
Republic of Vietnam

The final reports about the results of the one-day raid called Freedom Porch Bravo had arrived at the TACC, and Court's Special Projects group was compiling the official after-action intelligence report, to be signed by General Norman and transmitted to the Deputy Chief of Staff, Plans and Operations, United States Air Force, at the Pentagon. The CSAF would be provided an information copy.

While Court Bannister, confirmed and unrepentant fighter pilot to the core, would normally not care for the task, he worked carefully on the wording of the message. Part of the reason was caused by, of all things, the way he'd been so impressed by the B-52 raid.

Specific results of the April 16 raid had already been forwarded, by message followed up by two classified couriers traveling with complete sets of annotated bomb damage assessment (BDA) photos. The B-52 liaison officer, a brigadier general in the SAC ADVON office at Tan Son Nhut, had also forwarded a message to the Pentagon, with info copy to Strategic Air Command Headquarters, stating that the mission had been impeccably executed by the bomber aircrew, proving their tactics were valid. He'd hardly mentioned the massive support that had been provided by the tactical fighter aircraft.

Court had been brooding about that message. He had also been impressed with the results of the B-52 raid, but he was concerned when he remembered Major Smitty Smythe's estimates, and that the mission had gone precisely as he'd predicted. They could get away with it only once, Smitty had said. The next ones could be a bloodbath if SAC did not change its tactics.

In a single day, half of the petroleum reserves in the critical northern sectors of North Vietnam had been destroyed, which was a phenomenal feat. Phantoms had done superb work with laser-guided bombs at the Hanoi petroleum area, but to their credit, the B-52s had done even better at Haiphong. Of course the Phantoms had used only a dozen smart bombs, while the bombers had used thousands of dumb bombs. Still, he was impressed.

In the first paragraph of the message, Court reviewed the planning for Freedom Porch Bravo. In the second and third paragraphs, he regurgitated the results they'd sent in the bomb damage assessment report. It was the fourth paragraph that was difficult to write, the one synopsizing the raid and providing suggestions for future planning. After several attempts, he finally decided to make it short, sweet, and to the point.

4. (S) REMARKS.
A. (S) WITH PROPER USE OF B-52S IN THE HANOI AND HAIPHONG AREAS, IT IS MY VIEW THAT WE CAN IMPOSE AN EARLY END TO THE CONFLICT. MY CONCERN IS THE PREDICTABLE TACTICS SPECIFIED BY STRATEGIC AIR COMMAND IN THEIR CURRENT PLANNING, WHICH DO NOT ADEQUATELY REFLECT THE MAGNITUDE OR SOPHISTICATION OF THE NVN THREAT. SUBSEQUENT B-52 MISSIONS SHOULD BE PLANNED USING TACTICS AND LESSONS PREVIOUSLY LEARNED BY TACTICAL FORCES, AND BE EXECUTED WITH THE SAME MASSIVE DEGREE OF COORDINATED PROTECTION PROVIDED DURING FREEDOM PORCH BRAVO. IF THIS IS NOT DONE, I BELIEVE B-52 LOSSES WILL BECOME UNACCEPTABLY HIGH.

When the remainder of the message was completed, Court reread the paragraph. Finally he said to hell with it and sent it forward. If General Norman disagreed, he could change it himself.

For the fifth time Court tried the MAC-SOG telephone number Wolf Lochert had given him, and finally received an answer. A gruff sergeant said Colonel Lochert was in a meeting and would be there until fifteen-thirty hours. He hung up, grabbed his flight cap, and set out for the door. "I'll be gone for the afternoon," he told his admin sergeant. The noncom raised an eyebrow.

Court saw no reason to tell him where he was going. "I'll be back around eighteen hundred."

"Will you be flying in the Disco bird again tonight, sir?"

Court rubbed his eyes, then nodded. It was becoming an obsession, listening to the combat pilots on the radios as they flew only a few miles distant. He hurried out the door, determined to find Wolf and advise him that Smythe had been shot down. Intell had received an input from a covert radio operator at Monkey Mountain, at Da Nang Air Base. North Vietnamese Army patrols had radioed their headquarters in Hanoi that they'd captured all three men shot down during the Freedom Porch Bravo raid. An A-7 pilot, as well as the two "pilots" from a downed F-105. As he hurried toward the parking lot, Court wondered just what part Wolf Lochert was playing in the game.

Two hours after he'd departed, Major General Leonard Norman called Court's office and found that he was away for the afternoon. He'd sent the message just as Court had written it, and had especially agreed with the portion concerning the utilization of B-52s. Someone at the Pentagon had also been impressed, although Norman did not really know whether in a positive or negative sense. The Chief of Staff of the Air Force had fired a back-channel message to Norman, asking specifically who had drafted the message and requesting personal background information. General Norman wondered if it was wise to release Court's name, especially if the CSAF was pissed off about what had been said there. The informal manner the message was worded did not betray the Chief's feelings.

Since the response was requested ASAP, Norman sent the name of Lieutenant Colonel Courtland E. Bannister, and included a synopsis of his background, including the facts that he was a highly decorated veteran of two combat tours in fighters and had been credited with four and one half MiGs. He wrote that Court was a capable and dedicated officer with consistently superb officer efficiency reports. Finally, hoping he might blunt any anger the General might have that his precious B-52s were being maligned, he added the fact that Bannister was a relative of Lieutenant General Whitey Whisenand, who was presently a personal assistant to President Nixon.

The back-channel reply was received over the Blue Net within half an hour.

BETTER HIDE YOUR FEMALE SECRETARIES, LEN, the CSAF stated in the informal, eyes-only message. ANY SON OF SILK SCREEN SAM BANNISTER HAS GOT TO BE A THREAT TO WOMANKIND. THIS IS AN OUTSTANDING MESSAGE, SHOWING DEEP UNDERSTANDING OF THE PROBLEM OF B-52S BEING SENT UP NORTH—LET'S DISCUSS FURTHER AT LATER DATE.

1730 Hours Local, Monday 17 April 1972
MAC-SOG Headquarters
Rue Pasteur, Saigon
Republic of Vietnam

Wolf Lochert stepped out of his meeting as Court was being escorted down the hall toward his office in the two-story converted villa.

"I'll handle the Colonel from here," Wolf told the corporal. "How you doing, Court?"

Court noted that Wolf's face was grim. "We've been busy," he told him.

"Same here. Your guys are pounding the *Scheiss* out of the NVA, but there's a lot of 'em and they keep coming." He led the way down the long corridor.

"Think the ARVN can stop them?"

"Maybe. I'd be more positive if your pilots could cut off the supplies and reinforcements from up north." He led the way into a small office that was no larger than his cubbyhole at 7th Air Force.

"We're trying. The President's resolved, and we're finally being turned loose to fight."

"I heard about the B-52 hitting Haiphong."

Court gave him a grim nod. "That's why I'm here."

Wolf raised a puzzled eyebrow. "The B-52s?"

"Frizzell and Smythe were on the mission, protecting the bombers."

Lochert's face darkened. "Those two guys from Korat?"

"They were shot down."

"Damn!" Wolf exploded, then remembered and gave a quick upward glance, as if something might strike him for cursing.

Court sat down. "They got out okay. Both were captured within ten minutes of hitting the ground."

Wolf rubbed a big paw over his face, then shook his head resolutely. "Smythe's a definite target."

"Of what?"

Lochert stared at a wall map of North and South Vietnam, mouth tight. He was not going to respond.

"Thought you should know," Court said, rising to his feet.

"I'm going out to the field tonight," Wolf said. "Little place called Hoa An. Sixty ARVN Rangers with an NVA battalion looking down their throats, and I can't get the Viets in the headquarters here to reinforce them. Politics. The generals here are suspicious of the General who commands the Rangers—thinks he might not support President Thieu in the next election."

"What good are you going to do there? You can't personally fight off a battalion."

Wolf shrugged. "I trained the Viet Lieutenant there. He's a good guy."

"But why are you going?"

"I want to make sure the Lieutenant's doing things right. If things start falling apart, they'll send a chopper to pull me out. Maybe I can pull out some of the survivors."

"That sounds dangerous as hell, Wolf."

"Don't curse," Lochert counseled. Then he shrugged. "Dangerous? Fighting a war with one hand and a half-load of ammo is dangerous. Drawing your troop level down while the enemy is building up and preparing to invade is dangerous. Being a poor country like South Vietnam and relying on your best ally for support when they can't even make up their minds about charging some doped-up kid who burns up police cars with a misdemeanor—that's dangerous."

Court had never seen his friend in such a mood—hadn't heard the devout warrior philosophizing in such depth.

"Anyway," said Wolf, with a death's mask grin. "I fight with both hands, and with my eyes open. I'll be okay."

"I'd better be going. I've got a flight in a command and control bird tonight."

"Thanks for the information."

"Wish I could help more."

"Yeah. I guess that's what I'm trying to say. I wish they'd let us help more. Take that guy Smythe. I wish we could go in and take him away from harm, same as I'd like to do with my ARVN lieutenant friend at Hoa An."

Court tried one last time. "What's the Russian involvement with our POWs, Wolf?"

Wolf Lochert remembered the KGB senior officers at Son Tay. "I wish I knew," he finally responded.

Chapter 5

0900 Hours Local, Tuesday 18 April 1972
ARVN SF Camp, Hoa An
Republic of Vietnam

The ARVN Ranger camp at Hoa An had lasted longer than Wolf Lochert had thought it would, but that was only due to the methodical way the NVA was going about overrunning the camp. Wolf was brought in by Huey helicopter on Tuesday morning, along with the "replacements" authorized by the ARVN general staff in Saigon.

The sixty men holed up at the hilltop camp at Hoa An had been under siege by more than eight hundred North Vietnamese Army regulars, a battalion of the 371-I Division, for four days. They received periodic support by VNAF (Vietnamese Air Force) pilots flying T-28s and F-5s, but none from the Americans since ammo and food had been dropped in by C-130s from Tan Son Nhut two days before. ARVN Headquarters, Saigon, had told MAC-V that further airdrops wouldn't be necessary until they'd decided whether to reinforce or evacuate the camp. The hilltop location was strategically located and defensible, overlooking the lowlands on three sides, with a hill of similar elevation three kilometers to their west, and the ARVN officer in command, Lieutenant Hoang Lo Binh, had repeatedly radioed that if a second company of Ranger reinforcements were provided, and if the VNAF would attack the enemy troops and destroy the NVA medium artillery before it was transported up the rugged sides of the adjacent hill, and a couple of ARVN heavy weapons platoons were inserted on that hill, they could hold.

Wolf looked over the ARVN "replacements" during the wild chopper ride into Hoa An. All twelve were junior enlisted men, obviously green and untested in battle. They'd huddled in numb silence throughout the flight, clutching their M-16s, black eyes wide with fright. None were Ranger-trained or jump-qualified. When the VNAF pilot made his assault landing, they had to be prodded out the door by a crew chief brandishing a .45 Colt M1911A1 automatic.

Wolf jumped down last, carrying only a PRC-25 ground-to-air radio. He automatically ducked into a defensive crouch as a mortar round went off fifty yards distant.

The previous afternoon, following Court Bannister's departure, Wolf had flown to Nha Trang. He hadn't told Court that he also maintained a small office there, and still others at the Command and Control centers at Da Nang and Phu Bai. From those locations, six-man recon teams were sent to probe into Laos and North Vietnam, and they sometimes provided information about American POWs being held in those countries. Neither had he told Court the whole reason for wanting to contact the ARVN junior officer at the small camp at Hoa An. Lieutenant Hoang Lo Binh had been a team member on one of the latest audacious recon forays deep into North Vietnam. For a week they'd worn NVA uniforms and operated in the area immediately west of Hanoi, and when they'd finally been withdrawn, the team commander had reported the first signs of the buildup for the Easter invasion. He'd also told of sighting Caucasians who did not appear to be advisers. The report had been heavily censored by the ARVN before being released to MAC-V.

Wolf's suspicions had been whetted, especially when he heard that the team leader, an ARVN Ranger Captain, had been killed by a sniper three weeks after the recon team's return. That was the real reason for going to Nha Trang, and for the dangerous field trip to see his friend.

In the sixties, the base at Nha Trang had been headquarters for most of MAC-SOG's operational units; home of the Air

Force's 90th Special Operations Wing's command element, as well as the 5th Special Forces Group, under which Special Forces troopers trained and coordinated large numbers of U.S., Vietnamese, Laotian, Hill tribe, and other semifriendly irregular ground forces. With Vietnamization, op control was being passed to the ARVN, the best of their units being the battle-tested officers and men of the 91st Ranger Battalion, once the ARVN reaction group for projects Delta, Omega, and Sigma. First Lieutenant Hoang Lo Binh, Wolf's one-time friend and protégé, was now a detachment commander in the 91st Rangers.

Seven years earlier, Hoang had been a smart-ass young enlisted man, and Lochert had begrudgingly allowed him to accompany his seasoned III Corps Mike Force team on a few jungle patrols. The thing he'd immediately noticed about the ARVN corporal had been his cool, almost brazen, performance under fire. He was one of those rare soldiers who did not fear an enemy . . . any enemy . . . not out of disdain for the VC or NVA, but because of his faith in his own ability. Hoang had grown an intense loyalty to his self-chosen teacher, whom he'd decided was one of the few American long-noses who could provide valuable lessons about how to kill the enemy most efficiently. He'd studied and listened to Wolf, and learned well. It began quietly enough in 1967.

That year, Wolf had known Hoang Lo Binh as the noncommissioned officer in charge of an ARVN Ranger patrol, and had accompanied him on a short foray. On the second night, waiting in ambush, Hoang had told him not to trust the Viet Cong deserter serving on Lochert's secretive Dakota Team. But Lochert had reason to place faith in the man named Buey Dan—the stocky Viet had saved his life and single-handedly destroyed a VC squad on their first patrol together—so he'd ignored the advice. A year later, Buey Dan had attacked him with a stiletto. After Wolf had killed Buey Dan, he'd realized how many of his men, American and Vietnamese, had been betrayed or outright killed by the Viet Cong double agent and full colonel, code-named Lizard. Wolf had been outraged, both at Buey Dan's treachery and at his own hardheadedness. If he'd listened when Hoang had first told him . . .

The top ranks of the ARVN were filled with descendants of old Vietnamese mandarin families, the same greedy, insufferable bureaucrats who had ineptly run the country for a thousand years. But in the lower and mid ranks, a new breed of officer was emerging—battle-tested, capable, and with a desire to find out what real democracy was all about. Hoang Lo Binh was one of those, yet it was doubtful that he'd rise above the rank of lieutenant. His grandfather had made the error of marrying a girl of mixed Montagnard blood, and the Vietnamese hierarchy was as staunchly racist as Hitler's Third Reich's had been. Hoang's promotions had been born of combat necessity, but that went only so far with the suspicious people in Saigon. Now Lieutenant Hoang Lo Binh was in trouble, and at the mercy of the same general-politicians who distrusted him.

After the short mortar barrage ended, Wolf Lochert watched as the twelve green privates regained their feet, only to cringe at the sight of several body bags and four severely wounded ARVN Rangers who had been brought to the helipad for evacuation. An ARVN sergeant waved the replacements toward a sandbagged bunker, then turned to his task of getting the wounded loaded onto the helicopter.

A familiar figure approached. As Wolf greeted Lieutenant Hoang Lo Binh, a flare of hope flickered in his young protégé's face. It was quenched when Wolf told him he'd come unofficially, and was not the harbinger of an American force of combat advisers.

He didn't tell Hoang Lo Binh that his own superiors didn't know he was at the besieged camp, or that all Americans were under orders to withdraw from the vulnerable forward camps. Instead he began to methodically inspect the puny assets the Lieutenant had at his disposal, and the ways he'd deployed them. Wolf found only a small discrepancy, but when he'd suggested that two of the three M-60 .30 caliber machine-gun crews be pulled in closer to the command bunker for a wider field of fire during the inevitable assault, the Lieutenant ignored him and stalked past to give a sergeant hell for deploying the green replacements too slowly. The old rapport between American leader and Vietnamese protégé was unraveling.

Throughout the morning a small number of VNAF prop-driven T-28s arrived to drop 250-pound bombs and napalm in the general vicinity of the NVA artillery being hauled up the side of the heavily forested, steep hill less than two miles distant. At noon the intermittent stream of fighters stopped, diverted to a higher-priority attack some thirty kilometers to the south. Those in the besieged camp could hear the distant sounds of the bombs dropping there, as well as the more ominous sounds of the artillery pieces being hauled into place on the adjacent hilltop.

They did not get to talk until early evening, when the Lieutenant advised him to call in a helicopter and leave the camp. He said the NVA would begin their shelling during the early-morning hours. Wolf agreed. They were hunkered, staring over the sandbagged berm of the observation post trench at the western perimeter, the side closest to the enemy-infested hill. The noises of enemy preparations were metallic; of artillery rounds being stacked, adjustment wheels being cranked, and loading chambers being opened and closed; and they rang out clearly in the quiet semidarkness of early evening.

"We've been ordered to no longer call the Americans directly for air support," said the Lieutenant, wearing an impassive expression.

Wolf grunted in response as another clanging sound came from the adjacent hill.

Hoang's conversation turned bitter. "You Americans should never have come. We thought you would save us. Where are you now?"

Wolf didn't like the tone. "It's your own senior officers who are letting you down."

"Most of our generals are fools. You knew that from the first."

Wolf saw movement below and pointed it out.

Hoang narrowed his eyes and noted the position. "Many of us hoped you would set up an interim government, help us throw out the communist invaders, and when that was finished, show us how to set up a real democracy."

"Smacks too much of colonialism and imperialism. The American people would never stand for it," Wolf said.

"You did it during World War Two, each time you liberated a country in Europe. We felt you were prepared to do the same here—for us."

"Things are different now."

"Yes. Our enemy has invaded in full force, and we need you more than ever."

"We won't be sending more troops, Hoang. Forty-five thousand dead soldiers are enough. You'll have to do your own ground fighting. If you haven't learned in the past nine years—"

"We are willing to sacrifice," the Lieutenant interrupted crisply.

"Then we're willing to supply you and provide training and air support. Our government is committed, Hoang."

"For how long, Colonel? Until your politicians get tired of helping us? I trust you. I know better than to trust politicians, wherever they may be."

They both sat quietly, thinking about what the other had said. They'd had similar discussions in the past.

After a long pause, Wolf almost casually mentioned the purpose of his visit. "After you went on your last recon patrol with Command and Control, your team leader reported seeing Caucasians near the Son Tay POW camp."

"East of there," said Hoang Lo Binh. "They've not repaired the camp. They use it for propaganda, showing visitors how the Americans invaded and destroyed a schoolhouse."

Wolf stored that tidbit away.

"They were Russians, and there were not many of them. We saw others who were obviously advisers, but not these men. They had a small barracks and stayed to themselves."

Lochert's lips pulled back into a grin. "In uniform?"

Hoang nodded. "Some were in uniform." He touched his collar. "Blue service flashes."

"KGB," Wolf breathed.

"Yes. One was short and thick, with a large nose, and wore civilian clothing. A white shirt with a khaki jacket with the sleeves rolled up. He was the one in charge. He was driven wherever he went, and the others were quiet when he was around. He had many pens in his pocket."

Wolf painted a mental picture of the man and stored it away.

Hoang pursed his lips as he watched another movement in the trees below, then he glanced back at Lochert. "We saw an American prisoner brought there."

Wolf's heart raced. "How do you know he was American?"

"I heard him. He was frightened, but he shouted a lot at them."

"What did he look like? What did they do with him?" Wolf had a thousand questions. This was his first truly live sighting of what he had suspected.

The sergeant came up then and interrupted. "Observation post two reports movement."

The Lieutenant flashed eyes at Wolf, telling him they would talk later, then crouched and followed the sergeant back toward the command bunker.

Lieutenant Hoang Lo Binh had sixty-two fit men dug in within the prepared hilltop fortifications. Twelve of those were the green recruits, too inexperienced and frightened to function effectively. The heavy shelling began at 0400 hours, and lasted until 0900. More than one hundred and fifty 75mm high-explosive rounds and seventy 40mm mortar rounds impacted, and only thirty-eight men remained uninjured. Two of the observation posts and one .30 caliber machine-gun position had been destroyed, and a high-explosive round had landed squarely upon the poorly prepared position of the green replacements, killing or maiming nine.

Throughout the artillery barrages, the Lieutenant repeatedly called his headquarters unit at Nha Trang, telling them they were under heavy artillery fire and requesting assistance. Each time, he was told that no air support was available, and to try again in two hours.

At 1138, a bleating, staccato-sound of bugles rang out from below, immediately followed by movements of enemy troops, and the positions were noted by two of the remaining OPs. The Lieutenant ordered the four remaining mortar tubes into action. As the fifth outgoing round whistled overhead, the enemy responded with an intense, fifteen-minute counterartillery barrage that destroyed both firing positions. Four more Rangers were killed and five more wounded. There were now twenty-nine men left to fight off eight hundred of the enemy. Then a barrage of rockets struck ineffectually on the hillside below, and the three surviving green privates jumped from their prepared dugout and ran screaming toward the Lieutenant's command bunker. Two were cut down—most likely, Wolf felt, by their own unit's fire. The single remaining recruit replacement was left babbling in a corner of the Lieutenant's bunker. Twenty-six fighting men left.

Wolf was getting increasingly concerned, wondering when the hell the ARVN HQ was going to send help. Bugle sounds began to constantly ring out, bleating from all sides of the hill, signals to begin moving into position for the attack. *Blaaaaar! Blaaaaar! Blaaaaar!* Again the Lieutenant called the ARVN

Ranger battalion at Nha Trang. This time he was told they were too busy to even take his request.

The bugle calls quieted, and the utter silence was loud. Wolf knew the next time they began, the North Vietnamese would scamper up the hill. They'd taken a minimum of losses to this point, and it was doubtful they'd lose many more when they took the camp. The recruit continued sobbing in the corner until an ARVN Ranger noncom went over and kicked him and told him to be quiet or he'd shoot him.

"Bullshit!" yelled Wolf Lochert, and he strode into the rear of the bunker and pulled out the PRC-25 radio, hauled it to the entrance, and strung out the cable antenna, which he preferred over the whip. At 1225 hours, using the call sign of Wolf, Lochert made contact with Rustic Two-One, a forward air controller bird he'd seen orbiting in the distance to the southeast. He was asked to authenticate Tango-Whiskey to establish his credentials. When he told the airborne FAC that he had no code wheel, but that he was at Hoa An with an ARVN unit about to be overrun by NVA, he was told to route his request through proper channels, meaning the Viet Army chain.

"Look, *Scheisskopf,*" Wolf bellowed, "we're about to be overrun, and we're the good guys. Which side are you on?"

The FAC tersely told him to stand by. A few minutes later the OV-10 broke out of its orbit and flew in their direction.

"Not too low," Wolf cautioned over the radio as he watched. Too late. Streamers of 12.7mm and 14.5mm rounds erupted, waving in arcs about the sky and searching for the small observation aircraft.

"Hot damn!" cried the OV-10 pilot as he jinked out of their range. "I don't know who the hell you are, Wolf, but those bastards just gave me all the authentication I need. How many of 'em you got cornered down there?"

"Maybe eight hundred NVA, Rustic. They're on three sides of us here, and they've got four or five medium-artillery pieces and a bunch of mortars set up on the hill immediately west of us. You need their coordinates?"

The pilot's voice remained angry. "They gave me their cords when they fired on me, Wolf. I do not like being shot at. You got marker panels down there?"

The Lieutenant nodded vigorously.

"Roger that, Rustic Two-One. Where do you want us to lay 'em out?"

"Set up arrows in the directions of the heaviest troop concentrations. I'm going off your frequency for a couple minutes so I can rustle up some help on the UHF."

Ten scant minutes later two flights of four F-4 Phantoms began dropping napalm and cluster bombs on the adjacent hill. The remnants of the ARVN Ranger team came out of their bunkers, gawking and cheering as Lochert and the Lieutenant continued to lay down the long, fluorescent-orange panel markers. Sounds of jet engines roared about them, and in the silences between each attack they could hear shrieks of agony from the enemy soldiers on the nearby hill.

Rustic Two-One then called in a succession of fighters on the NVA troops who were now scurrying about madly below. A-7s and F-4s circled and pounded away with machine guns, bombs, and rockets for more than half an hour. The roaring of jets continued nonstop, with booming sounds made by the munitions being released upon the NVA troops.

At 1400 hours four NVAF F-5 fighters showed up, and the OV-10 FAC radioed Lochert.

"I've been told to put these guys on target, then to stop our bombing, Wolf."

"There's more targets down below, Rustic Two-One. A lot more. All you've done is slow them down."

"Sorry 'bout that. Orders from headquarters, Wolf."

Rustic Two-One fired a final rocket at a point east of their hill, and told the VNAF fighter leader to release his bombs on the red smoke. Then he banked away, and the orbiting American Phantoms were told to drop their napalm and rockets on enemy vehicle traffic that had been located twenty klicks to the south.

Wolf stared grimly as the fighters departed.

The Lieutenant came out of the bunker. "Headquarters advises they're going to reinforce and hold the hill." He did not appear overjoyed with the news. Hoang had been jerked around by his bosses before.

At 1600 hours a single bedraggled VNAF Huey brought in a six-man advance party. They briefed the Lieutenant that they would direct first a resupply airdrop, then the insertion of 200 ground troops using American H-53s, closely followed by 600 more. Saigon had decided that Hoa An must be held, and that the enemy troops below must be pursued and eliminated. Wolf did not ask why they had directed the American fighters to stop before they'd wiped out the battalion of NVA. Who, he wondered, were they trying to impress?

Wolf Lochert studied Lieutenant Hoang Lo Binh for his reaction, and noted the bitterness growing there. This time he decided to take his advice and hitch a ride back on the VNAF Huey, so he could get out of his way. Before he climbed aboard, the Lieutenant came over and told him very pointedly that he'd see him in a few days. The relief task force would be led by a colonel from ARVN Headquarters, and his Ranger team would be returned to Nha Trang. Hoang's wife and three children lived in Saigon, and he would visit them in a week or so. He asked if Wolf could send someone by and tell them he was coming. Lochert said he'd do it himself, since he was headed that way, and told him how to contact him at MAC-SOG.

"There is more to tell you about our recon patrol and the Russians."

Wolf nodded. "See you in Saigon next week, Hoang."

It was the following afternoon when Wolf Lochert was waiting for a C-130 ride to Saigon, that he heard the camp at Hoa An had been overrun by the NVA battalion before the ARVN task force had been brought in. The Lieutenant, his team, and the advance party from Saigon had been lost. There would be no American prisoner-of-war information forthcoming from the Vietnamese Lieutenant.

1030 Hours Local, Friday 21 April 1972
Hoa Lo Prison (The Hanoi Hilton)
Hanoi, Democratic Republic of Vietnam

Smitty groaned, blinked, and looked out at the gray walls through his foggy vision. He tried again to sit up on the hard platform-bed, but stiffened as shock waves of intense pain coursed through his body.

It was now five days since he and Frizzell had been shot down and captured, four days since he'd been shoved into the dreary room. He'd remained there in isolation, except when the guards would arrive to take away his waste bucket or bring the awful-tasting bowls of food. And except for the times he'd been taken to the strange room with mounds of plaster splotched on the walls. Up to neck-high, the mounds were darkly colored. For the first couple of days, Smitty's sessions had been sheer beatings, and he knew he could withstand those without giving away the farm. The questions had been more or less routine, asking about his unit and his hometown—things like that.

This morning had been different. The bushy-haired Vietnamese interrogator with the wandering eye stood dutifully off to one side. The new questioner was broad-shouldered and swarthy, wearing an olive-drab uniform without rank insignia, and a revolver secured in a black holster at his side. He was not Vietnamese. That was as much as Smitty could tell, because he'd lost his glasses during the ejection, and his vision was 90/20 in his *better* eye. The man greeted him in English with only a trace of an accent, which Smitty could not readily recognize. Hispanic?

After a short diatribe about the criminal acts of the Yankee pilots, he introduced himself, saying he was Señor Ceballos.

Cuban, Smitty decided. He'd heard that they were in North Vietnam.

Ceballos said matter-of-factly that he knew this miserable criminal standing in front of him, this Major Todd S. Smythe, was not a pilot, although he'd been wearing pilot's wings when he was captured. Ceballos leered and said Smitty was an *ee-wo-ah* who flew in the backseat of a special fighter called a Wil' Wizzell. Ceballos asked wonderingly why an ee-wo-ah would wear pilot's wings. When Smitty didn't answer, the Cuban told him in a conversational tone that they could do things one of two ways, and that Smythe would not like the second. When Smitty remained quiet, Ceballos sighed, as if he was truly sorry, then gave terse instructions to the bushy-haired Vietnamese. Smitty's elbows and hands were quickly tied tightly behind him. Then a rope was looped though a ring secured to the ceiling and fastened to his wrists. He groaned in agony as he was hoisted up to his tiptoes, and his shoulders began to dislocate. The Cuban picked up a wooden club and smiled.

"This is the second way."

He began to methodically beat Smitty, circling and swinging the club at his face, ribs and kidneys, each blow more agonizing than the last. There were no questions, just Smitty's shrieks and the sound of harsh breathing from the Cuban, as if he got some sort of sexual delight from what he was doing. After an eternity, the guy had finally stopped, chest still heaving dramatically. "You are ee-wo-ah?"

When Smitty's cries had subsided, he'd gasped, "My name is . . . Smythe, Todd S. . . . Major, United . . . States Air . . . "

The man had not waited for him to provide the rest of his litany of name, rank, and service number. He'd swung viciously, and Smitty had shrieked as the club impacted his testicles. Ten minutes later he'd babbled that he was an electronic warfare officer, not a pilot. Ceballos had smiled happily. Smitty was lowered, untied, and returned to his cell by the turnkeys.

Was that all they'd want? Smitty wondered. He tried again to sit up on the platform, and this time succeeded. A wave of shrill pain and nausea coursed through him, emanating from his swollen and battered gonads. A scrabbling sound then, and he watched something large and furry push under the cell door and pause to look him over. Smitty detested rats, and he let out a muffled groan as he tried to rise and chase the thing back out. New noises came from the corridor outside, and the huge rodent scurried under the door.

He knew there were other Americans in the prison, although he'd not yet seen them. Twice he'd heard their voices. Also—screeching loudspeakers periodically blared announcements about the numbers of American soldiers being killed each day in South Vietnam, and listed exorbitant numbers of Yankee airplanes being shot down. Those were obviously for the consumption of American prisoners, and Smitty wanted desperately to contact them, so he could learn how to best evade answering the questions. He also wondered what they'd done with Frizzell, and whether he was receiving the same awful treatment.

The door swung open and two guards came in and motioned. With great exertion Smitty slid off the platform, almost crumpled, then huffed his way in shuffling steps toward the door. As they led him down the familiar corridor, he saw a shadow at the peekhole of one of the cells. Another American? Frizzell?

"I'm Major Todd Smythe," he said in a croaking voice. "I'm being . . . " The guard behind him shouted in Vietnamese and struck him so hard in the back that Smitty stumbled forward and almost lost his balance. "I'm being tortured!" he cried out to end his sentence, and the guard shrieked and hit him again.

They led him into the same room he'd left two hours earlier, the one with the knoblike, bloody plaster bulges. This time there were three men waiting. The bushy-haired, walleyed Vietnamese and the Cuban had been joined by a squat, pudgy man in a khaki bush jacket. They spoke together in quiet tones, not bothering to look at Smythe, who was left standing beside a small table. On its top was an opened, leatherbound folder. The two guards asked a hesitant question. The bushy-haired Vietnamese with the walleye answered, then returned his attention to the conversation. The guards shuffled out.

Smitty bent slightly to get a better look at the words on the exposed page of the opened folder, but his vision was blurred and he had to read upside down. He bent closer, squinting.

A neatly typed list of names, in English, two of them underlined in green ink. He scanned and his brow furrowed, for he knew a couple of the men. Not well, but vaguely. Both were military officers, and both were electronics specialists, as he was. Then he noticed his own name, underlined in the green near the top of the page. Smitty felt numbed. He glanced and saw that the three men were still talking, still seemingly oblivious of his presence.

It was obvious that he'd made some sort of list. His mind churned with possibilities. Was it a roster of the American prisoners of war? Then he thought and wondered again, because as far as he knew, neither of the other officers he knew who were listed on the page was even in the combat zone. One was a nonrated engineer—not even a flier.

The pudgy man raised his voice angrily, and the bushy-haired Vietnamese was quick to reply in a conciliatory tone. Smitty slowly and cautiously reached down to turn the page, wondering if there might be other names he could recognize.

"Stop!" called out the Cuban, and he crossed the room and stood before Smythe, fists planted arrogantly on hips. He smiled, but the expression was more a sneer than one of happiness. "Haven't you learned yet, Señor Smythe the ee-wo-ah?"

The pudgy man came over and deftly snatched up the leather folder, then began to leaf through the pages. He stopped, eyes glittering then as he read and nodded. A pleased look grew on his face. He spoke almost under his breath, but Smitty could make out the inflection and even a few of the words. He'd taken a short course in Russian. That was when he knew what

he must do. He could not allow this man to interrogate him. It
was a simple decision that he'd known he might face. He pulled
in a long breath to muster determination as the Russian spoke to
the others in Vietnamese. It was time to die.

Ceballos had begun to answer when Smitty swung his right
fist in a roundhouse, directly at the Cuban's face, using every
ounce of his energy. A sharp snap sounded as he connected.
Then Smitty fell forward and began to fumble with the holster
on the Cuban's belt. The Vietnamese grappled behind him, and
he jabbed back with a sharp elbow and heard a sharp wheeze.
He had a firm grasp on the revolver's handle and was tugging
when a heavy blow smacked into the side of his head. Smitty
groaned, released his grip, and staggered, stunned for a few
seconds, then lurched toward the Russian and grasped arms
about him. *Come on,* his mind pleaded. *Get it over with. Shoot
me, for Christ's sake!*

The Cuban clawed and pulled Smitty away, and threw him
onto the floor beside the table. Then Ceballos stepped back and
pulled out his pistol. Smitty swung an arm toward him in a
threatening gesture, using his last reserve of strength. Ceballos
had the revolver free, and thrust it toward his head, pausing for
only a split second before his finger tightened. Smitty closed his
eyes tightly. The roar of the pistol was loud in the room, the air
from the muzzle blast hot on his face.

His ears rang with the sound and he waited for pain. When he
realized he was still alive, Smitty cautiously opened his eyes. The
Russian was grappling with Ceballos, shouting angrily. Ceballos
sullenly reholstered his weapon as the bushy-haired Vietnamese
began to tie Smitty's elbows and hands firmly together, as he'd
done before. The Russian smiled happily as Smitty was drawn to
his feet. As they left the room, first the Russian, then the Cuban,
and finally Smitty being pushed along by the Vietnamese, he drew
pleasure from only one fact. Ceballos held a brown handkerchief
to his nose, and was bleeding like a stuck pig.

An eye went to the small crack in the wooden shutter of the
window. A tall, gaunt, black man had painfully pulled himself
up to the high window to silently observe the procession as
four men emerged into the sunlight and continued toward the
gatehouse. He did not know the short, pudgy Caucasian in the
lead, but he'd heard reports of such a man. His eyes smoldered

with emotion as he observed them. Behind the squat man walked the one they called Fidel, the Cuban who delighted in torturing his helpless Yankee enemies, and he was holding a cloth to his nose. Pushing the bound POW along was Bug, one of the prison interrogators.

They passed into the building, and out of Major Flak Apple's vision.

Apple recited the prisoner's name. Major Todd Smith, the man had said as the turnkeys had led him down the corridor toward the Knobby Room. Or was it Smythe? Yeah, he remembered the "y" sound in there. *Smythe.* Tonight he would enter the name into the system, methodically tap it out so the others could start memorizing. The SROs, the senior-ranking officers, said it was important to memorize all the names of the prisoners who were brought to the Hanoi Hilton, and all the POWs fed the names to a central repository.

Flak wondered where they were taking the poor bastard. Out of the prison, for sure, and that was odd for a new guy in the system. Then he began to remember little things about what he'd seen. Like the fact that Fidel had been holding the bloody rag to his nose. Smythe had done a number on the Cuban's nose. Apple really began to like the guy. He remembered the startling sound of the gunshot from the Knobby Room, and wished he knew more of the story. It would be a good one to pass on to his prison mates—and to the outside world, if he ever got the chance again.

Flak Apple kept his eye to the crack in the window for a long while. He was about to take a pause from his vigil when he saw Bug come back into the prison yard, a frown etched on his face as he walked across to the admin building, passing a hand through a shock of hair that stuck out like it contained an electrical charge.

Where had they taken Smythe? Was the squat Caucasian who he believed he might be? A Russian?

Todd S. Smythe, Major in the United States Air Force, was never again seen nor heard from by the American prisoners. It was as if he'd dropped from the face of the planet.

0910 Hours Local, Thursday 4 May 1972
7th Air Force Intelligence
Tan Son Nhut Air Base
Republic of Vietnam

Court Bannister stepped through the doorway, eyeing the General who sat reading the draft copy of the message laid out before him. "Take a seat," Major General Norman said vaguely, and continued scanning. Finally he looked up and cast a quizzical eye on Bannister.

"Is there a problem with it, sir?" Court asked. The message Norman was reading had been on his own desk half an hour earlier. The results of the previous day's bombing sorties, and the status of the Freedom Train operation.

The two-star wagged his head. "None at all. It's a good synopsis."

"And my suggestion, sir?"

General Norman cracked a smile. "Your infamous paragraph four? This time suggesting that we proceed to step two and mine the harbor at Haiphong to restrict shipping?"

"Yes, sir."

"I'll sign it out, even if it's a bit presumptuous coming from a lieutenant colonel."

"They don't know that at the Pentagon. You sign off the messages, General."

"Half the swinging dicks at the Pentagon know by now just who's writing these reports. They stand in line to read the fourth paragraphs."

"They know I'm the preparer?"

"The Chief of Staff asked, remember?"

"I thought that was between the two of you? Back-channel messages, for your eyes only?"

"Yep, but the Chief's let the cat out of the bag. One of those he told was the three-star Deputy Chief for Ops and Plans. Another was Lieutenant General Whitey Whisenand. He told him you were doing good work over here, and he ought to be proud of you."

Court felt a sinking feeling. To be known by the top generals had its good points, but there were many more bad ones. High visibility was not always desirable, especially when what you wanted most was a third—quite illegal—combat tour in the cockpit of a fighter.

Withdrawn into the privacy of his reflection, he almost missed the General's next words. "What was that, sir?" he sputtered, wondering if he'd heard correctly.

"I said, we're going to miss you around here. You've done everything I've asked for and then some on the Freedom Train operation. You can feel good about that, Court. Even General Vogt says you've been doing great work, and he doesn't pass out compliments lightly. It's going to be hard to replace you."

"Replace me? Where the hell am I going, sir?" he blurted.

"Time comes in every good officer's life when he has to stalk the hallowed halls of the five-sided circus, Court. You're being transferred to the Pentagon."

All color drained from Court Bannister's face. It was the worst possible assignment for a pilot who loved to fly. Under the new rules, Pentagon people didn't get to fly at all—regardless—not even if they were a rated pilot with four and a half MiG kills to their credit. All the Pentagon offered was demeaning jobs and pasty skin from seldom seeing the sun during their atrociously long workdays. Full colonels and one-stars were relegated to corner desks in crowded offices that did important work like keeping track of the number of noise complaints from chicken farmers.

"Congratulations, Colonel," Norman said heartily.

Court's jaw tightened. "For what, sir?" he stammered.

"The Chief of Staff personally requested the transfer. That kind of attention does not come often to a lieutenant colonel."

Court slowly wagged his head from side to side. "No, sir! I most respectfully *decline* the honor of the transfer."

"They're cutting your orders right now at Personnel."

"Jesus!"

"He can't help you on this one either."

Chapter 6

"I don't care what you say," the heavyset pilot in pajama-style prison garb said in a low voice to the emaciated man seated beside him, "I think he's a collaborator."

"Nuts. You don't know what you're talking about," the gaunt man said. He looked to be more than forty years of age. He was in fact twenty-seven.

The two were among thirty American POWs trucked from Hoa Lo Prison to the place they called the Zoo, a run-down villa where prisoners were occasionally paraded in front of foreign propaganda cameras. Also in the compound, hidden from the view of the visitors, were dank, bug-infested prison cells.

Today they were the "audience" for a POW choral group. Only those who were relatively unmarked by torture had been selected to attend. They were seated on wooden benches, and warned to look happy and remain quiet. Of course, there was little the guards could do about their talking in the presence of the newsmen, even if they were mostly East Bloc. Punishment awaited the transgressors, but they were willing to accept the risk, for they were thrilled to see inmates from other buildings

121

and cells and eager to share information on what was happening in the system. It would be worth the beatings.

It was time and the choir was growing restless, waiting to sing. Flash bulbs were ready to pop, a movie camera on a tripod was poised to roll.

"Whaddya mean, 'nuts'?"

"Knock it off and listen," the second POW said. "They worked hard as hell to put this on."

"Knock it off, yourself. They're collaborators. Look at the candy and cookies on the table in front of 'em."

"That's to impress the media. They don't get those all the time. Besides, we'll get our crack at 'em just like they do."

"Yeah, while those commie assholes film us."

"Just stuff your mouth and look starved and unhappy."

"Fucking collaborators." The speaker was an RF-4 recce pilot who had been shot down two months earlier during one of the first Freedom Train missions. His backseater had been killed and he was permanently PO-ed.

"Listen," the thin POW hissed without moving his eyes from the singers. "You're a new guy and you don't know what the fuck you're talking about. If you'd been studying the tap-and-flash code like you should've instead of bitching at everything, you'd see the guys are already passing information. Now shut up. I don't want a beating for listening to your bullshit while I'm missing out on what they're trying to tell us."

An emaciated, tall black man with an oddly bent left arm served as choirmaster. He stood in front of ten fidgety songsters, all dressed in purple-striped POW pajamas. The singers were formed before him in two rows on a raised platform. They settled down when the black man raised his hands. When he deftly lowered them, they began to sing.

Flak Apple led the group into a special song about Hero Nguyen, based on a Vietnamese propaganda song. The words were Flak's own and the men sang Homer-and-Jethro style to accommodate the twangy Vietnamese melody. Flak always tried to open with a Vietnamese song to warm his captors with a sense of familiarity and security before he got down to business.

Then he changed tempo and brought the choir to a fervor with *"Give me some men who are stout-hearted men who will fight for the right they adore."* The singers' chests swelled and their voices emerged clear and strong. As the POWs sang, they swayed and moved their arms and hands in tempo-snapping rhythm, while the designated "receivers" in the audience translated and stored away the information the choir were signaling.

TORTURE AT PLANTATION AGAIN

HEAVY COMMUNICATIONS PURGE EXPECTED AT VEGAS

ROBINSON GAVE BIRTH TO 24-INCH TAPE WORM. FATHER FINE, WORM LOST HEAD

LATEST SHOOTDOWNS SAY NIXON SURE TO WIN ELECTION

Code flashing—seemingly natural motions of fingers, hands, and parts of the body—had evolved from the original tap code, where a series of taps on a wall or pipe could communicate letters of the alphabet. It was quite unlike the Morse code, with its dots and dashes. The number of taps indicated first a row and then a column of 25 letters of the alphabet (C was also used for the letter K to allow a 5×5 matrix). A quick thumping by the heel of a hand meant break it off.

	1	2	3	4	5
1	A	B	C	D	E
2	F	G	H	I	J
3	L	M	N	O	P
4	Q	R	S	T	U
5	V	W	X	Y	Z

The first taps referred to the number of the row reading across, the second to the column reading down. Tap tap was the F row, tap tap tap was the third letter in that row, or H.

As time continued, hand and finger flashes, body movements, wheezes, and just about any method to make a count were used. Even slaps of a broom as a POW swept a floor. The long-term POWs had become proficient and lightning fast. Words and phrases were abbreviated. SRO meant Senior Ranking Officer. GNGBU meant Good Night and God Bless You. Whole conversations could be flashed out in a minimum of time.

Life for the POWs had improved since the Son Tay raid. Slowly at first, then faster as the peace talks progressed in

Paris, the POWs were allowed more freedoms. In the States, the POW wives banded together, ignoring the advice of certain civilian officials of the Department of Defense and the State Department, and urged the world to hold the communists accountable about the plight of the POWs. As a result, more packages were allowed in, and more letters out. An ex-Navy man, Ross Perot, had loaded a Boeing 707 with packages for the POWs and gotten as far as Vientiane, Laos, before being turned back. Then one glorious day the POWs had been assembled and told they would begin living together, barracks-style. The men were ecstatic, and when they were first put together, talked nonstop for days. Unfortunately, the new "freedom" did not apply to all. Prisoners of higher rank and/or bad attitudes (by communist standards) were still singled out for solitary cells in a particularly evil place the POWs called Skid Row.

The choirmaster, Air Force Major Algernon A. "Flak" Apple, was an F-4 pilot shot down five years earlier, in late 1967, and had been consistently singled out for bizarre swings of treatment—from months of severe beatings and living in stocks in an isolated, filthy cell, to a hospital operation to mend his badly broken left arm. He'd also been forced to meet peace groups and pro-communist newsmen visiting Hanoi to drum up attention. It was noted by the 4th Allied POW Wing historian that he'd met with more Hanoi visitors than any other prisoner to date.

Why Apple's treatment ranged from savage to serene was frequently debated among the POWs. Perhaps it was because he'd been the first black POW, and the commies wanted to exploit his background. No, the old heads said, it was because he'd once escaped and the V (the POW term for their Vietnamese captors) were determined to make an example. During the escape, Apple had made it all the way to the French consulate, where he'd been turned back over to the Vietnamese. His partner, Ted Frederick, had been shot and then methodically beaten to death. Apple had also been severely tortured for several weeks. Then the V had decided not to kill him, but to indoctrinate their first black POW and release him as a witness to their humane treatment.

"How about this choir-directing shit?" the newer shoot-downs complained. "Look at all the privileges he gets." The speakers had not gone through the years of deprivation and rope torture, and felt *they* could not be broken. With sardonic smiles, the old heads tried to tell them *anyone* could be broken. The secret was to bounce back and make the V work just as hard during the subsequent sessions to wrench out another bit of trivia. Inside, the new guys quaked, while outwardly they were John Waynes. The old heads were Jimmy Stewarts, inside and out.

One group of old heads knew why Apple had been selected as choir director, for they'd made it happen. Quincy Collins, the original director, and Norm McDaniels, a later director, had been caught communicating with their fellow POWs, and had been beaten and placed in stocks for their crimes. In the efforts of the peace-loving North Vietnamese to help the black criminal USAF Major Algernon A. Apple become a visible manifestation of their humane policies, the V had decided to appoint him as the new choir director. It took three months of beatings to get him to agree, and then only because he was contacted by a POW with a message from an SRO.

The SRO had directed Apple to take the choir—and to communicate, as Collins and McDaniels had done. Having remained in solitary for so many years, Apple had no idea of what the choir had been about. Now that he knew, he was elated to take advantage of the situation.

The recent shoot-downs did not know about the torrents of information that flowed from the choir to the "receivers" in the audience, who passed it on to their cell and compound buddies. Until the new guys proved they wouldn't squeal under torture, they had to be kept in the dark. And so it was that the communications section of the 4th Allied POW Wing (Allied because there were three Thais and a South Vietnamese in the prison) was operating better than ever.

PEACE TALCS SLOW

V INVADED SOUTH VIET FULL FORCE

NIXON SENT MORE FIGHTER WINGS AND NAVY CARRIERS TO BOMB PISS OUT OF THEM

THEYRE USING SMART BOMBS NOW AND SOME USAF PUCE DROPPED THANH HOA BRIDGE WITH ONE

That caused a ripple among the receivers. The Thanh Hoa bridge crossed a gun-infested gorge that had, through the years, claimed nearly 100 Navy and Air Force airplanes attempting to drop a span.

ANYBODY SEEN FINGERS OFALLON OR NU GUY NAMED SMYTHE, a singer asked. This was a very important question.

NEG, NO replied the audience.

Flak, his back to them, couldn't "see" the words, so the singers transmitted the answer back to him. Apple then asked with eye motions if the camera was rolling. The choir said yes.

Flak was ready. He swung the choir into a rousing version of the main chorus from *Oklahoma!* His arm-swinging was vigorous, and only those close by saw the concealed grimaces as his bent left arm moved in concert with his right. He would transmit differently, for another audience than the POWs seated behind him. He'd deliberated long hours over message content, for he wanted to pack the important information into the fewest and plainest words possible.

He began . . .

Once before, Flak Apple had gotten information out via a communist television program. An American air attaché in Belgrade had made a copy and sent it to the POW tracking room in the basement of the Pentagon. The trackers had read the flash codes and deciphered names, deaths, torture, V attitude, messages to families, and that something fishy was going on with the electronic specialist POWs. Then came, very rapidly, the detailed information which had set up the raid at Son Tay.

Apple was assigned the code name Caruso. The men in the Pentagon tracking room had been thrilled at the decoding, for they'd not heard from Major Apple since Dancer had made contact when he and Dipper had visited Hanoi. Dancer was the code name of an Air Force officer who had gone under cover and become heavily involved in the antiwar protest movement. His name was Richard Connert.

Dipper was a California politician and activist son of a well-known movie actor. Early in the conflict, he'd become a war correspondent for the liberal *California Sun* newspaper and scored several journalistic coups. The first was an interview in the caves under Cholon, Saigon, with a Viet Cong colonel. The second came in 1968, when he had been invited to Hanoi in the dual role of peace delegate and reporter. He'd taken Connert with him. It was in Hanoi that Dipper had met USAF Major

Algernon A. Apple and tried, under North Vietnamese urging, to get him to accept an early release and return with them to the United States. Apple had refused.

Dipper hadn't known that Dancer was an undercover Air Force officer. He had not known his own code name was Dipper. His real name was Shawn Bannister, and he occasionally got so stoned he didn't even know that.

Flak Apple had been stunned during his interview with Bannister and Connert, when Dancer had begun flashing in expert POW code. After verifying that Connert was a "blue mailman"—the code Flak and a handful of other pilots had been taught in a special USAF course—Flak had passed names of POWs. The Pentagon had been elated with the new information, and that more would follow. Based on an official's promise, Flak and Connert thought they'd periodically see each other in Hanoi and be able to exchange information.

Although a North Vietnamese official had promised that Shawn could return to Hanoi once a year, the invitation had not materialized. The official, named Thach, had fallen from favor when he'd failed to break Flak Apple, and was exiled to porter duty on the Ho Chi Minh Trail. His invitation to have Shawn Bannister return was forgotten.

Flak became increasingly dejected as each year passed and Dancer failed to return. He'd attended propaganda sessions after only minimal beatings, on the theory that a new mailman might have replaced Dancer. He'd met Berrigan, Dellinger, Apteker, Robinson, and Hayden, but nothing other than sneers were passed. Then came the opportunity to lead the choir.

His first performance before East Bloc cameras had been two years ago. Several months later two carefully worded sentences in a POW wife's form letter confirmed that the right people knew what the choir was all about. "Some of your Air Force friends called," she wrote, "and said I should join them to watch an inspirational new TV music program. It was wonderful, full of hope and uplifting messages, and we look forward to seeing more of the same."

Now Flak had a message more important than any he'd tried to pass previously.

Flak Apple and a few of the other SROs believed American POWs were being taken by the Russians—possibly being questioned somewhere nearby, or even being shipped to another country. Through the years, little things had begun to add up to the outrageous conclusions.

A USAF B-66 electronic warfare officer, Captain David Bunker, was seen being captured in apparent good condition, but was not seen again. Same story for a Navy radar intercept officer, Lieutenant Thomas Ewonski, who had ejected from an F-4. He'd spent a few torturous nights in New Guy Village, then disappeared. Shortly after, a squat-looking Caucasian was seen coming from the administrative building, speaking to the Cuban they called Fidel. The same spotter heard the man speaking words in a Slavic language. It took months for the bits of information to reach the Personnel section of the 4th Allied POW Wing. The men assigned as record keepers tentatively concluded that some Americans with special backgrounds were receiving special treatment. At first it was thought to be isolation from the POW community, then the shipping-to-Russia theory took shape as other pieces of information surfaced.

One of the new shoot-downs, Navy A-6 pilot Lieutenant Rick Lorton, had been taken to the Knobby Room for his initial beating. Most POWs were taken there first and evaluated by the North Vietnamese, given varying levels of torture to see how well they could hold out, for the pain threshold varied from man to man. Lorton, determined by his captors to be a hardnose, had been thrown into a cell across the corridor, and heard the sounds of another man being dragged into the Knobby Room. The ugly sounds of the man being stuffed into the rope torture position had taken Lorton's mind off his own pain, for he'd recognized the outraged cries of his BN (Bombardier-Navigator), Peter J. "Fingers" O'Fallon, whom he'd last seen in his chute drifting into a treeline half a mile from where Lorton had come down. Lorton had been pleased O'Fallon was alive, but appalled at the sounds of his beating. Then an unusual event occurred. Having been in Hoa Lo only two days, Lorton hadn't realized just *how* unusual.

The door to the Knobby Room had been thrown open and someone had shouted angry words in a language other than Vietnamese. The beating had immediately stopped and O'Fallon was taken away. To keep his mind from his pain, Lorton had continuously repeated the foreign words in his mind, in a kind of trance-inducing mantra. Weeks later, when the V eased off on the beatings and put him into an eight-man cell, he'd recounted the experience.

"Sounds Russian," one of his cellmates had said. "A guy over in the Mint knows Russian. Let's ask him." While the foreign words were being carefully circulated, the Personnel section of the 4th Allied POW Wing discovered that O'Fallon was no longer in the known system. Finally the translation came back: "Stop beating him, you Oriental sister-fucker, he belongs to us." The POW linguist also confirmed the language was Russian.

Then had come the incident with Smythe, and the fact that he'd been taken away by the Russian and Fidel, and not been returned to the prison.

As a result, the SRO at Hoa Lo had instructed Flak to get the message out.

Since he wanted to ensure the mission, Flak reverted to a surer method of signaling. This one was so important that Flak wanted to use both visual motions and audible sounds, which could be decoded from either film or audio tape. While the choir used hand flashes and eye-squints, he began to wave his arms stridently, and then to utter staccato accompaniments in his deep and pleasant voice, accenting the harmony of the songs. Bum bum de . . . bum bum de de de de . . . bum bum bum bum bum de . . . bum de de de de de . . .

FIVE MEN POSITIVELY ID-ED MISSING. NO NOWN INJURIES. OFALLON USN, EWONSCI USN, DEHNE USAF, BUNCER USAF, SMYTHE, USAF. ALL R OLDER, MOST R EWOS, OR HAVE PREVIOUS ASSIGNMENTS IN SENSITIVE JOBS. THEIR QUIZES DIFFERENT FROM NORMAL. RUSSIAN SPOCEN BY FAT MAN IN BUSH JACET. QUESTIONS TECHNICAL. TWO SAID THEY SAW TAPE RECORDER.

It was difficult for Flak, and he was concerned that some real choirmaster would note that his arm and hand motions were not what would be taught at Juilliard, or that a code breaker might somehow catch on to the repetitions. He also hoped the microphones for the tape recorders were picking up his humming. Probably no need to worry there . . . the camera would have it on sound track and film.

0930 Hours Local, Monday 5 June 1972
Room 1D215, Pentagon Basement
Washington, D.C.

Three weeks later the men of the 1127th FAG received the bad news. There was no film of the Easter propaganda songfest in Hanoi. The Air Attaché in Belgrade had forwarded a coded message back to DIA with details of the screwup. The communist cameraman had returned the 16mm film directly to the lab at the Yugoslavian national television station and stood by while the technician prepared a fresh solution of chemicals to make sure the important film came out perfectly. One of the Soviet-supplied chemicals was so out of tolerance that the resultant mixture completely stripped the film—leaving a 150-foot strip of crystal-clear celluloid.

Lieutenant General Whitey Whisenand received one of the trackers in his Spartan and unmarked office in the Pentagon basement.

"Are you sure the AIRA got his straight story?" he asked.

"Yes, sir, we're sure."

"How did he get so many details?"

"The lab tech's one of the AIRA's prime contacts. He's been utterly reliable in the past."

Whitey grimaced. "How about the audio? You have the Radio Hanoi broadcast?"

"Yes, sir. The signal was weak and the weather gave us problems with reception, but we have some of it." The tracker placed an aluminum suitcase on the conference table, opened it, and snapped on the battery-powered reel-to-reel tape recorder.

After the standard Radio Hanoi orchestral piece, with its overtones of the communist *Internationale,* a thin female voice said in precise British English that this was Radio Hanoi calling. She went on to relate news stories about how poorly the running-dog lackeys of the imperialists were doing in South Vietnam, and how many Yankee imperialist air pirates had been shot down over North Vietnam. Her voice faded in and out as atmospheric conditions changed.

"To conclude our broadcast," she finally said, "we will present two musical selections made by American criminals so remorseful about their crimes they wish to provide reparation. Members of our listening audience must remember that it is only due to the humane treatment of our government that these criminals are allowed to gather together and sing their songs. Their first rendition will be their interpretation of the famous Vietnamese love song 'Chi, and Nguyen the Victorious War Hero Who Carried Supplies Down Victory Road to the Valiant Fighters of the South.' That will be followed by a traditional American song."

There was a scratchy pause, then the song began with a whining tonal background of male voices that swelled, then diminished and remained as accompaniment as two other POWs sang Hero Nguyen's song. They used a fast tempo, accented in the nasal twang of Homer and Jethro.

> *Oh, this little Nguyen, doncha know, doncha know, doncha*
> *neee-owe,*
> *This little hero, doncha know, doncha know, doncha neee-*
> *owe,*
> *Carried his load, carried his load, carried his leee-owed,*
> *Into the storm, into the storm, into the stee-orme,*
> *And they shot at him, shot at him, shot at heee-imm,*
> *So it was balls to the left, balls to the right, nuthin' but*
> *balls, balls, beee-awls,*
> *Hero Nguyen did not care, did not care, did not kee-air,*
> *Courageous Nguyen thought of no balls at all, no balls*
> *at all, no balls at eeee-awl,*
> *Fearless Nguyen faced the enemy and dropped his load,*
> *dropped his load, dropped his leee-owed.*
> *NO BALLS AT ALL NGUYEN DROPPED HIS LOAD.*

The tracker was laughing so hard he had trouble snapping off the tape. "Oh God, can you believe that? Those guys."

Whitey Whisenand wore a wide grin, but he also felt a thrill of reverence. "Those guys, indeed," he said. "Pulling that off right in their face, and slick enough to get it broadcast by Hanoi Hannah." He walked from his desk to the table. "Any more?"

The tracker snapped the recorder back on and the reels began to turn. The swelling chorus of "Oh What a Beautiful Mornin' " from *Oklahoma!* was tinny and clipped. The transmitter and antenna system of Hanoi Hannah was 1930s vintage. The tracker increased the gain and fiddled with the base and treble controls to break out the words as best he could.

". . . oh what a beautiful day . . . the corn is as high . . . elephant's eye . . . climbing clear up to the sky . . . " The tape spun for several minutes.

"Did you get anything from the words or rhythm?" Whitey asked in a dubious tone.

"No, sir. But listen to this." He replaced the tape with one on a smaller reel, and turned the switch. "This is Caruso, and he's sending tap code." The technicians had isolated and amplified Flak Apple's humming. Whitey bent closer over the machine to hear better.

"Bum bum de . . . bum bum de de de de . . . bum bum bum bum bum de . . . bum de de de de de . . . " The tape ran for five and a half minutes. Flak's humming alternately faded and boomed, interference and static overrode some of it, transmission noise interfered with other parts. Finally Whitey straightened.

"Okay," he asked. "What did you get from it?"

The tracker handed him a piece of paper.

FIVE . . . TIVELY ID-ED. MISSING. NO NOWN . . . FALLON . . . EWONS . . . HNE USAF . . . YTHE USAF . . . R OLDER . . . EWOS R HAVE . . . SENSITI . . . QUIZES DIFF . . . RUSSIAN . . . BUSH JACE . . . QUESTIONS TECH . . . TAPE RECOR . . .

"That's it?" Whitey said, his eyes drawn to the word "Russian."

"I'm afraid so, sir."

"Do you have any kind of reading on what he was trying to say?"

"Maybe. One of the guys brought up an idea, and so far it's the only way the words fit together that make sense. It goes along with what you and I discussed before."

"Show me."

The tracker pulled a classified folder from his briefcase and extracted a paper, which he spread before the General on the conference table. "First of all, we think he's talking about five men who were identified and are now missing from the prison. We think we've got four names from the word fragments we've got." He started at the top. "We believe this refers to a Navy

Lieutenant Peter O'Fallon. His parachute was seen, as was his pilot's, but so far neither has been reported in the system. We think he was referring to Navy Lieutenant Elmer Ewonski, here, and Air Force Major Richard Dehne, here. Both are backseaters, and both have extensive training and knowledge of electronic warfare. Then there's a Major Todd S. Smythe, who was shot down on April 16th, and he's not only knowledgeable in electronic warfare, but like O'Fallon, he once held a critical job in SIOP nuke targeting and operational war planning. What we think Caruso is trying to tell us, is that these men underwent some sort of special questioning—they call them quizzes—regarding their technical knowledge, and now they are missing. And, of course, the word 'Russian' is in there."

"What do you think that means?" Whitey's heart beat faster. He'd spoken to the tracker before about the possibility that foreign nationals might somehow be involved with the POWs, and told them to remain on the lookout for anything which might shed further light on the matter.

The tracker didn't bite. "No idea, sir. Perhaps he's talking about some Russian who wears a bush jacket? We really don't know why, unless—"

"Go on."

The tracker took an angry breath. "Unless the goddamn Russians have taken our men somewhere to interrogate them."

Whitey frowned, then walked to the window and stared out at the Potomac. Finally he turned back to the tracker. "I want to know where our men are being taken. What is the latest Gamma? Do we have any correlation?"

Gamma, under "G" clearance, was a project set up to glean useful scraps of information concerning the POWs from every possible source—including tapping the phones and reading the mail of war protesters who traveled to Hanoi.

The elaborate Gamma project was operated by the NSA (National Security Agency) and the DIA (Defense Intelligence Agency) and was expensive. There were two dozen Gamma targets, designated by four-letter words beginning with G. Thus Cora Weiss was Glob, Jane Fonda was Goat, Tom Hayden was Goof, and so forth. Shawn Bannister was the only one with a different code name. He remained Dipper, so named on another, earlier operation, as did Dancer.

The tracker shook his head. "There's nothing on any of the

Gamma intercepts relating to this problem. No mention of Soviets whatsoever."

"Is Dipper returning to Hanoi in the near future?" Whitey asked hopefully.

"We've got nothing to indicate that." He brightened. "Goat's going, probably next month." Goat, Jane Fonda, had an impressive record as an antiwar activist.

Whitey returned to the conference table and sat, feeling suddenly irritable. "That doesn't help. We need to get Dancer back into Hanoi so he can talk with Caruso and sniff around." Whitey tapped his fingers. His mind continued to return to the message he'd received from Wolf Lochert, telling what he'd found out about electronic warfare officers at Korat, and a major named T. S. Smythe in particular. Smythe had indeed been shot down, confirmed as captured, and now . . . he glanced at the paper and read the name again . . . now he just *might* be on his way to Russia.

He brought it out into the open. "Is there anything at all that indicates our men are being sent to Moscow?"

"Not a thing, sir, with the possible exception of Caruso's message, and our interpretation may not be accurate."

"Damn." Whitey slowly punched his left hand with his fist. "We've got to get somebody in there to find out what is going on." He stopped. "Fonda is going to Hanoi?"

"We've got intercepts from the North Vietnamese, the Czechoslovaks, and Goat herself saying it's all set up. First or second week of July, as it now stands."

Whitey mused. "Well, then, I'd say Mr. Shawn Bannister would be a natural to go along. They're both Hollywood types. And along with Dipper—we hope—will go Dancer. Where are Bannister and Connert now?"

"It's time for Dipper's yearly war correspondent junket. He's running around the media bars in Saigon getting his war stories."

"Is Connert with him?"

"Yes, sir."

Whitey nodded. "Thanks for the briefing. Tell your men to keep up the good work."

When the tracker had departed his office, Whitey sat at his desk for a few moments, thinking hard about the way things were going. Tomorrow he'd be tied up for much of the day at the White House, for he was to be in attendance when the Chairman of the Joint Chiefs, along with the Chief of Naval Operations and the Chief of Staff of the Air Force, provided an analysis of how the bombing campaign was faring, including initial results of the placement of antishipping mines in Haiphong Harbor for the previous month. The Freedom Train operation—the name was being changed to Linebacker—was progressing well, although the North Vietnamese were once again proving to be tough enemies. They were flying their MiGs down low, under American radar coverage, and popping up to attack U.S. fighter-bombers before they could drop their bombs on targets in route package two.

He hoped, following the official briefing, to get a few minutes of Nixon's time so he could play the tape of Major Flak Apple leading his audacious rendition about Nguyen the Hero. The President liked to be kept informed, and it might serve to keep him focused on the POW issue. Afterward he wanted to find time to meet and greet Lieutenant Colonel Court Bannister, who was scheduled to report in to his new Pentagon assignment. While all Court really wanted was to fly and fight, his nephew was reaping the results of his own good work. Whitey grinned at that one. Court would get to see the other side of the game—from the view of the bowels of the system. Perhaps he'd even grow new respect for the work done at the great puzzle palace. Likely not, though. His nephew was operationally oriented, and certainly too impatient for the play-by-the-rules Pentagon way of doing things. But first things first.

He began to write on his pad, then to change and add words. When he'd composed what he wanted to say, he called for the secretary and asked her to type it. "Go final," he told her. There was no need for a glossy piece of art. As he waited for her to finish, he thought again about what he was doing. The message instructed Lieutenant Colonel Wolf Lochert to insert an agent into the Saigon press community—to select the person carefully and ensure there were no repercussions or discoveries. Then he'd included very specific instructions for the agent.

He assumed Wolf would choose someone from the ASA, the Army Security Agency, which was the investigative arm of the U.S. Army. In his position as Whitey's eyes and ears, Wolf carried the clout to get that done. He could commandeer about anyone for his task. Inside his briefcase, Whitey carried a

note, typed on White House stationery and appropriately signed.
It read:

> I desire full national resources, to include all Department
> of Defense, Commerce, Justice, and State personnel and
> material, to be placed at the disposal of Lieutenant General
> Albert G. Whisenand and his designees whenever and for
> whatever period of time he so requires.
> *Signed: Richard M. Nixon, President of the United States*

Wolf Lochert carried a copy of the President's note, as well
as another, even shorter one, which identified him as Lieutenant
General Whisenand's designee. Whitey had signed that one.
Knowing the direct manner in which Colonel Lochert operated,
Whitey doubted he needed it.

He'd made a good selection when he had chosen Wolf for the
special project.

Next Whitey began to word a second message, quite different
from the first.

The first message had been classified Secret, with the guidance that it contained sensitive, compartmentalized information,
and involved appropriate special handling. Whitey would have it
taken to the National Command Center, which was conveniently
located near his office, where it would be specially encoded
and transmitted via special means. The second was even more
secretive. This one he would hand-deliver that afternoon, to
"certain people" at the British Embassy, on the other side of
the Potomac.

His other nephew, Shawn Bannister, who was code-named
Dipper, was at the focus of the efforts his two messages would
generate.

0730 Hours Local, Tuesday 6 June 1972
Room 3D317, Pentagon
Washington, D.C.

Court reported to his new superior officer, the full colonel who
ran XOOF, the Fighter Ops Division, whose office and name
were shown on the form he'd been given at the reception desk.

The Colonel greeted him aboard and told him in pleasant tones that he'd be running his own branch, to be designated XOOFL, which meant that Court would indeed work directly for him.

"Glad to meet you, sir," Court said. He wore summer blues and full ribbons with command pilot's wings and his parachutist jump badge.

The Colonel shrugged happily. "It's a new shop," he said, "and it's called the fighter liaison office." He smiled. "It's a great chance to pull down some top ratings on your effectiveness report."

Court ignored the remark. "And my duties?"

"*Way* over my head. I was told to set up the office by the two-star who runs XOO, which is what they call operations here, and he said the Deputy Chief of Staff for Operations and Plans, the XO, a three-star by the way, just told him to set it up."

"But you're my boss, right?"

"You might say that," the Colonel told him happily. "Yeah, you can say that."

"So what do you want me to do?" Court thought the man a bit slick and entirely too nice.

"Well, first, just get yourself settled into your office, then . . . uh . . . stand by."

"Just . . . stand by?" He was confused, and increasingly irritated about the assignment.

"Are you familiar with the Linebacker operation plan?"

Court said he was. Linebacker had been one of the older OPlans they'd updated for inclusion in the Freedom Train plan, with which he'd worked at Tan Son Nhut.

"Well, that's what they're calling Freedom Train now, and your job's going to have something to do with that. That's all I know. I was told to have all message traffic regarding Linebacker routed to your office."

At least, Court thought, he'd be involved with the war effort. As branch chief, he might have some say in how his office would provide support. "How many people do I have in my branch?" he asked.

"Just you for the present. Once you get rolling, and we find out what you're doing, we'll make out the appropriate manning requests and also get you secretarial support. You're in the room next door, three-nineteen. It's sort of small, but there's a desk and a chair, and I think there's a blackboard."

"Look, Colonel. When do I find out my duties?" Court asked.

"Soon as someone tells us what the generals have in mind," the Colonel said cheerfully. "Right now I'd say you should be reading all the summary reports about what's been going on in the bombing campaign, bring yourself up to speed on what's going on. And . . . yeah . . . maybe you can help us out answering a few of these congressional queries."

At the last remark, Court began to groan inwardly. His worst fears were being realized. He would have no real job, and would be assigned duties which could be done just as well by someone with half his rank and experience. He decided to start nosing around to find out how he could fill his time trying to support the guys flying combat.

The Colonel's secretary escorted him to his new office, the walls of which were painted the same puke-green of all military offices, and he deposited a thick tome, the Linebacker OPlan, and an armful of classified after-action reports. Then Lieutenant Colonel Court Bannister, fighter pilot and MiG killer, settled down in his new office to read. He had no earthly idea what the next step was to be. He wondered if anyone even knew he was there.

1430 Hours Local, Tuesday 13 June 1972
Loc Ninh City
Republic of Vietnam

"Wolf, you purple-people-eating son of a bitch," the soldier shouted above the roar of the helicopter blades and the crack of incoming rounds, "what in Christ's name are you doing here?"

"Shut up, *Scheisskopf,* I'm here to rescue you. Don't swear or I'll leave you right where you are." Lochert stood in the right door of a UH-1 helicopter gunship that had just touched down in a debris-littered dirt street on the west side of the village of Loc Ninh, III Corps, South Vietnam. Lochert wore a set of clean jungle fatigues only slightly stained by sweat. "Move it," he boomed at a soldier who had stopped in his run toward the helicopter to fire over his shoulder at a furtive motion near a ruined building. The helicopter door gunner, following the soldier's lead, opened up with his 7.62 Gatling at the same spot, and all movement stopped.

Two days before, the 5th VC/NVA with units of the 203rd Tank Regiment had charged out of Cambodia and quickly engaged the 9th ARVN Regiment at Loc Ninh. With only an ARVN Ranger battalion and a handful of American advisers, the 9th ARVN had beaten back five thundering tank attacks. But the communist troops outnumbered them five to one and the outpost and Loc Ninh were falling. Helicopters had been shuttling in and out since noon. Many had been shot down. The still-smoldering carcass of a Huey lay near a shattered concrete house. Lochert was on the last helicopter and it was already loaded with escaping ARVN troops.

A mortar round exploded forty feet from the chopper, then another, much closer.

"Move it, move it," Wolf again yelled to the running soldier, Sergeant First Class James P. Mahoney, now the last man alive in the compound. Mahoney's sweat-stained jungle fatigues were badly torn, his strained face was black with smoke. He had a radio strapped to his back and an M16 cradled under one arm. A mortar shell crumped close behind him and his weapon went flying as he was hurled to the ground. Wolf Lochert leaped from the helicopter and picked him up under one arm, grasped the M16 in his free hand, and jumped back on board.

"Okay, lift off," Wolf yelled to the door gunner, who spoke into the boom microphone on his helmet to tell the pilot to haul ass. The engine surged and the overladen helicopter strained, then limped nosedown over the trees, headed south to the relative safety of An Loc. Small-arms fire rattled underneath like popcorn.

Wolf held the dazed Mahoney in his lap with one arm as he sat in the door with his feet on the skids. His other arm circled the gunner's pedestal. He held the M16 in that hand. Mahoney shook his head as if awakening from a deep sleep, his eyes blinked open, and he looked around. Then he focused on Wolf's face.

"I didn't know you cared," he said, teeth gleaming from his dirty face.

"I don't," Wolf rasped. He nodded at the radio pack on Mahoney's back. "Just didn't want to see good equipment going to waste." Wolf looked up to see an object trailing smoke streaking toward them.

"Flares—pop some flares," he yelled at the door gunner. "Missile inbound from five o'clock."

The gunner released his grip on his Gatling, reached inside his fatigue shirt and pulled out a day-night flare, ignited an end, and tossed it out the door. At the same time he told the pilot to turn hard right. The hot flare fell rapidly away from the helicopter, followed quickly by another, confusing the missile's heat detector. With the abrupt turn, the missile broke lock on the engine tailpipe and dipped into a nosedive for the flares.

Six minutes later the pilot brought the helicopter into a semihard landing at the helipad at An Loc, fifteen miles south of Loc Ninh down Highway 13. Mahoney slid to his feet from Wolf's lap and stood, wobbly-kneed, by the side of the helicopter as the engine unwound.

"This place isn't all that safe, either," he said, pulling at his clothing and moving around to check himself for holes.

Wolf stepped from the skid, followed by fifteen ARVN soldiers who scrambled out of the helicopter as if escaping a chariot bound for hell. "Here's what knocked you down," he said to Mahoney, and pointed to a hole where a piece of mortar fragment had slammed into the sergeant's radio.

"Shit," Mahoney said, using the breezy affectation of a Philadelphia Irishman who had experienced more combat time than most men had spent in the service, "that's the third radio blown off my back in two days."

"Correction, shithead," Wolf said, "that's the third radio that's saved your life in two days. How come you were wearing one, anyhow? That's a job for some two-striper." He handed Mahoney his M16.

"He took an RPG in the belly," Mahoney said. An RPG was a 5-lb rocket-propelled grenade. "And my captain needed an RTO. I was the last guy alive, so . . . you know."

The job of an RTO (Radio-Telephone Operator) was to follow his officer and hand him the telephone-like mouthpiece when communications were required. Enemy gunners liked to zero in on RTOs, who were easily identifiable by the protruding radio whip antenna.

"How come you're the last man out?" Wolf asked in a suddenly gentle voice. "What happened to your captain?"

"He was in that crashed chopper you saw. I'm the only trooper who got out of it alive."

The An Loc helipad was teeming with movement as helicopters arrived and departed, shuttling wounded out and ammunition in. The air was hot and dusty and filled with the shouts of men at work. ARVN 105mm howitzers were booming out shells nonstop. Wolf and Mahoney walked past the operations shack to a makeshift first aid station, where they drank water from a Lister bag and tried to clean up. As he was wiping down with his bandanna, Mahoney looked up at Wolf. "Hey," he said, "where's your weapon?"

Lochert looked as shamefaced as a man whose normal expression was as expressive as the north face of the Eiger could look. "Didn't have time to, ah, *procure* one."

Mahoney hooted. "Wolf Lochert, without a weapon? That's like Sears without Roebuck."

"Well, I did have *this.*" Lochert partially pulled up his right pant leg, revealing a Mauser 7.63 in a small holster on his ankle. "And *this.*" He produced a Randall stiletto from a left calf holster. He sheathed the slim weapon and stood up. "C'mon, we gotta get a move on."

"What do you mean, get a move on? We just got here. I've got to make an after-action report. I'm the sole survivor from our advisory unit."

Wolf looked at his watch. "Go see your S-3, tell him all you know, then meet me back here. I've got a helicopter coming and you're going with me. We take off in an hour. Oh, yeah. Get rid of your radio and your weapon. You won't need them where you're going."

Mahoney took another look at Lochert's fatigues and saw, in addition to the Combat Infantryman's Badge and jump wings, the subdued black threads on his collar denoting a lieutenant colonel's leaves.

"Jees, Wolf, you're an Ell Cee now. Considering you were my first sergeant when I was a kid, I guess I should say congratulations. But, damn, I can't go running off with you. My job's up here. You want I should go AWOL or something?"

Lochert fished a folded piece of paper from his left breast pocket and handed it to Mahoney, who unfolded and read that E-7 James P. Mahoney was relieved of duties with the 5th Advisory Group and assigned for up to 179 days temporary duty with the 1127th Field Activity Group, United States Air Force, Fort Belvoir, Virginia. Above-named EM was cleared up to and including Top Secret and for SI, sensitive information, on a need-to-know basis. Transfer of household goods and POV were not authorized. It went on to state further that Mahoney could requisition any vehicle from any motor pool or rent any vehicle from any civilian outlet, fly on any airplane, civilian or military, and stay at civilian or military quarters. Wearing of civilian clothes was left to the bearer's discretion. Final word before the signature was that funds were authorized under PCN 4227910.

Mahoney grimaced and glared at Lochert. He'd been assigned to other undercover jobs, and knew what the orders were about. "Aw Christ, Wolf, what—"

"Swear once again, Mahoney, and I'll rip your face off and stuff it in your left boot."

Mahoney's map-of-Ireland face looked both amused and chagrined as he spoke. "Okay, I get your point. I forgot."

It was well known that Wolfgang Xavier Lochert, an ex-Maryknoll seminarian, abhorred anyone using the Lord's name in vain in his presence. Repeated use brought about dire consequences. A Southern artillery captain who once, just *once,* swore horribly in front of Wolf had required the therapeutic help of his mother before he could regain his ability even to say "God bless you" when someone sneezed. He kept seeing Wolf's menacing visage and simply couldn't speak that simple courtesy for the longest time. There were other examples talked of in hushed tones in the Army.

Mahoney tried again. "I don't think I'm going to want to do whatever it is you've got for me *this* time. I'm no good at this sort of thing."

"Sure you are." And he was. Mahoney had a natural and unassuming air about him that had always made him good at undercover work. His gift of the blarney and easy laughter allowed him to join in with any crowd, in a great variety of situations. Wolf Lochert had not considered an alternate choice after receiving General Whisenand's message.

"Well, what do you want me to do this time?" Mahoney asked gloomily, washing away the last of the grime, then replacing the bandanna.

"Can't tell you."

"Where are we going?"

"Mahoney, you ask too many questions. You're a soldier, correct?"

"I'm the best damned soldier in the Army."

Wolf glared at the curse word. "Then shut up, *Scheisskopf.*"

An hour later they were airborne in a war-weary Huey, headed for the sprawling Tan Son Nhut Air Base, which was adjacent to Saigon.

Lochert and Mahoney were dropped off at the Tan Son Nhut Base Operations, run by the 8th Aerial Port Squadron, Military Airlift Command. Inside, Wolf led Mahoney into what passed for the VIP lounge, then on, into a locker room.

"Wolf, will you please tell me—" Mahoney tried again as they walked in.

"Shut up."

Wolf Lochert eyed Mahoney's strained face and long, disheveled hair. He leaned forward and sniffed. "You look awful and you smell awful." He leaned back and grinned. "That's good." He went to a locker, spun the combination lock, removed a bundle of civilian clothes from the bottom, and tossed them to Mahoney.

"Put those on," he rasped.

Mahoney eyed the clothing cautiously. "I need a shower."

"No, you don't. Put 'em on."

Mahoney's face took on a pained expression as he held up a worn green J. C. Penny leisure suit, with bell-bottom pants, then fell as he picked up a pair of leather sandals. He looked like he wanted to speak, but Wolf said, "Shut up," before he could open his mouth.

Mahoney changed clothes and stood by as Lochert threw the old fatigues into a trash can. He docilely followed Lochert to the operations counter, where Lochert displayed orders to a bored Air Force lieutenant who instantly sprang to feverish activity. "Yes, sir, sir," he stuttered, "I'll get a staff car right away, right away." As he picked up a black phone on the ops counter, Wolf pressed the off button.

"No staff car. We just need a line jeep to drop us off at the main gate. We'll take it from there."

Mahoney trooped behind Wolf as he strode out to the ramp, feeling uneasy. He held his tongue as an Air Force airman second class eyed his clothes and made a mocking grin while he drove them in a jeep to the main gate. He only nodded when he started to get out and Wolf told him to wait. He was silent as Wolf told him to negotiate a cyclo ride to the Caravel Hotel on Place Lam Son. If he was surprised he was not to go to his old headquarters in the MAC-SOG villa on Rue Pasteur, he didn't show it. He *was* surprised, but didn't say anything except "Yes, sir," when Wolf handed him a large French-style hotel key and told him to continue by himself to the room listed on the key in the Caravel.

"After you locate your room and look around," Wolf said, "go to the American Embassy on Thong Nhut and have a seat in the cafeteria. A big guy named Chef Hostettler will bring you to me." Wolf checked his watch. "You got an hour. Be there at 1600."

Wolf watched Jim Mahoney walk toward the cyclos waiting nearby, then turned and motioned to the driver and told him to take him to the 7th Air Force Headquarters, where he kept the cubbyhole office.

Wolf remained confident with his selection of Mahoney, and felt that if anyone could pull off the deception, it would be his friend. They'd served together in combat, and although the Irishman was courageous to the point of recklessness, he was also bright and could think his way out of any situation, whether it required belligerence or blarney. He also knew what undercover was about. The combination—to Wolf—made him perfect for the situation at hand.

Mahoney had a robotic look on his face as he entered the hotel. A thin, ancient Vietnamese seated at the concierge desk looked away in disdain as the smelly American civilian with the unkempt clothing entered his territory. He certainly wasn't going to help him carry his baggage. Then he noticed he had no baggage. *Likely bound for the roof bar,* he told himself. *Rough-looking man. A construction worker in town to spend some money? Certainly not a reporter. But those awful clothes . . . obviously one of the long-hairs, the sleepy-faced ones the American soldiers call hippies.*

Mahoney took the elevator to the fourth floor and unlocked the door to view a modest room containing a single, white-linen-covered bed, a small wooden night table and lamp, a narrow

Formica desk and chair by the window, a straight-backed sitting chair, a tiny, tiled bath with a bidet, and a large teak armoire against a wall. He flipped a rotary switch, bringing an air conditioner mounted near the ceiling wheezing to life, and turned on the overhead fan. A carafe of water and two thin tumblers rested on an aluminum tray on the desk. Mahoney poured a glass and drank deeply. He took a breath, then drank the remainder of the water. Glass in hand, he stood at the window and looked out at the bustling traffic. Cyclos, small yellow and blue taxis, and Honda motor scooters vied with swarms of pedestrians for the right of way. He wished he had a cold beer, thought about going up to the bar on the roof terrace, and decided against it. Whatever Wolf Lochert wanted him for wouldn't include beer on his breath. He glanced at his watch, grimaced, then hurried downstairs and out into the heat and traffic, where he walked toward the American Embassy. The leisure suit jacket pulled at his shoulders and his feet felt naked and strange in the hard-soled sandals.

The fortresslike Embassy stood on well-manicured grounds, surrounded by a high wall that had been breached by the Viet Cong during the Tet offensive four years before. The quiet street outside was lined with tamarind trees.

The Marine Corps guards at the gate waved Mahoney inside after examining his military DD2A ID card. " 'Bout time for a haircut, isn't it, Sarge?" one said, and the other made a mocking grin at his clothes, saying, "Cute, really cute." Mahoney paused going through the gate and gave them the look the IRA reserved for British royalty. "Heh, heh, just kidding," a Marine said.

Mahoney entered the compound. After identifying himself to the Marine at the counter in the lobby, he was directed to the snack bar, where he seated himself with the latest *Stars & Stripes* and a cup of coffee. He heard the sounds of battle again, so fresh in his mind, as he read the headlines stating that the Reds were only sixty miles from Saigon. He made a derisive sound in his throat as he read further.

Glancing around, Mahoney noticed he wasn't dressed so differently after all. Not like the Embassy types, of course. Those guys wore creased, summer-weight slacks, form-fitted short-sleeved white shirts and clip-on ties, and sat in small groups, smoked, and drank coffee. But there was also a carelessly dressed group of three men and two women, who were loudly arguing at two tables which they'd pulled together. The girls' stringy long hair hung down their backs, and they wore jeans and sandals. The men were in loose-fitting shirts open to their navel, with gold chains, bell bottom trousers, and sandals like the ones Lochert had given him. The girls glanced his way and offered welcoming grins. Mahoney heard them laugh about some military briefing fiasco at the Public Affairs office, and how they'd better get going if they were to make today's five o'clock follies. They were newsies, Mahoney decided.

Five minutes later a broad-shouldered man in a short-sleeved white shirt and dark pants asked him if he was Jim Mahoney. He said he was. The man shook his hand and asked him to follow, said he was Chef Hostettler.

Hostettler led Mahoney out of the snack bar, up some stairs, then past another guard post, where he showed his badge and had to get a temporary one for Mahoney. Finally, he led the way through an unmarked, thick door covered on the inside with a fine copper mesh.

"Welcome to the safest room in Saigon," Wolf Lochert boomed. "Take a chair, Jim." Lochert was seated at the end of a ten-place conference table. He'd changed from fatigues to a light sport shirt and tan slacks, but still looked exactly like what he was: a grizzled combat veteran trying to look comfortable in incongruous civilian clothes. Mahoney noted the weapons' bulge at each calf. So far he had not said a word. He'd been told to shut up enough times that day.

"You met Chef Hostettler," Wolf said. "Examine his face and pay attention. You'll be seeing him from time to time. He's an Air Force light colonel who works for the Defense Intelligence Agency. He wanted to get out and become some kind of a gourmet cook, but he decided we had some unfinished business here."

"Yeah," Chef Hostettler growled. *Prisoners of war,* was what he was thinking.

Wolf waved his arm around the small room. The walls crowded the table, and it had a low acoustical ceiling with embedded fluorescent lights. "This is a safe room," Wolf said. "Walls are covered by copper mesh so it can't be bugged. They restrict access and sweep it every four hours just in case."

That was it! Enough dumb conversation. Mahoney couldn't stand it anymore. He felt as if he might explode, and the words came tumbling forth. "Colonel, sir, mighty Wolf, if you don't for good gracious, cripes almighty tell me what the macky smack is going on, I'm going to jump out of my macky smacking skin."

Wolf Lochert did a rare thing—he banged out a belly laugh. The last time he'd done that, combat-hardened GIs began diving under tables, thinking they'd heard incoming. Wolf got up and put his arm around Mahoney's shoulders.

"I was rough on you, Mahoney, and I'll tell you why. You were as close to a guy being shell-shocked as I've come across after that mortar went off behind you, and I needed you to get your act straight in a hurry. Then, out at the base, I didn't want to be seen coming here with you, and I couldn't tell you why till we got here. Sorry, but I had to do it the way I did."

Mahoney looked at him with a doubtful expression. "I think you just like beating on me."

"Sure, 'cause you're so cute." He took his arm from Mahoney's shoulders. "Here's how it is. You're working for me now, so you do as I tell you." Wolf pulled an identification card from his shirt pocket. He flipped it to Mahoney, who caught it and read that, according to MACOI Form 3, JOURNALIST IDENTIFICATION, he was a newspaper journalist accredited by MACV and was to be provided privileges accorded thereto by all military installations. Upon expiry, six months hence, the card could be renewed if subject journalist continued to meet all the requirements.

Mahoney made a cynical smile. "Okay, Wolf. What's the joke? This belongs to some hippie newsie."

"It's yours. And that room at the Caravel is yours. And so's the pot in a cigarette pack in a desk drawer there. Let your hair grow. You are now a hippie newsie—and it's no joke, Jim."

Sergeant First Class James P. Mahoney settled slowly into one of the chairs. "You've got to be out of your mind. Me, a hippie journalist? I broke one of them guys' arm in Givral's Cafe one time. I can never *be* one of them. And these clothes?" He held his arms out, displaying the despised leisure suit. "They're awful! I look like a Hollywood fairy."

Lochert dug a gold chain out of his pocket and tossed it to Mahoney. "Put that on. You know about cover and concealment. This isn't the first time we used you to snoop around."

Mahoney caught the chain with a deft movement. "Not as a *hippie*." His voice became brittle with indignation. "If you think I'm going to—"

"Shut up and listen, *Scheisskopf,*" Wolf said and nodded to Chef Hostettler, who began to speak.

"What we are about to talk about is SI, level three—which means not only is it compartmentalized and higher than Top Secret, but you've got to sign that you will *never* disclose *any* information at *any* time to *any*body whether you are on active duty or retired." He pushed a pen and paper at Mahoney that was ready for his signature.

Mahoney saw where failure to comply with the regulation could result in a fine not to exceed $10,000 and/or a jail sentence not to exceed five years. He made a snorting sound and slid the paper back to Chef. "Now I know you're outta your minds. I wouldn't sign that even if I could find out I'm the sole heir to the Pope's church."

"How about if it's helping our POWs?" Chef said quietly.

Mahoney's eyes narrowed and he grew a grim expression. He quietly pulled the paper back, lifted the U.S. Government ballpoint pen, and signed.

Chef shook his hand. "Welcome to Wolf Lochert's music appreciation course." He took his seat across from Mahoney and looked intent. "We'll start with lesson one. There's a choir in Hanoi, and Caruso is the choirmaster."

Chapter 7

The maître d'hôtel immediately recognized Angie Vick, but he required a few seconds more to flip through his mental Rolodex before placing her escort, Courtland Bannister. He beamed and personally led the way to a prominent table, where they would be on display. They made a handsome couple, the svelte, green-eyed English performer, and Court Bannister, scion of wealthy movie star Sam Bannister and . . . hmmm yes, some kind of military officer. Like most Americans, the maître d' had been entranced by Angie Vick in her popular television adventure series. Also like most Americans, he had no idea she was an accomplished Shakespearean actress, although he'd been told she was in town for a stage performance.

"I would prefer over there," Court Bannister said, indicating a secluded corner table. The maître d' looked pained but complied. Their waiter appeared instantly and took their order, while trying not to stare at Angie Vick. Tall, she was resplendent in a simple, off-white silk dress under a dark-blue jacket. Her shoulder-length auburn hair barely brushed the collar. An opera-length rope of pearls at her neck and matching bracelets completed her

149

ensemble. Bannister wore gray slacks, a blue blazer with four gold buttons on each sleeve, over a light-blue shirt. A dark-blue ascot was at his throat. He ordered a white wine, Angie Vick a piece of dry toast and a cup of Chinese tea. After the waiter departed, she reached across the table and squeezed his arm.

"Oh, Court, it's so *good* to see you again. I wish I could stay longer, but I must be there no later than seven. The curtain goes up at eight." She spoke with the accent of the sophisticated English upper class, yet her tone was rich and without nasalness. Her perfectly proportioned nose bore no trace of the elkine aristocracy which had become so prominent through the centuries.

It was early and there were only four patrons in the room. They, of course, also instantly identified her as the female star of the British TV series *The Adventurers*. Although her escort looked familiar, they could not place him.

Their order arrived. Court sampled the wine while Angie ate a small portion of toast and took the smallest sip of tea.

"Can't do any more, you see," she said. "Too much liquid and I have to spend a penny right in the middle of Act Two. Too much food and my body stocking bulges in quite the wrong places."

"Body stocking?" Court said.

"You haven't seen the play?"

He shook his head. She was in town to play Heloise in the play *Abelard and Heloise*. In a much-publicized major scene, she stretched out—seemingly naked—on the stage. Court had seen her name in an ad and left his name and telephone number at the theater. They'd known each other for years.

"It's a flesh-toned affair, and"—Angie raised an exquisite eyebrow—"it's frightfully tight. Let me know when you can come. I'll have a ticket waiting at the box office." She smiled, graceful curved lips with a hint of lipstick revealing even white teeth. "Or should it be 'two'?"

He shook his head. "Just one."

"No one special?"

"No."

"Sorry to hear about your divorce."

"That was a long time ago."

"Is she still on the stage?"

Court Bannister's former wife, Charmaine, had been a Hollywood dancer-actress when they'd married.

"Last I heard."

She looked at him over her teacup. "What happened, Court?"

He shrugged. "I was at the university, studying hard, and she decided she wanted her career back."

"No children?"

"No."

"Regrets? Recriminations?"

"Not really. We both had things to do. We're friends." He paused, and a shadow flickered upon his features. "There was someone, but that was later." Blonde Susan Boyle's image appeared in his mind.

"Marvelous. You *do* deserve a good woman, you know. Anything going to happen? Marriage, perhaps?"

"No. She, ah, died."

She showed immediate concern. "Oh, my dear . . . I'm *so* sorry."

"I'm more or less over it." *Liar. Four years and I still howl her name at the moon.*

She made an effort to change the conversation. "What were you doing at University?"

He leaned back. "You know how I was brought up: Europe, Hollywood. There were no financial worries and I never thought of college. After a few years in the Air Force I decided I wanted to get, I should say I *needed* to get, an engineering degree." He took a deep swallow of his wine.

"But why?"

"You have beautiful eyes. Such a deep green."

"So I've been told," she said, lightly discarding the compliment. "Why the late desire to get a degree, Court? You were what—early thirties?"

"Thirty-two. I wanted to be an astronaut. To do that, by regulation I had to be a graduate of the test pilot school at Edwards Air Force Base. And to be accepted at Edwards, I had to have an engineering degree." He smiled. "You're more beautiful now than you were at eighteen."

"I've been told that, too. I seem to remember reading someplace you were a test pilot, but I don't recall seeing your name on any astronaut roll."

He tossed his head back. "I suppose not. I didn't do any testing, much less get into space."

"Why?"

"I barely graduated from the test pilot school."

"Why?"

"Let me ask you a question. Why do you always say 'why'? You're pumping me, you know. Why so?"

She reached across and touched his hand. "We've known each other for so long, and I'm interested. You've led a fabulously fascinating life. You're a genuine hero, Courtland Bannister."

"Not in your country."

She laughed lightly. "Nobody's a hero in England anymore."

"Not even Bertrand Russell?"

She made a derisive snort. "As much as I am against your war, that old lickspittle is a loony. That phony trial of his in Sweden against America was the limit. *He's* the limit."

"This war has produced some weird ones on both sides of the Atlantic."

Angie picked at the tiny portion of toast. "You haven't told me what you are doing in Washington."

He made a sardonic face. "Sitting at a miserable desk when I should be flying."

"In Vietnam?"

"If at all possible. Look, let's get off me. Let *me* ask a few questions."

She gave a small laugh. "I've led a dull life, I'm afraid."

"Not according to the papers and magazines."

"They tend to exaggerate. You should know."

"I read that you married a volatile Hungarian." He grinned. "Let's see—the Hungarian Hurricane? Wasn't that what they called him?"

"Indeed." Angie rolled her eyes. "I felt I needed some direction in my life and thought he could provide it. I threw him out when he began trying to dictate my wardrobe and which cosmetics I should use." She looked at him. "You're amused?"

"I was thinking about us. When we met, what happened."

"You mean what *didn't* happen."

He pursed his lips. "Perhaps."

She arched her back nicely. "Bed can make or break a budding friendship. You spurned me, darling."

Court chuckled. "I didn't spurn you. I just didn't know what to do."

"You mean you hadn't *done* it before?" She gave him a disbelieving look as she replaced her teacup in its saucer.

"You were different. I wanted it right."

"So we ended up doing nothing."

"That was how it was . . . then." As he realized what he was inferring, a feeling of betrayal of Susan edged into his mind. *Why am I making such leading remarks?* he wondered. The implication hung heavy as musk in the air. Angie gave him a warm smile and allowed her fingers to rest on his arm. "I'll be here for three weeks." She made a contemplative gesture with her mouth. "Let's see, it's been twenty years?"

He nodded. "Twenty years since we met."

"Twenty years since we tried." She made a rich chuckle and circled his wineglass with a moist finger. "If at first you don't succeed . . ." She waited for his response.

"You want me to say, 'try, try again.' "

She arched a questioning eyebrow.

He responded with a short laugh.

She made a prim face. "Well, *excuse* me. There are, you know, men who simply *lust* for my body."

He took her hand, then lightly caressed the slender wrist. "You are very special." The difficult memory of Susan surfaced once more and he uttered a hardly audible sigh. "Look, you'll be here three more weeks, and we'll have time to talk. A lot has happened in the last few years."

"So serious?" She became contemplative and her forehead furrowed slightly. "Do you think I'm throwing myself at you? Perhaps trying to line someone up just for cuddles between shows?" Her eyes narrowed, green ice. "I could become very cross if that is what you thought."

He squeezed her hand lightly. "You know that's not what I think."

"Maybe I've had a lot happen to me as well, Court." She leaned forward to speak in a low voice. "Maybe I need the reassurance and warmth of an old friend. Perhaps . . ." She stopped herself. "Damn," she cried, "now that *does* sound like I want a few cuddles, does it not?"

"There's nothing wrong with wanting cuddles, Angie. I'm searching for the same thing."

She gave him a slow smile.

He cocked his head at her. "Remember just after we first met, how I taught you to play liar's dice. You were studying at the Royal Academy."

She laughed. "Quit trying to change the subject. But of course, I remember. We were at Columbia House."

"You became an accomplished liar in a very short time."

She laughed gaily. "Oh, I remember perfectly well. You were showing me the American Officers' Club on Oxford Street in London."

"God, we were naive."

"And innocent."

"That too, I suppose."

"Well, 'ow 'bout it, 'arry?"

" 'Ow 'bout whot, Liza?"

"If oi 'ave ter *tell* yer, it ain't."

He signaled for the bill, grinning. "I'll pick you up tonight after the last act. Then we'll take our clothes off and see what happens."

She gave him an exaggerated leer. "Your place or mine? I'm at the Hay-Adams."

"If you're going to argue about it, the hell with it."

She wore a happy smile as they left the dining room.

0145 Hours Local, Saturday 17 June 1972
John Jay Suite, Hay-Adams Hotel
Washington, D.C.

Angie's voice held a slight trill. "Court, that was a *very* good romp." She moved to where he sat, naked, in a red lounge chair. She was one of those few women who can walk about unclothed, yet maintain the poise and grace of a fashion model. She handed him a glass of Chardonnay and watched him sip. Actors and actresses speak on stage with timbre, to evoke emotion. Off-stage, some use tones best suited to subway chatter. Not so Angie Vick. As an eighteen-year-old, her voice had been rich. It was now even more so.

"A delightfully English word," he muttered.

"Romp?"

"Romp."

Her voice cooled. "That's all you have to say? 'A delightfully English word'?" She paused thoughtfully, then picked up the thick terry-cloth hotel robe and pulled it on. "I suddenly feel quite naked." She held herself, watching him with a thoughtful look.

He took a sip of wine, placed the glass on the side table, then rose and put on a matching robe. "Sorry," he said awkwardly. "It *was* a good romp. I'm not showing my appreciation."

She moved to his side. "Court, for God's sake, that isn't what I meant and you know it. What's the *matter* with you? We are old friends who just had a reasonably wonderful time in bed and you're being dark and broody. Did I *do* or *say* something wrong?"

He took her hands and pulled her into his lap as he sat back on the lounge, trying to display a wolfish grin. *"Au contraire,* dear Angie, you didn't do anything wrong. You were more than perfect." The grin faded and he became serious. "It's me. I'm only half here." He stroked her hair. "I'm not functioning well these days."

She nuzzled. "Well, there is not anything wrong with your . . . uhm . . . *apparatus.* That part of you is functioning *very* well, indeed."

"Thanks to you. You could melt statues with a touch, Angie."

She lay back, then reached over his shoulder and switched off the bedside light. The room was cast into semidarkness, illuminated only by a single dim light filtering in from the adjacent room. "You want to tell me about it?" Her voice was low.

He put her off. "It's two in the morning, and I put in a long day."

"Where did you say you work?"

"The Pentagon." He said it without enthusiasm.

"Oh yes. The big Yank war machine?"

"Something like that."

"You're not the type who sits well at a desk. Is that why you are so morose?"

"Partly." He grew evasive. "It's late—damn near dawn."

"Do you have to go to work?"

"Hah. We don't work much on weekends." He stirred and she got up. "We don't even work much during the week." He stood in the gloom and walked to the window. "That's not one hundred percent true. A few of the guys there work damned hard."

"I should think you'd be happy to be here, away from combat." She sat on the bed, a leg tucked under her—a still shadow in the dark room.

"You'd think so, wouldn't you."

"But that is not the way you are."

"That's not the way I am."

"God, but I'm glad I'm not in love with you." She leaned back.

"So am I." He'd said it without thinking.

"This is not a nice conversation. Are you sure we are friends?"

He nodded into the window. "Friends of the best sort, and I'm sorry I'm such a dead loss tonight." Lightning made a tentative flicker as a thunderstorm approached the city from the west.

"Then if we are friends and you don't have to work tomorrow, why not tell me what is going on in that devilish Yank brain of yours?"

He saw the first rain spatter in the lighted circles of the street lamps below. As the thunderstorm moved closer, he thought of other rains he'd watched. Rain dappling the beach at his Venice apartment in Los Angeles, the knee-high silver splash of Asian rainstorms at Bien Hoa and Ubon, the rain pellets thop-thopping on the broad leaves and drumming on palm fronds as he'd hidden in the Laotian jungle after being shot down.

"I love the rain," he said in a tentative voice, "but I also hate and almost fear it. We have this thing, the rain and I. It cleanses my memories and I feel better for a while, but I also know . . . someday I'll die in it."

"Good God, Court."

"You asked." He picked up his glass and drained it. "There was this girl, see, and—"

"Aha, I knew it. Whatever the problem, *cherchez la femme.*"

He picked up the wine bottle by the neck and took a pull. "And these guys, these military guys. I think about them."

"Guys?"

He returned to the window, bottle in hand, and stared out. "They're dead."

"You *are* the depressed war hero, aren't you?"

He turned, feeling a flash of anger. "Jesus Christ! I thought you wanted me to talk. So I'm talking and you're making fun of me. What's that quaint old Brit phrase? Fuck off. Why don't you just fuck off?" He was breathing hard and was surprised at his reaction.

"I can't, silly, this is *my* room."

He turned the bed lamp on, reached for the wine bottle, and

poured a fresh glass for her and for himself. "Then *I'll* just fuck off." *Christ, why am I doing this? I thought I had everything neatly put away.*

"When was the last time you talked about her? What is her name?"

"Susan, and it's not *is,* it's *was.* She's one of those gone dead on me." The image of her sleek body and long blonde hair swept over him, and for a moment he couldn't speak. Angie saw his eyes glisten.

"Was she killed in the war?"

"Cancer." He took another pull at his wine and told Angie the story of Susan Boyle. How she'd not wanted him around when the final stages set in, and had gone into hiding after the wonderful, final time together in Bangkok. How she'd left a note explaining what she was doing and why. How she'd written that she loved him too much for him to see her ravaged by disease.

"Your father could have located her for you, could he not?"

"She asked me not to try to find her." He was surprised how even his voice had become.

Angie frowned thoughtfully, then held up her glass. "To Susan."

"To Susan," he said. They drank and she tossed her glass at a wall, where it shattered.

"Why did you do that?" Court asked quietly.

"I love grand gestures, and from what you said, she must have been a grand girl."

Court flung his own glass into the same spot on the wall. Glass shards fell silently onto the thick rug.

"She'd appreciate this," he said quietly.

"You and I?"

"Yes."

"Making love?"

"Absolutely. She wanted me to go on." He felt more relaxed, as if talking about her helped mend his torn heart.

"But you haven't, have you?"

"Not really."

She frowned. "God, Court, I'm feeding you lines? Why don't you use your own script?"

"I don't even know if I have one."

She frowned.

"Let me explain." He sat on the lounge chair, facing her where she sat on the bed. "A lot has happened to me. Maybe more than I'm man enough to handle. I've put three years into this goddamned war and now Susan's gone, a lot of the guys I flew with are gone, and even my own father and I are at odds. As far as my half brother goes . . . well, that doesn't really count, I suppose. We never were close." He sipped his wine and frowned, knowing he was not getting to the point. "I guess . . . I'm only happy when I'm with the troops—my military friends—and we're . . . " He stopped and stared.

Angie spoke quietly. "You are hard on yourself, Court. You're man enough to handle anything, even the losses. As far as you say 'being with the troops,' I understand. I'm happiest when I'm caught up in a play, thinking of nothing else and dealing with those in the play or supporting it." She looked at him. "What about the people where you work?"

"At the Pentagon? Most are career-happy and perfectly satisfied to be right where they are—far, far away from the hostile gunfire in Vietnam. They keep themselves busy worrying about where their next top-block rating is coming from. The others, those like me, don't get along well with them. We see things in terms of what we can do to help the guys who are flying the airplanes, who are over fighting the war. We aren't considered realistic."

"If you dislike it so much, why did you come? Why didn't you simply stay in Vietnam?"

He chuckled. "It isn't quite like you, when your agent finds you a booking and you go somewhere to learn your lines and find out where front-stage is located. I have to go where they send me, and this time they sent me to fly a gray steel desk at the Pentagon."

"I should think they'd be happy to have experienced people like you in Vietnam. I read once where you are called the Ivory Ace."

He raised a sarcastic brow. "Do you even know what it means?"

"Yes, silly. You shot down four aircraft that were seen to hit the ground, and many more that were sort of *probably* shot down."

She'd surprised him with her knowledge. "You *are* informed."

"I do have a brother in the RAF, you know. He has been keeping me informed."

"Oh yes. Hugh. I remember." He rested his chin on his fists, then blew out an exasperated breath. "I haven't been all that nice to you, have I?"

"Do you feel better?"

He nodded. Angie was the first person to whom he had revealed his inner thoughts since his friend Flak Apple had been shot down.

They were silent for a moment, then she slid down and patted the bed next to her. "Want to spend the night?"

"What will the concierge think?"

"The concierge can get stuffed."

They'd made love, slept, made love again, and were talking the straightforward thoughts and ideas that occur at four in the morning. They veered through his love of opera music ("Mimi's Waltz" and "One Fine Day" were two favorites, he told her), her love of Shakespeare (she adored *Midsummer Night's Dream* and *Hamlet*), to the current political scenes in England and the United States (messy). They lay still for a while.

"These are not your basic after-love topics, are they?" Angie said.

He chuckled. "Not exactly."

Silence, then, muffled, "Do you do it for the glory?"

"No," he said, knowing what she was talking about. "There really is no glory. We like to shoot from ambush, from the sun, from their six o'clock. No more Marquis of Queensberry rules, like there were over France in the Great War to End All Wars and the cockpits were open."

"What about being scared? Haven't you been terrified once or twice?"

"No more than you."

"It's not the same thing. Sure, I get fearful sometimes before going on, or if something goes wrong on the stage, but it is not a life-threatening situation like yours."

"It's the same. If you have time to think about it, your hands get sweaty, your body gets clammy, your stomach starts churning and your heart begins to thump in your chest."

She made a lewd trill. "I get that when you touch me."

"You're a glutton."

"But you are right. I have had those feelings before a new

show, but of course, the show must go on."

"That's what we try to tell new pilots, Fear can paralyze you, but you must start moving, do something, *anything,* even if it's wrong. Start moving, then the brain will take over."

"You hope."

"That comes with experience. Often things happen so fast you haven't time to reason it out, you just react. Time seems to slow down, and everything is in slow motion. The shells come lazily floating up, or you see the plane you're fighting and it's as if you're viewing it all from above. It's as if you have some unique world you can slip into when danger threatens. Some seem to have that more than others."

"And you?"

"I'm still alive."

She cocked her head, a wing of auburn hair over one eye. "And others aren't. You seem so callous. Are you really that way?"

"When I'm flying combat I am. I need all my concentration focused on the mission." He made a derisive sound. "Of course I'm not flying those anymore."

"Get rid of your anger, Court."

"Anger?"

"You seethe with it. It boils just below the surface."

"Let's drop it."

She sat up and massaged his shoulders.

"That feels good. I'm coming to life."

She bent to touch him. "You are indeed."

For the next while, as they made love, Court Bannister forgot about anger and war. When they finished, they quickly drifted into deep slumber together, still entwined and one.

1712 Hours Local, Saturday 17 June 1972
F-105G—Airborne Near Vinh, Route Pack Two
Democratic Republic of Vietnam

The two huge fighters with their stubby wings and awesome power knifed through the warm air at the speed of sound, turning and twisting to create a difficult target for enemy gunners. Wild Weasels, searching for the elusive and deadly surface-to-air

missile sites which would threaten the twenty-four aircraft sent
to attack the well-camouflaged petroleum-storage area immediately northwest of Vinh. Offset to their right, back at their
five o'clock, flew Condor Two and Condor Three, two F-4E
Phantoms.

It was a true hunter-killer mission. The supply of big AGM-78
antiradar missiles (ARMs) was low at Korat, so the F-105Gs
were loaded with the much smaller and less capable AGM-45
Shrike ARMs. They were the hunters. Both they and the F-4Es,
the killers, carried CBU-52s, pudgy, bomb-shaped cannisters
packed with hundreds of baseball-sized cluster bomblets that
exploded on contact.

Unlike the other fighters and bombers flying combat, the Wild
Weasels were not restricted to a specific route or target. They
roved the area, searching for SAM sites, and when they found
one, they pounced.

The sky was deep blue, and a happy Captain Woodrow G.
"Bear" Woods scanned the airspace about the aircraft happily,
soaking in the beauty as he kept an eye out for MiGs. They'd
just passed over the verdant mountains near Keo Nua Pass, on
the Laos–North Vietnam border, and were heading directly
for the coast of North Vietnam. The redhead loved the thrill
of flying in the fighter, and he was a natural for the mission
to which he'd been assigned. In the front seat his pilot, Tuck
Tucker, kept up his own scan.

Woods had come to the Air Force from a migratory and modest childhood in various small lumber towns of the northwest
coast, but he'd brought with him a passion for learning and a
gift for understanding technical subjects. He'd been captivated
by flying and airplanes since age nine, when he'd gawked at Air
National Guard F-51 Mustangs and F-80 Shooting Stars dashing
about the skies near Portland, Oregon. After graduating from
high school early, he'd worked in a sawmill job for six months
until he'd turned seventeen, the minimum age for enlistment.
Woods had raised his hand and repeated the vow eagerly, for
he'd craved adventure and had visions of someday becoming
a pilot. After acing battery after battery of aptitude tests, Airman Woods was selected for and attended nucleonics training
in Denver, Colorado, and Livermore Labs, south of Oakland,
California, then was sent to the Armed Forces Special Weapons

Project, a Top Secret nuclear research and development facility located near Albuquerque. Although the AFSWP work fascinated him, he'd knuckled down to night school study, and by the time he'd been selected for Officers Candidate School, had finished three years at the University of New Mexico. After six frantic months of OCS at Lackland Air Force Base, Texas, he'd attended his final year at the University of Texas under Project Bootstrap, and earned a degree in physics.

Lieutenant Woodrow Woods (he'd not yet gone to Wild Weasels and gained the backseater nickname of Bear) had been ready and eager for flight training, and was utterly deflated when he found that the years of intense study had marred the vision in his right eye, and he could no longer qualify.

He'd worked for two years at Wright Patterson Field, applying his engineering skills to projects at the Wright Laboratory, and was known as innovative and bright, but he'd never lost sight of his dream. Then, in 1965, he'd learned about a combat test program involving a pilot and EWO crew, flying two-seat F-100s to locate surface-to-air missile sites.

He could not be a pilot, but Woods could become an electronic warfare officer, and in the Wild Weasel fighters, with his technical knowledge, he knew he had a lot to contribute. Even before a Weasel team located and destroyed the first SAM site, to show the concept worked, First Lieutenant Woodrow G. Woods had been accepted for navigator training at Mather Air Force Base, in Sacramento, California. He had finished the course in the summer of '66, and had learned that the Wild Weasels had converted to F-105 Thunderchiefs, when he was admitted into electronic warfare school. He'd graduated at the top of his class, and expected to get his choice of available assignments, as was the traditional right of the top grad . . . but it was not to be.

A colonel at Wright-Patterson had examined one of Lieutenant Woods' suggestions for a technical project, and immediately pulled the proper strings to have him reassigned there. His suggestion developed into a major project called Have Blue—and Woods had been disconsolate to learn that all participants in the project were permanently barred from flying combat. Which did not keep him from plotting a way. When program management was moved to a test base in Florida, he'd flown to the Personnel Center at Randolph Air Force Base, near San Antonio, Texas, and connived to have his orders changed. He'd pulled it off, first cajoling his way into an assignment as an instructor at the electronic warfare school, then—just three months later, since there was such a shortage of volunteers for the dangerous mission—he'd been accepted for Wild Weasels. The circuitous route had taken almost five years, and Woods was by then a fairly senior captain.

For the past month he'd been the chief electronic-warfare officer at Korat Air Base, replacing his friend Smitty Smythe. He was now teamed permanently with Captain Tuck Tucker, who had developed into one of the best pilots in the 17th Wild Weasel Squadron. The week before, they'd been credited with their third official SAM site kill, and just afterward he'd been told his name had been submitted for early promotion to major. Things were going very well for Captain Woodrow G.—alias "Bear"—Woods.

Does a bear shit in the woods? This Bear is the Woods!
Yeah!

Tuck Tucker broke into Woods' reverie, radioing for his second element, the pair of F-4E "killers," to drop farther back into trail. They were to fly behind and higher, and keep their eyes glued so they could eyeball the SAM sites the Wild Weasels might stir up.

"Got anything back there, Bear?" Tuck asked.

"Not much. There's a SAM at our ten o'clock, but he's distant. No threats yet."

"Nothing from Vinh?"

"Not yet." The Vinh area air defense commander was a cagey one. He had two SAM battalions, meaning four or five SAM batteries, each with six missile launchers, at his disposal, and he orchestrated their efforts like a maestro. Woods hadn't expected anything from him yet. He was likely sitting back and getting inputs from the acquisition radars and waiting until the Weasels came closer.

They could deceive some of the North Viet operators, but the commander at Vinh was damned good. He seemed to know precisely which flights were Wild Weasels, and he could use the waiting game—delay firing until the Weasels were running low on fuel or had departed.

"Thirty miles to go," Tuck muttered, although a Doppler

readout was available in both cockpits.

"You going to try the new tactic?"

"Yeah. We'll be pulling up in one minute."

Tuck wanted to try lofting a Shrike antiradiation missile in the direction of Vinh just as they came into the SAM firing zone. Tossing it, using the soaring speed of the aircraft, extended the Shrike's normal short range. It had been tried before, but not recently. If they hit a SAM radar with the missile, it was all the better, but that was not the only reason for the maneuver. Tuck felt the North Viets wouldn't be able to resist firing missiles at a fat target like they'd become. The F-4E killers would stay down at medium altitude and keep their eyes out, so'd they spot the firing.

"Condors Three and Four," called Tuck. "Prepare to swing out wide."

"Ah, roger, lead," the F-4E pilot responded in his Kentucky drawl.

They were flying at five-ninety knots. At twenty-two miles, Tuck pushed the F-105's throttle up and outboard. After a slight pause the big J-75 engine's afterburner caught, and they were booted forward. Tuck raised the nose 15 degrees and they began the long climb.

"Through twelve thousand," Tuck said, again unnecessarily.

"Still no signals," Bear Woods replied. He pulled his eyes from the receivers and scanned carefully outside. If MiGs were sighted, all the Thud pilot had to do was duck the nose. Nothing in the sky could keep up with a Thud headed for the deck.

They climbed through sixteen thousand feet, with five-eighty knots of forward energy. A signal rose on the primary scope in the SAM radar frequency. Woods deftly analyzed and correlated. "We've got a tracking SAM radar at eleven o'clock."

"Got it," muttered Tuck, easing into 20 degrees of turn. The preselected Shrike missile seeker began to chatter as it picked up the SAM's signal, and the Shrike needle quivered and pointed. He adjusted until the enemy radar was dead ahead.

"Condor Two, shoot with me," Tuck radioed, telling his Wild Weasel wingman to fly his wing and fire his missile when he did.

"They're preparing to launch," Bear Woods muttered conversationally. "They've got us centered and . . . they're boosting power."

SAM launch was imminent. Still Tucker delayed firing the Shrike. He wanted to be closer.

"Valid launch, twelve o'clock," said Woods over hot mike.

"Roger." Tuck continued to soar. They passed through 27,000 feet.

"Condor Three has the missile launch in sight at our ten o'clock. Three of 'em, one after the other. Prepare to drop, four," called the F-4E leader.

"Four," acknowledged the F-4 wingman.

"Better think of maneuvering, Tuck." Woods said it conversationally, but Tucker knew to trust him. Bear Woods was damned good.

"Prepare to take it down, Two," Tuck radioed his wingman. He fired the Shrike, then paused for a split second as the missile dropped away and he saw it arcing upward. "Shotgun!" he announced over radio, then wrenched the control stick, rolling the airplane upside down, and immediately pulled the nose into a steep dive.

"I . . . ngghh . . . got 'em . . . ngghh . . . in sight," grunted Bear Woods as they pulled G's.

"Nghhh . . . yeah," Tuck responded, gritting his teeth with the effort and trying to keep the lead SAM in view. The missile flashed by at two o'clock, and he pulled hard the opposite way.

"Second SAM's clear," gasped Woods. Tuck hadn't seen that one, but the third one was now damned close.

"Jesus," Tuck muttered as the last SAM exploded only a hundred yards after passing by. He began to pull out, breathing hard.

As soon as they'd leveled at 7,000 feet, Bear Woods began his analysis. "We stirred 'em up. Four SAM radars on the air now. Nine, eleven, two, and four o'clock. Whoops! The one at eleven just went off the air."

Condors Three and Four were pulling off their target at their eleven o'clock, so Tuck radioed that the SAM radar was off the air. "Good work," he told them. They'd obviously destroyed the site with their CBUs.

"We've got a tracking SAM at one o'clock now. He's launching," said Bear Woods.

Tuck radioed his wingman, "Condor Two, we've got a valid launch at one o'clock."

"Got 'em in sight?" asked the Bear.

Tuck saw the flurry of smoke and dust on the ground several miles distant. "Got 'em in sight," he confirmed. Another missile was launched, then another. Tuck pushed the throttle forward as he entered a slight dive. "Condor Two, we'll dodge 'em and bomb the site," he radioed.

"Roger." Two's voice was charged with adrenaline.

Tuck waited, eyeing the lead missile which dropped off its booster and accelerated to blistering speed. The closure rate was in excess of four times the speed of sound. He tried to keep the missile in the same spot on his windscreen, but the pursuit angle somehow seemed wrong.

"He's tracking Number Two," confirmed Bear Woods.

"He's tracking you, Condor Two," Tuck immediately announced. He pulled out wide, and the SAM continued to streak toward his wingman.

Condor Two's tone was high with fright. "Roger, I don't have—"

"Break, Two!" Tuck yelled.

Number Two turned hard right instead of into the SAM. "I don't—"

The missile detonated less than a hundred yards from Condor Two. The F-105 slewed sideways and torched as fragments sliced through the airplane.

"Jesus," someone radioed in an awed voice. A wing tore away and the fiercely burning airplane started to tumble earthward.

There were several seconds of quiet.

"Got the SAM site in view?" asked Bear Woods, his voice firm.

With effort, Tuck pulled his eyes earthward, away from the awful vision of his burning friends. He had trouble focusing for a moment, then peered hard and finally saw the drifting smoke and dust from the SAM launch. "Yeah," he muttered.

"We've got SAM signals at eleven, two, and four o'clock," said Bear Woods. "The one at two is tracking us. That's the one you're looking at. Same one that just fired."

Tuck began to climb to 10,000 feet to set up for bomb delivery, keeping his eyes glued on the SAM site. Large, dark flak bundles burst about them as they came closer.

"We've got correlation. He's preparing to launch SAMs," said Woods.

Damn! Tuck really wanted to get this one. The bastard had just killed his wingman.

"Get him, Tuck. We're too close for him to hit us."

"Yeah," Tuck muttered as he remembered the SAM battery couldn't hit a close-in target. They needed at least ten kilometers before the boosters fell away. A hard smile grew on Tuck's face as he rechecked his weapons-release panel. He rolled, pulled, and the F-105 nosed over into its dive. They were going to kill somebody.

On the way home, after Tuck had radioed their success code to Red Crown, telling them they'd scored a double SAM kill, the three crews of Condor flight were quiet.

When they'd pressurized the cockpit and checked for leaks, Bear Woods switched off his oxygen, let his mask swing free, and lit a cigarette. The day had not ended well. The confirmed destruction of two sites was a feat, but the loss of their wingman drove the score into the negative column, at least for him. He'd not known these two nearly as well as he'd known Frizzell and Smitty, but at least those friends had a chance. These were dead men. No chutes. Both of the others had ejected—he'd heard their beepers himself—and Frizzell had now been confirmed by Hanoi as a POW. Nothing yet on Smitty, but sometimes the enemy were slow about such things. A niggling fear coursed through Woods. Not of bullets or fiery death. He'd long since mastered those. Of all the men he knew who were flying combat—except one—Smitty Smythe had been privy to the most sensitive secrets. If they somehow were to find out, and break him, and ask Smitty the right questions—the result might be devastating to the American military planners.

What about you? an inner voice questioned.

What about the Have Blue project?

Chapter 8

1330 Hours Local, Sunday 18 June 1972
Washington Monument
Washington, D.C.

It was early afternoon, and they trotted side by side on the Tidal Basin path under the canopy of Japanese cherry trees. Jet airlines were sliding down final approach to land at Washington National airport. They'd left Court's car, an immaculate, five-year-old white Corvette, parked on Independence Avenue.

"If I'd only worn shorts," Angie Vick puffed. She was in black tights and a burgundy turtleneck sweater. The temperature was in the low seventies, and the sun shone brightly in a sky marred by a few drifting white cumulus puff-clouds.

Court Bannister easily kept pace, in red gym shorts and a white T-shirt with the faded red letters SOS 17. "Then you'd get all the publicity you could handle. I can see it now: a seventy-point headline reading, 'British Sex Kitten Bares All.' "

"No, silly," she panted, "my tights are entirely too warm. Let's slow down for a bit," she said. Sweat had darkened her sweater around her arms and her waist. They began to walk.

"You seem cheerful this morning," she said.

"I'm having a great weekend."

"I hope I am helping."

"You are. More than you think."

"Am I, now?" She hopped out in front and walked backwards facing him. "How so?" she asked with a big smile.

"You've made me realize I've been unreasonable and a little childish."

"You? Unreasonable and childish? The great Court Bannister?" She fell in at his side, grasping his arm.

"I've been too damn introspective, too wrapped up in losses, and not considering the gains. Time to reappraise. Get on with life."

"Demob from the Air Force?"

"Perhaps. I've given it thought recently."

"To pilot those?" She pointed to a nose-high 727 a few hundred feet over the river, landing gear extended and ready to touch down at National.

"Maybe."

"Back to Hollywood?"

"Never," he growled. "You can't believe that place."

"Oh, yes I can."

"Try this. When I was acting in those Westerns—and I use the term 'acting' loosely—one of the producers wanted me for a major part in a Viking movie with Kirk Douglas. Said it would assure my career. Said with my blond hair and blue eyes, all I had to do was have my rear teeth pulled and my jaw broken and reset to give me higher cheekbones, and *then* I'd be more Viking than Leif Ericsson."

"You are joking, of course."

"Not at all. No, I wouldn't go back."

They walked in silence for a while. The sun was warm on their shoulders and arms.

"So what would you do if you left the service?" she said.

"Perhaps I'll live in France a while. Relax. Kayak down the Loire, barge the Seine."

"You sound as if you really do want to drop out."

He stopped and looked out over the water, resting his arms on the upper metal railing and a foot on the lower. "Maybe. I'm full of it up to here . . . the war, the military, the politicians, pulling six mental Gs trying to dodge SAMs from the Pentagon. Fighting the press and the protesters, the whole damn world it sometimes seems."

"Fighting them about the war?"

"The war, everything. I've about had it." He straightened up and they continued walking.

"You sound like you've truly convinced yourself to leave it."

"One minute I think so, the next I'm not sure."

They walked a long block in silence to Court's Corvette, where they retrieved towels and her purse from the trunk. They dried off, put the top down, and climbed in. He drove west on Independence, then stopped to turn north on 17th Street, headed toward the Washington Monument. As they waited, they heard a faint but growing rumble, interspersed with metallic voices spoken over a loudspeaker system.

"What do you suppose that is?" Angie Vick asked.

"Probably another protest of one kind or the other. Last week it was a bunch of Vietnam veterans raising hell around the Congress and the Pentagon."

"I saw it on the telly. Threw their medals at the Capitol steps. That's serious stuff, isn't it?"

"They're angry. Vietnam-vet unemployment is a third higher than the national average, they don't get anything close to the benefits the guys from World War Two received, and those who return to college are heckled and spit on by students and teachers as well."

"You Yanks do have your problems, don't you?"

He shifted into low gear, and the engine rumbled as they crawled forward. The crowd was now across 17th Street, streaming about the convertible like a river flowing past a protruding rock. They were—for the most part—orderly. Many who passed the car flashed the two-fingered V signal. A significant percentage, Court noted, were old enough to have sons in Vietnam. The mob changed as a crowd of young men and women passed, carrying signs and chanting as they headed toward the Washington Monument. As he passed the car, a young man grabbed the arm of the girl with him and swung her about.

"What do we have here? Hey, everybody, look what's goin' down." He eyed the Pentagon parking decal. The group swarmed about the Corvette like horseflies around a sweating stallion.

"Ho, Ho—Ho Chi Minh," they chanted, and began to rock the car in time to the beat. "Ho, Ho—Ho Chi Minh, Viet Cong is gonna win." They held the doors pressed shut.

Overcome by sudden rage, Court lifted himself, as if on a steel spring, tagging the first man to his left on the jaw. Those immediately about him screeched loudly, clawing and trying to drag Court from the car. Shreds of T-shirt ripped away as he twisted in the confines behind the wheel. He grabbed the nearest body and pulled him close—a human shield—holding him by his hair and the back of his belt as he pushed and maneuvered him against the grasping crowd. A fist banged off Court's ear and another jabbed toward his groin. Court released his shield and punched his right fist out, catching a tormentor flush on the mouth, feeling the front teeth give. The crowd grasped, then roared with rage as it became apparent that they'd soon have him pulled from his car and be able to get at him.

"Ho, Ho—Ho Chi Minh . . . " they chanted, and the rocking became more pronounced. The wheels relentlessly rose in the air and smashed down with rubbery plops.

From behind, Court heard Angie's cry of dismay as he felt himself being dragged over the edge of the door. Her voice roared with the fervor of a cornered lioness: *"You bloody bastards."*

"Glove compartment, tear gas," he yelled over his shoulder, hoping she heard.

"Right," she responded in a loud voice.

Court was pulled farther over the door before he heard a hissing sound, accompanied by a terrible acrid smell. The crowd closest to the Corvette began choking and squalling with rage, backpedaling away as they rubbed at streaming eyes. The hands released Court as a blast of gas released past him. He pulled himself back in and sank into the seat. Angie was half standing, grasping the windshield with one hand, face determined as she held the aerosol can of tear gas extended in the other.

"One step closer, you bastards, and you'll get it again," she yelled and waved the can about menacingly. The attackers stood well out of range, shaking their heads and trying to wipe the gas from their faces.

Court blinked away his own stream of tears and put the car in gear, squinting to see better. He gunned the engine, but found they could neither go forward nor back up without running into the thick crowd. As he looked behind, he saw several brilliant flashes, as if someone was shining a mirror at them.

"Move on, leave 'em alone, cool it," sounded an authoritative

voice. The swarm surged then, and their attackers were swept
away toward the Monument and a barely visible platform there.
Four mounted policemen appeared and took up positions around
the car. One leaned down and shouted, "This street is closed.
Park that thing and lock it. You ain't going nowhere. We'll stay
here while you get it buttoned up." The four policemen kept the
crowd away while Court and Angie got out, pulled up the top,
then locked the doors. The lead horseman made a half salute
and the four gingerly moved off into the crowd, their horses
blowing and prancing.

"You were fantastic," Court said to Angie as he retrieved their
towels from the trunk.

"You look awful," she said. "Scratches and blood everywhere." She dabbed at him with her towel. His chest was
bare, with only a tattered ring of T-shirt around his waist. She
frowned suddenly. "Why were you carrying that awful-smelling
stuff?"

"You'd be surprised what I have hidden in the toolbox in the
trunk," he said.

She snorted. "Probably a loaded pistol." She scrubbed the last
bit of blood from his back. The crowd had thinned and they
could move about easily now. "You'd be surprised if you could
see your face. You're wearing the fiercest scowl. There was a
time back there when you actually bared your teeth and I heard
you growl."

He laughed, feeling tension drain away, remembered his sudden rage.

She checked her face in her hand mirror and smoothed her
hair. "You'd think you are at war here in the U.S."

"You saw what just happened when they found I was military.
This time we were lucky. Next time it might be worse. So,
yeah, I'm armed, and yeah, we're damn near at war here with
ourselves." All that was part of his anger.

She shook her head. "This is not the innocent Court Bannister
I knew years ago."

He shrugged. "Lots of blood over the dam since those days."
He slung the towel around his neck and looked in the distance,
at the wooden platform erected near the Washington Monument.
"Want to go over and see what they're saying?"

She checked her watch. "I have a few hours before matinee."

They walked at the tail end of the throng. As they drew closer they passed lawn chairs and spread blankets. There was a festive air and barefoot children darted about shrieking and laughing. Scattered applause rippled as a new speaker took the microphone. He was a tall, broad-shouldered black man wearing neatly pressed slacks and a dashiki. "That's Alexander Torpin," they heard someone say.

"Hey, hey, whaddya say; Ho Chi Minh all the way," Torpin chanted, and the crowd responded.

"Hell no, we won't go, hell no, we won't go," a rival group began to chant, as if in a contest.

"Tricky Dick, oh Tricky Dick," a third faction sang out.

"Marvelous," said the man on the stage. The sound system was good, and his voice boomed across the Monument grounds to drown out the opposition chanters.

"I'm so happy we're all here together today, and I see we can share our feelings," Torpin said in his cultivated and resonant voice. "That is so great." He repeated the chants, then added, *"You* are the force that makes this country great—" He was interrupted by applause. "And this is the greatest country and *you* are the people who own it and *you* have the power and I say power to the people, power to the people, *power to the people, power to the people. . . . "* He raised a clenched right fist over his head and the crowd did the same, roaring out his words even louder than Torpin could overcome with his sound system. They slowly quieted as he held his arms aloft.

Court and Angie had not yet had a good look at the platform. They threaded their way forward through the crowd, many of whom were seated or lying on the ground, until they arrived at one side of the platform, with a view of the structure and the men and women seated and standing on it. There were others on the stage, waiting for the chance to speak. Standing beside Torpin was a white youth with a bundle in his arms.

Torpin signaled to the young man, saying, "And now my good friends, I want to present to you the symbol of the courageous oppressed, I want to present the flag of that tiny nation struggling so valiantly against the bombs and napalm of American capitalistic aggressors. I want to present the symbol of the downtrodden of the earth, the symbol that unites us here today in our holy quest to end the genocide that we are perpetrating on our Asian brethren," his voice rose until he was yelling into the microphone, *"the spirit of revolutionaries everywhere."*

With that, he helped the youth unroll a large Viet Cong flag and drape it from the wood railing. A loud cheer erupted as they saw the yellow star on the blue background.

"Is that what I think it is?" Angie asked, awe in her voice. "Bloody hell. An enemy flag, here on your sacred grounds?" She turned to Court and drew her breath at what she saw.

Court Bannister had no idea that his lips were drawn into a snarl, or that his eyes flashed as cold as Arctic ice. He only knew of a pulsing, fiery rage at the sight of the symbol of terrorists who had taken the lives of so many of his friends. He started toward the platform, fists clenched, walking with slow, purposeful steps, totally uncaring of how he looked. The crowd took no notice. Just one more bare-chested man, this one in red athletic shorts rather than jeans.

"Court, I say, Court! What are you going to do? Stop," Angie cried behind him. She started after him, then had to trot as he increased his pace.

Court could see only the flag. Nothing else mattered or registered. His mind heard not Torpin's words, but the sounds of men fighting, falling, crashing, dying—giving all they had for their country. He did not hear Alexander Torpin saying that the people should *"rise and strike down the fascist leaders of Amerika, overthrow the murderers."*

Torpin was thumping the railing with his fist as Court stalked to the stand and, without pause, jumped up to grab the Viet Cong flag and rip it from the rail. Torpin had his hand on it and as it was torn away, he leaned down in an attempt to retrieve it. Court saw the grasping hand, and without further thought, stuffed the flag under his left arm, grabbed the hand and pulled the man's torso over the edge of the platform. Then, when he saw this was the same man who had been denouncing his friends, he reared back and slugged him in the mouth.

The crowd erupted—men shouting and pointing, women uttering loud shrieks, others gaping in fascination. Television crews, hitherto bored to distraction, ran pell-mell to get better shots and a view of the action while Angie Vick tugged at Court's arm, trying to pull him away as a group of hard-eyed men approached and the crowd began to surge forward.

Torpin vaulted over the rail, landed beside Court, and took his own swing. Court pushed Angie away, ducked and, still holding the VC flag, lashed out with his foot and caught Torpin full in the crotch. The man grasped himself, groaned, and then folded. The hard-eyed men arrived, hands outthrust toward Court. Angie gave a small shriek as one reached into a back pocket and pulled out a sap. As he raised his arm to swing at Court, she caught him full in the face with a shot of tear gas. Two other men tore the can from her hands while three more were punching at Court and trying to wrest the flag away. TV crews and still photographers were crowing with delight as they jostled for position.

Angie flailed and caught one man with an openhanded slap. "Bitch," the man rasped and drew back a fist. She stood her ground firmly, her own fists upraised, as the four mounted policemen entered the melee and deftly cut the attackers away from both Court and Angie. Her hair was awry, her blouse torn, one sneaker was missing, and mud was smeared onto her chin. Court had suffered a few more bloody scratches, and his face was smeared with a mixture of sweat and blood, but he now clutched the enemy flag in both hands.

"Back, goddamn it, *back*," the mounted policemen yelled at the crowd as they drew their horses sideways to form a barrier. "This way," cried out one of two park policemen on foot, and they led Court and Angie through the crowd to a patrol car. A black officer held the door open as the escorts pushed Court and Angie into the rear seat. The officer closed the door, piled in front, and the driver let out the clutch and growled the siren as he steered away from the Monument grounds.

"Whew, I say, that *was* exciting," Angie said. "Say, what time is it? I've got a matinee." She leaned toward the front seat. "Drop me off at the Hay-Adams, will you?"

"Lady, we're not dropping you off anywhere except at the Precinct. You and your chum here are under arrest for disturbing the peace, inciting to riot, causing a nuisance in a public place, and probably a few more things."

A voice sounded over the policeman's hand-held radio. "This is mounted patrol B-5. You get 'em out okay?"

They were passing the last of the demonstrators.

"Yeah, B-5," said the officer. "We're clear."

The voice chuckled. "Shake the guy's hand for me before you drop 'em off. B-5 out."

The policeman eyed Court inquisitively, then dropped his vision to the bundle he carried. "What's that?"

Court didn't answer, just continued to stare morosely out the window.

"That," said Angie, "is an enemy flag."

The policeman eyed the bundle closer, then looked at Bannister again. "Viet Cong?"

"Yes." Court didn't say more.

Angie spoke up again. "Colonel Bannister just tore that enemy flag from their silly platform."

The policeman looked over at the driver, who glanced toward the backseat.

"Four years ago I was a Marine corporal stationed at Cam Ranh," the driver said.

They drove in silence for a while.

The black policeman finally surveyed Court again, his expression quite different. He spoke hesitatingly. "My youngest brother was in the First Cav. Door gunner in a chopper."

Court drew his gaze into the car and returned his look. "Where was he flying out of?"

"Pleiku. Helicopter went down in the Ia Drang Valley."

"They bring him out?"

"Never found him. Located the chopper but no one was inside."

Court did not respond further. The Viet Cong hated and feared helicopters, and the crewmen who flew them were treated savagely when they were captured.

A female voice on the radio asked where they were located.

The driver answered that they were on their way to the . . . He glanced back at Angie Vick and raised an eyebrow.

"The Hay-Adams Hotel, please," she replied primly.

"The Hay-Adams Hotel," the driver said into his mike.

The female voice said the duty sergeant had heard about the incident at the Monument, and wanted to make sure their two *guests* were okay. So did the Captain. In fact, *everyone* at the Precinct wanted to make sure they were okay.

The driver replied that the two were safe and sound, but that they might be delayed because they had to drop off some garbage. He signed off, then pulled over to the curb, hit the button which released the rear door locks, and silently pointed to a Dempster Dumpster.

Court got out of the police cruiser and walked to the Dumpster, then chunked in his armful of flag atop a particularly smelly heap of refuse. He gave a single purposeful nod, then returned to the car and crawled back inside.

"Thanks," he said.

Both policemen stared at the trash receptacle with distaste.

"You ever get the urge to see some friendly faces," growled the black officer in the front passenger's seat, "just stop by any precinct in town. What's your name?"

"Court Bannister."

"I'll spread the word." He nodded at the driver. "We better drop 'em off and get on back. Who knows? Might be a couple more people with balls in the crowd there."

1830 Hours Local, Sunday 18 June 1972
John Jay Suite, Hay-Adams Hotel
Washington, D.C.

They sat side by side on the couch, feet propped up on the coffee table, drinks on the side table, watching the evening news on the console television.

Both local and network news had featured the incident with the VC flag and the ensuing battle. Court, war hero and son of Sam Bannister, received a healthy share of the coverage, but most of the video time was given to Angie Vick, the Adventurer, who had come to the rescue of American dignity. A still shot of her with her dukes up and an auburn curl over flashing eyes got the edge over Court's leap to rip down the Viet Cong flag.

Most of the coverage was complimentary. Two attractive and prominent people had enlivened an otherwise dull news day, and the announcers responded with happy sympathy. People on the street were interviewed, and several, older men vowed they would have done the same as Court. A group of burly hard hats applauded and said they wished they could have a few minutes with the men who tried to beat up on Angie Vick.

A local station showed the picture of Court landing his fist on Alexander Torpin's jaw and his foot in Torpin's crotch. They had an on-camera interview with Torpin, who said he would like to meet Courtland Bannister for a little one-on-one.

"That man gives me the creeps," Angie said. "You should have hit him harder."

"What about your career? This kind of attention can't help your image."

"You've been out of the business too long. As long as they spell my name right, any publicity is good. In fact, this *particular* publicity is *very* good. Look." Angie pointed.

Once again they were showing her pose with raised fists. They played clips of *Adventurers* scenes showing Angie Vick in action.

Court considered and nodded. "No doubt it can help you. Wish I could say the same for myself. It's not the kind of thing generals want shown on national television."

"Maybe not," she was saying, "but your ripping down the enemy flag, now *that* was proper."

He turned and raised an eyebrow. "Why did you back me up like you did, Angie? It's not even your war."

She smiled. "You were being threatened. We're friends, remember?"

He laughed. "You're a study." He looked back at the TV screen. "Well, that will probably make up their minds."

"What do you mean?"

"When the Air Force wheels see those shots, they'll realize I belong back in Vietnam."

"You must be joking."

Court realized he had resolved a difficult personal issue. After what had happened, he was determined to stay in the military. He was also determined to return, somehow, to Vietnam. That afternoon's experience had reaffirmed his commitment to his friends still in the war.

"Aren't you joking?"

He blew out a long breath, then abruptly shook his head. "I want to go back. I'm ready."

"Why?" she cried. "Why are you always trying to get back to Vietnam?"

Court looked at her. Angie's expression held a mixture of puzzlement and anger. He thought of Susan Boyle and how she'd asked the same question and worn the same look. With an inward groan, he knew how it would go. He would try to explain, and she wouldn't understand, and then the puzzlement would fade, leaving only the anger. But still he had to try. With a sigh, he began.

0650 Hours Local, Monday 19 June 1972
F-105G—airborne near Vinh, Route Pack Two
Democratic Republic of Vietnam

The morning Linebacker mission was again to the petroleum area on the northwest side of Vinh, in northernmost route package two. Bomb-damage assessment photos had shown that the strike force had destroyed less than half of the well-camouflaged tanks. They were to return and finish the job.

The routine, begun under the old Freedom Train operation, was established. Immediately before the first fighters arrived, EB-66s would set up in an orbit over the water and begin to jam the longer-range acquisition radars. The Wild Weasel flight would then enter the target area and attempt to neutralize the SAMs, from immediately before the chaff flights arrived until the bombing attack was completed. Next would come the chaff flight, call sign Snow, out of Udorn Air Base, Thailand—eight F-4s flying line abreast, releasing chaff from AN/ALE-38 dispensers. They would create a long corridor filled with drifting, feather-light strips of foil, from an initial point to the target, through which the strike aircraft could fly and remain immune from radar coverage. Since they had to fly straight and level during the entire time, the chaff-layers were vulnerable to attack by MiGs or SAMs.

"There they are, at our five o'clock position," said Tuck Tucker.

Bear Woods looked back, scanned, and finally saw the eight specks in the sky. Snow flight. He looked closer until he noted two other aircraft, flying higher and slightly aft, on either side of the chaff-layers. Those were MiG-CAP F-4s from Udorn Air Base, call sign Vega, with the mission to engage and destroy enemy interceptors found in the area.

"You got anything yet?" Tuck asked.

"Nope," Bear Woods replied. He'd picked up all sorts of radars north of them, both SAMs and AAA, but so far there'd been nothing at all in the target area.

"I don't like it," said Tucker, unusual concern in his voice.

"Maybe they're taking a break," said the befreckled red-head, peering hard at his panoramic receiver, the AN/ALR-35. He shook his head finally. "Still nothing." Tuck was right. It was eerie.

"They're up to something," Tuck said. "I can feel it."

"Relax and enjoy it." Woods looked out at the chaff-layers again. They were only five or six miles out now, and the specks were growing wings. Invisible from where they flew were the thousands of metallic strips which constantly fluttered earthward from small bundles ejected from the dispensers. A cloud was being issued, impenetrable by the radar beams. The fighter-bombers would be protected if they remained in the cloud. But of course the chaff-layers, their MiG-CAP escorts, the EB-66s, and the Wild Weasels were all at risk.

Woods looked carefully about the sky, thinking how the Have Blue project, the one he'd thought up and later worked on, might someday change all that. It had been the F-105 that had given him the idea for Have Blue. The Thud was so sleek and had such a small radar cross-section from head-on that a reflector had to be lowered for a ground-approach radar to see it. So what if they could build aircraft that were even more difficult for radar to pick up? Use radar-signal trapping baffles, diverse reflective angles, radar-absorbing material and paint, hide the engine intakes . . . if they could make it work, and if future military airplanes were built that way, there'd be few support aircraft required. SAM and interceptor radars wouldn't be able to see them, and you can't shoot what you can't see. If they had them now, Woodrow G. Woods could be back at the base chasing pussy, instead of here, hanging his skinny ass out as a target for the SAMs so they wouldn't shoot at the other aircraft. Yeah. And if . . .

He caught a glint of reflected light down low, a few miles to the southwest, and peered. A rice paddy? He thought he saw a movement.

"Tuck, take a look at our two o'clock low. Maybe five miles out."

"You got a SAM signal?"

"No. Something else. Dunno what."

Tuck was quiet for a moment as he also looked.

They saw them at the same time. Two delta-shapes, turning

and climbing toward the stern of chaff-layers.

"MiGs!" Bear Woods exclaimed.

Tucker was immediately on the radio. "Snow flight, this is Condor lead. You've got two MiG-21s at your six o'clock low, about two miles out."

The two MIG-CAP Phantoms flying off the leftmost chaff-layer's wing immediately turned hard right, but the eight-line-abreast aircraft continued straight ahead.

"Snow flight leader, this is Condor . . . "

A white smoke trail issued from one of the delta-winged fighters.

"Atoll, Snow, Atoll!" Tuck cried over the radio.

The small air-to-air missile darted forward, seeking the heat source of a Phantom's jet exhausts. The targeted aircraft began a turn—not in time, for the missile nicked a horizontal stabilizer and the Phantom immediately slewed.

"Snow Three's hit!" came a radio call.

"It didn't explode," Bear Woods said in wonder as the Phantom began to correct and recover.

The other seven chaff-layers had scattered like quail. The two MiGs continued to draw closer to the same lone F-4, which was back to a straight and level attitude, nose slightly high.

"Snow Three's got a stability-control problem," the Phantom pilot called in a high voice.

"The MiGs are still closing on you, Snow Three," Tuck called.

"Where are you, MiG-CAP?" Snow Three called in a frightened tone.

The leftmost MiG-CAP Phantoms were still turning, and the ones on the right were slicing upward to get an eye on the attackers.

Another flash and smoke trail.

"Atoll, Snow Three!" Tuck called, and the chaff-layer jogged to his right.

A clean miss.

A puff of smoke and white streamer from the second MiG.

"Atoll . . . "

This time the Atoll detonated properly, and the Phantom's aft section was momentarily engulfed in a small puff of gray. The airplane slewed once more, this time violently, and this time there was no response or correction.

"Ngghh . . . Snow Three's . . . nghh . . . hit!" The F-4 began a violent roll, still yawing badly, then flipped up on its back and began to tumble.

"Vega Two's got the lead MiG in sight," called a MiG-CAP bird.

Emergency beepers began to wail over guard frequency from the crew of Snow Three.

"Condor Two has two chutes in sight south of the Ca River."

Tucker was looking hard just then, for something new had caught his eye. "Condor Lead's got three more bogeys in sight just west of Vinh."

Yet another MiG seemed to come from nowhere, off the deck, and was soaring toward a lone chaff-layer. A puff issued.

"Atoll over the Ca River!" Tuck shouted because he didn't know the call sign of the Phantom.

The missile detonated and the F-4 immediately torched. Both of the crew ejected. They didn't see the seats come out, but they heard the beepers on the radio when the chutes opened. Someone said it was Snow Four.

Two birds down now. The first flight of MiGs had turned northward, diving for the dirt. A MiG-CAP Phantom fired an AIM-7 Sparrow. "Vega lead is Fox one!" he called.

The second flight of MiGs also turned northward, headed very fast for the deck.

"Vega four is Fox two," called another Phantom, meaning he'd fired a Sidewinder.

"This is Disco," came a booming radio call. "Bandits north of Victor. I repeat. This is Disco. Bandits at Victor, three five zero for six miles." It was the EC-121 radar controller, calling the MiGs.

"About bloody time," Tuck muttered.

"The MiGs came in low, under Disco's radar coverage," said Bear Woods.

"Jesus," said Tuck. "What a fire drill. You hear anyone call a splash?" Splash meant someone had killed a MiG.

"Not yet."

"Jesus," Tuck repeated.

Snow Leader called Red Crown control and canceled the strike mission, then called two flights of fighters to provide Res-CAP, to help find the downed aircrew members and then protect the search and rescue forces when they arrived. They spoke to one of the downed WSOs, Snow Zero-Four Bravo, but he said that soldiers were closing in and he was going to destroy his radio before they captured him. They tried, but could not make radio contact with the other three men. That night the intelligence section at 7th Air Force Headquarters said they were presumed captured. It had been one of the worst air-war days in the war.

Chapter 9

"Come in, come in," Richard Nixon called from his desk to Lieutenant General Whisenand, who stood outside the door to the Oval Office. "I'm . . . ah . . . sorry we couldn't get together earlier." He leaned forward in his chair, wearing his serious and tentative lawyer's expression. He was rather wooden-faced and had trouble showing emotions, a fact gleefully exploited by photographers and political cartoonists. They were increasingly successful in conveying him as wily and conniving, while Whisenand had thus far found him to be much more sincere than other Washington politicians he'd dealt with. Unlike Lyndon Johnson, Nixon often sought his generals' advice and took their recommendations regarding the war. He seemed to genuinely want to bring the prisoners of war home and to support South Vietnam by forcing an honorable solution to the war.

Nixon nodded energetically. "As you know, the summit went well. The Russians were surprisingly cordial . . . makes you wonder what they're after. You, ah, must excuse me. I've been extremely busy since I returned from Moscow last week."

"I understand. Welcome back, Mr. President," Whitey Whisenand said.

Nixon had met with Leonid Brezhnev, First Secretary of the Communist Party. The international press cautiously hailed the meeting as a success. A number of reporters had predicted that the Russians would call it off over the Freedom Train/Operation Linebacker raids. The reporters had waited expectantly for Brezhnev to publicly castigate Nixon for the bombing raids, and for the four Soviet ships known to have been damaged in Haiphong Harbor by U.S. warplanes. Instead, the two men had met, signed important arms control treaties, and parted cordially. Upon his return to the U.S., one of Nixon's first actions, as a sign of good faith, was to order a halt to ongoing antiballistic-missile research.

Nixon pointed. "Come, sit down. I must tell you what the media does *not* know." Whitey took a seat on the white upholstered chair to the right of the President's desk.

"An amusing event occurred," Nixon said. "We had dinner at the Ambassador's residence and dessert was Baked Alaska. When it was brought in, Brezhnev clapped his hands and said, 'Americans really are miracle workers. They've found a way to set ice cream on fire.' "

Whitey chuckled.

"The meeting went well. Brezhnev even volunteered to send a representative to Hanoi to see if he could get the peace talks moving at a faster pace."

"That's good news, Mr. President."

Nixon leaned forward. "Now to business. It's been several weeks since we talked about your POW project. Are there any developments?"

"Nothing since our people decoded the message from Caruso that I briefed you about."

"Ahhh . . . the songfest."

"Yes, sir. I'm still trying now to set up another meeting between our 'blue mailman' and Caruso, in Hanoi."

"No progress there yet?"

"We're still working on it."

"Are you getting all the cooperation you need? The CIA and the others?"

"Yes, sir." Whitey was not using those agencies at the moment, except to provide him with the latest intelligence briefings.

The President grew a brooding expression. His words emerged slowly, as if they were studied. "My visit to Moscow, and face-to-face discussions with our ambassador there, convinced me once again that the Russians might not . . . ah . . . hesitate at all to do something such as we fear. Take our men—perhaps brutalize and brainwash them—to gain our secrets. They are a highly secretive and compartmentalized group of bureaucrats there. These things could be happening . . . ah . . . unilaterally by the KGB, without the participation or blessing of either their military or Brezhnev himself."

Whitey frowned.

The President raised his hands. "Don't worry. I didn't give our suspicions away. The Russians don't know what we suspect."

"Perhaps they should, Mr. President. Perhaps that would stop it. Especially with your growing rapport with their First Secretary."

Nixon wagged his head vigorously. "No. It would only destroy that rapport. Our dealings are . . . ah . . . quite fragile. The timing's wrong."

"They've blatantly taken our fighting men before, Mr. President."

Nixon sighed. "After World War Two, you mean."

"And there are strong suspicions about our POWs in Korea, sir."

Nixon shook his head again. "The timing's all wrong. If we confronted them now with unfounded accusations, they'd pull back into their shell and deny everything, and there'd be nothing we could do about it."

Whitey lowered his voice, but the words still came out stronger than he'd intended. "It must be stopped, sir. And we must get our men back."

The President's eyebrows arched. "You are suddenly very positive they're doing it."

"So many puzzle pieces. But no, sir, I still have no real, smoking-gun proof."

"Let us proceed under the assumption it is indeed happening."

Whitey nodded, wondering.

"I agree with what you said. The first thing would be to stop the shipments of prisoners out of North Vietnam. Let me tell you something, General. After my visits to China and Moscow,

I made up my mind even stronger. The war must be stopped. It's like a cloud over all of our negotiations with communists. We have a window of opportunity to bring about an end to the cold war, to begin a new era. The leaders in Moscow and Peking do not like me, General, but they respect me. Yet although we talk, both they and I know that the war must be ended."

"I cannot agree more, sir."

Nixon's voice was low and full of conviction. "We will make it happen, General. The Linebacker bombing campaign is beginning to give us the results we desired. Fewer supplies are getting into North Vietnam. The North Vietnamese are finally negotiating."

"It may require more pressure, sir."

"I realize that, and I'm prepared to authorize whatever it takes. Not hastily, of course. I can't be seen to be impulsive."

An old Washington hand, Whitey could interpret political talk. He'd just been reminded that this was a presidential election year.

Nixon was nodding to himself, confirming some inner thought. "Our participation in this war will not continue much longer—perhaps . . . ah . . . six or seven more months."

Which meant, Whitey realized, that no real escalations would be made until after the November elections.

"So in the meantime, if the Russians are indeed taking American prisoners, we must contrive a way to stop it."

Whitey nodded. "Yes, sir."

"I believe a note from Henry to their negotiators, telling them in diplomatic terms that any movements of our POWs would be severely frowned upon, might suffice to make them pause. It will be vaguely worded, as such things . . . ah . . . must be, but enough to remind them that we value our men."

"Will that work, sir?" *Severely frowned upon? That's all?*

"I believe it will be enough to stop them long enough for you to find out more. With the end of the conflict in sight, you must hurry with your confirmations, General."

"Yes, sir. I'll certainly try." *Ah, God, how I'll try.*

"Good." Nixon smiled and nodded. "Good," he repeated.

"And what about any prisoners who might already be in Russia, sir?"

"When we have . . . ah . . . fully disengaged from Vietnam,

and our air power remains poised in Thailand to ensure the North Vietnamese honor the agreement and do not try to invade again, I will present Mr. Brezhnev with our proof, and offer a juicy inducement of some sort to get our men back."

"Yes, sir." *Juicy inducement? Politicians speak such pap.*

"Get me that proof, General," Nixon said (he had never called him Whitey).

"I am doing everything in my power to do so, sir."

"Good. Now then"—Nixon smiled vaguely—"to a lighter subject. May I assume you saw the flag incident on television yesterday?"

"Yes, sir, I did." It was a hot news item, and had run incessantly.

"What did you think of the young Air Force man who confronted Torpin?"

Whitey tried to keep his face neutral. "He was identified as Lieutenant Colonel Court Bannister, sir. He's a highly decorated Air Force fighter pilot."

The President's brow slowly raised. "I was told that he's your relative." As was often the case, he knew more than he'd initially let on.

"Yes, sir. A cousin, but we're closer than that. I'm his godfather and we spent time together when he was a youngster."

The President still hadn't let on whether he was pleased or angered by the incident. "All the world loves underdogs and lovers," he muttered.

"In this particular circumstance, they were certainly underdogs, sir. It was a dangerous situation. I'm just glad it didn't get more out of hand than it did."

Nixon made a "hmmm" sound. Finally: "Did you see Miss Vick with her fists raised? Extraordinary?"

"Yes, sir."

"Well, pass the word along, General. I don't want to make a public thing out of it, but . . . tell him well done."

Whitey felt pleased. His nephew's career in the Air Force could easily have been terminated over the incident if the President had felt it was in some way wrong or demeaning.

When Whitey left the White House fifteen minutes later, he checked with his watch. The Chief of Staff of the Air Force had his own message he wanted to pass to Court, and he had just enough time to make the appointment. He sighed. Court wasn't going to like it, but it was for his own good—and the military's.

0800 Hours Local, Tuesday 20 June 1972
Room 1D215, Pentagon
Washington, D.C.

Court's face blanched. "B-52s! You're not serious?"

They were in Whitey Whisenand's office, and Whitey had just delivered the bad news.

"First you'll attend a short familiarization course at Castle." Castle AFB was a Strategic Air Command training base near Merced, California. "Then you'll go on to the '52 Wing at Guam."

"You're serious," Court whispered, still unable to believe.

"It all started with your message, saying you felt more B-52 bombardments in the Hanoi area of North Vietnam were critical to winning, but that they should be using revised tactics and some of the lessons learned by the fighters. The Chief agrees then, and he still does. That's why he brought you here." He grinned. "And, frankly, after your little demonstration at the Monument, he thought it wouldn't be a bad idea for you to stay out of sight for a while."

Court's eyes were wide with a mixture of shock, and another emotion akin to fright. It was the worst fate that could befall a fighter jock. He could not contain it. "With all due respect, just what in hell would I do in bombers? I'm a fighter pilot, Uncle General Albert, and I live and breathe fighter tactics. You know what we call B-52s?"

"BUFFs."

"Yes sir. Big ugly fat fuckers. And 'aluminum overcasts.' And 'monkey killers.' And some more names that are unmentionable. Christ, you could park a squadron of fighters under a B-52's wings, load all the squadron personnel in the bomb bay, and still have room left over for card games in the cockpit. Me? Fly one of those? Be the copilot in command of elevator trim for five years before they let me make a landing? Fly something with more engines hanging under its wings than on the track at Indianapolis on race day? No! Enn bloody oh, no!"

"Are you finished?" Whitey's look had become amused.

"I'm probably *not* finished," Court muttered, thinking hard for an escape route.

"I take it," Whitey said with a wry smile, "you don't wish to fly Boeing's best?"

Court threw up his arms.

"Anyway, it's not *fly* them, exactly," Whitey continued.

"What does *that* mean?"

"It's a liaison position. That's what the L stands for in XOOFL, which is your new office. You'd go there as a fighter pilot, in an advisory capacity, for a six-month temporary duty tour."

Court was far from convinced. "You mean sit around and listen to all those SAC guys tell me how they're winning the war by dumping bombs on empty jungles from seven miles up." He snorted. "The only danger they face is the possibility of falling off their barstool at Guam. The mission? Seven hours of briefing, six hours of preflighting, four days in the air eating box lunches and crapping in plastic bags. That's not flying, that's more like serving jail time."

"The Chief's having trouble getting the SAC generals to understand that they must work on improving their tactics before they're sent back up to Hanoi or Haiphong again. He's going to be working from here at the Pentagon, but he wants your presence felt among the pilots who'll be out there flying combat."

Court tried a rather silly last effort. "They don't even wear G-suits. What kind of pilots don't wear G-suits? I'll tell you what kind. Lard-assed *bomber* pilots, that's who." He leaned forward, his eyes pleading. "Get me out of this, Uncle Albert. I've never asked you for anything, but *please* get me out of this."

"Write me when you get to California and then Guam," Whitey said cheerfully. "Sal and I always like to be in touch. Now if you'll excuse me, I have to arrange with Personnel for your TDY orders."

After his nephew stumped out, still in shock, the smile on Whitey Whisenand's face remained in place. He had confidence in Court's ability to help make the required changes in B-52 tactics. That's why he'd told the Chief of Staff that Court was the man for the job.

Chapter 10

2115 Hours Local, Saturday 24 June 1972
Officers' Club, George Air Force Base
Victorville, California

During the Middle Ages, monastic brotherhood was cemented in closed ceremonies. These rites were solemnized by warrior-monk societies, such as the Knights Templar, who used the occasion to celebrate military achievement. Upon the formation of the Royal Air Force in Great Britain, the ancient tradition was continued by flying officers, and during World War II, the rite called the Dining In was admired and adopted by officers of the United States Army Air Corps.

In the course of the thousand years, the protocols had been altered, but the function remained formal, strictly stag, and closed to anyone not in the brotherhood—a time for official boasting, followed by ribaldry and the celebration of masculine warrior camaraderie.

Ritual was fastidiously observed. Two men held critical positions: the President, who was the unit commander, and Mister Vice, a lowly lieutenant who served as official clever quipster, and who summoned the group to the dining room with a gong of a bell. Formalities included drinking much wine, an invocation, a series of grand toasts, a robust dinner fol-

lowed by cigars and brandy, presentation of awards, and a
windy speech by a long-forgotten aviator. As the President
made closing remarks, the pilots often hurled buns at him. If he
was unpopular, the buns would be buttered. The unit flag would
be sheathed, and the ceremony closed by another, single, bell
gong . . . which also signaled the beginning of revelry, games,
and singing.

The ladies of the various Officers' Wives Clubs, who gave
not a whit about the millennium of history behind the ritual,
were increasingly incensed at being excluded, and cast critical
eyes upon mates who returned home with happy smiles on their
faces. After a staunch stand, the male chauvinists folded. The
thousand-year-old tradition was altered and the Dining "Out"
was born. Women were admitted. Cigars were banned. Menus
were changed to Cornish game hen.

At George Air Force Base, when Captain Toby Parker and the
eighteen other members of his F-4 upgrade class had completed
their course, the grueling feat was acknowledged with a formal
Dining Out, with wives, girlfriends, and even a few parents in
attendance. The officers were dressed in mess dress uniforms,
with white jackets, cummerbunds, and black trousers with a
vertical silk stripe down each leg. The ladies wore floor-length
formals, and most sported corsages from Sand's Florists in
Victorville. The miniature medals Toby displayed below the
wings on his left breast were much more impressive than those
the instructors had won during their Vietnam combat tours. The
only pilots with more medals than Toby were those who had also
flown combat in Korea, and the senior colonels with World War
II experience. Those gentlemen's medals garnished their chests
from left shoulder to midwaist.

The wine had been served, the toasts made, and the meal
consumed. The smoking lamp was lit and Mister Vice declared
that the formal portion of the Dining Out was concluded. The
Top Gun award had just been presented to a husky blond captain
named Eugene J. O'Sullivan, whose easygoing manner belied
fierce aggressiveness in the air.

Toby and Ken Tanaka took a booth at the bar, each with
a glass of Coca-Cola in his hand. The two had become close
during their scores of mock combat sorties. They'd maneuvered
against each other so often and each had become so predictable to the other that the last few fights were draws—like

two wily tic-tac-toe players when both had learned how to use the middle against the other. They'd flown every combination, Parker v. Tanaka with and without GIB help, Parker v. Tanaka when Tanaka had a wingman, Parker with a wingman v. Tanaka solo or with a wingman or with a flight of four. They'd flown in the same airplane so Tanaka could monitor Parker's control movements while Toby recited the reasoning behind this or that maneuver. The few times they'd flown as a two-ship team against other students and instructors, they'd been invincible.

"If I were a nice guy," Tanaka began, "I'd say you were the best student I ever had. And I'd probably thank you for dragging me out of my funk. But as you know, the golden peacock never is."

"The golden peacock never is what?"

"Never is a nice guy."

"Course not, it's a bird."

"See." After a bit Tanaka muttered, "Thanks, anyway."

"No sweat. I'm the one who benefited and learned."

Ken Tanaka looked at his friend. "How come you don't have a date? I can understand you being too busy while you were here, but how about all those Southern belles back in Virginia?"

"All those Southern belles have been rung. They're married and have two-point-three kids, a dog, a mortgage, and a husband named Bubba. How about you? Why don't you have a date?"

"I haven't met my girl yet," he said.

"What the hell does that mean?" Toby asked.

"I have yet to meet the girl I want to spend my life with. Besides, I want you to get your buddy Court Bannister to fix me up with Liz Taylor. He told me he knew her."

Toby mused. "I think she's married right now."

"Just my luck. Can't last for long though. Soon as you hear she's between husbands, give him a call, okay?" Ken grinned. "Shit hot what Court did with that flag, wasn't it? How's Court doing these days? He and I had some times together at Ubon." Ken Tanaka had flown F-4s with Bannister in the Phantom FAC unit Court had commanded in Thailand. The pilots had flown only at night—their mission to seal off the Ho Chi Minh Trail from truck traffic. Once, when Court had been trapped on the ground atop a karst known as Eagle Station, Tanaka had saved Court's life with some well-placed ordnance.

"I called him this morning to tell him I'd finished the program here." Toby grimaced with distaste. "Poor bastard's en route to Castle for some B-52 time."

"Bannister in B-52s? I don't believe it."

"Court Bannister in B-52s?" repeated J. T. Neddle as he and his wife, Topsy, walked up to the booth. He had his arm around her waist. "Is this a private session or can anyone join?" he asked. He had an impressive array of medals from Korea, where he'd shot down three MiG-15s, and Vietnam, where he'd hammered a MiG-17.

Toby and Tanaka stood and invited the couple to join them.

"So what's this about Bannister going to bombers?" J.T. asked as he took his seat. "Anything to do with the VC flag thing?"

"I believe you're right, Colonel," Toby said.

"Vicissitudes of the service," Ken Tanaka said. "The lilac bush wears strange shoes."

They all laughed and Neddle went to the bar to get another round, scotch for him and Topsy, Cokes for the other two. It was common knowledge that Parker didn't drink, and Tanaka only rarely.

"Toby," Neddle said in a cheery voice when he returned, "you set a fine record here."

"Thanks, J.T.," Toby said.

"Quit talking shop, you guys," Topsy Neddle said. She was a buxom brunette who wore her hair swept up and back, revealing large ears and a sun-red neck. She and J.T. had been married for twelve years and had five children. She took in Toby and Tanaka. "You guys keep shooting your watches off your wrists when you talk flying. There's lonely ladies over there. Why aren't you guys up and chasing like normal fighter jocks?"

Topsy pointed to the bar, where three local beauties were ensconced, surrounded by a dozen or so young pilots whose collective tongues dangled to their brightly polished shoes.

On Friday and Saturday nights, most base NCO and Officers' Clubs were opened for town girls to drop in. Club managers tried to entice the young ladies by offering them half-price drinks and the chance to meet scores of eligible bachelors. Wing commanders were happy to keep their troops on base, and not racing at max RPM around the downtown gin joints, and therefore gave permission for the girls to be allowed on base. Parents near some bases became appalled and wrote letters to congressmen, but in barren Apple Valley, where George Air Force Base was located, husband material was scarce, and young women flocked in from as far away as Barstow and even San Bernardino.

"Why aren't I chasing?" Kenichi Tanaka repeated Topsy's question. He brightened. "I don't want to make the competition feel bad."

"Saving myself for a pure virgin," Toby said.

"Well, hell," Topsy said, "in that case you might as well talk flying. I know the look. Can't wait to get the gear in the well." She flung her ample arms around Toby's and Ken's necks. "I love you guys. You know that?" She cast a wifely look at J.T. "You can talk now, dear." With that she waved across the room, announced she was going to chat with someone more interesting than a bunch of fuddy fighter pilots, and strode off toward a gathering of wives.

J.T. watched as she walked away. "Old Acrocka Tanaka here hung it out for you, Toby. I hadn't planned on nearly that many air-to-air sorties. The curriculum calls for four practice dogfight sorties per pilot. Too dangerous, the wheels say. I let Ken badger me into setting up the extracurricular air work. You guys did so well, I'm going to see if I can use your record to get approval for permanent curriculum changes."

"For everyone that goes through?" asked Tanaka.

"I'd like to tailor the level of fighter instruction to a pilot's experience and ability. Our shoot-down record in 'Nam is lousy and we need better training. The Navy's into it at Miramar, but we're dragging our feet." Neddle sipped his drink and looked at Toby with an enigmatic smile. "By the way, I voted against you getting the Top Gun award."

Toby looked surprised.

"You had the best air-to-mud and the best air-to-air scores, your formation, refueling, academics, and all the rest were shit hot, but I voted against you," Neddle persisted, obviously trying to get a rise.

Toby shrugged.

"You also demonstrated leadership and fighting skills, not to mention superb situational awareness. I still voted against you.

You were the best pupil this squadron has seen," Neddle said, "but I voted against you."

Toby made an exaggerated yawn and looked in the direction of the bar. "Colonel," he said over his shoulder, "I get the distinct impression you're trying to tell me something."

J. T. Neddle leaned back and smiled. "Now that I've captured your attention, I'll tell you *why* I voted against you getting the Top Gun award."

Toby swung around. "What's all the mystery for?"

"Because the *why* is the most important lesson you can learn. I'm the world's greatest training squadron commander, and telling students *why* things happen goes with the job."

"Get it over with, Colonel," Toby said, irritation heavy in his voice.

"There are several reasons. The primary one is, you didn't earn it."

"Didn't *earn* it?" Toby's voice raised.

"You had an advantage none of your classmates had."

"Ken Tanaka?"

"Exactly. No one else in your class had him as their IP. You couldn't *help* being Top Gun."

Toby raised his glass to Tanaka, who returned the toast with a smile. "Even the Samurai weaves twigs," Tanaka said.

"There's another reason," Neddle continued. "Maybe more important." He paused, then asked, "Tell me again why you studied so hard and flew all those extra aerial antics."

"To learn how to fight the Phantom," Toby said.

"And to kill MiGs?"

"Absolutely."

"But not to become an Ace. You said you weren't concerned about that."

"It's not my most important goal in life. What's your point, Colonel?"

"I'll give you an example. On two separate occasions I know of, you had a clear kill in front of you and you didn't take the opportunity."

"Just a damn minute here, Colonel," Toby said, his voice tight. "In each case my wingman was in just as good position to make the attack as I was, so I told him to take the kill."

"That's my point, Parker. You don't have the killer instinct. You don't go for the jugular."

"I know I could have gotten the kills, but my wingmen were also in position and they needed the training too."

"Parker, you cut the odds on a shoot-down by giving it to someone not as good as you. You can't do that in combat. The mission's to shoot down MiGs, not train someone else. You're a student here, not an IP. You want to train pilots, we'll keep you here as an IP. You want that?"

Toby responded quickly. "No, sir, I don't."

"Then get over there and kill five MiGs, and make Ace. You don't do that, you're not doing your job—and our time training you was wasted."

Parker, eyes flashing, said, "Colonel, don't tell me what I can think. Don't talk to me about reasons why I do or don't do something. I'm motivated to fight. If I shoot down MiGs, so much the better."

Neddle studied him for a final moment. "You've got courage. I don't question that. Just let me know how you feel at the end of your tour. Tell me if your motivation's still the same." With that, Lieutenant Colonel J. T. Neddle excused himself and left to join his wife.

"Whew," Toby said.

"Just so you'll know," Ken Tanaka said, "I voted for you to be Top Gun."

Toby eyed him. "Thanks." He gave Tanaka a lopsided grin. "Sorry I spouted off to your boss. I'm shipping out, but you've still got to work for him."

"You've got him all wrong," Tanaka said in a businesslike voice. "J.T.'s job is to make sure every student who graduates here is overflowing with all the killer motivation the young stud can handle. He knows you are the best who's been through here for years, so he'd like you to be the most motivated. And he wants to make sure you don't pussycat out."

"Do you think I will?"

"Absolutely not."

"Then why does Neddle think that?"

"He doesn't. It's his job to push. He's like the bayonet instructor in the Marines who has to motivate kids to stick a knife in someone's belly. J.T. wants to build guys who'll be winners when they get into combat."

Ken Tanaka didn't tell Toby about the telephone conversation he'd overheard in Neddle's office that morning, when J.T. had told a two-star named Norman at 7th Air Force in Saigon that he was about to send over the Air Force's next Ace, a guy named Toby Parker. They needed an Ace, and as the Linebacker air campaign continued to pick up steam, they'd be presented the opportunity.

Parker was still brooding, muttering, "I've been in a lot of combat. I'll do it my way." He took a swallow of Coke, then turned to Ken. "I got my assignment. I'm booked out of Travis for Udorn on MAC next week."

"Yeah, I heard," Tanaka said. "Got some news for you, I'm going there too."

"Hey, that's great," Toby said with genuine joy.

"We'll both make Ace," Ken Tanaka said with confidence.

"Didn't you listen to what I just told J.T.?"

"I listened. Look, I'm a dumb-shit fighter jock like you, who wants to be the best. I just happen to think making Ace is a great way to prove it."

"Okay, partner. I'll just bet you'll become an Ace. In the meantime you taught me the fine points of fighting the F-4. Now I'm ready to go back over and put it all to work."

"Yeah, me too. Can't sit here while you and the other guys shoot down *all* the MiGs." Tanaka's voice faded as he looked at the bar. "Hey, fix me up with one of those girls, stud. I am still your IP, you know."

Toby glanced at his watch. "Not since two hours ago, you're not." He also looked. The local girls were still cute, and still holding the young jocks at bay. He drained his Coke and stuck his face next to Tanaka's. "You want to go over there with me and cut some bunnies out of the brood, or are you going to sit here and pontificate? If you are, you'll be talking to yourself."

Twenty minutes later the two fighter pilots departed the George Air Force Base Officers' Open Mess with the three bunnies, headed for Tanaka's less than spacious mountain cabin, which somehow had been transformed into a splendiferous lodge during their invitations.

0840 Hours Local, Monday 26 June 1972
Airborne in F-105G northwest of Hanoi—
Route Pack Six
Democratic Republic of Vietnam

"Shotgun!" Tuck Tucker announced over radio as he launched their last Shrike missile. They were flying at 11,000 feet, nose up, and lofting the radar homing missile toward a SAM site near Yen Bai, which was very close to the target.

The bomb-laden Phantoms were inbound, already past the Black River and now only thirty miles from the Lang Chi hydroelectric power plant, which generated the majority of power for northernmost North Vietnam. The SAM site must be neutralized before the F-4s arrived at the target, for it posed a definite danger to the force.

"He went off the air," Bear Woods announced from the backseat.

"Did we get him?" Tuck asked.

"Nope. He shut down before the missile could possibly have impacted."

"Damn," Tuck muttered.

"Condor Lead, Two has bogeys in sight at our eight o'clock, high."

"That's the MiG-CAP, Two," Tuck replied with a hint of sarcasm. The call had been made by a new guy, who was overly nervous because they were flying in Route Pack Six.

Bear Woods huffed a breath which sounded loud on the hot mike.

"You got something back there?" Tuck asked. They'd flown together enough that they almost knew what the other was thinking.

"The SAM signal's back on the air. He's not looking at us. Probably looking out west, toward the F-4s."

"Well, shit," said Tuck. He pulled in a breath. "Guess it's show and tell time, Bear."

"You going to try bombing him?"

"We've gotta."

"You know where he's located?" The rear cockpit receivers were good at analyzing signals, but they did not show the precise location of the SAM radars. They normally had to wait until a SAM missile was launched, and then keep the smoke and dust in sight so they'd know precisely where to place their bombs. Thus far the SAM site had refused to be suckered into firing SAMs at the Wild Weasels.

"I think he's set up shop in VN-521." The prepared sites were given VN numbers. The Viets moved SAM firing batteries around among the prepared sites, like knights in a game of chess. When a SAM battery was set up at a site, they called it "occupied." VN-521 was located immediately west of Yen Bai, as were more than sixty medium-sized antiaircraft-artillery guns.

"Makes sense," Bear Woods muttered. "The radar signals are coming from that direction. I'll keep tracking him while you're in your dive-bomb."

Tuck was turning slightly eastward, to offset a bit so he could view VN-521 as he set up to dive-bomb. "If you find it's not the right site as we get closer, tell me to break it off."

"Will do," Woods said.

Tuck pressed the radio transmit button on the throttle. "Condor flight. We're on the attack." He began to climb.

"Two."

"Three, roger."

"Condor Four."

The other F-105G and then the two F-4Es followed as he snaked upward through the sky, then leveled at 12,000 feet.

"Tracking guns at eleven and three," muttered Bear Woods from the back, meaning two Firecan radars were locked on to their aircraft, feeding position information to the big guns.

Tuck oriented himself, found first the city on the bank of the Red River, then traced back to where the site should be located. The area appeared indistinct, meaning the site was camouflaged, which might mean it was occupied—and so far there'd been no "break-it-off" call from the rear cockpit. Tuck glanced out to ensure his wingman was in proper position, then sucked a breath of apprehension, turned on his left wing, and rolled into his dive.

The flak, both 57mm and 85mm, began as soon as he stabilized in the dive-bomb maneuver. He reoriented and stared at the impact point, jinking and turning so they'd be hard to hit. As they passed through 10,000 feet, Tuck stabilized the aircraft in a 45-degree dive and positioned so the aiming pipper was just above the intended target.

Orange balls of fire flashed past the canopy. Too close. He gritted his teeth and kept the target in view, continued the wings-level dive.

Eight thousand feet. The pipper was stable, and the target was slowly moving up toward it. Almost . . . almost. There! He pickled, felt the lurch of the aircraft as the four CBU-52s released, then pulled and shoved the control stick against his left knee, to recover to the west.

Bam! The bird shuddered hard.

Bear Woods heard the huge 85mm explosion that got them, and felt the airplane begin to shake violently, like a car running on a flat tire. His first thought was, *Oh shit.* The shuddering dampened some as they entered a slow but constant left-hand roll, nose slightly low in a shallow dive.

"We're . . . hit," he heard Tuck say.

Woods tried to answer, but his own intercom was inoperative.

"You . . . you hear me, Bear?" he heard.

The altimeter showed that they were descending through 5,000 feet, and Woods tried to remember if there'd been mountains higher than that in front of them. Smoke was filling the cockpit. Northwest? He leaned forward to peer, and confirmed a fluctuating heading of two-ninety degrees. Yeah, there were mountains there.

"If you can . . . hear me, you'd . . . better eject, Bear."

Woods drew in his heels against the seat and braced, then waited as the airplane rotated. *Through four thousand feet?* It was difficult to see the instrument panel. He pulled his head back against the headrest, and when he felt the aircraft was upright, rotated both handles. The canopy was slow about it, but it flew away, and the wind blasted through the open cockpit. At least he could see clearly now. They were inverted—upside down—and getting close to the ground. Green everywhere, so they were across the Red River at least, which meant they had a chance of being rescued.

As the big airplane continued rolling, he waited until they were almost upright, tensed, and pulled the left ejection trigger. The blast of the seat rockets slammed hard into his buttocks. The next lucid thought was of tumbling through the air, then of being separated from the seat. Woods heard a mechanical sound, and the chute deployed, flapped wildly, then was filled with air.

He felt a tug, then was swinging in a wide arc, like a pendulum beneath the camouflaged parachute canopy. Everything was green below. He looked about, blinking hard to clear tears made by the windblast that had hit him in spite of the lowered helmet visor. He saw the wide, muddy river in the near distance, emitted a curse because he'd thought they'd come farther than that, then glanced below again. He was close to the ground—coming down smack on a damned thatch house! Until then he'd been so busy he hadn't had time to feel fear, but it caught up with him in the form of a wave of nausea which quickly degenerated into something akin to hysteria.

Woods pulled frantically on the forward risers, to steer clear of the house and surrounding fields, and heard himself begin to whimper uncontrollably as the adrenaline drained from his system. Even in the chute, he could hear the sounds of distant voices shouting in Vietnamese. The ground was rushing up at him. He bent his knees slightly, positioning and moving almost trancelike.

He hit, tumbled and fell, was dragged for a few feet as the chute caught a gust of air. He released one clip, then the other, disconnecting from the parachute, then tried to unfasten the lanyard that tethered him to the inflated life raft and survival kit. His hands were shaking so badly that he had trouble with the simple task. He shucked off his gloves and worked at the clip, and finally succeeded. On the ground the voices sounded more distant. He had very little time!

As he removed his helmet, Woods heard another, much louder voice. Tuck Tucker's. Higher then, shrill, yelling for them to stop. He heard cursing and a scream. A loud *pop-pop-pop*—not too distant. Woods released an involuntary sob, then leaned low, close to the ground, and began to run. He forgot about the survival kit contents, even about the extra radio in there, about everything except trying to get away and staying alive. He simply bent over and ran, and vowed not to stop until he could run no farther.

Chapter 11

1730 Hours Local, Tuesday 27 June 1972
British Consulate, Hanoi
Democratic Republic of Vietnam

"Could you please come down here, sir?" the cipher clerk inquired on the shielded internal telephone system in the British Consulate in the northern quarter of Hanoi. Relations weren't cordial enough to merit an embassy.

"Straightaway," the man on the other end of the line answered and replaced the heavy black phone on the cradle. He snubbed out a cigarette, rose from his desk, and walked at an urgent pace down to the code room and was admitted into the cramped facility. The clerk spun his swivel chair to meet him.

"Got an Eyes Only, sir," the cipher clerk said and handed him a tan envelope with red markings. The man signed a form, that he'd received it and promising to safeguard the information thereon. The clerk had decoded the five-letter groups and typed them out in plain text. Still standing, the man opened the flap, pulled out a single sheet, and read:

REQUEST ALFRED ARRANGE THAT D.R.V. EX-
TEND OFFICIAL GOV'T INVITATION FOR FOLLOW-
ING U.S. NEWSMEN TO VISIT HANOI SOONEST;

BANNISTER, SHAWN AND CONNERT, RICHARD.
BOTH PREVIOUS VISITED HANOI IN NOV 68. UT-
MOST IMPORTANCE. SECRECY AND CELERITY ES-
SENTIAL.

The man, code-named Cochise by the Americans, made a
quiet snort in the back of his throat and slowly tore the sheet
into several pieces. Those he dropped into the classified burn
bag before turning to speak to the clerk, who was the only
other person at the embassy who held the appropriate level of
clearance.

"I should like for you to arrange a foursome for the far court
at the *Cercle,* Evans. Yourself, our Vietnamese friend, Mr.
Doang, of the Central Committee, and of course, me. Make it
for . . . hmmm"—he checked his watch—"six p.m. if possible.
Yes, that should do it. The usual precautions."

"Very good, sir."

He parked the Consulate's Morris Minor under the tamarind
tree at the end of the lot of the *Cercle Sportif.* He and the cipher
clerk climbed out and went directly to the bar for an orange soda,
then to the locker room and changed for tennis. They smiled and
whistled and chatted aimlessly as they walked out to the farthest
of the four tennis courts. They said hello and shook hands with
Nguyen Van Doang and his young partner. Doang was near fifty,
and had light skin, short dark hair, and eyebrows so bushy he
looked like an Asian version of John L. Lewis. He was quite
thin. They decided the clerk would pair with the younger man
and he with Doang. He spun his racket, the young Vietnamese
said "Down," which it was, and he and the clerk selected the
shady side of the court. After a ten-minute warm-up, the game
was on.

They took a break at the end of the third game. Court boys
brought water and they drank and toweled down by the bench
in the shade. After the clerk and his partner had walked off
toward their side of the court, he spoke quietly to Nguyen Van
Doang.

"I trust you remember when the American reporter Shawn
Bannister and his photographer-friend Richard Connert were
here in November 1968."

Doang nodded vaguely. He was more slender than most

Vietnamese men, mere parchment stretched over bones, as if something inside were eating away at him.

"Could you see your way clear to invite them back as soon as possible?"

Doang nodded again, his anthracite eyes barely flickering at the request. Nguyen Van Doang, code-named Alfred by his Western case officer, was a senior official in the research office of the Communist Party's Enemy-Proselytizing Department.

The game resumed and the clerk and his partner, both younger men, lost to the cunning and wiles of Doang and his British diplomat partner.

1730 Hours Local, Thursday 29 June 1972
Juspao, Rue le Loi
Saigon, Republic of Vietnam

"That was the worst thing I've ever seen," James P. Mahoney said to Wolf Lochert. "You want me to go through with this, you got to figure some way I don't cold-cock some of those macker smackers."

Mahoney had just come from the JUSPAO building on Le Loi in downtown Saigon, where he'd attended the press briefing the journalists call the Five O'clock Follies. Briefers from the military, and from the United States Information Services, had stood before the 200-seat auditorium to give their version of how the war was going. The audience had been its usual rowdy and unappreciative self. At the close of the briefing, Mahoney had slipped away and climbed the stairs in the same building to meet Wolf in an empty USIS office.

"Don't blow your cover," Wolf Lochert said. "Do precisely as I said. Listen to everyone, don't talk, act spaced-out. I know you, Mahoney. You can get along with the devil himself. Just don't let yourself get serious about what's being said. It's a game, remember?"

"Let me tell you," Mahoney said. "It's a bitch not being able to say something to those assholes."

"I know, but tough it out. You know how. It's worth it, believe me."

Mahoney remembered the POW briefing and nodded. "Yeah."

"Anybody recognize you?"

Jim Mahoney snorted. "Looking like this? You gotta be kidding."

He sported a scraggly Jesus beard and mustache, and wore faded blue jeans, a tattered denim jacket, and sandals over bare feet. His plastic MACOI ID card was slung around his neck on a dog tag chain.

"You'll have to attend a few more of these to establish your face and reputation. How you doing at Givral's and Brodard's?"

The press people hung out at those two coffee shops on To Do Street to share the latest rumors and listen to the word from the few Vietnamese they trusted.

"I'm getting to be a regular. No one's making me, Wolf. My own mother in Philly wouldn't recognize me like this."

"What happened to your leisure suit?"

"Damned thing rotted and fell off . . . sort of." Mahoney had hated the leisure suit and felt more at home in the jeans. "So what's the next step?" he asked. "How does all this tie in with our guys up north, Wolf?"

"You know of Shawn Bannister?"

"Traitor newsie."

Wolf grinned his death's-head look. "Mahoney, with an attitude like yours, you'll never get along in this world."

"Who wants to get along with assholes like him?"

"You're going to have to. You want to help on this project, you got to get along with *Scheisskopfs*. I want you to start hanging out with one of his buddies, Richard Connert."

"Never heard of him."

"He hangs out with Shawn Bannister and you got to get next to him."

"Bannister. Okay, I got it."

Wolf nodded. "You're there, Jim. You look like a newsie. You got the right flavor there. Now listen. This Connert's one of us, and we gotta talk with him right up to the last minute."

"Gotcha." He frowned. "The last minute of what?"

"The last minute before they go on the Hanoi trip with Jane Fonda."

"Wolf, why the *hell* are they going to Hanoi?"

"Don't worry about why anyone's going. It's part of the whole thing, Jim. We're going to use the *Scheisskopfs*." Wolf stuck his face next to Mahoney's. "Bannister and Connert just got into town, and they're staying at the same place as you. We knew they usually put up there, so that's why we got you that particular room. Now, besides hanging out at Givral's and Brodard's, they also like the roof bar at the Caravel. I want you to make yourself known up there. Spend whatever it takes. We'll make it up to you." There was no funding for the operation. While cooperation from the brass could be assured due to the Presidential note, to apply for discretionary funding might invite undue attention and compromise. Wolf had decided to pay whatever it took out of his own pocket. Keep track of it somehow and maybe try for some sort of repayment when the operation was over.

"Gee, Wolf," Mahoney said with a mischievous grin, "you always told me no boozing on the job."

Lochert growled. "You don't want me to pull that beard off your face and stuff it up your nose, shut up and listen. Go up there and get to be pals with all the regulars, so when Connert shows up it'll be easy to get next to him. We hope to contact him and tell him about you. If not, you'll have to find the right time and identify yourself."

"How do I do that?"

"Just tell him you're a part-time green mailman, and you have some messages." Wolf fished some pictures from a blouse pocket and flipped them to the stocky Mahoney. "Here's what he looks like." Mahoney examined the photos. One was of a youthful-looking, blond Richard Connert in an Air Force lieutenant's uniform, the other was of Connert as a bearded man in a crowd of antiwar demonstrators.

"Does he still have the beard?" Mahoney asked.

"Yeah, and long hair. What I want you to do is set up a way for you to contact each other at a moment's notice while he is here in Saigon. He'll need to tell us exactly when he and Shawn Bannister are going to Hanoi, and we'll need to give him last-minute information to use once he's up there."

"What's he going to do up there?"

"Talk to Caruso if possible. He's to clarify what was in Caruso's last message, and what he meant about the connection between our POW and the Russians."

"Okay. So how do I let him know I'm one of the gang?"

"Mailmen are taught ways to ID each other." Wolf told Mahoney how it was done.

2130 Hours Local, Saturday 1 July 1972
Romeo et Juliette Roof Bar, Caravel Hotel
Saigon, Republic of Vietnam

Night had descended, and James P. Mahoney had been at the boisterous rooftop bar of the Caravel Hotel since two o'clock that afternoon. He sat on one of the tall bamboo stools at the long bar, which was covered by an overhang of thatch. He'd fastidiously alternated between the bar and his room since late Thursday night, and was getting bloated and queasy from booze. But he'd done as instructed, had established himself as a pal of the regulars, then as one himself, through the bounteous application of money to buy drinks for all. Tonight drunken contractors, newsies, and a few military men in civvies surrounded him, laughing and listening to his stale Irish jokes. He was a great guy; he was one of them. From a thatch-covered dais, a six-piece Filipino band imitated the latest American songs with reckless abandon. Before them was a small dance floor. The remainder of the open-air rooftop was filled with heavy wrought-iron tables and chairs. The place was dark, the only lighting provided by a string of colorful Christmas tree lights and a flickering candle in a hurricane cup on each table.

Vietnamese piasters were piled bountifully on the bar top before Mahoney, and whenever it diminished, he would dig into the right front pocket of his jeans and peel more large bills from a roll. He'd been "on duty," as he thought of it to suppress his guilt, since Thursday night.

Some fucking party, he grumbled to himself. He was pouring his beers into the handiest plants, which thankfully were plentiful, and he'd arranged via a daily five-dollar tip for the bartender to make his drinks a blend of Coke and soda water, to produce a rich whiskey color. His drinking pals, of course, received the real thing.

The five-dollar bills were illegal in South Vietnam, where the U.S. government forbade its employees to possess green, since it might further inflate an economy which was up 300 percent since the Americans had arrived. One could buy 50 percent more piasters with green than with funny money—the

Military Payment Certificates issued to the GIs.

Mahoney needed a break from his boozy vigil, so he disentangled himself from the crowd and walked around the bar, to stand by the railing and stare southward at the dark countryside. What a difference, he told himself, from the days when you could stand on the same rooftop and watch two or three firefights between American or ARVN forces and the Viet Cong. Long, looping streams of red tracers would duel with the green arcs from enemy guns, while bright explosions of rockets and artillery shells punctuated the night with loud explosions you could feel in your gut. It had been a great way to get a young lady new to the war zone excited enough to cast away inhibitions. Now 90 percent of the American troops had been withdrawn—from half a million down to 50,000. And since the Viet Cong had been eliminated as a fighting force in the 1968 Tet offensive, and because the North Vietnamese Army had been so soundly repulsed in its invasion last Easter, there were no more vivid firefights providing the evening's *son et lumière*.

Jim pushed away from the rail. He went to the French-style latrine, got rid of a vast amount of water and beer, and returned to the bar.

"Hey, Jimmy, where the hell you been?" a deeply tanned, potbellied contractor wearing a white T-shirt and khaki shorts bellowed in a boozy voice. He and several others had been drinking off Mahoney all day. The contractor pushed free of the crowd, belched, and flung a beefy arm around Mahoney's neck. "Lesh sing a song, hey whaddya say?" he bellowed, then whispered quickly, "Four stools to your right—both of them."

Chef Hostettler had told him he'd be backed up by a heavyset man. Without pause, Mahoney clapped him on the back and led off with a fractured version of "Irish Eyes." Others joined in, and they tried to drown out the Filipino band, which was blowing some light jazz. At the end of a second boozy Irish song, Mahoney swung into "Birmingham Jail" and the others tagged along as best they could as he bellowed about the inmate who wanted his sweetheart to "write him a *letter,* send it by *mail,* send it in care of the Birmingham *jail.*" The men worked hard on the song and actually came up with a little harmony, as Jim emphasized the key words.

"God, but that's *awful* singing," Shawn Bannister said, frowning, to Richard Connert. The two were similar in their slender builds. Bannister stood two inches under six feet, and had neatly coifed blond hair that covered his ears and protruded fashionably over his collar. He was tanned and, except for a clipped Errol Flynn mustache, smooth-shaven. He wore a safari suit with extra pockets sewn on the jacket, which was open to his navel. Around his neck hung a gold rope chain with a two-inch golden alligator dangling from it. The jade-eyed alligator was a functioning roach clip. Also hanging from the chain was an aluminum finger ring.

Shawn Bannister had grown up in the shadow of his half-brother Courtland, and had worked diligently to become, in every possible way, as unlike Court as humanly possible. He had succeeded.

"The singing? Yeah, terrible isn't it," Connert agreed, listening to the words and what they might signify.

"Hey, check the round-eyes," Shawn said, pointing out two Caucasian females at a table near the rail. Several men were standing near them, laughing and talking. "Let's see what we can do." He flashed one of his trademark dazzling smiles. Both of Sam Bannister's sons were well known, but Shawn's smile was regarded as the more appealing, and certainly more like his father's than that of the more somber Courtland.

"Go ahead," Connert said, "I'll be over in a minute." Richard Connert was tanned, with sand-colored hair and a beard that made him look older than his thirty-one years. He had hazel eyes and wore a light-blue safari suit. After Shawn left, he ordered another beer and elbowed his way toward the singers. The song ended as he arrived, so he stood at the periphery of the crowd, studying Mahoney and the contractor, wondering if one of them had sung the song with a special purpose in mind. Any mention of "mail," regardless of how innocuous, alerted "mailmen" to a possible contact.

"Drinks all around," Mahoney yelled at the bartender. The men applauded and surged closer as Mahoney pushed a wad of bills toward the bartender. Then he backed out of the melee as the men pressed in to order their drinks.

"Doncha wanna drink?" Mahoney said as he approached Connert.

"Got one, thanks."

"Like the song?"

Connert shrugged.

"Think she ever wrote him the letter?"

"Hard to say."

"Hell, I'll bet she did—and the mailman delivered it in a blue envelope."

"You do?"

"Yeah, only the guy's dog had just died, so he was a *blue* mailman. Heh, heh. Get it?"

Connert was indeed a blue mailman. "Yeah, but what a bad joke. Where you from?"

"Normally I work at the main post office but lately I've become a, uhm, journalist—but I also deliver mail once in a while . . . to dancers."

Because of the crowd's noise and the band music, Connert determined that they were unlikely to be overheard. The man's brashness was somewhat irritating. He'd worked very hard to maintain his cover, and the guy was cracking jokes. "You any particular color?" he asked conversationally.

"Yeah, I'm green, I guess. But I'm really only part-time, not a *real* mailman."

"I'd like to hear more. Any place we can talk?"

"Over there." Mahoney waved his arms in a drunken gesture to the railing behind the bandstand, overlooking the Saigon River. He led the way, grinning and stumbling some. They stood silently for a full half minute, looking across the buildings at the floodlighted river docks, where war material was unloaded from ships around the clock. Beyond, they saw the lights of planes taking off and landing at the huge Tan Son Nhut Air Base.

"What's up?" Connert asked. He knew better than to ask for a name.

"First, the Postmaster, whoever that is, wanted to pass on that you're doing a great job."

Connert shrugged. "I haven't done much the last few months except turn Bannister into a politician and help get the bastard elected."

"Well, anyway, the word from the Postmaster is that he thinks you're doing good work."

A couple walked to the railing several feet distant. Connert took a pull on his beer and fabricated a drunken voice. "So what else is happening, bro?"

Mahoney's voice was low. "They're trying to get Dipper

invited back to Hanoi right away, because they need you there—"
He stopped when he sensed a presence behind them.

"Hey, Richard, you old dick, get your ass over here," Shawn
Bannister grumbled as he grabbed Connert by the arm. "These
gals are dying to meet you. Want to know if your pubes are
sandy-colored like your beard." He ignored Mahoney.

"God, Shawn, I'm starting to feel crappy. I think I'll pass on
this one."

"Can't do that, old son." Shawn tugged forcefully at Connert's
arm to start him toward the table. "The redhead's hot for your
bod and the brunette won't go with me until her pal's taken care
of." He pulled Connert along.

"Hey, buddy," Connert yelled over his shoulder to Mahoney,
"come on along. You might find some laughs."

Mahoney followed them to the table and stood behind them
as Bannister presented Connert to the girls.

"See," Shawn said to the brunette wearing a polka-dot halter
that accentuated an awesome chest, "now I've got ole Dicky
here for Betsy-boo, so let's hit the road." He went closer and
took her by the hand.

The brunette looked with appraising eyes beyond Shawn, at
the stocky Mahoney. "I dunno," she pouted in a not very sultry
drawl. "Let's not be in a hurry, big boy. Who's your big-chested
buddy bringing up the rear?"

Bannister swung around to glance at Mahoney. "Buzz off,
tubby," he grumbled.

Tubby? Mahoney said to himself . . . *Tubby?*

"Naw, let him stick around," Connert argued. "He's my buddy. He's a journalist, too."

Shawn looked back at the brunette and decided she was worth
humoring—he could dispose of the stranger at his leisure, and
maybe even have fun doing it. He sat beside her. "Sure," he said
with joviality, and to Mahoney, "Grab a chair and sit down, old
buddy."

Mahoney found a chair and sat beside Betsy-boo, who was
indeed interested in Richard Connert's pubes. "Well, this," said
Betsy-boo in a slightly tipsy voice as she fingered his beard,
"is so sandy, and, uhm, smooth. Is the *rest* of you like that?
Your, uhm, *you* know." She giggled, and Connert allowed as
how she could probably find out if she was lucky and played
her cards right.

"Oh, you," she said, and touched his hand with her fingers.

Her brunette pal, who'd been introduced as Flo, looked past Shawn and asked Mahoney his name.

"Jimmy," he replied, and, not wanting to annoy Shawn, he offered to go to the bar and buy a round.

"Yeah," Shawn said, and everybody placed an order. After Mahoney left them, Shawn leaned toward Flo. "Okay, now you met him and Betsy's fixed up, so let's blow."

Flo, who worked for RMK construction and didn't read Hollywood fan magazines, or much of anything except the comic page of *Stars & Stripes,* had no idea who Shawn Bannister was. She thought he was kind of cute, but certainly not built as well as stocky and solid Jimmy, who was more like the construction workers she was used to.

"Don't be in such a hurry," she said in a petulant tone. "We just got here. We haven't even danced or *anything."* The whine in her voice indicated she was used to getting what she wanted.

Shawn tossed his head impatiently. "Okay, so let's dance." He was increasingly peeved about all this. Back in Los Angeles, and certainly in Las Vegas, Shawn Bannister was used to girls far more beautiful than this doggy creature breaking their necks to get next to him.

Flo watched Mahoney return with the drinks. "Not jes' now," she said to Shawn. "Don' wanna dance yet." She'd just about made up her mind whom she wanted to favor with her charms.

"Jee-*sus,"* Shawn said into the night, watching Mahoney hand out drinks. "Sure you can afford that?" he half-snarled.

"Sure," Mahoney said cheerfully and sat.

"Who you write for?"

"Des Moines Register."

Shawn snorted. "Never heard of it. Column? Features? What?"

"Features."

"Is this a lousy war or what?" Shawn was ready to dispose of this interloper.

"It's a lousy war."

"You think them guys are going to win?"

"What guys?" Jim Mahoney worked hard at keeping the amiable smile on his face.

"The North Viets. You think they're gonna win?"

"Hell, I don't know. I just write about soldiers, I'm not into the politics of all this."

"Well, I am. It's an immoral war and that's what I write. And so should you. Too bad Ho Chi Minh died. He was an okay guy. Here, look what they gave me." He lifted the aluminum ring on his neck chain. "Little souvenir from up there, made from the wreckage of the thousandth American airplane they shot down. Isn't that something?"

Yeah, it's something, motherfucker. I think I'll just poke it in your eye with a long stick. "Interesting," was the best Mahoney could say without strangling on his words.

Flo made a muzzy smile. "Whyncha dance with me. I wanna dance," she said to Mahoney.

"I'll dance with you. C'mon," Shawn said. He stood up and pulled at her arm.

"Let me go. I don't want to dance with you, I want to dance with Jimmy."

Shawn tightened his grip and she slapped at his hand. "Hey, you're hurting me." She turned to Mahoney. "Make him stop."

Shawn Bannister looked down and across the table at Mahoney. "Thanks for screwing things up, asshole," he snarled.

And a knee in the nuts to you, asshole. Mahoney carefully maintained the naive look. "Sorry. Really am."

"Sorry? Sorry this." Shawn Bannister snatched up Mahoney's beer and flung it in his face.

There was a horrifying second when Mahoney's eyes clearly signaled he was about to throw Shawn Bannister off the roof. Then he blinked. *Wolf, you'd be proud of me.* "Aw, I said I was sorry. You didn't have to do that." Mahoney stood and pulled a bandanna from his pocket to wipe his face. "You didn't have to do that."

"No, he dint," Flo said and flung her own drink in Shawn's face, who immediately swung a hand and slapped her with a resounding smack. At that, a man from the next table stood and chopped Shawn on the back of the neck, dropping him onto the table, sending glasses and beer bottles scattering. Bannister rolled onto the floor and came up with a bottle in his hand. He started to swing at the man. Connert deftly moved in behind and grabbed his arm.

Shawn struggled in his grip. "Goddamn it, let me go."

"Your reputation, Shawn. You can't do this."

Mahoney came around the table to calm the other man, who was ready to do battle. Flo looked at him—he was broad and craggy—and decided that *this* one was *really* nifty. She elbowed past Mahoney and told him just that. Betsy-boo eyeballed the guy's friends at the other table, decided they looked okay, and told Richard Connert he was a jerk to hang around with people as shitty as Shawn, and rose to join Flo and her new boyfriend at their table.

Shawn Bannister, chest heaving, glaring maliciously at Connert.

"You shit. I was going to take you along to Hanoi with me. Not now. Nothing doing. You're off the payroll. You're fired—got that?" He spun on his heel and stalked out.

2315 Hours Local, Saturday 1 July 1972
Apartment on Rue Thuong Nhut
Saigon, Republic of Vietnam

"Mahoney," Wolf Lochert said, "I don't know why I bothered dragging you out of Loc Ninh. At least up there you were absorbing mortar blasts that otherwise might have hurt somebody important."

The two were at the apartment of Greta Sturm, on a tree-lined street near the American Embassy. Greta, although a West German national, worked for the huge USAID office in Saigon. Wolf had been seeing her for several years, and had given Greta's telephone number to Mahoney in the event of an emergency . . . just like this one.

"Wolf, I'm telling you there was nothing I could do." They spoke in near whispers on the balcony of Greta's second-floor apartment overlooking Thuong Nhut Street. Trees towered over the balcony and rustled in the night breeze. It was midnight dark, the street lamps were dim, and the streets nearly devoid of traffic since the eleven p.m. curfew. A few bicyclists, their tires humming, scurried past, bound for home.

Wolf Lochert glared. "You were there to keep things on track and still it got screwed up."

"When will you two be finished?" Greta called out from inside. "I've prepared a little supper."

Wolf leaned into the living room. "Five minutes." Although he trusted her implicitly, the operation was far too sensitive to let Greta have even a hint of what was going on. Wolf and Mahoney had fabricated a sad tale and said Mahoney had requested Wolf's expert advice on the subject of unrequited love.

"What do I do now?" Mahoney asked.

"Let me think about it," Wolf growled, extremely unhappy at the latest glitch. He motioned with his head. "Let's go eat."

Greta's *little supper* consisted of great mounds of steaming noodles surrounding a huge pork roast.

Greta spoke as they ate. "Poor James. Did you have a lover's quarrel?" Greta was in her early thirties, and had flaxen hair and wide-set gray eyes. She'd seen the smoke and terror of battle at Wolf's side when he had rescued her from capture at Hue city. She was a stoic woman, very much in love with Wolf Lochert. She had no idea whether he returned the feeling.

"Uh, yeah. A bad quarrel." Jim shook his head. "Now she wants to go off on a, uh, business trip without me."

"Do you love her?"

"Well, maybe not exactly . . . you see—"

"Yes, he is in love with her," Wolf interrupted. He took a thoughtful bite of succulent pork. "Jim wants to go along on the trip, but he's got to convince her." He continued Jim Mahoney's game while his mind turned and pondered the question.

Greta frowned, then brightened. "Who is she seeing? Perhaps you can get them to tell her she should bring you along. Where is she going, James?"

"Well, unh, you see . . . " Mahoney tried not to look at Wolf for help.

"It's too painful for him to talk about," Wolf said.

Greta looked from man to man, her eyes squinting with suspicion. "You are . . . what you say . . . putting me on. I do not believe either one of you. I want to know what is going on. You sit here and eat my food, you must tell me." Her voice was heavy with Teutonic authority.

Wolf didn't answer as he shoveled his food in.

"Why do you think we are putting you on?" Mahoney asked.

"No one would ask my Wolfgang for help on a problem of the heart."

Wolf looked up and glowered from under his bushy brows. "Why not?" he rumbled.

"Oh, *liebchen.*" She patted him fondly. "You were in the seminary—and then you met me and I treat you good. So . . . where could you get experience in affairs of the heart?"

Wolf snorted, then lowered his head and resumed shoveling the food in.

"I do have a problem," Mahoney said, helping himself to the pork.

"But it does not have to do with a woman, does it?" Greta said.

James P. Mahoney remained quiet.

"Business?"

He frowned. "Maybe."

She heaped noodles onto his plate. "Then I understand why you cannot speak about it."

Wolf looked up sharply. "What was that advice? To convince her she can't make the trip without Mahoney?"

"But there is no such person," Greta replied.

A smile formed on Lochert's face as the answer came to him. He would get a message out to General Whisenand first thing in the morning, outlining a suggested course of action. Then he'd have Mahoney set up a meeting with Connert in the Embassy safe room to provide instructions.

0930 Hours Local, Monday 3 July 1972
British Consulate, Hanoi
Democratic Republic of Vietnam

"Another special message, sir," the clerk said as Cochise walked into the small room.

Cochise read the contents with interest:

ENSURE ALFRED SPECIFIES CONNERT ACCOMPANY BANNISTER. CONVINCE BANNISTER DUAL VISA REQUESTS WERE PROCESSED, THUS BOTH MUST COME OR NONE AT ALL.

He shredded the message into the burn bag.

"Another tennis game, sir?" the clerk asked.

"I think not. This time I believe a simple tea will suffice."

Chapter 12

The four F-4Ds of Rattler flight were in combat spread formation, looking for trouble as they approached Hanoi three miles
above the green countryside and close to the speed of sound.
Their mission was MiG-CAP, combat air patrols against MiGs.
When they heard the radio transmission for which they had
trained so hard and were so eagerly awaiting, each man's pulse
rate increased. The transmission was from Red Crown, a Navy
air-intercept controller on a destroyer in the Gulf of Tonkin.

"Rattler Lead, Red Crown, you've got two bogeys eleven low
for twenty, closing." Red Crown had just told Rattler flight that
two unidentified aircraft were approaching, at a lower altitude,
from their eleven o'clock, and at a range of twenty miles.

"You got them, Jerry?" Rattler Lead, Captain Kenichi Tanaka,
said to his backseater, who only had time to grunt "Yeah" before
the next powerful transmission.

"Rattler, Red Crown, you've got one more bogey at your ten
for twenty-five, closing. It may be friendly." The destroyer, USS
Chicago, cruised one mile outside the territorial waters of North

Vietnam, and carried a powerful aerial search radar.

"You see anybody on radar yet?" Tanaka repeated to his backseater.

"Rattler, two more bogeys at your ten for twenty-five, closing. Looks like you're in for it. I'll vector Python to your area."

"Hold off and use Python as backup," Tanaka radioed. "We'll give a call if we can't handle these. You got an ID on the bogeys?" Tanaka wanted to know if the approaching planes were friendly or enemy. A bogey was an unknown, a bandit an identified enemy.

"Negative, Rattler."

"Got 'em, Jerry?" Tanaka asked again on the intercom.

"Shit, yes, like crabs in a crotch. That Red Crown guy kept interrupting. I'll put 'em on your scope. Who do you want first?"

"We'll divvy with the rest of the guys." Tanaka punched his transmitter button. "Rattler Three, check out the three bogeys at ten and we'll take the ones at eleven o'clock. Get a positive ID before you shoot. Copy?"

"Rodge, Lead, Three's breaking off," Captain Toby Parker answered as he eased his Phantom slightly left. "Loose deuce, Four, push it up," he said. His wingman pulled abreast, 600 feet out from his leader, and they both increased their throttles. Toby's best flights were those led by Ken Tanaka.

"Good paints, dead ahead for fifteen," Toby's backseater, Ed Starr, said in an excited voice. "Locked on . . . you can select Sparrows."

"Negative," Toby said, "still need a visual. We'll press closer." He pushed the transmit button. "Four, get a good lock-on but hold your fire till we get a valid ID."

The Sparrow, a twelve-foot missile, weighed 450 pounds and carried a 66-pound warhead. Its top speed was just under Mach 4, range thirty miles. Although the radar-guided missile could blast an airplane out of the air well beyond the visual range (BVR) of the pilot, the rules of engagement required an eyeball identification of the bogey as enemy. Thus the long-range factor was negated. Also, a Navy A-4 and a MiG-21 looked similar beyond four miles. Only Red Crown or Disco, the orbiting EC-121 radar plane, could clear a BVR Sparrow shot, and then only if they'd tracked the MiG from takeoff on. If they hadn't, the pilot had to get the positive identification, which forced firing range down to four or five miles, which meant using the smaller, heat-seeking AIM-9 Sidewinder or a cannon for close-in dogfighting. Rattler flight had Sparrows and Sidewinders but no gun, for the centerline station was taken up by an auxiliary fuel tank.

The jets had a combined closing speed of 1,100 mph, three miles per second.

"I'm padlocked," Rattler Four said, meaning he had his fire-control system locked on to the approaching aircraft and a missile ready to go.

"Hold it," Toby replied, staring, "hold it." Then he was able to see the approaching planes clearly. "Don't shoot," Toby yelled, "the first one's friendly."

"There's three of them! Which one's the friendly?" Rattler Four asked, then immediately: "Oh, Christ, I see him, the lead bird's Navy, and the other two are MiGs attacking him."

The Navy A-7 in the distance was trailing smoke. Directly behind were two MiG-21s, diving and closing rapidly. A broken radio transmission sounded in their headsets.

". . . my antenna's gone and I'm hit bad. Red Crown, you read Beefeater?"

"Beefeater," Toby transmitted, "you the A-7 at 120 for forty from Bullseye?" They were forty miles southeast of the Bullseye . . . Hanoi.

"Affirm. Got one of theirs, but now I got two MiGs cornered at my six and I'm Winchester and a tad shot up." Winchester was the code word for out of ammunition. "You the Phantoms up ahead?"

"Ah, roger. Beefeater, break left, break left," Toby suddenly bellowed as he saw the MiGs begin their attack. "You got two MiGs at your seven." He pushed his throttles into afterburner and pulled the nose of his Phantom up to engage as a MiG-21 fired a missile at the A-7. "They're shooting at you, Beefeater! Come on, bend it around."

". . . hydraulics 'bout gone, can't . . . " The transmission quit when the missile struck the A-7 and blasted a hole in its fuselage. The plane slewed, shedding pieces in a sheet of smoke and flame. There were blurs then, as first the canopy, then the ejection seat flashed from the carnage. Toby pulled sharply up to try to keep the pilot in sight, while still tracking the MiG, but then smoke obscured his sight and he lost them. He punched his transmit button.

"Red Crown, Rattler Three. We got Beefeater going down at my location."

"Copy, Rattler, any chutes?"

"Can't tell, but he ejected. I saw the seat." Toby turned his concentration back to the delta-winged MiG, finger poised on the missile-firing button, but saw that he'd lost his radar lock during the maneuver. He switched to Sidewinders and heard a tone indicating one had picked up the enemy heat source.

"I see a good chute," Rattler Four said. He'd rolled inverted to keep the Navy pilot in sight.

"Oh, shit," Ed Starr yelled from Toby's backseat. "Rattler Four, break left, break left, you got one on your ass."

Just as Starr finished the radio call, Toby fired two Sidewinders at his MiG, then he made a quick visual search for Rattler Four. He cursed as he realized that between his concentration on MiG one and looking for Beefeater's chute, he'd lost sight of MiG two as it maneuvered in on his own wingman. Toby risked a quick look and saw one of his missiles blow up in MiG one's tailpipe, then lingered as that entire airplane came apart. Toby jerked his eyes back to the problem at hand, then pulled tighter to the left. He still had too much angle-off to shoot at MiG two, so he pulled straight up and rolled, floated, and stared down through the top of the canopy. Ken Tanaka's words about using the vertical rang in his ears.

"You got number-one MiG," Ed confirmed jubilantly. Then his voice calmed. "But you gotta bring the nose around or we won't get a lock on number two." The Sidewinder tone did not indicate a good track, nor could Ed get a radar lock on the MiG, still intent upon attacking their wingman, Rattler Four.

"I'm firing ballistic, hope to scare him." Toby grunted. "I'm sure he's got a lock on Four." Toby was surprised he didn't feel as excited as his backseater.

As he watched, MiG two squeezed off one, then another Atoll missile, and Toby immediately yelled over the radio, "Rattler Four, break hard right! Break right. You've got two Atolls back there." As he spoke, Toby fired a single Sidewinder, then pulled the nose through in an attempt to get a better radar angle on MiG two.

One of the MiG's Atolls detonated beside his wingman, who immediately transmitted, "Four's hit."

Toby shot another missile at the MiG that had completed his turn and was now in a full power dive running back in the direction of Hanoi. Toby let the speeding plane go and looked around to keep track of the crippled Rattler Four.

"I got him," Ed Starr said. "Three o'clock low, headed west." Court quickly maneuvered and slid down next to his wingman. The left rear of the Phantom was peppered with dark holes and shiny punctures from the exploding Atoll.

"You look like a sieve, Four. You guys okay? How does it handle?"

"We're okay but the utility pressure's gone, PC-1 is low, and I can't get my left engine above sixty percent without a fire-warning light coming on. Also, my TACAN and radar are out. Outside of that we're ready to party. We saw you get your MiG. Shit hot, Three."

"Yeah," said Toby. "Now let's go home. Red Crown, Rattler Three and Four are egressing. Four has battle damage but I think he'll make it to the tanker."

"Rattler, Crown, you got enough fuel to cap a SAR for Beefeater? You're the only ones who know where he is. The Sandys and the Jollys will be in the area in five minutes." A SAR was the name for a search and rescue operation.

Toby checked his gauges. "Red Crown, we've got ten minutes of fuel to spare, but I want to stay with our wingman."

"Go ahead, Toby," Rattler Four said. "We'll make it to the tanker okay. You can catch up. They'll never find that guy without your help."

Four's voice was collected and he sounded very positive. Toby was torn. Finally he asked, "Think you can climb up to the tanker's altitude?"

"Rodge, no sweat."

"Okay, start easing on up now. This is a good heading. See you at the tank, Four. Break, break, Red Crown, Rattler Three is heading back to cap for Beefeater."

"Thanks, Rattler, the package is thirty south of your position. How is the ground fire?"

"There's something down there east of us," Ed said. Toby looked and saw a small white streak against a green hillside. He pulled the throttles back slightly and zoomed down to 5,000 feet before he pushed them back up. They were over an area of green hills and rice paddies.

"So far so good. I got the chute in sight and nobody's shooting," he told Red Crown. He switched to Guard frequency on the radio. "Beefeater, do you read Rattler?"

"Gotcha, Rattler," a tinny voice replied as the Navy pilot spoke into his tiny survival radio. "I'm on the hill above my chute. The bad guys down below know I'm here, and I think they're on their way up. Get me *outta* here."

Six minutes later a flight of Phantoms, then the HH-53 Jolly Green rescue helicopter and supporting A-1s arrived, and took over the operation. Toby was released to RTB (Return to Base). Thirty minutes later Toby was at the tanker.

No one had heard from or seen his wingman, Rattler Four.

1315 Hours Local, Tuesday 4 July 1972
Intelligence Section, 432nd Tactical
Fighter Wing
Udorn Royal Thai Air Force Base
Kingdom of Thailand

In the intelligence debriefing room, Toby and Ed pored over the maps, correlating reports from other airplanes flying in the area at that time. No one had a clue as to the fate of the two men in Rattler Four. The intelligence officer typed up the Missing in Action reports while another took the data on the confirmed MiG.

Toby was numbed and shattered as he left the group and walked out the door, headed toward the Officers' Club. His flight suit was stained dark, drenched with sweat, his face was twisted, eyes squinty.

Ed Starr followed him for a way, then split off, saying he'd join him later, that he was going to buy and distribute the beer for the armorers and maintenance men, all of whom had contributed to the shoot-down as far as the crews were concerned. Toby nodded but said nothing.

Inside the Udorn Officers' Club, he ignored the calls of friends congratulating him for shooting down his first MiG, and took a seat at a table near the far end of the huge bar. On the other side of the club a cheer rang out as several men from the Air Rescue and Recovery Group entered and the F-4 crew members scrambled to get them drinks. It was a time-honored tradition that no fighter crew allowed a Jolly to buy his own drink. Jolly Green rescue people had the earned reputation of caring more for the life of the man on the ground than for their own.

Toby ordered a double vodka on the rocks as Ken Tanaka walked up and slid onto the stool next to him.

"Congratulations on the MiG, old buddy," Tanaka said in a quiet voice. "Nice job."

Toby made a disgusted sound in his throat. "It wasn't fucking worth it, Ken. If I hadn't been so intent after him, I'd have seen one that got my wingman." He hammered a fist on the bar top. "Remember Neddle telling me I didn't have a killer instinct? Well, today I was out there with fire in my eye, and what did I do? Lost a damn good wingman and his backseater."

"That's not *exactly* how it happened," Tanaka said.

"Bullshit. If I'd been alert, they'd be here now." The Thai barmaid placed his vodka in front of him and he threw a ten-dollar bill on the bar. "When it's done, keep 'em coming."

Tanaka's dark eyes flickered at the vodka. "Are you sure that's what you want to do?"

"And I let them go back by themselves, Ken." Toby stared at the glass and cupped his hand around it. "It just wasn't fucking worth it."

"Are you sure that's what you want to do?" Tanaka repeated, nodding at the glass.

"I just killed two guys. Why the hell not?"

"Maybe you should talk to someone first." He signaled to a man standing with the rescue troops, who walked over. He wore a torn and dirty Navy flight suit and a grin that stretched from ear to ear.

"Hi," he said, and stuck out his hand, "I'm Fred Lewis and I owe my life to you." He eyeballed Toby's untouched double vodka. "And I'd like to sort of return the favor. Ken Tanaka here has told me all about you."

They talked for two hours while Fred (call me Bad Freddie) and Ken dissected Toby's decisions and consumed gallons of iced tea. By the end of the conversation, Toby had eased up on himself. Bad Freddie and Ken Tanaka had argued that both of

Toby's decisions were correct and logical, and besides, it was unlikely that the two men in Rattler Four were dead. It made more sense they they'd bailed out somewhere along their route.

"You did the logical thing, Toby," Ken said.

"Maybe, but I'll bet they didn't think so."

"Look, they were—" Tanaka corrected himself. "They *are* mature and responsible. In war you have to make hard decisions and most often they involve taking a risk. Not everybody walks away. You made the most logical decisions under the circumstances."

"Something else," Bad Freddie said. "The reason you didn't shoot earlier was because neither Red Crown or Disco knew who was friendly and who was enemy. After I debriefed, I talked to the controller. He didn't know about the MiGs being on my ass because I couldn't talk to him. My antenna was shot up and only someone within a mile or two could read me."

Toby held up his hands. "Okay—enough, guys. You've accomplished what you set out to do. I'm not going to drink, and you made me feel a lot better."

"Good," said Tanaka. "Now I can get on with feeling good about my own kill." He too had downed a MiG-21.

"About fuckin' time," Bad Freddie said as he grabbed and tossed down Toby's now-warm double vodka. "Now *I* can celebrate." He sprang up on the bar and clanged the bell. "Drinks on me," he yelled to great cheers.

"About fuckin' time, squid," a Jolly pilot growled.

Toby pasted a smile on his face, rang the bell, and said drinks were on him, too.

"About fuckin' time, MiG killer," a fighter jock yelled. Then Tanaka followed suit for his confirmed MiG, and everyone settled down to a good time.

Toby grinned. "I did everything you taught me," he said later to Tanaka.

"Tell me about it," Tanaka said delightedly. For twenty minutes, as Toby told Ken Tanaka how it went, the club noise stopped and the Phantom crew members listened. Hangar flying was an important part of a pilot's life. A pilot could study all the books and, as his flying time mounted, learn many things. But not all the rules of success or all the odd circumstances that can and frequently do happen to a pilot are in the books. So pilots listen carefully and store away the experience of others because someday the very same thing may happen to them and they can pull the proper response from their memory banks.

As Toby spoke, he noticed a slender lieutenant colonel wearing summer khakis. He was listening intently. Standing next to him was a husky man in civilian clothes Toby thought he recognized as an intelligence officer from Ubon a few years back.

When he was finished, Ken Tanaka told the story of his own MiG shoot-down. Both men agreed the MiG-21s had seemed more powerful and maneuverable than those they'd been briefed to expect.

Then Bad Freddie told the story of his own shoot-down. He summed it up when he finished, then said, "My wingman and I got into a furball with three MiGs. I got one, took a couple hits, then couldn't find anybody to join up with, so I started back. I found out later my wingman's okay. Moral there is, don't get separated." He realized what he'd said and cast a hasty glance at Toby, whose face remained impassive. His concern was unwarranted, for Toby was now at home with the decisions he'd made. Lewis continued. "And what do I recommend you carry if you go down? Three radios and a lot of water." He answered a few questions, then, with a flourish, he led the way back to the bar and ordered more drinks for the Jollies.

The Lieutenant Colonel and the man in civilian clothes detached themselves from the crowd and walked over to Toby and Ken.

"Hi, I'm George Weiss and this is Chef Hostettler. He can answer your question about the MiGs being more powerful."

As they shook hands, Toby looked hard at Hostettler. "You were at Ubon in '67, weren't you?" Hostettler said he was. He was with Seventh now but didn't specify what job.

Weiss had a happy twinkle in his eye. "I'm from the PIO at Seventh."

Toby and Ken rolled their eyes. Seventh Air Force, at Tan Son Nhut, ran the in-country war and had more staff members, it was rumored, than the Pentagon. A vast number were thought to be assigned to the Public Information Office, grinding out chocolate-covered stories about how the USAF people in Southeast Asia were faring, for the consumption of the folks back home.

"We were sent here for two reasons," Weiss continued. "I've

got to get your MiG story, Toby. You're a pretty famous guy and we want to feature your shoot-down. There are some pretty unusual aspects about it. And I need Tanaka's story as well."

Hostettler spoke. "I'm here to brief the pilots on the new MiG-21 and about some better IFF features coming up." IFF meant Identification Friend or Foe, an electronic device initially developed in World War II that emitted coded signals when interrogated by a special radar set.

Toby frowned at Weiss. "Colonel, I don't care to be interviewed for any story. It was a tough day and we took losses. Besides, I don't want my face and name in the paper." Not many pilots did. If they went down and were captured, it provided the enemy information the pilots did not want them to have. The classic case was USAF Lieutenant Colonel Robbie Risner, whose face appeared on the cover of *Time* magazine a few weeks before he was shot down and captured.

"Look, make my job easy," Weiss said. "There's a lot of interest in you upstairs because of the Air Force Cross you won a few years back, and they want me to do a piece on you."

"Colonel, I just don't want to do it," Toby said. "I don't *care* what they think at Seventh—or any other place, for that matter."

"What's so important about getting this one interview?" Tanaka asked Weiss. "You act like it's a matter of life or death."

"Life or death of a good fighter training program, perhaps," Weiss said. "And you play a role in this too, Tanaka."

"What do you mean by that?"

"Let's find a table where the noise isn't quite so loud, and I'll tell you about it," Weiss said.

"I'd rather hear what Colonel Hostettler has to say about identifying MiGs," Toby said.

"It's classified," Hostettler said. "I'll be briefing it every four hours for the next day at Wing Headquarters so all the crews can get it. Meanwhile, I think you should hear what George has to say. You just might change your mind." He stood up. "Now if you kind gentlemen will excuse me, I've got to go set things up. First brief's at 1700." He walked away.

Weiss led Toby and Ken to a table farther from the ongoing party.

"Here's the situation," Weiss said. "Since the late fifties, neither the Air Force or the Navy has had realistic fighter-versus-fighter training. As a result, our shoot-down ratio over Hanoi has generally been dismal, almost a one-for-one trade-off."

"Tell me about it," Tanaka said. "In Korea we got twelve of theirs for one of ours."

"In the late sixties," Weiss continued, "Navy Captain Frank Ault made a study about how pisspoor Navy fighter training was. As a result, a couple of their best people got together and rammed through a whole new training concept at Miramar, their Naval Air Station outside San Diego. These guys have updated the old tactics that went out with the old prop jobs."

"I heard about all that at George," Tanaka said.

"He's being modest, Colonel," Toby said. "Ken ran me through a special air-to-air course, but very clandestinely. Very little we did was in the approved curriculum. His ass was stretched-out grass and TAC was looking around with their giant lawn mower."

"Exactly," Weiss said, "and that's my point. But perhaps you only *thought* no one knew about what you were doing. There were some midlevel guys watching very closely, and a few high-level guys too. They know we need to improve our fighter training, but they've run into roadblocks trying to get it approved in the Pentagon."

"You mean we were the patsies?" Tanaka said, an eyebrow arched.

"I'd rather call it the pathfinders," Weiss replied. "Of course if things had gone wrong, it sure as hell would have got you burned. Everyone who was watching would suddenly be looking the other way with innocent looks on their faces."

"Well, I'll be goddamned," Tanaka said.

"But you guys did great and it went good. And today, both teacher and pupil shot down one of their new, razzle-dazzle MiG-21s, and if we bring *that* to the attention of the right people, we can most likely get our training improvements."

Toby was impressed. "Colonel, for a PIO guy, you're awfully knowledgeable about all this. How come?"

"Son, ever since the big one, I've lived, breathed, and dreamed fighters, but I could never pass the Air Force flight physical. Bad eyes. Funny thing is, I got my commercial license and have logged more than three thousand hours. I've got half interest in a Cessna, but someday soon, after I get back to the States, I plan on picking up a Mustang." He looked at both men. "I'll buy a round, since I seem to be doing most of the talking."

As Weiss elbowed his way to the bar, Ken looked at Toby. "Sorta like we were test rats in a laboratory."

"Yeah. He seems to be sincere enough. Pathfinders?"

"I sure as hell like the idea of the improved training. Remember when we talked about it with J. T. Neddle? It's as if the two of them have been talking."

"I wouldn't bet against it. I'd be damned mad about it if I didn't agree."

Weiss returned with a round of drinks, including iced tea for Ken and Toby. As soon as he sat, he picked up where he'd left off. "Even now at the fighter training bases they haven't really gotten into the high-powered stuff the Navy is teaching, and they certainly don't do dissimilar. Can't get permission. Maybe we can help change that." "Dissimilar" meant practice dogfighting with different types of fighters.

"Are you trying to tell us the fate of the whole program depends on Toby and me?" Tanaka asked.

"There are a lot of others pushing and shoving in the background, but you two guys can be out front, adding a lot of practical impetus to the idea."

"Look," Toby said, "I go along with the upgrade idea, and even using Ken and me as proof of the concept. But how about at least keeping our names and photos out of the papers until we've finished our tours?"

"That would mean losing the impact with the public, the congress, and hence . . . with the brass. Specific tactics, of course, would be classified, but you guys, with all your special training, have to be on the front page."

Toby and Ken looked at one other. "Well, okay by me, I suppose," Toby finally said.

"Sure," said Ken, "if it will help get the job done."

"Okay, here's some real icing on the cake, then," Weiss said, "something I wasn't going to bring up unless you agreed to the publicity."

"I don't like the sound of this," Toby said.

"You will," Weiss said. "You two are to be scheduled only for MiG-CAP missions, no air-to-ground, no interdiction, nothing but MiG-hunting missions. Further, you'll be scheduled to fly nothing except F-4Es." The new F-4E was a much better fighting machine than the C or D model, with a new radar and an internal 20mm cannon. "Who knows, one of you might be the second Air Force Ace." Captain Steve Ritchie had made Ace earlier that year, and the Navy already had a pilot Ace in Lieutenant Randy Cunningham. Many USAF pilots had up to three MiGs, two of them—Robin Olds and Court Bannister—had four, but no one besides Steve Richie had gotten the elusive fifth. Two USAF backseat WSOs, Chuck DeBellevue and Jeff Feinstein, had been conferred Ace status when they had assisted different frontseaters shoot down a total of five MiGs. The way was now clear for a second USAF pilot Ace, and maybe the third.

The two pilots looked at each other. *"Shit hot,"* they said in unison.

"Come to think of it," Toby said to Tanaka, "you're ahead of me already." Tanaka had helped shoot down a MiG on his earlier tour at Ubon, and was credited with half a kill.

"Yesterday's memories are tomorrow's tennis balls," Tanaka said with a grin.

Weiss looked puzzled. "I beg your pardon?"

"To phrase it another way," Tanaka said, "the wise crow does not smoke cigars."

Weiss eyeballed Toby. "Does he always talk this way?"

"Only when his mind is clear."

1700 Hours Local, Tuesday 4 July 1972
Main Briefing Room, 432nd Tactical
Fighter Wing
Udorn Royal Thai Air Force Base
Kingdom of Thailand

"It's called Combat Tree." Chef Hostettler stood at the podium on the stage. Beside him were tripods holding blowup photographs of the equipment and the missiles. "Using it will triple your kill range because you will no longer have to get a visual ID before you shoot. With this, you can get a positive ID and fire your Sparrows beyond visual range."

There were murmurs of excitement in the audience of eager Phantom crew members as Hostettler lifted the cover of a display. All the big white poster board showed was a small black box and a keyhole-shaped image on a radarscope.

"What the hell is *that?*" a rough voice questioned.

"That, my friend, is the box that receives the MiG IFF squawk, and *this* is what the signal will look like on your scope."

The audience became spellbound when Hostettler told them about all the new information they'd receive from Red Crown and Disco.

"I'm not at liberty to tell you how they *get* their information, but I can tell you that you'll be receiving very detailed, I repeat *very detailed,* information about what the MiGs are up to. The source is highly classified and if you were to become, ahem, guests of the Hanoi Hilton, they might put your nuts in a vise until you tell them all about it, and it would go away. *Capiche?"*

The audience allowed as how they *capiched.* They no longer wanted to know.

What Chef Hostettler withheld from them was the complex aerial electronic signal processing that would go into action when the big bombing strikes were made.

The processing package involved five different types of aircraft that ranged from a U-2 at high altitude to a propeller-driven Constellation flying down at low altitude. The U-2, from SAC's 99th Strategic Reconnaissance Squadron (SRS) based at U Tapao, hovered fifteen miles in the thin air over North Vietnam, picking up enemy radio traffic. That was relayed to a collection center at Nahkon Phanom, Thailand, where it was rapidly analyzed and retransmitted. From SAC's 82nd SRS at Kadena Air Base in Okinawa, a Boeing RC-135M orbited off the border of North Vietnam. In its fuselage were thirty-five men and a host of electronic signal processing equipment, and that information was also forwarded. The propeller-driven plane, an EC-121D from the 552nd at Korat, was a radar picket plane, call sign Disco, which orbited over the South China Sea. A Navy EP-3B Orion from Da Nang was also part of the package. The Navy also flew EC-121Ms from Da Nang that carried a thirty-four-man crew which included four American linguists, fluent in Vietnamese, several Morse code operators, a Korean and Russian linguist (pilots from those countries were known to fly combat in North Vietnamese MiGs), and T-branchers who copied and interpreted enemy radar signals. Perched on top and slung from the belly of the Super Connie were two gray-painted radar radomes. The big ships orbited over the Gulf of Tonkin, east of North Vietnam.

All the planes worked as a team, feeding into the combat information center of the destroyer *Chicago,* call sign Red Crown, which correlated all the data and transmitted it to the American pilots as if only its own radar were providing the information.

Hostettler told them none of that, but only what they would see and hear, and concluded his briefing by saying most of their planes would be modified with Combat Tree black boxes before the end of the week.

Before that happened, Toby had shot down two more MiGs.

0810 Hours Local, Thursday 6 July 1972
Western Bank of Red River
Democratic Republic of Vietnam

Bear Woods crawled to the edge of the thicket of bushes and stared hungrily at the three scrawny chickens pecking away in the farmer's yard, wishing to hell he could get closer. If he could just get his hands on one, he'd be able to eat his first real meal in the past eleven days. So far there'd been only a single feast at a blackberry bramble which had obviously already been overpicked by farmers in the area. The berries had been small, paltry compared to the ones he'd known in the States, when he'd picked them as a child in Oregon with his ma and sister. But he'd stripped the bushes bare, eating each one as if it were a juicy steak at a fine restaurant.

There'd also been a handful of rice he'd scooped from where it had been spread to dry on a hard, bare area at the side of a farmer's house, but it had been dark and he'd swallowed as much dirt as rice, and what the hell was good about a mouthful of pebble-hard rice grains anyway? If he could get away from the damned river area, back into the jungle where he'd spent his first day running the wrong direction, he felt he'd be able to forage enough food to last for a while. Maybe give him enough energy to make it out someplace where he could be rescued. He had drunk water from banana trees he had cut into.

A withered and elderly Viet came out of the house, stared about for a moment as if he were getting his bearings, and scratched at his crotch. Woods sympathized. The area was infested with crawling insects, and of all sizes and descriptions, when you were anywhere near the river.

That first day he'd eluded the pursuers he'd heard coming after him. He'd been cagey as hell—completely baffled them—because instead of running toward the west and someplace rescuers might pick him up, he'd run like hell, passed right over a railroad track and two well-traveled dirt roads, even, until he'd damn near splashed right into the wide river.

Hell, he should have at least noticed a rough direction from the sun's position.

He'd run four miles the wrong damned way! Trick-fucked the enemy and himself as well. Between that fear and leaving his survival kit behind, the Bear's self-confidence was way down.

Since then he'd only gotten a mile or so away from the Red River. Every time he'd tried to make it farther west, he'd heard a multitude of voices on the roads, and the sounds of their working. Labor gangs, he'd figured. They'd been told there were half a million of them, working to keep the roads, railways, and bridges functioning. It hadn't helped to wait for darkness, because they brought in new gangs and used lantern light to continue working. Angry bosses screaming in shrill, singsong voices at the workers sounded incessantly every time he approached the roads. He'd thought they'd spend their time on this stretch and then move on, but they seemed to be taking forever, filling the huge potholes and such, he supposed.

He'd known not to walk south, because Yen Bai was not far in that direction. He'd tried going north, but he'd come to a congestion of stilted houses there too.

After dawdling through the night and hiding near the river throughout the second day, the remnants of the abject terror had left him, replaced with self-disgust. He'd left behind the survival kit, with its bars of pemmican, extra radio, water purification pills, medical kit, maps and such. All he had was a hunting knife sewn to the leg of his G-suit, and the gear stowed in the pockets of his survival vest, and he'd taken inventory so many times he knew it all by heart. One each ground-to-air UHF survival radio, two plastic bottles filled with drinking water (now refilled with murky, foul-smelling river water), a pouch of ammo for the .38 Special revolver, waterproof matches, a miniature pen gun flare kit, and a compass, which he'd been too stupid to use that first day or he wouldn't be in this terrible fix.

The old Viet farmer finished with stretching and scratching, and ambled lazily in his direction. Woods inched backwards, deeper into the brush, and watched. Two female children emerged from the hut, chattering and laughing. Woods cursed, knowing there was no way to get to the chickens. He slithered slowly backwards until he was well out of sight, then crouched and found the hiding place he'd used the previous day. A niche hidden between a small tree and a profuse bush. He pushed his way in, and wriggled until he was moderately comfortable. The bush gave off an obnoxious, sort of lemony, sour odor, but there seemed to be fewer of the awful swarms of insects here—probably because they didn't like the smell either. The redhead lay there and tried to adjust his priorities.

One, get food. There was no way he could go on much longer without sustenance. Already he was light-headed whenever he rose to walk. And he needed fresher water.

Two, get the hell across the roads somehow. It was the only way he could go west, and it was only to the west that he could go if he wished to be rescued. He'd heard sounds of jet engines several times in the past few days. Once even at night—most likely from an F-111. Still, he hadn't dared to use the radio because he was just too close to the humanity teeming around him. So get across the roads, tonight, if possible, travel west as far as he could, then use the radio to call for help. That thought was pleasant.

Three, do not let the Viets capture you. But if they somehow do—fake it that you're a pilot, maybe an A-7 pilot, because that was a single-seat bird. He remembered conversations with Smitty, that the Viets were doing something funny with EWOs, because entirely too few were shown on the captured list given by the North Vietnamese. More ominous was the fact that Smitty was known to be captured—intell had briefed them that Viet radio transmissions had told them that—yet he hadn't come out on the captured list either, and they'd had him for almost three months. Smitty had all that secret knowledge stored away, which made it worse.

A thought struck him. Smitty had said he'd kill himself if the bad guys started working him over for his secrets. Had that happened?

A familiar chill ran through him. He had information which would be at least as useful to the enemy as Smitty's. Smitty knew about the here-and-now stuff that affected warfare. Woods knew what the Americans would have tomorrow. If he was captured, would he be able to kill himself, like Smitty had talked about and maybe done? He wondered, then gave up, because the question was too hard and too painful.

A water buffalo moaned in the distance, and he blew out an angry breath. After cursing his luck for a while, Woods ignored his hunger and several swarming flies that didn't care how badly the bush smelled, and prepared to sleep until darkness.

Chapter 13

They'd started relatively early that morning, the men who were to fly MiG-CAP in the second go. They were up and shaved by the time the sun was a pink glow on the horizon at Udorn Royal Thai Air Force Base, and as they walked to the Officers' Club for breakfast, they'd heard the engines of the first wave running up, then felt the angry booms and watched the fire-plumes of the afterburners scorching the dark sky as the wave took off. They ate as dawn broke. By full daylight they were in the command post briefing room, studying the frag order for the second big Linebacker mission of the day. The first wave was on its way to the lower route packs. The second would fly to the red-hot zone—Hanoi. The scheduling board showed the strike force, the bombers, flak suppressors, chaff bombers, and MiG cappers. All would be F-4 Phantoms. "There will be sixty-four aircraft involved in today's second bombing mission," the briefer told, "with strike aircraft from Ubon and Takhli. We're putting up two MiG-CAP flights, Alamo and Buick, to protect them." Ken Tanaka was to be flight leader for the four-ship Alamo flight. Toby Parker would fly as number three, his element lead. It was Toby's last flight as element lead (two ships) before being upgraded to flight leader (four or more ships) status.

The F-4E MiG-CAP flights and F-105G Wild Weasel SAM killers from Korat would already be attacking when the strike force arrived. The briefer tapped his pointer on the target map near Hanoi. "The target is the Hanoi Vehicle Repair and Assembly Facility on the western edge of the city of Hanoi. The strike crews are under strict orders not to release their bombs outside of parameters, and to ensure they impact on the target. There is a lot of tension in the States over the Linebacker operation, and the wheels are mightily concerned that some nervous fighter jock is going to accidentally bomb civilians." He looked hard at the MiG-CAP crewmen. "That means you guys are to keep the MiGs off their backs so they can set up and do a proper job of it. We don't want any MiGs sneaking in and shooting up the guys so they have to jettison ordnance."

"Got it," the briefer said, and the two flight leaders nodded. "Good, now let's go over the rules of engagement one more time."

A stifled groan came from the pilots and backseaters. They were only too familiar with the ROE—the Rules of Engagement—that had severely restricted their actions when over enemy territory from the day of the first air attacks eight years before. A tremendous number of pilots had been lost due to the ROE, imposed by politicians, which stacked things in the enemy's favor and made their jobs both dangerous and difficult. While the American public read about pilots indiscriminately bombing hospitals and schools, the fact was that they fastidiously avoided any civilian targets, and even critical military targets that were deemed too close to areas where civilians *might* be located.

Pilots had to bypass the massive numbers of SAMs, weapons, ammo, trucks, and war supplies being off-loaded from ships, and even after they were stockpiled in nearby areas, for fear of harming ships and foreign sailors. They could not strike MiGs taxiing for takeoff at Gia Lam airport, because there were also civilian aircraft there. They could not hit SAM sites, gun emplacements, power plants, or warehouses located too close to civilians. They could not release bombs near dams or dikes, even if gun emplacements were mounted on top and shooting at them, because the subsequent flooding might endanger civilians. MiG-CAP pilots could not engage adversaries in restricted areas, and had to have positive ID before firing. The lists went on and on, and the pilots were made to memorize and sign off that they knew and understood each one. If they were caught ignoring any one of the rules, they were liable for court-martial and disgrace. That had already happened more than once.

Fully aware of the ROE, the North Vietnamese placed radars, antiaircraft guns, and communications centers onto the huge networks of dikes. They ordered civilians to build their shack homes crowded about power plants and weapons and ammo-storage facilities. MiG pilots flew down low, then popped up toward the bombers, attacked, then fled into the restricted areas.

The briefer brushed over the tactics which the MiGs were likely to use that day. ". . . a high-speed run from the rear, fire a missile, then dive for the deck and go supersonic. They have about twenty of the new MiG-21MFs that are faster than the older ones, so watch your collective asses. Also, we won't have the Tree-equipped airplanes ready until Wednesday, but you'll be receiving the additional intelligence support you were briefed about from Red Crown."

He reiterated all the briefing items: target information, TOTs (Time Over Target), radio frequencies, call signs, secret code words, E & E (Escape and Evasion) routes, KC-135 tanker tracks, threat info (7,000 guns and SAMs *everywhere*), intell photos, and weapons load. Finally he stepped aside for Stormy, the weatherman.

Stormy told them the skies over Hanoi were forecast to have scattered cumulus clouds with good visibility, winds at altitude would be easterly. They didn't have to worry about leaving contrails. The con altitude was 36,000 feet, and they'd be flying lower than that.

When the briefing was concluded, the Buick flight leader took his eight people off to one side of the room, while Ken Tanaka took Alamo flight off to the other. The final flight briefing.

"Standard MiG-CAP configuration," Ken told them. "Each plane will be loaded with two Aim-7 Sparrows, four Aim-9 Sidewinders, two 370-gallon wing tanks, one 600-gallon centerline tank, two ECM pods, and a full gun." They were flying F-4Es, and those came with an internal M-61 Gatling 20mm cannon.

Because the afterburners on the J-79 engines of the big Phantom could guzzle a railroad car of fuel in no time, their use was limited to takeoffs and to actual fighting, and the F-4s had to carry the three external fuel tanks (the big 600-gallon balloon under the belly and the two 370-gallon tanks under each wing) to extend their range after they were topped off by KC-135 tankers. The ECM pods provided limited protection against SAM radars, and a scope in both cockpits called RHAW, Radar Homing and Warning, showed the strength of the lock-on radar signal and from what direction SAMs were launched.

Tanaka covered emergency procedures, divert bases in case of emergency or combat damage, radio out signals, and the myriad of items pilots and WSOs come to know intimately but must cover fully in briefings nonetheless. When he was done, Ken took Toby aside as the others filed out.

"You've got enough missions now, so if all goes well, I'll recommend orders be cut to upgrade you to flight leader." Toby smiled and gave him a thumbs-up.

Two hours later the strike force was in action over Hanoi. The raid had been precise and the vehicle assembly plant was a smoking ruin. No bombs had fallen outside of the plant's confines. Several SAMs had been fired, damaging two F-4D bombers and scaring hell out of three others. So far no MiGs had been called out as being in the area. Just south of Hanoi, Ken Tanaka was leading Alamo flight in a fighter weave searching for MiGs when Red Crown called him.

"Alamo, Red Crown. You've got five bandits at your twelve for forty and closing. Four of 'em are blue bandits." A blue bandit was a MiG-21.

"You sure of that, Red Crown?" Tanaka asked. MiGs just didn't attack head-on, and seldom flew in such large formations. Their slashing attacks were almost always solo and from the rear quarter.

"Affirmative, Alamo. They're at thirty miles now and closing rapidly. What's your altitude?"

"Base plus twelve." Base altitude was changed daily so they could transmit their altitudes without giving anything away to the enemy. Today's base was 7,000 feet, which meant Tanaka had his Alamo flight at 19,000.

"Understand, Alamo is base plus twelve. I'm getting a better paint now. There are four fighters and a larger target we believe to be a transport. You are cleared to shoot, repeat, cleared to shoot." They avoided the mention of the word "fire" over radio, unless to indicate that an aircraft was burning.

"Roger, Crown, understand cleared to shoot. Three, you got anything yet?"

"How about it, Ed?" Toby asked his backseater. He was holding his two-ship element 2,000 feet above and a half mile to the left side of Tanaka and his wingman. On his repeater radarscope, Toby could make out four smaller blips and one larger. The four small green smudges were accelerating, leaving the larger one behind.

"I have them all," Toby said, after getting his backseater's confirmation that he could get a good lock on any of the enemy planes.

"They are attacking," Tanaka said. "Jettison centerline tanks . . . now." Simultaneously, the big white 600-gallon tanks fell away from all four Phantoms. The drag created by the big tanks was too much to fight with. They always drained that tank first since they knew they might have to drop it.

"Push it up," Tanaka continued. "Alamo Three, you and Four take the two on the left, we'll go after the two on the right. We've plenty of fuel, so let's get some kills. Fire when you get a good lock. Whoever finishes first go for the transport." As yet, no one had shot down a transport in the Vietnam war.

"We're padlocked on the lead of the two leftmost bogeys," Toby's backseater said almost immediately, meaning he'd locked the radar onto that target.

The radar in the FCS (Fire Control System) had acquired the MiG. Toby selected AIM-7 missiles number one and two. Once launched, the FCS kept track of the target and provided turn signals to the missile.

Toby waited four seconds for the radar to settle, then launched the two AIM-7 Sparrows. As the two missiles dropped out of their wells under the Phantom's belly, their rocket engines ignited, and they accelerated to Mach 4, streaking off toward an enemy that Toby could not yet see, etching white trails as they knifed through the air, directed by electronic pulses to impact with the enemy planes. From the corner of his eye, Toby saw

Tanaka fire two missiles, and those white trails paralleled those of his own.

Toby glanced out. Both Tanaka's and his wingmen were in proper fighting wing position.

"We still have a good lock," muttered Ed Starr from the backseat as they waited for the missiles to impact.

Toby gave orders to his wingman. "Four, get a lock on the leftmost MiG and shoot him."

"Roger," Toby's wingman replied, and two Sparrow missiles immediately dropped from his wells, showing he'd had a radar lock all the time, awaiting permission to fire. Some leaders would have tried for both MiGs and to hell with their wingmen. Toby was peering forward, following the missile trails, when he found he could just make out the tiny specks of the approaching MiGs. The cons of their Sparrow missiles passed through the formation, narrowly missing but causing them to scatter.

"I've got a tally and it looks like we missed," he said to his backseater. Ed had his head in his scope, and had no forward visibility, so Toby kept him informed. "There goes Two's—"

"Missiles inbound," Tanaka yelled. "Break as required."

Both flights of two were now flying parallel, Toby's at a higher altitude. All four had to wait for the air-to-air missiles, which looked like tiny, smoke-trailing bees, to commit on one or the other airplane before they knew which way to turn. Toby saw that two of the missiles were coming at his element . . . when the timing looked right, he pulled sharply up. Four followed, and the missiles streaked past underneath. A glance out at Tanaka's maneuvering twosome showed that they'd done the same.

"You're clear, Alamo lead," Toby transmitted as he recovered. "The missiles didn't guide."

"Yeah, our Sparrows forced the MiGs to maneuver after they fired," Tanaka said, "so their radars broke lock."

"Alamos, they're coming in," Four said in his distinctive Southern drawl.

Then the MiGs were diving on them and the close-up gunfight began.

Eight nimble jets flying in elements of two, swirling and diving, each trying to gain advantage on the enemy. They were so close that all the pilots quickly ruled out even the short-range heat-seeker missiles, and relied on guns only . . . the MiG pilots on the 23mm cannons in chin-mounted packs . . . the Phantom pilots on the internal, 20mm Gatling guns mounted under their own radomes. As the eight pilots finished a single shuddering turn, Toby Parker and Ken Tanaka somehow knew they had the advantage. Although the aircraft, systems, and weapons were more or less similar in capability, they had the knowledge and training. As they entered the second hard turn, Toby already knew what the adversaries were thinking, and what they would try, and where they would be next.

The MiG pilots were fighting in the blind. Russian advisers advocated only the slashing missile attack from the rear, and to avoid becoming engaged in close-in dogfighting, where the objective was to get into optimum attack position—6 o'clock at 600 feet. In the swirling, turning furball of eight airplanes, Toby and Ken had little trouble.

"Stay high and to the south, Toby," Tanaka transmitted, "and I'll drag them under you from the north."

Tanaka put the nose down and went into afterburner, his wingman with him, to draw the two leading MiGs into pursuit. In the process he gained speed advantage as well as bringing the enemy fighters under Toby, who could attack from above. Tanaka would then use his excess speed to climb into a head-on attack at MiG three and four, who'd be trying to get at Toby. He would thread the needle and they would swap opponents. The maneuver had worked over the high California desert.

And it worked in the skies of North Vietnam. In seconds, Toby had MiG one under his gun, his wingman was on MiG two, and Tanaka had zoomed up to shoot the face off MiG three.

"You got him, Lead . . . "

"Shit hot . . . "

"Good work, Tobes . . . "

"Nice shot, Three . . . "

"Where's the other son of a bitch . . . "

"Oh, shit, he's rolling in . . . "

"No, he's not, he's diving away, doesn't see you . . . "

"Jesus . . . "

"Shoot, shoot, shoot . . . "

MiG four had panicked at the carnage wrought upon his flight and had pushed over to dive away. Tanaka's wingman tried a radar missile shot, but both Sparrows dropped away without engine start. It was a hell of a day.

"Alamo Three, rolling in," Toby said calmly, then racked a wing up and dove for the gun kill. The MiG pilot never saw him. After a single two-second burst from Toby's cannon, the silver MiG spewed fire and shed parts as the fuselage tumbled through the sky. Hell of a day.

Four black smoke trails and two green parachutes. The fight was over.

Toby pulled up and away from his kill, looking around for the transport.

"Heads up, Alamo. Gimme a fuel check and report any damage, then join back up in spread," Tanaka ordered, his voice barely concealing his jubilation.

"Two, twenty-five over thirty-two, negative damage."

"Three, twenty-seven over thirty-five, negative."

"Four, twenty-two over twenty-nine, negative."

The three Phantoms closed on their leader in spread formation and went back on the lookout for MiGs. Tanaka turned to a westerly heading.

"Okay, guys, lets take it to the tank. Keep an eye out, we're still in Indian country. Everybody who got a MiG say, 'hot shit.' " Tanaka was exuberant. He now had two-point-five kills.

"Fuck shit, double damn," radioed his wingman, Alamo Two, whose missile had malfunctioned.

"Hot shit, hot shit," Toby boomed. He had just nailed his second and third.

"Well, hayut shee-it," said his wingman, Alamo Four, a lanky lieutenant from Tennessee who'd just bagged his first.

"Look out at two o'clock low," Toby's backseater said. "There's something down there."

Toby stared until he made out a four-engined turboprop airplane, and after a short mental pause identified it as an IL-28. "Got a tally on the transport," he transmitted, "two o'clock low."

"Go ahead and attack," Tanaka ordered.

"You're cleared for attack, Alamo Three," Red Crown immediately echoed.

Toby rolled up and in. "Cover me," he said to Tanaka.

"Rodge, take him out, Three. Get him." Tanaka and the wingmen were scanning the sky for more MiGs who might come to the rescue of the luckless transport.

With his wingman in trail, Toby rolled in from 11,000 feet. He estimated the transport's altitude to be 7,000 feet, and it was heading straight for Hanoi. It was an easy pass, from the transport's left rear, its 8 o'clock position.

"He sure as hell doesn't see us," he told his backseater, frowning as they closed.

"I've a good lock, range 6,000 and closing, 200-knot overtake."

"I've selected Heat," Toby said, meaning he'd chosen the number one Sidewinder.

"Good range, good angle off," his backseater said. As further encouragement, the selected Sidewinder sounded the lock-on tone.

The IL-28 transport grew larger until it filled the gunsight.

"Get it and we'll have three in one day," Ed Starr said jubilantly.

The big transport was silver. Toby saw a big red star on the tail and CCCP on the wings.

"Red Crown, Alamo Three, it's Russian."

"You're cleared in hot," Red Crown said. "Kill it."

"Alamo Three, this is Disco," a new voice said. "We confirm the target. Go ahead and kill it." The Disco controller on the EC-121 rarely came on the air unless something was important.

Toby frowned as he parked in position behind the lumbering transport. It was a sitting duck, an easy and sure kill.

"Shit," Toby transmitted on the radio. He pulled up from his firing pass without pulling the trigger. He couldn't do it. This would be murder.

"Want me to get it, Three?" his wingman asked, but his voice was not sure either. They'd had it ingrained in them to fastidiously avoid airliners—and the most horrible thought to an American fighter pilot was that he might cause the death of innocents.

"Negative, Four." Toby could not conscience shooting down a defenseless transport. "Let's get out of here." He led the way back up to rejoin Tanaka.

1145 Hours Local, Saturday 8 July 1972
Gia Lam Airport, Hanoi
Democratic Republic of Vietnam

Jane Fonda stood for several minutes at the top of the stairs leading from the door of the Aeroflot IL-28 airliner to the tarmac, looking out over Gia Lam airport outside Hanoi. She wore black pajama bottoms and a white blouse, and blinked in the sun. Those close by saw her wrinkle her nose at the incredible heat and humidity. She waved and smiled to the welcoming committee below, while photos were taken.

Alfred stood with the committee. They were uniformly dressed in dark trousers, white shirts, and tan-colored pith sun helmets with red stars. They moved closer as Fonda descended.

"Greetings," said the young actress, showing her toothsome smile as a microphone was thrust in front of her. "I bring greetings from your comrades in America to the peace-loving peoples of the Democratic Republic of Vietnam." There was enthusiastic applause as the translator repeated her words in Vietnamese.

The committee chairman motioned a young girl in blue skirt and white blouse to hand the flower bouquet to the American woman. He tried not to frown as Fonda patted the child on the head. The girl ducked away, and with a shy grin, presented the bouquet. Fonda smiled, then patted her on the head again as she accepted the flowers. Then the crowd of grinning officials surrounded her, each vying to be photographed shaking the hand of this fearless fighter of freedom for the communist government of North Vietnam.

A minor functionary nervously asked her for her passport and checked the number, C1478434, against his list. He nodded and handed it back. "Fool," his superior hissed into his ear, "this one *never* needs to be checked." The man blanched.

When Alfred's turn came to shake her hand, he pumped once, European-style, and noted the beads of sweat channeling down her cheeks. As he stepped back he wondered why Westerners never bothered to study Asian customs. The hand on the girl's head meant Fonda had placed herself between the child and her God. Alfred shrugged inwardly. Religion was the opium of the masses, Marx had decreed, so what difference did it make if a child was patted on the head?

The committee would take the "progressive and celebrated American actress and freedom fighter," as the *Nhan Dan* newspaper called her, to see ruined sites around villages, hospitals, and schools. Alfred watched from the edge of the entourage, almost anonymously, although his Party position was quite high. This one was like the others who had come to visit. Never questioning what they were told, agreeing with the propaganda words that had been so carefully contrived. He wondered if she would realize that the wreckage and ruins she was about to view were fallen aircraft or made by antiaircraft rounds and missiles that had dropped back onto the city. Or if she'd notice that Hanoi was full of life and bustle.

Alfred had been the one who had first suggested her invitation. And when word came back that she'd accepted, the Party elders had poured out their congratulations. It would be a very good year for his career. Unfortunately, the nation he'd loved and the cause which had once evoked emotion that burned fervently in his breast had betrayed him. The men with whom he had met on the Central Committee were no longer great in his eyes. They were self-centered and cruel, and would utterly destroy the Democratic Republic, which was not democratic at all, but an oppressive farce.

But of course, the men with whom he worked daily must never know how he felt, or that he was doing more and more to thwart them. They must never know that his code name was Alfred.

1315 Hours Local, Tuesday 4 July 1972
Intelligence Section,
432nd Tactical Fighter Wing
Udorn Royal Thai Air Force Base
Kingdom of Thailand

The intell room was in bedlam. Not since the days of Olds and Titus had so many MiGs been bagged by a single flight. The debrief was over and three bottles of champagne had been bootlegged in and uncorked to great cheers. Someone thoughtfully provided the grinning Toby with a soda. Another took a slug of bubbly, then sprayed the heroes with what was left.

When they were asked to tell their stories again, Tanaka said, "Off to the O'Club, serfs, where we'll once again tell all for your edification and knowledge . . . but only after we visit our crew chiefs and the armorers." He and Toby linked arms and started for the door when it swung open and a full colonel entered, closely followed by a two-star general.

"Not so fast, gentlemen," the wing commander growled, "you have a bit more debriefing to do for the General."

As they found a briefing room to themselves, the Colonel told them the General had just arrived, and asked to see them. He'd made the trip from 7th Air Force for that purpose.

The Major General motioned them to sit. He waited, then paced a bit before swinging around to face them.

"I'm General Norman, Chief of Intelligence for Seventh Air Force, and of Air Intelligence for Military Assistance Command—Vietnam."

After a short pause, Toby remembered Norman from long before, when he'd been a full colonel and Court and Toby had visited him in Saigon to help set up a new FAC program. Yet the General had shown not the slightest sign of recognition.

"What the hell happened up there today?" the General asked, a trace of anger in his tone.

"What happened," Toby said stiffly, "was that between the two of us we shot down three MiGs . . . sir."

Norman almost snarled his next words. "Why didn't you shoot down the Soviet transport?"

Tanaka looked at Toby. It was his to answer.

Toby took his time with it. "Because it was an unarmed transport."

"Goddamn it, they don't hesitate to shoot down *our* transports. Lure them off course any way they can, like that C-130 in Turkey. Their fighter pilots didn't hesitate to shoot it down."

"Well, *we* don't do that."

"What if it was full of MiG pilots or bombs and bullets to kill GIs?"

"We don't shoot down unarmed transports."

"What if it was a railroad boxcar full of bombs and bullets?"

"I'd have blown it up."

"But not a transport?"

"Not a transport."

Norman grunted and sat back in the chair. "Good thing."

Toby's eyes widened in confusion.

"An American entertainer was on board."

"Whew," Tanaka breathed.

"Jane Fonda. Can you imagine what would have happened if you had flamed *her?* She'd be a bigger martyr than Joan of Arc. So . . . it's a good thing you didn't." He leaned forward again. "But you know what that tells me?" He was looking directly at Toby Parker.

"Sir?" Toby asked.

"That just perhaps, you *still* don't have a proper killer instinct."

It was J. T. Neddle all over again. *"Dammit, General—"*

Norman raised an eyebrow and Toby cut himself off.

Norman nodded. "Okay, gents, let's talk." The two-star nodded his head for the wing commander to leave, then looked back at the MiG killers. "Get yourselves relaxed. This'll only take a few minutes, then you can get back to your party."

The two captains spun chairs around and sat facing him over the backs.

"I'm here to follow up what George Weiss spoke about. We need you guys to help prove that your type training is the way to go. To do that, you've got to get more MiGs. One of you has got to make Ace."

"Hell, General," said Tanaka. "We're shooting 'em fast as we can. Four a day's not bad."

Norman nodded. "Those opportunities won't come your way often. Take all you can get. Go find 'em. Just make damned sure you don't get shot down yourselves."

"They didn't even come close today," Toby said.

"Which also proves your training was right on track, wouldn't you say?"

"Yes, sir." Toby nodded thoughtfully. "There was a time, just after we started, when I realized I knew just what the MiG drivers were thinking. Yes, sir, my training was right on."

"I'm in a unique position, gentlemen. I talk to people up and down the ladder. The Chief of Staff, for instance, tells me that as soon as the November election is over, we're going for the jugular. That means we're going to bomb the piss out of the Hanoi area and end this damnable war. And when it's over, we'll go back to being a peacetime Air Force. That will mean cutting back on pilots and assets and other things that cost money. Combat training is a big cost factor, and people are going to take a hard look at cutting back there too."

"We can't do that!" Toby blurted.

Norman flinched at the outcry, then smiled as Toby continued.

"We're training like milquetoasts, General. Like I told Colonel Weiss, my training was unique. *That's* why I'm shooting down MiGs."

"Precisely my point. When I heard what had happened up there today, destroying the four MiGs, I couldn't resist making this trip so I could reemphasize what Colonel Weiss was sent to tell you. We've got you in the spotlight now, and that must continue until we win or lose this training program. All the rest of us, the generals and staff officers and instructor pilots in the States, are on the sidelines. We're cheering you on, but that's all we can do. You're carrying the weight, but of course there is also a certain amount of attendant glory which might help."

"For making Ace," Toby muttered, as if hearing the same old record.

"For that, yes, and for being known as the men who paved the way for a realistic training program."

"I agree with the training concept, but the rest of it's bullshit. General, I don't give a damn whether I—"

General Norman cut him off. "I'd like to speak alone with Captain Tanaka," he said.

Toby rubbed his jaw angrily, then abruptly nodded and left the room.

Ken Tanaka sat in silence, regarding the two-star.

"Do you think Parker's going to be able to get two more kills?"

"If they show up, we'll kill them, sir."

"That's my point. We got to make sure *he* gets them."

Tanaka frowned. "I do have a few MiGs myself, you know."

Norman's glance softened. "I know. But you're the teacher, a high-time fighter jock who's developed into one of the best. Parker is a low-time fighter pilot who very recently was a student. He's got less than two hundred hours in fighters, while you've got more than two thousand. If a low-time guy can make

Ace using the teaching methods you came up with, then so can a lot of others."

Ken Tanaka frowned at the unfairness of what he was hearing. "How 'bout we *both* do it?"

Norman leaned forward. "This war is about over, and then there won't be MiGs to shoot down to prove our point. We're not going to get a second chance at this game. Parker first. You copy?"

Tanaka stared. "That's what you really came for, wasn't it, sir? To tell me to back off and let Toby take the kills."

"I just want you to understand precisely what we're trying to accomplish."

Ken Tanaka watched narrowly, then followed the General as he rose to his feet.

"Thanks for your time, Captain."

Five minutes later, Toby Parker came back into the room, sipping on a Coke. "What else did the asshole General have, Ken?"

"Just wanted to know how we were doing." Tanaka kept a bland face.

"Speaking about that, how did I do on my flight lead checkout?" Toby grinned. "Did I pass?"

Tanaka was slow to smile. "With orange trees and typewriter keys."

Chapter 14

"You *will* meet with her," the Vietnamese man screamed.

"Nuts to you," Flak Apple said through gritted teeth, and immediately wished he hadn't been so impetuous, for the Vietnamese, named Bug by the POWs, tightened the rusty iron bar that pressed against Apple's shins. Flak barely stifled a groan as electric pain shot up his legs into his brain. *Oh God, when will I learn to keep my big mouth shut.*

"You Americans think you are so clever," Bug sneered. He had a smooth, round face and a wandering right eye. Unlike most Vietnamese, his black hair was bushy and stood up as if charged with electricity. "That criminal Stockdale, so smart he thinks. We fix-ed him."

It had been passed between cells via the tap code that Navy Commander Jim Stockdale had torn his face against a stool in his cell rather than appear with Jane Fonda. The V had realized the ploy and now beat people where it wouldn't show in an effort to get them to appear with her. Flak had a delicate road to tread. He mustn't upset his captors so much they would take away his leadership of the choir, but he was determined not to appear with her.

251

They were in the Knobby Room, known as the Star Chamber, where many of Flak Apple's past quizzes had taken place. He sat on the floor, back against the wall covered with large plaster mounds to absorb the cries of the tortured. The knobs were splashed with blood to eye level. Bug sat on a low, three-legged stool next to the bar on Flak's legs.

"Another famous person be here, too. Mr. Shawn Bannister. He come soon, yes. You must see him also, Apper."

Flak was electrified and concealed his joy with difficulty, even though he'd learned the merits of remaining expressionless during his years of captivity and torture. If Shawn Bannister was present, maybe Richard Connert, the Blue Mailman, would be with him.

Now Flak knew he'd have to see the delegation. Still, he couldn't be seen to fold too easily, to appear suddenly eager to change his mind. There would have to be more pain to endure, and although he'd been tortured off and on for his entire stay, there was no getting used to it. He set his teeth.

By midmorning, Bug had his way and Flak agreed to appear with them. Bug smirked in victory and sent him back to his cell.

Flak began to worry as soon as they'd shut the door behind him, *Connert's got to be there also. He's got to. I need to know if my message got through. Someone has to know about the guys who're disappearing.*

That night a guard walked in carrying a fresh set of purple-striped prison pajamas, new sandals, and a razor blade and soap. Behind him another guard carried a tray with a heaping bowl of hot rice and a real spoon.

"Eat," the first said. "Then shave, then new clothes."

"No," Flak said. He seldom did anything they ordered the first time. He grunted as the guard punched him, knuckle-extended, in the kidneys. Then he bent to eat the food. The rice was warm and covered with a thick layer of real sugar. It tasted wonderful.

You can't just give in and give the V satisfaction, the SROs had tapped out as part of the POW's personal code of conduct in the Hoa Lo Prison. *Make them work for everything, and, when you are forced to yield, bounce back and make them work just as hard the next time.* But Flak knew he had to be careful. It was a thin line he was treading. To back down from his normal, hard-nosed attitude would be discussed and probed by the suspicious V, and he might be put back into solitary until he revealed what was in his heart (*never*, he knew) and miss the meeting with Connert. He almost dared not breathe the name, for he had an abiding, deep fear that if he were put back in the ropes he might scream out something beyond his control and give it away. A fine line. He could not give away the one sure tie the POWs had with their government.

He ate the rice, savored the taste, and sucked every grain from his teeth. That had once been another fine line. No one was to accept favors geared just for the individual. They were to refuse everything unless everybody else got the same. Then the SROs had decided that if you had the opportunity to improve your health without giving anything away for it, it made sense to do so. So he ate with enthusiasm.

When he'd finished eating, he was led to the slimy bath area, where a trickle of tepid water ran from a rusty tap. He removed his worn POW shorts and cupped his hands to splash as much water as he could on himself. They gave him a small tin mirror and he stood in the sun, painfully shaving the bristly black hairs from his face. Finally he donned the new pajamas and was ready.

At 1830 hours they left.

Bug and two guards took him under the arches and through the administrative area to a small compound just inside the main gate to the Hoa Lo Prison. There they climbed into a small Russian automobile. Inside, the July heat was scorching and oppressive. Thirty minutes later Flak found himself standing in a high-ceilinged parlor. On a long table were trays of fruit and thin waferlike biscuits. He had been through this before. On one side of the table a worn French couch was set against a wall, on the other side a straight-backed chair. Two floor fans stirred the air.

The door opened and two Vietnamese men entered and went about setting up a 35mm movie camera on a wooden tripod. They found a narrow-holed French-style socket, plugged in a flood lamp, and turned it on.

"Sit here," Bug demanded, pointing to a straight-backed chair. "No, no, not yet," he yelled when Flak began to seat himself. "After they are themselves on the sofa. Then you sit."

The cameramen rearranged the lamp and spoke a few Vietnamese words to Bug, who went to the double doors and threw them open, a broad smile creasing his brown face.

A young woman entered the room, wearing black Viet Cong pajamas and a frown. On either side were Viet party officials. Their narrow faces split into wide, toothy grins as they led her to where Flak Apple stood. Her frown deepened as she looked at him, then she quickly replaced it with a wide smile, stuck out her hand, and said, "Hi, I'm Jane Fonda. How are you?"

As Flak decided whether to shake her hand, he flicked a glance about, looking for Shawn Bannister or Richard Connert. *Damn, where are they? Shit, if I shake this broad's hand I'll never hear the end of it.*

So he decided to do what Jack Bomar and Dick Stratton had done in front of the cameras, and what he'd done himself so successfully on previous forced meetings—act brainwashed and programmed like a robot. Flak assumed a position of servile attention, head slightly bowed, and allowed a blank look to wash over his face as he stared at her hand.

Embarrassed, she thrust it farther toward him, and Flak twisted his head like a quizzical animal examining some strange object.

She returned her arm to her side in some confusion, then grew a bright expression and said, "Why, let's get something to eat," and walked to the table with the condiments. She picked up a tray of biscuits and held them out to Flak.

Again he was faced with the problem, and since he didn't think he could pull the robot trick again, he said in a voice too low to be picked up by the sound equipment, "No, I cannot eat."

"Oh, you get well fed here, then?" she said in a warm, full voice, half-turning to face the cameras. "There are those who say you don't get enough food, and here you are, turning some down. They are liars, aren't they?"

Flak refused to go along, yet he knew better than to say something that might alienate Bug and scuttle the chance to see Connert. *Damn, where are they?* "Uh, I'm sick, too sick to eat," he said in the same low voice.

"Oh, do you get medicine? Of *course* you do. How long have you been here? Do you want the war to end? What message do you have for the people back home?"

His dilemma continued. He knew he must answer, but was desperate to ask if Connert was with her. Flak tried another tack. Afraid she might leave, he said the first things that came to his mind, babbling childlike to keep the conversation alive in other directions. "Is this your first visit? Did you come alone? Is there anyone with you? Where are they? What did they talk about?"

She put her hand to her throat. "Well, my goodness, so many questions. Yes, this is my first time here, but"—she looked up at the Vietnamese officials and smiled, and they smiled back—"I hope to return many times. Yes, I came alone but I hear there is another American here and we are to meet or something."

Flak's heart speeded up. He let an infantile grin grow. "That's nice. Who?"

"His name is Shawn Bannister. Ever heard of him?"

"Yes, I have. Is anyone with him?" He cursed himself for that one. Too obvious.

"No, not that I'm aware of." She frowned.

Flak's heart plummeted. "Unh, are you *sure?*"

"Am I sure of what?" Her frown deepened. "Why are you asking so many questions? I don't think you are supposed to do that." She looked at the Vietnamese officials and asked, "Is he?"

After she left, they immediately returned Flak to Hoa Lo Prison, where the turnkey put him back in his cell. He sank to the floor in a corner and placed his head on his knees. *Ah, God, it was all for nothing. I met with her and I know damn well the camera got shots of us together.* He sat motionless for long moments and felt himself sliding deeper into despair. So much had happened. The shoot-down, the torture, the escape, Ted Frederick shot and beaten to death, Co Dust in the hospital, so much. The heat was oppressive. He heard footsteps on the concrete leading to his cell. There was a noise at the door and he looked up as Bug and the Vietnamese official entered the tiny cell.

"Apper, we heard you talk to the woman. Yes, there is someone else here in Hanoi that we want you to see. It will be arranged for tomorrow." Bug spoke normally instead of screaming.

"Who is it?" Flak's nerves were tingling.

"Tomorrow is Sunday. You will go to church."

"Who is it?" Flak repeated, trying hard to keep himself from screaming.

"It will be a little surprise for you, so spend your night thinking of how sorry you are about your crimes against the innocent people of the Democratic Republic of Vietnam."

When Bug had left the cell, Flak felt a heavy weight in his chest, wondering about all he was trying to do. Was it worth losing his dignity as a man? He pondered the question long into the night, until he remembered other things, like Major Todd Smythe, who had shouted his own name so someone might know, before he'd been pushed out the prison gate, only to disappear.

God help me! Flak thought in his turmoil. Then he prayed that there would be no more prisoners, and then that there would be no more who would be taken to an even darker future.

He would have to continue. There was no alternative.

2245 Hours Local, Saturday 15 July 1972
Foothills—Route Pack Five
Democratic Republic of Vietnam

Bear Woods found a growth of giant ferns near the pathway, ghostly-appearing in the subtle moonlight, like a scene from a fairy tale. He plucked and piled several fronds together and rested, lying back on the nature-made bed, then drew the last small chunk of meat from the pocket of his G-suit and gnawed on it. It was the last of the monkey. He sipped his banana-tree water.

Things were considerably better for Woods than they'd been a week earlier, when he'd finally made it across the roads and staggered westward on hunger-weakened legs, hallucinating from starvation. Then he'd known it was only a matter of time before he collapsed and either died or was found and captured. But after crossing the roads he'd left the populated area and entered a new world of dense forests, with sources of food everywhere. He'd found a sprawling mango tree on his first day in the jungle, and ate the juicy fruit until his stomach threatened to burst, grinning and belching happily as the juice trickled through his inch-long red beard. He'd puked it up, but as soon as the stomachache subsided, he'd eaten again, then slept there.

The next morning he'd contacted an A-7 pilot flying overhead. He'd given his call sign, Condor Zero-One Bravo, and told the guy he was alive and well, but was still too near civilization for rescue. He'd advised that he would keep going for another few days until he found a suitable location. The A-7 jock had told him he'd pass on the information and wished him good luck. When the flight had gone on, Woods had put the radio away again and hadn't turned it on since. He wanted the batteries to remain strong.

He'd traveled slowly, pushing through the jungle, crawling up the sides of steep hills, but each day had found food. He estimated that altogether he'd come only ten miles in the dense growth, for travel was difficult, but there was no longer the great fear and sense of urgency.

Three days before, he'd spotted a small monkey with a wizened grampa's face, skittering about in a tree. He'd watched closely and salivated over the memory of the taste of meat. Woods had thought it over, mentally measuring the distance he'd traveled from civilization, and decided to break a rule he'd set for himself—not to fire the noisy pistol unless absolutely necessary. He'd missed on the first shot, wincing at the loud report that echoed through the rain forest. The monkey had frozen at the sound, stood stock-still, and tried to become invisible. He'd killed it with the second shot. Then he'd broken another rule and built a small fire, which gave off entirely too much smoke because of the green wood he was forced to use. He'd cooked the monkey, which when skinned looked entirely too much like a human baby. All squeamishness was forgotten as soon as he'd taken his first bite of meat.

Throughout that night and the next day he'd worried, angry that he'd broken the rules about the gunshots and the fire, but there was no new pursuit that he was aware of, and his concern slowly dwindled.

Tomorrow he'd forget about worrying completely, for he'd find a clearing, pull out the hand-held survival radio, and call the fighters that passed overhead daily—and be rescued. He'd told them he would be doing that, and he hoped they were waiting.

Bear Woods liked to prepare carefully for the challenges of life.

Just a year earlier, for instance, he'd briefed the people at the Defense Advanced Research Projects Agency (DARPA) at the Pentagon, explaining the sensitive project which had just been given the nickname of Have Blue, and the Air Force's need for aircraft that would be difficult to track on radar. He'd been speaking to the choir, so to speak, for he knew DARPA had been working with stealth projects since the fifties. Then he'd gone down the hall and briefed the people in the Air Force's Special Projects Office, and the next day he'd gone to Langley and briefed the folks there who were running the SR-71 Blackbird development, and told them about the progress they'd been making in defining a stealth fighter.

His bosses at Wright Patterson had told him it was entirely too early for such a briefing, that he'd just let the cat out of the bag about the breakthroughs they were making, but they'd been wrong. Before he'd left the Washington area a week later, he'd been able to collect insights that would make their task much easier.

He'd thought that one out very carefully, for the series of briefings had been his swan song in the Have Blue project. Soon thereafter he'd taken the circuitous route to fly Wild Weasels.

Well, he thought, he hadn't thought *that* one through too well. If he'd been captured when he was scurrying about down near the river the previous week, the entire Have Blue project, which he felt would someday become one of the most important development programs in the Air Force, would have been jeopardized.

As soon as he was rescued and returned to Korat Air Base, Woods planned to go to the squadron commander and tell him that he possessed knowledge that made him ineligible to fly further combat, and that he could verify the fact with a single phone call to the project director at Wright Patterson. The pilots and bears in the squadron might think he was a candy-ass, but he knew it was the right thing to do—both for his country and his own sanity.

Woods finished the meat and carefully wiped his hands on his filthy flight suit, which was beginning to rot at the seams. The suit was fabricated out of tough Nomex, a material which refused to burn, but it was rotting nonetheless. Which proved that Mom Nature's jungle could get to anything. His underwear and socks hadn't even made a struggle, had deteriorated into ragged strips the first week.

But tomorrow, after his rescue, he'd get a good shower, douse himself with insecticide to kill the lice, and shave away the three-week growth of beard that he was sure made him look like an orange-hued wolfman.

Woods curled up on the bed of giant fern leaves, catnapped fitfully for a few hours, then woke up at 0500 hours, well before dawn, realizing it was impossible to sleep when he was so hyped up about being rescued. He cautiously gained his feet and stretched out the kinks, then repositioned the fern leaves to mask signs of his stay. Finally he tried to push on through the undergrowth, but the moon was down, and it was simply too dark to move. He waited for an impatient hour, until there was a smattering of light in the sky.

It was time to find the proper place.

His heart beat faster as he pushed through the undergrowth. A new sound caught his attention and he paused and heard a systematic, thwacking noise. He furrowed his brow, listening for another moment, then nodded grimly. Machetes were being used to hack a path through the jungle. The redhead waited for a few heartbeats longer, until a distant high voice confirmed the noises were being created by humans. They could be hunters, he told himself, or even farmers clearing an area. It was unlikely they were tracking him. Still . . .

The noises stopped as suddenly as they'd begun, followed by quiet.

Woods waited for five long minutes before proceeding on through the dense thicket.

Twenty minutes later, he heard the sound of airplanes, but he did not try to call them. Not yet. He wanted to put more distance between himself and the human noises. He continued to push his way through the ferns and bushes, circumventing a thick stand of bamboo, then emerged into a small open area, and paused, examining. It was not big, certainly not large enough for a Jolly Green HH-53 helicopter to set down in, but it would give him plenty of room to crawl onto one of the tree-penetrator devices they dropped down, and be hoisted to safety.

He glanced at his watch. It was six-forty, and he'd traveled for fifty minutes since hearing the machete sounds.

It should be enough, if they were not following him, and he'd heard nothing further to indicate they were.

After fifteen minutes he heard aircraft in the distance, and he pulled the radio from the pouch in his mesh survival vest, extended the antenna, and for the second time in three weeks selected the TRANSMIT-RECEIVE position on one wafer switch and EMER-GRD 243.0 on the other.

Woods radioed in the blind, giving his call sign. On his second try he got a response.

"Roger, Condor Zero-One Bravo, this is Slam Five-One and I'm hearing you weak but readable."

He was talking to an A-7 pilot, as he had the first time. An involuntary smile began to grow on Woods' face. "I'm in a small clearing down here. Request you advise search and rescue that I'm ready for pickup." The sound of himself speaking the words thrilled him.

"Zero-One Bravo, hold down your transmit button and give me a long count."

Woods' heart began to thump even more wildly, yet it was somehow important that he not betray his emotion. He tried very hard to keep his voice steady as he held down the trans-mit switch. "Ah, roger, Slam Five-One . . . " He counted, very slowly, to ten, and then back to one.

The sounds of the jet engines grew louder as the aircraft approached. Woods again counted to ten and back to one. Two flights of four small, pudgy fighters passed high overhead, then banked away. He interrupted his count and said, "You just went over me," but could not keep his voice from trembling. Woods released the switch and waited, his heart pounding so hard he could hardly contain himself. He wanted to shout and laugh, maybe even dance.

"I think I've got a position on you, Zero-One Bravo. You're in a thick forest about a half mile from a road?"

Woods frowned. "I'm in jungle, but I don't know anything about a *road.*"

"We're rustling up the rescue people now, Zero-One Bravo."

"Which way's the road?" Woods called, and this time his voice was entirely too shrill.

"North of you. Soon as we get things moving with the search and rescue people, we'll drop down and take a closer look."

Woods squinted suspiciously into the jungle toward the north, which was to his right. He saw only dense foliage and under-growth. He frowned, wondered if he shouldn't move farther south, away from the road. He decided to stay in place, since he might not find another clearing. Woods listened to the sweet sound of the A-7s orbiting high overhead, but now it was not without concern. Ten minutes later he heard the droning sounds of the jets changing pitch, and listened harder. Were they leaving him?

"What's happening up there, Slam Five-One?" he called.

"I contacted Red Crown and they've got the Jolly Greens on their way in, Zero-One Bravo. We're dropping down to take a better look at the area so we can tell them what to expect."

The engine noises receded, then grew louder as the A-7s turned to fly toward him.

Woods held his breath, increasingly happy that the process was under way. It wouldn't be long now. Not long at—

Boom-boom-boom-boom. Woods cringed. The big-gun sounds were deafening and were interspersed with heavy automatic weapons fire. Jesus! Woods turned then and began to run across the small clearing.

He saw movement, then two soldiers in green uniforms and brown pith helmets stepping out of the jungle directly in his path, rifles raised, shrieking in Vietnamese.

Woods slowed, and uttered a single loud sob of despair.

Can't let 'em take me!

He gritted his teeth and again began to run, straight toward the soldiers.

Chapter 15

Bug led Flak through a door at the rear of the room filled with several benches before a raised dais with a cloth-draped altar. To one side he saw the same movie camera crew as the day before. There were also two other men wearing the maroon-and-gray-striped POW pajamas already seated. He knew who they were. Navy Commander Eugene Wilbur and Marine Lieutenant Colonel Eddison Miller, both collaborators. They interrupted their casual chat and turned to greet him, but he ignored it and took a seat on the bench behind them, uneasy in the company of these men who gave the enemy so much of themselves.

A small, elderly Vietnamese man in Christian religious garments came in and struck a pose in front of the altar, which had no cross or other religious symbol.

"I am the Correct Reverend Pastor, Chairman of the Evangelical Church of Hanoi." The man immediately launched into a sermon in which he likened his beloved and respected former leader Ho Chi Minh, now dead, to Jesus Christ; and Richard M. Nixon to Herod, the baby killer. He assured his congregation of three that just as Jesus Christ had led his people to a great victory over the Roman imperialist aggressors, so had Uncle Ho's teachings assured the Vietnamese people that they would reach a great victory over the American imperialist aggressors. Bug nodded appreciatively at the words.

"Now," the Correct Reverend Pastor said, looking at the three men without making an attempt at further services, "we have a very important visitor from the United States who wants to help you."

The door opened and Shawn Bannister walked in, followed by . . . Richard Connert.

"See, Apper," Bug said, "I told you there would be a surprise. Now you see we keep our promises. We told them they could visit you every year and here they are. Now, Apper, you must tell them how happy you are to see them and how well you have been treated."

Flak was stunned, for it was impossible to shift emotions so completely, so quickly. Then elation began to blossom within and he had to fight to keep it from his face.

Connert did not hesitate, but immediately began to flash signs in their tap code. He tried to gather his wits and concentrate on talking one subject while reading and signing another.

"Ah, yes, yes indeed, I am very happy to, unh, see these, unh, men," Flak stammered.

"How are you, Apple?" Shawn Bannister said perfunctorily. When he saw the camera he brightened, shifted slightly to ensure he was in good position, and showed his trademark smile. He grasped Flak's hand and pumped it energetically, and placed his arm around his shoulders. "You're looking good, old boy," he said in a hearty tone, showing pearly teeth.

"Yes, welcome back," Flak said, just as heartily. "And how are you, Mr. Connert?" Flak said and shook his hand, concentrating hard as he decoded, yet maintained the proper vacant expression.

HAD BITCH TIME GETTING HERE . . . BEST HURRY . . . WHAT U GOT RE POWS N USSR . . . Connert signed as he said, "Good to see you again, Apple."

"Did you get to see Jane Fonda?" Shawn asked almost too casually.

Flak hardly registered the question in his concentration.

DIDNT U GUYS GET MY CHOIR MSGE

NOT ALL... HOW MANY... WHO FOR SURE MISSING... WE COULDNT READ NAMES...

FIVE WE SURE OF DISAPPEARED EARLY... OFALLON USN... EWONSCI USN... DEHNE USAF... BUNCER USAF... SMYTHE USAF... QUIZZES DIFFERENT FM NORMAL... TECNICAL QUESTIONS... TAPE RECORDR... ONE MAN HEARD RUSSIAN... SAW FAT MAN THINK RUSSN... NOW OTHERS DISAPPEARING... MAYBE TWENTY...

"Fonda? Why, yes, she was here." Flak's mind whirled as he maintained the two vastly different conversations. Even as he spoke with Bannister, he continued signaling.

OTHERS...

WE BELIEVE YES... BUT NOT YET SURE

HOW...

NEW MOVEMENTS... SEVERAL PULLED OUT... HEALTHY GUYS... TOLD ROLL UP SLEEPING MAT N FOLLOW GUARD... THEN GONE

ANY IDEA WHERE...

NO... WHAT CAN U DO...

MAY SEND SOMEONE IN...

IN JAIL... U GUYS NUTS... WHAT WOULD HE DO HERE...

Shawn was beaming happily. "What did she say? What did she do? Do you know where she went from here, I mean, how she's getting back to the States?" Shawn Bannister saw Jane Fonda as an excellent political companion.

"What did who say?" Flak frowned, having difficulty tracking both conversations.

"Jane Fonda," Shawn said with obvious annoyance at his denseness. "I want to know all about her." His political position in California would certainly be strengthened with her in his corner.

"Well, ah, how would I know anything about her?"

Shawn turned to Richard Connert. "This guy's an idiot." Connert smiled in response, continuing to sign.

CANT GIVE U MORE INFO... I BRIEFED IN BROAD TERMS CASE SOMETHING WENT WRONG... U GOT ANYTHING MORE...

LESS TORTURE NOW MORE GUYS IN TOGETHER

BUT SOME SENIORS STILL HELD ISOLATION . . . TELL
NAVY NOT SEND MORE RADIO PARTS . . . FOUND
WHEN PACAGES ALLOWED . . . FOUND THEM N CUT
US OFF . . . Just as more packages were being allowed to the
POWs, the Navy had tried to smuggle in parts for a miniature
radio receiver. They were immediately found, and the new pack-
age program was cut back severely.

GOT IT . . .

N TELL NAVY SENDING PROMO LIST WAS DUMB
. . . WE WASTED DAYS TAPPING IT THRU CAMPS JUST
TO FIND USAF GUYS NOW OUTRANCED BY SQUID
CELLMATES . . .

WHAT CAN I DO FOR U . . .

SEND USAF PROMO LIST . . .

U SERIOUS . . .

NAH . . .

"Are you going to come home with us this time?" Shawn
asked Flak.

It took Apple a second to register what had been said to him.
"Well, ah, you see, the situation is the same as last time. I really
can't go."

Shawn Bannister looked exasperated. "Then why should we
even talk to you?"

WHAT MORE INFO U HAVE . . . Connert rapidly signed.

NOTHING . . .

CHOIR GOING ALL RIGHT . . .

CANT SAY . . . V MAY NEVER LET US MEET AGAIN
. . . NOT SCEDULED . . . JUST CANT SAY . . .

"You tell me. Why should we stay and talk to you?" Shawn
persisted.

Flak balked at ending the conversation with Connert, but he
had nothing more to give him and nothing whatsoever to say
to Shawn Bannister. Still, he wanted to leave hope for another
conversation someday and must leave that opening.

"Who knows," he said darkly, "maybe next time I *will* go
home with you."

With little fanfare, Flak Apple was hustled away as the
Vietnamese ushered the two men out.

As they were being driven back to their hotel, Shawn
Bannister took out a large handkerchief and wiped the sweat
from his face. Connert pulled out a red farm bandanna and

did the same. Then he tied it around his forehead, hippie style.

Shawn took a swat at a hovering insect, then used the handkerchief again as he peered at the bandanna on Connert's forehead. "That thing work?"

"Some," said Richard Connert.

The car bumped along in the scorching midday heat. He pulled down the red farm bandanna, soaking up the beads of sweat on his forehead, and thought about Alfred as he pushed it back in position.

"We will not tell you who or what Alfred is," he'd been told. "You can understand why. But he's up there, and he'll know to watch for the right signal."

They'd been in a safe room in the Saigon Embassy. The man named Jimmy, the fake drunk with the awful voice who'd sung about "send it by mail," had established contact again and told him when and where to go for the meeting. The briefer's name was Chef Hostettler, another Air Force spook on detached duty, whom he'd met before, now going under the name of Mr. Thomas.

"What kind of signal am I supposed to make?" Connert had asked.

"You're not, unless you have an emergency, a bona fide emergency, like you're about to be compromised or something has happened that you feel he must know immediately. What you do is, it's hot up there, you tie a red bandanna around your head. He'll identify himself to you when he can."

"How reliable is he?" Connert had asked. "I mean, how far can I trust him to keep his mouth closed?"

"Put it this way. If his bosses found out, they'd cut his balls off and parade him around People's Victory square up there."

Connert had frowned, for that had been no real answer.

Chef Hostettler had seen his hesitation and shrugged. "You play it by ear. He's a pretty secretive fellow. We think you can trust him but who really knows?"

0830 Hours Local, Monday 17 July 1972
Victory Hotel, Hanoi
Democratic Republic of Vietnam

Shawn Bannister groaned at the knock on his door, then wiped sleep smear from his eyes and peered at his watch. It was after eight. His head throbbed, he was terribly thirsty, and there was a foul, sour taste in his mouth. All that beer the previous night, that horrible Vietnamese beer brewed and made just outside of Hanoi. He and Connert had chugged back a few too many.

The knock sounded again, even more insistently.

"All right, I'm coming." He pulled on his shorts and opened the door to see Richard Connert. "What in hell do you want?" Shawn rasped.

"You wanted a chance to meet Fonda?"

"Yeah," Shawn rasped as he yawned.

"I set it up. We can go along on a trip they've set up for her out to some of the local villages. You up to it?"

Shawn began to feel better. "Goddamn right I am."

Twenty minutes later they stood outside the hotel entrance. The heat was rising and Connert casually took out his red bandanna and tied it around his head.

Shawn eyed him and grinned. "That's a good idea," Shawn said and pulled out his own and tied it across his forehead. It was red.

Nguyen Van Doang sat near the front when they picked them up in the wheezing old army bus. Several other Party functionaries and a few high-ranking military men were also on board. Doang's dark eyes flickered when the two Americans climbed the steps, and he saw each man wearing a red bandanna. He signaled the driver to continue, wondering what to do about the dilemma. Certainly there were not *two* of them.

The bus bounced and picked its way among the terrible potholes the Vietnamese called hen's nests. Soon they arrived at one of the dikes surrounding the southern portion of the city, where the bus shuddered to a halt. The Vietnamese hosts climbed down and stood outside with the two Americans. Then, filing from the back of the bus, the Vietnamese photographers and cameramen also dismounted.

Alfred, standing to one side, motioned for Bannister and Connert to join him. He was confused and a bit worried. Both men were giving the distress signal. Were they both American agents? The British diplomat had told him to invite both, and he'd done so, but he'd been somehow led to believe that only one would be an agent. He sighed inwardly, supposing he'd erred. Now he must find a way to identify himself to them and determine what the emergency communication was about. He edged over beside Shawn and murmured, "The red scarf. Does it mean much to you?"

"Well, yeah, sure," Bannister said lightheartedly. "Like, it does the job, you know what I mean?"

Alfred studied him, noting he didn't appear apprehensive, as one would expect under the circumstances. He also wondered that the seemingly callow Shawn Bannister was doing such important and dangerous work for his government. A very good role player, he concluded.

"Yes, I know what you mean." Alfred spoke quietly, so no one close could hear. He started to identify himself, but paused out of long-ingrained caution. Finally he asked, "What is the problem?"

"Eh? Problem?" Shawn snorted. "Yeah, I got a serious problem. I've been here ten days and I haven't gotten laid yet."

Alfred drew back as if struck. This man was as callow as he had thought, and certainly not the one he was looking for. He'd almost made a serious, perhaps fatal mistake. He murmured excuses and stepped away, wondering if he should speak with the other man.

He didn't get a chance until near the end of the afternoon. They were riding back to Hanoi, Bannister in Fonda's car, the rest of them in the bus. Connert had taken a seat near the rear, entertaining the thought of catching a few winks on the return trip. It was a bad idea. The hot air blowing through the opened windows was full of fine dust, and the rear chassis springs were shot and so were those of the bench seat. Each hen's nest jarred his teeth and catapulted him into the air. He was about to move forward when Nguyen Van Doang came back, holding on to seat backs and swaying against the movement, to take the seat beside him.

"You should ride up where it is more comfortable," the Vietnamese said.

"I'm about to do just that."

"It is very hot, is it not?"

"Yes, it is."

"Does the bandanna help?"

Connert felt charged with electricity, and his senses went on full alert. He felt the blood pulsing in his ears. "Yes," he said cautiously, "the bandanna helps a great deal. I have a blue one, but I prefer the red."

"Your friend also wears a red bandanna."

"So he does, but it means nothing to him."

"Ahh," said Alfred, nodding his understanding. "Tell me, do you know anyone named Alfred?"

"I would surely like to."

"Is it important?"

"Very."

Doang cocked his head almost mischievously. "I was once called Alfred by a schoolmate."

Connert took a deep breath and faced him. "Are you Alfred?"

"If I were, would you have something for me?"

Connert felt as if he were about to explode. "Jesus Christ, I need to know!"

"Lower your voice, please."

"Okay. If you're Alfred," Connert said, "I definitely have something for you."

"I am Alfred."

Connert did not hesitate. "We believe a number of our people are being taken from the prisons. We feel it is being done by the Russians."

The Vietnamese grunted. "I am not aware of that."

"Could it happen without your being aware?"

Doang thought it over. He knew many things, yet so much in the communist government was done secretly. Prisoners taken by Russians? It was possible, of course, but seemed unlikely. The majority of the Party elders did not like, and certainly did not trust, the Russians. But of course the Russians supplied them with essential war material, so . . .

He nodded finally. "It could happen without my knowledge—especially if our most powerful men, like Le Duan or General Giap, are involved. Why do you think it might be so?"

"I can't answer that question, but believe me when I say it is a possibility."

Doang nodded vaguely. "And what did you want me to do about it?" Thus far Alfred had been little more than an agent of influence, one sympathetic to the American cause who could sway events in small ways.

Connert had planned for this moment ever since he had spoken with Flak Apple and confirmed their fears. "Find out what they are doing, how they're doing it, who is involved, and where they are taking our men. We *must* get them back, and stop them from sending more. It would be best if you can tell me these things before I leave. If not, then pass the information on through your channels when you find it."

The Vietnamese sucked his teeth and hissed, suddenly terribly afraid. These actions seemed so . . . so blatant. He'd been content to play a small role in protest of the awful actions of men like Ho, Giap, and the militants as they continued to destroy his beloved Vietnam, but to actively perform espionage duties? That was something entirely different. The bus gave a lurch and both had to grab the seat back before them to keep from being thrown to the floor.

"You are asking too much," he finally said. "I cannot do these things."

Connert drew a breath. "Look, I realize that you're a patriot, and you want only to help your country. But think of how badly Hanoi will appear to the world when they learn you're exporting American prisoners to Russia."

Alfred looked at him in amazement. "They are taking them there?"

"We believe they've already taken some, and now they may be about to take more. Maybe also North Korea and Czechoslovakia."

Alfred nodded glumly. It was indeed something the militants might secretly conspire to do. Nothing was beyond them. They sent so many sons off to die in the evil war, and even plucked girls from the farms to serve as communal whores for the soldiers. Why wouldn't they sell or trade hated American pilots?

"The war may soon be over," Connert continued. "Even now the peace talks are under way in Paris. While I can't speak officially for my government, I am sure President Nixon would

view most favorably anyone who would help get our Americans
back."

A thought surfaced in Alfred's mind, one he'd entertained
only with caution and no real plan to bring it about. He had
to ask.

"If . . . if I help, would my daughter and grandson be welcome
in America?"

Connert looked at the man, and saw hope flare in his eyes.

"It is very important to me. They are all I have."

Connert shook his head slightly. "You must know I can't
promise something like that."

The flame dwindled from the man's eyes.

"I'll try to get them to agree. I promise I'll try," said Connert.
"Will you help?"

Van Doang was staring out of the window without expression.
He did not respond.

0730 Hours Local, Saturday 22 July 1972
Gia Lam Airport, Hanoi
Democratic Republic of Vietnam

They stood in the morning shade, under the crumbling overhang
of the old French air terminal. The whitewash was crumbling
and peeling. The Russian Aeroflot IL-28 was there, ready to take
the Americans to Vientiane.

The final week had passed slowly for Connert. There were the
obligatory tours of ruins and war museums, which he dutifully
attended, hoping to again see Alfred, but the man had not made
an appearance and Connert could not ask questions or show
undue interest. He felt that part of his mission had been a
failure. Flak Apple had corroborated what the analysts in the
Pentagon and Fort Belvoir suspected, that POWs had been taken
away by Russians, possibly shipped there, and that they might be
gathering more now. But if someone were to be inserted to find
out and document details, he still had no suggestions on how to
direct that investigation. Flak's question had been valid—where
would they start?

Connert, code name Dancer, was pondering all of that when

Alfred walked out from one of the terminal's doors and came up to him.

"I will help," he said simply.

Alfred—Nguyen Van Doang—had spent the week in introspective study. He had come to the conclusion that if he were to help, his actions must not cause his country to lose the war or the loss of any of his countrymen's lives. He'd also concluded that helping the Americans to prevent their young men from being shipped to Russia would do neither of those things, and might make the American government aware that there were North Vietnamese who were compassionate, who didn't subscribe to the hard-liners' brutal methods of doing things. Alfred wasn't sure precisely *why* he wanted the Americans to think this . . . he simply knew he did.

"What have you found?" Connert asked quietly.

"I am an official in the Department of American Studies in the Enemy-Proselytizing Office, one of many departments in our Ministry of External Affairs. I study American journals and newspapers to see what your people think, and distribute my findings to the Party and to other government agencies. I have learned there is a new and secret office that reports directly to the Central Committee. It has no real name, but is referred to as the Transportation Division."

Connert memorized the office's name as Van Doang continued.

"A woman who works in my office as a translator of Russian documents also works in the new Division, and after I showed interest, she began to pay visits to this poor widower. She also talks to me, for I am an adviser to the Central Committee, and if not me, who else can she trust?"

Connert's head came around. Alfred was indeed an important man.

"She does not know if any Americans have yet actually been moved to Russia, but believes it may be so. Some previous agreement between Giap's generals and the Russians, perhaps. But now this new office is involved, and they are indeed gathering prisoners, those identified by a Russian official, at a secret location."

"How many?"

"I do not know. Perhaps as many as a dozen."

Flak Apple had guessed even more. "Perhaps twenty?"

Van Doang shrugged. "I simply do not know. Some are being moved there, and others are being examined and isolated, and will likely be moved later."

Connert's excitement grew. "Where are they holding them? How are they being moved?"

"I do not know the answers to either question, but I will try to find out. The move will not be soon. Perhaps as late as December or even January. It is somehow tied to the timing of the peace conference in Paris, and somehow to the resolutions reached there."

"How?"

"I do not know."

Connert blew out a breath, thinking hard, and was about to speak when the group leader walked up with a serious look on his face.

"Mmmm, you two speak together so much, maybe you would like to stay longer, Comrade Connert?" Richard's heart lurched, then started to pound. They'd been overheard . . .

". . . and study the war," the leader concluded with a wide smile.

Connert managed a ghastly grin. "Well, that's a thought."

"But come now," the leader said, "it is time for you to board your plane. See, here come the pilots." He put a friendly hand on Connert's arm and tugged him toward the rest of the group preparing to mount the stairs. Three Caucasians in ill-fitting airline uniforms, with the Russian red star on them, walked from the terminal toward the big transport.

Connert needed more time with Alfred, who followed close behind, but the leader was insistent and remained with him until they were at the foot of the boarding steps, where the others were making their goodbyes.

Connert turned. "I thank you for your help," he said, shaking Van Doang's hand, only too aware of their crowded surroundings.

"My daughter and grandson send their farewell," Alfred said in response.

"I will try very hard to see them someday."

Alfred nodded. "I can ask no more of a friend," he said.

"Perhaps I may send you a package someday," Connert said. He wanted to tell Alfred the next man, whoever it might be, would also identify himself as a "mailman," but there were too many people about them to risk the words.

"A package? Yes, that would be nice. Do you know how to address such a thing?"

"No, I guess I don't."

"I will write it for you." Alfred produced a cheap ballpoint from a shirt pocket and Connert handed him a small spiral notebook he carried in a cargo pocket. Alfred scribbled a few words before handing it back. Connert didn't risk looking, but replaced the notebook into his pocket. As he turned to mount the steps, he saw the leader had been watching them closely. He turned away finally, a thoughtful look on his face.

Inside, the seats were austere and uncomfortable, damp from accumulated humidity, and the airplane had already grown hot under the unmerciful sun. The passengers blew long breaths and mopped their brows as they settled back for the ride. After a very short pause, the aircraft taxied to the end of the runway, ran up the engines, and took off. In the cockpit, the pilots called Victory Control to verify they had a MiG escort to accompany them to the Laotian border. As they climbed out and turned to a westerly course, toward Vientiane, they discussed the MiG escort they'd lost just before landing a few weeks back, when they had brought the American actress to Hanoi. They concluded the Vietnamese had either lost them somehow or probably gotten bored and simply flown back to their base. "Not trustworthy, these flat-faces," the pilot grunted.

In the cabin, Connert finally had a chance to pull out his notebook and read what Alfred had written: "I play tennis at the *Cercle Sportif* each Wednesday. You may send your package there."

Chapter 16

1330 Hours Local, Monday 24 July 1972
Bachelor Officers' Quarters (BOQ)
Castle Air Force Base, California

Court Bannister wheeled his white 1967 Corvette toward the front gate of Castle Air Force Base, outside Merced. He idled down near the flight line, stopped, and let his senses take in the alien surroundings.

He immediately noted that arriving at a B-52 bomber base was quite unlike going onto a fighter base. There were the noises of flying. The tremendous boom of a fighter's afterburner as raw fuel sprayed into the A/B section of the exhaust pipe—the ripping roar of its jet engine on takeoff—were loud. But the shuddering, thrumming thunder of the big bomber he watched on takeoff roll, with its eight engines roaring at full throttle, was near deafening.

Another major difference was visual. Fighters left small or no smoke trails, whereas lifting off, the B-52 billowed clouds of dark effluvia from all eight engines. The black smoke, he knew, was poorly combusted fuel, most of which was consumed in the afterburner of a fighter, but the B-52, without an afterburner, had no way to consume the stuff.

Court slowly looked about at the flying operation, taking

mental notes, and he realized that another obvious visual difference was in the landing patterns. Every fighter pilot draws a breath at the sight of four sleek fighters, staggered in perfect echelon, as they pass over the runway at 500 miles an hour only 1,500 feet above the ground—then, as the lead plane racks into a 90-degree left-hand bank, bangs out his speed boards, reduces throttle, and completes a 4-G, 180-degree turn to the downwind leg to set up for landing. Three seconds later his number-two man makes the same break; three seconds later number three; and finally number four, all seeking perfect symmetry. The turn radius is tight, about a quarter of a mile—the emotional effect is gut-wrenching and somehow satisfying.

Fighter jocks said that being at a bomber base was like being at a commercial airport, watching airliners, but Court had been told that was not at all so. B-52s were behemoths compared to airliners, were designed for maximum operational efficiency, not safety, and were equipped with few aids or frills.

He watched a B-52 on final, flying a sedate, straight-in approach from ten miles out, almost hovering in the distance as it flew at less than 200 miles per hour. Fighters did that only if the weather was bad and they were forced to make an in-the-blind radar approach . . . and even then they often flew in two-ship formations and landed side-by-side on the runway. He'd been told that the wings of the B-52 were so large they actually overlapped the sides of most runways. He remembered fighter pilot bantering about the bombers' cautious 200-feet-per-minute rate of descent, and how the crew had time to play a hand of cards, their approaches took so long.

Before he'd left the Pentagon, Court had spoken to a couple of bomber pilots there to get a feel for the new environment. They'd told him that in the landing phase the bomber pilots had to exercise utmost skill. All a fighter pilot had to do was aim his steel arrow at the runway, making sure his flaps were down and landing gear in place, and slam onto the concrete. His plane was small, heavy, and easy to control, and brought a sneer from bomber aficionados, for the B-52 pilot faced true adventure upon landing.

A bomber pilot had to place over 200 tons of aircraft, with its ten massive wheels, onto what appeared on approach like a very slim strip of concrete. His feet and hands were very, very busy, Court was told, and, if it was a bad day, so were those of his copilot. It was a bit like landing a sprawling warehouse on a four-lane highway, they'd told him.

A new world, Court decided as he looked at the ramp and the rows of B-52s there. During discussions at the Pentagon, speaking with both fighter and bomber pilots, he'd tried to examine the differences in personalities. The perceptions of fighter jocks were that they were the daredevils, but Court had not been so sure. He'd talked with senior officers who had flown in World War II, and heard tales of pressing on, straight and level at 35,000 feet, flying into flak so thick they could get out and walk on it. Holding the plane steady on course until the bombardier took control from below and made his turns and corrections until bombs-away. Then they'd taken back over and made an immediate post-target turn toward England and safety. B-52 pilots said nothing had changed since then, that they were prepared to do the same. In fact they had done the same thing during the Freedom Porch Bravo raid on Haiphong three months earlier.

Those things took big balls, Court had decided. But if they went back to Hanoi and Haiphong . . . he remembered Smitty Smythe's forecast that unless they changed tactics, the results would be disastrous.

Which was why he was here. To try to make a difference when the balloon went up . . . if it did. Court tightened his jaw and forebade himself from growing bitter.

He started the engine and headed back for the main road that bisected the base, then followed the signs.

Court parked his Corvette in the parking lot and checked into the BOQ. His room was on the second floor, with a distant view of the flight line. As a lieutenant colonel, he rated a private bathroom (shower, no tub). There was a wood-framed bed, a chest of drawers, a sitting chair, a desk and chair, a small refrigerator, a closet, a single print on the wall (a World War I–vintage biplane bomber), and a clock-radio. The clerk had told him his telephone would be connected once his deposit (which he'd paid by check) was forwarded to the telephone company.

He put his B-4 bag and leather suitcase on the bed, hung his clothes bag in the closet, and began to unpack. The final item, from a compartment in his leather suitcase, was a hand-carved rosewood box with a trick latch and a silver pint flask inside.

He opened it and stared moodily, then lifted the flask, unscrewed the top, grimly saluted the ungainly appearing old bomber on the wall, and took a long pull of smooth scotch.

Court sat on the bed and slowly pulled items from the box. A light-blue aviator's scarf. He held it, felt the texture and memories of that long-past day return as sharp and clear as when they'd happened. He'd shot down a Russian pilot in a MiG over the border area between Laos and North Vietnam, then had to bail out of his own airplane when it ran out of fuel. He'd landed hard and was knocked unconscious, and when he'd come to, the Russian pilot stood over him, wearing the blue scarf and wielding a pistol. As they spoke in halting sentences, the Russian pilot had revealed himself as a man of compassion. In the distance were sounds of approaching enemy ground troops, coming to rescue the Russian and capture Court. As they drew closer, the Russian had told him his name, Vladimir Chernov, and after deliberation had turned him free. "The bastards torture," Chernov had explained. Then Chernov had gone down, a bullet in his own chest fired by attackers who'd thought him an American. As yet, Court had not told anyone of the loss he felt for the man who had returned him his life, or what the blue scarf he'd taken from the Russian pilot meant to him.

"Tovarich," he said aloud, "if not for you, I'd be dead or in the Hanoi Hilton."

The thought of the Hanoi Hilton made him remember his times with Flak Apple, one of his instructors at the Test Pilot School at Edwards and, later, a fellow combat-flight leader at Ubon when they'd gone up for MiGs together over the skies of North Vietnam. Now Flak was in the Hilton. So many of his friends were there. He sighed deeply and had a drink for them.

Next—carefully wrapped in tissue paper—was Stately Horse, an exquisite, two-inch golden horse that reared from its ebony base on tiny golden legs. He remembered the joy of buying it for Susan Boyle when they were in Bangkok, the last time he was with her. His sleek California girl, who had flown with American Airlines, shuttling soldiers to and from Vietnam, and whom he had loved as no other. With Stately Horse was the letter, now worn and heavily creased, she'd left on his pillow before disappearing from his life. In it, she'd written that she loved him and didn't want him to see her die of an ugly, fast-acting cancer. He removed the small brass frame with her picture and placed it on the dresser. She was poised on a large sailboat, grasping the forward lines with one hand and waving with the other, golden hair streaming in the wind, eyes alive and sparkling, her smile infectious and full. *To my very own,* was written on it, and the signature, *Your Susan.* Court picked up the picture and stared into Susan Boyle's eyes. His former wife, Charmaine, for all her happy, bubbly ways, had never given him so much, nor made him as content as Susan. And now she was dead.

He stood again and stared out the window—heard the voice of Susan. "I love you, but why do you keep going back to Vietnam?" it asked. And he heard the words of Angie Vick, "Why are you doing this? Why are you always trying to get back to Vietnam?"

As always, the ghostly faces of missing comrades provided the answer.

Court walked next door to investigate. The Officers' Club at Castle was a long, low rambling brick structure. Inside was thick carpeting; paintings of stern SAC generals and ludicrously big airplanes adorned the hallway walls. Linen and china were laid out on the dining room tables. In the next room a brass rail ran the length of a dark bar—the main lounge. There was also a stag bar with sawdust on the floor, and a manager who hurried about in a bow tie and spoke with a European accent. At five P.M. a few officers began to drift in. Those in Class A uniforms went into the main lounge—those in flight suits found the ambiance more to their suiting in the stag bar.

Court, wearing slacks and a sport shirt and preferring to mix with fliers, chose the stag bar. He propped himself at one end of the bar and ordered a Budweiser, and by the time he'd half finished the bottle, the bar was crammed with aircrew members who filled the air with the hum of their talking. A few of the men in flight suits briefly glanced his way, but made no attempt to introduce themselves. The crewmen were somewhat different, Court mused, from what one would find in a fighter club. These were larger and bulkier men, and some wore glasses, which vanity would never allow even the oldest fighter pilots to do. It also seemed they wore more serious expressions.

An unexpected clamor arose from the other end of the bar. The place was now quite crowded, the men standing four deep, and he couldn't see what was happening. A loud quack pierced the air, and a broad smile immediately opened Court's face.

He sprang from his stool and elbowed his way to the other end, where the noise had originated. A sickeningly sweet odor, like burnt plastic, became more pronounced as he drew closer. A knot of people were gathered around one-foot-high flames, and oily smoke issued from something burning on the bar. Standing beside the burning mass, cigarette lighter in hand, was short, wiry, black-haired . . . yep . . . Duckcall Donnie, alias USAF Captain Donnie Higgens.

Hands in descriptive motion, as always, a huge grin plastered on his face, animated eyes agleam—the duckcall sound—it could be no one else. And on the shoulder of his flight suit was a—Court Bannister almost gasped—a SAC patch.

Years back, flying F-100s out of Bien Hoa, Higgens had acquired two of his many sobriquets: Higgens the Homeless and Duckcall Donnie. The former for being banned from the O' Club for asking a visiting minister's wife to "show us your tits." The latter for his habit of carrying a duckcall and blowing flatulent quacks whenever he felt the time was appropriate. Few mature people, a title seldom attributed to Donnie Higgens, agreed with his definition of what was appropriate. Later, Court had flown with him at Udorn in F-4s, where Higgens had a MiG to his credit.

As he approached, Court noticed Donnie still wore the rank of captain. He had obviously been passed over for the rank of major.

"Donnie," he yelled over the crowd.

Higgens looked up and his grin widened. He waved. "Holy shit, it's Court Bannister." He snatched up his duckcall and let out several quacking peals of sheer duck enjoyment.

Court saw what was burning—a foot-long plastic model of a B-52 mounted on a narrow chrome pedestal. The wings were melting, drooping, and two of the engines had already fallen off.

Donnie pumped Court's hand and slammed him on the back. "Goddamn," he said, "but it's good to see you. Great job on that VC flag, great job. Gotta tell me about it, Court." He waved his hands at the smileless crowd. "You're the first fighter pilot I've found in this fairy farm. Hey, listen to this, it's a good one. Know how a bomber pilot finds a navigator for his crew? By trolling. Hangs his pecker out and walks backwards down the flight line."

There were no comments from the crowd.

"Good God, Donnie," Court said, grimacing. "There're guys around here big enough to pinch your head off for remarks like that." He looked around and noticed the crowd around Donnie was not with him, was now in fact trying to thoroughly ignore him. Several of the men glanced at Court with frowns. Cataloguing him along with Donnie Higgens? Court wondered.

Just another obnoxious fighter pilot. He couldn't afford that kind of tag if he wanted to get anything across to them.

"Well, some tried," Donnie was admitting. "But these guys don't like to fight. Look at that." Higgens pointed to the model, now completely burned and being scooped up by a neutral bartender with a wet towel. "Hell, they don't even defend their airplanes."

A giant of a man, wearing lieutenant colonel's leaves on the shoulders of his flight suit, turned and grabbed a fistful of Donnie's flight suit collar, face red with emotion. "Little man, we heard every word you said. You're just a pimple on the ass of humanity. We ignore guys like you because soon you'll turn to pus and ooze away. And if you think you're going to put a crew together around here, you're nuts. No one will fly with you. They'll take a court-martial first." He released Donnie's collar and snarled at Court. "And since you're his buddy, that goes for you, too." He turned back to the group that had been watching in silence and motioned with his head. They moved several feet away and resumed their talking.

"Nice work, Donnie," Court said with a trace of disgust. He took Donnie's arm, noting the strong smell of bourbon on his breath, and said, "There's a table over there. Let's go get caught up." Donnie grabbed a dark drink off the bar as Court tugged him away.

When they were seated, Court cocked his head at his friend. "What in hell are you doing here? Last I heard, you were getting out and going with the airlines."

Donnie took a pull at his drink and wiped his mouth. "Shit, Court, I decided I didn't want to leave, not yet. Too much good flying left to do, I told myself, so I volunteered for a third tour, hoping someone would overlook the rule about no third combat tour. Someone at the Personnel Center had a sense of humor and the next thing I knew, I had orders to SAC for B-52 upgrade. I've done that here at Castle."

"And you're a bit uptight about it, I'd say," Court observed.

"You couldn't pound a greased pin up my ass." Donnie took another drink. "This is most *definitely* not my bag. That big asshole over there's right. No one wants to fly with me. I'll never get a crew, and they know it, so they put me to shuffling papers over in the Wing Personnel section." He sighed and looked in the distance. "And you probably noted I'm still a captain. Hell, my contemporaries are going up for light colonel. Offhand I'd say I've fucked things up." He turned to Court with a smile. "But I've had a great time doing it."

"You're one of the best, Donnie. I'll fly your wing anywhere, anytime."

"Coming from you, those words mean a lot." He took another drink and grinned. "Hey now, what are *you* doing here?"

Court told him he was assigned to the Pentagon, but for some reason had trouble with the next part. "I'm . . . ah . . . assigned to six months of temporary duty to an . . . ah . . . flying unit."

"I see," said Donnie Higgens. "You're just passing through. You bring a fighter in on a cross-country flight?"

"Not exactly."

Higgens frowned.

"I'm going over to the bomber wing at Guam. I'm here for B-52D familiarization."

Donnie stared in disbelief.

Court shrugged, but he wondered if he was turning red-faced.

"So you're being checked out here?"

"Only a few fam rides so I'll know what they're up to over there. It's not a flying job, just liaison work."

Donnie Higgens snorted. "Sounds like you're double-A priority on somebody's shit list—just like me." He waved at a waitress. "Let me buy you another beer, and let's talk over good times and try to forget where we are and about all this depressing bomber crap."

Yet even as he spoke about the old days with his friend, Court Bannister remained determined to make his visit to Castle Air Force Base useful—to keep an open mind and to learn all that was possible about the B-52 operation. He sincerely hoped his

friendship with Duckcall Donnie Higgens hadn't destroyed the
rapport that he'd hoped to build.

After they'd talked for two hours in the bar and had ambled
into the dining room for supper, Donnie came out with something that surprised Court.

"You know," he said reflectively, "I've discovered something
here. They use these Buffs right, turn 'em loose up in Hanoi,
for instance, they can make a hell of a difference, Court. Give
'em a week up there, bombing the hell out of things, and Uncle
Ho, or whoever it is up there that took his place, is gonna yell
uncle."

Then Donnie realized he'd just said something good about
B-52s and frowned.

He added, grinning, "I just don't think it oughta be me doing
it."

1145 Hours Local, Wednesday 26 July 1972
Hoa Lo Prison (Hanoi Hilton), Hanoi
Democratic Republic of Vietnam

Bear Woods groaned a muted sound, which was the loudest
he could issue from his parched and strained throat. He'd first
begun to scream an hour after they'd started the beatings the
previous day, but now all he could do was whimper and make
low animal noises.

After the soldiers in the clearing had battered him with rifle
butts and not shot him as he had planned, there'd been beatings.
Then, after they'd stripped off the G-suit, vest, flight suit, and
boots, and he'd been made to stand in the filthy strips of rags
which had once been undershorts, a soldier had methodically
struck him with his fists. He'd been a runty little twerp, so it
had been no big deal. But Bear had wanted to die.

The five-day, start-stop trip, hog-tied in back of a truck, first
down the dusty back roads, then along the potholed highway
paralleling the Red River, hadn't been that bad. They'd holed up
during the daytime while the fighters passed overhead, fed him
periodically, and only berated and pounded on him when bombs
were heard going off in the distance. The redhead had expected

worse, and was almost lulled into thinking it wasn't going to be so bad after all. Then they'd arrived at the prison, and he'd been pushed into a room by himself and chained to a wall beside a concrete platform bed. The food they brought was shitty, but except for not knowing how to balance on the once-white bucket to relieve himself, it was all bearable. Yesterday morning they'd brought him to the strange room with the lumpy, stained walls, and he'd met the interrogator with the wandering eye and bushy hair. The party was over. It was bad.

He'd learned to shriek louder than he ever had before, and found that when the pain was excruciating for long enough, and when you're tied into an impossible position and they pull your arms back farther than you thought was possible while a foot is stomping down on your head for leverage, you tell them what they want to hear.

He remembered babbling, "Oh God I'll tell you oh God I'll tell you oh God I'll tell you oh God I'll tell you . . . " on and on until the bug-eyed guy finally had the others ease up. That first time it had been his unit and how it was located at Korat, Thailand. Then he'd stopped cold, realizing what he was doing. Two hours later he'd shrieked again, over and over like before, that he'd talk. That time he'd admitted he was an electronic warfare officer, which they already seemed to know. The next time it was that he flew in F-105s, and the next that he was a Wild Weasel. And it was then, through the fog, that Woods realized that someone else, a swarthy Caucasian type, was doing the questioning, but it did not matter. Only the pain mattered. His shoulders were both dislocated, maybe permanently, he figured, and the skin on his belly and face and a few other places was raw and seemed afire. Every possible joint in his body was swollen and sore as a boil. He didn't know if both legs were broken, but the right one emitted constant sharp pain.

There was no letting up, and it was like no one slept. Not only did the bastards torture relentlessly, they seemed to truly get satisfaction from doing it. They laughed among themselves and made pleased little sounds when they succeeded in really hurting him. There was no way to accurately estimate time or tell if it was night or day, for the single overhead light burned dimly throughout, but he felt it had been more than twenty-four hours. It had to be. They were alternating their questions now, first one then the other leading, while other men did the twisting and tying and beating and levering him about.

Woods was now tied into a bow, his feet at the back of his head and his arms twisted unnaturally behind and secured tightly at the elbows, his chestbone protruding like a chicken's, his face digging into the hard concrete floor.

Babbling in tiny gasps.

An hour into it—a day ago?—he'd decided again to die. That had been a joke. The bastards wouldn't let you die, and he'd found that you cannot expire of sheer pain—you can only continue to hurt. He'd also found that no matter how badly you hurt, it could always be worse.

The door slammed and he heard a new voice, this one deep and angry, speaking in a new tongue he vaguely understood. Consciousness dwindled. When he wafted back to lucidity, the ropes were being removed, and a face was bent down close to his own, peering hard, as if trying to penetrate his thoughts. A reddened, pudgy face, the blush more likely gained from booze than from the sun. The nose was bulbous, pitted and webbed with small red veins. A W. C. Fields face that grimaced from Woodrow Woods' stench. When Woods' thin legs were released, he uttered "ah-ah-ah-ah," in ever higher notes as the blood began to flow, and pain to throb in pulse after relentless pulse. The face slowly nodded, then left his view. He heard outraged words, and knew them.

"Fuck your mother, you fools. This one is *mine*. I *told* you he might someday be here, and not to mistreat him, but you did not listen. Getting this man is like getting a rare diamond." The voice was thick with excitement. "The others tell us secrets of the past and present. This one will tell us about the future!"

The northwestern U.S.A. contained several moderately sized Russian immigrant communities. Woods' mother's side was Kievan. His maternal grandfather had never learned English. Woods had spoken Russian haltingly as a child, then had taken three years of it in college to become relatively fluent. "What do you want with me?" he whispered in the fat man's language, then whimpered and faded as the pain grew unbearable.

One hour later Bear Woods was escorted to the door by the swarthy man, supported on either side by an attentive guard, crying out with each painful step. The Russian watched carefully from the rear, exuding an air of triumph.

This time there was no one who had heard his name, but

an American had hoisted himself and watched quietly from his solitary cell as the slender, nondescript man with the bushy red hair and bright beard was dragged through the yard toward the gate.

0945 Hours Local, Friday 28 July 1972
U.S. Embassy, Thong Nhut Street, Saigon
Republic of Vietnam

They gathered in the office of the Air Attaché, known in diplomatic jargon as the AIRA, on the second floor of the American Embassy, to listen as Richard Connert, code name Dancer, debriefed his Hanoi trip. As an excuse to make the meeting, Connert had told Shawn Bannister he wanted to check a detail on his passport. He wore his safari suit, Mahoney blue jeans and a loud shirt. Both had long hair that looked out of place in the room. As Connert and Mahoney walked in, Chef Hostettler, in yellow T-shirt and brown shorts, was sitting on the edge of the desk. He was known at the Embassy as Mr. Thomas of the FAA. Leaning against a wall was Wolf Lochert, wearing slacks and a white polo shirt that looked as if it were painted on his muscular body. He was known as Mr. Johns.

Hostettler rose to his feet and held out his hand and they shook. "Richard, I'm Mr. Thomas, remember? I briefed you before you went in. It's good to see you back."

"Thanks." Connert's face was tense.

"Since we talked last, I've been assigned as your local field supervisor. You know Mahoney. This is Mr. Johns."

Lochert came forward and as they shook hands, studied his face and decided Connert was a man close to burnout. "You're quite a warrior, lad," he said in a deep, gentle voice, "and I know how difficult it is for you. You must understand how valuable your work has been for us."

"I wish I believed that," Connert said in a strained tone. He knew Thomas' real name was Hostettler, and Johns' face looked vaguely familiar.

"Believe it," said the powerful man called Mr. Johns, noting that Connert was haggard and drawn, and acted entirely too nervous.

Chef Hostettler pointed to the straight-backed chairs around a small conference table. On the table beside his briefcase rested a large Teac reel-to-reel tape recorder, arranged with two microphones. The AIRA had to be content with donating his office in the secure DAO (Defense Attaché Office) wing of the Embassy. He could not attend because he didn't have the need to know what would take place there. Connert settled heavily onto a chair and leaned toward a microphone, ready to begin the debrief. Hostettler held up a finger. "We have one more coming."

They chatted of inconsequential things until ten o'clock, when a portly, distinguished-looking man with burn scars on his face entered and closed the door softly behind himself. Connert noted that both Mr. Thomas and Mr. Johns quickly gained their feet, so he followed their lead.

Hostettler made introductions, "This is Mr. White, gentlemen. Mr. White, this is Mr. Johns." Wolf Lochert had worked for Whitey Whisenand for the past three years, but they shook hands as if meeting for the first time. "And this is Captain Richard Connert, Office of Special Investigations, and Sergeant James P. Mahoney, of the Fifth Special Forces Group."

After the men finished shaking hands, Whisenand continued to regard Richard. "Your intelligence isn't all that good in this case, Mr. Thomas. This is not Captain Connert at all."

Richard frowned. He opened his mouth to set him straight.

"This is *Major* Connert." Whitey smiled and put his hand on his shoulder. "If you hear somewhere that the promotion board results aren't out yet, don't worry. Your promotion was decided a few weeks ago by . . . ah . . . another authority."

Connert was stammering. "I—I really . . . " He gulped a swallow and grinned nervously. "Thanks."

"You've been doing a damned fine job. I wish we could do more for you."

"Major?" Mahoney said in surprise, frowning. "Hell, I didn't know you were in the military."

Wolf Lochert fired a 100-watt glare at James Mahoney for his verbal transgression.

"My intell wasn't all *that* bad, Mr. White." Hostettler reached into his briefcase and handed the surprised Connert the pair of major's leaves he'd bought at the embassy PX.

Richard Connert cautiously accepted them.

"Now," Whisenand said to the group, "let's talk about the prisoners of war up north."

Connert had been examining the shiny gold oak leaves. His smile faded. "Ah, God," he sighed. "All those guys up there. I couldn't help them and I felt like shit." His shoulders slumped.

"Let's sit down so you can start your debrief," Whisenand said in a kind voice. "And we'll see if there isn't something we can do." Hostettler started the tape recorder.

It took Connert more than an hour to cover the details of his trip. There were a few questions about Fonda and Bannister, and in-depth examination of Flak Apple's responses, but the bulk of the queries were about Alfred and his disclosure about the new "Transportation Division," and his attitude of cooperation. At the end there was a contemplative silence. Finally Whitey Whisenand spoke.

"I'd say one very important revelation is the probability Mr. Doang spoke of, that they won't move the men for a while."

"He mentioned December or January, and said the delay is somehow tied to the Paris peace talks and"—Connert frowned in recollection—"somehow to the resolutions they agree to. He was vague about that point. I don't think he knew."

"But you believe he was telling the truth?" It was the dozenth time he'd been asked.

Connert nodded, slipping into his earlier display of nervousness.

Whitey was doodling on a pad, deep in thought. He glanced at Lochert, then Hostettler. "We need to stop it. Stop the transfer of the men to wherever it is they're being taken."

Hostettler nodded. "Yes, sir."

"We need to go in and get them out," Lochert rumbled, and Mahoney brightened.

Whitey wagged his head. "No way the President's going to screw up the peace talks. You can rule out another Son Tay–style raid."

"How about using what we've got now? Tell the North Vietnamese negotiators about our information. That we believe they're turning our guys over."

"You've got part of it. The Paris negotiations are the appropriate vehicle to pass on our demands, but we've got to have more than speculations. They'd simply laugh at us and call us liars. We need positive proof: one, that the men are alive, and two, that they're being held wherever they are."

Hostettler-Thomas spoke up. "So we put a man into Hanoi, like we originally thought we'd have to do."

"Perhaps. What are your estimations of Cochise's cooperation level? Think we could convince him to find our people and get the proper proof?"

Chef considered what he knew of the British MI-5 contact. "Doubtful. I don't think they're going to do anything at all outside of Hanoi. They're pretty closely monitored."

Whitey turned to Connert. "What about Alfred? Would he do it for us?"

Richard Connert remembered Nguyen Van Doang and his hesitations. To travel somewhere and take photos? Too overt. He shook his head. "I don't think so."

Whitey nodded abruptly. "Then it's settled. We must insert someone to find out exactly where they're holding our men and, if Alfred finds they really are going to be moved to Russia, then we make a move."

"A rescue in downtown Hanoi?" Mahoney blurted. "Count me in."

Wolf Lochert fixed him with a 500-watt glare. "Mr. White already said a raid is out of the question." Then Wolf had a thought. "We could send in a long-range patrol. We've done it before, just not that far."

"No," said Whitey. "That would be a military ground operation and you can rule it out."

Hostettler tried another tack. "The ARVN Rangers sent a team to the Hanoi area just six months ago, the one Mr. Johns spoke to Lieutenant Hoang about. We could request they send another."

"I don't trust them with information this sensitive," Wolf said immediately. "There's soldiers there I've trusted with my life and would again, but to request something like this through their official channels? No way. They're riddled with leaks."

"And," said Whitey, still staring at his doodling, "we've got the meetings set up with Mr. Doang. He's too good a contact not to use on something like this. Would he even work with the South Vietnamese?"

"No, sir," Richard Connert said with conviction. "He's a patriot. Dealing with us is hard enough for him. Working with the South Viets would be too much to ask. Anyway, part of the reason he's working with us is to get his daughter and grandson to the States."

"Which I'll work on, as I said I would," said Whitey.

They listed the various methods: aboard a Quaker boat delivering supplies to the communists, go in with a Swedish or American peace group, go in as a media member, parachute in during a raid, masquerade as a Canadian ICC member, walk or helicopter in from Laos. All were rejected as unrealistic.

"Well, gentlemen, we seem to be going in circles," said Whitey Whisenand.

That was Chef Hostettler's prearranged cue. He turned to Richard Connert. "Maybe you'd better be getting on back to your hotel. We wouldn't want to blow your cover by keeping you here too long."

Connert started to rise, but Whitey raised his hand. "Before you leave, we need to name our operation. I would like you to have the honor of providing the nickname, Major Connert, since you were the one to return with the critical information."

"I thought they used computers at the Pentagon for that sort of thing," Connert said.

Whitey chuckled. "We leave it to the computer boys, they'll likely end up with something entirely inappropriate. You name it, son."

Connert's troubled brow became knitted as he thought.

"Combat Shamrock," Mahoney suggested hopefully.

Richard Connert looked up. "Both times I've gone up there, we had to fly through bad weather, and I don't see clear skies ahead for this difficult operation. How about 'Storm Flight'?"

They looked at the man who was so depressed and felt so inadequate, who had gone into the tiger's den twice with great success.

"That's it," Wolf exclaimed, and Chef nodded. Even Mahoney liked the sound of it.

"Agreed," Whitey said. "Operation Storm Flight."

Connert stood then, saying he had to pack to leave. He and Bannister were to take a Pan Am flight to San Francisco in the morning. Hostettler phoned the OpsCo (Operations Coordinator) for someone to escort Connert from the secure area to the consular section.

USAF Lieutenant General Albert Whisenand stood and placed his arm over the shoulder of USAF Major (Temporary) Richard

Connert and went to a corner of the room.

There was a knock on the door. Chef looked out and told the escort to wait.

Whitey spoke to Connert in a low tone. "I don't think we're going to have to worry about our prisoners much longer. Things are to be resolved one way or the other in the near future, what with the talks in Paris and all. Start thinking about yourself, son. What you want to do in the Air Force, in particular. When this is over, come see me and we'll work out whatever you want."

"Sir, I don't even know who you are."

"You will, when the time comes, and it will not be long."

Connert nodded, thanked him, and went out the door.

"There goes a very tired man," Wolf said.

"He was never trained for this sort of prolonged deep-cover work," Hostettler said. "It requires a special kind of guy."

"Yeah," Mahoney piped up, "one who can pick flowers with one hand and strangle kittens with the other."

Wolf became so red-faced it looked as if he'd strangle. He gave him a 1,000-watt glare. "Go to the cafeteria and have a root beer. We've got work to do. I'll send someone for you later."

Chastened, Mahoney left the room.

Wolf looked apologetic. "Sometimes we get a little crude," he said, and the three men immediately fell to organizing Operation Storm Flight.

"Which option?" Whitey asked.

Chef Hostettler mused. "Cochise is with the British Consulate in Hanoi. How about if we inserted our own man there?"

"Mmmm. Perhaps." He nodded more vigorously, liking the idea. "The Brits have been cooperative. We could send in one of ours as a member of their staff, and maybe someone else as a backup aboard one of their cargo ships that's going to be in port. Wouldn't have to act unless needed."

"Meanwhile," said Hostettler, "we have Cochise continue to work the problem with Alfred."

After fifteen more minutes of discussion, they'd completed the rough details of the plan. When they were finished, Whitey said, "By the way, I like Connert's suggestion for a nickname."

"Sort of catchy," Wolf agreed. "I hate cutesy little names. I was on a deep strike once that was called Lavender Trees." He snorted.

"Okay," said Whitey. "Let's go over it one last time."

An American agent (code-named Geronimo and preferably a military man) would be assigned to the British Consulate to work for Cochise. Geronimo would establish himself as an Oxfordian with communist tendencies, and would meet with Alfred for weekly tennis matches. The usual comm net via Cochise would be in place, and in emergency he could contact the second man on the British ship.

"Good," said Whitey. He went over the coordination which would be required. He'd made contact with the MI-5 before, but that was for a simple bit of information. This time he would ask for much more—an American to pose as a British subject. He would return to Washington, get a go-ahead nod from the President, then gain approval from the Departments of Defense and State, and *then* contact MI-5 to arrange permission for the cover, both in the consul and on the boat. It would take time to go up the line for approval on the American side, and the British would likely take as long. At each level he would have to prove the plan necessary and feasible. He thought Dennie Blaine would be the best man to send to the British Consulate.

"I'd like to see Jim Mahoney as our man on the boat," Wolf said. "Maybe with an Irish passport."

"You have that much faith in him?" Whisenand asked, surprised after the way Lochert had seemed so angry at his man an hour before.

"I'd stake my life on Jim. I've been able to in the past. He's good under cover. He's just no good in polite company. Anyway, the fewer people we have to brief in on this thing—"

"Storm Flight," interjected Chef Hostettler.

"Yeah. The fewer who know about Storm Flight the better."

Whitey nodded his acceptance of the idea, then pushed his chair back. "The Storm Flight plan hinges on Defense and State Department acceptance, as well as British approval and cooperation. If I can't get those, there'll be no man in place in Hanoi unless we can come up with a workable plan B, something for which we need no outside support."

The men before him frowned.

"We must somehow use our own assets to get into Hanoi."

"Mahoney from the boat?" asked Hostettler.

"Maybe."

"Only as a last option," said Wolf. "I think we should use someone else and keep Mahoney as backup."

"I've been playing with a thought," Whitey said. He hesitated, then sighed and continued. "In case the British prove difficult, is there any way we could either put a man ashore or parachute someone in at night? Colonel Lochert brought both ideas up, and in case plan A fails, I feel we should at least explore them."

"I should be the one to do that," Wolf said.

Chef frowned, uneasy with the idea. "Explore the alternatives?"

"Study the problem, help pick the best alternative, and if the need arises, be inserted."

"We'll see," said Whitey Whisenand with a sigh. "If everything works out properly, we'll handle the problem through the British Consulate." He checked his watch. "I've got a series of meetings at Seventh Air Force headquarters. The President wants an estimate of how things are going with the Linebacker bombing campaign, and he likes his information from the horse's mouth. Then I'm to go over to U Tapao to meet with the wing commander. That one's for the Chief of Staff."

Whitey didn't tell them that a minor hassle was continuing between the Chief of Staff and the Commander of SAC. That sort of thing was for the generals to brood over. Neither did he tell them that their friend and his nephew, Court Bannister, might end up a casualty of that argument.

They arose to shake hands and depart separately. They didn't smile and there was no jocular conversation. Wolf walked down to the OpsCo's office and asked him to send someone for Mahoney.

When Mahoney arrived, Wolf took him back to the room.

"Jeez, I'm sorry, Wolf, I mean Colonel, sir," Mahoney began.

"Shut up and listen. Once that airplane gets airborne for San Francisco tomorrow with Connert on it, you don't have a job."

Mahoney brightened, and his smile returned. "This was no job, it was bullshit. Now how about I cut off this hair, have a little I and I in Bangkok, then off to an A camp?"

Wolf frowned. I & I was GI slang for Intoxication and Intercourse, a takeoff on the official R & R (Rest and Relaxation) term. An A camp was a Special Forces remote fighting unit in the wilds of Vietnam, and those had mostly been turned over to the ARVN.

"I have something else in mind. How long will it take you to polish up your Irish accent?"

Chapter 17

General Whisenand had reported to President Nixon immediately upon his return from Saigon, and was told, rather absently, to proceed with his Storm Flight plan as he thought best. Nixon had a lot on his plate and had taken to spending much of his time in a hideaway office in the Executive Office Building.

Whitey had not pressed his busy Commander in Chief further, and had proceeded. Very soon, however, he'd learned that his task was not to be easy. It began when the Chairman of the Joint Chiefs of Staff, Admiral Tom Moorer, had said, "I'll have it staffed and get back to you."

"Sir," Whitey had said to the JCS Chairman, "I must ask you not to staff this in the normal manner. There is too sensitive material involved here, and the consequences to our POWs would be grave if a leak develops. I request you discuss this only with your chief of intelligence."

Moorer had fixed him with a gimlet eye, then dismissed him. That conversation had taken place two weeks previously, and there'd been no response since.

Tom Moorer was a tough man, who'd been CINCPAC—the

man next up the convoluted chain of command from COM-MUSMACV, now General Fred Weyand, who had replaced Abrams in June when he'd stepped up to become Chief of Staff of the United States Army. Now Moorer was head of the JCS, which had working for it the Joint Staff, a multiservice, overmanned bureaucracy full of inter- and intra-service rivalries and a maze of perplexing staffing procedures. On the outside, each service fought for bigger slices of the two big pies—the appropriations pie and the Vietnam combat-operations pie. On the inside, the submariners fought the airedales in the Navy, SAC fought TAC in the Air Force, Infantry fought Artillery and Armor in the Army, and the Marines argued within about how and with what they should fight.

Aware of all that, Whitey had debated taking the plan around the Chairman to the Secretary of Defense. He had that authority, but without military support things could go awry, so he decided against it and time wore on. It was not that his military cohorts were against any plan to assist American prisoners—they were too preoccupied with the difficult tasks of following the President's orders to withdraw troops from South Vietnam, while conducting increasingly large-scale air operations against North Vietnam. In the meantime Whitey was left with no answer to his request for support and assistance regarding the Storm Flight operation. He would have loved to discuss the thorny problem with his wife, Sal, but the security level was simply too high. This time he had to ponder it alone.

Chastened by the experience at Defense, he'd gone directly to the intelligence branch of the State Department in an effort to coordinate his request with as few people as possible. He'd described the plan in general terms with the intelligence chief and requested the two of them meet with the Secretary and no others. The Secretary, William P. Rogers, was enthusiastic about anything that might help the POWs and told his intelligence chief to cooperate fully with Whitey.

The intelligence chief proved less enthusiastic. "Peace talks are under way," he'd said, referring to Henry Kissinger's meetings with North Vietnam's Le Duc Tho in Paris, "and the atmosphere is tense. The slightest slipup and we may receive a setback where we get *nobody* back. Let's wait for a month and see what happens."

"I can't do that," Whitey had replied, huffing a sigh of exasperation, and had reluctantly shown the man his note of authority from the President, demanding full cooperation. "Now," he'd said, "I intend to notify the MI-5 contact at the British Embassy and forward my request to insert a military agent in Hanoi. I've met with him on previous occasions."

The intelligence chief had smiled thinly at his display of power. Then, to Whitey's dismay, he'd learned that there had been a shakeup at the British Embassy in Washington, and the man he'd previously worked with regarding Cochise had been reassigned.

The chief of intelligence had provided the new man's name and set up the meeting—but for one week hence.

On that day, Whitey had gone to the British Embassy on Massachusetts Avenue and been ushered into a small room (which he was assured was secure) where he'd had his first meeting with the new representative of MI-5. The man listened politely, seemed skeptical about the USSR's involvement, and said Whitey's plan had *intriguing possibilities*. He'd get back to Whitey as soon as he'd spoken to the Ambassador. Whitey knew the man was not fully aware of the situation in Hanoi when he asked him if he knew of Cochise. "Not outside of your nineteenth-century Western history," the British intelligence officer had replied. Whitey had asked him to please forget everything he'd told him and to take no further action.

In the past, the DDO at the CIA had cleared Whitey to deal directly with the MI-5 contact at the Embassy regarding communication with Cochise in Hanoi. When Whitey drove across town to Langley and spoke with the deputy director for operations (DDO) to find out what was afoot, he was told they would now have to deal through the CIA Chief of Station in London, thence to his counterpart in MI-5, who would message his man at the consulate in Hanoi. Whitey asked him for his support regarding the Storm Flight operation, to plant an American agent on the staff of a British consul. The DDO had been as enthusiastic as the Secretary of State had been, and said he'd brief the Director and get moving on it right away. The operator must, of course, be one of their men and not from the military side. Fine, Whitey had said. The DDO had then told him that the request would likely require approval from both the British Foreign Office and from 10 Downing Street . . . and that would take time.

But time was running out.

Whitey messaged to Wolf Lochert in Saigon that progress in Washington was proceeding very slowly, and that he should begin preparations to implement Plan B of Storm Flight—the insertion of one of their own men. He asked Wolf to examine their options and recommend the best way to insert someone into Hanoi.

1300 Hours Local, Tuesday 22 August 1972
Dogpatch
Democratic Republic of Vietnam

The place they'd taken Bear Woods—and he still didn't know the real name—had been a full night's ride from Hanoi in a Soviet-manufactured six-by-six. They'd left Hoa Lo Prison in the afternoon, paused at the edge of the city until darkness, then crossed two bridges. Although he'd been transported in a covered truckbed from which he'd been unable to see out, he could tell, because they'd swayed some, and because of the clanking and humming sounds, like they were riding on steel-mesh matting. They used the stuff to repair their bombed-out bridge surfaces. That likely meant they were going north, over the Doumer and Canales bridges. Then they'd ground slowly along, uninterrupted through the night, and didn't stop when it grew light. And *that* meant they were somewhere they could drive in the daytime and get away with it, like up near the Chinese border. Finally they'd labored up and down several steep hills. By the time they finally stopped, it was midmorning.

Woods had been scared shitless throughout the truck ride. The bug-eyed Viet asshole had been mean, and he'd made the redhead hurt in places he'd not known were possible. The Cuban—he found out later that the guy was nicknamed Fidel—had been an even meaner shit, and had hurt him even worse. But it was the goddamn Russian—the guy who'd resembled W. C. Fields—who'd brought Woodrow G. Woods' mind to the verge of numb terror. Where were they taking him?

After they'd finally stopped at the nameless location far north of Hanoi, his two armed guards had prodded him down from the truck, a painful feat because he'd been tucked into a cramped position in the back of the bouncing vehicle for some eighteen hours, with only two stops to refuel and allow him to urinate. He'd stood on the ground, grimacing and tottery on trembling legs, and darted his eyes about.

They were in a fenced, hillside compound, with guard towers set about the periphery, in the midst of pleasant, green-clad, rolling mountains. There was no dense jungle that he could see, like the one into which he'd tried to escape. It looked more like the view might be in Vermont or New Hampshire, with different and lusher flora. Then he'd been greeted by a pleasant, English-speaking Viet, who seemed more like a summer camp official than a prison boss, and ushered into his office. There he was offered a smoke, and asked how the trip had been.

For Chrissakes, the guy had acted as if he was truly concerned that his trip might have been uncomfortable.

They'd both lit up, and Woods had eyed him like he was some kind of nut.

The lull before the storm, he thought. *The guy's going to soften me up, then show me next door, and that will be another funny room with soundproofed walls, and they're going to use ropes and beat the shit out of me again.*

"Is diff-runt here dan in Hanoi," the Viet said pleasantly as if reading his thoughts.

And it was. He'd been told the rules, like he had to bow correctly (sharply at the waist, with head bent forward at a 90-degree angle) when an officer entered the cell or passed by, he must follow the rules of the guards and not those of his fellow prisoners, and he must take a shit (he learned the word "bo") and cleanse himself daily. Any questions would be answered and problems settled by the prison authorities, and not by his fellow prisoners, who were criminals like himself. He was again told to do precisely as told by the jailers. The biggest thing he noticed was that there was no railing or even threats of beatings.

It was downright eerie.

Woods was taken to a washroom, where he was doused with water, then with disinfectant, then with water again. He was allowed to shave under the scrutiny of a quiet but watchful guard, then provided gray-and-maroon-striped pajamas that bagged in the wrong places and were too short, but which were clean.

Finally he was issued a blanket, mosquito net, and porcelained bucket, and marched to a plain wooden building, from which he heard American voices. Their sounds had died down as the guard opened the door, and he'd been shown into the large, open-bay room. As soon as the turnkey departed, he'd been surrounded by grinning, chattering fellow Americans, and Woodrow G. Woods, Captain USAF, felt his heart soaring for the first time in a month.

The euphoric feeling had lasted through the first few days, but now that Bear Woods had spent almost a month at the nameless place the Navy and Air Force aviators called Dogpatch, the elation had been replaced by new emotions. They weren't mistreated. Prisoners could spend a considerable amount of time in the sunlight, walking around the compound, and every few days they were even allowed to form up teams and play volleyball. There were no beatings that amounted to anything, even for the worst transgressions. If you refused to bow, for instance, the guards would fuss and glare, but they'd not really beat you, so the practice was modified. You bowed only when someone big was around or the V would lose too much face. Even the food, while bland and tasteless, was plentiful enough. Beans and rice flavored with flecks of meat were standard, and each man was given a scrawny green banana, but there was enough to nourish them and the V encouraged·them to maintain their health. But the sense of elation Woods had felt was entirely gone.

All of the indoctrination briefing rules, except those dealing with hygiene, were ignored or at least bent by the prisoners. This was especially true of the directive not to follow rules set down by fellow prisoners. The Senior Ranking Officer (SRO) was a major, a dour and sad-looking pilot who'd been shot down in a Thud back in 1967, and the others scrupulously followed his orders. He'd come out of the Pentagon's fighter requirements office before upgrading to F-105s, and the scuttlebutt was that he'd been working on some very advanced, very secretive projects. He was a studious type, not at all your typical fire-eating fighter jock, and had a PhD in engineering. None of the sixteen guys had run-of-the-mill backgrounds. Nine were electronic warfare officers, and seven of those were Wild Weasels like Bear Woods. The university education level was high—the average held a masters degree in a technical field with substantial work toward a doctorate. There were a large number of those around the Air Force, but seldom had Woods seen this many gathered into a single group.

A few days after his arrival at Dogpatch, Bear Woods brought up the strangeness of the situation to the SRO, and he was told to be quiet about it and then was utterly ignored. Finally, after another week had passed, the SRO had taken him to a corner of the room to talk.

The guys knew that Woods was a no-shit POW, but there was another new guy, a captain named Tracey, who was now out in the yard, whom they had reservations about. Do not talk about sensitive subjects when Tracey was in earshot, he was ordered. Don't talk freely about the uniqueness of the prisoners at Dogpatch in front of either Tracey or jailers who understood English. That was a subject the V would not allow them to discuss. If they caught you mentioning backgrounds, their response was to quickly usher you out for a few weeks of isolation in solitary cells in the shedlike building at the far corner of the camp. There were two people there now. The SRO said the standing order was to get the word about what was going on out to the other camps, especially to the big one where the majority of the guys were being held—Hoa Lo, the Hanoi city jail, which the guys also called the Hanoi Hilton. So far, though, they'd been unable to.

When Woods had asked what it was all about, he was given a shrug. No one knew. He'd asked if the SRO had heard of a major named Todd Smythe, and he'd nodded. Smythe was known to have come through Hoa Lo, but then had disappeared. He was the last of several who had vanished from the system. After Smythe, there'd been some sort of change. Now no one was disappearing. But—he said ominously—he did not believe the people at Hoa Lo knew about the existence of Dogpatch and who was there. He was also concerned that they were incarcerated in one of the barracks, but two more had just been built. That could mean that others might be on their way to join them.

When Bear Woods asked if anyone else had seen the red-faced W. C. Fields look-alike, the SRO had quietly nodded. More than half the internees at Dogpatch had seen the man hanging around before they'd been shipped north.

"He's Russian," Woods had told him, and then he'd explained that he spoke Russian, and what the guy had said when he'd been in the torture room at Hoa Lo. The SRO had huffed a sigh, and

said that confirmed a lot of suspicions. The senior officers at
Hoa Lo had believed that to be the case, but hadn't been a
hundred percent sure.

"Where the hell are we, sir?" Woods had asked. Somewhere
up north near the Chinese border was all the SRO knew. There
was a village and a man-made lake with a small dam not far
away, he added, and one of the prisoners had learned from a
guard that the town was called Don Kee, or something like that,
so the POWs called them Donkey Town, Donkey Dam, and
Donkey Lake. In their boredom, they'd even made up a song
about Ramblin' Round in Donkey Town. Bear Woods had tried
to remember the lake on his aeronautical charts, but could not.
They hadn't studied the area in the Chinese buffer zone, since
it was off-limits to the fighters.

But he decided now to examine it all very closely, every time
he got out to the yard, even though the SRO was saying he'd
ordered the men to forget about trying to escape, because the
rumors at Hoa Lo had been that it wouldn't be long before the
Americans and the Viets came up with some kind of agreement
and the prisoners were released.

Woods had been about to ask another question when Captain
Tracey and some of the other prisoners were ushered back into
the barracks cell from the yard where they'd been playing
volleyball. They'd immediately changed the conversation to
something more mundane.

Woods had spoken with the SRO a couple of times since then,
and now was about to help him with a project. He was going to
use his Russian-speaking ability to catch a rat.

Captain Rick Tracey said he was a recce systems officer, a
backseater in an RF-4C who'd been shot down two months
earlier near Haiphong. He said his frontseater had been killed.
He'd also said he was from Chicago, and had gone to school
with Jimmy Hoffa's son. Another POW, a Navy Lieutenant JG,
had come from nearby Gary, and said Tracey was full of shit,
because from what he remembered, the junior Jimmy Hoffa was
older than Tracey. He'd had an idle conversation with him, and
slipped in a few ringers. Captain Tracey had fucked up
when he'd agreed that the Drake was a superb discotheque.
The Drake was an elegant downtown hotel, and anyone from
Chicago should know that. The POW from Gary had been

tight-mouthed when he'd told the SRO. He said he wanted to kill the fink bastard.

So who was Tracey? Before they took more drastic measures, the SRO wanted to know.

Woodrow Woods was playing chess with Tracey, with a couple of others looking on. The prisoners had scratched out a checkerboard on a wooden box and used carefully selected stones of different shapes and colors for chessmen.

"Guard your king," Tracey said, moving his rook. They'd been playing intently. Both were fairly good at the game.

"Damn," Bear Woods muttered, brooding.

Tracey's eyes were glued to the situation on the boxtop.

Woods sighed. He moved a knight into jeopardy to block the rook.

It was Tracey's time to get serious. His queen had been placed in harm's way, threatened by a protected bishop after the removal of the knight.

"Damn," Woods said again. He muttered that he hadn't considered Tracey's own knight, which was poised to take the bishop and remove the threat.

Tracey grinned and immediately took the bishop. The smile faltered. Woods had spoken his words in Kievan Russian, and was staring coldly at him.

The two onlookers were also looking at Tracey.

Captain Rick Tracey smirked. "So what's wrong with you guys? I learned some Russian in college. How about you, Woods?" His look narrowed in accusation. Perspiration beaded and glistened on his forehead.

Bear Woods looked down, then calmly took the queen with his own knight. "Check. I think you're in deep shit, Tracey."

"Where'd you learn your goddamn Russian, Woods?" Tracey asked in a louder tone.

"In Cottage Grove, Oregon. That's in the U.S.A. *How about you, Ivan?*" The last sentence had been spoken in Russian.

Tracey abruptly stood, shouting, "I won't stand for that kind of insinuation!" His voice was shrill and very loud.

One of the onlooker POWs clamped a heavy hand onto his shoulder. "Asshole!"

Tracey tried to rise, but the hand held him firmly in place as others in the room began to converge.

"Stop!" Tracey shrieked. "What the hell are you guys doing?"

The guy from Gary spoke up. "The Drake isn't a discotheque, Tracey. It's a hotel."

"It's also a disco!" the man cried out, eyes widening as the men continued to gather.

"You don't know fuck-all about RF-4s, Tracey," said another. "How about MiGs? You fly MiGs, Tracey?"

"Get the hell away from me!" He was shrieking very loudly now.

The door flew open and two Viet guards hurried in.

The guy from Gary took a wild swing, but the man who had called himself Tracey pulled away and the fist grazed off his forehead.

The guards were screaming. They'd brought AK-47s and one lifted his and aimed.

"Okay, guys, back off!" yelled the SRO. The men slowly shuffled clear. One hawked and spat at Tracey, then another.

The guards looked questioningly at Tracey, who was reluctant to give up his role. "What the hell are you guys talking about? Woods knows some Russian and so do I. For Christ's sake, what's wrong with that? And there *is* a discotheque called the Drake."

One of the taut-faced POWs started to edge forward.

"Back off," barked the SRO in his authoritative tone.

Tracey sighed and motioned. The guards came over and stood protectively as he first stood, then took a hard look back at the staring group.

"This is not the last you'll hear of me," he said in a calm, bell-clear voice. He disdainfully wiped a gob of spittle from his pajama top and flicked it onto the floor, then turned to Woods. He nodded slowly, grew a hateful smile, then strode haughtily out of the room.

The guards held their positions for a while, then backed toward the door.

At dusk a huge, double-bladed, Soviet-built helicopter landed in the flat area immediately east of the Dogpatch compound. Before it departed a few minutes later, guards came into the room and herded the prisoners into the back of the barracks cell so they couldn't watch through the grate over the opened window.

"Betcha that chopper's for our good buddy Tracey," said the prisoner from Gary.

• • •

A few days later, the men in Dogpatch learned two items of interest. The first was from a prisoner who had been held in one of the solitary cells at the shed. He'd peered through a crack and seen Tracey, now wearing a khaki jacket and civilian clothing, climbing aboard the big chopper. The second revelation came from a new arrival, an A-7 pilot who had a masters degree in electrical engineering, and who Bear Woods remembered from Wright Patterson as a project engineer who'd specialized in fuzing systems for reentry-vehicle warheads. The A-7 jock had visited his parents in Chicago before being shipped to the combat zone. The hottest new disco in the windy city was a place called Drake's Inferno.

The same day the A-7 fighter jock/engineer had told them about the discotheque and set them to thinking, half of the twenty-one men now held at Dogpatch refused to eat the evening meal because it gave off a sour smell and tasted bitter. The other half were older heads, who'd been imprisoned much longer and gone through lean times, and had learned to eat whatever food was available. Within half an hour they'd become sick as dogs, and one, the Navy JG from Gary, Indiana, was hurting so bad that all he could do was writhe about and howl in pain. By night-fall he and two others seemed even more ill, and were carted away in Russian-built utility vehicles. The camp commandant told the slowly recovering and concerned SRO they were being taken to Hanoi for treatment at the Bach Mai hospital.

1030 Hours Local, Wednesday 6 September 1972
Hoa Lo Prison (Hanoi Hilton), Hanoi
Democratic Republic of Vietnam

Flak Apple lifted himself and peered out at the courtyard through the tiny slit between boards covering the window. He wore the standard POW garb of ragged maroon-striped pants and large pajamas. His mind wrestled with the problem of what to do, for another prisoner had just been ushered into the gatehouse, making it two in the last hour. More men were being culled out. If there was a new common thread (and that was hard to determine because of the difficulty of obtaining information and passing messages), it was that the men were younger and more recent shoot-downs. They were still the ones with the secretive backgrounds and higher education levels.

Since the Son Tay raid almost all the POWs had been brought directly into the Hoa Lo Prison Complex and placed in larger, more communal cells, yet many of the older types, those more senior in rank, and those known to be hard-line resisters, were still kept isolated. Flak was one of those. He stiffened when he heard the familiar tap code call-up rapped on his cell wall.

Tap ti-tap tap . . . Tap ti-tap tap . . .

He sprang to the wall and answered . . . tap tap.

Shave and a haircut . . . six bits.

BIG NEWS . . . the caller tapped.

GO . . .

ONE OF THE MISSING JUST CAME FROM HOSPITAL TO THE BIG ROOM SAID WAS ONE OF THREE VERY ILL GUYS BROUGHT IN FROM NEW CAMP N AFTER MEDICINE SOMEHOW TURNED LOOSE OUR COMPOUND FOR FEW HOURS BEFORE THEY FOUND HIM AGAIN . . . SAID TWENTY-ONE MISSING GUYS IN NEW CAMP THEY CALL DOGPATCH NEAR CHINESE BORDER . . . GAVE NAMES . . . NO TORTURE . . . GOOD TREATMENT . . . COUPLE MEN THEY NO R RUSSIAN SEEN UP THERE . . .

WHERE DOGPATCH . . . WHAT V NAME . . .

DONT NO V NAME . . . DOGPATCH MAY BE NORTH NEAR BORDER CHINA . . . SRO WANTS U TO GET THIS INFO OUT . . . SEZ U MUST GET CHOIR GOING . . .

MAYBE I CAN BUT THAT NO GUARANTEE WILL BE FILMED . . .

Flak heard a guard coming and gave three quick thumps to break off the conversation. He'd heard enough. There was only one way to get the choir going again and that was to show willingness to cooperate.

When the guard brought his evening pumpkin soup, Flak made him understand he wanted to see someone higher up. Two days passed before Flak was brought before Bug, who seemed unusually agitated.

"What you want, what you want?" the little man with the bushy hair screamed into Flak's face. He wore the greenish-tan uniform with no insignia.

"I think we should have the choir sing some more."

"That make you happy, Apper?" Bug asked in a dangerously quiet voice.

"It's not just for me. It's for the rest of the fellows, too."

"I not make any of you happy," Bug screamed. *"You kill my mother, you air pirates kill my mother."* Bug had frequently screamed that his mother had been killed in an air strike. His wandering right eye followed invisible birds somewhere over Flak's shoulder. "There will not be choir, Apper. No."

Flak regarded the Vietnamese and took a breath, mentally switching to an alternative plan to get the vital information out to his government. It would be a shameful thing in the eyes of his fellow prisoners, but he would just have to endure their contempt, his message was vital.

"I want to live better," Flak said. "I want better food, better quarters, better clothes."

Bug's head jerked and his eyes almost popped. "Live better," he said. "Live better? You are a criminal, you have no *right* to live better. Why should you live better?"

Flak said and swallowed, "I repent of my crimes, I am sorry for what I have done and want to make atonement."

"Apper, you . . . you *sorry?* Why I believe you? You have many chances before to be sorry. We give you too much, too lenient and humane to you. You never pay us. No, Apper, I cannot believe you."

"Will you believe me if I make a tape?"

Bug looked at him suspiciously. "Maybe I believe you if you make live broadcast over camp radio." Bug knew what he was doing. It was one thing to be tortured into making a tape with words full of agony and pain. It was quite another to make tapes and broadcasts with words and banter as easily rendered as if they were in the ready room on board their ship.

Flak thought quickly. He could formulate his message text in such a way as to convey the news about Dogpatch, but he wanted his words to be aired over Hanoi radio so American monitors could record his message. The camp radio was a very low power, short-range system that couldn't be picked by even the northernmost communications monitoring stations in Laos and South Vietnam.

"I'll do as you say," he said. "I just want to . . . to live better."

"Apper, you are smart man. You will live better. You will make broadcast, but maybe not too soon. I will tell you when it will be."

"I will need paper and a pencil to write my . . . my *talk.*" It would take time for Flak to formulate the exact words he needed to give the cadence that would form the POW code.

"Oh, no, Apper, you do not need paper and pencil. All you have to do is read. We will write everything for you. You wait and repent your sins. We will let you know when it is time."

Bug was pleased when he reported to the new Party liaison officer and a representative from the Central Committee that criminal Apper finally appeared to be ready to give in to the system. "After all the years of being a problem," Bug said, "the black man will now do as I—" He made a dramatic pause, then corrected himself with a deprecating smile. "As *we* say."

"You have done well, comrade," the liaison officer said. "But do not give anything to the criminal just yet. Make him worry some more. We have interesting negotiations ongoing with the imperialists and it is possible we will have a special statement for the black criminal to make."

"I will do as you say, comrade," Bug said, trying to keep the disappointment from his face.

The other man, Nguyen Van Doang—Alfred—remained silent, anthracite eyes revealing nothing.

1030 Hours Local, Thursday 7 September 1972
Camp David
Catoctin Mountain Park, Maryland

Dressed in a charcoal suit and carrying the overcoat and the overnight bag he'd been advised to bring, Lieutenant General Whisenand was met at the southwest gate of the White House grounds by the President's scheduler and office aide-de-camp. It was a clear, crisp day.

"May I carry your bag?" The aide hefted and turned. "This way, sir."

Whitey followed him up the long circular driveway of the South Lawn, then across the lawn to a Marine helicopter, rotors still and drooping, impeccable guards in place.

"Sorry for the secrecy," the aide said, "but the press has been on full alert ever since Henry disappeared from Claridge's this morning." Henry Kissinger had made a highly visible trip to London to confer with British Prime Minister Edward Heath, then had ducked out, leaving a Do Not Disturb sign on his door. The press maintained one contingent at Claridge's, another in Paris waiting to see if he'd show up for another round of talks with Le Duc Tho.

The aide saw Whitey to the helicopter and stepped back as the engine was brought to life and the big blades began to churn. The helicopter took off and climbed to 1,000 feet and followed the Potomac north to the mountains. Whitey watched the towers of the Healy Building at Georgetown University slide under the craft and mused about the times he'd been a guest lecturer in their history department. Then he thought of his upcoming visit with the President and the difficulty he'd had just making an appointment. It was as if Nixon's Chief of Staff did not want anyone who wasn't part of the inner circle seeing the President. He sipped absently on decaffeinated coffee served by the steward as the helicopter droned on for another twenty minutes.

Past Thurmont, Maryland, the pilot headed for a forested mountain, its trees turning autumn golden, then pulled up sharply to climb like an overhead tram. He settled sharply down the other side into a field cleared in the midst of the forest. Whitey caught a quick glimpse of a field house and skeet range before the helicopter settled with a slight bump. Armed Marines in camouflage fatigues stood guard at the edge of the pad as a uniformed Navy commander opened the helicopter door. The commander snapped a salute and led Whitey to a waiting bulletproof limousine. He chatted about the weather as they were whisked up the narrow tree-lined road, past more armed guards, to a small guest cabin labeled Elm. Inside, a cheery fire was already burning in the fireplace. An Air Force enlisted aide welcomed Whitey and took his bag.

Whisenand accepted a soda and walked to the window to look over the manicured paths winding through the trees to other guest houses and to Aspen, the President's lodge. He'd been here twice before, while working for Lyndon Baines Johnson. LBJ had started renovation of the cabins on the 143-acre estate before he'd decided not to run. Richard Nixon had finished the job and added the large-scale communications capability, similar to that available at the White House.

Whitey checked his watch, twenty minutes to go before his luncheon date with the President.

"So good to see you, General Whisenand," said Richard Nixon in his ever-serious mien. "You're just in time for lunch. I apologize for not seeing you as often as we would both like, but you understand things have . . . ah . . . been moving very quickly these days. Even now Henry is in Paris preparing for another meeting with Le Duc Tho." He smiled. "He does like his intrigue." The President wore a soft smoking jacket and dark trousers, and appeared more relaxed than he had recently. Sun streamed in through the wide picture window, through which Whitey could see the pool and, beyond, the valley overlooking the Maryland countryside.

Bob Haldeman made a brief appearance to show, Whitey guessed, he was still very much the Chief of Staff. His crew cut was as fresh as a Quantico drill sergeant's. He left after saying he was delighted to see General Whisenand.

Nixon led the way to a small table set up near the front window. In moments, stewards served the President his customary lunch of pineapple and cottage cheese, and the small tossed salad requested by General Whisenand.

When the room had emptied, Whitey began without pause. The President was simply too busy these days to waste his time with glossy niceties. "Sir, I will be brief. I still need to get a man into Hanoi to verify that a number of American prisoners are being singled out by the Russians for possible transportation to Russia." While Whitey had briefed the President on all that upon his return from the Saigon meeting, he wanted to refresh his memory.

Nixon was frowning even more than usual.

"You do remember, don't you, sir? The Storm Flight operation."

Nixon brightened just a bit. "Ah, yes, go ahead, General."

"Our plan is to first locate the secret camp where the men are being held, then obtain positive proof of where and how those men are being held."

"And what would you propose to do with this . . . proof?"

Whitey felt strained. He'd told the President about all of this in the previous meeting.

"Sir, that would be your decision, of course. One course of action might be to provide the film, or whatever, to Le Duc Tho or his top people in Paris, with the admonition that if our men are moved one inch toward Russia, it would be released to the world press, and that we reserved the right to take appropriate retaliatory action."

The President put down his fork, wiped his lips, and took a sip of coffee. He looked up to Whitey. "These are indeed critical times," he said. "The balance is . . . ah . . . delicate, very delicate. We think, that is, *Henry* feels that we are close to an agreement with the North Vietnamese. Of course we've had our setbacks, but I believe the communists are beginning to believe our resolve. Unfortunately it is difficult to get that across with all the shrill, critical voices being raised."

Whitey was in no mood for a lesson on the obvious, but he listened politely.

"We have prominent Americans like Ramsey Clark ignoring our directives and going to Hanoi, then coming back and telling the public that if McGovern's elected, North Vietnam will release all the POWs. We've got McGovern sending a man to Paris to approach the communist delegation about releasing some of our boys to them to prove the point, and of course, they'd be foolish not to. I tell you, all of this leaves Le Duc Tho wondering not only who is in charge here and what our policy really is, but if they shouldn't just wait a bit longer." He stood and walked across the room, hands behind his back, head bowed thoughtfully.

He turned to face Whitey and shook his jowls vigorously, come to a decision.

"Therefore—I cannot feel . . . ah . . . comfortable authorizing you to put a man into Hanoi, nosing around the countryside to locate a prisoner camp and film it. At least not just now. Obviously you can't guarantee that he wouldn't be found out and captured. Were that to happen, it would give the North Vietnamese added leverage for their demands at the peace table."

"I see, sir," Whitey said in a muted voice. A roaring sound built to a crescendo in his ears.

If Nixon sensed his helpless outrage, he did not show it. "Just now, concentrate on other means to find out where the new camp is located, and about the Russians' intentions."

"Yes, sir."

Nixon peered then, as if seeing something in Whitey's face. He cleared his throat. "Don't believe for a moment that I've softened my resolve, General Whisenand. Your plan is not canceled. Oh no. It's just placed on hold while you find out more, and we can find a better . . . time to implement it." He waved his hand. "Meanwhile, enjoy Camp David. It is a wonderful place to get away from it all."

Lieutenant General Whisenand did not wish to get away from it all. He excused himself, and as soon as he had returned to his cabin, Whitey called the Navy commander and requested a Marine helicopter return him to Washington.

He looked down as the helicopter flew over the trees of Maryland. The autumn colors. Burnished gold and brilliant reds and yellows. His eyes rose to the skies and he saw the invisible Phantoms and Crusaders and Thuds, the faces of hundreds of pilots who languished in communist prison cells. His brow furrowed and hot tears scalded his eyes as the frustration overwhelmed him. He thought of men being readied to be shipped to Russian interrogation cells and labor camps. Whitey pounded a clenched fist on his knee, upsetting his coffee.

"Are you all right, sir?" the steward inquired as he blotted with a napkin.

That night, Lieutenant General Albert G. "Whitey" Whisenand retired to the music room in the home he and his wife shared in Falls Church. It took Sal's quiet words, a half bottle of a dry red, and some Grieg on the stereo to soothe him.

Tomorrow he would send notes to the State Department and the CIA that the Storm Flight operation had been placed on hold, and to forget about anyone's being placed into the British Consulate in Hanoi. But he would also send a second note—that one to Wolf Lochert—telling him to continue work on his Plan B options and to keep him advised of his progress.

It now seemed unlikely that the President would ever give approval—but if he did, Whitey wanted to be ready to move quickly.

Chapter 18

To a KC-135 pilot, the island of Guam is a mere dot in the vast Pacific Ocean his navigator must find for him. It is a bit closer to Hanoi, 2,900 miles, than Hawaii, 3,800 miles. Until the pilot has sight of the 30-by-12-mile, footprint-shaped island, he must trust his navigator to get him there.

It was a long, grueling haul to Guam from their jump-off base at March Air Force Base, California. Five hours en route to Hickam AFB in Hawaii, where they'd landed and refueled, then a butt-sore, mind-numbing leg to Anderson Air Force Base on the northeast end of the Guam footprint.

Although the KC-135 had the same basic Boeing airframe as the Boeing 707 airliner, at that point all resemblance stopped. Besides having no passenger windows, the most obvious external difference (besides the USAF white-and-silver paint job) was the long aerial refueling boom hanging from the rear end, under the tail like the extended stinger of a wasp. The "stinger" had two vanes attached so the Boomer, an enlisted crewmember, could "fly" the boom into position over a receiving aircraft. Above the boom was a podlike affair, built into the tail of the tanker, wherein the Boomer lay on his belly facing aft, looking out a window at whatever airplane was in position to receive fuel. He then flew the boom into place over the open receptacle of the receiver and toggled a switch to extend the nozzle into place. He then transferred fuel at a rate of 1,000 gallons per minute.

Internally, the KC-135 was an even more radical departure from its cushy airliner cousin. Instead of rows of seats and pretty stewardesses, the KC-135 was a vast cavern, with tie-down space for cargo and uncomfortable canvas seats along the sides, stretched into shape by aluminum tubing. This particular cavern was filled with jet engines, spare parts, and mechanic's tool kits, for tankers flying to the SEA combat zone hauled their own spares and mechanics. Thus the seating was uncomfortably crowded. Instead of a stewardess, a gruff male crew chief informed the passengers how to eat (from a box), sit (strapped in), shit (don't), piss (in a portable john), and save themselves in event of a ground emergency on takeoff or landing (out the doors or emergency ports, one at a time, no yelling or pushing). He did not mention in-flight emergencies other than how to put on the oxygen masks in the event of depressurization at altitude, and where the big inflatable rafts were located in the event of ditching at sea.

There were six bunks in the forward part of the airplane, but they'd become occupied immediately following takeoff by KC-135 augmentee crewmembers. The big tankers were rotated back and forth across the Pacific under an operation code-named Young Lion. Because of the primitive conditions, the passengers could wear flight suits or fatigues, as they wished.

At a point eighteen hours into the multileg Young Lion flight, and with two hours remaining, the thirty-two passengers were bone-weary and so bored they were ready to chew hubcaps for something to do. The crew chief had taken pity and allowed them to walk around in shifts . . . which was no big deal because of the tiny space remaining between outstretched legs and cargo.

Court Bannister had long since run out of candy bars, pocket novels, clean socks, clean breath, and patience. For the tenth time he got up and made his way through the obstacle course, to finally stand by a small, round window built into one of the rear doors. He stretched and did a few limbering knee bends.

A lieutenant colonel with a formidable handlebar mustache and a pleasant face looked on. They exchanged "awful, isn't it" eye rolls.

"You're Court Bannister?" the light colonel asked. He was a stocky six-footer who wore a rumpled flight suit. Court glanced at his cloth name tag: ROBERTS, C.R. was printed over an embroidered set of master navigator wings.

"Yep, how'd you guess?"

Roberts stuck out his hand. "Says so on your name tag. Hi, I'm Clem Roberts."

Court grinned at this cheerful man who seemed to be making the best of a bad trip. "Where are you stationed?"

"I'm the DON at Andy."

Court wasn't sure he heard him correctly. "Don?"

"Wing navigator, Directorate of Operations. Office symbol Dee Oh Enn. DON." That meant Clem Roberts was the top navigator for the B-52 Bomb Wing stationed at Anderson AFB. "How about you? Where you stationed?"

Court kept the frown he felt from showing. "I'll be staying with you guys for the next six months. I've been assigned as the tactical liaison officer with your Bomb Wing."

Clem raised an eyebrow. "We had a fighter jockey from Saigon over for a three-month stint, supposed to look over our procedures and help us with our in-flight reporting. Poor bastard went home in a bottle. DTs. Couldn't stand not flying and the heat, not to mention a definite lack of girls to chase. I take that back. There are a few nurses and female officers, but they hate fighter pilots. Knew beyond doubt they were untrustworthy and would steal the brassiere off their chest."

It was Court's turn to raise an eyebrow.

Roberts shrugged. "Well, it *is* a bomber base and we *did* get there first. Sort of indoctrinated the ladies to the proper way of thinking."

"No flying, you say?"

"None. Our deputy commander for operations, the DCO, wouldn't stand for it. Told him that unless he was a mission-qualified SAC aircrew, he had no business taking up a slot in one of his airplanes. Didn't matter the guy had orders signed by a two-star at Seventh Air Force. We don't report to them. Our bomb wing reports to General Austin at SAC Headquarters, and the DCO told the guys so."

"Any chance he'll change things for me?" Court asked with a frown.

"Unless you go through the full SAC crew upgrade course, you are not qualified."

"I just finished up at Castle."

"You went through the whole course? They declared you combat-ready in the B-52D?"

"Just through the familiarization course."

"Not enough, according to our DCO, and he's in charge. Our wing commander's a one-star, but he walks lightly around Colonel Gartley. Gartley's got an in with General Austin, and the wing commander knows it."

"Not even to just fly along on the missions? I mean, I wouldn't be at the controls or anything."

Roberts put his hands up. "Not my policy. I think it's dumb. How can a TAC man liaise if he doesn't fly with us and experience our problems firsthand?"

"Doesn't give me much to look forward to," Court said dismally, and peered glumly out the tiny window.

It was late afternoon when the big tanker swooped down to land. Large, rolling blue waves lapped at the rugged coast and numerous white, sandy beaches. Large hotels on the western end of the island in the city of Agana made an incongruous skyline for the multitude of Japanese newlyweds who visited Guam for affordable honeymoons. The dense vegetation of the island's interior was penetrated by narrow, winding dirt roads and tiny villages, and there were a thousand places to be "discovered" by the lovers. Japanese with money went to Hawaii.

When they landed, thunderstorms had just swept the base and left steam in the air. Blue Air Force buses met the exhausted passengers as they deplaned and took them to the MAC Terminal. Like all USAF buses, theirs was seemingly without springs or shock absorbers. From the terminal, Clem Roberts called a friend, who was quick to arrive in a Guam bomb, a 1953 DeSoto four-door with a push-button transmission, rusted-out rear flooring, and corroded fenders flapping in the breeze.

"Sit up front," Clem told Court in his cheerful tone. He nodded at the driver, who wore shorts, thongs, and a wild Hawaiian shirt. "This is Captain Beep Beep Bentley, our crew EWO. Best in the business." Bentley was a tall, thin young man with unruly

brown hair, a prominent Adam's apple, and gigantic earlobes.
He nodded to Court's hello. Court noticed an olive-drab steel
ball dangling from a dog tag chain around his neck. Bentley
punched the Reverse button on the control panel. The car lurched
back, then jolted forward as Bentley hit the Drive button.

"Won't go ahead any other way," Roberts said by way of
explanation as they rattled away from the terminal.

Roberts continued. "We'll get you squared away at Billeting,
get you signed in at Wing Headquarters, then pour a beer down
your throat at the O' Club."

1715 Hours Local, Thursday 14 September 1972
Officers' Club
Anderson Air Force Base, Guam

An hour later Roberts picked up Court at his BOQ room and
the two men walked to the nearby club and ordered beers from
the Filipino bartender at the circular bar. Both had showered,
shaved, and wore fresh flight suits.

"You don't seem too bothered by the heat," Roberts observed
as the beer was served. "Acclimatized by all your tours in
Vietnam?"

"This is Arctic weather compared to Vietnam," Court said. He
took a swallow of beer. "You seem to know a lot about me."

"You've been good copy for newspaper and magazine articles
these last few years."

Court made a brief, grimacing nod. "I suppose so."

"I haven't read anything you should be ashamed of," Clem
said, "and ripping down that goddamn enemy flag earned you
this free beer."

Court grinned. "My turn to buy. Thanks for helping me get
settled. Ready?"

"Damned right."

Court ordered two more and they drank with relish. Court
noticed there seemed to be a slight stir in the club, kind of an
undercurrent of meaning rippling through the men by nudges
and winks. He saw a woman in her mid-thirties make her way
to the bar. She walked very purposefully to a vacant barstool
and was greeted by the bartender. She had a triangular face

with obvious pores, and wore her brown hair short in page boy style.

Clem perceived Court's interest. "Who does she remind you of?"

Court chuckled. "Sounds silly, but she looks just like Prince Valiant from the comics."

"Congratulations," Clem said, "you've just joined the ancient and medieval rustic order of Who Fucks the Prince."

Court's eyebrows shot up. "Certainly not *me,*" he choked.

"Wait until you've been here a few months. She gets better-looking each week."

They sipped slowly as Clem told Court about Anderson Air Force Base. "We call it the Rock because it's the top of a seven-mile-high mountain that comes up out of the Mariana Trench. The highest point here is thirteen hundred feet above sea level. This base was designed for only a max of four thousand Air Force people. Now, with Bullet Shot in full swing, we're up to twelve thousand souls."

"Bullet Shot?"

"That's the code name for the TDY our guys from the States pull over here. It runs 179 days at a time, one day less than enough to qualify for an overseas tour, so the guys can be rotated in and out like clockwork. Bitch for families. Lots of divorces."

Court had just signaled for two more beers when a tall, ramrod-straight full colonel in the summer blue uniform came up behind them. He wore command pilot wings over two rows of World War II ribbons, and his blue name tag identified his last name as Gartley.

Both lieutenant colonels slid off their stools, and Clem tried to make introductions.

"Colonel Gartley, I'd like you to meet—"

"I know who he is," Gartley snapped. "Bannister," he said, "I want things to get off on the right foot from the first. We were sent a copy of your TDY orders, and they make clear that you'll be working for me while you're here. I tried to reclama and get your orders canceled, but your Pentagon people insist you stay the full six months. So you're here and there seems to be nothing I can do about it."

Court's mouth tightened at the man's vitriol.

"I want it *clearly understood*—you are not to start any trouble.

You've got to understand we don't want you here, we don't need you here, and we will be very happy when you leave here." He clenched his jaw.

Court said, "Colonel, with all due respect to the eagles you wear, I don't know what you're talking about or what it is about me that has you so upset. If you must know, I am no more pleased to be here than you are to have me. I will happily leave anytime you can arrange it."

"I wish I could. I'm tired of you ego-stuffed fighter jocks coming in here and trying to tell *me* how I should run *my* planes. This is *my* unit, dammit, is that clear?"

"Of course, Colonel, I have no intention of—"

Gartley cut him off. "Report to me at the command post tomorrow morning at 0700. Be in proper uniform. No flight suits. Roberts, you be there, also." Colonel Kieffer Gartley spun on a heel and walked away.

Court glared at his beer. "You guys really know how to make a man feel welcome," he said to Roberts.

"Sorry about that."

Court fingered his flight suit. "Be in uniform, the man said. I thought flight suits *were* the uniform of the day on combat bases."

"Only for the aircrews. He doesn't see you as a crewmember. We guys on the wing staff are the same way. Have to wear class-Bs to work. He's kind of a . . . stickler for that," Roberts said. From his tone, Court could tell he did not care much for his boss.

Court drained his beer and checked his watch. "I'm jet-lagged out. Going to rack out." He and Clem agreed to meet for breakfast at six the following morning. Court left the club and walked back to the BOQ. The night air was heavy, full of salt and humidity.

In his room he finished unpacking and stretched out on the bed, thoughts of Gartley swirling through his head. He switched out the light and tried but couldn't sleep. He got up in the dark and stared out the window toward the flight line. Ramp lights illuminated the maintenance area, and the tails of the B-52s rose up like huge shark fins. The planes themselves looked like hulking, ungainly prehistoric birds of prey.

Court Bannister wondered just what the hell he was doing here.

0700 Hours Local, Friday 15 September 1972
Wing Headquarters
Anderson Air Force Base, Guam

Dressed in short-sleeved summer blues, Lieutenant Colonels
Court Bannister and Clem Roberts reported in a military manner
to Colonel Kieffer Gartley in his office. Gartley sat behind a
polished oak desk, bare of all except a nameplate, two empty
wooden baskets marked In and Out, and one black and one
red telephone. He returned their salutes and let them remain at
attention.

"As Roberts can tell you, Bannister," he began without pre-
amble, "I run a tight ship around here. I brook no nonsense, no
excuses, no failures. We are under a management-control system
and I run the top shop on the ship. You do exactly as I say and
we'll get along. You slip up in any manner, and I'll add a report
to your record that will ensure you'll never be promoted again."
Since he was assigned on Temporary Duty, Court would not
receive an Officers Efficiency Report. Although Gartley was
not in a position to write Court's OER, his report to the colonel
in the Pentagon who did could be influential.

Court refrained from telling Colonel Gartley his philosophy
regarding OERs: worry about those of the men working for you,
but never read your own. You might believe it.

Gartley stood up. "Come with me. I'll show you where you'll
work."

The two men followed him out of his office downstairs to
the operations room, the nerve center of the SAC command
post. Dimmed overhead lights cast a glow on work positions.
Officers and enlisted men in neat, short-sleeved khakis manned
the radio/telephone consoles and tracking boards. The Battle
Staff sat at a separate table. A Boeing representative was at
a corner of the room, on call for consultation regarding any
inflight emergency requiring knowledge about the big bomber
not contained in the manuals carried aboard.

Without explanation of the room or its purpose, Gartley
threaded his way past consoles and status boards and stopped
near a dark corner. He pointed. "You'll use that desk."

Court looked grimly at the small desk and chair. "My duties?"

"Stay put and don't make noise. I'll see to it that you have plenty of reading material."

"Colonel, I was briefed by the Air Force Chief of Staff about what he wants me to accomplish here. He wants me to sit down with your people and study your tactics, and make suggestions and—"

"Bannister," Gartley snorted. "When I want your suggestions, I'll ask for them. Chief of Staff or not."

"Colonel, I—"

"I've heard *enough,* Bannister." Gartley turned to Lieutenant Colonel Clem Roberts. "Roberts, make sure he gets the current *Daily Intelligence Summaries,* the *Stars and Stripes,* and the base newspaper." He faced Court. "You want anything more, there's a bookstore at the Base Exchange. You *will* be at your desk every day, pulling twelve-hour shifts like everyone else here. And I *don't* want to see you *away* from your desk, bothering people who're trying to do their jobs." He could not contain a small smile of sheer pleasure before turning on his heel and stalking back toward his office.

As soon as the DCO was out of earshot, Roberts rolled his eyes. "I'll be the first to apologize."

Court looked glumly about at his new home.

Clem sighed. "Gartley's an ex–command post weinie who flies only minimum time and then only in the jump seat. I doubt he's even taxied the bird since he got here three months ago. He's what we call a mattress colonel, and none of the aircrews like him."

"Mattress colonel?"

"Yeah, he climbs on board, sits in the IP seat for takeoff and landing, then spends the rest of the flight sacked out on the six-by-eight rubber pad behind the pilots."

Court studied the small, gray steel desk. "No way," he said. "There is absolutely no way I am going to chain myself to that desk." He made a wry smile. "And to think I talked myself into thinking I might be able to do some good here."

Roberts also stared. Finally he shook his head. "Look, Court, it doesn't have to be this way."

"You're damn right about that. That guy can write me up for AWOL, but I'm not going to sit here and do absolutely nothing."

"Well . . . " said Roberts, thinking. He nodded. "Let's fix it so you can do some of the things you want—*and* sit at your desk."

"I don't understand."

"At least Gartley will *think* you're sitting at your desk."

Court positioned the chair, then sat down with an indignant huff. "This is the most ridiculous thing I've been told to do in all my years in the Air Force."

"Welcome to SAC. I know brigadiers who pissed off the brass and are chained to a desk with very little to do."

"Dammit, Clem, I'm supposed to be briefing you guys on what it's like over Hanoi."

"We're not fragged to fly to Hanoi. We just bomb below the twentieth parallel."

"The Chief of Staff of the Air Force believes you're going to be tasked to hit Hanoi, not long after the election. That's why I'm here."

Clem whistled. "Chief of Staff himself, huh? You weren't putting him on?"

"I didn't mean to imply we're buddies or anything, but he did send me. He's concerned that the bomber force is holding on to World War Two tactics too long, that they need to listen to what's been done by the fighters. I've been there, Clem. I know what it's like flying up near Hanoi with the whole world shooting at you. And when you guys are sent up there, it's silly to have to learn it all from scratch."

Clem Roberts nodded very slowly. "Makes sense. Beep Beep Bentley and some of the other EWOs keep trying to get it across that we're using bad tactics."

"Between the USAF, Navy, and Marines, we've lost a couple thousand tactical airplanes in Vietnam, and a lot of those were up near Hanoi. We've learned a lot of ropes over there, and I was sent to pass them along for what they're worth. Now this idiot wants me to sit here and keep my mouth shut?"

Clem gave him a sideward look. "So where did you want to start?"

"By getting a look at your tactics. The ones you'll be using up in pack six if you're sent there. Then I wanted to fly the mission and take a firsthand look at how you're doing it now."

Clem was nodding. "That we can easily handle. Your orders show you're cleared for top secret, and I'll set it up with the plans shop. I know the people there and I'll vouch for you."

"They won't run to Gartley?"

"Hell, like I said, no one here likes Gartley, Court. We've got some bastards in SAC, just like you've probably got a few of your own in the fighter game."

Court nodded. "Problem is, this particular bastard is the man in charge here."

"Well, we'll see, won't we? I'm of a mind that it's the middle managers that make a place work or not, no matter what the top dogs think. NCOs on the enlisted side, and the majors and light colonels for the officers. And as modest as I may seem to your tender eyes, I'm probably the big daddy of the light colonels on the Rock. You want to fly the mission, you said?"

"Yeah."

"Then we'll work on it. But right now, let's split for a special place I know." Clem Roberts led the way past a duty controller, who was frantically handling two microphones and two telephones at once.

"What?" he said over the telephone marked BICYCLE WORKS over a Maintenance logo. "Complete electrical failure? Green Three? Okay, that's a legitimate abort." He scribbled furiously on a pad, consulted a sheet, then picked up a microphone. "Red One, you are now Green Three, Red Two you are Red One, Red Three you are now Red Two. Green One and Two retain your call signs. Blue One hold your position while Charlie Tower revises the taxi schedule. All other Wave One aircraft continue taxiing. There will be no, repeat *no* revised takeoff times." He sat back to run his fingers through his hair, then rocked forward as a telephone jangled. "Duty officer." He listened intently then answered, "Yessir," "nossir," and "Idunnosir," in rapid succession. He hung up and shouted, "Harry, anyone else wants to know how many of 'em got off when the mess is over, tell 'em to call the Skunk."

Clem Roberts' dour look turned into an amused grin as he overheard the conversation. "What that was," he explained, when they were outside and walking toward a nearby BOQ, "was the usual clusterfuck when someone aborts after the birds are taxiing. We have an intricate plan to get thirty or forty airplanes to the runway, each with call signs that go with a position. Each three planes are called a cell. For instance, Red One, Two, and Three make up Red Cell. If someone aborts, the next bird has to roll forward and take his spot. That happens two or three times in the half hour or so it takes to get thirty planes airborne, so the controller doesn't always know how many actually got into the air until the maintenance guys out in Charlie Tower tell him. Meanwhile he says to ask the Skunk."

"Who or what is the Skunk?"

Roberts barked a laugh. "That's the Russian trawler that sits in the water off the end of the runway, counting our takeoffs and bomb loads."

They stopped by an office, where Roberts stuck his head inside and signaled Beep Beep Bentley to come out and join them.

"Take us to the Rum Shack, my good man," Roberts told Bentley as they climbed into the DeSoto. In the rear, Court had to brace his feet on the chassis to keep them from dangling through the rusted flooring of the Guam bomb.

Bentley punched the Reverse button for a quick back trip of five feet, then forward as he hit the Drive button. A man of few words, Court observed.

Twenty minutes later they were seated in Ninny's Store in Agana City, drinking beer brought directly from a walk-in cooler.

"Delicious," Court said, as he took a long pull on the beer labeled *Three Horses*. He looked at the label. "Now suppose you tell me how you propose to get me out of this mess."

"Deck Asshole Gartley," Captain Beep Beep Bentley said in a sepulchral voice, the first words Court had heard him speak.

Roberts ignored the EWO. "It goes like this. I'll tell Gartley I've put you on the work shift opposite his. You come in and he sees you at your desk before he goes home. When he comes on duty, you'll be there. But in the meantime, while he's gone, you get the things done you have to."

Court chuckled. "You're devious. Think it'll work?"

"Sure. You can get in all the tactics studying you want and still have time for some of the serious stuff. Skin-diving, tennis, golf, chasing the schoolteachers living in Menopause Manor."

Court shook his head. "Clem, you have an empire here. Don't you ever fly?"

"Hell yes, as often as possible."

"You seem to have a lot of playtime available."

"Not really. This is the first time in this man's life I've taken off and had a beer in the middle of the morning. Gartley got me that pissed off. Shouldn't have let it get to me, but I did."

"Okay," said Court. "I get put on the night shift and Gartley sees me when he comes and goes. How do I get to fly, with him checking up like that?"

"I figure he'll check for a week . . . two at the most. After that he'll forget. Asshole Gartley's limited intelligence is only rivaled by his attention span."

"So for the next two weeks I study your tactics and war plans."

"Yep. Something else, too." Clem nodded thoughtfully to himself. "Any real criticisms or ideas you've got about changes we ought to make, I'd appreciate you talking them over with me."

"I'd be happy to."

"Good," Clem said. "And then we'll start working on getting you in the air."

"I owe you."

"You'll just be going up as a Blob at first. You won't be a real crewmember. You're not checked out as an aircraft commander, copilot, or navigator, so you'd just be a Blob."

"What the hell's a Blob?"

"Big lump on board."

Court shook his head as he ordered more ice-cold Three Horses.

Beep Beep Bentley, while watching and listening to the conversation with interest, remained silent. Court meant to ask about the ball suspended on the chain around his neck.

"Gotta question," Clem Roberts said.

"Shoot."

"You say the Chief of Staff of the Air Force wanted you to come here, right?"

Court nodded.

"Why not send him a message telling him about Asshole Gartley and the way he's treating you? He ought to be able to handle things with a phone call."

"Maybe, but calling generals for help is just not my way."

A moment of quiet settled over the trio, and Court stared into the distance. He'd tried to put it all into perspective on the long ride over to Guam. A certain Air Force general had been on his case since 1966, when an F-100 pilot Court had flown with had crashed and been killed on a combat mission in South Vietnam. The general/father had felt it was Court's fault. Richard L. "Tex" Austin now had four stars, and was the Commander in Chief of the Strategic Air Command. Although the Chief of Staff of the Air Force was responsible for Court's temporary duty to bombers in Guam, and although the two generals seemed at odds, Court knew Tex Austin and the Chief had been World War II buddies, and now he'd heard that Colonel Gartley was a sort of protégé of Austin's. It was all enough to make Court wonder.

Clem Roberts spoke up. "So. Two weeks of desk time, and I'll set up your first flights."

Court nodded.

"First as a Blob on a KC-135 tanker, then on a Buff, then, who knows, maybe as a real crewmember on a Buff."

Court sighed inwardly. *Christ amighty. In the last few years I've gone from an up-and-coming fighter commander to a guy exiled to a small island trying to snivel a ride on SAC tankers and bombers.* "That'll be great, Clem." *Shit.* He managed a weak smile. Court turned to Bentley and asked, "What's that ball around your neck?"

Bentley fingered the heavy camouflaged ball. "It's my bearing," he said solemnly. "My military bearing."

Chapter 19

The schedule Clem Roberts had set up for Court had worked. For the first few days, Colonel Gartley, although he hadn't acknowledged Court's presence, had viewed Court at his corner desk as he'd arrived and departed. After eight days he had stopped the practice, just as Roberts had forecast, as if he'd completely forgotten about him. During the first two weeks, Court had gone to the plans shop each night and, with Clem vouching for him, had no problem obtaining the highly classified documents he sought.

As he'd pored over them, he'd realized just how valuable Major Smitty Smythe had been when they'd worked together earlier in the year to perfect the Freedom Porch plan at the Saigon headquarters. Smitty's tactics descriptions had been easy to follow, and full of explanation and common sense. The SAC OPlans and contingency plans he read at Guam were filled with gobbledygook and confusion. The thing that struck him most was SAC's rigid control of all actions the aircrews were to perform in combat. Everything was in black and white, and done precisely the same way—every time. There was no tailoring of tactics to individual skills, no small surprises a pilot could toss into the game. Each tactic was rigidly dictated. If the crew ran into an unforeseen problem in flight, they were to contact the command post on HF radio for guidance. There was little discretion left to the pilot and crew.

The cells flew in the same precise pattern and at the same altitudes—approached the target the same way—bombed the same way—made the same post-target turn the same way—and exited the same way. They were . . . *predictable* . . . a word which made fighter pilots who had flown repeatedly in route pack six shudder and do a couple of Hail Marys. To be predictable when you faced an enemy equipped with radar and computer-controlled artillery, MiGs and Mach 3 SAMs was the surest way to be shot down.

Which to Court Bannister meant these were not tactics at all. They were *procedures*. And as he read the SAC plans he knew that he'd been wrong and that the Chief of Staff of the Air Force had been right. As much as he hated to say it, and as much as the bomber environment was an alien world, he was needed, doing just what he'd been sent to do. Not because he was brilliant, like Smythe, or because he knew anything about bombers—he didn't—the reason was because *he'd been there,* dodged the flak and SAMs, hassled with the MiGs, and learned how to survive and succeed. He hoped the Chief of Staff was making headway in his task of convincing General Tex Austin that he should listen. Court's advice, if heeded, could indeed save a lot of lives.

If heeded. That was the ringer. Somehow he had to convince the people at the SAC base on the Rock that they should listen to a fighter jock. The DCO was an impossible hurdle, so he'd have to do it without him. He decided to work directly with the people who counted: the bomber pilots and crews. And of course he would continue to share insights with Clem Roberts, as he'd done from the first.

He knew that the only way the aircrews would listen to him was if he proved himself to be one of them. To do that he had to fly with them, listen to them, drink with them in the bar, and, perhaps cautiously at first, insert his tactical expertise.

At the end of the second week, Clem had also been true to his word, for Court flew on two six-hour night missions with the local KC-135 tankers to top off B-52s bound for Arc Light missions in South Vietnam. The tanker crewmembers had been polite but busy, and he'd confirmed that they were just as professional and efficient in their duties as the fighter jocks in the combat theater had always believed.

He also confirmed that he'd only scratched the surface of what he had to learn if he wanted to talk with any degree of authority to the bomber pilots.

After one flight, he put on Bermuda shorts, T-shirt and thongs, and walked to the Officers' Club, where he was to meet Clem Roberts. The bar was moderately filled, and Prince Valiant was seated in her usual spot, giving the men her normal once-over examinations. Roberts joined Court and they ordered beers.

"Got a Buff hop set up for you tomorrow," Clem said.

"Does Gartley know about it?"

Clem snorted. "He's too wrapped up with self-importance and sending heroic messages back to SAC headquarters to notice what we drones are doing. Meet you here for breakfast, four-thirty in the dark, Aye Em." He took a sip of beer, then nodded at the other end of the bar. "One of the new guys is zeroing in on the Prince. She'll get rid of him quick, 'cause he's way too old for her. Prince Valiant goes for the young lieutenants."

Court smiled in surprise as he saw Duckcall Donnie Higgens striking up a conversation with the woman. He was in tan shorts and a black tank top, had a drink in both hands and a glassy look on his face. Court watched for a long moment, wondering if he shouldn't go over to welcome his old friend to the Rock, since this was the first time he'd seen him at Anderson. He decided to leave things alone—to hook up with Donnie later.

"You know him?" Roberts asked.

"We flew together at Bien Hoa and Ubon. Last I saw of him was at Castle, where he was trying to drum up a crew. He wasn't very successful while I was there. What's he doing here?"

"Still doesn't have a crew. They use him as a standby replacement pilot. We need everybody we can get. He's a fully qualified B-52 aircraft commander, so we use him to fill in as needed. Been here two weeks now. Already got his combat checkout, and he's flown two Arc Lights and a Linebacker mission to Route Pack One."

"This is the first time I've seen him here."

"That's because you're on that night schedule and you've been working so hard." Roberts hesitated. "Oh . . . how well do you know him, Court?"

"Well enough. He worked for me at Ubon and did a good job. Shot down a MiG. Why?"

"I think Gartley's gathering material on him for an Article 15 at best, a court-martial at worst."

"What for?"

"Conduct unbecoming an officer. Drinks a lot, noisy—his damn duckcall drives people nuts, and he actually used it on the radio once. The guys do their damnedest to be professionals here, so he's not the most popular guy around. Still can't get a regular crew, so we're thinking of forming one using him and mixtures of new guys and old staff heads from Wing Headquarters."

Court paused before he spoke his next words. While he was hesitant to give the people here advice until he'd proven himself, he felt loyalty toward his friend. "You guys may be making a mistake by not using him on a regular crew, Clem. He was a fine combat pilot when I flew with him. A bit on the wild side on the ground even then, but damn good in the air. He didn't want B-52s, but I looked into it and found he burned up the Combat Crew course at Castle. Smooth as glass, his instructors said."

Clem looked down the bar thoughtfully.

"Anyway, if Gartley's so down on him, how come Donnie's still flying?"

"Like I said, we're hurting for pilots. We'd put you in the left seat if we could." Roberts paused as he stared. His eyes widened. "Well, I'll be damned," he said, real surprise in his voice.

Duckcall Donnie and the woman known as Prince Valiant walked out the door together. She grasped his arm possessively and was giggling at his words.

0800 Hours Local, Sunday 15 October 1972
U.S. Embassy, Thong Nhut Street, Saigon
Republic of Vietnam

"General Whisenand," Wolf Lochert said in a serious tone, "maybe I'm dense, but I don't understand the problem." Lochert and Chef Hostettler sat across from Whitey at the small conference table in the Air Attaché's office. All three were dressed in casual civilian clothes.

"Politics, that's the problem," Hostettler said bitterly and laid down the latest copy of the Pacific *Stars & Stripes,* the daily newspaper that sold worldwide to GIs for a dime and contained no advertisements. Inch-high headlines told the story.

VIET CEASE-FIRE RUMORS FLY

WASHINGTON (AP) Rumors were circulating in Washington that an internationally supervised cease-fire has been agreed upon in the private talks at Paris. According to these rumors making the rounds, China, Russia, and France would serve as the supervisors of the cease-fire.

"That would be ludicrous," Hostettler said, "like using starving wolves to guard the lambs."

"What does that have to do with Storm Flight?" Wolf grumbled. "Three months have gone by since we decided to put a man into Hanoi and nothing's been done." He caught himself glaring at Whisenand and quickly softened his look. "Pardon me, sir," he mumbled contritely. "Been out of the field too long." Wolf Lochert had remained in Saigon, waiting for a call that never came. When Jim Mahoney had started coming apart at the seams with boredom while waiting to be flown out to a British boat, Wolf had dispatched him on temporary duty to the 1st SFG in Okinawa for a brushup on his training. The *Scheisskopf* was likely making parachute jumps, practicing his hand-to-hand combat techniques, and doing other things that Wolf would have given his eyeteeth to be doing himself.

"As I said in my message," Whitey said patiently, "the President put a hold on Storm Flight. We're supposed to be working on finding the camp the POWs are being sent to and gathering more evidence that the Russians are preparing to move them to the motherland."

Hostettler shook his head grimly. "I've personally gone over every debriefing form from new NVA prisoners, and examined every recce photo the RF-4Cs and SR-71s bring back. Without knowing where to look, it's like searching for a needle in a haystack. There's some fuzzy areas where we know they've put up camouflage netting, but nothing to tell us if one of 'em's what we're looking for. How about our contacts in Hanoi, General? Do Cochise or Alfred have anything yet?"

Whitey blew out a breath. "We've got a delay there. My usual contact in Washington has moved along, and now I'm having to get everything through a more circuitous route. I've requested the information but nothing's come back so far."

"Anything out of Caruso?" Wolf asked.

"We haven't been in contact since the Dipper and Dancer visit. Seems there haven't been any choir sessions taped by the media recently."

All three men looked troubled. They wanted to act, but were frustrated by the brick wall they'd encountered.

After a long pause Whitey spoke to Wolf Lochert. "Let's discuss Plan B."

"We're dropping Plan A?" Hostettler asked.

Whitey thought about it for a short moment, then made his decision and nodded. "If the President turns us on again, we're simply not going to have time to complete all the coordination required to put the man into the Brit Consulate. We go with Plan B. We'll put our own man into Hanoi. Wolf, what have you come up with?"

"I called in some of the guys at Nha Trang and we talked. A year ago it would have been relatively easy to put a man ashore using a small watercraft to drop him off. In fact they did just that several times. That's not possible any longer. The SEALs say the North Viets have their coastal watch militia beefed up so much that the chances for a successful insertion is way down."

Whitey sighed. "So what are we left with?"

"We drop someone out of a plane at night, and he parachutes in."

Both of the others grimaced at the thought.

"Sounds dangerous as hell," Chef Hostettler said.

"We'd have to set up a diversion," Wolf said, "so the North Viets have other things on their minds than looking for our agent."

"Like a fighter strike?"

"Maybe. I thought about sending . . . ah . . . *someone* up in the backseat of an F-4 Phantom during a night attack, then having him eject over Hanoi. Problem there is all the stuff that goes out with the guy. The seat itself, for instance. They find an ejection seat in downtown Hanoi, they know someone went out and the alarm's going to be sent out to look for him."

"How about a Special Ops C-130?" asked Hostettler.

"If we're to place the agent where we need him, we'd have to get the Herky bird to fly over downtown Hanoi. We had 'em fly around the periphery of Hanoi during the Son Tay raid, but they were generally down in the weeds and they never went right downtown. But don't toss the idea out yet. I've got the Special Ops guys over at Nakhon Phanom looking at the idea."

Whitey Whisenand had looked on quietly as the two men spoke together.

"What's our best bet on timing, sir?" Hostettler asked the General.

"I feel that two things must happen before the President will turn us back on." The others waited as Whitey cleared his throat. "One, the President has to be reelected. Two, we've got to find out where they're holding our men. That's become a prerequisite. I heard it in the President's tone when we last spoke. He won't approve sending someone up there to nose around. We must have a well-thought-out plan to get him into Hanoi, then to wherever the prisoners are being held, and then out of the country."

"I'll come up with that last part. Getting in and out," said Wolf Lochert.

Whitey nodded, then set his jaw grimly. "There's a definite possibility that we're not going to get to do any of this, you both understand. If the talks continue to go smoothly, no one is going to take a chance on screwing things up . . . and we lose our men for *political* reasons."

Chef Hostettler tapped on the newspaper article. "Is this true?

Are we really this close to signing an agreement with the North Vietnamese and Viet Cong?"

Whitey shook his head sadly. "Who knows? The negotiators are saying one thing today and another tomorrow. Then there's President Thieu and the South Vietnamese government. They're hesitant to take the communists' word on anything." Whitey looked at the two men. His words emerged slowly. "Part of the reason for my visit was to bring President Nixon's reassurance to President Thieu that we'll continue to back him in the future. Last evening I briefed him that in the event North Vietnam breaks any of the treaty agreements, the United States will respond with massive air attacks, just as we've been doing since we discovered the spring invasion."

"What was his reaction?" Hostettler asked.

"He looked me in the eye and said, 'I hope you are correct.' "

"So do I," said Wolf very soberly.

"Anyway, right now it's a wait-and-see game for Storm Flight." Whitey slowly gained his feet. "In the meantime I've got a ten o'clock meeting at MAC-V. The President wants another reassurance that we'll have all our people out on schedule." The last American ground-fighting unit, the Third Battalion of the Twenty-first Infantry, had been deactivated in early August, two months before. The President was determined to be drawn down to a total strength of 27,000 by the first of December.

Both of the other men had politely followed the General's lead and were standing.

"I'll continue to work on a way to get our man into Hanoi when the President changes his mind," said Wolf.

"It's *if,* not *when,*" said Whitey.

Wolf shook his head. "Those lying *Scheisskopfs* in Hanoi won't be that easy to deal with. It's going to take more than nice words to get them to agree with *anything,* and then it's going to take a lot of watching so they don't cheat after they *do* agree."

Hostettler cocked his head quizzically at Whisenand and asked the question that had plagued him. "Who are we sending in, if we get the okay?"

Whitey glanced at Wolf. "Any suggestions?"

"Yes, sir," Wolf Lochert rumbled. "The most qualified man we've got."

1135 Hours Local, Thursday 26 October 1972
White House Press Room
Washington, D.C.

"Ladies and gentlemen," Henry Kissinger began in a slow voice to the accompaniment of the whirring of cameras and the heavy double clicks of single-lens reflex cameras, "we have now heard from both Vietnams and it is obvious that the war that has been raging for ten years is drawing to a conclusion. We believe that peace is at hand."

Whitey Whisenand had returned from Saigon only a week before. He sat unobtrusively in civilian clothes in the rear and frowned inwardly.

Despite his reassurances, Thieu had not signed the agreement. He remained incensed over two points. South Vietnam would be partitioned off, with the North Vietnamese–dominated Viet Cong, as well as 120,000 NVA troops, remaining in place in South Vietnam. As a result, Kissinger had not gone to Hanoi for final approval, and the promised bombing halt never came about. *Peace is at hand?* Kissinger sounded like Neville Chamberlain returning from his talk with Hitler, saying, "Peace in our time." Did he mean peace at all costs, regardless of their ally's fate?

A beeper sounded in his pocket, and Whitey eased out the back door to a telephone. It was Bob Haldeman, saying the President wanted him to proceed to the Oval Office ASAP.

"I don't know why Kissinger said that," Nixon fumed, his anger evident in the set lines on his troubled face. Haldeman stood against the wall, nodding vague agreement. The President continued. "Now our bargaining position with the North Vietnamese is eroded, and the problem of bringing Thieu along will be doubly difficult." He rose to his feet and paced, periodically shaking his head, each time setting his heavy jowls aquiver. "Henry's put us in a box, damn it all. The North Vietnamese will think we *must* have peace. The press will run hard with it, and false euphoria is bound to set in with the public." Nixon took off his dark suit coat to reveal a sweat-stained white shirt. He hung the coat over his chair.

"The market is already rising," Haldeman added in his monotone.

Nixon continued to brood. "All based on a false statement. And if we release a statement to set them straight, I'm the one who will suffer in the polls. The timing is . . . ah . . . *incredibly* poor." He shook his head darkly, muttering, "That phrase was not cleared with me. The day will *never* come when I back down like that."

"It's not you, sir," Haldeman urged, then grew quiet, as if embarrassed by his words.

Nixon sat again, and looked at Whitey. "This war cannot be resolved until we discourage future aggression by the bullies in North Vietnam." He nodded, liking his choice of words. "So!" He glanced at his desk calendar. "General, I want you to accompany Henry on his next trip to Paris in three weeks. Work closely with him and assure something like this does not happen again. Henry means well, but he sometimes . . . ah . . . loses sight of the bigger picture and is . . . drawn to grand gestures." He again rose from his chair and this time stared out the tall window, still obviously restless. "My critics will say I've told Kissinger to reach a settlement at all costs before the election. I don't need that," he scoffed, "to beat the pants off McGovern."

Haldeman smiled his agreement.

"But they'll say it, and I don't need Henry out there making more statements that will make it look as if we're negotiating from desperation."

Whitey spoke cautiously, phrasing carefully. "I may not be able to influence Mr. Kissinger as much as you might like, sir."

Nixon dismissed his words with a deft motion of his head. "Henry will listen. You're a stabilizing influence, General. Perhaps you can modify his . . . ah . . . *grand* gestures. Sit in on the meetings and speak with him before he makes public statements. If he starts to make another *faux pas,* tell him to clear it with me first."

"Tell him, sir? Do I have that authority?"

Nixon pondered that one. "Advise him, shall we say. Henry is a bit too high-strung to suggest you have any kind of real authority over him."

"He already has a military adviser, sir. Major General Haig."

Nixon frowned. "And you are *my* adviser. I don't trust Al Haig. Something impulsive about the man. It's obvious he's not the sort of moderating influence Henry needs." He nodded. "I want you to go along, General."

The task seemed difficult and not a bit confusing, but the man before Whitey was his Commander in Chief. "I'll try to help, sir."

"Try to keep him from making this kind of 'peace is at hand' statements without thinking it over first. As much as I'd like to, I can't go to Paris with him—wouldn't look right—so I need someone along to ensure reason is applied." The President smiled mirthlessly. "Of course, in *two* weeks I may find that I no longer have a mandate from the people." He shook his head grimly. "But even if I were to lose this election, I still would not alter my policy, General. I intend to end this war before I leave office, and end it with America's honor intact." His face was bulldog firm.

"Sir," Whitey began, "may I bring up one more subject before I leave?"

The President looked up at him.

"I would like to have your permission to implement Storm Flight."

Nixon frowned, then brightened as he remembered. "Have you discovered this . . . ah . . . camp you suspect the prisoners are being taken to?"

"No, sir."

"Like I told you the last time we spoke about it, have your people locate the camp, *then* come to me. In the meanwhile I want you to prepare to go to Paris in three weeks."

"I still don't fully understand why he wants me in Paris," Whitey told his wife that night.

"Perhaps it's not only Al Haig he doesn't trust," Sal replied. "He may have reservations about Henry Kissinger too."

Before he slept, Whitey thought about what she'd said. Sal was often correct in such observations.

Chapter 20

"Colonel," said the staff sergeant at the door, "you got a call on the number two autovon line."

Wolf picked up. It was an SF supply sergeant at the Nakhon Phanom command and control (C&C), telling him a couple of bundles had arrived from Wright Patterson Air Force Base in the States, with instructions that they were to be opened only by Lieutenant Colonel W. X. Lochert, U.S. Army, presently on extended temporary duty to MAC-SOG in Saigon.

"That's me," Wolf said in an amiable tone. "I'll be there tomorrow." During the thirty-second discussion, his spirits had risen several times over. He would go out to NKP, which was what the Special Forces and Air Force men stationed there called Nakhon Phanom. From NKP the Air Force ran a dozen highly classified operations, including the Jolly Greens—the Search and Rescue helicopter effort for pilots shot down over North Vietnam—and Igloo White, which was the placement of listening devices and seismic sensors along the infiltration routes. The Special Forces presence had once included such efforts as placing Kit Carson (North Vietnamese turncoat) scouts and SF

338

long-range recon patrols into Laos and North Vietnam to watch the trails.

The SF had access to a restricted flying zone east of the base, sometimes used by the Thai Army for parachute jumps training. Two DeHavilland Otter aircraft, piloted by Army warrant officers, were parked on the NKP ramp to take the SF troopers up. Wolf called the U.S. Army liaison office at the NKP Air Force base operations and reserved one of the Otters for two jumps each on the following Thursday and Friday. Satisfied with that arrangement, he called Nha Trang and was connected to the operations officer in the C-130 squadron of the 90th Special Operations Wing. They'd been speaking together a lot recently. Planning to try out a new gimmick designed to snatch down pilots out of harm's way. It was called the Fulton Recovery System.

"I'd like to set up for Friday afternoon. Fourteen hundred. Place and method same as we spoke about last time we talked."

"Let me check," said the Air Force Lieutenant Colonel. After a two-minute pause he was back on the line. "I've got you set up. Everything as we discussed. No surprises." He chuckled. "I'll be the pilot. Wouldn't miss it for the world. We got a six-pack bet, remember?"

"You told me the thing would work."

The ops officer laughed again. "If it doesn't, we'll give you your money back. See you Friday afternoon. If things go right, we'll do it again that night."

"What if things don't go right?"

"We-ell. Let me put it this way, Wolf. We've only had one of those so far, and he's not around to complain about it."

An odd sense of humor, Wolf thought. "One question I forgot to ask last time we talked. How many of these have you tried so far?"

"Two. Cheers."

"Yeah, see you," Wolf said, wondering at the man's warped sense of humor.

He went back to his notes.

There was a new parachuting technique he wanted to look into. HAHO—High Altitude, High Opening—had been proven to work, but was not yet adopted by the Army, as was the older HALO—High Altitude, Low Opening. Since he didn't yet know what kind of aircraft he'd be jumping from, or how close to the target he would be released, he'd decided to test variations of both techniques.

Wolf always said to himself *when*, and never *if* the Storm Flight operation would be approved—he could not comprehend a world in which Americans did not try to save their own.

Wolf began to hum a lively (to him) Wagnerian tune, in anticipation of getting away from the office and the headquarters. He would not be operational, but in two days he would at least be training as a Special Forces officer should. Greta Sturm had been complaining about how grumpy he'd become in the past weeks of inactivity. Tonight he'd do something special for her—perhaps take her a couple of the colorful little birds the street vendors sold along with small wicker cages. She'd said she was thinking of getting one for her apartment, so two should be even better, and keep each other company to boot. He pushed out of his mind the picture of Frenchy, years back, biting off their colorful little heads.

He paused in his humming and a frown tried to form. It was increasingly difficult to think about life without Greta. He had always considered her as a sort of interlude, and their relationship as a convenience. Yet somehow his feelings had slowly, almost insidiously, become something deeper and more . . . content? That sort of human frailty was for others. He was a warrior to the core. Certainly nothing had changed there. He nodded firmly to himself, and forced himself to resume the humming.

In two days he'd jump from the Otter and feel the wonderful freedom a man could feel only when parachuting. Five jumps would be required, he decided. Three to test the three candidate parachutes and two more with the one he selected. Wolf began to scribble down the desired parameters. Within seconds he again became engrossed in the planning.

And somehow, planning for it made the upcoming Storm Flight operation feel all that much closer. American warriors took care of their own.

**1140 Hours Local, Monday 30 October 1972
Airborne in Dehavilland Otter
Royal Thai Army Parachute Zone
14 Miles West of Nakhon Phanom
Royal Thai Army Base
Kingdom of Thailand**

Wolf sat in the back of the Otter with three Special Forces NCOs, who were also going to jump. The door had been removed from the airplane, and the noise from the engine and the whistling wind was loud. Like them he wore strapped-down jungle fatigues, jungle boots, and a leather bunny helmet. He'd stuffed his green beret into a cargo pocket.

The master sergeant beside him eyed the primary parachute on Wolf's back, with its dark-colored, elongated pack. "That the new seven-gore?" he asked in a shout.

Wolf nodded. He'd used a five-gore on the previous jump, three hours earlier, trying for maximum soar distance, and had reached an estimated seventeen miles per hour forward impetus.

"We're leveling at four thousand feet," said the chief warrant officer at the controls of the airplane with its huge single engine. "We'll be at the drop zone in twenty seconds."

The master sergeant gave his helmet chin strap a tug and nodded to the other two sergeants, both much younger. He pulled off his headset in preparation and glanced at the copilot/jumpmaster in the right cockpit seat, who flashed five fingers. The master sergeant tapped the first of the jumpers on the shoulder.

When the three were away, Wolf spoke into his mike. "They're out. Let's take it on up." They began to circle and ascend.

The pilot called out when they passed through 10,000. At 12,000 they leveled and the pilot eased back on the throttle. This was as high as they were authorized to go without use of breathing oxygen.

"Fifteen seconds," the pilot called.

Wolf pulled off the headset and poised at the opened door, staring down at the bull's-eye etched into the earth more than two miles below.

Now.

He pushed away, started to tumble, but righted himself with outstretched arms. A grin formed beneath the goggles as he stared about for a short moment. Wolf peered at the altimeter on the aux chute on his chest, which was winding down rapidly. As it approached 10,000 feet he ensured that he was in proper position—spread-eagle and facedown.

The automatic opening device (AOD) activated, and he heard a mechanical sound, like a clock winding down, and a gentle tug, then a harder one as the chute fully opened.

He looked up to see a properly deployed canopy—the same one he'd packed himself the previous night. It was quite normal except for the single fact that the rearmost seven panels were not connected to shroud lines—which gave him forward motion. Wolf grasped the forward two risers and pulled, tugging the air-filled panels farther down and adding to the jet effect of the air passing behind. When he felt he had reached the configuration providing fastest momentum, he held the risers steady and watched the earth slide slowly beneath his feet.

At 5,000 feet on the altimeter he approached the 3,000-meter mark, meaning he'd soared three kilometers, which was very good. He was traveling at fifteen miles per hour. Six or seven miles an hour faster than the five-gore chute. The other had been a Model-A; this one was a '57 Chevy with a four-barrel carb.

When he was at the distance above the ground his gut told him was appropriate, Wolf released the forward risers and yanked hard on the rear ones—not enough to collapse the chute, but enough to slow the momentum. He continued to pull back until he was moving forward at a crawl, then bent slightly at the knees, anticipating impact. As his feet touched down, he began to shuffle along, and remained on his feet as he came to a halt.

Not bad for an old man. Wolf was grinning as he began to collect his parachute. An M-151 jeep pulled up and braked in a cloud of the fine red dust that permeated the countryside.

"You're not far from the six-thousand-meter marker, Colonel," called out the driver.

Wolf nodded, thinking as he continued to pick up the dark olive-drab chute. From 10,000 feet up he'd soared five and a half kilometers in the fourteen minutes of descent. That would be a difficult feat to match in the ridiculous parachute sent from the Air Force research and development center. He wondered if he should even try the silly thing.

He stuffed the nylon and the bunny helmet into the bag he'd carried between his legs, pulled out his beret and put it on.

"Back to the base, sir?"

"Yes," he said, deciding. "I'm going to make one more jump today."

The third time he jumped that day, he did so alone. He liked it that way because he wanted a minimum of people to observe the silly configuration the Air Force idiots had sent for him to test.

The five- and seven-gore chutes had been cut away in the back, but they'd still looked like parachutes. What kind of trooper would use a silly-looking thing without either front or rear, and shaped like the foresail of an old Yankee square-rigger? *Good thing Mahoney's out playing sailor,* he told himself. Jim would have given his eyeteeth to be along, and Wolf would never have heard the end of it about this goofy-looking USAF chute.

The engine's roar lessened, and the pilot announced that they were at 12,000 feet. "Twenty seconds."

As Wolf pulled off the headset and braced in position at the door, a fleeting thought ran through his head. He definitely did not trust the thing on his back, regardless of how bright the men were who had thought it up. Lochert watched the target crawl beneath and launched himself forward. He was glad he had a reserve chute on his chest.

Again he was in good position when the AOD sensed 10,000 feet and buzzed. He waited. Only a single gentle tug, but then Wolf found himself swinging forward like a pendulum weight until he was almost parallel to the canopy. It seemed forever before he began to swing back, but then a single sharp pull and there was no more oscillation. He looked up. When filled with air the square canopy looked unseemly, like several fluffy ribs. He pulled gently on the fore risers and, when he sensed no change, shook his head grimly. Enough was enough. If the parachute gave him one more surprise, he vowed to pull the releases and fall away, and then deploy the reserve chute on his chest. The normal, *round* one.

Approaching 5,000 feet, Wolf looked down. Couldn't be. He'd already passed the 4,000-meter mark. When he looked again, he found that he was hurtling along over the ground like a race car at Indy.

Ho boy. How do you stop this thing?

He pulled the rear risers too early and quickly slowed.

When he touched down and trotted along, the chute caught a gust and he had to release it to keep from being pulled away. He watched as it collapsed fifty feet distant, then started for it.

The jeep pulled up and the driver was staring, mouth agape. "We're almost nine klicks from the bull's-eye, Colonel. What the hell is that thing?"

"A race car," Wolf rumbled happily, continuing to walk, "and don't curse." *How could those Air Force guys have come up with such a chute?*

After repacking the three chutes, Wolf spent the night in the NKP bachelor officers' quarters. The next morning he was up at four. By six he was airborne in the Otter. By ten-thirty he'd completed his second jump of the day with the square parachute, which was easily the most maneuverable he'd ever used. It was also very fast—reaching an estimated twenty-five miles per hour on the best drop. On his longest run he'd soared more than 9.3 kilometers.

Wolf Lochert had found the parachute that would get him into Hanoi. Next he had to find a way to get out of the country alive.

At 1350 hours, Wolf waited at the paradrop area. A radio warning had been announced an hour earlier, advising all aircraft in the area to remain above 5,000 feet. The only humans there were the driver of the jeep and Wolf, who stood near the center of the etched target, extending the legs of an aluminum tripod. Next he affixed a small device on top of the thing and examined his work.

"Looks good to me, sir," called the driver, who had become his official kibitzer.

Wolf flipped on the device's two toggle switches, waited until he'd seen several strobe flashes, then backed off a hundred feet.

The box contained an electronic homing beacon which could be seen on a C-130's radar and transmitted a tone which could be tuned in on the radio direction finder. Those and the strobe light marked drop zones for the aircrew.

The Herky bird, this one modified with two large antenna-like "whiskers" that protruded forward in a vee from the nose, was late by six seconds. It came in low and slow, and as it passed the target, a chute blossomed and tugged out a small pallet from the opened rear cargo door.

Wolf pushed the button of his stopwatch, handed it to the jeep driver, then began to trot toward the small cloud of dust that marked the pallet's impact.

It took two quick swipes with the razor-sharp Randall stiletto to free the packages on the pallet. He pulled out a sealed bag, ripped it open, and awkwardly fingered the contents.

Gotta learn it better than that.

"Four minutes!" cried out the jeep driver, who manned the stopwatch.

Connect it to the rope first, he remembered. Wolf clipped the lanyard of a half-inch-thick nylon cord to the deflated balloon, then carefully threaded the balloon's tube onto the nozzle of an aluminum bottle of compressed helium gas.

"Eight minutes!"

Wolf double-checked his work, then grabbed another bag, pulled out a five-pound hammer and a long anchor rod, which he pounded securely into the ground.

"Thirteen minutes!"

Wolf heard the distant sound of engines.

Time was racing by. *Hurry!*

He clipped the other end of the nylon rope onto an eye at the top of the anchor rod and twisted the handle atop the helium bottle. He heard a hissing sound, but also another noise. The C-130 Herky bird was inbound.

"Sixteen minutes!"

Wolf picked the final package off the pallet and ripped it apart, then fumbled with the straps. It took precious seconds to lay out the harness and get the straps straight. There was also a bulky protective suit with rubber padding, but he had no time for that. He shrugged into the harness and clipped the crotch strap into place.

The balloon was only half-filled, but he had no more time, for the C-130 noises were growing louder.

Wolf shut off the helium flow and secured the tube end.

"Nineteen minutes!"

The balloon rose into the air.

Lochert was breathing hard, not from the exertion but from

worrying about the ridiculously compressed schedule he had to perform in his allotted twenty minutes. *Have I finished with everything?* Wolf raced through the mental checklist. *Yeah. Everything but the protective suit—and there wasn't time for that.* He was now attached by his own cord to the anchor, which also tethered the balloon, which floated ever higher on its hundred feet of line. He faced the direction of the incoming C-130, which was half a mile distant, flying very low and approaching fast. The idea was that the whiskers would capture the balloon and pull out the anchor from the ground—and then pull Wolf from the . . .

"Your chest straps!" screamed the jeep driver.

Wolf didn't hesitate. He released the leg straps and stepped free.

The Herky bird was overhead, catching the balloon squarely. The anchor rod pulled out of the ground as advertised. A few seconds later Wolf watched as the apparition disappeared, the empty harness fluttering behind the C-130.

"Forgot your chest straps, sir," the jeep driver called in a cheerful tone.

Wolf glared maliciously at him, and had a delicious thought of walking over and ripping off his head. Instead he reached into the secured pocket of his jump suit and lifted a hand-held VHF radio.

"This is Wolf, Herky," he growled.

A chuckle sounded over the radio. It was the ops officer light colonel from the special operations squadron with whom he'd been setting up the Fulton Recovery System snatch operation.

Wolf spoke through gritted teeth. "Drop another pallet and let's try it again."

"You owe me a six-pack, Wolf. I told you you wouldn't get it right on your first try."

"Just drop the pallet, *Scheisskopf,*" he growled, face burning. Wolf Lochert was not known as a fuck-up.

As the C-130 came around and dropped down for another approach, Wolf wondered what it was going to be like to be snatched off the ground at more than one hundred miles an hour, like the empty harness had been.

Twenty minutes later he found out.

0920 Hours Local, Thursday 2 November 1972
MAC-SOG Headquarters
Rue Pasteur, Saigon
Republic of Vietnam

Jim Mahoney stuck his head in the door.

"I'm busy," Wolf grunted, looking at the notepad. He'd created a rough scale, interpolating from the results of his test, showing altitudes, drop times, and soar distances using the new parachute:

30,000'	41 min.	25,800 meters
20,000'	28 min.	17,200 meters
10,000'	14 min.	8,600 meters

Mahoney remained at the door. "Colonel Hostettler wants me to go over to the Embassy for a meeting."

Wolf nodded. "Okay. But while he's here in Saigon, call him Mr. Thomas. Don't mess up his cover, *Scheisskopf.* You don't know a colonel named whatever it was."

"Hostettler."

Wolf glared daggers, and Mahoney abruptly left, closing the door behind him.

Lochert shook his head at the distraction, then retrieved a map from the opened drawer of the safe beside his desk. He examined the detailed depiction of Hanoi, then, with a blunt forefinger, quickly found the location of the *Cercle Sportif.* Wolf stared at the spot on the map for a full minute, as if seeing the structures and open areas on the paper before him. He'd studied detailed reconnaissance photographs so thoroughly that it was not a difficult thing to envision. He knew the location within the sprawling urban mass from a number of prominent reference points, such as the Doumer Bridge—the Citadel—Ho Tay Lake—Ba Dinh Square—Gia Lam Airport—the rail station—the thermal power plant—a dozen more which might be visible at night.

He picked up a compass on the tabletop and carefully drew a series of circles about the target, spaced one kilometer apart. Then he penned in figures from his scale, showing the altitudes from which he had to be dropped to be able to soar those distances.

Following an abrupt nod to himself, Wolf laboriously wrote out his message, addressed to General Whisenand at his Pentagon office.

1. (C/SF) ANALYSIS PROVED TEST SQUARE PARACHUTE PROVIDED BY USAF TO BE BEST CANDIDATE FOR OPERATION STORM FLIGHT. SUGGEST CHANGE TO NORMAL AF-410 HARNESS.

2. (S/SF) WILL REQUIRE ANTI-EXPOSURE SUIT WITH FULL BODY PROTECTION AND SUFFICIENT HEAT AND OXYGEN FOR 60 MINUTES OF FALL TIME (THIS PROVIDES SAFETY FACTOR OF AT LEAST 20 MINUTES).

3. (TS/SF) WILL NEED AIRCRAFT AT MINIMUM OF THIRTY THOUSAND (30,000) FEET, MAXIMUM OF TWENTY KILOMETERS (20 KM) FROM THE TARGET LZ.

4. (S/SF) HAVE NOT YET DETERMINED TYPE OF AIRCRAFT TO USE. PERHAPS YOUR SPECIAL PROJECTS PEOPLE CAN MODIFY A USAF OR USN FIGHTER?

5. (TS/SF) EXTRACTION METHOD IS DETERMINED TO BE SPECIAL OPERATIONS C-130 & FULTON RECOVERY SYSTEM IN APPROPRIATE LOW THREAT AREA.

As Wolf reread the message, he felt a glow of satisfaction. He'd done all he could. Now it was up to the people at a place General Whisenand called the Special Projects Office at the Pentagon to get him the required equipment, the Air Force to provide the jump aircraft, and the President of the United States to authorize the mission.

No reason to waste the time all of that might take, he told himself cheerily. Practice makes perfect and keeps troopers alive, as he liked to impress upon his men. Next week he'd return to the training area near Nakhon Phanom and make a few more jumps using the new chute. He would continue to do that until he received word from the General, telling him they had approval. He had to train with the square parachute in the darkness, and locate a specific spot on the ground, maybe a dim flare, from altitude. That would be more realistic and give him practice for the real thing. What he would do over Hanoi was different from anything he'd done before—like his night combat jump into Laos several years before.

Wolf had risen to his feet and was heading out his office door to take his report to the comm center for encoding and transmission when the phone jangled.

It was Jim Mahoney, calling from the Embassy, and he did not sound pleased. "I'm . . . uh . . . going on a trip for Mr. Thomas, Colonel. You got any objections?" he asked hopefully.

"No," Wolf said, staring at his message with a critical eye.

"I . . . uh . . . gotta leave right away, and I thought I remembered about you wanting some work done there. I mean, you ain't in such good shape right now, Wolf, and—"

"It'll wait," Lochert rumbled forcefully.

"Well . . . uh . . . *au revoir,* Wolf." Mahoney hung up.

French? Most of the old head SF troopers had picked up gutter French during their early days in Vietnam, when that had been a second language for a large number of Viets, but they seldom spoke it anymore. Now the Vietnamese second language was English.

He vaguely wondered how long Mahoney would be gone. Wolf slowed his step, thinking Chef Hostettler might have sent Jim out on his Storm Flight assignment. Mahoney had not looked forward to being in close quarters on a British ship with a bunch of *Limey sissies,* as he'd called them.

Wolf decided to drop by the Embassy and ask "Mr. Thomas" about it. It didn't seem fair, even if Mahoney was going out on an op he didn't look forward to. Anything would be better than sitting on your tailbone in an office, like he was doing. Especially if your tailbone was as sore as his particular one presently was, along with sundry other parts of his body.

He decided to call NKP as soon as he returned from the comm center, to set up the jumps for next week. Maybe late next week, he thought, reconsidering. And no more practicing the awful snatch by the Herky bird. The next time he did that would be from inside North Vietnam.

Wolf Lochert hobbled down the hall very gingerly, aching from more places than he'd deemed possible and grumbling to himself about how he'd not only been yanked from the ground by an airplane lumbering along at more than a hundred and fifty miles an hour, he'd flailed around in the air for five horrible minutes and suffered a thousand bruises when he bounced against the metal door-ramp as they winched him into the cargo bay. And *then* he'd had to buy the *Scheisskopf,* no-good, split-ear grinning Air Force light colonel a six-pack.

Maybe tonight Greta Sturm would help soothe some of the rough edges, especially if this time he remembered to buy the colorful birds he'd promised her the week before and had continuously forgotten.

Chapter 21

At dusk the silver and white Air Force VC-135 skimmed the tops of the poplar trees to land at the French Air Force base. A large American flag adorned the tall rudder, and the words UNITED STATES OF AMERICA were emblazoned clearly on the band of white above the windows. It was the same plane used to transport the President of the United States; one of many assigned to the 89th Military Airlift Wing, based at Andrews Air Force Base, outside Washington, D.C.

The U.S. Ambassador and several members of his staff stood at the bottom of the wheeled staircase. Surrounding them were Secret Service agents who had been flown in earlier. Kissinger bounded off the aircraft without a backward glance and was swept toward a black Cadillac limousine. Whitey descended the stairs, wearing the USAF blue jacket provided by the plane's pilot, over a white shirt and tie. He carried his suit coat over an arm and toted a bulky briefcase. The Air Attaché intercepted him, saluted smartly, and led the way to a dark Ford sedan. They both crawled into the backseat, and the attaché gave instructions to a driver wearing civilian clothing. Escorted by French police on motorcycles, the caravan roared off.

"I've heard a lot about you, General," the attaché, a full colonel, said politely, "and I'm delighted to meet you. The DIA back-channel message said to render all services. What can we do to make your stay productive?"

"Help me keep track of Mr. Kissinger."

"Yes, sir."

Except for a number of somber looks in his direction, Henry Kissinger had totally ignored Whitey's presence during the long flight over. It was apparent that he was unhappy to have a nonmember of his staff along to look over his shoulder.

Fortuitously undetected by the press, the motorcade sped away.

"According to the DISUMS [Daily Intelligence Summaries] my old unit in Thailand is really being pumped up with airplanes," the attaché said by way of conversation. Whitey had read the youthful Colonel's file on the way over. He'd earned his early promotion the hard way, by serving two tough combat tours with distinction. He had amassed 900 hours of combat flying time in Southeast Asia, completing 100 fighter missions over North Vietnam and more than 200 over Laos and South Vietnam. He had been shot down twice, recovered once from the Tonkin Gulf, and the other time from the Plaines des Jarres, in Laos. His name was Marc de St. Gall.

Whitey nodded vaguely, keeping his eye on Kissinger's limo two cars ahead. "We've built up a real air arsenal over there," he said. "Last Thursday we flew eight hundred tactical strike sorties in route packs one and two. I believe it was a record number over the North."

The attaché whistled at the figure.

"We're stinging them."

The attaché glanced at Whitey, then cleared his throat. Finally he could hold it in no longer. "We've *never* really been allowed to sting them, General. They still don't know what we could *really* do to them if we were turned loose. We could turn Hanoi into something resembling the face of the moon, but we just peck away at the edges."

"We'd never do that, Colonel."

The attaché muttered something that Whitey did not hear.

"What was that?" he asked.

The Colonel looked penitent. "I was out of line. Sorry, sir."

"No, repeat it, please." Whitey wanted to hear what the young war hero had to say. He was too insulated, listening to the politically correct views of the senior officers at the Pentagon.

The attaché sighed, as if wondering if he wasn't about to immerse himself into a pot of hot water. "I said we're still running a screwed-up air war, sir."

"And what would you recommend?"

Colonel de St. Gall swallowed, then nodded his conviction. "We should do just as we did in World War Two when the Nazis wouldn't listen. We keep trying to get their attention, but to really do that we'd have to break a few eggshells. They still think we're a bunch of dumb shits who're scared to death of world opinion, and know we'll never really hurt them."

"Ahh," Whitey said in understanding of his bitterness.

The attaché was quiet for a moment as they entered the traffic of the city. As they slowed, he gathered his brows. "I hear we're shipping a lot of weapons to the South Viets."

Whitey nodded. "In addition to tanks, armored personnel carriers, ammunition and bombs, we're sending one hundred twenty more F-5s, ninety A-37s, thirty C-130s, twenty AC-199 gunships, and two hundred seventy helicopters."

"You have quite a memory, sir."

"I just presented the list to the President yesterday. He wants us to have it all in place before the peace agreement is signed."

"And the NVAs are doing the same for their troops and the VC."

"Trying to."

"Think the South Viets will really be able to handle the commies by themselves if things get serious again, General?"

At first Whitey decided not to share his opinions with the young attaché. Then he realized he was speaking to a taxpaying Vietnam veteran, who had as much right as anybody to know what he thought.

"No, I don't," he said, and the attaché nodded in grim agreement.

"Does the President know this like we do, sir?"

"We've never discussed it outright, but I think he does."

"Then why the buildup? Isn't it just a waste of money?"

Whitey smiled at the Colonel's dogged attempt to inject common sense into a political situation. "Part of the President's policy is to show the world that America stands by our allies."

The Colonel brightened with understanding. "That's important."

"If we come to a fair agreement here, and if the communists adhere to the terms, then everything will work out. The other part of the President's plan is to keep American air assets in place and let the North Vietnamese know we'll stop future aggression with swift and sure force."

Colonel de St. Gall pondered that over and finally agreed. "Sounds like the most logical plan we could come up with, given the situation."

Whitey noticed their car was breaking off from the motorcade. "Where are we going?"

"Excuse me, sir. Here's your itinerary." The neatly typed sheets showed Whitey was staying at the home of the attaché and would be dining at diverse times with various embassy officials and French military men.

Whitey frowned. "I was instructed to accompany Mr. Kissinger to all functions and meetings."

The Colonel cast him an odd look, then released a long breath. "Sir, I was advised that if you asked questions to play dumb about it all, but I guess I'm not very good at lying or playing games with superior officers."

"Go on," Whitey snapped.

"We received two different notes from the National Security Council, with instructions to make certain we kept you busy and away from Mr. Kissinger, both socially and during any negotiations."

"Me specifically?"

"Yes, sir. By name."

A tremor of anger trilled in Whitey's voice. "So I'm relegated to the back burner, regardless of what the President wanted."

The Colonel looked out the window, then back to Whitey. His voice was low, but very sure. "You're the General and I'm the Colonel, sir. Whatever you say, I'll do. It's going to be damned difficult to get you on Mr. Kissinger's schedule, though. The protocol people and the Chief of Operations have the same instructions."

Whitey thought for a moment, then pulled a pad from his briefcase. "No, I don't want you to get in any kind of trouble with these people needlessly." He scribbled words on the paper, squinted to read it once, then folded it and handed it over. "I

want you to back-channel this through the USAF to the Air
Force military aide in the White House."

"Classification, sir?"

"Eyes only. Now let's proceed to the Embassy so you can get
it on the wire immediately."

"Yes, sir." The attaché leaned forward and gave instructions to the driver, then drew himself back. His eyes dropped
quizzically to the folded paper, then darted away as if he were
forbidden to look.

"Go ahead and read it."

The attaché unfolded the paper.

```
TO: POTUS
FM: WHISENAND
DATE: 192245ZNOV72
FYI: NSC ORDERS PRECLUDE MY ACCOMPANYING HK
     TO ANY FUNCTION, SOCIAL OR BUSINESS.
```

Major General Whitey Whisenand had his answer the next
morning, when at 1000 hours Colonel Marc de St. Gall delivered
General Whisenand to a villa owned by the French Communist
Party in the village of Gif-sur-Yvette. Both he and the attaché
wore dark suits for the occasion.

"Here we are, sir," the attaché said cheerfully as they pulled
up. He had just passed on Whitey's new agenda, which simply
read that he was to attend any and all functions, interviews, and
even meals, as did Henry Kissinger. The attaché had not been
able to keep a straight face during the recital. The Colonel's
instructions had been issued directly from the Ambassador to
the AIRA office at an ungodly hour that morning. The office
rumor was that there had been a very short and succinct phone
call made from the White House to the Ambassador's residence,
where Mr. Kissinger was staying as a guest.

Inside the villa once owned by French cubist Fernand Léger,
Whitey was escorted to a waiting room, where he was met by
two members of Henry Kissinger's advance party. Both men
wore black suits and muted ties.

"Good morning, General," the taller one said in a cheerful voice before introducing himself and his partner. "Sorry about the mixup in communications but, uh, I hope all is squared away now. Let me explain the protocol of the situation. We are the Doctor's translators and general factotums, and as such, the only persons on his staff allowed with him when he actually sits down with Le Duc Tho. Tho, of course, has his two men. As we have just been directed, you are to be available for consultation with the Doctor at any time before, during, or after the meetings." A servant entered with coffee and dry toast. "Today's proceedings start in one hour, at eleven. The Doctor will be here in thirty minutes and would welcome it if you wish to confer with him."

Whitey nodded pleasantly. "I'd like that."

They spoke about Léger's art until Dr. Henry Kissinger swept through the door. It was precisely 1030.

"Ah, General Whisenand," he said, hurrying over, hand extended as if they hadn't been on the same airplane coming over, and it had been *such* a long time. "Let me tell you how much I value your presence. You will be of inestimable assistance—especially on any, ehhh—military questions." They sat and were served coffee. Kissinger, having now forgotten about snubbing Whitey on the airplane, seemed jubilant. "I think it will go very well today—verrry well. We almost had things nailed down on the 8 October meeting. A few misunderstandings since, nothing substantive. Of course, I do have a few minor requests from Thieu in Saigon, ehhh—some sixty-nine, if I remember. We'll see how they go. But . . . " He smiled. "Of course I'm prepared to negotiate on everything." He chuckled in a low, Teutonic rumble. "The press hasn't caught on to my presence yet, but they will." He nodded somberly, as if that were a certain, awful thing, and of course he did not wish for another sage statement—or, as the President had put it, *grand gesture*—to sweep the nation's headlines. "If questioned," Kissinger continued in his most pleasant tones, "your role is as an assistant. Try not to mention your name, and *certainly* not your service affiliation. Avoid the press, and making any statements, and—"

Whitey raised a hand. Kissinger frowned at the interruption but held his tongue.

"Sir, let me say this. Regardless of what *anyone* says to *anyone* else, I *am* a military man. As such I take orders, and my

Commander in Chief has provided those. I am to accompany you where you go, see what you see, and he would like for me to lend an ear and generally help keep things on track. I am not a spy. If you tell me something in confidence, I will not betray your trust unless national security or the President's interests are threatened. If you need any military information or advice, I will try to provide it, and if I cannot, I will get it from the Pentagon. If you want me to be stand back and be quiet, as you are suggesting, then I will do that, so long as I continue to be informed and not shuffled off elsewhere."

Kissinger was listening, but his face had continued to darken as Whitey spoke. "I take it you are sent along as a, ehhh—moderating influence."

"I believe that is the President's intent."

Kissinger stared, then nodded his head abruptly. "Then it is done. It seems we both have our orders."

"Yes, sir."

"As for my betraying national security, I—"

Whitey quickly interrupted. "I cannot imagine such a thing, sir. I was speaking in generalities. My charge is to defend the national security, but I am sure you feel just as strongly as I do on that issue."

Kissinger slowly brightened. His voice strengthened. "But this is *my* meeting, and I *am* in charge."

"Of course, sir."

"Doctor?" One of the factotums hurried over to alert Kissinger that the meeting was about to begin.

More than six hours passed before General Whisenand saw Henry Kissinger again. "Come, ride back with me," he said, and he was not smiling. They were escorted to the main door and were greeted by raucous sounds and flashing bulbs as they stepped from the entryway toward Kissinger's car.

"Kiki, oh, Kiki, over here . . . "

"Doctor, I say, Doctor, do you have an agreement yet?"

"Allô, Kiki, a leetle smile . . . "

Photographers and TV cameramen were jammed three deep outside the fence, and several figures with large still cameras were perched in the trees bordering the iron-fenced grounds.

Kissinger's face lit up and he pasted a smile into place. "Frank and earnest," was all he would say in response to the inquiries as to how the meeting had gone. "Frank and very earnest."

The smile disappeared as soon as they were seated in the anonymity of the dark-windowed automobile, a white sedan driven by a quiet, broad-shouldered man.

"Tho has done another about-face," Kissinger rasped moodily. "He's not nearly as cordial as before. He questioned our sincerity, our airlift to South Vietnam, and complained about our failure to keep our commitment to sign on the 31st of October. He refuses to bend at all, and says we *must* abide by the old provisions, regardless of what the South Vietnamese government wants." He pounded his fist on his knee. "It's all poppycock, of course. *They* are the ones who reneged on the original provisions, who ignored the cease-fire and launched the biggest rocket and mortar attack ever on Tan Son Nhut Air Base. *They* are the ones who keep 150,000 combat troops in South Vietnam, while we now have only a handful of advisers." He sighed heavily and shook his massive head. "I had no opportunity even to present Thieu's demands. We were so close, so *close.*" Another sigh. "We meet again tomorrow."

There was nothing for Whitey to say.

They returned to the massive stone American Embassy building on the tree-lined street just off the Champs-Elyseés. There, Whitey listened as Kissinger drafted a cable to Nixon, summarizing the results. He then listened as Dr. Kissinger telephoned Haldeman and made banal and trite comments about the meeting. "Never know who's listening," he muttered after hanging up.

The next morning Whitey stood by as Kissinger read his message traffic, spoke briefly to reassure the South Vietnamese ambassador that their points would be included in the day's agenda, then looked on as Kissinger escorted a pretty blonde out the door, going, he said, to lunch at Chez Tante Louise on Rue Boissy d'Anglas. He asked if Whitey would please pick him up there afterward to attend the afternoon meeting.

Late that afternoon, when the meeting was concluded, Le Duc Tho escorted Kissinger to his car. They posed for photographers and shook hands warmly. Another failure, the Doctor told Whitey later, but tomorrow was promising. That night Kissinger and Whitey flew to Brussels to talk with visiting Indonesian President Suharto about his country's participation in a four-nation commission to supervise the cease-fire once it took effect. Indonesia, Canada, Hungary, and Poland had agreed to join such a contingent. Hanoi protested Indonesia's inclusion, saying they were anticommunist and a lackey of the West. Suharto assured the two men that Indonesia would remain on the force regardless of Hanoi's obnoxious trumpeting.

Henry Kissinger's original ebullience faded as the days ground on. The word from Saigon was disturbing, for their government-controlled press called Kissinger "an ambitious person," and accused him of "haste," making "mistakes," filled with "overconfidence and ambition."

On the 22nd, a Wednesday, Whitey was shattered by a report from the attaché. A B-52 had been hit by a surface-to-air missile near Vinh, in Route Pack Three of North Vietnam, and went down very close to the American base at Nakhon Phanom, Thailand. It was a psychological victory for the enemy, for although the crew was picked up, it was the first of the big bombers to be lost in combat. The Paris newspapers ran big spreads on the shoot-down, and *Le Monde* printed an outrageously false claim by the North Vietnamese news agency that nineteen of the bombers had thus far been downed. Whitey had to grit his teeth and bear it the next morning, which was Thanksgiving back in the States, for when he entered the outer room with Kissinger, they were met by unsubtle boasts from the North Viet delegates.

The Thanksgiving Day meeting produced no results, but the principals agreed to meet again on the 25th. As that meeting opened at a North Vietnamese residence on Rue Darth in Choisy-le-Roi, Tho immediately blasted the entire American concept, and Kissinger warned that Nixon had suspended bombing above the 20th parallel only in expectation of satisfactory negotiations. The atmosphere was chilly and there was no progress. Finally, the two men decided to recess for several days so they could return to their respective countries for consultation.

Whitey and Henry Kissinger arrived in Washington late the morning of the 26th.

"I believe the leaders in Hanoi ordered Tho's shift of position," Kissinger began in his verbal report to his President. Whitey, Haldeman, Melvin Laird, and the Chairman of the Joint Chiefs of Staff were present. "I suspect they intend to stall until

January, when they feel Congress will vote the United States out of the war."

"Well," Nixon said, lips pursed, "Congress is certainly surrender-minded." He nodded absently. "And that would mean abandoning the POWs."

"They would be used as bargaining tools to obtain economic aid."

"Or even reparations," the President said quietly, entering a tentative mood.

"Exactly," Kissinger replied.

A moment of silence followed.

The President leaned forward, eyes slowly coming alive with some inner fury. Kissinger blinked uncertainly. Nixon's voice quavered with new emotion. "I want those accords *signed,* and I want it done by the 15th of December. I *demand* that the POWs be released and sent home no more than ten days later. I want them here for Christmas. We will agree to reasonable terms, and we will do so *with* or *without* Thieu."

"Yes, sir," the Doctor said. The President had not left room for another response.

Richard Nixon regarded Melvin Laird and the Chairman of the Joint Chiefs. His voice was forceful and filled with icy determination. "Draw up two contingency plans using air power. One in the event the talks are broken off, the other in case the North Vietnamese sign and then violate the agreement. We must maintain sufficient force in the area to do the job. I am not speaking of a weak response. I want every industrial and military target in that miserable country targeted, and most especially those in and around Hanoi."

"Shall we include B-52s up there, sir?" the chairman asked quietly.

"Most specifically, General." Nixon's voice faded, but the ice remained. *"Most* specifically."

A small, involuntary thrill ran through Whitey Whisenand, even overriding his concern for the airmen who would be placed in jeopardy if the plans were executed.

The eagle had been pushed far enough.

Instead of going directly home from the White House, Whitey Whisenand took time out to visit his office in the basement of the Pentagon, located near the National Military Command Center.

There he glanced through the correspondence his secretary felt was most important. Before taking any other action, however, he penned a short message to Lieutenant Colonel Wolfgang X. Lochert, in Saigon. He told him that the Storm Flight operation was not yet approved, but that he had identified the aircraft to be used to drop Wolf over Hanoi. He went into more detail then.

Next Whitey contacted the Special Projects office upstairs and asked them to make a specific aircraft modification, posthaste. He also told them to go ahead and ship out the antiexposure suit Wolf Lochert would require for his jump at altitude over Hanoi. Yes, he knew it was still experimental. Ship it out, he said.

Finally, Whitey Whisenand went home to Sal. It had been entirely too long since he'd seen and sought solace from the woman he cherished.

0730 Hours Local, Friday 1 December 1972
Hoa Lo Prison (Hanoi Hilton), Hanoi
Democratic Republic of Vietnam

"Too much time has passed since I made my offer," Flak Apple told the leering Bug. "I don't want to do it anymore. I don't want to make a tape, and I don't care if I live any better. Forget the whole thing." Flak was betting on a hunch, a final desperate gamble.

During the preceding three months, Flak had sunk ever lower into despair. He knew where they'd taken the POWs selected by the Russians, but could not get the information out. From tap-code conversations, he had learned that designated prisoners had tried to get the information into their letters home, using pin pricks near certain letters, slightly backslanting others, raising them slightly above the line, but no one ever knew which few would actually be sent. Now, out of the blue, Bug had called him out to talk. The conversation was definitely not the usual confrontation between prisoner and torturer.

"We have been very good to you, Apper. Now you must be good to us."

Flak had not been tortured or quizzed during the last three months. He had remained in his solitary cell, but the food had been adequate and he'd been allowed to bathe weekly. He had also been allowed to perform his physical exercises without interference, and now was able to do hundreds of sit-ups and 100 push-ups, even with the badly twisted arm. He was even relatively current on camp news, passed through finger-flashing and the tap code. But many of the messages from the SRO told of his frustration at not being able to get the information about the detention camp for the special POWs to the U.S. government.

Now Flak felt an anxiety in Bug, and something else . . . perhaps even a desire to please. He wanted to know why. The answer was soon revealed.

"Apper, our minister, Mr. Le Duc Tho, is even now talking to your Mr. Henry Kissinger. They talk in Paris about the end of the war. Your president does not want to end the war. He does not want peace. You want peace, don't you?"

Flak sighed, the old routine. "Yes, I want peace."

"Then, Apper, you must make broadcast to your fellow criminals. You must broadcast to them that you want peace and they want peace and then you can all make a broadcast to the people of the world you criminals all want peace."

Flak frowned at the bug-eyed Vietnamese. "You mean you want me to get on the camp radio and convince the others to make a big broadcast over Radio Hanoi asking for peace?"

Bug shifted uncomfortably. He'd been told explicitly not to "punish" this prisoner—no matter what happened. But he *must* get him to make the plea to the other prisoners. The delegate from the Central Committee had directed it. Bug was sure the Central Committee knew something big was about to happen. They'd ordered partial evacuation of Hanoi and an increase in the gun platforms within and around the city. They acted, he thought, scared.

"Yes, Apper, you *mus'* do this thing," Bug said almost plaintively.

Flak studied the man's face. The eye was wandering frantically. *You son of a bitch, you need me, don't you?* "All right," he finally said, using his weary tone. "I'll make a camp broadcast. But I must be allowed to choose my own words."

"Oh no, Apper." Bug smiled nervously. "We have it all written out for you."

Flak knew the weak camp broadcast could not be picked up by the American monitoring stations, but he wanted to see just how far he could go. And—if his words were good enough—they'd likely rebroadcast the tape over Radio Hanoi. And if *that* didn't work, he would surely join the others in making the mass appeal over Radio Hanoi Bug was looking for. It was a chance.

"No," he said firmly, "I will write the words to make the camp broadcast."

"No!" Bug looked sullen. A moment later his shoulders dropped and he caved. "Ah, all right, Apper. *You* write the words."

The next day it was different. "No, Apper," Bug said when he read Flak's speech. "This is *not* what you can say. This is like prayer. You must rethink what you say. Unh, what is this thing, this 'dog patch'?"

"Oh that is just a way of referring to a bad, ah, a difficult place. You know, where only dogs can be happy."

"Oh, very *bad* place."

"Yeah, that's it."

"What is this 'donkey' word mean?"

"That's an animal. A very dumb animal. We use it to describe stubborn people."

Bug nodded knowingly. "Ahhh. Like the criminals who will not make a statement?"

"Yeah."

Bug pushed out his lower lip thoughtfully. "It is still too much like prayer."

Flak's next words were softer. "Americans believe in prayer," he said. "It is the most important thing we do."

He seemed even more nervous than last time, Flak thought as he was led out of the interrogation room. *Things must be going to hell in Paris.*

Flak was returned to his cell, not yet knowing if he'd won—whether the critical words had been acceptable. *Dogpatch,* their name for the new prison camp, was located near someplace the Viets pronounced similarly to *donkey.* But even if they scratched the words out of this one, he was determined to get them out on the subsequent Radio Hanoi broadcast.

1430 Hours Local, Wednesday 6 December 1972
Neuilly-sur-Seine
Near Paris, France

The emissaries met once more, on the 6th of December, at a new
site in Neuilly-sur-Seine, the home of a wealthy American-born
jeweler. Against an expensive backdrop of tapestries and paintings, the two sides seemed once again to be coming together.
On the 9th they had narrowed their difficulties, but the next
day, Sunday, Tho's clerks presented seventeen new outrageous
changes.

By Wednesday, the 13th, the negotiations had reached total
deadlock. Tho would not agree to a continuation of the demilitarized zone between North and South Vietnam, and demanded
there be only a token international supervisory force which
would be dependent on the Viet Cong for supplies whenever
investigating an incident. They also refused to make even a
token withdrawal of their 150,000 North Vietnamese troops
from South Vietnam.

Dr. Henry Kissinger, Whitey observed, was no longer the
urbane, brilliant, and sure diplomat he'd been a few weeks
before. He seemed much more nervous, and even ready to
accept any scrap of advice. There were no more attempts at
"grand gestures" with the press.

On Thursday, the 14th day of December, they returned to
Washington, where Kissinger explained the North Vietnamese
intransigence to his president. "Tho even has phony fainting
spells," he concluded bitterly. He gritted his teeth and clenched
his fists. "They're shits. Tawdry, filthy shits."

"We have now gone the distance," the President said. "I'm
going to cable Hanoi, demanding they reopen negotiations within seventy-two hours or face the consequences." His words were
very calm, and Whitey knew he had mentally prepared that
message on the day his voice had first turned to ice.

An hour later Whitey heard the Chairman of the Joint Chiefs
advise that "the military option is prepared, Mr. President."
The briefing of that option, which was to become known as
Linebacker, Phase Two, was thorough.

The eagle's talons were sharp, and his eyes were coming alert.

0600 Hours Local, Thursday 14 December 1972
Hoa Lo Prison (Hanoi Hilton), Hanoi
Democratic Republic of Vietnam

"Up, Apper, up," Bug commanded from Flak's cell door. "You must broadcas' now, yes, you mus' broadcas'."

Flak could tell he was rattled and distraught. "My words," he said.

"Yes, yes, *your* words. Hurry."

Flak sat before the ancient desk microphone and began to read his prepared speech:

> "My fellow prisoners, we are gathered here today in the sight of Almighty God to make a wedding between His mind and ours. We send winged prayers about our dogpatch on this earth of travail to Thy heavenly brain in hopes Thou canst see and know of what we want. What we want is peace, a just peace where everyone gets exactly what is coming to them, particularly the North Vietnamese men who guard us so well at this camp and their leaders. The men of this camp call to You in unison to make Thy will known and save Thy faithful servants who are soon to be dispatched to the gates of hell. They no longer wish to be as stubborn as donkeys. We all here broadcast to the world that we want peace and justice for all and for all a hearty good night."

At both nine and noon they played the tape of Flak's speech over the camp radio. As the second repeat began on the loudspeakers, Bug visited Flak's cell, a guard bearing a tray with steaming hot rice and vegetables behind him.

"You make strange speech, Apper, but all other criminals say they understand you and will make a broadcast to the world. Now you have good food. Tomorrow maybe you move to room with other prisoners. But Apper, our high command say they not sure you make broadcast to world. They say you and your other criminals not sincere. You must think on this."

"We will not make a broadcast?"

"Not yet, Apper," Bug said and left the cell, followed by the guard.

Flak kept his face impassive until the cell door was closed, then hot, bitter tears spilled down his face and he found his throat so constricted he could not eat any rice.

Twenty miles over Hanoi, the pilot of the SR-71 monitored his gauges as he eased the giant spy plane around its wide orbit over North Vietnam. The height was so great that he and the man in the back cockpit saw darkness and stars at noon. They both wore full-pressure suits, like spacewalk astronauts. The two men were part of operation Giant Scale, the highly classified program that made photo, radar, and signal intelligence flights so high over enemy territory that no SAM could threaten, no MiG could fly even four miles below them. The pilot checked his flight plan to match mission accomplishment to fuel remaining.

"That's about it," he said on the intercom to the reconnaissance systems officer in back.

"Rodge," the RSO agreed, "we can return to base."

"Got anything good cooking?" the pilot asked.

"Never really know until analysis. The usual from the Air Defense center, some junk from ground units." He was silent for a moment. "Just now getting some sort of a low-gain transmission from downtown Hanoi. Probably one of those hand-held radios the diplomats use 'cause the telephones are so bad."

"Want to break it off and start back?"

"Nah. You never know."

The pilot checked the fuel flow. "We've got enough for one more orbit."

The systems officer moved a gloved hand to ensure the low-band recorder switch was on.

Chapter 22

In his three months at Guam, Court Bannister had sniveled a total of twenty-one KC-135 rides, but had only been successful in getting two B-52 flights in—one a low-level training flight, where the big Buff had bounced along at 300 feet above the water on a route circumnavigating the Mariana Islands chain, then simulating a bombing run on Tinian Island—the other had been a short test hop. On neither of those had they carried bombs or made heavyweight takeoffs, and there hadn't been time or opportunity for the busy pilots to allow him to fly the airplane, had they been so inclined. The previous evening Roberts had passed a message for Court to meet him at the dining hall at 0400 hours, wearing his flight suit.

Court Bannister, Clem Roberts, and Beep Beep Bentley ate a wordless breakfast at the all-night mess. Afterward, he walked with them toward a building called Arc Light Control.

"I've finally got you aboard a combat mission, Court," Clem said. "That means you've got to attend the mission briefings. You'll be flying with our crew."

"Is it wise to be seen in the briefing theater?" Court asked, remembering Colonel Gartley's insistence that he do nothing but sit at the assigned desk.

"Yup. All nice and legal. This first time you'll be going on an Arc Light mission to South Vietnam, and there's not much for the crew to do except follow the radar nav's directions to the target. No one'll be shooting at us, and they're mostly all milk runs. But keep your eyes open, because after a few of these you'll be going along on the Linebackers up north." Missions to South Vietnam fell under the Arc Light OPlan. Those to the southern portions of North Vietnam fell under Operation Linebacker. The B-52s had flown to Route Pack Six, the deadliest area of North Vietnam, only once, in the massive single-day Freedom Porch Bravo raid on the Haiphong petroleum-storage area, when Court had watched and listened from the EC-121 called Disco.

Court was cautiously optimistic over the turn of events. "This is a switch. Why the sudden difference, Clem?"

"You are now on official flight orders."

"I'll be damned," Court said. "What about Gartley? Won't he shit when he sees me in the briefing room?" On both of his B-52 sorties, Court had felt like an illegal alien on the run.

"He won't be there this morning." Clem wagged his head sadly in the darkness. "Anyway, there you go giving the good Colonel too much credit again. I told you, the man's got a memory like a sieve and an intellect to match."

"No balls, either," muttered Beep Beep Bentley.

"Hush, Beeper. Anyway, I floated a sheet of paper across Gartley's desk the other day with your name about halfway down the list, showing you as a member of the wing staff. I even used your real title, *tactical liaison officer,* and showed you as a flight member on casual status, getting ready to upgrade."

"Jesus," said Court, admiring Clem's audacity. "What did he say?"

"Looked at your name kind of suspiciously, like it ought to mean something, so I brought up another subject. He chewed my ass for some trivial bullshit, then he signed it and took off golfing with some visiting general. Hell, he's forgotten who you are. We're home free, long as we don't wave a red flag in front of his face to remind him."

"Dumb shit," piped up Beep Beep Bentley.

"So I can fly legally now?" Court asked cautiously.

"Still as a Blob for a while longer, but yeah, you can now legally fly. We'll get you upgraded to aircraft commander status eventually, but we've gotta go softly so no one will get pissed off and remind Colonel Gartley that he's supposed to hate you. The guy we're flying with today is an IP, and just also happens to be the AC of our crew and a good guy. He's agreed to take you on and get you upgraded. He'd do anything to fuck up Gartley. They're both West Point grads, and he thinks Gartley is an insult to the cadet corps. Says he can't understand how Gartley got through the four years there anything higher than mascot mule third class."

"Hell, I'm just sorry it took so bloody long. Come on, let's get to the briefing."

DEPARTMENT OF THE AIR FORCE
Flight Order 72-5122-3

1. Crew Members listed below will proceed in aircraft indicated and upon completion of flight will return to: CLASSIFIED
2. Effective on or about: CLASSIFIED
3. Return on or about: CLASSIFIED
4. From: (Place flight will originate): CLASSIFIED
5. To: (Itinerary, list complete address, variations in itinerary authorized) CLASSIFIED
6. Mission: Higher Headquarters Directed
7. Special instructions/Remarks: Brfd on customs proc by 48SW, Anderson AFB, Guam
8. Crew No: S-13
9. Take-off time: HHD
10. Duration of Flight: Classified
11. Security Clearance for period: Top Secret
12. AIRCRAFT

		TACTICAL	
TYPE	TAIL NBR	CALL SIGN	FUEL LOAD
B-52	57101	TBA	Full

13.

Crew	Posit	Name
BEA	AC	Norwich, Pierre L, Major
S-13	CP	Gilland, Peter B, 1Lt
	RN	Roberts, Clement H, LTC
	NN	Robbs, Alton J, Capt
	EW	Bentley, William B, Capt
	G	Slater, Elmer R., Tsgt
	P/PX	Bannister, Courtland E, LTC

I have read and understand ALIF through item number 12 signed:

Pierre L. Norwich, Major, USAF, Pilot in Command

There were three designations for crews in the SAC structure. When crews were first formed and passed several rigorous hurdles, they received the basic R prefix, meaning they were Combat Ready. Once they'd proven themselves to be *highly* capable, they were given an E designation, and were called a Lead crew. They could lead the three-ship cells. The highest crew designation was S, which stood for Select. Those were the cream of SAC's crop, the best, and all such designated crewmembers were eligible for spot promotions to the next-higher rank.

The tactical forces had tried the same system for a while in the fifties and early sixties, but as Court well recalled, it had turned disastrous, breeding contempt among the group of individualist fighter jocks, most of whom felt they were the best in the world. SAC stuck to its designations, and it seemed to work much better with the crew-coordination-oriented group. Each SAC crew strove hard to make the elitist Select status. Few made it.

Court studied the men of Select aircrew 13. Norwich was stocky, Gilland tall and thin, Robbs heavyset, and Slater, the gunner, was a smallish, silver-haired man in his late thirties. Outside of Roberts and Slater, they all seemed very young, especially Norwich, the aircraft commander, who appeared about college sophomore age. Court took a second look at him. His face was pale and sweaty. While the others nodded and offered pleasant words of welcome, Norwich swallowed a lot and looked as if he was about to vomit.

"You okay, Major?" Court asked.

"Don't feel wonderful, but I'm good enough to fly. Got up too early, maybe. Anyway." He drew a deep breath. "I'm sorry, Colonel," Norwich said, "that I can't put you in a crew position, but SAC regs don't authorize that."

"I understand," Court said. "I've got a lot to learn."

"We'll take care of that once we get you on upgrade status. Today, after we're airborne and en route to the tanker, I'll let you fly the bird some and get the feel." As he spoke, the youthful Major pulled a handkerchief from a flight suit pocket and wiped sweat from his brow. Court thanked him, wondering. He'd seen too many pilots keep themselves on a schedule when they were too ill to fly.

The crew moved as a unit and took their seats, three in one

row, the other three directly behind. They did it in SAC's unofficially prescribed pecking order: AC, copilot, and RN in front; EWO, nav, and gunner in back. Court took a seat in the second row, beside Beep Beep Bentley.

After the regular crews were seated, several other men in flight suits, among them Donnie Higgens, filed into the room from the rear and sat down. When Duckcall Donnie saw him, he grinned and waved.

"The standby crew," Bentley muttered to Court. Taciturn on the ground, Clem had told Court that Beep Beep became a regular chatterbox when they were airborne and things got exciting. It would be interesting to see the transformation, Court thought.

The auditorium's stage sported a briefer's podium and pullout racks of 4 × 8-foot briefing boards. A tall lieutenant colonel who walked so stiffly he looked as if a rod had been inserted in his butt minced his way to the podium and adjusted the mike. He introduced himself. "I'm Lieutenant Colonel Merriwell, and I will be the mission commander for our three-ship Arc Light cell. Our call sign is Gold."

Roberts whispered back to Court, "As a Select crew we'd normally be leading the cell. Merriwell's only a fair pilot and doesn't like to make decisions in the air, but he's one of Colonel Gartley's fair-haired boys." Merriwell made roll call, gave the crews their individual call signs (Norwich and crew were Gold Three), and told them they were to fly a standard Arc Light mission to a target in the II Corps area of South Vietnam. Then he pulled out a large map with an acetate overlay that traced the 2,400-nautical-mile route from Guam to the Vietnam land mass.

The essence of the target intelligence was that Gold cell would be dumping bombs on a VC base camp area which had been reported by an ARVN ground-reconnaissance team. They could expect to find as many as 500 enemy troops there.

Court leaned toward Beep Beep Bentley, whose eyes were almost closed. "How do—"

Bentley started, jumping in his seat, his eyes opening wide. "Ngh," he grunted. "You woke me up," he mumbled in an accusing tone. He slumped back down and his breathing evened.

Roberts turned back toward Court, smiling. "Beep Beep says these guys just waste his time on the Arc Light missions. There's no threats down there to speak of. He's only attentive if we're on Linebacker missions."

Court kept his voice low so he wouldn't interrupt the droning briefing officer. "I wanted to ask him what kind of postmission report you guys get. How do you know if you hit anything?"

"They send in a team to check half an hour after we're off the target. Used to be U.S. Army Hueys with recon teams. Now it's ARVN in their own choppers."

"What kind of report do they give you on something like this?"

"Body count. Of course there's not much left to see after we dump more than three hundred bombs on a place." He frowned. "I suppose they count arms and legs. Maybe heads. 'Course they inflate the hell out of the numbers, especially now that the ARVN's handling it. According to them we've killed half the population of the known world." Clem grinned and turned back forward.

Beep Beep's head was fully down on his chest now, and he did not stir when the intelligence briefer told them there would be no anticipated threat from enemy weapons. "But," he added, "you pilots keep an ear out for phony divert orders, and you EWOs keep an eye out for false navigation signals." He droned on.

Roberts leaned back and again whispered to Court. "We've heard American-sounding voices on our cell frequencies, trying to get us to change heading or strike another target. And a couple times they've transmitted phony TACAN signals from the wrong side of the border, trying to fake us into turning the wrong way. The Russian trawlers do some of it too, along with some mediocre jamming of my radar set. No big deal—just irritants."

The intell officer left the stage.

As the weather officer took his place, Beep Beep began to snore so loudly that the nav punched him in the ribs. Bentley smacked his lips, turned his head to the other side, and was immediately back asleep. The weather briefer showed charts displaying the winds aloft, temperature and pressure information, and cloud cover. He then took the easy way out, forecasting a late-afternoon rainstorm. That was a safe bet. It would rain every afternoon in South Vietnam until they were later into the dry season.

Court remembered it from the ground at Bien Hoa—rainwater

splashing down so heavily it sounded like a noisy waterfall. Warm rain in the spring, quite chilly in the fall.

The weatherman finished by giving the expected weather at U Tapao, their primary divert base, and then back at Guam for the time period they were expected to land. It was all good.

Merriwell returned stiffly to the podium, flipped on a projector, and showed a vu-graph displaying aircraft tail numbers and parking locations. Then he raised his wristwatch to eye level and primly counted down the seconds so all could coordinate their watches: "Seven, six, five, four, three, two, one . . . now," he said.

Merriwell then outlined the complex procedures and coordination required to launch the three bombers.

As the mission commander droned, Court looked about, sensing something was amiss. It took a moment before he realized what it was. No one had a knee board strapped to his leg. For all of his flying career in fighters he'd used a knee board, with flight plan, lineup and data cards, and maps clipped in place. Here, the pilots and EWOs carried satchels, and the navigators dragged along two of the biggest, heaviest, leather briefcases Court had ever seen. It seemed odd, in this modern age of electronic wonders, that anyone would require all of that material just to tell the pilots when to turn and a heading to fly.

The men stood when the briefing was concluded and started to go next door for their individual crew briefings. Court cast a concerned glance at Major Norwich, who was now soaking with sweat and looking pained. The mere act of standing was too much for him. "I've had it," the green-faced aircraft commander grunted. Then he groaned aloud and bolted for the men's room.

"Now he thinks it might be food poisoning," said Lieutenant Pete Gilland, the copilot, as they watched him stumble away. He turned to Lieutenant Colonel Clem Roberts, who was the senior member of the crew. "We'll need one of the replacement pilots, sir."

Roberts nodded toward the rear of the room. "Make it Captain Higgens," he said. A groan sounded from both the nav and EWO, and Gilland frowned at the choice. Although senior in rank, Clem was not senior to the copilot by crew position. As a fellow pilot, Gilland would likely be able to get his way if he took it to Merriwell, the mission commander. Court frowned, for the First Lieutenant did indeed immediately walk over to Merriwell.

"He's just letting him know what's going on," Roberts said, looking on.

"You sure you want Donnie, Clem? He's still not winning any popularity contests here."

"You said he was good . . . right?"

"He was damn good when I flew with him in fighters."

"Then we want him."

Both Beep Beep Bentley and Robbs the navigator groaned. "You'll be sorry," the nav said. "I met the guy and he's a walking disaster. Makes fun of everything we're doing here."

"Hell," observed Court, "he made fun of everything we did in fighters too."

Gilland returned. "Our new aircraft commander is Captain Higgens," he said.

"Oh, boy," Beep Beep breathed unhappily.

"I'll get him," Court said, and walked back to where Donnie and the other spares were gathering their notes and briefing cards and placing them into satchels.

"Hi, Court," Donnie said, all smiles. They shook hands.

"Donnie, you're our new AC."

"Of S-13?" Donnie asked with surprise.

"I recommended you." Court didn't have to add that his credibility was now on the line.

"How 'bout that," Donnie Higgens said in a quiet voice after a pause. He picked up his briefcase and followed Court over to where the crew of Gold Three waited, then they all walked next door and found an empty crew-briefing room. There they spread out around a large table and the crewmen slapped down their notes and manuals.

The others were dead quiet as Donnie slowly placed his own notes on the table. He looked at each man in turn before he spoke.

"Okay, guys," he said, "I know you probably aren't chomping at the bit to get to fly with me, and I suppose it's my fault, because I haven't exactly endeared myself to the people in the wing. But the fact is, this is the United States Air Force, we have a fine plane and a mission we're all trained for, and we are going to put our bombs squarely on the target and do it as a team." He formed a big smile. "Tell you a secret. You may not want to fly with me, but I sure want to fly with you guys. I've seen you all around and listened to the talk, and I'm impressed. Pete"—he looked at Gilland—"you graduated number two in your pilot class and they say you're as smooth as they get. And you, Bill," he said to Beep Beep Bentley, "are the best EWO in the combat theater, and the commies probably have a price on your head. Al Robbs, you helped this bunch become a select crew with your superb navigation. Colonel Roberts"—Donnie shook his head—"you're the wing DON, and we all know you don't get that position by sharpening pencils. I hear you can thread needles with your bombs." Finally he turned to Elmer Slater. "And you, Sergeant Slater, always arrive early, stay late, and outshoot all the other gunners in the simulator. Therefore, gentlemen, I'm honored to fly with you. I will do my utmost to get us into the air safely and back home again, but I don't have any illusions about who it will take to find and put our bombs on target or to protect us if things go bad. That'll be you guys all the way." There were grudging glances among the crewmembers. Finally Clem Roberts spoke.

"For everyone's benefit, Captain Higgens graduated at the top of his own pilot class, gained a reputation as a steady and superb fighter pilot with a MiG kill to his credit, and then graduated at the top of his B-52 upgrade class at Castle."

Donnie gave his own look of embarrassed surprise.

"I have my sources." Clem smiled. "I have no doubt we'll all work very well together today. Shall we get on with the briefing?"

It was quiet in the predawn darkness as the six crewmembers and Court Bannister boarded the standard Air Force blue bus with hard seats, no shocks, and a worn interior. Court had wondered why each six-man crew needed an eighteen-passenger bus. He soon found out.

Their first stop was at the personal equipment shop, where each man picked up his helmet, headset with boom mike, .38 caliber revolver, and green-mesh survival vest. Court was given a twenty-pound seat-pack survival kit, which he would strap to his parachute and sit on, like a cushion. The other crewmembers' survival kits were an integral part of their ejection seats. They all stowed their personal effects and wallets, carrying only an identification card and Geneva Convention card. Court cheated a bit, as he'd done when flying other combat birds, by carrying a set of underwear and a shaving kit tucked into his helmet bag and three hundred dollars in a clip zippered into the right leg pocket of his flight suit. It had come in handy when he'd had to divert to other bases and his buddies found themselves without enough cash to even buy a twenty-cent drink at the bar.

From the PE shop, the bus took them to the in-flight kitchen where Robbs, the junior navigator, went inside and collected the box lunches and then distributed them among the men. Court had ordered two small Number 3 Snacks for the eleven-hour mission, and was surprised to see the others with shoe-box-sized cartons that he figured must carry enough food for a week. By then nearly all the seats in the bus were filled either with a crewmember or his gear. Sergeant Slater came out with a big metal box with a spigot, which contained hot coffee for the officers in the forward compartment. Then he went back and brought out a large metal cylinder of iced water, and two metal Thermos containers of coffee for himself.

Dawn was draining the black from the sky as they started down the flight line. Clem told Court there was more than five miles of ramp space, with just enough revetments to park the 150 assigned B-52s and twenty-odd KC-135 tankers. The crew bus pulled into the revetment of B-52 tail number 57101. The men stayed put, the driver turned on the interior lights, and two crew chiefs entered the front door with the maintenance books from their big bomber in their hands.

"Your airplane is 101, the wonderful one, gentlemen," the lead crew chief said in a cheerful voice. "It has 7,735 hours on the airframe. We call her the Guam Queen because she was a hangar queen up in Okinawa before we got her here and tweaked her up. Now she's Miss Reliable herself." Since aircrews weren't assigned to specific airplanes, the crew chiefs gave them their names. "She's full up on gas and oxygen, has eighty-four Mk-82 bombs in her belly and twenty-four on the wing pylons. She has a few discrepancies but none affect safety of flight." The chief read through the list, and Donnie Higgens said he had no trouble accepting them. "You guys have anything?" he asked the crew, and each man had a minor technical question or two that the chiefs easily answered.

Donnie Higgens stood and announced, "Rings and scarves." The crewmembers removed and stowed them in flight suit pockets so they wouldn't catch on any of the scores of protuberances inside the crowded airplane. As they dismounted from the bus in the gloom of dawn, Court was astounded, as always, at the sight of row upon row of the giant, camouflage-and-black bombers. He followed Donnie and Gilland as they walked around the huge aircraft performing their preflight inspection, each carrying a flashlight. A large power cart supplied electricity to the airplane, and lights were turned on to illuminate hatches and such. The aircraft loomed over them, dark and brooding.

"It's not like in fighters, Court," Donnie said. "Because of the Buff's size and complexity, there are just too many items to check. You can't shake every bomb or check every bomb fuze setting, can't rap each fuel tank to make sure it's filled and check that its cap is tight." Donnie hoisted himself up to peer down an engine's maw to ensure there was no foreign matter there. He huffed as he dropped back to the tarmac. "Like I say, you can't check everything. You've just got to trust the crew chiefs, and mostly look for major hydraulic or fuel leaks."

After a few more minutes of this, it was time to board. Court followed Higgens up the ladder built into the hatch under the navigator's seat. They stopped at the first level, which the crewmembers called "downstairs" or the "bilge." The RN sat on the left, the nav on the right. Two ejection seats faced control panels, each with two large radar screens, several smaller scopes, and a complete set of flight instruments.

"Guess you've been briefed about how both of these seats eject downward," Donnie said. "We've got to somehow give 'em at least two hundred fifty feet of altitude or these guys won't make it. Since you won't have an ejection seat, if I set off the alarm, hustle down here and dive out one of the open hatches after these guys go out. As AC, I'll stay with the airplane as long as I can and try to keep it stable so you can jump. Anything catastropic happens, everyone has to get out quick, bam—bam—bam, so we can all make it."

A few feet up a set of metal stairs and they were on the flight deck. Opposite the top of the ladder was the EWO's position, where Beep Beep Bentley stared intently at his confusing maze of scopes and switches, as if they made sense.

From the bilge downstairs, Clem Roberts and Al Robbs handed up satchels, helmet bags, and box lunches for the upper-deck crewmembers. The passageway became clogged with the gear until Donnie, Gilland, and Bentley claimed and stowed their material.

"How do you get back to the gunner?" Court asked. He'd flown his missions in G models, where the gunner sat up forward beside the EWO and controlled his guns via television and long-distance.

"Very carefully," Donnie said. "Just behind the nav's seat there's a small hatch, and you have to crawl a hundred feet down a narrow catwalk that passes through the bomb bay. We don't go back and forth unless there's an emergency. The gunner's got his own cockpit back there, facing aft, of course. He doesn't have an ejection seat. Bails out by jettisoning the back half of his turret, then leaning forward and falling out. He's handy back there. Not only does he keep MiGs off our tail, he keeps track of airplanes behind us. We're last in the cell today, so it doesn't matter, but if we were first or second, and the airplane behind us lost its radar, the gunner positions 'em with his radar so they're precisely two thousand feet back and our radar nav tells 'em when to drop their bombs."

"Are they accurate?"

"A good nav team like Rob and Clem Roberts?" Donnie grinned. "They can bomb the spot off an eight ball from thirty thou."

"I mean the second B-52, when they're telling them when to bomb."

"Just as good, Court. Wait'll you see a crew like this working together." Donnie Higgens, confirmed fighter pilot, was grinning from ear to ear. Court followed Higgens forward, slithered over a rubber mat, and lowered a small hinged IP seat behind Higgens, who manned the left, forward ejection seat. At Donnie's right was a center pedestal, filled with eight throttles, a wheel that controlled the flaps and trim, and sundry other levers and control knobs.

Court lugged his backpack parachute into place nearby, then struggled into the awkward shoulder harness and seat belt. Next he pulled on his helmet and plugged it into an oxygen-hose receptacle and intercom socket on a panel on his left.

"You 'bout ready back there?" Donnie called to him over his shoulder.

"Yeah." Court leaned forward to watch him flip switches as Pete Gilland read aloud from a yellow-paged book the size of a pocket novel. As Gilland droned on, they covered eighteen line items for the *Interior* check, 57 for *Before Start Engines,* then 23 more for *Starting Engines* and *Before Taxi* checklists. Donnie finally released brakes and Gold Three waddled down the taxiway behind Gold One and Two. Donnie leaned back toward Court.

"Watch this," he yelled and moved a large control knob on the pedestal. The huge airplane swiveled first left, then right, following the directions of the knob. The 240-ton airplane could be turned, *crabbed* they called it, directly into the wind for takeoff or landing as the eight giant landing-gear wheels tracked straight ahead. That way they could rise from or descend onto the runway without dipping a huge wing and possibly dragging it into the ground.

Court looked out the side window and saw that the ninety-two-foot wings extended well beyond the sides of the taxiway. The outrigger trundled along at the very edge of the asphalt, almost in the grass. At the end of the taxiway they turned onto a concrete apron adjacent to the active runway and held position. Anderson control tower gave takeoff clearance to "Gold cell, with three." Gold Lead trundled onto the runway, ran up engines, and slowly moved into the distance. Gold Two followed suit. Black smoke poured so thickly from the eight jet engines of the bombers that they became obscured from their vision.

Fifteen seconds after Gold Two released brakes, Donnie brought their B-52 into position with great squealing of brakes and hydraulic systems and lined up meticulously with the white center stripe. At sixty seconds Donnie pushed the eight throttles full forward. A foot in front of the throttles on the instrument panel were 32 two-inch gauges, in four neat rows of 8 each, indicating engine performance. As Donnie moved the throttles, the needles on the gauges moved clockwise. The engines roared and the airplane shook violently. Higgens held the throttles until Pete Gilland placed his left hand under the throttles to lock them into position so they wouldn't creep back. Then Donnie released the brakes and they began to creep forward.

The airspeed indicator needle moved with agonizing slowness. Donnie hit switches—water sprayed into each engine to cool the inlet air—engine-pressure ratio increased. The big craft moved a little faster. Court looked out the windscreen at a mile-long rolling dip in the runway. As they started down the long decline, they gained airspeed and the vibration frequency grew.

The airplane reached the bottom and started up the long incline, and the airspeed needle slowed its movement. Higgens calmly called seventy knots, and Clem Roberts, down in the bilge, began timing the roll. A long minute later Clem called, "Coming up on S-one speed."

Gilland said, "S-one."

"Committed," Donnie Higgens replied. Now they had to continue the takeoff, because there wasn't enough runway remaining to stop the giant bomber. Engine failure, a blown tire, or any one of many problems could spell disaster for airplane and crew.

Court noted that the gauges of all systems were in the green as Roberts said, "Coming up on unstick speed."

"S-two," Gilland called out, and Donnie pulled back on the control wheel.

Nothing happened.

An eternity later the bomber rose slightly into the air. There was none of the nose-high climb attitude Court was accustomed to in high-thrust fighters. Then all eight wheels left the pavement at the same time and the giant airplane lifted straight up, much like an elevator.

They were established in their climb, the airplane was pressurized, and the crew had removed helmets and put on headsets. "Want to give it a try?" Donnie asked, pointing to the control wheel. Court nodded. With much contortion, they exchanged seats. Court strapped into the ejection seat and took the controls from Gilland, who dropped his hands into his lap. All went well for the first few minutes until Court tried to make minor heading corrections.

He entered a wing-rocking sequence he couldn't break, then made it worse by trying to catch up and control the unplanned roll movements. As the left wing would go down he'd twist the wheel to the right—sufficient, he thought, to bring the wing back up to level flight. Then, when nothing happened, he'd give it more right wheel, and about that time the left wing would come up and the right wing would start down.

Ho boy! When Court tried centering the controls, nothing

happened, so he gave exaggerated left wheel, and the wing that had dipped low to the right started up and the left one started down. Each oscillation became more exaggerated than the one before, as Court chased the elusive wings-level position. Finally his test pilot training asserted itself—he released the controls and let the big airplane assume its own stability. *It worked.* Then he cautiously took over again and his control movements, while large, were anticipatory of what the big airplane *should* do, not what it was actually doing at the moment. Then he heard the cell leader's high voice on the radio.

"Gold Three, this is Gold Lead. You got . . . *ehh* . . . control problems back there?"

"No sweat, Gold Lead," Donnie radioed back in a jolly voice, "all is well."

"Sorry 'bout that," Court muttered.

Donnie leaned forward in the IP seat. "I want you to try something. Very rapidly give me full left and full right ailerons."

Court frowned. "You kidding me?"

"Nope. I want you to see what happens."

Court rapidly moved the wheel full left, then full right, then back to center. Aside from a barely perceptible wing rock, there was no response.

"Now you know what the spoilers do for you on a bird this big," Donnie said on the intercom to Court.

Court slowly nodded his understanding. Most airplanes' ailerons responded instantly to pilot input, and there was an instant response. The spoilers on the wings did not generate sufficient effect to roll or bank the B-52 quickly. It was a new world for Court, who was accustomed to instant response. By then he had settled down to hold the airplane level and on course as Gilland maneuvered the throttles to keep them at the proper airspeed and the proper distance relative to Gold Two. After an hour of the backbreaking work, Court gratefully yielded the pilot's seat to Donnie.

Three hours later they were north of the Philippine main island of Luzon and were pulling up behind their assigned tanker to refuel. Donnie ordered the crew to buckle up and put on their helmets, as he eased the eight-engined bomber into position underneath the aft end of the KC-135. He had to lower his ejection seat as far as it would go so he could look up and through the clear glass panels over his head.

"I can't believe those inputs," Court said to Donnie over the intercom as he watched him wrestle the wheel from side to side and drag the two inboard throttles back and forth. "And it's smooth up here. You look like you're trying to refuel in a thunderstorm."

"Nothing to it." Donnie grinned. "After a hundred or so tries."

When they were in position, Donnie reached up and hit the switch to open the refueling door, located over Court's head, and they heard the rushing sound of disrupted air flow. Higgens continued his exaggerated control movements, holding the bomber in rock solid position beneath the tanker. There was a loud thump as the boom's probe locked into position, and the boomer flipped a switch to begin transferring fuel.

When Gold Three was filled with 89,000 pounds of jet fuel, the boomer withdrew the probe. Donnie thanked him for the gas and slowly eased his big ship back and down. Within five minutes they were back in formation with Gold One and Two, headed for South Vietnam. Shortly after, they were boring in on the bomb run at 37,000 feet on a perfectly clear day.

Gold One flew at 36,000 feet. Gold Two was staggered slightly right, one mile back and 500 feet higher. Donnie Higgens kept Gold Three aligned slightly left of the leader and one mile aft of Gold Two, at 37,000 feet. Clem Roberts was viewing the two other aircraft on his scope, and crisply advised Donnie to ease forward or back so they precisely maintained the mile separation. Court would have taken a bet that they were not more than ten feet out of position in the cell formation, a feat he would have thought impossible with the airborne behemoth. Donnie periodically grinned back at Court, who realized he was thoroughly enjoying himself.

Gold Two and Three were flying formation directly on Gold Lead's airplane. Merriwell's radar nav would give a countdown, and each ship would release simultaneously. The 324 bombs would fall in a one-by-six-kilometer rectangular pattern onto the jungle seven miles below.

Donnie and Clem Roberts completed their pre-bombing checklist. They waited, with bomb bay doors opened. Gold Lead began the countdown. Court watched as the bombs began raining from the two aircraft before them, but felt little sensation from their own bird. But Clem muttered bombs away, so he assumed they'd also dropped. Immediately thereafter, Donnie cranked the wheel to the right and they followed the other two aircraft in the post-target turn, the PTT.

"Got a problem," Clem announced at the same time the copilot pointed to an amber light on the panel, then turned and pulled a tome the size of a small doghouse from his satchel.

"Our bomb bay doors are still open," Donnie said.

"Roger. I'll try recycling," Clem answered.

"Negative response," Donnie said on the intercom, staring at the lights.

"I heard them come partway closed the first time," Clem said. "When I tried 'em this time there was nothing at all."

The copilot muttered the location of the circuit-breaker panel, and the row and number of the breaker button.

Beep Beep Bentley spoke up. "I'll check them, AC. Am I cleared to unstrap?"

"Roger," Donnie replied.

Court turned and watched as Bentley came forward and worked at a panel in the open space just behind him. He finally plugged in his headset to a receptacle there. "AC, EWO. I found the circuit breaker, but it keeps popping out when I try to reset it."

The copilot continued reading from the huge tome. "There's another circuit breaker back in the crawlway just forward of the bomb bay."

"I know where it is," said Bentley. "Want me to try resetting it?"

Donnie hesitated. If they tried that, he'd have to descend below 10,000 feet and depressurize so the EWO could open the hatch and crawl down the narrow passageway. He'd be hanging there above the open bomb bay doors. "Negative, EWO. Go back to your position and strap in," Donnie said.

He pressed the radio switch on the control wheel. "Gold Lead, Gold Three. We can't get the doors closed."

"Ahhh . . . roger, Gold Three. Did you . . . ehh . . . try recycling?"

"Doesn't work. The circuit breaker is popped and it won't close. There's an electrical problem with the system."

"Ahhh . . . roger . . . ehh . . . stand by." The cell leader went off radio.

"Aww," Beep Beep complained over the intercom. "Couldn't get that idiot to make a decision if you begged him. Notice how he makes that *ehh* high sound when he has to think? He couldn't lead a pack of Cub Scouts to the rest room."

"What's normal in this instance?" Court asked.

"It's not a big problem," Donnie answered, "but they won't want us flying all the way back with the doors hanging open. We'll have to divert to U Tapao and wait there until they fix the door actuators."

"So what's he doing?"

Beep Beep Bentley snorted over the intercom. "Merriwell's calling the command post at Guam so someone else will make the decision. He's a weak dick. That's why Asshole Gartley likes him so much."

A moment later the radio sounded. "Gold Three, Gold One. Go ahead and divert to UTP."

UTP was the designator for U Tapao, the B-52 base on the southern tip of Thailand. It was ninety miles south of Bangkok and had its own sandy beach on the Gulf of Thailand.

1715 Hours Local, Friday 15 December 1972
U Tapao Royal Thai Navy Airfield
Kingdom of Thailand

As they approached the big base in southern Thailand, Donnie had received the forecast that scattered thunderstorms were approaching the U Tapao area. He and Gilland busied themselves studying the letdown procedures and going through the pre-landing checklists. Half an hour later Donnie descended, avoided an ominous thunder-bumper cloud, made a smooth approach, and kissed the tires onto the wet runway.

"I'm impressed," Court told him as they were directed to a parking area, where they were chocked and then shut down engines. As he unstrapped, stretched mightily, and then climbed out and followed Beep Beep down the ladder, he felt as if he'd been shut up in a steamer trunk for a week. He stood under the plane, massaging and moving his arms as Donnie and the crew debriefed the maintenance people. A bus pulled up shortly thereafter and took them to the office of the three-story concrete BOQ. There they were assigned rooms by a bored clerk wearing three stripes on his fatigue sleeves.

The telephone jangled. The command post, calling for Captain Higgens. Donnie spoke for a few minutes, then handed the phone back to the clerk and turned to the others with a grin.

"Tough luck, guys. They say we can't go back right away, that we've got to stay here until the bird's fixed, then fly a mission and take the bird back to the Rock."

"How long?" grunted Beep Beep, who had reverted to being a man of few words.

"That's the terrible part." Donnie's grin widened. "Maintenance says it will be a few days before they get the bird fixed, so to be safe they're not scheduling us until Wednesday morning. And *that* means we've got the next three days off. All we have to do is keep the Command Post informed of where we are." The crew, except for Lieutenant Gilland, gave out a joyous whoop.

"The BX is open twenty-four hours," the clerk said, "if you want to buy any clothes."

"So who's got money?" Gilland said unhappily.

Clem shook his head sadly. "You mean you listen to them when they say you can't take *anything* along on a combat mission?" Gilland frowned.

"You'll learn, son. You'll learn." Roberts asked the rest of them. All had secreted cash in a flight suit pocket. They pooled and provided the copilot with fifty bucks, which in the base exchange and on the Thai economy would go far.

After consultation, three decided to stay on base, two decided to go to the local Riviera called Pattaya Beach, with maybe a short side trip to the massage parlors at Buffalo Junction.

"Let's you and I head up to Bangkok," Donnie said to Court.

"Let me think about it," Court responded in an unsure tone. His last time in Bangkok had ended tragically, when Susan had left her note of farewell.

The crew made a BX run and bought toilet articles and some basic wearing apparel of sport shirts, shorts, bathing suits, and thongs.

When they returned to the BOQ, Donnie again asked Court about going to Bangkok. "Think about it," he said pointedly. "I'll shower, then stop by your room." He grinned and pulled his duckcall from his pocket. "If you agree to come, I'll play a serenade with this."

Court slowly climbed the stairs and walked down the concrete halls to his room, thinking of that time in Bangkok with Susan.

The pleasures they'd shared, the note about her fatal illness, the fact that he had never seen her again. He unlocked the door and walked in the room, switched on the overhead, and sat on the bed.

They had stayed in a terraced penthouse suite overlooking the Chao Phaya River at the Oriental Hotel and had had a week of each other and shared the joys of Bangkok. Then there was that final day when she was gone and all he was left with was the handwritten note that spoke of her love for him, her carcinoma, and that she wanted him to have only the best of memories of her because her time was now so short. His eyes stung as he remembered her last lines.

Fly high and fast, my beloved. And once in a while, when you see the right cloud, think of the girl who loves you so much.

Your Susan

He sat stock-still for a long, tortured moment, then nodded very slowly to himself.

He showered and shaved.

"Let's go to the Command Post before we head out," he told Donnie when he showed up at the door. "I want to call an old buddy of ours up at Udorn and see if he can meet us in Bangkok."

"Glad you decided to come along. You need the time off. What's our friend's name?"

"Toby Parker."

Chapter 23

The seventy-two hours of the President's ultimatum had not yet passed, but only twenty-four hours remained, and thus far Henry Kissinger had received only a terse and insulting note. The President had called in Melvin Laird, the Chairman of the Joint Chiefs of Staff, and Lieutenant General Whisenand. When the three men entered the office, only the President and Bob Haldeman were there. Whitey had in his briefcase the message for which he had waited so long that he could barely concentrate on what was being said.

"There has been no response from the North Vietnamese thus far," Richard Nixon began, his face grim but composed, "and we have received word that there will be none. If anything, they've only intensified their land-grabbing tactics. I have reluctantly decided . . . that we have now reached a point where only the *strongest* reaction will succeed in settling this . . . ah . . . affair."

The Chairman looked on calmly, his narrowed eyes the only indication of the gravity of the moment. "Shall we implement Linebacker Two, sir?"

Nixon nodded. "But, of course not before the full seventy-two hours have passed. You can wait for nightfall in Vietnam, but not more. They must have come to realize that we mean precisely what we say. Any questions?"

"No, sir," Laird and the Chairman echoed.

"Then get on with your preparations."

As the others filed toward the door, Whitey raised his voice. "Mr. President?"

Nixon looked up at him.

"I have just received a decoded transcript of a message from Hanoi. An SR-71 recorded a low-power transmission from the camp radio at Hoa Lo Prison. Caruso has confirmed POW movements to a place the prisoners call Dogpatch."

"Do you have the location yet?"

"We believe it may have something to do with the word 'donkey,' which was also contained in the message. Fort Belvoir is working on it now."

"Mmm. But no specific location yet?"

"I'm convinced we will know very shortly. We also have confirmation from an agent in Hanoi, code name Alfred, who if you will remember is a member of the North Vietnamese government, that the selected prisoners are indeed about to be moved to Russia."

Nixon's face turned to stone.

Whitey continued in a low voice. "I respectfully request we implement Storm Flight, sir."

President Nixon hesitated for only a short pause. He rubbed his eyes as if he were very weary, and muttered two final words: "Go ahead."

By midnight the Joint Targeting Office had triple-checked the target list they'd provided the White House. Thirty-one near Hanoi, nineteen near Haiphong, and fifty-three others.

Whitey had helped to draft the JCS message to CINCPAC (Commander in Chief, Pacific), CINCSAC (Commander in Chief, Strategic Air Command), and subordinate operational commanders, directing them to proceed with planning and preparations for a three-day maximum-effort air strike to begin at 1200 hours, Greenwich Mean Time, on 18 December, 1972. They were to plan to extend operations beyond the third day if so directed.

● ● ●

After the Chairman approved the message for transmission, he asked Whitey to remain. "Before I left the President's office, I overheard you speaking about prisoners of war."

Whitey explained the basics of Storm Flight's Option B, and that the President had given his approval to proceed. He apologized for not keeping the chairman fully up to date while remembering how bureaucratic staffing had threatened to slow everything down to a crawl.

The Chairman looked troubled. "How are you going to get one of our men into Hanoi?"

"I believe we've found a way. I'll need your support, sir." He explained.

Whitey returned to the Sit Room in the basement of the White House at four in the morning. He was haggard and drawn. He drew a fresh cup of coffee and spent thirty minutes having the DAO in Saigon get Lieutenant Colonel Wolfgang X. Lochert to the secure phone. Four a.m. in Washington time was five in the afternoon of the same day in Saigon.

"Lochert, sir."

"It's a go, Wolf. Everyone's on board. Get yourself and your equipment to Uniform, and have Chef go with you as launch chief, as I discussed in my last message. I also just learned that Court Bannister will also be at Uniform. You can use him also, since he's been briefed in on part of the program. Check in with me here when you're ready and I'll handle any final details."

"Yes, sir. Understand we'll use launch site Uniform. Anything else?" His voice was utterly expressionless.

"One last thing. The President said it."

"Yes, sir?"

"Godspeed."

Wolf's voice remained neutral. "Thank you both, sir. Out."

"Out here."

The connection was broken.

2100 Hours Local, Sunday 17 December 1972
Siam Intercontinental Hotel, Bangkok
Kingdom of Thailand

Court, Toby, and Donnie rendezvoused at the inside bar of the Siam Intercontinental Hotel at nine o'clock that evening and decided to make a run on the Cat's Eye, the An An Room, the Montien Hotel, and wind up at the Garden Cafe. Each place was well known for its Filipino band and cruising round-eyed women of all nationalities—out for as much of a good time as the men. Many were stewardesses, but there were also vacationing teachers, retail buyers, executives, and others from all over the world, most of them able to keep the most sophisticated of men interested in something more than their body . . . for at least half an hour.

By one in the morning, Court, Donnie, and Toby, along with four Swedish girls they had latched on to at the Montien, were settled in at the Garden Cafe, listening to a jazz quartet do great things with some vintage Getz. The ladies were schoolteachers from Göteborg; two of whom wanted to bed and spread the "cude" Donnie. The other two had paired off with Court and Toby. All four awaited only an invitation for a nightcap at the pilots' hotel.

Finally it was time, and it required two small blue Thai taxis to get them all back to the Siam Intercontinental. They strode across the broad, carpeted lobby to the desk and took turns asking the clerk for room keys. The clerk smilingly complied, then nodded pleasantly to a man sitting in a chair. As he approached, the pilots saw that he wore the uniform of a technical sergeant in the Air Force.

"Colonel Bannister and Captain Higgens?"

When they said yes, the man in uniform said, "I'm Sergeant Bowan from the Air Police Detachment at U Tapao." He looked at the girls and the clerk, who was leaning forward with interest. "Sirs, can we go someplace and talk?"

Court smiled at the girls, said, "Excuse us for a minute," and led the way to an array of potted palms in a corner of the lobby.

Sergeant Bowan spoke awkwardly. "You gentlemen are to

accompany me back to the base right now. I'll tell you why in the van. We must hurry because I've got to pick up several other officers on the way."

Toby came over to join them, waving a note. "I've been ordered to catch the first Khlong back to Udorn." He looked at the sergeant. "What's up?"

"All I know is there's a big push to get everyone back to the base. And, sirs," he said to Court and Donnie, "would you mind checking out right the fuck *now* so we can hit the road? I'll have the van waiting in front."

The girls and Toby accompanied them to their rooms and helped them pack their meager belongings. Donnie, who had disappeared into his room with his two ladies, took a little longer, but emerged soon enough with a smile on his face. When they hurried outside the front door of the hotel, the van was waiting. Their girls gave Court and Donnie long kisses, then they all waved goodbye as the van quickly pulled away.

"Son of a bitch," Donnie said in awe as he stared out the rear window.

Court looked. Toby was going back into the hotel, his arms about all four girls.

0500 Hours Local, Monday 18 December 1972
U Tapao Royal Thai Navy Airfield
Kingdom of Thailand

It was still morning-dark outside the control tower. Inside, muted light from glowing panels illuminated the air traffic controller. "Park a lousy little T-39 in a B-52 revetment? Must be something special. Look at the sedans headed that way."

"Just do as the command post says," the senior controller growled. "Ours is not to question why."

Yellow ramp lights glistened off the silver-and-white twin-engined executive jet as it taxied into the high-walled, huge revetment normally used to house a B-52. It bobbed to a stop and shut down the left engine. A blue staff car and two security police pickups drew up to the airplane as the door was let down, and a burly man dressed in dark slacks and an off-white guayabera immediately descended. He was handed two bulging parachute bags, one after another. Another man in civilian clothes, a pouch chained to his wrist and wearing a .45 caliber side arm, stepped down carrying a third bag. From the sedan, a husky colonel in a flight suit emerged, walked over and said, "Welcome to U Tapao, Colonel Lochert. I'm Mike Thompson, Director of Intelligence." He nodded to the second man. "You must be Colonel Hostettler."

"Yes, sir," Chef Hostettler replied.

The copilot in a flight suit pulled up the door and the left engine started to spool up. In seconds the plane was taxiing out, red and green nav lights flashing.

Thompson picked up a bag. "Colonel Lochert, if you'll come with me, we'll motor over to the command post. I'm assigned to see that you get whatever you need." As they walked to the sedan, they were enveloped in the hot jet exhaust of a taxiing B-52. "They're taking off on an Arc Light mission," Thompson shouted above the noise.

It was quiet in the small intell room off the main section of the CP. Wolf and Chef sat in chairs next to a battered gray steel desk where Mike Thompson had seated himself. Next to him stood the wing crypto officer, a bespectacled and portly major. The overhead fluorescent shed its merciless light. The Major signed for Chef's pouch and removed a thick brown envelope, from which he extracted a smaller envelope with red bands and the words TOP SECRET—TRINE. He handed it to Thompson, who thumbed open the envelope and silently read the contents, paging through the document. Finally, he whistled and handed it to the crypto officer.

"I guess you gentlemen know," he said to Wolf and Chef, "what's in there."

"We wrote it, sir," Wolf rumbled. "It's our operations plan for Storm Flight."

Thompson sat back and snapped the top paper. "Can't believe it, but I'll set it up. You want to parachute from a B-52 into down-town Hanoi"—he shook his head and made a wide grin—"then so you shall. It will require some modifications to the hatch, but we'll do it."

0945 Hours Local, Monday 18 December 1972
Dogpatch Prisoner of War Camp
Democratic Republic of Vietnam

The numbers of prisoners at secretive Dogpatch had now swollen to forty-six, and it still was not known what their fate was to be. But as Bear Woods and the others crowded about the window of the barracks-cell, they felt they were closer to the truth.

They'd been in the yard, milling about in the sun after the morning meal of rice and bananas, when they'd heard the rumble of vehicles arriving outside the gate of the compound, and turned to stare.

Guards had then brusquely herded them all, including one who was squatting in the shithouse, into the open-bay cell. It was serious when they interrupted a man taking a crap. The guards at Dogpatch might not give a damn about human rights, but they encouraged the men to defecate as often as possible. The stuff was used in the vegetable gardens about the periphery of the compound, and it was held by the women who collected it and the farmers who tended the crops, that American excrement was firmer, richer in nutrient, and therefore better than that from the shitter used by the guards.

There were five big, Soviet-built vehicles, diesel-powered six-by-sixes, and one smaller, box-nosed utility vehicle. They parked in neat rows beside two new wooden buildings a Viet work gang had been scrambling to complete just outside the compound fence, not far from the helicopter pad. One structure was long and low, the other boxlike and constructed with more care. When the vehicles' engines were switched off, one backfired in a loud belch that startled the onlookers. As the men began to dismount, a titter ran through the prisoners. They were all Caucasians and wore dark-green Soviet field uniforms—the drivers, the twenty-odd soldiers with slung rifles who unloaded from the backs of the trucks, and the two officers in the utility vehicle.

"I'll be damned," said the SRO. He turned to the men behind him. "The drivers are wearing black-colored collar flashes and epaulets. Anyone know what that means?"

"Combined arms," piped up a Navy aviator lieutenant who

had been in Intelligence. "They're Soviet Army."

"The officer and the ones carrying the weapons have blue epaulets. What's that?"

"Soviet Air Force."

Bear Woods stared closer, squinting. He shook his head. "Nope. Air Force color's light blue. These guys are wearing royal blue."

"Shit," grumbled the naval aviator, pushing his way through the crowd to peer out.

"What's that mean?" asked the SRO.

"KGB," said Bear Woods, and a queasy feeling began to run through him.

The SRO was staring. "What rank are the officers?"

"One's a *kapitan*. A Russian captain," said the naval aviator. "The other's a *starshiy leytenant,* a senior first lieutenant."

"Wonder what they're here for?" mused a new-guy major.

A *clop-clop* sound was heard from the south, accompanied by a loud whining sound of a jet engine.

They waited expectantly as the big green chopper arrived. The star on the tail was blood red. As the rotors were still whining to a stop, a figure stepped out, then bent over and hurried. The tails of his khaki bush jacket flapped like wings until he was clear of the downdraft.

"I'll be damned," the SRO muttered again.

The Russian Captain was saluting smartly. The fat man who resembled W. C. Fields nodded and arrogantly placed his hands on his hips. They spoke together for a while, then the fat man turned and stared at the building where the Americans were incarcerated.

Chapter 24

Hundreds of aircrew members—pilots, navs, EWOs, and gunners—stood in groups and talked excitedly.

"Jeez, there I was in Satahip working on the railroad and this air policeman . . . "

"Maybe the war's over . . . "

"Hey, we're going home . . . "

"None of the above. We're gonna hit Hanoi . . . "

"Or Moscow . . . "

Court stood with Donnie Higgens, Gilland, Beep Beep Bentley, and the rest of the crew. A thoughtful look crossed Bentley's face. "You don't suppose the war *is* over, do you?"

Court shook his head and made a wry smile. "I really doubt it. What I've been reading about the Paris peace talks doesn't jibe with the Viets giving up so easily."

Another man spoke up. "Yeah, and I just heard all the guys living off-base have been told to move back on-base."

"What about Norwich?" Gilland asked. "Think they'll fly him over here to take the crew?"

Duckcall Donnie Higgens looked pensive.

"Probably not," said Clem Roberts. "They probably need max crews right there at Andy."

A tall colonel in khakis strode out to the podium on the stage and leaned forward to the microphone. "Seats, gentlemen, seats." The logo on the podium read 307th Strategic Wing.

The crowd milled, then sat by crews.

"For you new guys, I'm the DI, the Director of Intelligence for the Wing." Mike Thompson swept his eyes slowly around the room. He was not smiling.

"Uh oh," Bentley whispered, "doesn't look like we're going home."

Thompson took a sip of coffee and adjusted a chart. "If you haven't guessed by now, we're targeted on Hanoi for the next few days, starting tonight."

There was much stirring and movement in the crowd.

"No shit . . . "

"About time . . . "

"Sweet Jesus . . . "

"Hey, I'm due to rotate next week . . . "

"We at U Tapao are on the first wave. Forty-eight birds, which means a big effort. Target folders and wave information will be broken out after this general briefing. We've got a lot of ground to cover, so stay with me." He adjusted the microphone.

"You old heads know this, but you new guys who haven't been up on a Linebacker mission need to have it hammered into the old concrete. The bad guys have three primary ground-to-air defenses that can harm us at the altitudes we fly: SA-2 SAMs, fifty-seven and eighty-five millimeter antiaircraft artillery, and MiGs. For all those weapons, enemy radar searches for us, and if it finds us it then guides the SAMs, AAA, or the interceptors to try to bring us down. Talk to your crew EWOs about how the radars perform their functions. We can defeat these defenses in three ways: by flying where they can't see us, using electronic countermeasures, or using physical force. Hide from 'em, jam 'em, or use ordnance to take 'em out.

"Now, we're so damned big, it's hard to hide. The trick there is to use electronic warfare in such a way that we *can* hide, like have the fighters drop a bunch of chaff in a corridor and fly in the stuff. Sometimes that's easy, sometimes it ain't. Right now the prevailing winds over North Vietnam at our altitude are around a hundred knots, and that means the chaff corridor blows away fast, and *that* means we've got to be smart—know where it's blowing to so we can fly there and hide. That's why you want to listen closely when the weatherman gives the winds aloft.

"We've also got a lot of other ECM support packages here to help us survive." He placed a vu-graph onto the overhead projector.

"And here," the DI said, "is another chart showing other folks trying to help out. We now have better radar and eavesdropping coverage over North Vietnam than ever before." He pulled back the drop-sheet on a board.

"These guys'll tell you what the MiGs are up to and when they're about to attack." The DI pointed from the vu-graph to the briefing board. "Study these two and think of ways to use all that information to your advantage."

"This guy's got his act together," Court said in admiration of the briefer.

" 'Course he does," said Beep Beep. "Before Colonel Thompson got into intelligence, he was a Buff EWO. He and General Johnson at Eighth Air Force have done a lot of planning for this day. You're a tactics guy. Wait'll you see the changes they've made." Beep Beep Bentley was so charged up over the upcoming mission that he'd entirely forgotten to be taciturn. Or perhaps, Court thought, it was because the previous missions had mostly been milk runs, and this one definitely was not.

SECRET

Electronic Counter-Measures Order of Battle

ACFT	Location	Mission
EB-66	RP 5 NVN Orbits	Ingress and egress ECM
EA-3A	Tonkin Gulf	Provide ingress and egress ECM
EA-6A	Hanoi, Haiphong	Radar jamming
EA-6B	Hanoi, Haiphong	Radar jamming
A-7E	Target Area	SAM Suppression
F-4	Target Area	Chaff Corridors
F-105	Target Area	SAM Suppression
F-111	Target Area	Night SAM Suppression
B-52	Target Area	On-board Jamming/Chaff

SECRET

Friendly Air Radar Order of Battle

Call Sign	Platform	Location	Mission
Luzon	EC-135	Orbit over Tonkin Gulf	Radio Relay
Disco	EC-121	Orbits over Tonkin Gulf	Control Friendly Acft
			Decode Enemy Radio Talk
Red Crown	USN CV	Tonkin Gulf	MiG Warning
Teaball	WCC	Nakhon Phanom	Weapons Control Center

Court studied the unveiled board. "Teaball wasn't up and running when I flew F-4s at Ubon. With all the info they provide, our MiG shoot-down ratio ought to go up."

"You fighter guys, always thinking about shooting airplanes down," Bentley quipped.

"You bomber guys, always thinking about burning some country down," Court retorted.

"There are presently more than two hundred MiGs based in North Vietnam," the DI continued. "Almost half are MiG-21s. They're fast and highly maneuverable. You EWOs and gunners keep your eyes out for 'em. The first birds on target tonight will be F-111s hitting three of their airfields, but as of right now they're operating from nine known locations, so you can expect a number of MiGs to be airborne.

"Then there are SAMs, and I expect those to be your biggest headache." The DI placed a negative on the projector—a map of North Vietnam—showing a profusion of bright-red dots. "We know of about four hundred prepared locations, and presently suspect there are as many as two hundred firing batteries for them to play chess games with. They move them around quickly, so we're never sure where they all are. Watch out for them. Begin a slight weave when they're locked on and listen to your EWO. SAM radars are tough to handle. If they know your altitude, they can turn down their gain and send a SAM up your jamming strobes."

Thompson gave a mock sigh then. "I would put up a slide showing antiaircraft gun locations, but *that* vu-graph would be solid red. There are guns about everywhere in the area you are flying to. Fortunately, at your altitude they shouldn't be a big problem. The chaff will screw up their radars, and your EWOs will jam the rest. Triple-A radars aren't that hard to jam."

Colonel Thompson put away his pointer and stepped forward, surveying them.

"Here comes the good part," Beep Beep said.

"Gentlemen, this is the big one. You're going to fly to the most heavily defended area in the world, and I include Moscow and Washington, D.C., in that comparison. But if we are smart—damned smart—we can minimize our losses. That ends the general portion of the briefing. Now let's get down to the specifics of how we're going to fly tonight's missions."

The DI slid out a briefing board and drew back a drop cloth.

A loud murmur went up from the aircrews when they saw the big red arrows pointing to the Hanoi and Haiphong target area.

"As I told you," he said in a deep, resonant voice, "your targets tonight will be in Hanoi." He stepped aside and watched as the operations briefer brought out the raid composition chart.

"There will be three waves in the attack," the operations colonel said, "with approximately four hours between waves. A total of one hundred and twenty-nine B-52s." Another loud murmur and several whistles sounded at the magnitude of the effort. "The first wave will consist of forty-eight aircraft, using airplanes from both Guam and U Tapao. The next wave will be from Anderson only, so we won't be involved. The last will be from both bases again."

The Colonel spoke at length about the 118 aircraft tasked to support their first wave. He finished and nodded to Colonel Thompson. "Mike will now brief some changes in our normal tactics that he's worked hard to come up with to screw up the enemy."

Colonel Thompson took the podium again and pointed to the route chart. "Now listen up hard, because this is indeed new. First, we're attacking at night to preclude optical and visual tracking. We will fly at a base altitude of thirty-six thousand feet, but the various cells will be at varying heights, so the enemy will not be able to discover one and know them all.

"You'll note that all the fragged inbound routes are from the west and northwest, to take advantage of the tailwinds at altitude and coincide with the chaff corridors laid down by the F-4s. The actual axes of the attacks are based on availability of radar bombing aim points, proximity of targets to civilian centers, and, last, enemy defenses. We will have the chaff-layers drop five different corridors into the target area, and we will use all five, so the enemy won't be able to concentrate on a single one."

Court found himself nodding in agreement. This was much better than SAC's old plan of using a single chaff corridor and flying one cell directly behind the next.

"We'll strike all five targets simultaneously, all TOTs at the same time, to add confusion to the enemy's problem. And lastly, we are going to modify the post-target turn procedures because studies show that is our most vulnerable time for enemy radars to burn through our jamming."

Clem Roberts leaned toward Bannister and whispered. "Court, you didn't know, but when you looked over our tactics and then started criticizing and suggesting changes, I forwarded them all to General Johnson at Eighth Air Force, and he shared 'em with Colonel Mike Thompson up there. You'll notice they're implementing some of them."

"So *that's* why you wanted to know." Court was startled, yet pleased at the revelation. He nodded toward the stage. "And they're adding more that I didn't think of. Maybe I shouldn't have complained. Looks like they listened, after all."

"Now, about our formations," the DI continued. "We're going to make some changes there too. First of all we will compress our—"

A major hurried into the auditorium from the side door and made a beeline for the stage. He hurried onto the podium and whispered to Colonel Thompson, whose face betrayed sudden dismay. He made a grim line with his mouth and leaned toward the microphone. "Gentlemen, I've just been told that the tactics you will use will be covered during your wave briefing." Thompson walked from the stage without further ceremony and stalked out the side door, his face a frozen mask of anger and dismay.

The ops Colonel looked at the departing DI without expression, then retook the podium.

"Wonder what that was about?" Donnie Higgens asked.

Beep Beep shook his head. "Nothing good, I'd say. I noticed a couple of our Anderson crews showed up a few minutes ago."

Court was frowning. "I hope they're not going to change what he was saying about using surprise and confusion tactics."

Higgens agreed.

"Now," the ops briefer said when the DI had left the room, "let's talk about the 'press-on' policy for this raid—and this one comes straight from the head shed in Omaha. In simple words, outside of the failure of critical-to-flight systems before takeoff, and loss of engines or water injection during takeoff, there will be no ground aborts." A few crewmembers gave mock groans.

"Once airborne you can lose two engines, all your ECM, and your guns and you will still press on. Only if your flight-stability systems or radios go out will you turn back."

The room grew quiet. "These guys are *serious,*" a crewmember finally breathed in awe.

The Colonel turned off the overhead projector. "You can break up now and draw your target folders. The first-wave briefing will begin—in here—in twenty minutes." He paused, checked a clipboard, and looked over the audience. "Will Captain Higgens and crew report to the podium immediately."

Donnie went first. As soon as he was out of earshot, Robbs, the nav, piped up.

"*And* crew?" he muttered. "Sounds for sure like Norwich isn't going to be in on this."

"I watched Higgens fly," Gilland, the copilot, interjected. "He's as good as I've seen. *Plus* he's seen combat. I'd say we're lucky to have him."

"I'll fly with him," said Beep Beep Bentley.

"We all will," Clem Roberts said with finality.

All but me, Court thought unhappily, for it was unlikely they'd allow passengers to go along for a ride on something as big and dangerous as this.

They pushed through the dispersing crowd and walked toward the podium, where Donnie waited for them. Colonel Mike Thompson came back in through the side door and approached Higgens. His grim look had not changed.

"Captain Higgens," the DI was saying as the others approached, "you and your men from 57101 are going to participate in wave three of tonight's show, in the lead cell with two other B-52Ds that were flown in from Anderson. Ash cell will rendezvous with the tankers over the Gulf of Tonkin, and assume the lead position. You'll coast in with the Anderson birds, and our people from U Tapao will join formation as you enter the chaff corridor."

"How many airplanes in *that* wave?" Donnie asked.

"Fifty-one, the biggest attack of the night. Thirty from Guam and twenty-one from here. Here's your target folder. As I said, you'll be in the first cell in the wave. I don't know which position within the cell. Two other B-52s from Anderson landed here this afternoon, and altogether you will make up Ash cell."

"Ash cell," Donnie repeated, as if memorizing it. He cast Thompson a hopeful look. "Same tactics as you briefed up there?"

Thompson huffed a pained sigh. "A colonel arrived from Anderson with the two B-52s an hour ago, hand-carrying a directive from SAC headquarters. He'll brief you and your guys on what to do up there. That briefing's at 2145 hours, in squadron briefing room number two, next door."

The DI referred to his clipboard and looked at Court. "You must be Lieutenant Colonel Bannister." He gave Court an odd look. "You're also to sit in on the Ash cell briefings."

"I'm flying on the mission?" Court asked hopefully.

"You'll find out everything later, Colonel."

Donnie turned to the crew. "We've got four hours of downtime until the briefing. You guys go on to your BOQ rooms and try to get some sleep. I'll try to pick up on what's going on, then join you over there."

When Higgens located the other Anderson aircraft commanders to try to pick up on what was going on, they could tell him nothing. They didn't know anything except that Colonel Gartley and Lieutenant Colonel Merriwell had come with them, and that Gartley was acting more obnoxious than ever. Donnie finally gave up and went to his own room to try to get a couple of hours of rest. Like the others, he had trouble dropping to sleep with all that adrenaline sloshing about in his system.

1630 Hours Local, Monday 18 December 1972
Main Briefing Room, 432nd Tactical Fighter Wing
Udorn Royal Thai Air Force Base
Kingdom of Thailand

The scene at Udorn was the same as it had been for their colleagues at U Tapao. Scores of fighter pilots and WSOs in flight suits stood around talking with excited words, waving hands and flashing eyes.

"Air Police all over the place. Cleaned out the bar at the Charon in two minutes."

"Same at the Chao Phaya and Intercontinental in Bangkok."

"They got the SAC crews first. Wonder why it took our guys another three hours to start the recall?"

"Maybe we go north again."

"Damn right. That's what this has got to be all about."

"How do you know?"

"They sure as hell wouldn't recall us to tell us the war is over."

Toby Parker, a look of great contentment on his face, stood with Kenichi Tanaka.

"Four Swedes, eh?" Tanaka said.

Toby's face flamed. He had come a long way since his days with Tiffy Berg.

"One more and you'd be a Swedish Ace." Tanaka grinned.

The men fell silent and took their seats as the wing commander walked out onto the briefing stage.

"Gentlemen, this briefing is classified Top Secret." He paused and looked over his men, a curious smile on his lips. "I have the pleasure to tell you . . . we're going back to Pack Six."

A sustained roar of approval went up from the aircrew.

"Shit hot."

"At last."

"Hey, Parker. Maybe now you'll get your fifth MiG. We need another Ace so we can show those Navy pukes a thing or three."

The wingco held up his hands. "One big change. This time the main attraction's not going to be our fighter guys. The President has ordered the B-52s to strike Hanoi. This one's big time. One hundred and twenty-nine of them, in three big waves, and that's only the first night. Our job's to try to protect them."

The room grew silent.

A fighter pilot from Mobile put it best then, summarizing the feelings of the rest of the men. He shook his head with sheer, awed amazement and muttered, "Well, ah'll be gaw-dammed."

The pilots were then split into three groups, to protect the three different waves. The pilots supporting the second and third waves would do their initial planning and immediately go to their quarters for crew rest.

Toby and Ken were selected to support wave number three. They were told they'd be awakened at midnight. Their station time over Hanoi would be at 0345.

2145 Hours Local, Monday 18 December 1972
Squadron Briefing Room,
U Tapao Royal Thai Navy Airfield
Kingdom of Thailand

The two other B-52s from Anderson had arrived at U Tapao in the late afternoon, bringing Colonel Kieffer Gartley, who had hand-carried a directive from SAC headquarters. They, and 57101, would make up Ash cell, which would join the incoming B-52s from Anderson at the refueling tankers near the Philippines, and lead the massive third wave. Clem and Gilland had impressed upon Court that the other two crews were not only good, they were *extremely* good. Both aircraft commanders were majors, but both had won spot promotions to lieutenant colonel.

The three crews sat in the theater-style seats, sipping coffee and talking with one another. The mood was tense because of the upcoming dangerous mission, but the men were thorough professionals and did not appear overly nervous. The other two crews had also sat in on the briefing given by Colonel Thompson, and they, like the men of S-13, had totally agreed with the new tactics. Also, like them, they worried about the changes Gartley had brought from Anderson.

There was a commotion at the door as three men in flight suits entered. Court saw a brigadier general, followed by Colonel Gartley and the ramrod-straight and prim Lieutenant Colonel Merriwell, whose face was very pale. Donnie Higgens called the room to attention.

"At ease," the Brigadier said. His name tag read McBurney. He was the wing commander at U Tapao and, Court smiled to himself, a former operations officer he'd once served under in fighters. "There have been a number of changes in the briefing you heard my people give," McBurney said. He took a breath and glanced at Gartley with a neutral expression. "Please disregard everything that was said by Colonel Thompson. My own people are being told the same thing. I apologize for the confusion, and will leave the remainder of the briefing to your deputy commander for operations." McBurney gave a crisp nod and left the room without further words.

Gartley watched the wing commander leave, his eyes narrowed, then walked to the front of the room and gave the group a smirk and wag of his head. "Seems things got out of hand here. Tactics changes made at the last minute are dangerous . . . damned dangerous. The potential for midairs and accidents would rise dramatically. And . . . there is seldom a need to alter proven tactics. As soon as I heard what they were doing this morning, I telephoned General Austin, and he immediately dispatched a message, which I briefed to our people at Anderson and then hand-delivered here." He glanced about the room. "General Austin knows more about flying combat than *anyone* in this combat theater. We will be flying business as usual, gentlemen, using the same proven tactics which have minimized our losses since they were developed in World War Two. There will be only one ingress route and chaff corridor, a fact I'm sure the fighter people are happy about, and our target times will be staggered, not simultaneous. We will also fly in our standard formations and at normal altitudes, each cell flying in trail, just as we've always done."

Court bit his tongue and tried to repress the flash of anger that surged over him. He could not. Men's lives were being jeopardized. He gained his feet. "May I speak, Colonel?"

Gartley's eyes flashed. "No, you may not." He glared at Court, and a vague flicker of recognition crossed his face before he returned his attention to the group. "I will be wave commander, and will make any required airborne decisions. Lieutenant Colonel Merriwell will be cell commander, and therefore fly in the lead aircraft."

Merriwell turned and cast a nervous smile at the aircrews.

Gartley walked brusquely over to the aircrew lineup for Ash cell which was printed on the blackboard, and gazed, then brusquely wrote numbers 1, 2, and 3 above the crews. S-13 was selected as Ash One.

CREW S-13—AIRCRAFT B-52D 57101

AC Higgens, D. (NMI), CPT	NN Robbs, A. J., CP
CP Gilland, P. B., ILT	EW Bentley, W. B., ILT
RN Roberts, C. H., LTC	AG Slater, E. R., TSGT

Gartley then slashed through Gilland's name. "You're off the mission, Lieutenant." He frowned at Donnie's name as if there were something he should remember about it, finally shook his head, and spoke over his shoulder. "Captain Higgens, you're now copilot. Colonel Merriwell will take the left seat, since he's cell commander. I'll fly in the IP seat as wave commander." He nodded at the wisdom of his changes, then motioned to Merriwell to give his cell briefing and took a seat in the front row.

Merriwell took the podium. When he spoke, his voice came out so low and tremulous that it was difficult to understand. He also injected a periodic squeaking *ehh* sound to his speech.

"Speak up," called an aircraft commander from one of the other crews.

"I . . . *ehh* . . . I said that everything will be pretty . . . *ehh* . . . standard. You're all select crews here, and . . . *ehh* . . . you know wh-what to do. We'll fly the standard route inbound, and . . . *ehh* . . . sh-shouldn't have any surprises."

"Jesus," groaned Beep Beep. He stood and waved an arm. "I'm going next door to get the latest threat intelligence."

Merriwell nodded. "Yes, uh, that . . . *ehh* . . . sounds like a good—"

"Me too," the EWOs from the other two crews chimed in, and followed Bentley from the room.

Clem Roberts leaned toward Court. "Since there'll be no changes in tactics, the EWOs know the entire problem of crew survival is going to fall on them and the gunners."

Merriwell was going on about how the pilots should hold their bombers utterly straight and level throughout the last four minutes of the attack, from the initial point to the target, so the RNs would be sure to have good target pictures and good bombs.

Court could stand it no longer. He gained his feet and shook his head. "No! You can't fly straight and level for that long and get away with it. I know. I've been there."

Merriwell's jaw drooped at the rude intrusion.

Gartley immediately stood and turned, then glared at Court. His frown deepened. Recognition and remembrance flooded across his face and he whispered, "Bannister."

Court doggedly continued. "I can understand holding the aircraft steady for the final thirty seconds before bomb release so the gyros will be stable, but four minutes would be suicidal."

Merriwell swallowed. "Then perhaps—"

"Out!" Gartley shrieked, staring at Court and pointing at the door. "You are not part of this briefing, or even on a crew. You are simply a troublemaker. Out!"

Court felt his jaw muscles working in his rage, but as much as he would have liked to walk forward and deck the red-faced, angry man before him, he turned and slowly made his way down the aisle. This wasn't the Air Force, this was mayhem.

"Colonel Gartley," he heard Roberts say behind him. "Lieutenant Colonel Bannister is correct. We don't need four minutes. We do that over South Vietnam, but that's a low-threat area, and I believe if you read the general war plans, they only call for thirty seconds of stabilization before release in a high-threat area."

An RN from another crew stood and added his agreement.

This time Gartley brusquely disagreed. "I do not care what is in some disassociated war plan. We will fly as we have practiced on the Arc Lights, and that means we hold the aircraft perfectly straight and level from the IP to the target. If any of you pilots should dare to move the aircraft even slightly during that period, and endanger innocent civilians, I will *personally* see to it that you are court-martialed . . . and these are General Austin's orders."

The RNs sat back down. No one else argued.

"You may proceed with the briefing," Gartley told Merriwell.

The door before Court opened and General McBurney strode in, with Colonel Mike Thompson at his side.

"Colonel," the General asked Merriwell in a loud voice, "how much longer do you have with your cell briefing?"

"We . . . we've still got . . . *ehh* . . . weather to cover." Merriwell's voice was even more tremulous. Gartley's eyes were narrowed suspiciously as he stared at the intruders.

"You can get that later, just before takeoff. We're going to have to interrupt for a few minutes here." He motioned to Thompson, who raised his own voice.

"We'll need to speak with Colonel Gartley, as well as the crew of the lead aircraft in your cell." He looked at Court. "And you as well, Colonel Bannister."

Captain Robbs hurried out to retrieve Bentley from the intelligence section next door. Then Gartley, the puzzled crew, and Court trooped behind McBurney and Thompson out the door and down the hall to a briefing room guarded by two air policemen.

They crowded in and saw two men in civilian clothes standing beside a blackboard. Brigadier General McBurney took up a position against the far wall.

Court's mouth curved into a welcoming grin as he recognized Chef Hostettler and Wolf Lochert.

2215 Hours Local, Monday 18 December 1972
Crew Briefing Room, U Tapao Royal Thai Navy Airfield
Kingdom of Thailand

Colonel Mike Thompson introduced Wolf and Chef to Crew S-13 as Mr. White and Mr. Jones. Hostettler immediately launched into his spiel.

"Gentlemen, the operation we're about to discuss is of a higher classification than any of you possess." He looked at the serious faces of the crew staring at him, smiled, and said, "Therefore, this briefing and what happens on this mission never took place." He waited a moment. "You are to take Mr. White along with you to Hanoi, but you won't bring him back. He will not be listed on flight orders nor on any manifest."

There was dead silence as the crewmen digested the information. Court wondered why they'd brought him in.

Colonel Kieffer Gartley spoke, his tone imperial. "*Mister* Jones, why on *my* airplane?"

"Because, Colonel," Hostettler said, "yours is the lead ship in the wave, and you're striking the right target at the proper time. If you haven't guessed, it was arranged that way for this purpose. What is your target and TOT?"

Gartley frowned at the demanding tone. "Those are highly classified."

"Kieffer, these gentlemen are cleared for everything you have and then some," McBurney said in a soft voice.

Gartley gave Mr. Jones a hostile look, then sighed and nodded. "Our target is the Hanoi railroad siding. Time over target is oh four hundred hours."

Hostettler looked at Wolf.

"Move it up five minutes," he said in his deep voice.

"Your new time over target is zero three fifty-five."

"That's ridiculous! You can't—"

"Yes they can, Kieffer," said General McBurney. "Consider it changed," he said to Hostettler. "I'll notify the proper people for the change in scheduling."

Gartley almost glared at McBurney until he remembered the difference in rank. He regarded Hostettler. "I should think you'd want your man to use the last ship in the wave, to avoid falling bombs."

"We chose the lead ship because of the diversion created by the wave's bombing, so their attention will be focused on other things and not Mr. White. He'll be well off to the side of the bombs." Hostettler quickly drew a cross-section of the wave on the blackboard. "Here we have the cells of the third wave. Number two and three planes in each cell will be one mile in trail, each stacked up five hundred feet behind the plane in front." He held up a strip map. "This is a copy from your target folder of the final run-in on the Hanoi railroad yard." Chef placed a forefinger at a point midway on the strip map. "There is a four-minute period between your turn over the initial point and bombs away over the target. Mr. White will exit the plane here, two minutes after the turn and one minute before the bomb bay doors open. Your radar navigator will give him the go sign."

Clem Roberts took the strip map from him and examined it. Finally he nodded.

"*Before* the doors open?" Higgens said. "Why not jump from the bomb bay?"

"Can't. The door from the crew compartment to the bomb bay is too small for Mr. White in his antiexposure suit and parachute. He'll go out the hatch beneath the navigator at the bottom of the forward crew compartment."

"You can't open that hatch in flight," Robbs said. He was correct. The hatch beneath his seat swung down and forward, so the slipstream would keep it forced closed in flight.

"We've got maintenance installing a modified door right now. This one has a special three-by-three-and-a-half plug that fits in the hatch, which can be pulled up and back in flight. Mr. White will arrange his equipment over his body in such a way he can get out without a problem."

"I don't like *any* of this," Gartley said. "I don't know why you want to do this and I don't think you can make it, but in any case I *am* not going to allow this man on my aircraft."

"I agree," Lieutenant Colonel Merriwell said in a more cautious tone.

McBurney pushed forward from his slouched position against the wall. "Kieffer," he said, ignoring Merriwell, "will you come outside with me for a moment?" Without waiting for an answer, he stepped out the door.

Gartley walked stiffly out the door behind the General, who turned and said, "Look, it doesn't make any difference *what* you think. Mr. White is going on your airplane."

Gartley drew himself up. "General McBurney, *I* am wave commander and *I* decide who or what goes on *my* raid."

McBurney made a low chuckle. "Kieffer, you are a true pain in the ass, and I'm getting a perverse sort of satisfaction from this little scene. Now, if you wish to *remain* as wave commander, you will do as Jones and White request. They both carry a paper signed by the highest authority—and by that I mean someone who can tell the JCS and CINCSAC what to do and how to do it. So you will do precisely as they say or you will likely not only be relieved of duty, but wind up as commissary inventory officer in Thule, Greenland. Do you understand?"

Gartley was suddenly extremely uneasy. He swallowed with some difficulty. "Well, yes, sir, since you put it that way. I only meant—"

"I don't care *what* you meant. I also have to follow orders or you wouldn't be wave commander. I know you, Kieffer, and I personally wouldn't trust you to lead a kiddy-car parade. But you're from another unit, and seem to have General Austin and your wing commander buffaloed." He started for the door to the briefing room, then paused. "I notice you aren't even flying the aircraft—you're leaving that to Merriwell and Higgens." He cocked his head thoughtfully then. "Probably just as well, come to think of it."

McBurney and Gartley reentered the room and Hostettler picked up the briefing as if nothing had happened. "There are technical details we need to go over. One is that the aircraft will have to be depressurized so Mr. White can open the plug in the hatch prior to leaving, and you may have difficulty closing it. That means you must ensure your oxygen system is full and that you have extra walk-around bottles in the event of problems. Mr. White will use aircraft oxygen before he exits, then switch to the two bailout bottles he has attached to his rig." He looked around. "Now, you men are probably wondering who we are and why Mr. White wants to visit Hanoi, but I'm sure you'll understand that I can't tell any of that. And . . . if you're shot down and captured, I hope you remain as closemouthed." The crewmembers made small nods.

Hostettler looked at Court. "Although I am the official launch officer for Mr. White, I'll be turning my job over to Colonel Bannister when you board the aircraft. That will give him the same level of authority I presently exercise. He will fly on your mission with you."

Higgens grinned, Merriwell frowned, and Gartley made a guttural croaking sound in his throat, as if he might strangle. He opened his mouth to argue, glanced briefly at McBurney, and subsided, reverting to hostile glares.

Hostettler nodded. "Court Bannister has a hell of a lot more time than I do wearing an oxygen mask in an unpressurized aircraft. Further, I am not a pilot and have never been over Hanoi. Nor am I jump-qualified. Colonel Bannister has done all of that. You never know, his experiences might prove useful. At any rate, he will go along and make sure that Mr. White is dropped off on time and at the proper location, and I will debrief him after you've landed."

"I don't know," Merriwell tried, in a valiant attempt to help Gartley, who was still glaring daggers at Court. "There simply isn't . . . *ehh* . . . enough room for all of us."

"Colonel," Brigadier General McBurney said, "I am increasingly impatient with the negative attitudes in this room. I don't know about you people on the Rock, but we at U Tapao have a can-do attitude. Just as I advised these gentlemen, Colonel Gartley will sit in the instructor pilot's seat behind the pilot, Colonel Bannister will occupy the instructor's seat next to the EWO, and Mr. White will sit down below in the instructor navigator seat. Now, if you wish to retain your position as the aircraft commander of the lead ship in this wave, I suggest you cooperate."

"Yes, sir, sorry, sir," Merriwell stammered. "We'll make it." He glanced at Gartley, who remained tight-lipped.

"About that negative attitude, General," Clem Roberts said in a quiet voice. "Mr. White doesn't have to worry one bit about this crew getting him to the right place and out the door at the right time. If anyone can do it, we can."

"Damn right," muttered Beep Beep Bentley.

"I agree," said Donnie Higgens, fighting a powerful impulse to pull out his duckcall and make a loud, flatulent noise at Gartley and Merriwell.

McBurney couldn't resist a smile. "Sorry 'bout that, guys. I think you're probably right."

0115 Hours Local, Tuesday 19 December 1972 Main Briefing Room, 432nd Tactical Fighter Wing Udorn Royal Thai Air Force Base Kingdom of Thailand

Toby Parker and Ken Tanaka had briefed their flights together. Toby was leading Alamo, a flight of four F-4Es, and Ken was leading four more with the call sign Zippo. The wing commander had appointed Toby as MiG-CAP leader for the obvious reason that he wanted him to get first crack at the MiGs. It was a long-standing unofficial rule that when a pilot reached the threshold count of four enemy aircraft shot down, his commander would try to feed him the fifth. Toby was summing up their mission.

"We are the only two MiG combat patrol flights from this wing. We don't have experience in night MiG-CAP, so much as I hate to do it, we'll have to talk to each other once we are in the MiG-CAP area. Until then I want radio silence, and everyone will try to stay together, using their radars. We'll go into a racetrack between the MiG force and the bombers. And you backseaters are the most important guys on this mission. Without your radar eyes, we frontseaters are blind. Any questions or comments?"

"Yeah," Tanaka said, "one comment."

The others looked at Ken, for his experience and guidance were invaluable.

He nodded sagely. "Remember, night owls never wear galoshes at noon."

Chapter 25

The big ship had been leader of the three–B-52 congo line that lumbered out to the runway at U Tapao, eased all eight throttles forward, and disappeared into the dark sky. Throughout the night, people in the simple fishing villages for miles around had heard the roaring of the heavy bombers as they'd cleaved the black night air, clawing for altitude with their bellies full of bombs. The Guam Queen was one of those.

Colonel Gartley had remained uncommonly quiet during start-engine, taxi, and takeoff. As they'd leveled at 30,000 feet, Merriwell instructed the crewmembers to switch their oxygen-panel settings. Since part of the mission would be made in a depressurized state, they would pre-breathe 100 percent oxygen. If they did not, when the hatch-plug was opened, nitrogen would quickly form in their bloodstreams and collect in their elbows and other joints, causing excruciating pain. Only the gunner, Sergeant Slater, in his private rear-turret compartment, was exempt from the pre-breathing rule. The other precaution was that they all wore heavyweight flight clothing because with the hatch-plug open at 37,000 feet they would be exposed to the

415

outside, minus-50-degree temperatures. Mr. White did not have to adhere to that rule, for soon after crawling aboard, Court had helped him don an ungodly-looking contraption called an antiexposure suit (experimental), contrived by the Air Force's Special Projects Office.

They leveled six miles above the earth, in moonlight so bright it made a smooth white glacier of the cloud layer beneath. The pilots of the aircraft behind them saw the fat condensation trails from the jet engines etch the dark sky with white billows which were several miles long and hundreds of feet wide. Radio silence prevented them from commenting on the hazards of such beauty, but that didn't stop Sergeant Slater from coming up on the intercom of Ash One.

"Jesus Christ, but those cons are bright."

No one answered for a moment. The navigators were looking for the distant tankers on their long-range radar, and the EWO was studying the jumble of enemy radar signals emanating far north of them. He'd commented that the other bombing raids had stirred them into a frenzy.

Higgens waited for Merriwell to say something, then finally took the initiative. "Guns, Copilot, keep us advised about the contrails."

"Roger. Cons won't do the bastards much good, though," Slater continued. "They can't see up through the solid over-cast."

"Unless they're MiGs," Higgens said. "Let us know if we're still laying contrails as we approach the target."

Ash cell made their rendezvous with the tanker orbiting west of Luzon on time, and dropped off with full tanks, wallowing their way back westward, now with twenty-nine heavy bombers behind them in a fifty-mile tail. One mile between cell members—three miles between cells—all flying westward toward their individual fates. The tail would grow longer when they were joined by the twenty-one bombers from U Tapao as they approached the North Vietnamese coast and turned into the chaff corridor.

In the bottom part of the forward crew compartment of Ash One, down the ladder and behind Al Robbs and Clem Roberts, who were seated at their green-glowing consoles, Wolf Lochert sat on the floor, bathed in the red light of passageway lamps, checking his equipment one last time.

His first layer of garments was civilian black pants and white shirt. Next came an electrically heated jump suit to protect him from the cold. During flight it was heated by aircraft power. Once he leaped into the darkness, a battery pack would take over the task. His outer garment was a black canvas, billowy affair, designed to provide camouflage as well as a certain amount of stabilization as he assumed the free-fall position. In his backpack was the odd square, silk parachute, the same one he'd tested. It was also dyed black, and would provide glide speeds of up to twenty-five miles per hour. On Wolf's chest, attached to his reserve chute, were several battery-powered, red-lit instruments that provided altitude, heading, and countdown time. He could not open his chute at 37,000 feet, the altitude to which they were now climbing, and from which they would bomb. His forward speed would be too great. He had to stabilize in both position and speed. He'd set the AOD (Automatic Opening Device) to 24,000 feet.

Also on the instrument panel was a dial with a needle which would point toward the powerful Radio Hanoi transmitter. He would not be going near there, for that was the target of the twenty-one bombers sent from U Tapao. But Wolf had calculated the heading from the Radio Hanoi tower to his drop zone, and would use it to navigate in the blackness. There would also be a small, dim, green-colored signal light blinking in the drop zone.

On his head Wolf wore a thick leather cap that looked like a World War II flying helmet. Because of its design, the men of the Special Forces referred to it as a bunny helmet. Attached to the helmet was an oxygen mask, and a face plate so large that no part of his skin would be exposed to the icy blast. He was currently plugged into the ship's oxygen and intercom systems as well as to aircraft power to preheat the suit. Everything seemed to be working. He carried two small oxygen bailout bottles secured to his right side for his descent. The hatch-plug was closed and would remain so until one minute before the drop.

Clem eyeballed the landmass radar return. "AC, Radar, three minutes to checkpoint alpha."

"Roger." Merriwell's voice wavered, but it seemed no worse than it had been throughout the flight, and he'd done a good enough job with the air refueling. Maybe he had settled down.

When they'd first approached the tanker, Colonel Gartley had called the lead cell of the bombers approaching from Guam to ensure everyone was on time. Since then he'd not uttered a word. There had been periodic harsh, ragged breathing sounds over the intercom, and Clem believed they came from that source.

"AC, EWO, we've got three distant SAM radars and a GCI up north of us," muttered Beep Beep. "My gear checks out okay."

"Roger," Merriwell replied. His voice had still not changed.

"SAMs?" came a trembling voice.

"They're no threat," muttered Bentley. "That was just an equipment check to make sure the receiver's working, Colonel."

There was no response from Gartley.

"AC, Radar, we'll be turning in one minute," Clem said, leaning forward toward the big radarscope, as he did when he became intent on his work. They were now approaching the first turn point, which would take them toward a second turn point, and then the initial point (IP), where the bomb run would begin. This turn was critical, so they'd be properly lined up to enter the chaff corridor. It was also the rendezvous point for the twenty-one B-52s from U Tapao.

As they approached the turn, the lead U Tapao bird called the wave commander. "Ash Leader, Ruby One, we've got you at checkpoint alpha."

Gartley did not answer. After a full minute, when they were well into the turn, Donnie Higgens' voice sounded over the radio. "Roger Ruby One, Ash is at alpha."

They crossed the coast and continued toward the second turnpoint. "AC, Radar. We're entering the chaff corridor. Six minutes to turn point bravo."

Merriwell muttered something unintelligible. A few minutes later Clem ordered the second turn, and he complied. They rolled out, now headed for Route Pack Six, the deadliest and most heavily defended area in the world.

"AC, Radar. Seven minutes to the initial point," Clem Roberts grunted over the intercom. He was alternately eyeing the radar and map, and clutched his stopwatch. "We're still in the chaff corridor."

"AC, EWO, we've got a sweeping Firecan triple-A radar directly ahead." Beep Beep Bentley's voice was distinct and matter-of-fact.

Upstairs and in the nose of the bird, Lieutenant Colonel Merriwell rogered and hunkered lower in his seat, wondering what it was like to be shot at. He flexed his fingers on the control yoke and felt an overwhelming desire to urinate. He swallowed twice and calmed himself by reviewing in his mind the Before Initial Point checklist.

Captain Donnie Higgens periodically looked over at the aircraft commander, waiting for him to respond to the EWO's call. Finally he yanked his duckcall from the elongated left sleeve pocket and pulled down his oxygen mask, which while on a bomb run was in violation of every known regulation, and managed a single, strong, and very loud quack. He jammed the mask back to his face, latched it, then pressed the intercom switch. His voice emerged as clearly and calmly as if he were ordering a drink at the club. "Beeper, you can give us countermeasures anytime, old buddy." Because neither Gartley nor Merriwell had been shot at, it escaped them that they needed to clear the EWO to activate countermeasures. ECM wasn't necessary on Arc Light missions, since no enemy radars tracked them there. Here ECM was the one thing most likely to save their collective lives. Donnie then began going through the Before Initial Point checklist, keeping his voice light. Clem responded readily as they set up for the attack.

"Five minutes to IP," Clem announced. "Time to begin depressurizing."

"Roger," said Merriwell, finding his tongue. "Depressurizing to . . . *ehh* . . . twenty thousand feet."

Ears popped as the atmospheric pressure inside the compartment was reduced to that which would be found at 20,000 feet in the air.

Colonel Kieffer Gartley heard the timing count, felt the pressure inside his eardrums increase, and a wave of terror swept over him. He had not flown in World War II, and had successfully avoided combat in Korea, and never during his one hundred Arc Light missions had he been shot at—at least not that he'd *known* about. Yet up ahead he could see bright explosions of antiaircraft-artillery rounds. It did not matter that the few brilliant bursts were going off several thousand feet below their altitude.

"Four minutes to the IP."

Roberts and Robbs worked their instruments steadily and might have felt twinges of apprehension had they not been so preoccupied with their well-rehearsed duet.

Beep Beep Bentley hunched over his ALR-20 scope, eyeing the enemy radar signals, which rose and fell, flipping jammer switches, and moving dials so the jamming noise covered them.

Slater sat wide-eyed and alert in the tail turret, intently scanning the dark sky, guns and radar on and ready.

Wolf Lochert heard the four-minute count and prepared himself for the drop.

His launch officer, Court Bannister, lifted the seat next to Bentley back into the stowed position, disconnected from his panel, and descended the ladder to the bottom compartment. He had only thirty seconds to get back on oxygen before he would begin to lose consciousness. His oxygen hose and intercom cord dangled free until he deftly reconnected to twenty-five-foot hose and cord extensions at the spare station belowdecks. He was glad for the movement, the feeling of being able to do something. A fighter pilot, accustomed to being able to view the world about him, was not comfortable shut up in an airborne closet, even if the wingspan was 185 feet. He switched on more red dome lamps for better visibility.

"AC, Radar, we're at the edge of the chaff corridor. It's drifted too far to the east."

Captain Beep Beep Bentley watched the sweeping search signals on his screen from the enemy radar, then studied two new, steady ones. "Pilot, EWO. We've got two tracking SAM radars and we're being scanned by GCI." He quickly adjusted dials to feed noisy energy onto the proper frequencies to try to blind the enemy radarscopes. More radars began to rise and fall on the scope. "We've got eight threat signals and I've only got six jammers to cover them," he said.

"Well, do something, do something," Gartley shouted into his mask. "Where's the chaff? Get in the chaff!" His voice became strangled with emotion.

No one answered. It wasn't worth the effort. If they returned to the chaff corridor they would no longer be headed toward the target. The chaff spread by the F-4s had been blown away by the strong winds.

"*Visual SAMs, Visual SAMs, five o'clock,*" Slater yelled into his mike.

Court felt his bowels tighten. He'd seen and dodged too many SAMs not to feel the involuntary stomach jump that accompanied each one. *Thank God Donnie's up there,* he thought as he bent over Wolf and helped him stand beside the still-closed hatch and make final preparations for the jump.

"AC, EWO," said Bentley in his businesslike voice, "disregard the SAMs coming up at five o'clock—they're not locked onto us. Oh, oh, another SAM launch, eleven o'clock, three rings and he's locked up. I'm jamming, but you better start your TTR."

Merriwell began to move the big bomber in a weaving motion called the Target Tracking Radar maneuver, similar but much more ponderous than the random jinking of a fighter.

"AC, Nav, two minutes to IP," said Captain Robbs. Clem was busy picking the target out of the mishmash on his radarscope.

The pilots' cockpit lit up like daylight as the rocket motor of one of the eleven o'clock SAMs tore by the left side of the B-52, but thankfully didn't explode. A muffled boom sounded as the second one detonated at their eleven o'clock, and there was a simultaneous patter, as of BBs on a wall. The left wing rocked up.

Merriwell made no move, so Donnie grabbed the controls and leveled the big craft. When Merriwell still didn't speak, Donnie continued to fly the bird. "Okay, guys, give me a damage report. None up here. Instruments OK . . . oh oh, losing number-one engine, but that's no big deal. Gimme your damage, guys."

"EWO, none, systems okay."

"Nav, okay."

"Radar, okay."

"Guns, okay."

Donnie poked Merriwell and pointed. "We should shut down number one. All the gauges are zeroed out. No fire." When Merriwell was slow to react, Donnie pulled back the throttle of the leftmost of the eight engines and shut off the fuel.

Merriwell shook himself, adjusted his oxygen mask, and looked over at Donnie—as if he'd emerged from a deep sleep. He squirmed to look over his shoulder at Colonel Gartley. "You okay, sir?" he asked on intercom. There was no response, although Gartley was crouched into a ball and making odd motions with his hands. Merriwell looked back at Donnie. "I'm okay now. I'll take it."

"Court, how're you and Mr. White doing down there?" Donnie asked over intercom.

"Everything's fine here."

"Pilot, Nav, forty-five to the IP." Forty-five seconds to the initial point, where the airplane would make its final adjustment turn into the four-minute bomb run. Clem Roberts was carefully comparing photos showing predicted radar returns with the actual returns on his scope. He and Robbs then activated the systems, one by one, to tie them into the bombing computer.

"Guns, searching." Slater had set his fire control system to perform a preprogrammed radar search of the sky behind them. He saw the blips of the B-52s in the cell behind them on his five-inch screen. Then a new blip appeared, moving in rapidly from the side. He punched his mike button. *"Oh, shit . . .* something's back there."

"AC, we're approaching the IP," Roberts said in a mechanical tone, as if they were on a practice radar bombing run back in Michigan. Clem slewed and positioned electronic crosshairs over the radar return he knew to be the target, at the upper right side of his scope. The crosshair input provided range and heading to the bomb computer. "Ready . . . *now.* Start your turn."

"Turning right," Merriwell said, voice calmer now, "to zero eight five degrees." His eyes were glued to an instrument on the panel before him, the FCI, Flight Command Indicator. Its needles were driven by the computer and indicated direction to target.

Clem Roberts continued to fine-tune the crosshairs. Their input, along with drift, temperature, altitude, ground speed, and pre-computed bomb ballistics, would provide a precise release point for the bombs. The system was so automated that the computer would even open the bomb bay doors before tripping the bomb release, then close them afterward.

Merriwell held the aircraft in the turn, then rolled out on the 085 heading. "What you got, Guns?" he asked. His voice was calmer now than it had been at any time on the mission. He was holding the aircraft rigidly straight and level, as he'd briefed he would do.

"Two blips, wide at five o'clock, going away now . . . *Uh oh,* visual SAM seven o'clock . . . and there's another one."

"I got it," Beep Beep Bentley said. "We're jamming and dropping self-protection chaff."

"AC, Nav," said Captain Robbs. "Time to complete depressurization."

"Roger. Watch your ears." The pressure difference between the inside of the forward compartment and outside air was zeroed. The oxygen regulators sensed the change and began forcing oxygen into their lungs in a process called pressure-breathing, making it difficult to talk against the constant oxygen flow. When you did so, you had to speak in small bursts.

"AC, Radar, gimme . . . three more degrees left and . . . hold it. We've got very . . . little drift, but there's . . . more than a hundred knots . . . of tailwind. Hear that . . . Mr. White?"

"Thanks," Wolf replied. That much tailwind would indeed have made a difference if they'd not been forewarned by the weatherman before takeoff, and adjusted his jump-timing schedule accordingly.

Merriwell rolled out exactly on track, as indicated by the FCI.

"Very nice, very nice," Roberts said. "Okay, Colonel Bannister, thirty . . . seconds before Mr. White . . . steps out. Hatch open."

"Roger," Court answered, moving to the hatch and kneeling.

Wolf heard the call, unplugged from aircraft power, intercom, and oxygen, and pulled a small lanyard with a tiny wooden knob to start the flow from his self-contained oxygen bottle. He stood and adjusted the kit bag strapped to his thighs in such a way that it hung between his legs, then slowly waddled to the hatch.

Court, on his knees and bent forward, released two clasps and cracked the hatch-plug open. He swung the plug off its hinges and lifted it free. The noise was terrific.

"What's going on?" Gartley screamed, unheard. He hadn't been able to speak with the others since the SAM bursts, when he'd inadvertently unplugged his intercom cord as he'd cringed and thrashed wildly about. The sound of the opened hatch added to his panic.

Wolf positioned himself over the hatch, checked the instrument panel on his parachute one last time, and glued his eyes on Court. He was crouched, facing aft, and couldn't see the timing signal from Roberts.

Court looked at the giant swathed in high-altitude clothes, face made monster by faceplate and oxygen mask and hose running to oxygen bottle. He wondered at the internal strength that allowed this man to jump into the night to make a landing in downtown Hanoi. The jump itself was something most crewmembers would do in an emergency situation, but to do so deliberately, and to land in Hanoi *intentionally,* was something which took extraordinary courage.

Court's eyes were then drawn to Clem Roberts, who gave him a countdown with his gloved fingers. Court repeated the one-second intervals with his own fingers so Wolf could see. It came to zero and he was gone, dropped out the hatch-plug so fast he seemed to vanish before Court's eyes.

Court had bent to place the plug back into position when the next SAM hit. The explosion made a tremendous clanging sound, like something heard in a locomotive-repair shop, and blew him sideways against the aft bulkhead.

Upstairs, shards of cold-rolled steel ripped through the cockpit from top left to the bottom right, tearing away the left quarter panel from Merriwell's window, as well as his throat and face. They slashed into the center pedestal and opened an artery in Donnie Higgens' left leg.

Frigid air blasted through the broken window, whipping a great gust of glass and debris down onto the IP position, where Colonel Kieffer Gartley had crouched and whimpered. The storm of debris cracked his helmet visor, ripped the left sleeve of his heavy coveralls, and tumbled him back six feet, to settle beside Bentley's EWO position. He slid partway into the opening over the lower compartment. Shrieking and confused, he looked down and saw a crumpled body by the aft bulkhead, and then—the opened hatch-plug. His mind gave way to basic survival instincts, and without conscious thought he clawed his way headfirst down the ladder, moaning and screaming, fell headlong onto the corrugated metal floor, then scrambled forth and unhesitatingly flung himself through the open hatch-plug into the frigid night air. His screams were immediately muted by the blast. In a daze nearby, Court watched the spectacle of Gartley diving through the still-gaping, black hole.

Kieffer Gartley's body tumbled and twisted through the mind-numbing cold air. He was out, and now had only one thought . . . to open the parachute. He screeched and clawed at the front of his harness, searching for the D-ring. He tumbled and spun. The forward motion of his body slowed and he fell more in a downward course, through thirty, then twenty-five, then twenty thousand feet, and was losing the final vestige of consciousness from lack of oxygen. By now the fingertips of both gloved hands were bloody, as he'd torn away his nails scratching and clawing for the ripcord. At eighteen thousand feet a thumb hooked the D-ring and his parachute opened with paralyzing shock, momentarily stunning him. When he came to, he was above the overcast, swinging in the chute, gasping for air. He saw several large round glows in the clouds from the missile rocket motors as they shot up through the layers. He was whimpering as one ring grew larger, larger yet, and he heard an express train sound—the missile burst through the clouds roaring its rocket fury and tore through Gartley's parachute as it sped to its rendezvous with a bomber. Kieffer Gartley's cry was lost in the night as he fell three miles to the earth, the shredded parachute fluttering like a ragged flag in a gale.

Wolf Lochert held his spread-eagle position and, by slight body movements, steered away from the bomber stream as he fell, the wind loud as it rustled through the loose canvas overalls. The B-52's true airspeed had been 360 knots, but due to the tailwind their actual speed over the ground was 465 knots, which provided much potential for error. He oriented himself to the Hanoi radio signal and commenced looking down at the faint glow of the city through the undercast. For reasons known only to the North Vietnamese, Hanoi Radio never went off the air during a raid. There was a single hole in the cloud coverage, and there he saw many lights, and thought that their blackout procedures must be very poor. He checked his compass, then his altimeter, and again the position of Radio Hanoi, and realized that the strong wind had carried him even farther east than anticipated. Approaching 24,000 feet, he switched off the AOD to further delay the parachute opening, and angled his free-fall farther toward the west. When he felt he was back on the glide track, he deployed his parachute, at 18,000 feet and in the midst of the cloud cover. He felt the comforting pull of the canopy opening, and settled into the harness as he grasped the toggles on the risers.

The oxygen from the first bottle depleted and the oxygen flow stopped, so he pulled the round knob on the second bottle. Nothing. He pulled his oxygen mask free and sucked in the thin air. It would be enough, he decided, although he felt decidedly giddy.

As soon as Wolf broke through the clouds, still high above the partially lighted city, he practiced steering this way and that, then cast his eyes about for the landmarks in an effort to pinpoint the *Cercle Sportif.* He noted the crash of bombs and the hissing roar as rocket after rocket roared into the sky, with their blinding bright flames, launched from a dozen sites around the city at the planes far overhead.

In the bomber, Ash One, Court roused himself from where he'd been blown by the exploding SAM, pushed himself from the bulkhead, and checked his oxygen hose and mask. As he slowly recovered his wits, he was immensely relieved to feel the blast of life-giving oxygen over his face. The roar of the wind by the open hatch was deafening. He hefted the plug, dropped it into place, and latched it down, vividly remembering Gartley's wild screams as he'd dived out the gaping hole. Plugging the hole diminished the air flow through the compartment but did not lessen the loud roaring sounds, so he knew the airplane must be holed. He looked up at Robbs and Roberts at their consoles. Robbs was slumped in a welter of black, which Court immediately realized was blood, the color transformed by the green glow of the console light. Roberts was shaking his head, also bleeding profusely and spraying blood, but seemed to be slowly rousing himself. As Court gained his feet and started to lean forward to examine the men closer, the airplane lurched and the nose pitched up. Roberts pointed topside and made frantic flying motions with his hands, as if grasping a control yoke. Court nodded his understanding, and quickly made his way to the ladder, then climbed to the top deck against a strong flow of frigid air, coiling and pushing the long oxygen hose ahead of himself. When he reached its limit, he quickly disconnected and reconnected into the instructor EWO's position. Bentley was still at his console, deftly working knobs. Court patted him on the shoulder, and received a thumbs-up. The wind was icy cold as he worked through the blast in the passageway toward the AC and copilot's seats. The area was brightly lit with glaring white light from the thunderstorm lights which were recessed into the side bulkheads and came on automatically in case of emergency. Higgens, slumped low, weakly motioned him toward the left seat. Court leaned over Merriwell and saw only gore where his face should have been. He felt—there was no pulse. He unfastened the dead man's harness straps with gloved fingers which were quickly soaked with blood, and hauled the lifeless body back to the center of the passageway, marveling at how light the lanky man now seemed. He returned to the AC's position and maneuvered himself to sit in the welter of blood. As he strapped in, he noted that the ejection mechanism was mangled. He unplugged from the stretched oxygen cord and into the pilot's system, then did the same with the intercom, and heard a couple of intermittent sounds.

Court grasped the controls, then searched the instrument panel for the gauges that would tell him the attitude of the big bomber relative to the earth's surface, and what height and speed they were holding.

"Court, hey . . . Court, do you . . . read?" He could barely hear Higgens' voice. He looked over and saw a tortured look on his friend's face. His ejection seat was twisted to one side, and his legs looked bloody and mangled. "You got to . . . fly this thing," Donnie Higgens said as his eyes rolled up and his head fell to his chest.

Court looked back at the panel, found the flight gauges and saw they'd lost 5,000 feet of altitude and were in a descending left turn. He brought the big ship under control, but continued the descent, for he had no idea if Donnie or the others could breathe or whether their oxygen systems might be shredded. His first task was to get down below 20,000 feet so they'd be able to draw oxygen from the thin air. Court brought the throttles back and found he had to increase right rudder to keep the bird's wings level. He looked grimly at the rows of engine indicators. The number-one engine was dead, and number four was at reduced thrust, with high exhaust-pipe temperature. He retarded the number-four throttle further, then looked carefully at the compass to get a heading. Best he could tell, it was south, and he knew there were big guns that way. He turned east, the fastest course to the South China Sea, and ordered the crew to check in.

Bentley and Slater said they were okay. Roberts said Robbs was hurt bad—he had reached over and found a weak pulse. Roberts said he'd also been hit, but didn't elaborate.

"Do what you can for Robbs, Clem. EWO, you got any more SAM lock-ons?" Court asked.

"Negative."

"Then come on up here and help Donnie," Court ordered. "Use a walk-around oxygen bottle until we get a bit lower."

In seconds Beep Beep Bentley was bent over Donnie Higgens.

The plane was descending through 25,000 feet. A streak of light, then another and another outside Court's shattered window caught his eye.

"We got a MiG-21 on our tail and he's shooting," Slater yelled over intercom. Two 23mm rounds struck the left wing and ignited a fire in the number-two engine. The wing dropped.

"Shoot him down," Court yelled. He fought to bring the wing up but the big airplane didn't want to respond.

"Can't. My guns are jammed and off-line."

Chapter 26

Wolf hung in his parachute, his kit bag dangling on a lanyard ten feet below. He was still a half mile over downtown Hanoi and had never felt more alone or isolated. East of the city, guns boomed and rockets roared from their launchers at the bomber force above the cloud layer. Those gunners were deathly afraid of Navy and Air Force flak-suppression and hunter-killer teams, with good reason. Within the city other big guns, those mounted on dikes, in parks, and at street intersections, around and atop of all sturdy structures—schools, warehouses, hospitals, and hotels alike—blasted away with impunity, for the Americans never attacked their positions so near civilians. They did not realize that they were also safe from the fighters for another reason, for a twenty-minute block was built into the frag orders of the fighter aircraft, imposed by the Storm Flight operational plan to allow Wolf to descend into the city without fear of being overrun by a jet fighter zooming past at the speed of sound.

Wolf had known and accepted the high element of risk associated with the Storm Flight operation, but now, peering down frantically from above, it appeared as if it were all coming to naught. He shivered in the cold as he looked about the darkness, unable to find the landing zone, the tennis court at the *Cercle Sportif.* Lochert felt a jolt of apprehension, not due so much to fear as the specter of failure. At chute opening he had known precisely where he was, so for the next five minutes he had concentrated solely on flying eastward, for that was the direction of the target. Then, when Wolf had looked back at his instruments, he'd found the transmitter at Radio Hanoi had gone off the air. Never mind, there were the landmarks—right? He'd searched in vain for the big open area of Ho Tay Lake, then for Ba Dinh Square. Although he'd made them out from high above, after breaking through the cloud cover they were nowhere to be seen.

He was hopelessly disoriented and increasingly filled with despair. Within the next few minutes he would land in some unknown location and most likely be captured.

Four miles over Wolf's head and forty miles toward the coast of North Vietnam, a MiG-21 pulled up in the night air to make his second run on the crippled and flaming B-52. The MiG pilot, a seasoned *Thieu-ta,* a lieutenant colonel in the North Vietnamese Air Force, had determined that the four .50 caliber guns mounted in the tail turret of the big plane were not firing. He pressed the radio button and transmitted to Victory Control what he was about to do, but all he received in return was a noisy buzz in his helmet headset. He continued to maneuver for the kill, doing well without their radar vectors and warnings. The *Thieu-ta* made a thin smile behind his mask as he pulled back toward the bomber, now several thousand feet below and clearly outlined against the lower cloud layer. It was in a constant left bank, and a long stream of flames trailed from an engine on that side. He knew the plane was doomed, for it was obviously uncontrollable, but he wanted to fire another long burst of high-explosive 23mm cannon fire into the left wing root of the Yankee criminal and watch the wing break off and the flaming craft spiral down to a fiery ruin. He was pleased that he'd insisted on the gun pack on his airplane. He had long ago learned from his Russian adviser, Vladimir Chernov, to appreciate the value of guns. A few minutes ago he had fired the last of his aerial rockets, but he still had rounds in the cannon. He rechecked his radar and began his firing pass, finger poised over the firing button on the control stick.

Forty-five miles behind the North Viet fighter pilot and directly over the city of Hanoi, a SAM rocket streaked toward Rose One as the bomber began its post-target turn, bomb bay doors still wide open and EM energy no longer directed at the ground. The proximity fuse of the SAM detonated the 288 lbs of explosive in the thirty-five-foot-long missile just six feet from the aircraft's fuselage, causing hot metal fragments to slash into the main structure, rupturing tanks and igniting the fuel. The huge craft stayed intact for long moments as it arced downward through the night sky, trailing hundreds of feet of brilliant flames which lit the sky and earth below like early dawn.

The light revealed the city below Wolf's feet with the clarity of a map, and he became instantly aware of features and street intersection angles he'd studied so intently before the mission. He easily picked up the tennis courts of the *Cercle Sportif,* even the dim, green blinking light, and tugged on a riser toggle to head in that direction. There was just enough time to maneuver the square parachute onto a base leg and final approach before he ran out of altitude. His kit bag hit the ground and skittered along below as Wolf flared nicely and touched down on the surface of the courts in the middle of downtown Hanoi. He'd done it. He felt a new surge of adrenaline, higher than any he'd felt in his life. Two men moved toward him from the shadows. An unseen third, crouching on the roof of a combination apartment/sweets shop outside the sport complex to watch the aerial bombing show, had also seen the strange parachute and the man who hung from it disappear behind the trees.

"Here he comes again," Slater yelled when he saw the winking of the cannon under the attacking MiG's chin. Yellow-white tracers curved toward the big bomber, then fell away. In his eagerness, the pilot had begun firing too soon—still out of range. To his right, Slater, facing to the rear, saw the long thin flame trailing from the number-two engine. He frantically tried his guns again, but to no avail. The plane descended through 18,000 feet. He put his hand on the turret jettison lever. It was time to leave.

"Mayday, Mayday, Mayday," Court transmitted over the radio, hoping it was working. "Ash One about fifty miles east of the

Bull's-eye at one eight thousand, left engine on fire, under MiG attack from the stern." He transmitted the message twice over the emergency guard frequency, not so much because he thought someone could do anything to help, but so Disco would at least know what had happened to the big craft.

Red Crown heard the call and searched for a flight of MiG-CAP F-4s in the vicinity. His return call to Court went unheard.

Beep Beep Bentley was still bent over the semiconscious form of Donnie Higgens. He'd stopped the awful blood flow from his leg and was now trying to loosen his straps. Donnie blinked his eyes open and cried out. He said his legs hurt.

"I'm going to bail out and take him with me," Bentley yelled to Court over the roar of wind from the shattered windows. His oxygen mask hung from the side of his helmet.

Court ripped the mask from his own face. "Not yet. Get Donnie's attention so I can find out how to put out the engine fire." Court frantically searched the instrument panel, then saw what he'd missed . . . two small red lights above the engine instrument panel, over the column of gauges monitoring the number one and two engines. Beside the glowing lights were fire pull-switches. Court tried to hold the drooping wing up with his left hand, gripping the control yoke while he reached with his right for the switches that would dump CO_2 into the burning engines. He couldn't do it. He needed the strength of both hands on the yoke.

"Bentley," he shouted over the roar, "pull the fire switches on one and two!" He risked a quick point to their location.

Beep Beep Bentley raised and pulled the two buttonlike switches.

Then they both heard the banging impact of 23mm cannon rounds.

The Vietnamese who had watched the strange parachute descend into the *Cercle Sportif* complex had seen other parachutes of the enemy who bombed his city. They'd been round and white or brown, while this one, illuminated by the bright glow of the falling bomber, was black and rectangular, almost square. Perhaps this was a North Vietnamese pilot, or maybe even a Russian. He decided to look and lend assistance. Perhaps there would be a reward for his help.

• • •

"Avon, this is Red Crown."

"Crown, Avon, go."

"Big brother under stern attack, your nine for twenty."

Toby Parker swung his F-4E around to an easterly heading, told his backseater to begin a search, and radioed, "Crown, Avon. We're headed that way."

Ken Tanaka heard the call. "Press on, buddy, I've got you covered." He also turned his flight of Phantoms to the east.

Wolf spun, crouched, and pulled a long-barreled, silenced automatic pistol from a leg pocket of the antiexposure suit as the two men approached with noiseless steps.

"Storm," Wolf whispered.

"Red Bandanna," Nguyen Van Doang replied quietly. He and the other man helped Wolf roll up his parachute and strip off his bulky flight gear from his civilian clothes. The night was cool and humid. Wolf was still shivering from his night drop, for the batteries had not properly heated the suit. Under Wolf's direction, the men quickly pulled a pair of shoes and a special carrying case, shaped and covered like a well-used valise, from Wolf's kit bag. They stuffed the parachute, helmet, and drop clothes back into the now empty bag. Inside the valise was a 35mm camera with an assortment of powerful lenses, an attachment to convert what the camera recorded into digital format, and a burst transmitter to send the product to an orbiting Giant Scale SR-71 aircraft. There was also a miniaturized 16mm camera which could be used in low light conditions, but that film could not be transmitted and had to be returned to the U.S. for processing. Wolf sat and grunted a couple of times as he replaced his jump boots with high-sided Italian shoes. The boots went into the well-stuffed bag, and the silenced .22 automatic into the valise. He checked the Mauser 7.63 in the small holster strapped to one ankle and the Randall stiletto on the other. He made a grim smile as he remembered promising in all sincerity not to carry a weapon on Storm Flight. His fingers had been crossed behind his back. Only REMFs would ask a man to go into combat without a weapon.

When Wolf was ready, they quietly stepped across the court into the trees and took the path to the ground maintenance shed. There, Van Doang pushed a barrel from atop a wooden grate, pulled up the grate, and dropped the parachute-filled kit bag into the hole he had prepared underneath. He motioned in the darkness for help and the three men pushed dirt from the nearby pile to fill the hole. Van Doang made no attempt to introduce the man at his side. Wolf determined he was a Caucasian by his bulk and the smell of his after-shave lotion. When the hole was filled and the grate and barrel were in place, they crept out of the shed and helped one another over the high wall to the street below.

"Choi oi?" The two words of exclamation came from a shadowy figure in the middle of the street.

Wolf made an instant decision to kill. He could tell by the grunts and exertions of the other two men as they'd gone over the wall that they were not warriors and would not react to a threat in the manner required. Wolf gingerly dropped the valise and attacked from a loping crouch, killing the man instantly with the Randall stiletto, with a single puncture under the rib cage into his heart. He heard gasps of horror from his two companions as he deftly dragged the body to the sidewalk and placed it facedown, as though the man had suffered a heart attack. Wolf rejoined the two men and they hurried away in the darkness. He'd just done what he had been forbidden to do—kill a civilian. The planners had decided that the critical meetings in Paris precluded the use of deadly force on the ground in North Vietnam, which might harm innocent civilians. They didn't seem to realize that civilian workers in the railroad-yard targets were being killed daily in the bombing raids, or that their efforts fueled the war and made it possible. War was like that, and Wolf Lochert knew war as well as he knew his mother's face.

"Bentley," Court yelled, "I can't get the left wing up. What do you know about the hydraulics systems?" The plane was now in a wing-low descending left turn which was becoming steeper with each second.

Because of the increasingly tight left turn, the MiG pilot had to maneuver once more to rearrange his final attack pass.

Toby Parker saw the B-52 just as the flames from the number one and two engines were extinguished, but he didn't have the attacking MiG-21's return on his radar.

"You got that MiG?" he yelled at his backseater.

"Coming up now. Your ten o'clock for five. You gonna use missiles?"

"Negative. Too close to the Buff, might home in on them. Going guns." Toby Parker bent forward and by feel switched to GUN on his fire control panel. He could barely make out the bulk of the big bomber. "Oh, oh," he said to his backseater, "it's going in."

"Sir, should I bail out?" Sergeant Slater asked from the tail. He could feel the big plane entering a death spiral as the MiG was setting up for another pass.

Court had his hands full at the controls. Higgens couldn't bail out. Like his own, the seats of the two men downstairs were wrecked, and one of them was badly wounded. For Slater to bail out meant he'd have to jettison the tail turret, and Court didn't know how well the airplane would fly without it.

"Negative, not yet. Hang in there." He leaned toward Bentley and Higgens. "Donnie, where the hell is the hydraulic backup?" he yelled. The wing was down 45 degrees now, and still dropping, and Court couldn't bring it up. The compass was slowly swinging in the turn. Bentley bent over Higgens and repeated the words the wounded pilot was saying.

"Light above directional gyro . . . is it on?"

Court found it. "Yes."

Higgens grabbed Bentley's sleeve and spoke urgently, and Bentley repeated his words, shouting. "Check the hydraulic pack and standby pump circuit breakers." As soon as he said it, Bentley realized Court was too preoccupied to find or set anything, so he reached over and did as Higgens said to do with the switches. Court felt the ailerons come to life under his hands, but he still couldn't bring the wing up more than a few degrees. More right rudder didn't seem to help.

"It's not working, Donnie," Court yelled.

Higgens shook his head and blinked rapidly, but couldn't seem to understand the words. Court scanned the engine instruments and the crux of their problem dawned. The four engines on the right were providing full thrust, while on the left wing only numbers three and four were operating. The right wing wanted to fly faster than the left—and it was. Court eased the four throttles of the right engines back until the wing came back up to level flight.

"Hey, we got it," he said happily. "I can fly this thing."

Behind and high to Court's left in the darkness, the MiG rolled in on its final deadly pass.

The three men climbed into a small official car Van Doang had parked around the corner, beside the wall of the *Cercle*. Wolf sat in back, the valise on his lap. "All right, where are we going?" he asked in English as the Vietnamese man started the engine. Wolf did not yet want to reveal that he was fluent in Vietnamese. He opened the valise, then repositioned and snapped the silenced .22 automatic into the special holder he'd built there. As he pondered the situation, he also remained very conscious of the two other weapons he carried. He would not hesitate to use any of them should the occasion prove necessary, regardless of what the staff idiots in Washington believed. He was determined to make a success of the mission.

"We are going to a house until daylight," Van Doang answered. "I cannot tell you where." He drove slowly, with only the dim illumination provided by the blue blackout headlamps to show his way.

Wolf understood the need for secrecy. Were he to be captured he could reveal nothing, not the house, not even who the men before him were. He was impressed by the calmness of both men. If they remained upset by the killing of the civilian, they no longer showed it.

"After dawn you will be driven to the place where you can use your camera." He nodded his head to the right as he spoke, indicating that the other man would be taking him. They drove cautiously for a few more blocks, then Wolf looked ahead as Doang braked, the vehicle coming to a halt touching a barbed wire barricade. He barely made out a blackout lantern and several soldiers, all carrying rifles that were pointed at them.

The *Thieu-ta* held his MiG-21 steady on a proper firing course, listening to the frantic buzz in his headset that he knew was Victory Control trying to be heard. He still could not make out the controller's words. They made no difference . . . as he drew closer he picked up the big bomber's return on the intercept radarscope. He swooped closer and pressed the firing button. A spray of 23mm rounds began to impact the left wing root of the bomber.

• • •

"We gotta get out of here," Bentley yelled.

"I've got one last trick!" Court reached over with his right hand and snatched the throttles back, then moved his fingers an inch to the left and pulled the air brake lever, which actuated the barn-door-sized panels on each wing and caused the aircraft to immediately slow down.

The MiG pilot cursed as he released the trigger, overshooting the target. He brought the aircraft sharply about to set up for another firing pass. He was soon again in position, with the B-52 precisely where he wanted it. One more second and he would shoot.

Court Bannister felt the big craft shudder on the verge of a stall as he pushed the throttles back up and retracted the air brakes. The plane responded sluggishly. He leveled at 12,000 feet.

"Locked on," Toby Parker's backseater cried. Toby looked intently into his scope, saw the MiG-21, and maneuvered very slightly to place it where he wanted it—dead ahead. Bright flashes at his twelve o'clock showed the MiG had again started to shoot. Toby bored in closer until the dark shape of the MiG was clearly before him and mashed the trigger of his 20mm Gatling cannon. Pieces of the MiG flew away, and a gout of flame instantly shot from the exhaust pipe. The MiG spun away to their left, out of control, and disappeared toward the ground. It was all over in a record five seconds.

"Toby, baby, you got him," the backseater exulted. "That's number five. You are now an Ace."

Toby briefly reflected on J. T. Neddle's words, and knew he felt no differently. Elated as he was, he felt no ambition to be an Ace. It was his job to protect bombers, and he did it.

"Holy shit," Slater whooped. "Somebody back there just shot the MiG off our ass." He withdrew his hand from the rear turret jettison lever as if it were suddenly very hot.

"Now let's see if we can get this thing on the ground," Court shouted to Bentley. "Get Donnie comfortable, then check the other guys and tell 'em to find me a place to land. Also, see what you can do about the intercom. It just went dead." Bentley bent over Donnie Higgens, loosened, then retightened the tourniquet he was using to stop the flow of blood from his leg. Donnie gave him a weak thumbs-up.

Bentley rose, snugged up his parachute straps, climbed over Merriwell's mangled body, and scuttled to the rear, where he descended the ladder to the lower compartment. The shrieking wind noise from the holes there was as deafening as it had been upstairs, and the emergency white lighting created eerie shadows in the compartment. Beep Beep made his way to the nav consoles. Robbs was slumped over his display and Roberts was splayed back in his ejection seat, huffing from exertion. Blood ran from a slash wound across Clem's cheeks and nose, but his eyes were alert. He had been working with the medical kit, trying to wrap a pressure bandage about Robbs' torso. Bentley took over, disconnecting the nav and pulling him back onto the flight deck. Robbs' face was gray and he did not stir. Beep Beep pulled another first aid kit from where it was clipped to the bulkhead and bound a wound in Robbs' arm, then pulled the pressure compress tighter on his chest. He plugged Robbs' hose into the receptacle and made made sure the oxygen was flowing, then went to Clem to see what he could do there.

Roberts shook him away. "I'm okay," he yelled. He pulled off his mangled helmet, pulled on the headset, and tried the intercom. "Damn thing's dead," he yelled.

"You're bleeding," Bentley yelled back. He noted that Robbs' intercom box had been shattered and was now smoking, so he disconnected the power plug, then tried the intercom. "AC, this is the EWO."

"Yeah," Court responded. "I can hear you now. How're the guys down there?"

"Robbs is in bad shape, but Clem had the blood stopped and I've got him as comfortable as possible." Beep Beep leaned over to try to examine Clem's wound closer, but the RN shook his head to show he was okay.

"You okay?" Bentley yelled anyway. Clem was bloody and looked awful.

"Yeah," Clem said over intercom. "I passed out back there for a bit from lack of oxygen when my mask got blown from my face, but I'm okay."

"Radar, this is Court. Can you work your nav gear?"

Roberts tried a few switches on the console. "Nothing's operational down here," he said. He looked at Bentley, who hovered nearby. "Stay here and keep an eye on Robbs," he ordered. "I'll go upstairs and see what I can do to help get this old bird home." He unstrapped and started toward the ladder, but was flung to the floor when the bomber gave a ponderous and violent lurch. Something was happening, and it could not be good.

Wolf kept his finger on the trigger of the automatic concealed in the valise as Nguyen Van Doang spoke to the guard on duty at the barricade. He listened and translated in his head.

"You are out very late, comrade," the guard said.

"No," Van Doang snapped testily, *"I am up very early. These two are inspectors from Sweden to make sure everything is in order at a new water dam the Swedish Peace Committee has helped us to construct far to the north. The American criminals bombed the railroad yard near their hotel and I am taking them to my home so they will be safe for the night."*

"You have papers?" The guards all looked very nervous, and periodically cast fearful looks at the sky, although the bombers were now long gone.

"Of course." Van Doang produced several sheets from a large wallet on the seat beside him, and carelessly unfolded them. Wolf could tell the examining guard was a peasant who could not read the words, but he leafed through them as if he were an important man.

"Pass, comrade. But be very careful of the enemy bombers."

"Imbecile, can't you see who I am? Do you think I am not aware? Remove the barricade immediately and let us pass." Van Doang said his words in an imperial, angry tone to discourage further questioning and delay. Two guards hurriedly pulled a portion of the barricade aside and stood back. Another bowed low as Van Doang drove through.

"I suppose I should introduce myself," the man in the front passenger seat said as he turned to face Wolf. "I am Mr. . . . ah . . . Andres, with the Swedish Peace Committee. I do not know or wish to know who you are. I have a water dam to inspect, and you may accompany me if you wish. It is a nice place to take photographs."

Wolf grunted his understanding. He decided the man's name was likely not Andres, but that he might indeed be with the Peace

Committee. Otherwise he could not travel so easily through the tightly controlled city. Soon they arrived at a small, one-story whitewashed house, built square in the French style, and pulled through the open gate. The tiny compound was dark except for the faint glow of a single lantern beyond a side door.

"We will wait here for a short time," Doang said as he got out and noiselessly closed his car door. Wolf and Andres climbed out and followed him through the side door, into a small room that Wolf guessed functioned as a kitchen. Doang indicated for the men to sit on the floor. He extinguished the lantern. "Now we wait until the light of dawn," he said.

"Then what?" Wolf asked.

Doang looked thoughtful. "You will get what you need."

Wolf nodded and sat. He heard sleep sounds from the other room. Van Doang was taking a great risk to provide a safe house for a few hours.

"Remind the people you work for of one thing," the Vietnamese said quietly. "My daughter and grandson."

Wolf remembered Connert's debriefing about the favor the man wanted. "I will tell them."

Wolf settled down to a short nap and kept his mind blank until sleep came. He came fully alert as the others stirred and dawn illuminated the earth. Andres motioned, and they went outside and crawled into an even smaller vehicle. Shortly thereafter they were making their way through checkpoints and creeping along heavily potholed roads.

"A Cuban," Wolf said as he examined the papers while they moved out of the city. "I'm a Cuban?"

"Yah, sure. You don't look very Svedish."

0545 Hours Local, Tuesday 19 December 1972
Airborne in a B-52 Over Gulf of Tonkin
Republic of Vietnam

"Stall," Court yelled to himself. As he'd bent over to see how Donnie was doing, the yoke had begun to shudder violently as the airplane had approached a low-speed stall. Court pulled himself back up, pushed the yoke forward, and added what few RPMs he could get to the engines without their going asymmetrical on him again. The shaking subsided and Court leveled the nose. None of the pitot-static system worked, so he had no idea of airspeed or altitude.

Early dawn flooded the shattered cockpit with gray light. Court had leveled the crippled bomber at what the radar altimeter intermittently said was 8,000 feet as he headed in the direction he and Clem Roberts had determined was south, using the standby compass and the direction of the sunrise. Now it was confirmed that they were flying south, for off to their right they could see they were paralleling the coast of North Vietnam. The warmer air at the lower altitude had brought life to the crewmembers' chilled fingers and bodies, but Clem continued to chafe Donnie's hands. The slash across Roberts' face had stopped bleeding, but he looked grotesque in his mask of blood. Court looked out to his left and saw the same two F-4s that had accompanied them all the way. He again tried the radios on various channels and received no reply—not even a side tone indicating he was producing a carrier wave.

"Clem," he yelled across his shoulder. "Get Bentley up here." Roberts nodded and went below. Then Court went onto intercom and raised the gunner. "Come on up forward, Sarge," he said. "We can use the help of another able-bodied man."

"Yes, sir. See you in a few minutes."

Bentley came up, a bleak look on his face. He bent to pat the shoulder of Donnie Higgens, then plugged into intercom. His voice emerged strained and unnatural, and he shook his head woefully. "Al Robbs is in really bad shape. He's going to die unless we get him on the ground." He looked dully about the smashed cockpit, and his eyes lingered on Merriwell's faceless body. He was moving and speaking slowly, his face twisted into a caricature of a frown. "We're not going to make it, are we?"

The young officer was exhausted, dejected, horrified and near defeat. Court decided on shock treatment. He released his mask and let it dangle. "Of course we're going to make it, you dumb shit. Now how about you quit whining and whimpering, and make these radios work? Or is that too much for your delicate little electronic mind to handle?"

Bentley blinked a few times, then his head drew back as if he'd been slapped. Anger flared in his eyes. "What the hell's wrong with you? Don't you have any feelings for these guys, Bannister?"

"That's *Colonel* to you, kiddie. The only feeling I have is that if you don't do your job and fix those radios, I'm going to kick your ass all the way down the flight line after we land. And we *will* land. Now get to work."

Bentley straightened, fury in his eyes. "Yes, *sir*," he yelled with heavy sarcasm. When they got on the ground he'd show this asshole light colonel a thing or two. He turned back to his compartment, dug out his manuals, and opened them to the electrical schematics.

Slater popped through the small crawlway hatch, dog-tired from the night's activity and the miserable journey through the bowels of the bomber. He wearily climbed the ladder to the upper flight deck.

"Get over here and gimme a hand, Sergeant," growled Captain Beep Beep Bentley as he leafed through the thick manual in control again.

Ten minutes later, Bentley, unwinding a thick intercom cord, brought forward a headset with boom mike and clip-switch and handed it to Court. "Everything's working now except your control head. This puts you into my jackbox. We're still on guard channel, which is what we were on when the radio took a round from the MiG. Since we can't tune to any other frequency, that's all you'll get." American military airplanes and ground stations monitored the emergency guard channel on 243.0 Mhz in addition to other frequencies, which made it a good choice. Court adjusted the set over his head, fastened the heavy clip-switch to the control yoke, and pushed the transmit button. Sergeant Slater was below with Robbs. Clem Roberts and Bentley dragged Merriwell's body farther back, then hovered close behind Court, watching and listening as he pressed the transmit switch.

"F-4s escorting the Buff somewhere northwest of Da Nang, this is Ash One on Guard." Court got an immediate response.

"Ash, this is Alamo Zero One, glad to finally hear from you, old buddy. You look pretty ragged over there. Tell us what we can do to help."

Another voice came up. "Ash One, this is Waterboy Radar on Guard. If able, change to frequency 254.7 and we'll give you vectors."

"Sorry," Court said, "Guard's all we have." Pilots hated to stay on Guard and clutter up the air. The Navy called it Air

Force common, the Air Force called it Navy common, and the Marines said they'd use any damn push button they wanted, Guard included. Alamo Zero One turned on his transponder and the Waterboy Radar quickly located the three planes.

"Ash One, you are on the 340 radial for sixty-five nautical from Da Nang field. What are your intentions?"

"First I'll need a damage report from Alamo, and do a controllability check. Then I'll land this thing at your location."

"Roger, Ash, we'll have things set up. What is your status?"

"Total of seven souls on board. We've got one KIA, two badly wounded, and one walking wounded."

"How about your airplane?"

"My number one and two engines are out, number four has reduced thrust, and we're pretty badly shot up. We have many holes. I'm on alternate hydraulics, and our primary radio system is out. We've also lost ejection capability, so we've got to put her down."

"Alamo confirms the external damage, Ash One," the F-4 pilot called. "Your Buff looks like a sieve, but I don't see any smoke or indications of a fire. That's good, because you're streaming fuel from the left wing. Control surfaces look like they're all working."

Court radioed. "Waterboy, Ash One, give me a few minutes and I'll tell you if the gear and flaps are operational."

"Ash, Waterboy, standing by."

"Clem," Court yelled out, "see if Donnie's lucid. Find out the airspeed we should be flying to lower the gear and flaps."

"Two-fifty," said Beep Beep, kneeling beside Court as Clem queried Donnie. Bentley was back in action. The therapy had worked.

Roberts put his head next to Donnie's mouth and relayed. "That's what Donnie says. Slow to two hundred fifty knots," he yelled over the wind noise.

Court pressed the transmit button to call the F-4 pilot. "Alamo, Ash, I want to start a controllability check. First with the gear then the flaps, but my airspeed indicator is inop. I need to indicate two-fifty. I'll start slowing down. Tell me when I've got it."

When Alamo responded that he was at the proper speed, Court told Bentley to put the gear handle down. Nothing happened.

Clem relayed to Donnie, who told him what to do.

"These emergency switches will probably get everything down," Clem yelled to Court as he leaned forward, "but we won't be able to get them up."

Court calculated they were less than fifteen minutes from Da Nang, close enough to fly there with everything hanging. "Put 'em down," he ordered.

Clem Roberts flipped up the red covers on the six individual switches and snapped each one up. The plane shuddered and rocked from side to side as the gear came down, very slowly and unevenly.

Again the plane shook at the beginning of a stall. Court power-rammed the throttles forward and immediately had to jam in right rudder until he could ease the thrust of the two right outboard engines back. It was like trying to roll a pencil straight ahead by pushing on just one end.

"What am I indicating?" Court yelled at Alamo.

"One-sixty . . . you stopped dead when all that crap came down."

"This thing is a pig, I've got to lower the nose," Court transmitted.

Toby finally recognized the voice. "Court?"

"Yeah, who's this?" Court was wrestling with the controls.

"Toby."

"Hi. What's our altitude?" No time for social amenities.

"Passing through six thousand."

"Airspeed?"

"Up to two hundred now."

"Gonna try the flaps." Court started to lower the flaps, and when the airplane started a ponderous roll, he quickly slammed the lever back up.

"The left ones didn't extend," Toby radioed.

Donnie said something to Clem, who told Court what his final airspeed would be.

"Great," Court said. "Waterboy, this will be a no-flap landing. I need a straight-in approach and a GCA. There'll be no go-arounds." Court had just told Waterboy he had to land as close to straight ahead as possible, with help from a ground-controlled approach radar, and that if the attempt failed, he could not take it around the landing pattern to try it again.

"Ash, Waterboy, copy. Crash crews standing by. Remain this

button for GCA." There was a pause, then a calm, deep voice transmitted.

"Ash One, this is Da Nang GCA, how do you read?"

"Da Nang, Ash, loud and clear."

"Ash, I have you twenty-two miles north, turn to heading one forty-five for modified base leg for runway two-seven, descend to four thousand feet. Understand you have hydraulic and controllability problems. Set up your landing configuration now."

"Ash, roger." Court didn't have to do anything, the gear was down and he could not use the flaps.

"Ash, slow to proper approach airspeed."

"Donnie," Court yelled, "what approach speed, what touchdown speed?"

With Clem's support, Donnie drew himself up in his seat and looked around Bentley, who moved back and out of the way. "What's our fuel?" he yelled hoarsely.

Court risked a surprised glance. "Hey, you back on line?"

"Between the two of us . . . we'll get 'er on the ground. You handle the rudders, brakes, and throttles, I'll . . . I'll do ailerons and elevator. Turn them over to me when I say." His face was ashen and he was in obvious pain. "What's the fuel?" he asked again.

Court found the unfamiliar gauges and did some rapid calculations. "About sixty thousand pounds."

Donnie tried to add that to the 180,000-pound static weight of the B-52 and failed. "Court, I'm fuzzy as hell. What's best flare speed? Add thirty knots to it."

"Best flare? What's that?"

Clem Roberts calculated in his head the best flare speed for the gross weight of 240,000 and added the thirty knots. "Don't let it get below one-sixty on final and hold it until Donnie lands. There is no flaring for a no-flap landing in this beast."

"Start the approach at two hundred, then . . . then decrease to one-sixty as we get lower," Donnie said. "I'll take it the last couple hundred feet."

Court called Toby on the radio. "We need you to give us airspeed readings. We want to start down at two hundred, then bleed off to one-sixty over the fence." Over the fence was pilot slang for the approach end of the runway.

"Rodge, you're two-ten now."

Court eased the throttles back a fraction. From the corner of his eye he saw Donnie's head droop. For a moment he seemed to have passed out, then he slowly raised up and wiped his eyes. "Where's my duckcall?"

Clem Roberts found it on the floor of the cabin and stuck it into Donnie's special sleeve pocket.

"You're at one-ninety . . . now one-eighty," Toby transmitted.

The plane was slower and less responsive. Court felt the left wing begin to drop and rolled in right aileron. When nothing seemed to happen, he rolled in more until the wing started up. He centered the controls when the wing was level, but now the right wing started to drop and Court rolled in left aileron but the right wing kept dropping.

"You got one-seventy, Ash," Toby said.

Court had gotten the sluggish airplane into a wing rock. He was used to the instant response of jet-fighter controls on wings a quarter of the size of the 185-foot span of the B-52. *Basic damn mistake,* he said to himself, *an Edwards graduate and I'm overcontrolling.* He centered the yoke and held it steady, and added power to stop the rate of descent and increase airspeed.

"You're level at sixty-two hundred at two-ten," Toby said. "GCA wants you at four thousand."

"God almighty," Court bellowed in disgust at his inability to make the big aircraft do as he wanted. Without an instrument indicating rate of descent, Court could only guess. He pulled a fraction more power back.

"What's my descent?" he asked Toby.

"You got one thousand," Toby answered, meaning the B-52 was losing altitude at the rate of one thousand feet per minute. Court held that rate until Toby said he was at four thousand. He advanced the throttles a fraction.

"Ash, Da Nang GCA. You're at fifteen miles, turn right heading two-sixty and descend to two thousand."

"Right two-sixty, descend to two thousand," Court answered. He put the right wing down and again eased back on the throttles, careful to keep the left throttles at higher settings than the right.

Toby called out the altitudes and Court leveled at two thousand. Seconds later Da Nang GCA told him to descend to one thousand. He started down and Toby told him when to level, then when he was holding 190 knots.

"Ash, Da Nang, I have you at five miles, turn right to two-seventy . . . you're on glide path, start normal rate of descent." Almost immediately then, Da Nang said, "Ash, you're way below glide path, stop rate of descent."

"You're up to one-ninety," Toby said and Court tried to level off to intercept the glide path.

"There's the field," Clem called out. "Dead ahead."

"God, that's a good sight," Court said as he looked up and saw the Da Nang runway. Now he could judge his descent much better and, in fact, would drop below the glide path to land on the exact approach end of the runway. The big B-52 was very clean without flaps and was going to land thirty knots faster than normal. They needed all the runway they could get.

"Da Nang, Ash has the runway in sight."

"Ash, Da Nang GCA. Tower clears you for landing. Winds two-eighty at five, altimeter 30.12."

"All right, Donnie," Court said out of the corner of his mouth, "we're pretty close. Get ready to put your masterful touch on this beast."

"Okay . . . I'm ready. I got it. Use the rudders to keep the ball centered. Get her down to one-sixty, no slower. After touchdown stay off the brakes until I tell you, then just tap them. Pull the drag chute handle at a hundred and forty knots . . . no faster or we'll lose it."

"Toby," Court transmitted to the F-4. "Got a problem. You got to stay with us. We want one-sixty until touchdown, then we need to know when we're at one-forty."

"No sweat, I've got everything hanging, I'll keep you honest. You're at one-sixty-five now."

Now that Donnie had the control yoke, Court was able to take a quick look and see Toby's F-4 with gear and flaps hanging, nose held high as he flew formation with the bomber. Court turned his attention back to the instrument panel and the end of the runway.

"All right, guys," he yelled, "get back there and brace yourselves." Bentley hurried back to his seat to strap in while Clem Roberts went below to join Slater in holding Al Robbs as best they could in a protective crash-landing position.

Donnie Higgens held the wings level as they descended. Court gave some right rudder and moved the engine throttles slightly as Toby called out airspeeds. Court didn't need the altitude or rate-of-descent calls now that they were this close to the end of the runway. Da Nang GCA wisely stayed off the air.

Word had spread over the fighter base when the fire crash crew and hospital crash ambulance were scrambled that a shot-up B-52 with half power was on final approach without flaps. The control tower had gotten airborne what planes they could, landed others, and told those with fuel to orbit until the emergency was over. All the planes close to the runway moved away. No one knew what it would be like when something as enormous as a B-52, with thirty tons of fuel aboard, splashed itself all over a runway.

Court had the needle centered and, according to Toby's radio calls, his throttle manipulation had them on speed at 160 knots. He saw Donnie out of the corner of his eye, holding the controls steady. It felt odd, sitting in the left seat, just using the rudders and throttles, having someone else steer. He stifled an urge to put his hands on the control yoke just to balance out his body. At 100 feet above the ground, Court could see they would be touching down very close to the end of the runway.

"Looking good, looking good, right on one-sixty," Toby said, wallowing in the air beside the B-52.

The left wing went down a little, then a little more than Court was comfortable with. "Hey, Donnie . . . " he said, looked over, and saw him slump to the left.

Court grabbed the control yoke with his left hand, corrected the wing drop, tried not to overcontrol, knew if he could just hold what he had the airplane would touch down by itself and it would be all over except the stopping. Then the yoke went forward in a manner that would plunge them into the ground, for Donnie had slumped forward. Court tried but could not pull back against the weight on the yoke. With bare seconds to go, he snatched the throttles to idle with his right hand, then reached over and jerked Donnie back off the yoke so he could pull back. He felt the airplane drop like a runaway elevator . . . but he could not take his hand from Donnie to add power.

The airplane hit rear trucks first. Then, immediately, the front trucks slammed down and the wings flexed down so violently that both tip gears punched up through the wings. The empty outboard fuel tanks bounced off the runway, creating a fireworks of sparks. An incredible noisy vibration shuddered through the whole aircraft—but Court remembered it as not much noisier than the landing they'd made when it was—migod, only three days ago. Court pulled the air brake lever to six, the position that would extend all there was into the air, to help slow the plane. His mind was operating at blurring speed.

Court sawed the rudders back and forth, trying to keep the behemoth on the runway, and Toby called out 150 airspeed and *oh shit where was the drag-chute handle?* No drag chute and they'd go off the end of the runway in a big fireball but Christ where was the drag chute that Donnie was supposed to pull? Must be on his side. Toby called 140, then 135, and Court found the handle to the right of the throttles and jerked it back. There was an agonizing two seconds, then the tremendous deceleration as the huge chute blossomed behind and slowed the aircraft and Court began tapping the brakes and wanted to shut all the engines off to stop even the thrust they gave at idle but knew one or more of them powered the hydraulic pumps that gave him brake pressure but he didn't know which ones then he saw the 6,000-foot marker go by meaning he had more than a mile in which to stop and he saw Toby adding power and roaring by as he went around. Then the 5,000-foot marker and *Jesus they were going fast* and he bore down on the brakes then 4,000 and he felt they hadn't slowed a knot then harder on the brakes and harder and the 3,000 marker went by but it didn't seem as fast then the 2,000, definitely slower *but God they were still moving fast* then 1,000 and there was the end of the runway, *ho ho,* they had put up the barrier that could stop a little fighter but not 120 tons of bomber but the plane was slower and slower and only twenty knots over the barrier, felt a slight tug then slower and slower and there was the end of the runway and onto the sand and . . . it stopped.

Court let Donnie go, pulled off the throttles, and shut the engines down.

As he leaned over to check Donnie, he smelled smoke through the shattered windows, then saw the first tendrils of flame reaching up the outside of the cockpit. Beyond he saw the crash vehicles rocking to a stop and aiming their turrets like guns on a war tank as aluminum-clad men rushed from the trucks, grabbed hoses and axes, and ran to whatever was burning under the airplane.

"Clem, Bentley," he yelled, "don't open the bottom hatch. We got a fire under there." He unstrapped and climbed back of the throttle pedestal and bent forward to Donnie. His face was white and his eyes were closed, but he had a weak pulse in his neck. Court heard a sharp noise over his head. A large portion of the overhead hatch was pulled away, revealing an aluminum-clad firefighter standing on a ladder. He leaned in and spoke in a muffled voice under his helmet.

"Sir, we'll have you all out in a minute. Just sit tight while we put out a small brake-and-hydraulic-fluid fire."

A few minutes later the fire was out and the crew began descending through the hatch and staggering out into the air on leaden legs. Medics went in for the wounded Higgens and Robbs, and emerged with them a few minutes later. The corpsmen carrying Donnie's stretcher popped their eyes when he managed a weak quack.

Chapter 27

0730 Hours Local, Tuesday 19 December 1972
Road Between Honoi and Dong Khe
Democratic Republic of Vietnam

The tiny car bounced along on a rough road consisting of ancient asphalt covered with compacted layers of dirt and the droppings of water buffalo. The larger potholes had to be negotiated with care. Andres, the Swede, drove with due heed and methodical precision. "Break anything," he said, "and there is no repair depot." There were many bicycles and several military trucks on the road, but no private vehicles whatsoever.

Wolf marveled at the life along the roadside and within his range of vision. The busy rice paddies and small villages looked so normal! Much more so, he thought, than in South Vietnam, where soldiers and villagers alike lived in constant fear of a mine, booby trap, or sniper.

They followed French Route National 3 toward the northeast, paralleling one of the two major rail lines to China, and passed railheads and yards, many of which had been hit in the bombing campaign. Only a handful of bulldozers and trucks were being used to make repairs. The majority of the cleanup work was being done by teeming hordes of peasants wielding hand-hoes and shovels while others passed wicker baskets of rubble from hand to hand. Watching them, Wolf was reminded of the time-delay fuses on a number of the bombs dropped by the Air Force and Navy to prevent such repair. Delays could be varied from a few minutes up to seventy-two hours to keep repair crews off the roads. One- and two-thousand-pound bombs would go off at random times, killing those near them and scaring into trembling wrecks those who were not. Wolf had seen the effects on road recon patrols along the Ho Chi Minh Trail with his special teams. He wondered if, since these were civilians, the repairs were being delayed the seventy-two hours. Likely not, he supposed. Life was cheap to the communist leaders.

Wolf held on over a particularly bad bump and muttered *Scheiss* under his breath.

"Sorry," Andres said, his words crisp and spoken with a British accent.

"It wasn't the driving. I was thinking about the war."

"It's not like World War Two," Andres said.

Wolf took a better look at him. Andres was a thin, sparse man with sharp Nordic features and eyebrows of tangled silver wire. "I thought Sweden was neutral in that war."

"Officially we were neutral. But when our government allowed the German troops to pass through our country to invade Norway, it was simply too much for many of us, so we crossed the border and fought with the Norwegian resistance."

When Wolf didn't respond, Andres continued, as if it was somehow necessary to explain to this man he'd likely never see again. "We fought differently then. I went out on sabotage missions in Norway before I was called home. Then I was sent as a junior diplomat to our embassy in occupied Paris. There I helped the French resistance wherever I could."

"But your country wasn't at war. You didn't have to fight."

Andres snorted. "Anyone who values freedom and democracy should fight when they are threatened. Tyranny anywhere in the world must be snuffed out. We in the free world should have learned that in the 1930s, when bullies began to rear their heads in Germany, Italy, and Japan. Tyranny feeds upon itself and spreads like a great cancer. If we do not stop it, then who will?"

"Then you agree with what the Americans are doing here in Southeast Asia?"

"I agree with your intent, but I do not understand the way you go about it. Back in my war, armies fought to win. The dams and everything else were targets. It was how wars were fought—to win. You Americans don't do that here. You lose the lives of your airmen rather than allow them to destroy targets that are lethal to them."

Wolf nodded. "A lot of Americans don't understand that part either, Andres."

"Many of us in Sweden, especially those of us who fought the war, do not agree with our government's policy of encouraging Americans to desert their units and come to our country. No one in Sweden knows of your strict rules to not endanger civilians here. Why don't your newspaper people tell them—why don't they tell the world how your government sacrifices your own young men to keep their enemy's civilians safe? Surely you know it will be much more difficult to win that way, but could you not at least explain that you are making such sacrifices?"

Wolf mused. "A few try," he finally said, "but no one listens."

Andres humphed, as he turned onto another rough highway. They took Route National 1A past Kep to Lang Son, then turned north, up the RN 4 through the mountain valley toward the dam. Using the Swede's papers, which he took from a large brown envelope he kept on a pocket in his door, they easily passed through two more roadblocks. Each time Wolf took note of a guard ringing a call box. Andres said they were calling ahead so the army could track their progress. They'd been driving for four hours when they stopped to refill the tank from petrol cans placed where the rear seat had been. Then they took turns drinking from the plastic water bottles Andres had thoughtfully brought along, and munched on a stale loaf of French bread.

"Where are we going?" Wolf asked. "What will I see?"

Andres looked about, then regarded him somberly. "We are far enough along the route and safe enough for me to tell you. There are more than fifty Americans in a new camp located nine kilometers from the Chinese border. It's near a village called Dong Khe, in the mountains."

"Dong Khe?" *There it was,* Wolf thought excitedly. Caruso had mentioned the word *Donkey* in his last transmission. "The camp is near there?"

Andres nodded. "That is what you must film. There is enough camouflage netting at the camp to make satellite photographs indistinct, so your government may not know of it. I was going there to examine the repairs one of our Swedish engineering companies is making on a nearby earthen dam when I saw a truck bringing in a few American prisoners. I was curious and went to a vantage point and looked closer." He nodded. "They're there."

"Fifty? I thought only a few were being singled out."

"Perhaps *more* than fifty now. They bring in more each week. At one time Mr. Van Doang told me they had so many prisoners, they were prepared to sell large numbers of them to *many* countries for their knowledge. North Korea, Czechoslovakia, East Germany, and others. Now they've altered the—"

"Red China?" Wolf interrupted.

"At first that was considered. Now Van Doang doesn't believe so. The Chinese are trying to get along with the Americans. But all of those plans were changed when the negotiations began and the Vietnamese Central Committee realized how valuable a bargaining tool the American prisoners had become. Now there are only the ones selected by the Russians. The military attaché at our embassy has found that they have identified these fifty-odd prisoners from a list sent from Moscow. He says there is a fat Russian KGB colonel who wears civilian clothing, who is in charge of the operation. I haven't seen him yet, but Mr. Van Doang confirmed it."

"A list of names?" Wolf asked.

"God knows how Moscow got it. Possibly from Soviet spies in the United States. At any rate, the prisoners at this camp are believed to be very special. By the way, my man at the dam telephoned yesterday and said several trucks have arrived at the camp with Caucasian drivers and guards."

"They're about to take them!" Wolf exclaimed.

"It would appear so. Mr. Doang says he will do what he can to delay the transfer. He has his friends on the Central Committee." He shrugged. "But as you know, the Russians have great influence over the North Vietnamese. They're the ones supplying most of their arms."

"I've got to hurry with my mission. Get the information out right away," Wolf snapped. "I just hope I'm not too late."

"One other thing is in your favor. The Chinese and Russians are increasingly hostile to one another, so I doubt the Russians can take out the prisoners that way. It's also doubtful they would take them out though Gia Lam airport, since it is so visible. They're more likely to truck them to one of the ports and transfer them to a Soviet ship. Since many of the ports are being mined, they are likely under pressure to hurry."

"Scheiss!" Wolf roared at the outrageous thought.

Andres raised an eyebrow. "How are you leaving once you've finished your mission?"

Wolf shrugged noncommittally. After he'd transmitted his photographic proof to the Giant Scale SR-71 orbiting high overhead, he was to add a code word indicating one of several times and remote locations. On their first pass, a black Special Forces C-130 would drop his balloon and harness rig. He would have to move quickly in the darkness, for precisely thirty minutes later the C-130 would return for a second pass and scoop him up with the Fulton Recovery System, as he'd practiced in Thailand.

Wolf told the Swede none of that. "Just help get me where I can take the photographs," he said to Andres. "I'll take it from there."

1100 Hours Local, Tuesday 19 December 1972
Dogpatch Prisoner of War Camp
Democratic Republic of Vietnam

The fat Russian had left the previous evening in the helicopter, but the trucks and men had remained. Periodically, a Russian soldier would wander over to the fence and stare with inquisitive eyes.

Something was definitely happening.

The previous night they'd heard distant thunder, far to the south, but there had been no thunderstorm clouds in the sky either the previous evening or this morning. It was puzzling.

The A-7 pilot from Chicago cautiously said he thought it was a B-52 raid on Hanoi. He said he'd been in Saigon once when the B-52s had bombed a target fifty miles away, and it had sounded like that. The other prisoners were dubious. The B-52s had come that far north only once before, last April on the raid on the Haiphong petroleum area, and that had been a sort of token raid to show resolve.

A tight-lipped and obviously frightened camp commandant

had cleared the issue shortly thereafter, when the SRO had gone to see him, trying to find out what the Russian presence meant. The commandant told him in an emotional tone that the huge American bombers had destroyed hospitals, schools, and residential areas in Hanoi the previous night. Many innocent people had died. Several hundred bombers had attacked, but more than half had been shot down. It was a terrible day for the Democratic Republic, he'd said, but even more tragic for the foolish Americans. Vietnamese men and women would now fight to the last. It was the beginning of victory. He'd heard all of that on Radio Hanoi, when they'd begun transmitting again after the final raid. The telephone lines were all down, and no one had yet called him on the radio. And no, he would not tell him why the Russians were here.

When the SRO had returned to tell the others that the B-52s had indeed bombed Hanoi, a tremendous cheer erupted from the prisoners. One old head began to laugh with uncontrolled glee. Two new guys shouted at the guards and turnkeys, taunting them. They waited for retaliation, but the guards only cast nervous looks in their direction and did nothing.

The prisoners began an energetic volleyball match.

The Russian First Lieutenant was standing near the fence, watching the session, so Bear Woods walked over closer. The SRO wanted him to find out what was going on—why they were here. They were still thirty yards apart when he introduced himself in Russian.

The young Russian looked at him without responding, then regarded the game again.

"It's called volleyball," the redhead called out.

The Lieutenant came closer, glanced up to the nearest guard tower, then leaned on a truck fender and lit a cigarette. "We heard that one of you spoke Russian."

"My grandfather came from Kiev," Woods said.

"Ahh. He went from the motherland to America."

"Yes." Woods pointed toward the south. "Our bombers attacked last night. The war will not last much longer."

"Perhaps." He shook his head in disbelief. "We thought you would do that years ago."

"Politicians. You have the same problems."

The Soviet youth wagged his head. "Ours are better."

"You have to say that."

The Russian shrugged. "We would have used our bombers long ago."

The *Kapitan* came out of the officers' quarters and hailed the *Leytenant*.

The Russian Lieutenant waved that he'd heard and pushed off of the truck fender. "It is time for us to start, American." He smiled. "We will have more time to talk together, you and I."

"Time to talk?" the redhead called to the KGB *Leytenant*. "What are you going to do with us?"

"You will learn all that soon enough, American."

Just ten minutes later the prisoners were ordered by a Viet guard to form into a single long line. There were now fifty-seven of them, and they fastidiously fell in by rank, major to lieutenant, then by date of rank. The POWs listened to and strictly heeded the orders of the SRO. Such things were important—it reminded them that they were military men, a recognition the Vietnamese had tried long and hard to quell by calling them common criminals.

The Viet camp commandant stood looking on, wordless and without expression until he was called into his office by a Viet clerk. The English-speaking guard settled down to await his return, but the Russian *Kapitan* went over and spoke to him in a low tone. The Viet guard nodded, then looked down at a roster and began calling out prisoners' names. As each name was called, the man was assigned a number, one through five. "Rimembah you numbahs," he shouted to them.

There were five trucks. Bear Woods was not the only prisoner to realize that, nor the only one to frown and begin to worry in earnest.

The Russian Captain leaned and spoke to the Viet guard again. He nodded vigorously and shouted for the criminals to go to the barracks and collect their belongings. He told them to roll their individual bedrolls and mosquito nets into a single tight bundle.

The POWs looked at one another.

"We're going nowhere," the SRO called out.

The Americans who had broken ranks returned to the formation. All the men came to stiff attention, chins tucked in tightly, faces immobile, eyes staring resolutely straight ahead.

As the Russian Lieutenant and Captain glared, Bear spoke out. "Where do you intend to take us?" he asked in their language.

Both men looked at him without expression. The Captain finally spoke, using American-accented English. "Just do as you are told," he said.

"Woods," the SRO barked out.

"Yes, sir," the redhead replied crisply.

"Did you find out what they want to do with us?"

"No, sir. The Lieutenant said we will have time to talk together. I believe they intend to take us somewhere."

The SRO regarded the Russians. When he spoke his voice was firm. "You are not our superior officers and you are not our captors. You have no authority over us. We will not get into your trucks."

The *Kapitan* whispered more urgently to the Viet guard, who frowned and peered out at the prisoners he'd been told not to harm. Then he turned his head and looked at the headquarters hut, obviously wanting direction from his own superior officer.

"Beat them, I tell you, you Asian monkey fool!" the *Kapitan* raged in Russian.

"He's cursing the guard now," Woods announced for the benefit of the SRO. "Telling him to have us beaten."

"Quit that!" the *Kapitan* screamed at Bear Woods.

"He wants me to stop translating for you," Woods said.

The Russian *Kapitan* unholstered his side arm, a medium-bore automatic.

"Do not move," the SRO told the men resolutely.

The Russian Captain regarded the SRO with blazing eyes. "Do as you are told or I will begin executing your men." He glared at Woods. "Starting with this man."

The SRO winced. For a moment it appeared he would fold, for he began licking his lower lip as he considered. He gave a final shake of his head and turned his head toward the men. "Don't move," he ordered. "Don't do anything this asshole says. He has absolutely no authority over us."

The *Kapitan*'s face had become a deep red color, and he trembled with rage. He regarded the bewildered Viet guards, then turned to the *Leytenant* and shrieked. "Get our own men and bring them here." He was losing control.

"Yes, *Kapitan*." The *Leytenant* hurried away.

Bear spoke up, translating again. "He just ordered the lieutenant to get the KGB troops."

"Quiet!" the *Kapitan* screeched, and raised the pistol, aiming at Woods' head.

Woods gritted his teeth and could not help wincing in anticipation. "He just told me to be quiet," he told the SRO.

The *Kapitan* walked closer to Woods, the automatic trembling in his hand.

The prison commandant called out sharply as he hurried from his office. He walked to the KGB *Kapitan* and spoke in halting Russian. "Our orders are not to harm any prisoners."

"These are ours!" The hand that grasped the pistol was still quivering with rage.

"Not yet," said the commandant. He explained that the People's Army headquarters in Hanoi had ordered him to delay the transfer. Certain members of the Central Committee wanted to coordinate further with Moscow. It would not take long, he said. The prisoner transfer would take place as soon as they cleared up some political matter or other.

The *Kapitan* snorted in disgust, jaw still taut and the barrel still pointed at Woods' head. He lowered it slowly, then nodded in acceptance and reholstered his weapon. "I will radio my superiors," he snapped over his shoulder as he walked away.

When the group was dismissed, Woods walked over to the SRO. "We've got a reprieve," he said, and told him what had transpired.

The SRO nodded and huffed a long breath. "Do you think he would have shot you?"

"No, sir," Woods replied. "He was bluffing. We're too valuable."

"I wouldn't be too sure. He's got a short fuze." The Major narrowed his eyes and shook his head. "Man, if there's ever been a time for the cavalry to arrive, I'd say it's about now."

Woods watched the SRO return to the barracks, shoulders hunched by years of torture and now the weight of command. From the rear, he appeared like a very old man.

Woodrow G. Woods looked about the small camp, eyes lingering on the different men he was getting to know. Like the SRO, every man in the place was married, and most had children.

Every man except him. Woods had a semiserious girlfriend back in the States, but there was no family except for his widowed mother and an older brother who had elected to stay in Oregon. He was the nomadic adventurer in the family.

Somehow, someone had to get the word out to the Americans about what was happening here. He glanced casually about the camp, examining details for the hundredth time. He'd talked it over with the SRO, and been told flatly not to try to escape. The odds of capture were simply too great, he'd said.

But the SRO didn't know about the Have Blue project or what the Russians could learn from Woodrow G. Woods when they used the drugs and interrogation methods he'd heard about.

Yes, he told himself again. *You'll have to try.*

Try, hell, replied his brain. *You've got to make it.*

Can I make it?

He stared again at the steep mountainside and the small valley, and the tall grass along the route he'd picked for himself. Directly eastward, past the Donkey Dam, then on toward the South China Sea. Tonight.

Can I make it?

He grinned to himself. *Does a bear shit in the woods?*

This Bear is the Woods!

1430 Hours Local, Tuesday 19 December 1972
Road Between Hanoi and Dong Khe
Democratic Republic of Vietnam

Andres turned off RN 4 onto 169, a secondary, single-lane dirt road. This one was steeper, yet in better condition because, Andres said, it had been smoothed for trucks traveling through to repair the dam, and didn't get much daily traffic. For nearly an hour they crawled up the narrow road, negotiated the switchbacks, until they drew up to the guard post at a side road.

Two Vietnamese in dark-olive uniforms and pith helmets walked out from a small thatch shack. One, wearing the rank of sergeant, limped and had a broad smile. The other, a young corporal, carried an AK-47 and was scowling. Hair rose on the back of Wolf's neck and his body tingled. He prepared himself for action. He'd go for the Mauser on his leg first. The automatic in the valise in the backseat would be too hard to get to.

"Ah, Meestair Andres, you come back. How you?"

"Hello, Vong," Andres said. He reached in back and pulled out a small mesh sack of vegetables. "Here—for you and your friend."

The scowling man with the gun rattled off words that Wolf understood to be an insult about a man who would accept bribes from the long-noses.

"No lissen that man," Vong said. "He new, never fight in war." Vong had told Andres about his time as a soldier on the Ho Chi Minh Trail and of his wounds from an American airplane before his first week was finished. He'd been very lucky, Vong told Andres, to be chosen to be sent home to North Vietnam, and be assigned to this easy job near where he came from.

Vong leaned down and peered at Wolf. "Who this man?"

"An inspector who wants to see if I am doing a good job. Maybe I do bad job."

"Meestair Andres *never* do bad job," Vong chided, and waved his finger at Wolf. "He do good job, you see. You be nice." He nodded abruptly, stepped back and waved them through, his black eyes crinkling in merriment.

"He's like others here in the mountains," Andres told Wolf. "They don't like the flatlanders, consider them altogether too serious and no fun. Communism isn't entrenched up here."

Soon they were at the dam, where Andres conferred with a Swedish foreman named Kiga, who gave Wolf a firm handshake and speculative glance. Andres then led Wolf about the area. "We must appear to be inspecting," he said as they looked at the equipment, the small generator building, the spillways, and the top of the dam. The dam was small, hardly eighty feet in height, and produced little electrical power. The North Vietnamese considered its repair essential, however, for the Americans had severely damaged their electrical power facilities in their bombing raids the past few months. Andres explained all of that before stopping at the eastern end and pointed down to the water.

"If you look straight up from my finger, you'll notice a large tree with a double fork. To the left of the fork you'll see a few buildings in the distance." He lowered his arm. "That is where they are being held."

Wolf looked at his watch. "It'll be dark in an hour. The lens on this camera is good, but not that good." He looked up at the sun. "I'd like to get in position to shoot from east to west before sunup, then get my pictures at first light."

Andres smiled. "I think you'll be pleased with what is arranged."

"Where do we spend the night?"

"We have a house in Dong Khe village. It isn't much."

"I don't need much."

That night, under the casual scrutiny of two Vietnamese houseboys squatting in the shadows cast by a dim kerosene lamp, the three men ate an excellent meal of cooked vegetables and trout. Kiga had prepared the fish, and said he'd caught them in a mountain stream that he fished every morning. Would Wolf like to join him tomorrow?

Wolf said he'd be more than happy to accompany him.

The small house had four equal-sized rooms, with windows enclosed only by wooden shutters, and water supplied from large urns filled daily by the houseboys. The two Swedes had cots and mosquito netting. Wolf slept on a bamboo mat, under a net draped over chairs, his valise at his side. *This rounds the circle,* he thought as he fell asleep. He'd spent a thousand nights in Laos and South Vietnam, and a considerable number in Cambodia and in the southern mountainous regions of North Vietnam. Now he could say he'd slept north of Hanoi.

They were up and out the door before dawn, breathing chilly mountain air. Andres told Wolf that Kiga had followed this same routine for the past three weeks. At first, he said, a suspicious houseboy had trailed along. Now they did not. The climb was strenuous, and there was little pleasure in watching someone else fish.

The Swede led Wolf up a steep trail toward the stream. There was a very good view from there, he huffed pointedly. They climbed steadily, both men carrying long rods and creels. The plan was to cast the first fly at first light, and make sure they caught a few trout. Then Wolf would make the short trek to the viewpoint, alone.

By sunrise they'd already taken the fish and placed them all in Kiga's creel, for his own was filled by a small but powerful monocular and the two cameras. Then, following Kiga's instructions, he slipped into the trees and climbed his way through the

scrub brush toward the ridgeline. Just short of it, he lay down
and inched forward on his belly.

He eased to the top and looked down. Wolf did not need
the monocular, and he stifled a shout of joy when he easily
spotted the American prisoners in their gray-and-maroon stripes.
They were in a gravelled courtyard beside a half-dozen crude
buildings located on small plateaus jutting out on the steeply
slanted mountainside. Wolf looked down upon the panorama,
less than a quarter mile distant. He pulled out the 35mm camera
from its protective case, screwed in the heavy telephoto lens,
and was about to begin shooting when he noted that the men
were gathered near the perimeter fence, staring into the valley
below.

He followed in that direction with his eyes, then hoisted the
monocular to his right eye.

Vietnamese soldiers were fanned out, moving slowly up the
valley in the direction of the dam, some wielding machetes on
the tall grass, others with weapons at the ready—all searching.

He lifted the binoculars and scanned farther out, then paused.
Taller men, these wearing caps, not the NVA pith helmets, were
also fanned out, staring and holding unslung machine pistols.
He focused better, then drew a breath as he recognized Soviet
uniforms.

As he lowered the monocular and picked up the camera once
more, he wondered what the soldiers were searching for. He
began photographing the Americans lined up at the fence below.
Perfect, he thought. It was as if they'd come out to display
themselves for the pictures. Next he took pictures of the NVA
guards and Russian searchers. Finally he made two panoramic
sweeps with the movie camera, of the valley, the searchers, and
the camp.

When he'd taken his final photos, and after putting the cameras away, he scanned the valley one last time with the monocular.

Whatever, or more likely, *whoever,* the soldiers were looking
for was obviously still on the loose.

1130 Hours Local,
Wednesday 20 December 1972
Officers' Club, Da Nang Air Base
Republic of Vietnam

The party was not going to end. The B-52 and the two F-4s had been on the ground five hours and the Wing intell officers were still going berserk trying to debrief the aircrews, who insisted on opening more and yet more champagne and cognac to build what they called French 75s. Carrying clipboards, the debriefers followed the crewmen around, trying to get their questions answered. It was official, short of the actual paperwork, that Toby's fifth MiG was confirmed and he was the second Air Force pilot Ace of the war. Even though he was from Udorn, the Da Nang crew was as ecstatic as if he were one of their own, for now he belonged to the entire United States Air Force. They didn't know who'd pulled off the biggest stunt, Toby making Ace or Court Bannister and Donnie Higgens landing the shot-up B-52. They decided both feats were of equal but separate merit.

Toby thought again of J.T. Neddle. Making Ace was *not* the goal; doing his job the best he knew how to accomplish the mission *was*. Assholes like Jim Low proved what little character there was in a pilot who wanted *only* to make Ace . . . at the expense of the mission and of wingmen.

They had stolen a woozy Donnie Higgens from the hospital shortly after his deeply gashed leg had been sewn up and his body had guzzled a couple of pints of transfused blood. He sat in a wheelchair with a silly grin on his face, and had a hard time focusing his eyes. He clutched his duckcall and from time to time let go with quacks that, while feeble, were loudly applauded. Clem Roberts was also in attendance, even though his slashed face had been sewn and he'd been sedated and was so swathed in gauze that he was unrecognizable. The two wounded men, Court Bannister, Beep Beep Bentley, Gunner Slater, Toby Parker, and Ken Tanaka, all sat at a long table which was well-slopped with spilled booze. Toby and the two sedated wounded were drinking 7-Up from champagne glasses, with shots of Coke added to lend them a brandy color. The partygoers about them were crews who had already completed their mission for the day, and their drinks were not simulated. In attendance there were also several Marine pilots from across the field and two Navy A-6 crewmen who had landed their own shot-up plane an hour previously.

Beep Beep Bentley was standing on a chair, his glass raised high. "Here's to a hell of a lady. A beat-up old broad with too many miles and too much makeup. To the Guam Queen, who brought us home." A rousing cheer went up from the collection of fighter pilots.

Unnoticed, a brigadier general in fatigues and a stocky man in civilian clothes walked in the front door, surveyed the club, and eased into chairs at a table in the corner. They ordered iced tea from the waitress and Hostettler sent a note to Court, stating that Mr. Jones would appreciate a moment of his time. Court read it, grinned, and started over, but as he approached, his smile faded.

Beside Chef Hostettler was the same SAC brigadier general from the SAC ADVON office at 7th Air Force who had sent out the message the previous April stating that the bombers had used such wonderful tactics during the Freedom Porch Bravo raid that nothing should be altered. More than any other, this man was the source of his problem, the reason Court had been sent to the Pentagon, and then to the Rock to try to make the bomber leaders understand the gravity of the problem they faced. Court suppressed his flash of anger as he nodded to the men.

"Court," Hostettler began, "this is General—"

The Brigadier did not wait for introductions. He rose from his chair and demanded, "What the hell happened to Colonel Gartley? He telephoned me before you took off from U Tapao, and said he'd just been coerced into taking a passenger along. I demanded to see the flight orders." He pulled a copy of the orders from a folder and waved them in Court's face. "And there's no mention of a Mr. White in here. And furthermore—"

The Brigadier stopped talking then, and his hostile gaze turned to Hostettler. "Wait a minute," he said. "Why did you call Bannister over? According to these orders he was just an observer—a passenger. Maybe I didn't explain myself well enough, Jones. I am here under the direct orders of General Austin,

Commander of SAC, to find out just what happened aboard his
airplane. Colonel Gartley was one of his . . . ah . . . protégés."

Chef remained expressionless. "General, Colonel Bannister
was aboard Ash One to assist on an operation detailed in one
of those purple-banded folders that only two people at Tan Son
Nhut and very few others have access to. You are not on that
list, and neither is General Austin. When you insisted on coming
here to make this inquiry, I made certain that I accompany you,
so you wouldn't screw up the—"

"How dare you!" the Brigadier began.

"—so you wouldn't screw up the operation and destroy your
and a few more careers in the process."

The Brigadier sputtered, so upset he was unable to formulate
words.

"Now, before you continue, please look at this directive."
Chef showed him the note, written on White House stationery
and signed by their commander in chief.

The Brigadier swallowed. "I'm . . . ah . . . " He swallowed
again and slowly took his seat.

Chef also sat, and motioned for Court to join them. "Just
after they landed, I contacted Lieutenant Colonel Bannister by
telephone and got a short debrief. I'm sure he can answer your
questions about Colonel Gartley."

The Brigadier swung a gaze to Court. When he spoke, his
tone was much more reasonable. "What happened up there,
Colonel?"

Court turned and looked out the window. Years before, Court
had watched Austin's son crash on a combat mission because
he'd rolled in too low and slow on a strafing pass. In deference
to the man's family, he had reported that the loss was due to
enemy ground fire. Ever since, Austin had blamed Court for his
son's death, saying it had been Court's fault for not warning his
son about the nonexistent ground fire. Now he faced a similar
agonizing choice with Gartley, with a new twist. Whereas Court
had known young Paul Austin as an eager and courageous but
inexperienced pilot, Gartley had been a horse's ass of an officer
who hadn't deserved to command anyone—a cowardly pilot
who'd come apart the first time he'd been shot at. A wave
commander who not only had not flown the airplane, but who'd
been so terrified that he could not speak to the other pilots.

"Well—say something," the Brigadier persisted.

Court looked at the Brigadier. "Did Gartley have a family?" he asked quietly.

"Yes, he had a family. Now, what happened to Colonel Gartley?"

"Children?"

"Two, if I remember correctly, both teenagers. A boy and a girl."

Court turned away from the searching eyes and looked back out the window. He spoke in an official voice, like a recitation before a board of inquiry. "Sir, Colonel Kieffer Gartley was lost when he tried to close a hatch that was blown open. The plane was hit by a surface-to-air missile and he was thrown out. His actions reflected well upon himself and the Strategic Air Command. He died as he had lived his career."

The Brigadier was silent for a long moment. When he spoke, he did so with heavy emotion in his voice. "By God, that's worth an Air Force Cross, if not a Medal of Honor."

When the SAC ADVON General had departed to call General Austin with his findings, Chef pinned Court. "Did everything go on schedule?"

Court nodded. "Wolf went out on time, at the right place."

Chef stood to leave. "I'll send that message to General Whisenand."

Court also stood. "It's been quite a night."

"By the way, General Norman asks that when you finish up here, you catch a flight over to Seventh Air Force and drop by his office. He's got something he wants to talk over."

"I'd like to stay with these guys for a little longer while we all wind down."

"He'll understand."

Court cocked his head thoughtfully. "When I get to Seventh Air Force, I'd like to send out a couple of messages."

"Like your old after-action reports that got you in all this trouble in the first place?"

"Something like that."

"Hey, Court!" yelled out Clem Roberts. "Come on over here and tell these fighter guys what it's like to fly a real airplane."

Chapter 28

Wolf and Andres were again inspecting the dam. He checked his watch. Beginning today, and for the following two days—at one in the afternoon and one in the morning, local time—he was to make burst transmissions, sending digital camera information to the orbiting Giant Scale SR-71 aircraft, along with any messages he wished to put on their voice wire recorder, such as the time and location for the Fulton Recovery System snatch.

"I must transmit soon," Wolf said, squinting at the sky. The angle was bad, for the mountaintops cut off his line-of-sight to the SR-71 orbit, a large, elongated loop southwest of Hanoi. He grimaced. "But I can't get a clear shot from here. I'll need to be on the other side of the mountain, past Dong Khe village."

Andres said they would go straightaway. Ten minutes later, as they made their way around the tortuous turns, Wolf spoke again. "I can transmit voice. Do you have anything new from Van Doang?"

"We spoke for a short time this morning. The Central Committee is delaying the prisoner transfer with Moscow, as I told you yesterday."

Wolf did not ask how Andres had spoken with Van Doang in Hanoi. "Won't the Russians be upset?"

Andres shrugged. "Possibly, but the Russians have always found the Vietnamese difficult to deal with. They know they'll get their way eventually."

"Anything else?"

"Mr. Doang confirmed what I said about the Red Chinese not wanting to get involved any further with American prisoners. They're anxious for a new rapport with America and don't want to bollix it up. That doesn't mean they aren't holding a few from years past, of course. They already have several Americans we know about, including two civilian pilots captured several years ago, as well as a South Vietnamese who flew too close to their border."

Wolf smiled at the man who called himself Andres. "For a member of the Swedish Peace Committee, you're awfully well informed on what is happening around here."

Andres gave a shrug and said nothing.

"You've given me the last piece of the puzzle," Wolf said. "Now all I have to do is get the word out. I am grateful."

Andres snorted. "I am happy to have helped. What they want to do is despicable." He drove beyond the village, to the road leading to RN 1. There he pulled over on a small plateau on a mountainside facing to the south, just short of the intersection where they'd met the guards the day before. At ten to one, Wolf had the transmitter set up on a small tripod, hooked to its battery and a strange, curlicue antenna. He plugged a wire from the camera into the transmitter device, then activated a switch. There was a low hum as the photographic information was electrically transformed into a digital format. He wasn't at all sure how the thing worked, but had faith that it would. They'd described something vague about charge-coupled devices. He'd been told to destroy the camera and associated transmitting equipment, using a built-in destructive device, rather than try to bring it out on the C-130. He would take the miniature movie camera along.

At five to one, Wolf was squatting on the overhang, ready

to turn on the transmitter's power switch, the small automobile at his back, between him and the roadway. He looked about at the pleasant evergreen trees surrounding them, down the steep mountainside into the valley below, then scanned across to the next ridge. The mountains that rose and fell in ripples before him were like the Adirondacks might appear if they were laced with a few sharp karst ridges.

"Ssssst." He heard Andres' urgent hiss from the driver's seat. "We have visitors."

Wolf quickly pulled the silenced .22 automatic from the opened valise and dropped flat beside the car. He peered cautiously beneath, toward the winding dirt road. The two guards were advancing down the incline from the switch-back, rifles poised as they prodded an American prisoner along before them. The POW was slight, with blazing red hair, and he shuffled uncertainly, right hand held at shoulder height, grunting painfully with each lurching step. Blood was soaked into the striped pajama top and down the left side of his cotton trousers—it dripped freely from his dangling left hand. He was only ten yards from the car when he moaned, then dropped to his knees, head hanging low.

The corporal prodded the American with his AK-47 and shrieked for him to get to his feet, but the prisoner remained on his knees, chest heaving in small, rapid movements.

The sergeant pulled his eyes away and surveyed Andres. "What are you doing here?" he asked, flashing the same smile he'd shown the previous day.

The corporal bent down to examine the prisoner, then noticed the transmitter perched on its tripod and frowned. "What is that?" he demanded, pointing with his free hand, clutching the AK-47 with the other.

Wolf cradled the automatic in his left hand, body prone, elbows firmly on the ground.

"Sergeant Vong," Andres said, his voice too loud with apprehension. "We are—"

The sergeant came closer. Then his smiling eyes swung down and widened when he saw Wolf beside the car. He'd started to raise his assault rifle when Wolf fired twice in rapid succession, putting one round in the man's chest, the other in his head. The corporal froze, his youthful glower turned to a rictus of fear, then he whirled and started running back up the road. Wolf dropped him with two rapid-fire shots into his back. The dense forest absorbed the coughing of the gun like the drop of summer leaves.

Wolf ran over and deftly jabbed the sergeant once in the heart with his stiletto to be sure he was dead. The corporal was sprawled unnaturally, half turned toward him, eyes glistening. Wolf started for him, but paused as he heard a pitiful moan from nearby. He hurried over to where the American prisoner still knelt.

Bubbles formed at the corner of the redhead's mouth. He'd been hit with several rounds, but one had obviously taken him in the lungs.

"What's your name, son?" Wolf tersely asked the dying man. The eyes opened and stared, focused finally. "Woodrow . . . G. . . . Woods. Captain . . . United States . . . Air . . . " The pupils dilated and the words stopped.

"You're with friends, son," Wolf said softly, placing a hand on his shoulder to hold him upright. No man should die thinking he was with enemies.

There was no response. Then a single low moan sounded and the redhead slowly toppled forward. Wolf put his fingers on the carotid, felt a single flutter, then nothing.

Lochert gritted his teeth resolutely, then rose and started toward the transmitter. It was time.

Andres climbed out of the car, a shocked look on his face. "One forgets what it is like. That boy—"

Wolf ignored him. He was walking around the car when a burst of automatic-weapon fire sprayed the area, slugs thumping into the dirt and whanging into the car. Wolf went down with a sledgehammer blow to his left thigh and rolled back behind the vehicle, but as quickly as the firing had started, it stopped. Wolf peered around a tire and saw the corporal sprawled over his AK-47. He'd crawled to his rifle and held the trigger back as he passed out. Wolf walked forward, pulled his Mauser and shot the boy in the head. The body jerked and lay still. Wolf was angry. He'd known better than to leave an armed enemy at his back, even a wounded one.

Wolf tottered back on the bad leg and leaned against the car. He had to turn on the transmitter power switch. He heard a groan. "Andres, you okay?"

"I . . . I've been hit. How silly of me."

"Be right there," Wolf said and hobbled to the transmitter. Then his heart fell once again, for a single, wayward round had shattered the device. He closed his eyes for a helpless moment, then dragged himself to the other side of the car where Andres lay.

Wolf hastily bandaged them both. The bullet in his thigh was painful and bloody, but had fortunately not hit bone or artery. Andres was in worse shape. The bullet had slammed into his lower right rib cage, and although not bleeding heavily, he was in great pain. Wolf packed cloth in the hole and helped Andres into the passenger seat.

"Do not worry about me yet," Andres said in a forced whisper. "We must get away from here . . . who knows who heard those shots?"

Wolf hobbled to the two Viet bodies, painfully lugged them to the edge of the cliff, and pushed them over. They disappeared into the green foliage hundreds of feet below. After a moment's hesitation he tossed the AKs after them. Better not to have anything tying them to the dead guards. What he did next was much harder, but just as necessary. He pulled the body of Captain Woodrow Woods to the precipice.

The face beneath the swatch of red hair was at peace. Wolf crossed himself, staring and memorizing the features. "You did good work getting away this far, son. Wish I could have known you."

He shoved, and seconds later heard the body impact far below.

Wolf hesitated for a heartbeat, then went to the equipment, disconnected the camera, and kicked the shattered transmitter and battery pack over the side of the cliff. He placed the camera back in the valise, put it on the floorboard at Andres' feet, and painfully climbed in behind the wheel. Bare minutes had passed.

Wolf turned the key. The starter made a terrible grinding noise, but did not turn over the engine. Without bothering to check the problem, Wolf opened his door and pushed off with his foot until the car started to roll down the mountain road. As it gained speed, Wolf put the lever into gear and eased out the clutch. The motor caught and chugged to life.

Before leaving the secondary road, Wolf pulled into a thicket and examined Andres again. His breathing was shallow and rapid.

"Go to the port of Cam Pha," he said with effort. "We have a contact there. Use the papers in the door. They will get you through. Remember—you are now Cuban. Cam Pha—straight south of here."

"We're not going to get through any roadblock looking like this." Wolf's pants were bloody and Andres' shirt was a red sponge.

"My . . . my overnight bag . . . in the backseat."

Stifling a groan, Wolf leaned in back, found the man's case next to a gas can, and pulled it forward. He pawed through it and found a clean shirt and a pint bottle of schnaps. He also found a towel, which he carefully wrapped around Andres' middle. He helped the partially comatose man into the shirt and buttoned it over the bulky bandage. There were no trousers, so Wolf had to hope the dark stain of his blood would be sufficiently camouflaged by his dark pants. He looked about, supposed they were ready, and pulled back onto the road.

They came to the first barrier an hour and twenty minutes later, a time of pain and sweating for Wolf, of drifting in and out of consciousness and coherency for Andres. A thought came to Wolf as he crept the small car forward in low gear behind bicycles and trucks. He pulled out the schnaps, took a healthy swig, then dribbled some over Andres' face and the front of his shirt.

"*Sí, Cuban, por favor. Mi amigo es loco, whiskey loco, comprendo?*" Wolf spoke the few Spanish words he knew, waved the papers, gave a drunken laugh and blew schnaps breath in the direction of the Vietnamese with the rat face who was peering in the window. The man grew a sour look, drew back, and waved him on. In the rear mirror Wolf saw him ring the landline box telephone.

Soon the sun made the car a steam box and both men were dehydrating. Wolf had to stop to help Andres get some water down his throat. Before continuing, he drank some himself. An hour later, when he stopped to pour gas into the tank, militiamen with rifles slung on their backs rode by on bicycles and looked longingly at the car.

Wolf's mind moved slowly in a haze of pain, and his thoughts were becoming fuzzy. He had to stop again outside of Lang Son to fumble with an old French road map and discovered he should continue straight down RN 4.

It was late afternoon when he finally descended from the mountains north of Cam Pha. Bicycle traffic had picked up, and older women trudged along at the side of the road, poles over their shoulders supporting baskets filled with the produce they'd picked for their families. In the distance he saw the old French port authority buildings and the squat deckhouses and funnels of cargo vessels beyond. He was surprised at the ships in harbor, for Andres had believed the ports had been mined. Only Haiphong, he supposed. Andres had been wrong. The Russians could transfer their prisoners directly to the boats here. Then he noted that the ships were all tied up, and wondered if they'd not been stranded there, the crews fearful of moving out into the mined harbor. He wondered if the man Andres had spoken of who would help them was a foreign crewman from one of the stranded ships.

Foot traffic was increasingly heavy, and his progress was reduced to a crawl. People going home from work, Wolf imagined, and hallucinated himself going home to the Saigon apartment where Greta waited. He missed her.

He was upon the barbed wire barrier before he realized it, and had to jam on the brakes. Nervous soldiers with raised rifles immediately surrounded his car in a wide circle. Wolf chuckled, thinking all he had to do was fire a single round and the *Scheisskopfs* would shoot one another to death. Then he noticed a French Gazelle helicopter off to one side, blades lazily turning as if it had just landed. A swarthy Hispanic stepped out and strolled toward him. He was broad-shouldered, with dark hair and eyes, and wore an olive-drab uniform with no rank insignia. A .38 was strapped to his side. He stopped at Wolf's window and looked down at him, a quizzical smile forming on his face.

"Alto! Cubano? Buenos, señor. Mi nombre es Alvaro Ceballos." He paused, then looked more carefully into the car. *"Que haces aquí? Que le pasa al borracho?"*

When Wolf didn't answer, Ceballos said, *"Deme los papeles por favor."*

Wolf remained silent, wondering if he could get to the valise and if so, how many of the shitheads he could kill before they gunned him down. Particularly this Ceballos character. He was known as the torturer of American POWs.

Ceballos realized something was greatly out of place. He drew back, pulling out his revolver. *"Salga muy despacio, señor, con las manos altas."* He peered at Wolf. "You are an American, an American pig!" He motioned curtly with his head. "Hands up, pig—and get out slowly."

"I'm wounded," Wolf stalled, partially opening the door. He pretended to be worse off than he was. Then he wondered. He *was* wounded, for *Scheiss* sake.

"I don't care if you're dying, pig. Get out of there." Ceballos sprang forward and yanked Wolf out, then slugged him on the back of the head with his pistol. He said something in Vietnamese and the soldiers jumped forward and pulled Andres from the car. The Swede fell, moaning and bleeding profusely.

Ceballos leaned over Wolf's prone body, put the .38 to his head, and thoroughly searched him. He quickly found both the Mauser and the stiletto. "Well, well, what have we here, pig?" He motioned, and a Vietnamese came forward and bound their stunned prisoner's hands behind his back. Wolf was groggy and unresisting.

Ceballos told the soldiers to put the two prisoners in the helicopter, and began to strut about happily. He searched the car and found the valise. A smug smile crossed his face, and his eyes flashed happily as he examined the 35mm and the small movie camera. He didn't know precisely what it was, but knew it must be very important. Something his government would see first, not these yellow-skinned turds. He toted it to the helicopter and jauntily climbed aboard as Wolf and the unconscious Andres were strapped into the backseat. "It is a good thing we were alerted about the drunken Cuban driving south," he gloated to the pilot. "I have now found two American spies." He laughed. "I will have much *delight* in getting them to talk. Let us get back to Hanoi."

"Very well," said the pilot, French Air Force Colonel Henri Beaudreaux. "We are on our way." He pulled pitch and the helicopter lifted off.

1730 Hours Local,
Wednesday 20 December 1972
Airborne in Helicopter Over Port Cam Pha
Democratic Republic of Vietnam

Wolf Lochert's mind was now functioning at full speed. He knew about Beaudreaux. He'd studied the dossiers of every military attaché in Hanoi and knew Henri Beaudreaux, from the French Legation, as the man who had turned the escaped Major Flak Apple over to the Vietnamese. Flak had flashed out his message about his attempt with Ted Frederick to get to the British Consulate. Frederick had been wounded, then beaten to death. Apple had made it to the French and asked for sanctuary. Beaudreaux, a fellow fighter pilot, had turned Flak Apple back to the Vietnamese authorities. After that story, confidential as it was, had swept through the halls of the Pentagon, DIA's Attaché Affairs had had a hard time keeping the disgust from their attitudes when they dealt with bewildered and unknowing French attachés to Washington.

Lochert tested his ropes and seat belt. He was directly behind Ceballos, Andres behind the pilot. This was the perfect opportunity to kill two enemies at once, although it meant sacrificing his own life. Wolf intended somehow to get loose and cause the helicopter to crash. He found he couldn't yet free his hands, but he'd been strapped in with them in his lap and could snap the seat belt open whenever he wanted. Yeah! He'd shrug the harness off and throw himself over the pilot. Helicopters were hard enough to control in normal circumstances—with a kicking, squirming body draped over the pilot it would be impossible. The helicopter was far too unstable for the pilot to release the controls, like a fixed-wing pilot, and tend to the problem. The rotary-wing craft would go out of control and crash. They were still low as the craft sped across the water. Now was the exact instant to act. Wolf put his bound fingers on the lap buckle and tugged.

Beaudreaux leaned back and saw what he was doing.

"Where are you going?" Ceballos asked Beaudreaux with a frown. "This is not the way to Hanoi."

Wolf levered the belt open and bunched his muscles to plunge forward.

"What is going on here?" Ceballos cried in alarm and clawed for his pistol.

"Just a little change in plans," Beaudreaux said and put the helicopter into a steep climb, forcing Wolf back in his seat and paralyzing Ceballos long enough for Beaudreaux to snatch the gun from his hand. "Just a little change in plans," he repeated as he leveled the craft. "Mr. White," he called over his shoulder, "I saw you loosen your belt. Would you—"

Ceballos lunged for the pistol and the helicopter went into a steep dive as Beaudreaux wrestled with him. Wolf flung himself onto the back of Ceballos' seat, then pushed his bound hands over the Cuban's head and pulled a wrist into his throat. The Cuban flailed wildly as Beaudreaux regained control of the helicopter. Wolf tightened his grip and Ceballos slumped.

"Poor way to fly a helicopter," Beaudreaux said as he leveled very close to the water's surface. He pulled his right hand from the control stick long enough to fish a knife from his pocket and saw through Wolf's ropes. "Do you like red bandannas?" he said to the surprised American.

"You're the third man in Hanoi," Wolf muttered as he tugged Ceballos' inert form around the right side of his seat to tie him up with the ropes.

"Something like that."

When Ceballos was halfway into the back, he suddenly twisted and smashed a fist into the wound on Wolf's leg, then jabbed stiff fingers into Wolf's face. *"Chinga tu madre!"* the Cuban screamed.

Wolf's world went red and hazy, flashing with waves of pain and nausea. He couldn't see, but he felt Ceballos clawing for the pistol. Then the helicopter lurched sideways as Beaudreaux fought with the crazed Cuban. Wolf drew his good leg up and launched a powerful kick at Ceballos. He heard a click then a rush of wind and . . . Ceballos was gone. Wolf wiped the blood from his face and looked out the door that had sprung open. The Cuban was clinging to the sill with both hands, feet wildly feeling for purchase on the skids. The gray water of the Tonkin Gulf swept by far below.

"Help me, for the love of God. Help me!" He looked pleadingly into Wolf's eyes.

"Do we need him?" Wolf yelled over his shoulder at Beaudreaux.

Ceballos couldn't hear the answer. "That's it," he said with renewed hope as Wolf reached down toward him. Then Wolf extended his digit and middle finger and poked them into Ceballos' eyes. With a protracted scream he let go and fell screaming and spinning toward the water below.

"Fuck *your* mother," Wolf said, and pulled the door shut.

Beaudreaux stayed low, heading toward a cargo vessel that, as they drew closer, Wolf saw flew a British flag.

"You and your *equipment* will get off here," the Frenchman said. "They are waiting for you."

"What about Andres?" Wolf asked as he sat back and checked Andres' wound and pulse. He seemed stabilized though still unconscious. "I must take him with me."

"That would be best."

"How did you find out about us?"

"The reports were phoned in about your progress. Alfred called me to the tennis court and told me that the Central Committee thought at first it really *was* a berserk Cuban and notified Ceballos. I volunteered to fly him out in the helicopter we maintain at Gia Lam. I felt it had to be you."

"What about you? What will you do?"

Beaudreaux gave a laugh. "I will say you overpowered Ceballos and threw him from the helicopter, then forced me to take you and your friend to the ship."

"Will they believe you?" Wolf asked dubiously.

The French pilot nodded, pain in his eyes. "I have shown them where my loyalties lie . . . although it was not easy. Your Major Apple paid the price for me."

Beaudreaux took his hand from the collector long enough to fish an envelope from his pocket and hand it back to Wolf. "Maybe this will help your pilots."

Wolf put it in the valise, too woozy to read. The cargo ship grew larger as they approached and descended.

"Andres said he had a contact in Cam Pha."

"He thought so, but he does not. His contact was to be a man who is on this ship. One of yours, I believe. But the authorities feel the Americans will soon mine this port, and are denying port entry to all foreign ships."

Beaudreaux hovered over the cargo deck, then gently touched down. Several men hurried to the helicopter and eased Andres to the deck, then helped Wolf down. It was awkward, for his leg was in pain and he clutched the valise to his chest. The adrenaline that had kept him going was draining rapidly, and he had to force himself to keep going. As he stood on the wallowing deck, Wolf's chin drooped to the valise clutched in his arms like a pillow.

The helicopter's engines surged. Wolf looked up, and watched without expression as the chopper lifted off. Beaudreaux threw him a very smart French hand salute as the craft rose, then dipped and flew away toward the distant coast.

The ship's captain approached.

"Permission to come aboard, sir?" Wolf croaked, remembering his protocol.

"Geez, Wolf," said the sailor who had hurried up to support him, "you're already aboard."

The Captain smiled and nodded as James P. Mahoney helped Wolf toward the infirmary.

Chapter 29

1600 Hours Local, Thursday 21 December 1972
Special Projects Branch
7th Air Force—Tactical Air Control Center—
Annex F
Tan Son Nhut Air Base
Republic of Vietnam

As much as his hours there had been as exciting or made him feel as natural as any of the cockpit jobs Court had held, his old office in the small converted warehouse beside the TACC made him feel sort of at home. A major who had worked for him had taken over the "Special Projects" branch and was doing a good job of delving through all the BS and getting the straight word out to the men who counted, the guys in the cockpit, while keeping the generals aware of how the latest operation, now Linebacker Two, was going.

And it was going very well. For the third day they were hitting the North Vietnamese where it hurt the most, right in Hanoi. At night the F-111s and A-6s gave the North Viets nightmares by popping up out of the murky sky, utterly unexpected, and taking out targets. B-52s delivered their massive numbers of bombs on area targets. By day the F-4s dropped smart bombs on point targets in downtown Hanoi, right next to civilian neighborhoods, but with such surgical precision that nary a civilian hair was harmed.

But Court still had to finish the task he'd begun when he'd called upon Major Smitty Smythe to give him the best way for the B-52s to perform their mission in Hanoi and take the minimum of losses.

Court began by digging out Smythe's old summary and then adding the lessons he'd learned serving at the Rock, and then during the eventful mission on the first night of the massive raids, in the now-destroyed Guam Queen. He took it all, everything he had about what he'd learned and what he'd suspected. Then he added what he'd heard at the briefing given by Colonel Thompson at U Tapao, before he'd been stepped on by the report brought in by Colonel Kieffer Gartley, and went to see General Norman in Intelligence. Norman waved him into his office with a wide grin.

"Good to see you again, Court. That was quite a show you put on for the guys at Da Nang."

Court saluted smartly. "Definitely off the cuff and unrehearsed, General."

Norman laughed and motioned toward a chair. "Everything I heard about your actions was laudatory, Court. The new DCO at the Bomb Wing at Anderson called. He's putting you in for a medal. I don't think they've decided quite yet, but I suspect it will be quite high. Perhaps an Air Force Cross."

Court shook his head. "It'll never get past the SAC Commander. That doesn't matter. I've never paid much regard to medals anyway, sir."

"Except for those who work for you. I heard about you writing up the entire crew of the Guam Queen for Silver Stars."

"They earned them."

"Have you . . . ah . . . changed your mind about the bomber people now that you've seen them up close?"

Court nodded. His voice was quiet. "I suppose I have, sir. Most of the men I met there were very dedicated. Don't get me wrong. I'd rather fly fighters than drive a bus through the air, but they have their place."

"Anything I can do for you before we get down to business?"

"Well, sir, I'd like to beat the same old dead horse. I want to make sure the B-52 tactics are changed before more good men die needlessly."

Norman raised his hand to stop him. "Give them to my newest assistant here at Seventh. He's putting them all together now."

"Your new assistant, sir?"

"A fellow named Mike Thompson. General McBurney from U Tapao sent him over here yesterday on extended temporary duty. He's collecting ideas from the aircrews at Anderson and U Tapao after they land from the missions, and they're planning to very judiciously implement the smartest ones. General Austin at SAC headquarters was . . . ah . . . shall we say *persuaded* by the Chief of Staff, after the Chief read your mission debrief about the rigid tactics."

"He *personally* read it?"

"He's the one who sent you to Anderson, if you'll remember. Of course he read it. He sent a back-channel message last night, and I guess a lot of changes are about to take place in our Air Force. For one, there's going to be a series of new realistic training programs established in the Tactical Air Command for our young fighter pilots."

Court shook his head in utter disbelief. "Toby Parker told me about something he's hoping for in that line."

General Norman kept a straight face, as if so many people like himself, J. T. Neddle, Ken Tanaka, and even the Chief of Staff had played no part in that. "Ah, you mean our latest Ace?"

"Yes, sir."

"Captain Parker will return to the States to play a role in establishing that training."

"He'll like that, sir."

"So what do *you* want to do now, Court?"

"Right now I'd like to stay here until Linebacker Two is completed, General. I'm sure you have something for me to do that's worthwhile."

"Stay close to the action, you mean?"

"Yes, sir."

"No more combat flying for you, you understand."

"I understand, sir."

Norman acted as if he were coming up with the idea, and did not let on that it was precisely what the Chief of Staff of the Air Force had already suggested. "How about going around to the bases and looking into how the missions are going? Maybe helping out with the after-action reports like you did before. I'm sure we can swing that with your office at the Pentagon."

"I'd appreciate that, sir."

"I suppose you'd like to confine your trips to the fighter bases as you did before."

Court immediately shook his head. "I'd like to visit with them all, sir. It's all one Air Force. The bombers, the tankers, the fighters, the FACs and the transports. They all make it work."

1345 Hours Local, Saturday 23 December 1972
Apartment on Rue La Fayette
Paris, France

The peace talks had been officially postponed by the Americans, who after spending years of continuously butting their heads against the rock wall of North Vietnamese intransigence had chosen to bomb the hell out of them. From the fourth day of the bombing, the 22nd of December, the North Vietnamese, while continuing to scream about the injustice of the bombing, had frantically sought to speak with the American delegation. To no avail. Until there was clear indication that their terms were met, the Americans refused to meet—even informally. The atmosphere was quite changed for the men and women from Washington. The Vietnamese were now beating on *their* doors with ever-increasing urgency, and the American negotiators simply waited, smiled a lot, and shopped in Parisian stores for mementos to take home to their wives.

There was a nondescript two-bedroom apartment on Rue La Fayette, however, which only selected members of the negotiating teams knew about. Once a KGB safe house, the apartment's location had been discovered by the CIA two months previously. Rather than give up their lease, the Soviets had magnanimously offered it to both sides as a place where they could go for more private discussions. It was one of three such places the negotiators had at their disposal.

A light rain fell on that blustery Saturday afternoon in December, when a dark Peugeot pulled up in front of the semifashionable apartment complex.

"We'll be twenty minutes," said the younger of the two men

in the backseat. "No more than that."

"Yes, sir," said the driver, glancing back as the two crawled out and hurried through the mist toward the entrance of the gray-stone building.

The men stopped in the foyer for a moment, then gave each other a short glance. The older of the two was a State Department official, a senior member of Henry Kissinger's negotiating team who had been selected for his ability to hold his tongue. The younger, Special Agent Chef Hostettler, was from another governmental agency. The broad-shouldered man had flown into Orly International only ninety minutes earlier, in a Boeing 707 sometimes designated as Air Force One and reserved for the President of the United States of America. He had not allowed the leather case in his hand to leave his possession throughout that flight.

"Third floor," the older man said.

Chef nodded. They waited for the elevator.

The concierge on the third floor was a kindly-looking elderly lady. She was also a KGB operative, her cover blown at the same time the CIA agents had learned about the safe house. She examined both men quietly as they produced official identification cards, then pointed down the hall. "They are waiting," she said quietly, and went back to reading her magazine.

There were four men in the room. All North Vietnamese, from the negotiating team. They waited, standing in the small living room. No one shook hands or allowed any semblance of expression to mar their faces.

"We are willing to . . . " began the Viet team leader, an especially hard-faced man who was known to be Le Duc Tho's chief aide.

The State Department official raised his hand. "I believe we called for this . . . ah . . . get-together. It is for one purpose only."

A frown swept over the stone face of the Vietnamese diplomat, then disappeared as quickly as it had come.

The State Department negotiator turned to Chef. "Mr. Thomas has just arrived from the United States. He has information which may severely impact any further discussions we may have in the future. I say may, because your government has the power to move in either direction."

"I assure you—" the hard-faced man began, but he was cut off by another raised hand.

Chef Hostettler placed the briefcase on the table, then reached in and removed a fat manila folder. He opened it and placed five eight-by-ten glossy photos on the table.

The hard-faced Vietnamese shifted around some and stared.

Chef pointed to one. "This is a prisoner-of-war camp outside the village of Dong Khe, near the Democratic Republic of Vietnam, Chinese border." He shifted his finger. "These are American aircrew members. There are fifty-one men shown. We've positively identified forty-two of them so far. None of these were listed in the last prisoner-of-war list you provided."

The Vietnamese narrowed his eyes at the superb definition of the photography. The features and concerned expressions on the prisoners' faces were easily discerned. These did not come from any satellite they'd previously known of.

Hostettler snapped his briefcase closed. The State Department negotiator nodded to the hard-faced man. "I assume you will take all appropriate actions."

"First I must—" the Vietnamese man began, but the two Americans were already stalking toward the door.

0645 Hours Local, Saturday 30 December 1972
B-52G Airborne Over Hanoi
Democratic Republic of Vietnam

"Bombs away," came the radar navigator's crisp intercom call.

The aircraft commander immediately began to make small, jinking maneuvers, but not violent enough to disturb the radiation pattern of the on-board jammers. "We're holding this heading for forty more seconds," he said to the crew.

"There are two SAM radars up," the EWO muttered. "None are locked on." There had been no MiG attacks and no flak at their altitude.

Gray Three was the last of fifteen bombers to release on the Trai Ca SAM maintenance and storage area, which held the final vestiges of the North Vietnamese supply of Guideline missiles.

"Yeah!" exclaimed the RN, who was viewing the target using times-ten magnification through his video tracker. "Bombs on target!"

"Eight seconds until post-target turn," the pilot said.

"We've got a SAM launch," said the EWO, "but they're not tracking us, and the missile's not guiding. That one'll end up in some farmer's field." He paused. "We're out of range of the closest SAM site now."

"Turning," announced the aircraft commander. He reefed the big bomber up onto its right wing, and the crew grunted as they pulled Gs. It was a violent turn, much as a fighter might make.

"Leveling," said the AC twenty seconds later as the bomber settled on a route toward the coast, heading directly into the brilliant morning sun.

"No threats," the EWO announced.

Nine minutes later the radar navigator spoke up. "We're feet-wet," he announced, for they'd just passed over the coast and were now flying above the South China Sea. The old tactics were out, and the new ones were saving lives while getting the job done.

For eleven days the air armada of the United States Air Force and Navy had relentlessly pounded targets in the Hanoi and Haiphong areas. Meaningful targets, which destroyed the North Vietnamese military and industrial infrastructures. Wild Weasels had diminished their stock of AGM-78 and AGM-45 radar-seeking missiles on SAM sites. Air Force and Navy F-4 Phantoms had beat up on Mig-17s, 19s and 21s with great success. F-4 pilots and WSOs from Ubon had dropped amazingly accurate smart bombs on laser-designated point targets, destroying power plants, barracks, and warehouses and not harming adjacent civilian housing. A-7 jocks had dropped unerringly throughout the daylight hours. A-6 and F-111 crews had continued the tactical bombing work during the night. But most telling, and most destructive, had been the awesome tonnages released by the B-52 crews as they'd dropped devastating bombloads upon built-up military and industrial areas and rail sidings. They'd altered their tactics after the first two days, and more and more of the crews survived the impossible defenses. Flying in Route Package Six had begun as a nightmare, with terrible tolls paid by the aircrews. By the final day it was more or less of a milk run.

Fifteen B-52s were among the twenty-eight aircraft lost during Linebacker Two, one of those during a crash landing upon returning to an American base. Major Todd Smythe had forecast the loss of sixteen bombers.

On the fourth day of the Linebacker Two raids, the North Vietnamese delegation began to send messages that the talks might be resumed if the Americans stopped the bombing campaign. There were no concessions from their original position, however. The massive raids continued. On the eighth day, the North Vietnamese spokesman stated before the French press that they were definitely willing to talk, and might consider concessions. The bombing had continued. On the tenth day, a secret note was received by the American delegation in Paris. All conditions, including a complete list of all prisoners of war and a timetable for their release, as well as all other demands, would be met upon cessation of the bombing.

The bombing attacks in northernmost North Vietnam were ordered suspended by presidential order at 0700 on December 30th. Gray Three, the final aircraft in a three–B-52G cell from Anderson Air Force Base, Guam, ended Linebacker Two when their final bombs impacted squarely upon the Trai Ca SAM maintenance and storage area. They landed back at Anderson at noon, to cheers from the ground crews. When they entered the intelligence debriefing room, they were read the message sent from the President of the United States, which had been sent to all the units participating in the grand eleven-day war.

"I would like to commend those who have so skillfully executed the air campaign against North Vietnam . . . the courage, dedication, and professionalism demonstrated by our men is a source of enormous satisfaction to me as their Commander in Chief."

"Yeah," exulted the pilot of Gray Three. "This time they let us do it right."

0700 Hours Local, Monday 1 January 1973
Dogpatch Prisoner of War Camp
Democratic Republic of Vietnam

"Hey," yelled the POW, the once-A-7 driver from Chicago. He was standing at the window of the barracks-cell. "The Russkies are taking off."

The SRO hurried over, and the other intrigued prisoners made way for him. He peered out, and a grin slowly formed on his face. The last of the Soviet KGB troops were packing into the back of one of the Russian-built trucks. A belch of black smoke signaled that the engine had been started.

The KGB *Kapitan* strode out of the officers' quarters and climbed into the utility vehicle beside the driver. He did not look toward the POW camp, as the *Starshiy Leytenant* was doing, but only gave an abrupt head nod to the driver. First the utility vehicle, then the truck eased out of the parking lot and down the steep hill road.

"Good riddance," a POW growled.

The SRO was still too suspicious for that sort of display. For the past forty-eight hours there had been no thunder of B-52 bombings heard from the south, and since there had been no word from the camp commandant, he wondered what was going on. Still, the sound of the truck changing gears as it descended the hill was encouraging.

He turned and was walking back toward his bunk when the door opened and a guard stepped inside. No one made any semblance of bowing to the V any longer.

The SRO eyed him. The guard motioned for him to follow.

Less than an hour later, the SRO returned to the huge cell and lifted his arms for silence. As he spoke then, a grin surfaced on his own face. "I just came from a meeting with the commandant. Get ready to move out."

"Where?" a suspicious captain asked.

"Hanoi. They're taking all the prisoners there. We load up in one hour."

"They're moving us in the daylight?" asked an incredulous lieutenant.

"There's a bombing halt," the SRO said.

"Shit!" exclaimed a captain.

The SRO continued to smile. "This time I think it's different." His smile almost warped his face. "This time I think we'll be going home."

A rumble of cautious glee began to spread in the room.

"Too bad Bear Woods isn't here to go with us," said the Lieutenant. They'd heard absolutely nothing from him since he'd disappeared during the night two weeks earlier. They knew the Viets and even the Russians had searched for him, but it was as if he'd vanished from the face of the earth.

"Maybe," growled the A-7 driver, "he'll be there to meet us when we land in the States."

No one responded. The mood was mixed as the men began to gather their bedrolls, mosquito nets, eating utensils, and bo-buckets.

Chapter 30

It was a quiet ceremony, no press, no photographers, and no outside dignitaries. Although all of the honored guests were military, only USAF Lieutenant General Albert Whisenand wore his uniform. The other four wore civilan attire, as Whitey had suggested would be best for discussions of a covert operation such as theirs had been. Army Lieutenant Colonel Wolfgang X. Lochert looked ill-at-ease in a tight seersucker suit, while USAF Lieutenant Colonel Richard Hostettler and USAF Major Richard Connert appeared composed and rather sharp in gray flannel suits. Army Master Sergeant James P. Mahoney wore a Western-cut sport jacket and looked about with wide eyes and grinned a lot.

President Richard M. Nixon stood before the men, beaming. Flanking him were Henry Kissinger, the Secretary of Defense, the Chairman of the Joint Chiefs of Staff, the Commander in Chief of the United States Army, the Chief of Naval Operations, the Commander in Chief of the United States Air Force, and the Commandant of the Marine Corps. Bob Haldeman leaned against a wall in the background.

"You, ah, you might wonder why I requested all of you here," Nixon said to the distinguished group at his side. "These men have performed tasks for their country . . . ah . . . specifically for their imprisoned fellow countrymen, some at *great* personal risk, and I wanted to shake their hands . . . and I'd like you to do the same." He stepped forward then and grasped Whitey's hand. "General Whisenand was the spark plug behind the idea that American prisoners of war might be in special jeopardy. If he's been a thorn in your sides . . . as he's been in mine at times, I must say . . . it has been due to his unflinching dedication to those men. Thank you, General, for continuing to remind us of the realities of this terrible war."

Nixon looked at the next man in line. "Major Connert here, has endured great revilement . . . yes, *revilement* . . . because of his actions with those trai- . . . ah . . . those who disregard our nation's rules and go to Hanoi." He continued down the line, clasping each man's hand as he spoke of them. "Colonel Lochert actually worked deep behind enemy lines. His actions there read like chapters from an almost unbelievable adventure novel." He nodded gravely. *"Great* peril, there. And Sergeant Mahoney consistently volunteered for dangerous and quite . . . ah . . . unique tasks, and never once quibbled."

Volunteered? Never quibbled? Mahoney gave the President a frown and almost voiced his objection. He settled upon a confused expression as Nixon shook his hand.

"Finally, we have the planning efforts by Lieutenant Colonel Hostettler, who kept this entire effort on track and on time."

The President stepped back, beaming, and shook his jowled face for emphasis. "Terrific work, gentlemen. Superb."

Nixon paused and looked at the military chiefs. "Because of the utter secrecy of their assignment, they can never receive public acclamation. And it is not enough to merely award them medals, although I certainly believe those are in order. But you men who hold the highest positions must know who they are, to insure they all prosper in their careers, and suffer no discrimination."

The Secretaries and Generals surged forward, clasping hands and nodding their congratulations on a job well done, although none of them understood fully.

"There are others who helped on this project," the President said, looking on, "but they are unable to be with us quite yet. But they will be." He chuckled. "Oh yes. We've received word from Henry's negotiators that the date for the POW release . . . and, I . . . ah . . . mean *all* the POWs . . . is being discussed as we talk."

When the men had stopped shaking hands, the President cleared the room of all except the five men who were being honored.

Mahoney looked after the departing generals with awe. "Jeez. I never saw that many stars in one room except in a Hell's Angels reunion."

Wolf Lochert stiffened. "You've been to that sort of thing?"

"Aw, Wolf. I was joking, for Chri—" Mahoney stopped himself, looking at the dark expression which was forming. "I was just joking, sir."

"Scheisskopf," Wolf muttered.

"I believe refreshments are in order," said the President. A troubled expression was growing on his face. "Bob?"

Haldeman took orders and went out to ensure drinks would be provided.

"In five days I am sending Henry back to Paris to conclude the agreements which are being made by the two teams. We're assured of success this time. It seems the North Vietnamese are much more willing to talk reasonably than ever before. This has been a shining time for our airmen, but just in case they don't understand, we're maintaining a considerable force in position in Thailand."

The military men nodded at that wisdom. The knee-jerk reaction of Congress had been to bring all the airmen home immediately.

"There is an issue at hand, however, that is of some . . . ah . . . great concern to me. That is our growing rapport with the Soviet Union. I feel it is of paramount importance to keep the fact of what transpired in this incident completely to ourselves. The revelations about Soviet involvement, this Storm Flight operation, must never be discussed. It did not occur."

Whitey became grim-faced. "Sir, we still have questions concerning other men who—"

"It did not." The Commander in Chief said sternly, then looked at them one by one until each man nodded.

"Good," the President said. "Good." He looked at Whitey.

"General Whisenand will be named as overall coordinator for the release of our prisoners of war. Colonel Hostettler?"

"Yes, sir," Chef said, standing straighter.

"You will assist by debriefing the men who know about the Soviet involvement. The media of the world will be upon the men as they are released. None of this will be brought to light."

Hostettler became thoughtful. "What about the Cubans, sir?"

Nixon grimaced. "Their actions were despicable. Sending their officers over to teach the North Vietnamese how to torture our men." He nodded. "Tell our men they can . . . ah . . . mention them, but in a rather low key."

"It may be difficult to get the returning POWs to agree to all of this, Mr. President."

"How many are we talking about . . . who know of the Russian intent?"

"Sir, it may have been more than intent. There's the distinct possibility that some of our men may actually have been taken."

"I promise I will discuss that with Mr. Brezhnev during my next opportunity following the POW release, and I'll get to the bottom of it. Now let's return to my question. How many of the POWs know about the Russian intent, General?"

"I'd say sixty. Perhaps a few more. Mainly the senior officers and the men who were taken to the place called Dogpatch."

Nixon nodded calculatingly. "They're patriotic men. Surely we can convince them to remain quiet, especially if their nation's security is involved."

Haldeman returned with a tray of drinks.

They all took a glass.

"Gentlemen," Nixon said, looking gravely at his glass, then raising his eyes to meet those of the military men. "Let us toast our American fighting men."

Ten minutes later, as they were filing out of the rear entrance of the White House, Mahoney turned to Wolf Lochert. "That guy's okay."

Wolf nodded.

"I heard some scuttlebutt yesterday when I was checking into the NCO Quarters at Andrews. Some guys working for the President broke into the Democrats' headquarters over at the Watergate building during the election and tried to steal some of their secrets. The word is that the President's in trouble."

"Things like that happen all the time in politics. They just got caught."

"Think anything'll come of it?"

"Naw. He'll just tell the truth and it'll blow over. The public expects things like that."

"Good," said Mahoney, relief on his face. "This guy's a hell of a lot better'n the last one we had."

"Don't curse, *Scheisskopf.*"

1020 Hours Local, Monday 19 February 1973
Gia Lam Airport, Hanoi
Democratic Republic of Vietnam

The 587 prisoners of war were being released in batches, and those were selected by the order of their shoot-down. The earliest shoot-downs, guys like Alvarez, Denton, Risner, Day and Guarino, had gone out on the first flights, on February 12th, and when they left the parting was nostalgic, for the camaraderie among the old heads had become particularly close. Like the others, Flak Apple waited impatiently through that week, until his own turn arrived. By then he was numb and not a little stoic.

His group had received their special "release clothing"—shoes, socks, underwear, trousers, and shirts—the things worn by real human beings—the day before, and that night Flak had great trouble sleeping. Then, at eight this morning, they'd boarded buses and were hauled all around the big city, to avoid their seeing areas the V didn't want them to see. What Flak *did* see was that every single military target of any consequence had been flattened with uncanny accuracy. Finally they crossed over the Red River on a long, shaky pontoon bridge, because all the regular ones had been demolished beyond repair during the December Linebacker raids.

"Out," a Viet guard squealed, but this time he was smiling and trying hard to look pleasant, like the past four years had been a great old time.

Flak gained his feet and shuffled toward the door with the rest of the group.

"Hear that?" one of the guys whispered.

He listened closer. There was a distant rumble, like low thunder.

"There," another guy yelled out, pointing.

A small dot in the sky, growing as it approached. Becoming a silver bird. Distinctive as it neared, with its high tail and long, sleek body. A C-141 Starlifter. The big bird made a long final approach, then touched down with a *squeak-squeak* that was the nicest sound Flak could remember. He heard someone laughing as it taxied toward them, then as it turned and braked to a stop. Without pausing, the rear cargo door started down, and Flak heard the jolly laughter again.

It was his own!

He glanced around to see if anyone had noticed, but found everyone else making their own noises of pleasure.

A few minutes later they'd lined up and were trooping forward, stepping onto a red carpet that had been produced and rolled out by the military flight crew, eyeballing the pretty flight nurses in their eye-catching uniforms, and even the flight crew, who looked unbelievably sharp after years of seeing one another in ill-fitting, grotesque pajamas. A couple of men shook each prisoner's hand as he boarded. One from the State Department, another an Air Force major Flak didn't know.

Just before ascending the ramp, Flak turned and searched with his eyes until he found the V with the popeye and shock of straight hair.

"See something back there?" asked the guy from the State Department.

"Not really," said Flak. "I'm looking at nothing." He stared at Bug for another moment until he knew the man was looking back at him. Then Flak's lips came back in a wide grin. He wanted Bug to know. He was leaving while the miserable son of a bitch was staying in this godforsaken land.

The cargo deck was filled with airline-style seats, and as the prisoners continued forward in an orderly fashion, their excitement became subdued, pensive, as if it was a dream. They remained like that, answering the nurses' and crew's questions even as they taxied toward the active runway.

Takeoff roll.

The POWs held their collective breath.

The nose rotated upward and they were racing on two gear. Lift-off.

A great soaring feeling of elation filled them, and the men began a swelling cheer that filled the body of the beautiful, big bird.

1615 Hours Local, Monday 19 February 1973
Clark Air Base
Republic of the Philippines

As the silver C-141 touched down and taxied in, Courtland Bannister's heart pounded and he could not help wondering still if it was only a dream.

He wouldn't believe it until he saw the big guy.

The Band of the Pacific was on a stand beside the base operations building, playing patriotic tunes, and they were very good at it, but Court didn't need anything to make his heart swell, or for tears to threaten.

Court had made the trip from Tan Son Nhut that morning. Nothing could have kept him away. If he'd missed the arrival of his friend, he'd never have forgiven himself.

The ramp lowered and one by one the men began to emerge, each carrying a kit bag in his left hand, stopping and rendering a sharp salute to the two-star general who greeted them.

Court craned his neck, looking.

A tall, gaunt black man appeared, looking pensively out at the cheering crowd of Air Force members and their dependents and the welcoming banners strung across the front of base ops.

Court frowned, then whoofed out his pent breath.

Flak Apple walked hesitantly forward, then stopped suddenly, as if he'd almost forgot, and saluted. The two-star returned it, then shook his head happily, grinning from ear to ear.

"Welcome home, Major."

Flak mumbled something and was past him.

Court lifted the restraining rope and stooped underneath.

"Sorry, Colonel," a security policeman called out. "Can't do that."

Court ignored him. "Flak," he hailed.

Apple turned, watched as he approached, then tried to salute him, but Court grabbed him and hugged hard.

Court laughed. "Jesus, it's good to see you!"

"Yeah," Flak said. He laughed and hugged him back. "Yeah!" he repeated with more gusto.

Court held him at arm's length, grinning, laughing, and shaking his head in wonder, all at one time. "It's over!" he said.

Flak Apple was grinning hard, but then the look faded some and he looked out toward the western sky, toward Hanoi—beyond—thinking of others who were not there. Some were dead and gone—some just gone, disappeared, like Major Todd Smythe and the others.

"No," said Flak softly. "It's not over."

Epilogue

Court Bannister served in many interesting places (including a stint as air attaché in Cambodia, where he ran into his Russian counterpart, Vladimir Chernov) and retired a full colonel. Later he married Angie Vick. They own homes in London, San Tropez, and Rancho Santa Fe, California. They leisurely fly around the States in Excalibur, a converted B-26. Toby Parker married Tiffy Berg, earned three stars, and played a major role in the Gulf War. He was highly regarded for his incredible ability to reach and inspire younger troops. Wolf Lochert retired a full colonel and, with his wife, Greta, started an outreach program on a lake near Detroit Lakes, Minnesota, for youngsters in trouble. He performs security consulting work from time to time. Flak Apple retired in Sacramento, entered politics, and defeated Shawn Bannister for a seat in the state legislature. He found Co Dust and brought her to the U.S. After a year, they married. Flak later became a U.S. senator. Chef Hostettler had many adventures (most still classified) including a trip into the Iranian desert, two weeks before the rescue attempt, to install clandestine marker beacons for the landing C-130s. After retirement, he earned his *Cordon*

Bleu and opened a restaurant in Fort Walton Beach, Florida. Duckcall Donnie Higgens recovered from his wounds, was retired as a major, and joined United Airlines during the '80s. He married a female first officer and made captain in record time. He and his wife bought "his and hers" Tiger Moth biplanes and perform most Sundays with the Bealeton Flying Circus in Virginia. James P. Mahoney retired as a sergeant major and eventually found himself in Hollywood as a technical advisor to war movies and TV series. He once spent the night in jail for breaking the jaw of Oliver Stone, a man, Mahoney said, who detested his country and proved it by making brilliant but untruthful movies. Whitey Whisenand and his wife, Sal, trapped in the MGM Hotel fire in Las Vegas, died of smoke inhalation in each others' arms. It was obvious to investigators they had donned formal clothes (Whitey in his mess dress, Sal in an ivory-colored formal) and had had a last drink of champagne together. They were unmarked and looked peaceful.